A MOUNTAIN WALKED

GREAT TALES OF THE CTHULHU MYTHOS

EDITED BY
S. T. JOSHI

DRP

Published by
Dark Regions Press, LLC.
—2015—

ACKNOWLEDGMENTS

"The Franklyn Paragraphs," by Ramsey Campbell, © 1973 by Ramsey Campbell, for *Demons by Daylight*. Reprinted by permission of the author.

"Where Yidhra Walks," by Walter C. DeBill, Jr., © 1976 by Edward P. Berglund, for *The Disciples of Cthulhu*. Reprinted by permission of the author.

"Black Man with a Horn," by T. E. D. Klein, © 1980 by Arkham House Publishers, Inc., for *New Tales of the Cthulhu Mythos*, edited by Ramsey Campbell; copyright © 1985 by T. E. D. Klein, for *Dark Gods*. Reprinted by permission of the author and the author's agent.

"The Last Feast of Harlequin," by Thomas Ligotti, © 1990 by Thomas Ligotti, for the *Magazine of Fantasy and Science Fiction* (April 1990). Reprinted by permission of the author.

"Only the End of the World Again," by Neil Gaiman, © 1994 by Neil Gaiman, for *Shadows over Innsmouth*, edited by Stephen Jones. Reprinted by permission of the author's agent.

"Mandelbrot Moldrot," by Lois H. Gresh, © 1996 by Lois H. Gresh, for *Miskatonic University*, edited by Martin H. Greenberg and Robert Weinberg. Reprinted by permission of the author.

"The Black Brat of Dunwich," by Stanley C. Sargent, © 1997, 2002 by Stanley C. Sargent, for *The Taint of Lovecraft*. Reprinted by permission of the author.

"The Phantom of Beguilement," by W. H. Pugmire, © 2006 by W. H. Pugmire, for *The Fungal Stain*. Reprinted by permission of the author.

Trade Paperback Edition

Introduction copyright © 2014 by S. T. Joshi
The House of the Worm© 1933 Mearle Prout
Far Below © 1939 Robert Barbour Johnson
Spawn of the Green Abyss © 1946 C. Hall Thompson
The Deep Ones © 1969 James Wade
The Franklyn Paragraphs © 1973 by *Ramsey Campbell*.
Where Yidhra Walks © 1976 *Walter C. DeBill, Jr.*
Black Man with a Horn © 1980 *T. E. D. Klein*.
The Last Feast of Harlequin © 1990 *Thomas Ligotti*.
Only the End of the World Again © 1994 *Neil Gaiman*.
Mandelbrot Moldrot © 1996 *Lois H. Gresh*.
The Black Brat of Dunwich © 1997, 2002 *Stanley C. Sargent*.
The Phantom of Beguilement © 2006 *W. H. Pugmire*.
The Man with the Horn © 2014 *Jason V Brock*.
… *Hungry* … Rats © 2014 *Joseph S. Pulver, Sr.*
Virgin's Island © 2014 *Donald Tyson*.
In the Shadow of Swords © 2014 *Cody Goodfellow*.
Mobymart After Midnight © 2014 *Jonathan Thomas*.
Beneath the Beardmore © 2014 *Michael Shea*.
A Gentleman from Mexico © 2014 *Mark Samuels*.
John Four © 2014 Caitlín R. *Kiernan*.
Sigma Octantis © 2014 Rhys *Hughes*.
[Anasazi] © 2014 *Gemma Files*.
The Wreck of the *Aurora* © 2014 *Patrick McGrath*.
"Beneath the Beardmore © 2014 Michael Shea

Editor: S. T. Joshi
Cover and interior illustrations: David Ho
Cover design: Irina Summer
Interior Design by Cyrus Wraith Walker

ISBN: 978-1-62641-114-2

Publisher: Chris Morey
Dark Regions Press, LLC
6635 N. Baltimore Ave. Ste. 245
Portland, OR 97203
www.darkregions.com

Contents

INTRODUCTION

The publication of my *Rise and Fall of the Cthulhu Mythos* (2008) has had several unintended consequences, the most noteworthy of which is that I have plunged into contemporary Mythos writing far more deeply than I ever imagined I would. It would be unfair to say that in my book I came to bury the Cthulhu Mythos and not to praise it; any careful reader will have discovered that I end up praising a substantial number of works, early and late, that have elaborated upon Lovecraft's pseudomythology, and I am confident that we may well be entering upon a period of revitalized Mythos writing—chiefly the result of the widespread dissemination of more accurate views of Lovecraft's own goals and purposes in the writing of mythopoeic fiction, and a vigorous cadre of younger writers who refuse to engage in mere imitation but instead use Lovecraft's themes, imagery, and conceptions as a springboard for the expression of their own ideas.

The extent to which, even in Lovecraft's own day, some writers quite dissociated from Lovecraft himself used his work as a trigger for their own conceptions is illustrated by the curious item we know as "The House of the Worm" by Mearle Prout, published in *Weird Tales* for October 1933. Almost nothing is known of this author, aside from the fact that he published three other stories in later issues of *Weird Tales,* none of which is Lovecraftian in any regard. Prout published no books and, apparently, no work outside of these four stories in *Weird Tales.* (One scholar of science fiction maintains that Prout is a woman, but I doubt that this is the case.) In any case, this strange little specimen not only unintentionally echoes the title of a novel that Lovecraft purportedly conceived (but probably did not even begin) in 1920, but contains some patent borrowings of phraseology from both "The Call of Cthulhu" and "The Dunwich Horror," and perhaps also from "The Colour out of Space." Lovecraft took note of the story when it appeared, writing to Clark Ashton Smith: "This latter [Prout] is a newcomer, but to me his story seems to have a singularly authentic quality despite certain touches of naiveté. It has a certain atmosphere and sense of brooding evil—things which most pulp contributors lack." Incredibly, this passage does not suggest that Lovecraft was even aware of Prout's patent borrowings from his own stories; but I find it hard to imagine that he was not. And yet, the critical issue about "The House of the Worm" is not that it lifts passages from Lovecraft's stories but that it is, indeed, a largely original tale in no way weakened by its Lovecraftian touches. It may in fact be an exaggeration to classify it as a "Cthulhu Mythos" story, or even a Lovecraftian story in the strictest sense; but that it reveals a deep and creative reading of Lovecraft's work and is an effective and thought-provoking tale in its own right can hardly be denied.

Contrary to popular belief, I have never maintained that post-Lovecraftian Mythos writing is obliged to adopt his cosmic perspective to be powerful or legitimate. It may well be that cosmicism is the single most distinguishing feature of Lovecraft's own work as a whole (not just his "Mythos" tales), but that very fact makes any attempt to duplicate it a hazardous venture. Indeed, one of the ways in which neo-Lovecraftian authors can carve out a place for themselves, aesthetically speaking, is to use Lovecraftian elements in stories of a very different sort. Lovecraft was, it is widely admitted, not very strong on characterization, and his attempts to portray domestic conflict (as in, say, "The Thing on the Doorstep") are not markedly successful. Here, then, is an area where writers can establish their own viability, and we have examples of that in two very different tales, Robert Barbour Johnson's "Far Below" (*Weird Tales*, June/July 1939) and C. Hall Thompson's "Spawn of the Green Abyss" (*Weird Tales*, November 1946).

"Far Below" has oftentimes been referred to, somewhat flamboyantly, as the greatest story ever published in *Weird Tales*—an honor that might well be challenged by Lovecraft's own "The Call of Cthulhu," "The Whisperer in Darkness," or several other tales. But that it is a triumph in every way is manifest. It is assumed that this harrowing account of the horrors that can be found in the New York subways is a take-off of the hints of similar horrors in the Boston subways in Lovecraft's "Pickman's Model" (*Weird Tales*, October 1927), and probably this is the case; but that Johnson was well aware of much of the rest of the Lovecraft corpus is plain. The pregnant phrase "the charnel horrors of this mad Nyarlathotep-world far underneath" is extraordinarily potent; and the climactic revelation suggests that Johnson had read "The Shadow over Innsmouth" with care. This story in particular embodies exactly the kind of "imitation" that Lovecraft himself endorsed when, in a letter to

August Derleth, he wrote: "The more these synthetic daemons [Cthulhu and Yog-Sothoth] are mutually written up by different authors, the better they become as general background-material! I *like* to have others use my Azathoths & Nyarlathoteps—& in return I shall use Klarkash-Ton's Tsathoggua, your monk Clithanus, & Howard's Bran." The key phrase here is *background-material*—and that is exactly how Johnson treats Lovecraft's Mythos, with that veiled and ultimately inexplicable dropping of the cryptic name Nyarlathotep. Johnson's suggestion that Nyarlathotep is associated with darkness, and perhaps with chaos and entropy, is not only an accurate reading of Lovecraft's own view of his enigmatic Egyptian god but a means by which he can draw upon Lovecraft's legacy without in any way compromising the originality and vitality of his own tale.

As for Thompson's "Spawn of the Green Abyss," this able novella succeeds in vivifying a genuine emotional conflict, involving the physician James Arkwright and the woman he marries, Cassandra Heath, the daughter of the recluse Lazarus Heath; Cassandra finds herself torn between love for her husband and the call of her dubious ancestry. It may be true that Thompson's invented New Jersey town of Kalesmouth— meant to signal, no doubt, the tale's borrowings from "The Shadow over Innsmouth"—is not a very felicitous coinage; but the tale as a whole is richly textured and emotionally resonant in a way that few of Lovecraft's own are, and to this degree Thompson has carved out a genuine niche for himself. It is not surprising that August Derleth apparently badgered Thompson to give up the idea of any further pastiches—not because Thompson had failed and was somehow tainting Lovecraft's reputation, but precisely because he had succeeded, and succeeded far better than Derleth himself in any of his own Lovecraftian imitations.

The work of Lovecraft's own late colleagues, Robert Bloch and Fritz Leiber, certainly deserves commendation, but their Lovecraftian tales are sufficiently well known that they do not need to be included here. It took another generation or so for vital Mythos writing to get underway, but by the late 1960s some signs of life were evident. Ramsey Campbell, now perhaps the leading author of supernatural fiction in the world, got the ball rolling—not by the juvenile tales in *The Inhabitant of the Lake and Less Welcome Tenants* (1964), but by those narratives that he wrote in the years and decades following that early volume. The landmark story "Cold Print" (1967) has now become celebrated because of its inclusion in August Derleth's *Tales of the Cthulhu Mythos* (1969), but another story written at about the same time, "The Franklyn Paragraphs"—which did not see print until its inclusion in Campbell's revolutionary second collection, *Demons by Daylight* (1973)—is far less known than it should be. This tale perhaps embodies the use of the "documentary style" about as well as anything in Lovecraft, including as it does letters by the enigmatic Errol Undercliffe to Campbell himself, a review from the *Times Literary Supplement*, and even a British National Bibliography catalogue entry for Roland Franklyn's *We Pass from View*, one of the many "forbidden books" in the neo-Lovecraftian library. Just as in "Cold Print," although in an antipodally different manner, Campbell has revitalized the very notion of the "forbidden book"—a conception that had already become hackneyed and stereotyped in Lovecraft's own lifetime.

James Wade's "The Deep Ones" also had the honor of appearing in *Tales of the Cthulhu Mythos*, but to my mind Arkham House's James Turner erred in omitting it from the revised edition of the volume (1990) and including any number of inferior tales (even if some were by such noted writers as Stephen King and Philip José Farmer) in its stead. There may be a certain callowness in Wade's deployment of "hippies" in this updating of "The Shadow over Innsmouth," but the richness of the tale's California setting—a setting that Henry Kuttner had tried but failed to use effectively in his early Lovecraft pastiches—and its incorporation of other contemporary social elements make it a noble effort, and I am glad to bring it back into print.

Another means of engendering novelty in neo-Lovecraftian writing is the choice of setting. Campbell had attempted, in his *Inhabitant of the Lake* tales, to establish a British parallel to Lovecraft's imaginary New England towns (Arkham, Innsmouth, Dunwich, etc.), with such locales as Severnford, Brichester, Goatswood, and the like; but the general tenor of these tales was not significantly different from Lovecraft's own. But we are certainly in a very different environment in Walter C. DeBill, Jr.'s "Where Yidhra Walks," which brings the American Southwest—touched upon by Lovecraft only in the ghostwritten stories "The Curse of Yig" and "The Mound," and then only from second-hand information, since he had never visited that locale—within the framework of the Cthulhu Mythos. As with Thompson, Campbell, and others, DeBill has rendered his characters crisply and vividly in a manner that is poles apart from Lovecraft's own array of sober professors and half-crazed "searchers after horror," and it is precisely through the vitality of this characterization that Lovecraftian cosmicism can insidiously enter in.

Lovecraft, even in his own lifetime, became something of an icon, even a kind of fictional character, at least among his colleagues. No one needs to be reminded that Frank Belknap Long ("The Space-Eaters") and Robert Bloch ("The Shambler from the Stars") made patent use of Lovecraft-like characters in their tales; and the pattern has continued up to the present day, culminating perhaps in such works as Peter Cannon's *The Lovecraft Chronicles* (2004) and Richard A. Lupoff's *Marblehead* (2007). T. E. D. Klein's "Black Man with a Horn" may not exactly place Lovecraft himself on stage, but his first-person protagonist, manifestly based on Frank Belknap Long, comes to realize that he has spent much of his life in Lovecraft's shadow and, as this richly textured novella progresses, finds that he has apparently fallen into one of Lovecraft's own stories. Some of the horrific touches in Klein's tale constitute the very acme of subtlety in the display of the supernatural; and this tale becomes a triumphant success not merely as a Lovecraftian imitation but as a modern horror tale in its own right. Even some of Lovecraft's lesser colleagues have now become viable figures in fiction: Mark Samuels ingeniously uses R. H. Barlow's work as a Mexican anthropologist for the basis of his tale, "A Gentleman from Mexico."

Among contemporary writers, few have captured the essence of a certain type of Lovecraftian narrative than Thomas Ligotti. "The Last Feast of Harlequin," although not published until 1990, is an early work that set the standard for Lovecraftian pastiche—in this case, a pastiche of both "The Festival" and its more expansive rewrite, "The Shadow over Innsmouth"—so high that few can meet it; it would, indeed, be an insult to refer to this tale (now enshrined in the Library of America's *American Fantastic Tales*) as a mere pastiche, for it reveals Ligotti's distinctive vision of a world gone mad.

As for Stanley C. Sargent's "Black Brat of Dunwich," I can only echo what Rudyard Kipling once said after reading a tale by Lord Dunsany:

"I am not thinking for the minute of anything except the audacity of it."
I have frequently criticized mediocre Mythos writers who seem content
to do nothing more than rewrite one of Lovecraft's own tales; but what
Sargent has done here is to take a celebrated but (to my mind) seriously
flawed Lovecraftian narrative and turn it upon its head, thereby resolving
a number of its more problematical features. Audacity is the least of this
story's virtues, but the boldness of Sargent's conception carries the story
forward in a manner that is just on this side of parody.

Lovecraft's Mythos tales were written at a point in his career when
he had largely abandoned the nebulous prose-poetry of his earlier work
for the clinical precision of his later, scientifically driven narratives.
One way to revitalize neo-Lovecraftian writing is to hark back to that
earlier style, and that is something that W. H. Pugmire accomplishes
in "The Phantom of Beguilement," a delicate story of Kingsport—a
town first created in "The Terrible Old Man" (1920) and identified with
Marblehead, Massachusetts, in "The Festival" (1923), but that otherwise
does not play a central role in Lovecraft's later Mythos tales. Pugmire
is perhaps the leading prose-poet of contemporary weird fiction, and
the delicacy and pathos of his writing is on full display here. A very
different type of prose-poetry is evident in Joseph S. Pulver, Sr.'s "…
Hungry … Rats." Here again, the story, which uses "The Rats in the
Walls" as its springboard, can hardly be said to be a Mythos tale in the
strictest sense, unless Lovecraft's almost casual and unexplained mention
of Nyarlathotep toward the end of his narrative somehow renders "The
Rats in the Walls" a Mythos tale *ex post facto*. Some of the scenes in
Pulver's impressionistic work might have given Lovecraft apoplexy, but
it shows how even hard-boiled crime and erotica can be grafted onto a
Lovecraftian subtext.

Caitlín R. Kiernan has distinguished herself as perhaps the finest
prose stylist in contemporary weird fiction, and her "John Four" is
as brooding a vignette as one is likely to find—but at its core is the
Lovecraftian topos of entire worlds of terror and wonder lurking on the
underside of life. Neil Gaiman's "Only the End of the World Again"
takes "The Shadow over Innsmouth" as a springboard for a scintillating
and complex tale of werewolves, Deep Ones, and much else besides.
Another great novella by Lovecraft, *At the Mountains of Madness*, has

been the springboard for a number of splendid tales in recent years, and Michael Shea's "Beneath the Beardmore" carries on the tradition of Antarctic horror in a compelling manner.

Science remains the essence of the Lovecraftian worldview, and two recent writers—Lois H. Gresh in "Mandelbröt Moldrot" and Rhys Hughes in "Sigma Octantis"—use various elements of science (chemistry and astronomy, respectively) for their imaginative extrapolations on the Mythos. Gemma Files's richly textured novella "[Anasazi]" utilizes anthropology for its searching examination of humanity's fragile sinecure on this planet.

Donald Tyson, author of the splendid historical novel *Alhazred* (2006), has chosen to write a lengthy and substantial narrative based on one of the last entries in Lovecraft's commonplace book. The entry—which is largely a quotation from a 1935 article in the *New York Times*—is cited in the story itself, and Tyson's first-hand knowledge of the Nova Scotia setting of his tale is evident from first to last. August Derleth embarrassed himself and tarnished Lovecraft by writing incompetent "posthumous collaborations" based on Lovecraft's commonplace-book entries, but Tyson shows that the job can not only be done creditably but result in a tale whose fundamental originality is evident.

Cody Goodfellow's "In the Shadow of Swords" updates the Lovecraftian idiom in a striking manner, using the Iraq War as a grim backdrop for a tale as cosmic as anything in Lovecraft's own work. The malleability of Lovecraft's core images and conceptions is clearly on display here, and augurs well for future writings that can allow any number of contemporary social, political, cultural, and military events to be re-envisioned through a Lovecraftian prism.

Jonathan Thomas's "Mobymart After Midnight" wryly satirical tale takes potshots at the Walmart culture but gradually and insidiously turns to horror as it progresses. Jason V Brock's "The Man with the Horn" deliberately plays on T. E. D. Klein's now-classic story but veers in a very different direction, concluding in dreamlike prose poetry of the sort that Lovecraft repeatedly sought in his more ethereal tales.

Contemporary mainstream writers, as well as writers of the "New Weird" or "New Gothic," have also fallen under the sway of Lovecraft's siren song, and in this volume we present a scintillating original tale by

Patrick McGrath that draws upon Lovecraftian themes in a narrative that in some senses seems very far from the standard Lovecraftian pastiche, but whose undercurrent of weirdness is unmistakable.

What this anthology—which I will not hesitate to declare contains many of my favorite Mythos tales of the past and the present—seeks to establish is the continuing relevance of Lovecraft's work and thought for today's supernatural writing. So much is now known of Lovecraft's own motivations for his tales that there is no longer any reason to engage in the unimaginative mimicry of August Derleth and Brian Lumley. H. P. Lovecraft's work stands as a monument in the literature of supernatural horror; but it can continue to nurture future work so long as writers seek to borrow or adapt the central essence of the Lovecraftian vision rather than its occasionally flamboyant, and by now overused, externals. That the writers in this volume do just that is, I trust, evident; that much more work of this creative and dynamic sort can be expected in the future is my fervent hope.

—S. T. Joshi
Seattle, Washington

THE HOUSE OF THE WORM

MEARLE PROUT

But see, amid the mimic rout
    A crawling shape intrude!
A blood-red thing that writhes from out
    The scenic solitude!
It writhes!—it writhes!—with mortal pangs
    The mimes become its food
And the angels sob at vermin fangs
    In human gore imbued.

                      —Edgar Allan Poe

For hours I had sat at my study table, trying in vain to feel and transmit to paper the sensations of a criminal in the death-house. You know how one may strive for hours—even days—to attain a desired effect, and then feel a sudden swift rhythm, and know he has found it? But how often, as though Fate herself intervened, does interruption come and mar, if not cover completely, the road which for a moment gleamed straight and white! So it was with me.

Scarcely had I lifted my hands to the keys when my fellow-roomer, who had long been bent quietly over a magazine, said, quietly enough, "That moon—I wonder if even it really exists!"

I turned sharply. Fred was standing at the window, looking with a singularly rapt attention into the darkness.

Curious, I rose and went to him, and followed his gaze into the night. There was the moon, a little past its full, but still nearly round, standing like a great red shield close above the tree-tops, real enough....

Something in the strangeness of my friend's behavior prevented the irritation which his unfortunate interruption would ordinarily have caused.

"Just why did you say that?" I asked, after a moment's hesitation.

Shamefacedly he laughed, half apologetic. "I'm sorry I spoke aloud," he said. "I was only thinking of a bizarre theory I ran across in a story."

"About the moon?"

"No. Just an ordinary ghost story of the type you write. *While Pan Walks* is its name, and there was nothing in it about the moon."

He looked again at the ruddy globe, now lighting the darkened street below with a pale, tenuous light. Then he spoke: "You know, Art, that idea has taken hold of me; perhaps there is something to it after all...."

Theories of the bizarre have always enthralled Fred, as they always hold a romantic appeal for me. And so, while he revolved his latest fancy in his mind, I waited expectantly.

"Art," he began at last, "do you believe that old story about thoughts becoming realities? I mean, thoughts of men having a physical manifestation?"

I reflected a moment, before giving way to a slight chuckle. "Once," I answered, "a young man said to Carlyle that he had decided to accept the material world as a reality; to which the older man only replied, 'Egad, you'd better!'... Yes," I continued, "I've often run across the theory, but—"

"You've missed the point," was the quick rejoinder. "Accept your physical world, and what do you have?—Something that was created by God! And how do we know that all creation has stopped? Perhaps even we—"

He moved to a book-shelf, and in a moment returned, dusting off a thick old leather-bound volume.

"I first encountered the idea here," he said, as he thumbed the yellowed pages, "but it was not until that bit of fiction pressed it into my mind that I thought of it seriously. Listen:

"'The Bible says, "In the beginning God created the heavens and the earth." From what did He create it? Obviously, it was created by thought, imagery, force of will if you please. The Bible further says: "So God created man in His own image." Does this not mean that man has all the attributes of the Almighty, only upon a smaller scale? Surely, then, if the mind of God in its omnipotence could create the entire universe, the mind of man, being made in the image of God, and being his counterpart on earth, could in the same way, if infinitely smaller in degree, create things of its own will.

"'For example, the old gods of the dawn-world. Who can say that they did not exist in reality, being created by man? And, once created, how can we tell whether they will not develop into something to harass and destroy, beyond all control of their creators? *If this be true, then the only way to destroy them is to cease to believe.* Thus it is that the old gods died when man's faith turned from them to Christianity.'"

He was silent a moment, watching me as I stood musing.

"Strange where such thoughts can lead a person," I said. "How are we to know which things are real and which are fancies—racial fantasies, I mean, common in all of us. I think I see what you mean when you wondered if the moon were real."

"But imagine," said my companion, "a group of people, a cult, all thinking the same thoughts, worshipping the same imaginary figure. What might not happen, if their fanaticism were such that they thought and felt deeply? A physical manifestation, alien to those of us who did not believe ..."

And so the discussion continued. And when at last we finally slept, the moon which prompted it all was hovering near the zenith, sending its cold rays upon a world of hard physical reality.

Next morning we both arose early—Fred to go back to his prosaic work as a bank clerk, I to place myself belatedly before my typewriter. After the diversion of the night before, I found that I was able to work out the bothersome scene with little difficulty, and that evening I mailed the finished and revised manuscript.

When my friend came in he spoke calmly of our conversation the night before, even admitting that he had come to consider the theory a rank bit of metaphysics.

Not quite so calmly did he speak of the hunting-trip which he suggested. Romantic fellow that he was, his job at the bank was sheer drudgery, and any escape was rare good fortune. I, too, with my work out of the way and my mind clear, was doubly delighted at the prospect.

"I'd like to shoot some squirrels," I agreed. "And I know a good place. Can you leave tomorrow?"

"Yes, tomorrow; my vacation starts then," he replied. "But for a long time I've wanted to go back to my old stamping-grounds. It's not so very far—only a little over a hundred miles, and"—he looked at me in apology for differing with my plans—"in Sacrament Wood there are more squirrels than you ever saw."

And so it was agreed.

Sacrament Wood is an anomaly. Three or four miles wide and twice as long, it fills the whole of a peculiar valley, a rift, as it were, in the rugged topography of the higher Ozarks. No stream flows through it, there is nothing to suggest a normal valley; it is merely there, by sheer physical presence defying all questions. Grim, tree-flecked mountains hem it in on every side, as though seeking by their own ruggedness to compensate this spot of gentleness and serenity. And here lies the peculiarity: though the mountains around here are all inhabited—sparsely, of course, through necessity—the valley of the wood, with every indication of a wonderful fertility, has never felt the plow; and the tall, smooth forest of scented oak has never known the ax of the woodman.

I too had known Sacrament Wood; it was generally recognized as a sportsman's paradise, and twice, long before, I had hunted there. But that was so long ago that I had all but forgotten, and now I was truly grateful to have been reminded of it again. For if there is a single place in the world where squirrels grow faster than they can be shot, it is Sacrament Wood.

It was midafternoon when we finally wound up the last mountain trail to stop at last in a small clearing. A tiny shanty with clapboard roof stood as ornament beside the road, and behind it a bent figure in faded overalls was chopping the withered stalks of cotton.

"That would be old Zeke," confided my companion, his eyes shining with even this reminder of childhood. "Hallo!" he shouted, stepping to the ground.

The old mountaineer straightened, and wrinkled his face in recognition. He stood thus a moment, until my companion inquired as to the hunting; then his eyes grew dull again. He shook his head dumbly.

"Ain't no hunting now, boys. Everything is dead. Sacrament Wood is dead."

"Dead!" I cried. "Impossible! Why is it dead?"

I knew in a moment that I had spoken without tact. The mountaineer has no information to give one who expresses a desire for it—much less an outlander who shows incredulity.

The old man turned back to his work. "Ain't no hunting now," he repeated, and furiously attacked a stalk of cotton.

So obviously dismissed, we could not remain longer. "Old Zeke has lived too long alone," confided Fred as we moved away. "All mountaineers get that way sooner or later."

But I could see that his trip was already half spoiled, and even fancied he was nettled with me for my unfortunate interruption. Still, he said nothing, except to note that Sacrament Wood was our next valley.

We continued. The road stretched ahead for some distance along the level top. And then, as we started the rough descent, Sacrament Wood burst full upon our view, clothed as I had never before seen it. Bright red, yellow, and brown mingled together in splashes of beauty as the massive trees put on their autumnal dress. Almost miniature it appeared to us from our lookout, shimmering like a mountain lake in the dry heat of early fall. Why, as we gazed for a moment silently, did a vague thought of uncleanness make a shudder pass through my body? Was I sensitive to the ominous words of the old mountaineer? Or did my heart tell me what my mind could not—that the season was yet too early to destroy every trace of greenery, and replace it with the colors of death? Or was it something else?—something not appealing to the senses, nor yet to the intellect, but yet sending a message too strong to be dismissed?

But I did not choose to dwell long upon the subject. The human mind, I have long known, in striving to present a logical sequence of events, often strains the fabric of fact for the sake of smoothness. Perhaps I really felt nothing, and my present conceptions have been altered by subsequent events. At any rate, Fred, although unnaturally pale, said nothing, and we continued the descent in silence.

Night comes early in the deep valley of Sacrament Wood. The sun was just resting on the high peak in the west as we entered the forest and made camp. But long after comparative darkness had come over us, the mountain down which we had come was illuminated a soft gold.

We sat over our pipes in the gathering dusk. It was deeply peaceful, there in the darkening wood, and yet Fred and I were unnaturally silent, perhaps having the same thoughts. Why were the massive trees so early shorn of leaves? Why had the birds ceased to sing? Whence came the faint, yet unmistakable odor of *rottenness?*

A cheery fire soon dispelled our fears. We were again the two hunters, rejoicing in our freedom and our anticipation. At least, I was. Fred, however, somewhat overcame my feeling of security.

"Art, whatever the cause, we must admit that Sacrament Wood *is* dead. Why, man, those trees are not getting ready for dormance; they are dead. Why haven't we heard birds? Bluejays used to keep this place in a continual uproar. And where did I get the feeling I had as we entered here? Art, I am sensitive to these things. I can *feel* a graveyard in the darkest night; and that is how I felt as I came here—as if I was entering a graveyard. I *know*, I tell you!"

"I felt it, too," I answered, "and the odor, too.... But all that is gone now. The fire changes things."

"Yes, the fire changes things. Hear that moaning in the trees? You think that is the wind? Well, you're wrong, I tell you. That is not the wind. Something not human is suffering; maybe the fire hurts it."

I laughed, uncomfortably enough. "Come," I said, "you'll be giving me the jimmies, too. I felt the same way you did; I even smelt an odor, but the old man just had us upset. That's all. The fire has changed things. It's all right now."

"Yes," he said, "it's all right now."

For all his nervousness, Fred was the first to sleep that night. We heaped the fire high before turning in, and I lay for a long while and watched the leaping flames. And I thought about the fire.

"Fire is clean," I said to myself, as though directed from without. "Fire is clean; fire is life. The very life of our bodies is preserved by oxidation. Yes, without fire there would be no cleanness in the world."

But I too must have dropped off, for when I was awakened by a low moan the fire was dead. The wood was quiet; not a whisper or rustle of leaves disturbed the heavy stillness of the night. And then I sensed the odor.... Once sensed, it grew and grew until the air seemed heavy, even massive, with the inertia of it, seemed to press itself into the ground through sheer weight. It eddied and swirled in sickening waves of smell. It was the odor of death, and putridity.

I heard another moan.

"Fred," I called, my voice catching in my throat.

The only answer was a deeper moan.

I grasped his arm, and—my fingers sank in the bloated flesh as into a rotting corpse! The skin burst like an over-ripe berry, and slime flowed over my hand and dripped from my fingers.

Overcome with horror, I struck a light; and under the tiny flare I saw for a moment—his face! Purple, bloated, the crawling flesh nearly covered his staring eyes; white worms swarmed his puffed body, exuded squirming from his nostrils, and fell upon his livid lips. The foul stench grew stronger; so thick was it that my tortured lungs cried out for relief. Then, with a shriek of terror, I cast the lighted match from me, and threw myself into the bed, and buried my face in the pillow.

How long I lay there, sick, trembling, overcome with nausea, I do not know. But I slowly became aware of a rushing sound in the tree-tops. Great limbs creaked and groaned; the trunks themselves seemed to crack in agony. I looked up and saw a ruddy light reflected about us. And like a crash of thunder came the thought into my brain:

"Fire is clean; fire is life. Without fire there would be no cleanness in the world."

And at this command I rose, and grasped everything within reach, and cast it upon the dying flames. Was I mistaken, or was the odor of death really less? I hauled wood, and heaped the fire high. Fortunate indeed that the match I had thrown had fallen in the already sere leaves!

When next I thought of my companion the roaring blaze was leaping fifteen feet in the air. Slowly I turned, expecting to see a corpse weltering in a miasma of filth, and saw—a man calmly sleeping! His face was flushed, his hands still slightly swollen; but he was clean! He breathed. Could I, I asked, have dreamed of death, and the odor of death? Could I have dreamed the *worms?*

I awoke him, and waited.

He half looked at me, and then, gazing at the fire, gave a cry of ecstasy. A light of bliss shone for a moment in his eyes, as in a young child first staring at the mystery of cleansing flame; and then, as realization came, this too faded into a look of terror and loathing.

"The worms!" he cried. "The maggots! The odor came, and with it the worms. And I awoke. Just as the fire died.... I couldn't move; I couldn't cry out. The worms came—I don't know whence; from nowhere, perhaps. They came, and they crawled, and they ate. And the smell came with them! It just appeared, as did the worms, from out of thin air! It just—became. Then—death!—I died, I tell you—I rotted—I rotted, and the worms—the maggots—they ate ... I am *dead*, I say! *Dead!* Or should be!" He covered his face with his hands.

How we lived out the night without going mad, I do not know. All through the long hours we kept the fire burning high; and all through the night the lofty trees moaned back their mortal agony. The rotting death did not return; in some strange way the fire kept us clean of it, and fought it back. But our brains felt, and dimly comprehended, the noisome evil floundering in the darkness, and the pain which our immunity gave this devilish forest.

I could not understand why Fred had so easily fallen a victim to the death, while I remained whole. He tried to explain that his brain was more receptive, more sensitive.

"Sensitive to what?" I asked.

But he did not know.

Dawn came at last, sweeping westward before it the web of darkness. From across the forest, and around us on all sides, the giant trees rustled in pain, suggesting the gnashing of millions of anguished teeth. And over the ridge to eastward came the smiling sun, lighting with clarity the branches of our wood.

Never was a day so long in coming, and never so welcome its arrival. In a half-hour our belongings were gathered, and we quickly drove to the open road.

"Fred, you remember our conversation of a couple of evenings ago?" I asked my companion, after some time of silence. "I'm wondering whether that couldn't apply here."

"Meaning that we were the victims of—hallucination? Then how do you account for this?" He raised his sleeve above his elbow, showing his arm. How well did I remember it! For there, under curling skin and red as a brand, was the print of my hand!

"I sensed, not felt, you grip me last night," said Fred. "There is our evidence."

"Yes," I answered, slowly. "We've got lots to think of, you and I."

And we rode together in silence.

When we reached home, it was not yet noon, but the brightness of the day had already wrought wonders with our perspective. I think that the human mind, far from being a curse, is the most merciful thing in the world. We live on a quiet, sheltered island of ignorance, and from the single current flowing by our shores we visualize the vastness of the black seas around us, and see—simplicity and safety. And yet, if only a portion of the cross-currents and whirling vortices of mystery and chaos would be revealed to our consciousness, we should immediately go insane.

But we can not see. When a single cross-current upsets the calm placidness of the visible sea, we refuse to believe. Our minds balk, and can not understand. And thus we arrive at that strange paradox: after an experience of comprehensible terror, the mind and body remain long upset; yet even the most terrible encounters with things unknown fade into insignificance in the light of clear day. We were soon about the prosaic task of preparing lunch, to satisfy seemingly insatiable appetites!

And yet we by no means forgot. The wound on Fred's arm healed quickly; in a week not even a scar remained. But we were changed. We had seen the cross-current, and—we knew. By daylight a swift recollection often brought nausea; and the nights, even with the lights left burning, were rife with horror. Our very lives seemed bound into the events of one night.

Yet, even so, I was not prepared for the shock I felt when, one night nearly a month later, Fred burst into the room, his face livid.

"Read this," he said in a husky whisper, and extended a crumpled newspaper to my hand. I reached for it, read where he had pointed.

MOUNTAINEER DIES

EZEKIEL WHIPPLE, lone mountaineer, aged 64, was found dead in his cabin yesterday by neighbors.

The post-mortem revealed a terrible state of putrefaction; medical men aver that death could not have occurred less than two weeks ago.

The examination by the coroner revealed no sign of foul play, yet local forces for law and order are working upon what may yet be a valuable clue. Jesse Layton, a near neighbor and close friend of the aged bachelor, states that he visited and held conversation with him the day preceding; and it is upon this statement that anticipation of possible arrest is based.

"God!" I cried. "Does it mean—"

"Yes! It's spreading—whatever it is. It's reaching out, crawling over the mountains. God knows to where it may finally extend."

"No. It is not a disease. It is alive. It's alive, Art! I tell you, I felt it; I *heard* it. I think it tried to talk to me."

For us there was no sleep that night. Every moment of our half-forgotten experience was relived a thousand times, every horror amplified by the darkness and our fears. We wanted to flee to some far country, to leave far behind us the terror we had felt. We wanted to stay and fight to destroy the destroyer. We wanted to plan; but—hateful thought—how could we plan to fight—nothing? We were as helpless as the old mountaineer....

And so, torn by these conflicting desires, we did what was to be expected—precisely nothing. We might even have slipped back into the even tenor of our lives had not news dispatches showed still further spread, and more death.

Eventually, of course, we told our story. But lowered glances and obvious embarrassment told us too well how little we were believed. Indeed, who could expect normal people of the year 1933, with normal experiences, to believe the obviously impossible? And so, to save ourselves, we talked no more, but watched in dread from the sidelines the slow, implacable growth.

It was midwinter before the first town fell in the way of the expanding circle. Only a mountain village of half a hundred inhabitants;

but the death came upon them one cold winter night—late at night, for there were no escapes—and smothered all in their beds. And when the next day visitors found and reported them, there was described the same terrible advanced state of putrefaction that had been present in all the other cases.

Then the world, apathetic always, began to believe. But, even so, they sought the easiest, the most natural explanation, and refused to recognize the possibilities we had outlined to them. Some new plague, they said, is threatening us, is ravaging our hill country. We will move away.... A few moved. But the optimists, trusting all to the physicians, stayed on. And we, scarce knowing why, stayed on with them.

Yes, the world was waking to the danger. The plague became one of the most popular topics of conversation. Revivalists predicted the end of the world. And the physicians, as usual, set to work. Doctors swarmed the infected district, in fear of personal safety examined the swollen corpses, and found—the bacteria of decay, and—the worms. They warned the natives to leave the surrounding country; and then, to avoid panic, they added encouragement.

"We have an inkling of the truth," they said, after the best manner of the detective agency. "It is hoped that we may soon isolate the deadly bacterium, and produce an immunizing serum."

And the world believed.... I, too, half believed, and even dared to hope.

"It is a plague," I said, "some strange new plague that is killing the country. We were there, first of all."

But "No," said Fred. "It is not a plague. I was there; I felt it; it talked to me. It is Black Magic, I tell you! What we need is, not medicine, but medicine men."

And I—I half believed him, too!

Spring came, and the encroaching menace had expanded to a circle ten miles in radius, with a point in the wood as a center. Slow enough, to be sure, but seemingly irresistible ... The quiet, lethal march of the disease, the *death*, as it was called, still remained a mystery—and a fear. And as week after week fled by with no good tidings from the physicians and men of science there assembled, my doubts grew stronger. Why, I asked, if it were a plague, did it never strike its victims during the day? What disease could strike down all life alike, whether animal or vegetable? It was not a plague, I decided; at least, I added, clutching the last thread of hope, not a normal plague.

"Fred," I said one day, "they can't stand fire—if you are right. This is your chance to prove that you are right. We'll burn the wood. We'll take kerosene. We'll burn the wood, and if you are right, the thing will die."

His face brightened. "Yes," he said, "we'll burn the wood, and—the thing will die. Fire saved me: I know it; you know it. Fire could never cure a disease; it could never make normal trees whisper and groan, and crack in agony. We'll burn the wood, and the thing will die."

So we said, and so we believed. And we set to work.

Four barrels of kerosene we took, and tapers, and torches. And on a clear, cold day in early March we set out in the truck. The wind snapped bitterly out of the north; our hands grew blue with chill in the open cab. But it was a clean cold. Before its pure sharpness, it was almost impossible to believe that we were heading toward filth and a barren country of death. And, still low in the east, the sun sent its bright yellow shafts over the already budding trees.

It was still early in the morning when we arrived at the edge of the slowly enlarging circle of death. Here the last victim, only a day or so earlier, had met his end. Yet, even without this last to tell us of its nearness, we could have judged by the absence of all life. The tiny buds we had noted earlier were absent; the trees remained dry and cold as in the dead of winter.

Why did not the people of the region heed the warnings and move? True, most of them had done so. But a few old mountaineers remained— and died one by one.

We drove on, up the rocky, precipitous trail, leaving the bustle and safety of the normal world behind us. Was I wrong in thinking a shade had come over the sun? Were not things a trifle darker? Still I drove on in silence.

A faint stench assailed my nostrils—the odor of death. It grew and it grew. Fred was pale; and, for that matter, so was I. Pale and weak.

"We'll light a torch," I said. "Perhaps this odor will die."

We lit a torch in the brightness of the day, then drove on.

Once we passed a pig-sty: white bones lay under the sun; the flesh

30

was decayed and eaten away entirely. What terror had killed them while they slept?

I could not now be mistaken: the shade was deepening. The sun was still bright, but weak, in some strange way. It shone doubtfully, vacillating, as if there were a partial eclipse.

But the valley was near. We passed the last mountain, passed the falling cabin of the mountaineer who was the first to die. We started the descent.

Sacrament Wood lay below us, not fresh and green as I had seen it first, years before, nor yet flashing with color as on our last trip the autumn before. It was cold, and obscured. A black cloud lay over it, a blanket of darkness, a rolling mist like that which is said to obscure the River Styx. It covered the region of death like a heavy shroud, and hid it from our probing eyes. Could I have been mistaken, or did I hear a broad whisper rising from the unhallowed wood of the holy name? Or did I feel something I could not hear?

But in one respect I could not be wrong. It was growing dark. The farther we moved down the rocky trail, the deeper we descended into this stronghold of death, the paler became the sun, the more obscured our passage.

"Fred," I said in a low voice, "they are hiding the sun. They are destroying the light. The wood will be dark."

"Yes," he answered. "The light hurts them. I could feel their pain and agony that morning as the sun rose; they cannot kill in the day. But now they are stronger, and are hiding the sun itself. The light hurts them, and they are destroying it."

We lit another torch and drove on.

When we reached the wood, the darkness had deepened, the almost palpable murk had thickened until the day had become as a moonlight night. But it was not a silver night. The sun was red; red as blood, shining on the accursed forest. Great red rings surrounded it, like the red rings of sleeplessness surrounding a diseased eye. No, the sun itself was not clean; it was weak, diseased, powerless as ourselves before the new terror. Its red glow mingled with the crimson of the torches, and lit up the scene around us with the color of blood.

We drove as far as solid ground would permit our passage—barely to the edge of the forest, where the wiry, scraggly growth of cedar and blackjack gave way to the heavy growth of taller, straighter oak. Then we abandoned our conveyance and stepped upon the rotting earth. And at this, more strongly it seemed than before, the stench of rottenness came over us. We were thankful that all animal matter had decayed entirely away; there only remained the acrid, penetrating odor of decaying plants; disagreeable, and powerfully suggestive to our already sharpened nerves, but endurable.... And it was warm, there in the death-ridden floor of the valley. In spite of the season of the year and the absence of the sun's warmth, it was not cold. The heat of decay, of fermentation, overcame the biting winds which occasionally swept down from the surrounding hills.

The trees were dead. Not only dead; they were rotten. Great limbs had crashed to the ground and littered the soggy floor. All smaller branches were gone, but the trees themselves remained upright, their naked limbs stretched like supplicating arms to the heavens as these martyrs of the wood stood waiting. Yet in even these massive trunks the worms crawled—and ate. It was a forest of death, a nightmare, fungous forest that cried out to the invaders, that sobbed in agony at the bright torches, and rocked to and fro in all its unholy rottenness.

Protected by our torches, we were immune to the forces of death that were rampant in the dark reaches of the wood, beyond our flaring light. But while they could not prey upon our bodies, they called, they drew upon our minds. Pictures of horror, of putridity and nightmare thronged our brains. I saw again my comrade as he had lain in his bed, over a half-year before; I thought of the mountain village, and of the three-score victims who had died there in one night.

We did not dare, we knew, to dwell on these things; we would go insane. We hastened to collect a pile of dead limbs. We grasped the dank, rotten things—limbs and branches which broke on lifting, or crumbled to dust between our fingers. At last, however, our heap was piled high with the driest, the firmest of them, and over all we poured a full barrel of kerosene. And as we lit the vast pile, and watched the flames roar high and higher, a sigh of pain, sorrow and impotent rage swept the field of death.

"The fire hurts them," I said. "While there is fire they cannot harm us; the forest will burn, and they will all die."

"But will the forest burn? They have dimmed the sun; they have even dimmed our torches. See! They should be brighter! Would the forest burn of itself, even if they let it alone? It is damp and rotten, and will not burn. See, our fire is burning out! We have failed."

Yes, we had failed. We were forced to admit it when, after two more trials, we were at last satisfied beyond any doubt that the forest could not be destroyed by fire. Our hearts had been strong with courage, but now fear haunted us, cold perspiration flooded our sick, trembling bodies as we sent the clattering truck hurtling up the rocky trail to safety. Our torches flared in the wind, and left a black trail of smoke behind us as we fled.

But, we promised ourselves, we would come again. We would bring many men, and dynamite. We would find where this thing had its capital, and we would destroy it.

And we tried. But again we failed.

There were no more deaths. Even the most obstinate moved from the stricken country when spring came and revealed the actual presence of the deadly circle. No one could doubt the mute testimony of the dead and dying trees that fell in its grip. Fifty, a hundred or two hundred feet in a night the circle spread; trees that one day were fresh and alive, sprouting with shoots of green, were the next day harsh and yellow. The death never retreated. It advanced during the nights; held its ground during the day. And at night again the fearful march continued.

A condition of terror prevailed over the populations in adjoining districts. The newspapers carried in their columns nothing but blasted hopes. They contained long descriptions of each new advance; long, technical theories of the scientists assembled at the front of battle; but no hope.

We pointed this out to the terror-ridden people, told them that in our idea lay the only chance of victory. We outlined to them our plan, pleaded for their assistance. But "No," they said. "The plague is spreading. It began in the wood, but it is out of the wood now. How would it help to burn the wood now? The world is doomed. Come with us, and live while you can. We must all die."

No, there was no one willing to listen to our plan. And so we went north, where the death, through its unfamiliarity and remoteness, had not yet disrupted society. Here the people, doubtful, hesitant, yet had faith in their men of science, still preserved order, and continued industry. But our idea received no welcome. "We trust the doctors," they said.

And none would come.

"Fred," I told him, "we have not yet failed. We will equip a large truck. No! We will take a tractor. We will do as we said. Take more kerosene, and dynamite; we will destroy it yet!"

It was our last chance; we knew that. If we failed now, the world was indeed doomed. And we knew that every day the death grew stronger, and we worked fast to meet it.

The materials we needed we hauled overland in the truck: more torches, dynamite, eight barrels of kerosene. We even took two guns. And then we loaded all these in an improvised trailer behind the caterpillar, and started out.

The wood was dark now, although it was not yet midday when we entered. Black as a well at midnight was the forest; our torches sent their flickering red a scant twenty feet through the obstinate murk. And through the shivering darkness there reached our ears a vast murmur, as of a million hives of bees.

How we chose a path I do not know; I tried to steer toward the loudest part of the roar, hoping that by so doing we would find the source itself of the scourge. And our going was not difficult. The tractor laid down its endless track, crushing to paste beneath it the dank, rotting wood which littered the forest floor. And from behind, over the smooth track crushed through the forest, lumbered the heavy trailer.

The gaunt, scarred trees, shorn of every limb, stood around us like weird sentinels pointing the way. And, if possible, the scene grew more desolate the farther we proceeded; the creaking trunks standing pole-like seemed more and more rotten; the odor of death around us, not the sickening odor of decay, but the less noxious yet more penetrating smell of rottenness complete, grew even more piercing. And *It* called and drew. From out of the darkness it crept into our brains, moved them, changed them to do its will. We did not know. We only knew that the odor around us no longer nauseated; it became the sweetest of perfumes to our nostrils. We only knew that the fungus-like trees pleased our eyes, seemed to fill and satisfy some long-hidden esthetic need. In my mind there grew a picture of a perfect world: damp, decayed vegetation and succulent flesh—rotting flesh upon which to feed. Over all the earth, it seemed, this picture extended; and I shouted aloud in ecstasy.

At the half-involuntary shout, something flashed upon me, and I knew that these thoughts were not my own, but were foisted upon me from without. With a shriek, I reached to the torch above and bathed my arms in the living flame; I grasped the taper from its setting and brandished it in my comrade's face. The cleansing pain raced through my veins and nerves; the picture faded, the longing passed away; I was myself again. If only we had obeyed the call, gone forth into the shrilling forest! Yet, always after that, we could feel the obscene mind toying with ours, trying still to bend us to its purpose. And I shuddered when I recalled that those thoughts could well have been those of a worm!

Then, suddenly, above the roar from without and the steady beat of our engine, we heard a human chant. I idled the motor, jerked out the gears. Clear on our ears it smote now, a chant in a familiar, yet strangely altered tongue. Life! In this region of death? It was impossible! The chant ceased, and the hum among the poles of trees doubled in intensity. Someone, or something, rose to declaim. I strained my ears to hear, but it was unnecessary; clear and loud through the noisome darkness rose its high semi-chant:

"Mighty is our lord, the Worm. Mightier than all the kings of heaven and of earth is the Worm. The gods create; man plans and builds; but the Worm effaces their handiwork.

"Mighty are the planners and the builders; great their works and their possessions. But at last they must fall heir to a narrow plot of earth; and even that, forsooth, the Worm will take away.

"This is the House of the Worm; his home which none may destroy; the home which we, his protectors, have made for him.

"O Master! On bended knee we give thee all these things! We give unto thee man and his possessions! We give unto thee the life of the earth to be thy morsel of food! We give unto thee the earth itself to be thy residence!

"Mighty, oh mighty above all the kings of heaven and of earth is our lord and master, the Worm, to whom Time is naught!"

Sick with horror and repulsion, Fred and I exchanged glances. There was life! God knew what sort, but life, and human! Then, there in that forest of hell, with the odor, sight, and sound of death around us, we smiled! I swear we smiled! We were given a chance to fight; to fight something tangible. I raced the motor, snapped the machine into gear and pushed on.

And one hundred feet farther I stopped, for we were upon the worshippers! Half a hundred of them there were, crouching and kneeling, yes, even wallowing in the putrefaction and filth around them. And the sounds, the cries to which they gave vent as our flaming torches smote full upon their sightless, staring eyes! Only a madman could recall and place upon the printed page the litanies of hate and terror which they flung into our faces. There are vocal qualities peculiar to men, and vocal qualities peculiar to beasts; but nowhere this side of the pit of hell itself can be heard the raucous cries that issued from their straining throats as we grasped our tapers and raced toward them. A few moments only did they stand defiantly in our way; the pain of the unaccustomed light was too much for their sensitive eyes. With shrill shouts or terror they turned and fled. And we looked about its, upon the weltering filth with which we were surrounded, and—smiled again!

For we saw their idol! Not an idol of wood, or stone, or of any clean, normal thing. It was a heaped-up grave! Massive, twenty feet long and half as high, it was covered with rotting bones and limbs of trees. The earth, piled there in the gruesome mound, shivered and heaved as from some foul life within. Then, half buried in filth, we saw the headstone—itself a rotting board, leaning askew in its shallow setting. And on it was carved only the line *The House of the Worm*.

The house of the worm! A heaped-up grave. And the cult of blackness and death had sought to make of the world one foul grave, and to cover even that with a shroud of darkness!

With a shriek of rage I stamped my foot upon the earth piled there. The crust was thin, so thin that it broke through, and nearly precipitated me headlong into the pit itself; only a violent wrench backward prevented me from falling into the pitching mass of—worms! White, wriggling, the things squirmed there under our blood-red, flaring light, writhed with agony in the exquisite torture brought to them by the presence of cleansing flame. The house of the worm, indeed....

Sick with loathing, we worked madly. The roar of the alien forest
had risen to a howl—an eldritch gibber which sang in our ears and drew
at our brains as we toiled. We lit more torches, bathed our hands in
the flame, and then, in defiance of the malign will, we demolished the
quivering heap of earth which had the form of a grave. We carried barrel
after barrel of fuel, and poured it upon the squirming things, which were
already spreading out, rolling like an ocean of filth at our very feet. And
then, forgetting the machine which was to take us to safety, I hurled the
box of black powder upon them, watched it sink through the mass until
out of sight, then applied the torch. And fled.

"Art! The tractor—the rest of the oil we need to light our way out—"

I laughed insanely, and ran on.

A hundred yards away, we stopped and watched the spectacle. The
flames, leaping fifty feet into the air, illumined the forest around us,
pushed back the thick unnatural gloom into the heavy darkness behind
us. Unseen voices that howled madly and mouthed hysterical gibberish
tore at our very souls in their wild pleading; so tangible were they that
we felt them pull at our bodies, sway them back and forth with the
unholy dance of the rocking trees. From the pit of foulness where the
flames danced brightest, a dense cloud of yellow smoke arose; a vast
frying sound shrilled through the wood, was echoed back upon us by the
blackness around. The tractor was enveloped in flames, the last barrel of
oil spouting fire. And then—

There came a deep, heavy-throated roar; the pulpy ground beneath
our feet waved and shook; the roaring flames, impelled by an irresistible
force beneath them, rose simultaneously into the air, curved out in long
sweeping parabolas of lurid flame, and scattered over the moaning forest
floor. The powder!

The house of the worm was destroyed; and simultaneously with its
destruction the howling voices around us died into a heavy-throated
whisper of silence. The black mist of darkness above and about shook for
a moment like a sable silk, caught gropingly at us, then rolled back over
the ruined trees and revealed—the sun!

The sun, bright in all his noonday glory, burst out full above us,
warming our hearts with a golden glow.

"See, Art!" my companion whispered, "the forest is burning! There is nothing now to stop it, and everything will be destroyed."

It was true. From a thousand tiny places flames were rising and spreading, sending queer little creepers of flame to explore for further progress. The fire, scattered by the explosion, was taking root.

We turned, we walked swiftly into the breath of the warm south wind which swept down upon us; we left the growing fire at our backs and moved on. A half-hour later, after we had covered some two miles of fallen forest and odorous wasteland, we paused to look back. The fire had spread over the full width of the valley, and was roaring northward. I thought of the fifty refugees who had fled—also to the north.

"Poor devils!" I said. "But no doubt they are already dead; they could not endure for long the brightness of the sun."

And so ends our story of what is perhaps the greatest single menace that has ever threatened mankind. Science pondered, but could make nothing of it; in fact, it was long before we could evolve an explanation satisfactory even to ourselves.

We had searched vainly through every known reference book on the occult, when an old magazine suddenly gave us the clue: it recalled to our minds a half-forgotten conversation which has been reproduced at the beginning of this narrative.

In some strange way, this Cult of the Worm must have organized for the worship of death, and established their headquarters there in the valley. They built the huge grave as a shrine, and by the over-concentration of worship of their fanatical minds, caused a physical manifestation to appear within it as the real result of their thought. And what suggestion of death could be more forceful than its eternal accompaniment— the worms of death and the bacteria of decay? Perhaps their task was lessened by the fact that death is always a reality, and does not need so great a concentration of will to produce.

At any rate, from that beginning, that center, they radiated thought-waves strong enough to bring their influence over the region where they were active; and as they grew stronger and stronger, and as their minds grew more and more powerful through the fierce mental concentration, they spread out, and even destroyed light itself. Perhaps they received many recruits, also, to strengthen their ranks, as we ourselves nearly succumbed; perhaps, too, the land once conquered was watched over by spirits invoked to their control, so that no further strength on their part was required to maintain it. That would explain the weird noises heard from all parts of the forest, which persisted even after the worshippers themselves had fled.

And as to their final destruction, I quote a line from the old volume where we first read of the theory: *"If this be true, the only way to destroy it is to cease to believe."* When the mock grave, their great fetish, was destroyed, the central bonds which held their system together were broken. And when the worshippers themselves perished in the flames, all possibility of a recurrence of the terror died with them.

This is our explanation, and our belief. But Fred and I do not wish to engage in scientific debate; we only wish an opportunity to forget the chaotic experience which has so disrupted our lives.

Reward? We had our reward in the destruction of the vile thing we fought; yet to that satisfaction an appreciative world has added its wealth and its favor. These things we are thankful for and enjoy; what man does not? But we feel that not in adulation nor yet in pleasure lies our ultimate recovery. We must work, must forget the experience only by assiduous toil; we are stamping the horror, if not from our minds, at least from our immediate consciousness. In time, perhaps....

And yet we cannot entirely forget. Only this morning, while walking in the fields, I came across the dead carcass of a wild beast lying in a furrow; and in its thin, decaying body was another life—a nauseous, alien life of putrescence and decay.

FAR BELOW

Robert Barbour Johnson

With a roar and a howl the thing was upon us, out of total darkness. Involuntarily I drew back as its headlights passed and every object in the little room rattled from the reverberations. Then the power-car was by, and there was only the "klackety-klack, klackety-klack" of wheels and lighted windows flickering past like bits of film on a badly-connected projection machine. I caught glimpses of occupants briefly; bleak-eyed men sitting miserably on hard benches; a pair of lovers oblivious to the hour's lateness and all else; an old bearded Jew in a black cap, sound asleep; two Harlem Negroes grinning; conductors here and there, too, their uniforms black splotches against the blaze of car-lights. Then red tail-lamps shot by and the roar died to an earthquake rumble far down the track.

"The Three-One Express," my friend said quietly, from the Battery. "On time to the minute, too. It's the last, you know—until nearly dawn."

He spoke briefly into a telephone, saying words I could not catch, for the racket of the train was still in my ears. I occupied the interval by staring about me. There was so much to be seen in the little room, such a strange diversity of apparatus—switches and coils and curious mechanisms, charts and graphs and piles of documents; and, dominating all, that great black board on which a luminous worm seemed to crawl, inching along past the dotted lines labeled "49th Street," "52nd Street," "58th Street," "60th ..."

"A new wrinkle, that!" my friend said. He had put down his phone and was watching the board with me. "Lord! I don't dare think what it cost to install! It's not just a chart, you know. It actually records! Invisible lights—the sort of things that open speakeasy doors and rich men's garages. Pairs of them spaced approximately every twenty-five yards along five miles of subway tunnel! Figure that out on paper, and the total you'll get will seem hardly believable. And yet the city passed the appropriation for them without a murmur. It was one of the last things Mayor Walker put up before his resignation. 'Gentlemen,' he said to the Finance Board, 'it doesn't matter what you think about *me!* But this measure must go through!' And it did. There wasn't a murmur of protest, though the city was almost broke at the time … What's the matter, man? You're looking queer."

"I'm *feeling* queer!" I said. "Do you mean to say the thing goes that far back? To Walker's time?"

He laughed. It was a strange laugh, that died eerily amid the dying echoes of the train far down the tunnel.

"Good Lord!" he gasped. "To his time—man, Walker hadn't served his first term as mayor when this thing started! It goes back to World War days—and even before that. The wreck of the train, I recall, passed as a German spy plot to keep us from going in with the Allies. The newspapers howled bloody murder about alleged 'confessions' and evidence they claimed they had. We let 'em howl, of course. Why not? America was as good as in the war anyhow, by then. And if we'd told the people of New York City what really wrecked that subway train—well, the horrors of Chateau-Thierry and Verdun and all the rest of them put together wouldn't have equaled the shambles that rioting mobs would have made of this place! People just couldn't stand the thought of it, you know. They'd go mad if they knew what was down here—far below."

The silence was worse than the roar had been, I thought—the strange echoing, somehow pregnant silence of empty vastness. Only the "drip, drip" of water from some subterranean leak broke it—that and the faint crackling noise the indicator made as its phosphorescent crawling hinted at "68th Street," "72nd," "78th …"

"Yes," my friend said slowly. "They'd go mad if they knew. And sometimes I wonder why we don't go mad down here—we who *do* know, and have to face the horror down here night after night and year after year—I think it's only because we don't really face it that we get by, you know, because we never quite define the thing in our own minds, objectively. We just sort of let things hang in the air, you might say. We don't speak of what we're guarding against, by name. We just call it 'Them,' or 'one of Them,' you know—take Them for granted just as we took the enemy overseas, as something that's just down here and has to be fought. I think if we ever really did let our minds get to brooding on what they are, it'd be all over for us! Human flesh and blood couldn't stand it, you know—couldn't stand it!"

He brooded, staring out into the tunnel's darkness. The indicator crackled faintly on the wall. "92nd Street," "98th," "101st ..."

"Beyond 120th Street things are pretty safe," I heard my friend's voice as I watched. "When the train reaches that point you'll see a green light flash 'all clear,' though that doesn't mean absolute safety, you understand. It's just what we've established as the farthest reach of Their activities. They may extend them at any time, although so far They haven't done so. There seems to be something circumscribed about their minds, you know. They're creatures of habit. That must be what it is that's kept Them in this one little stretch of tunnel, with all the vast interlocking network of New York's subway system to rove in if they chose. I can't think of any other explanation, unless you want to get into the supernatural and say it's because they're 'bound' to this particular locality, by some sort of mystic laws; perhaps because it's lower than the other tunnels—chiseled far down into the basic bedrock of Manhattan, and so near to the East River you can almost hear the water lapping on quiet nights. Or maybe it's just the awful dankness of the tunnel here, the fungoid moisture and miasmic darkness that suits Them. At all events they don't come up anywhere else except along this stretch. And we've got the lights, and the patrol cars, and three way-stations like this one, with ten men on constant duty from dark till dawn—oh yes, my boy! It's quite a little army I command down here in the night watches—an army of the Unburied Dead, you might say; or an army of the Eternally Damned.

"I've actually had one of my men go mad, you know! Two others had to be placed in sanitariums for a while, but they got over it and are serving here still. But this fellow—well, we had to machine-gun him down like a dog finally, or he'd have got one of us! That was before we got the 'dark lights' placed, you see, and he was able to hide out in the tunnel for days without our being able to find him. We'd hear him howl sometimes as we patrolled, and see his eyes shining just as Their eyes do in the darkness; so we knew that he was quite 'gone.' So when we finally ran him down we killed him—just like that. No bones made about it. 'Put-put-put!' and that was the end. We buried him down in the tunnel, too, and now the trains run over him as he lies. Oh, there was nothing irregular about the business! We filled out full Departmental reports, and got the consent of his relatives, and so on; only we just couldn't take the poor fellow above-ground and run risks of people seeing him before interment. You see, there were certain ... alterations. I don't want to dwell on it, but his face—well, the change was just beginning, of course, but it was quite unmistakable; quite dehumanizing, you know. There would have been some excitement up there, I'm afraid, just at sight of that face! And there were other details—things I only found out when I dissected his body. But I think I'd rather not go into them either, old boy, if you don't mind ...

"The whole point is, we have to be rather careful down here, all of us in the 'Special Detail.' That's why we have such unusual working conditions. We wear police uniforms, of course, but we aren't subject to ordinary police discipline. Lord! What would an above-ground 'cop' make of having every other night off and every day all to himself, and with a salary that—well, a corporal down here gets as much as does an Inspector up there!

"But, at that, I think we earn our pay ...

"I know *I* do. Of course I can't tell you what my salary is—they made me promise never to disclose it when they hired me from the Natural History Museum back in—well, I don't like to think about how long ago that was! I was Professor Gordon Craig in those days, you know, instead of Inspector Craig of N.Y.P.D. And I'd just returned from Carl Akeley's first African expedition after gorillas. That was why they brought the Thing to me for examination, you see, after that first big wreck in the subway that'd only been opened less than a year. They'd found it pinned down in the wreckage, screaming in agony from their lights on its dead-white eyeballs. Indeed, it seemed to have died from the lights as much as from anything else. Organically it was sound enough, save for a broken bone or two.

"Well, they brought it to me, because I was supposed to be the museum's leading authority on apes. And I examined it—believe me, I examined it, old boy! I went for six days and nights without sleep or even rest, analyzing that dead corpse down to its last rag and bone and hank of hair!

"No scientist on this earth ever had a chance like that before, and I was making the best of it. I found out all there was to be found before I collapsed over my laboratory table and had to be taken to the hospital.

"Of course long before that I had told them the thing wasn't an ape. There was vaguely anthropoid structure, all right; and the blood corpuscles were almost human—quite shockingly so. But the head and the spade-like appendages and the muscular development were quite unlike any beast or man on this earth. Indeed, the thing had never been on this earth! There was no doubt of that! It would have died above ground in half a minute, just like an angleworm in the sun.

"And I'm afraid my report to the authorities didn't help them much. After all, even a fellow scientist would have found it a bit difficult to reconcile my classification of 'some sort of giant, carrion-feeding, subterranean mole' with my ravings about 'canine and simian developments of members' and my absurd insistence on 'startlingly humanoid cranial development, and brain convolutions indicating a degree of intelligence that—'

"Well, there's no use going into all that now! I firmly expected them to order me up before a Sanity Commission when I reported my findings. Instead, they offered me a position as head of the 'Special Subway Detail,' at a salary that was, to say the least, fantastic. It was more a month than I'd been getting a year from the museum.

"Because, you see, they'd deduced much of the stuff for themselves without needing me to tell them! They had facts they'd deliberately withheld from me, not wanting to influence my report. They knew that that train had been deliberately derailed—the mutilated track proved that beyond all doubt. No less than three ties had been taken up and laid some distance away down the tunnel. And the condition of the earth about the wrecked cars showed conclusively that extensive mining and sapping had taken place there—it was like a gigantic mole-hill, only worse. And while I'd been analyzing stomach fluids and body tissue to try to find out what my subject fed upon, they'd been burying, secretly and with most elaborate precautions, the half-desiccated corpses of half a dozen men and women and children who—well, they hadn't died in the wreck, old boy! They hadn't died in the wreck, any more than had that screaming thing that hid its eyes from the lights when they found it pinned in the wreckage where it had been caught while trying to drag a dead victim out—God! What a hideous shambles that place must have been before the wrecking-crews got there.

"Mercifully, of course, there was total darkness. The poor devils who were merely injured never knew what charnel horrors were going on in the Stygian depths about them—nor cared, no doubt, in their agony! A few of them gibbered afterward about green eyes, and claws that raked their faces—but of course all that was set down to delirium! Even one man who had his arm chewed half off never knew—surgeons amputated the rest immediately and told him when he regained consciousness that he'd lost it in the wreck. He's still walking the streets today, blissfully ignorant of what almost happened to him that night.

"Oh, you'd be surprised, old boy, how you can hush a thing up if you've got a whole city administration behind you! And believe me, we *did* hush matters up. No newspaper reporter was ever allowed to see the wreck—freedom of the press or no freedom of the press! The Government wanted to appoint a commission to investigate—we squelched it! And by the time the crews had cleaned out the smashed train and removed the last victim, the Special Subway Detail had gone into action. And it's been on steady duty ever since—for the last twenty-odd years!

"We had a terrible time at first, of course. All these modern improvements weren't available then. All we had were lanterns and guns and hand-cars—with which to patrol nearly five miles of tunnel. It was Mrs. Partington sweeping back the sea all over again—only worse. A handful of puny mortals against Hell itself, in the eternal darkness of these long gloomy tunnels far below the city.

"There were no more wrecks after we took over, though; I'll say that much. Oh, an accident or two. How could we prevent them? We did everything we could think of! How we worked in those early years! Once we sank a shaft fifty feet deep in the earth, where we'd seen queer disturbances beside the train-tracks and heard queerer sounds. And once we blocked up both ends of the tunnel for a mile stretch and filled it with poison gas. And once we dynamited—but why go on? It was all useless, utterly useless. We just couldn't get to grips with anything tangible. Oh, we'd hear sounds sometimes on our long dismal patrols in the darkness, our little lanterns mere pin-pricks of light in these vast old concrete vaults. We'd catch glimpses of glinting eyes far off, find fresh earth piled up where only a moment before there'd been hard-packed cinders and gravel. Once in a while we'd fire our guns at something whitish and half seen, but there'd be only a tittering laugh in answer—a laugh as mirthless and savage as that of a hyena, dying away in the earth....

"A thousand times I was tempted to chuck the whole thing, to get back above ground to sunshine and sanity and forget the charnel horrors of this mad Nyarlathotep-world far underneath. And then I'd get to thinking of all those helpless men and women and children riding the trains unsuspecting through the haunted dark, with Evil out of the primeval dawn burrowing beneath them for their destruction, and—well, I just couldn't go, that's all. I stayed and did my duty, as the rest did, year after year. It's been a strange career for a man of science, and certainly one I never dreamed I'd be following during all the years I prepared myself for museum work. And yet I flatter myself that it's been rather a socially useful career at that; perhaps more so than stuffing animals for dusty museum cases, or writing monstrous textbooks that no one ever bothers to read. For I've a science of my own down here, you know: the science of keeping millions of dollars' worth of subway tunnels swept clean of horror, and of safeguarding the lives of half the population of the world's largest city.

"And then, too, I've opportunities for research here which most of my colleagues above ground would give their right arms for, the opportunity to study an absolutely unknown form of life; a grotesquerie so monstrous that even after all these years of contact with it I sometimes doubt my own senses even now, although the horror is authentic enough, if you come right down to it. It's been attested in every country in the world, and by every people. Why, even the Bible has references to the 'ghouls that burrow in the earth', and even today in modern Persia they hunt down with dogs and guns, like beasts, strange tomb-dwelling creatures neither quite human nor quite beast; and in Syria and Palestine and parts of Russia ...

"But as for this particular place—well, you'd be surprised how many records we've found, how many actual evidences of the Things we've uncovered from Manhattan Island's earliest history, even before the white men settled here. Ask the curator of the Aborigines Museum out on Riverside Drive about the burial customs of Island Indians a thousand years ago—customs perfectly inexplicable unless you take into consideration what they were guarding against. And ask him to show you that skull, half human and half canine, that came out of an Indian mound as far away as Albany, and those ceremonial robes of aboriginal shamans plainly traced with drawings of whitish spidery Things burrowing through conventionalized tunnels; and doing other things, too, that show the Indian artists must have known Them and Their habits. Oh yes, it's all down there in black and white, once we had the sense to read it!

"And even after white men came—what about the early writings of the old Dutch settlers, what about Jan Van der Rhees and Woulter Van Twiller? Even some of Washington Irving's writings have a nasty twist to them, if you once realize it! And there are some mighty queer passages in 'The History of the City of New York'—mention of guard patrols kept for no rational purpose in early streets at night, *particularly in the region of cemeteries;* of forays and excursions in the lightless dark, and flintlocks popping, and graves hastily dug and filed in before dawn woke the city to life …

"And then the modern writers—Lord! There's a whole library of them on the subject. One of them, a great student of the subject, had almost as much data on Them from his reading as I'd gleaned from my years of study down here. Oh, yes; I learned a lot from Lovecraft—and he got a lot from me, too! That's where the—well, what you might call the *authenticity* came from in some of his yarns that attracted the most attention! Oh, of course he had to soft-pedal the strongest parts of it— just as you're going to have to do if you ever mention this in your own writings! But even with the worst played down, there's still enough horror and nightmare in it to blast a man's soul, if he lets himself think on what goes on *down there,* below the blessed sanity of the earth's mercifully concealing crust. Far below …

"We've figured out—we who've been studying Them all this time, that

They must have been pretty numerous once. No wonder the Indians sold this place so cheaply! You'd sell your home cheaply, too, if it were fairly overrun with monstrous noxious vermin that—but with civilization's coming they were decimated, killed off, pogromed against, blasted with fire and steel by men whose utter ruthlessness sprang from soul-shuddering detestation, who slew and kept silent about their slaying, lest their fellow men think them mad—until finally the blasted remnant of the Things went far underground, burrowed down like worms to charnel depths that—well, we daren't conjecture just where, but we think that there's some fault in the basic bedrock of the Island, some monstrous cavern whose edge this lowest of all the subway tunnels taps, and which lets them through somehow into the tubes ...

"Oh, it took us a long time to find all that out. At first we thought we had to patrol the whole subway system of the city! We had guards even out under the river, and over in Brooklyn and Queens. We were even afraid they'd get into upper levels of the tunnels, perhaps into the very deserted streets of Manhattan during the pre-dawn hours. We had half the police department down here in those days, even the mounted force. Yes, indeed; though God knows what even a trained police horse would do if it ever came face to face with one of those things! But horses were faster than the hand-cars we used then, and could cover more territory.

"But as time went on we got things pretty well localized. It's only in this one stretch of tunnel that the danger is, and only here in certain hours of the night. Don't ask me why they never come up in daylight; for it's always night down here, you know, hundreds of feet below the surface. Maybe it's the constant passage of the trains—they shuttle by at two-minute intervals all day long, you know, and until the Broadway theatres close at night. Only for about four hours of the night is there a lull when long miles of tunnel are lifeless and deserted and silent, when anything could come and go at will in them and not be seen.

"And so it's only during these hours that we really worry, you see. It's only now that we're vigilant and ready. Although of course it's no longer warfare, you understand. We hunt them now, they don't hunt us anymore! We run them down howling with terror, kill them or capture them as we will—oh yes, I said capture! A half-dozen times we've had a sort of mad 'Bronx Zoo' of our own down here—or perhaps it would be more accurate to say a living 'Madame Tussaud's Chamber of Horrors.' I have cages in my laboratory, and there have been times when it seemed judicious for influential people above ground to—well, to realize just how important is the work we're doing down here! So when we have a really stubborn skeptic to our program we'd take him in there, hand him a flashlight and let him train it himself on what was prisoned there in total darkness—and then we'd stand by to catch him as he fainted! Oh, a lot of city officials and politicians have been down here. Why not? They couldn't possibly speak of the experience afterward—they'd just be locked up as lunatics if they did! And it made them much more liberal about funds. Our menagerie was a great success, only we just couldn't keep it going for very long at a time! We'd get so soul-sick at the very proximity of the creatures that we'd have to kill them finally. There was just no putting up with them for any length of time!

"Oh, it's not so much the appearance of the Things, or even what they eat—we got an unlimited supply of *that* from the city morgue; and to anyone who's spent half his life in dissecting-rooms, as I have, it might be a lot worse. But there's a sort of cosmic horror the Things exude that—well, it's quite beyond description. You just can't breathe the same air with them, live together in the same sane world! And in the end we'd have to gun them and throw them back underground to their friends and neighbors—who were waiting for them, apparently. At least we've opened the shallow graves a few days later and there'd be only a gnawed bone or two there....

"And then, of course, we kept them alive in order to study their habits. I've filled two volumes with notes for my successors who'll carry on the fight when I'm gone—oh, yes, old boy! It'll always have to be carried on, I fear! There's no possibility of ever really wiping them out, you know. All we can do is hold our own. The fight will go on so long as this particular tunnel is occupied. And can't you just see the City Fathers consenting to abandon twenty million dollars' worth of subway tunnels for nothing? 'I'm sorry, gentlemen; but, you see, the place is infested with—' God! What a laughingstock anyone would be who even suggested that—above ground! Why, even on our own furloughs, when we walk sunlit streets among our fellow men, with God's own blue sky above and God's own clean air about us—even *we* wonder whether all this foulness isn't just a bad dream! It's hard, up there, to realize what can go on down in the crepuscular earth, the mad gnawing eternal darkness far below—Hello!"

The telephone was ringing.

Somehow I didn't listen as he spoke briefly into it, perhaps because I was listening to something else—to a faint crackling from that great blackboard on the wall, where one little light (no glowing worm this time, but only one minute spark) kept flicking oddly on and off and on again. "79th Street" it marked, over and over. "79th Street—79th—"

My friend hung up the phone at length, and stood up. "Queer," he said softly. "Very queer indeed! The first in months; and tonight, now, while we were talking. It makes one wonder, you know—about those supernatural telepathic powers that they're said to have …"

Something went past in the tunnel outside, something that moved so fast that I could scarcely make it out; just a little low platform on four wheels, with no visible engine to propel it. Yet it scudded along with the speed of a racing car. Uniformed men rode the bucking thing, crouching with glinting objects in their hands.

"Riot Car Number 1!" my friend said, grimly. "Our own version of the 'squad automobiles' above ground. Just one of the little electric hand-cars used in subway construction—but 'souped up' by our engineers until it'll do nearly eighty miles an hour. It could traverse the entire sector in less than five minutes, if it had to. But it doesn't, of course. Another one, also with machine-gunners aboard, left 105th Street at the same time. They'll meet somewhere along the tunnel's length—with the—er, disturbance in between. Let's listen to them!"

He crossed the room to the strange apparatus, threw switches and adjusted dials. There was a burring and crackling from what looked like an old-fashioned radio amplifier that stood on one of the cabinets.

"Microphones every hundred feet along the tunnel!" said my friend. "Another small fortune to install, of course; but another great step forward in our efficiency. A man listens all night long at a switchboard—and you'd be surprised to know what he hears sometimes! We have to change operators pretty often. Ah! there we are. Microphone Number 290—approximately a thousand feet below one of the busiest corners, even at this hour of the night, in all a great metropolis. And—listen! Hear that?"

"That" was a sound that brought me out of my chair, a strange high tittering, blasphemously off key, that merged into a growl and a moan....

"There we are!" my friend grated. "One of them, certainly— perhaps more than one. Hear that scratching, and the rustle of the gravel? All unsuspecting, of course, that they're broadcasting their presence; unaware that we modern human beings have got ourselves a few 'supernatural' powers of our own, nowadays; and unaware that, from both directions, death is sweeping down upon them on truckling wheels. But a little moment more and—ah! hear that shriek? That howling? That means they've sighted one of the cars! They're fleeing madly along the tunnel now—the voices get fainter. And now—yes! Now they double back. The other car! They're trapped, caught between them. No time to dig, to burrow down into their saving Mother Earth like the vermin they are. No, no, you devils! We've got you! Got you! Hear 'em yell, hear 'em shriek in agony! That's the lights, you know. Blazing searchlights trained on dark-accustomed bodies; burning, searing, withering them like actual blazing heat! And now 'Brrr-rat-tat-tat!' That's our machine-guns going into action—silenced guns, with Maxims on them so that the echoes won't carry to upper levels and make men ask questions—but throwing slugs of lead, for all that, into cringing white bodies and flattened white skulls.... Shriek! Shriek, you beasts from Hell! Shriek, you monsters from the charnel depths! Shriek on, and see what good it does you. You're dead! *Dead!* DEAD— Well, you blasted fool, what are you staring at?"

To save my life I couldn't have answered him. I couldn't look away from his blazing eyes, from his body crouched as if he would spring at me across the room, from his teeth bared in a bestial snarl ...

For a long moment that tableau held. Then suddenly he dropped into a chair, flung his hands up over his face. I stood regarding him, my mind sickly ticking off details. God! Why had I not seen them before. That lengthening of jaw, that flattening of forehead and cranium—no human head could be shaped like that!

At last he spoke, not looking up. "I know!" he said softly. "I've felt the change coming on me for a long time now. It's coming over all of us, bit by bit, but on me the worst, for I've been here the longest.

That's why I almost never go above ground any more, even on leave. The lights are dim down here. But I wouldn't dare let even you see my face in sunlight!

"Twenty-five years, you see—twenty-five long dragging years down here in Hell itself. It was bound to leave a mark, of course. I was prepared for that. But, oh, Great Powers above! If I'd for one instant dreamed what it was to be! Worse, oh, how much worse than any mark of the beast! ...

"And it's spiritual, you know, as well as physical. I get ... cravings, sometimes, down here in the night's loneliness; thought and charnel desires that would blast your very soul if I were to whisper them to you. And they'll get worse, I know, and worse until at last I run mad in the tunnel like that poor devil I told you about and my men shoot me down like a dog as they already have orders to do if—

"And yet the thing interests me, I'll admit; it interests me scientifically, even though it horrifies my very soul, even though it damns me forever. For it shows how They may have come about—*must* have come about, in fact, in the world's dim dawn; perhaps never quite human, of course, perhaps never Neanderthal or even Piltdown; something even lower, closer linked to the primeval beast, but that when driven underground, into caves and then beneath them by Man's coming, retrograded century by uncounted century down to the worm-haunted darkness—just as we poor devils are retrograding down here from very contact with them—until at last none of us will ever be able again to walk above in the blessed sunlit air among our fellow men—"

With a roar and a howl the thing was upon us, out of total darkness. Instinctively I drew back as its headlights passed; every object in the little room rattled from the reverberation. Then the power-car was by, and there was only the "klackety-klack, klackety-klack" of wheels and lighted windows flicking by like bits of film on a badly-connected projection machine.

"The Four-Fifteen Express," he said heavily, "from the Bronx. Safe and sound, you'll notice, its occupants all unsuspecting of how they were safeguarded; of how they'll always be safeguarded ... but at what a cost! At what an awful cost!

"The Four-Fifteen Express. That means it's dawn, you know, in the city overhead. Rays of the rising sun are gilding the white skyscrapers of Manhattan; a whole great city begins to wake to morning life.

"But there's no dawn for us down here, of course. There'll never be a dawn for poor lost souls down here in the eternal dark, far, far below...."

SPAWN OF THE GREEN ABYSS

C. HALL THOMPSON

I

I am not writing this to save my life. When I have set down, in the sanity of plain English, the strange story of Heath House, this manuscript will be sealed in an envelope, to be opened only after my execution. Perhaps then the accounts that have filled the papers during my imprisonment and trial will be more easily understood. Today, in his effective baritone, the attorney-for-the-State told a mixed jury: "This man, Doctor James Arkwright, is the cold-blooded murderer of his wife, Cassandra, and her unborn child. You have seen the evidence, ladies and gentlemen; you have seen the murder gun. The State and the voice of the dead woman demand that this killer pay the extreme penalty." It was a very forceful plea; I could not have asked better. You see, I want to die. That is why this will not be read until the prison medic his pronounced me dead of a broken neck. If it were read while I lived, I might never be granted the release, the nothingness of immediate death; instead, I should spend endless, remembering years in the State Asylum for the Criminally Insane.

Do not misunderstand me. No feeling of remorse prompts me to seek forgetfulness. Should all this happen again—God forbid!—I know I should do the same. I destroyed Cassandra because it was the only thing left to do. Undoubtedly that sounds callous, but when I have told the entire, horrible story, it will seem the inevitable conclusion of a sane man. For, I am sane. There were times when I doubted my senses during those ghastly months on Kalesmouth Strand, but, now, I can only say I am convinced. I know what I saw and heard, and I pray God no other mortal will ever be cursed with such a revelation. There are things beyond the veil of human understanding, strange, antediluvian monstrosities that stalk the shadows, preying on dark, lost minds, waiting at the rim of the Great Abyss to claim their own. These are the things I must escape. And, for the mind that has come to realize their existence, the only avenue of retreat lies through the quiet labyrinths of death.

Haunting, half-facetious dribblings of truth have seeped into the feature stories which various local newspapers ran on the trial. The Kenicott *Examiner* mentions briefly the strange manner in which Lazarus Heath died; a precocious young reporter who visited ancient Heath House in Kalesmouth makes note of the nauseous effluvia that hung like a caul over the staircase, leading to the chamber where I shot my wife; he mentions, too, a trail of dried sea brine which streaked the floor of the entrance-hall, and the carpeting of that same stairway. Those were only thoughtless ripples on the loathsome, scummed surface of abominable truth. They did not touch upon the fluting, hypnotic music that echoed in those decadent halls; they did not dare to dream of the slobbering, gelatinous horror that seethed by night from sightless, watery depths to reclaim its own. These are the things of which only I may speak; the others who witnessed them are mercifully dead.

In the night, lying on the hard stickiness of my prison cot, staring into soundless dark, I sometimes wonder whether I would have gone to Kalesmouth last fall, had I guessed at the horror that awaited me. All and all, I think I would. For, at that time, I should have scoffed at such legends as haunted the antiquated village sprawled on a forlorn peninsula off New Jersey's Northeastern coast. As a medical man, and a mildly successful brain surgeon, I would have set them down to antique folk-lore whispered by wintry firesides, told in the ghostly tongue of superstitious nonagenarians. Then, too, there were brief moments with Cassandra that were worth any price I had to pay; and, had I not gone to Kalesmouth, I should never have found her.

As things were, I suspected nothing. During that summer, I had been exceptionally active, and, my profession being as exacting as it is, toward the end of September I began to feel the effects. The only answer to the problem of a surgeon's trembling fingers is a complete rest. I do not know what prompted my selection of Kalesmouth; it was not a resort. But, then, I did not want amusement. When I saw that advertisement of a cottage to let in the seclusion of a rocky-coasted seaboard town, it seemed ideal. From childhood I had loved the salt-freshness of the Atlantic. Today, when I think of the greenish waves smashing at the beach, clutching it with watery fingers, I can never repress a shuddering chill.

Kalesmouth is little more than a sprinkling of cottages with a single general-store and a population in the low fifties. The small white houses are scattered along a narrow finger of sand-and-rock land that juts defiantly eastward into the sea. There is water on three sides and a single highway to the mainland. The people talk little to strangers, and one senses an aura of great antiquity in the solitary sun- and sea-swept life they lead. I will not say I noticed any sign of evil in the secluded settlement, but there was an air of tremendous, brooding age and loneliness about the homes and the people alike; the land itself seemed dry and barren, a forgotten relic of earlier, more fruitful days.

But quiet and rest were what I needed after the strenuous turmoil of antiseptic-choked corridors and operating amphitheaters. Certainly, no town could offer better chance for these than did Kalesmouth, redolent as it was of a Victorian era when life moved through leisurely, hidden channels. My cottage was small but comfortable, and Eb Linder, taciturn, wind-dried proprietor of the general-store, helped me lay in a good supply of staple foods. Long, salt-aired days were spent wandering the bleached stretch of a rocky shoreline, and in the evenings I turned to my collection of books. I saw few people and talked with fewer. Once or twice, when we chanced to meet at Linder's store, I spoke to Doctor Henry Joyce Ambler, Kalesmouth's only general practitioner. He was a florid, white-haired individual, full of shop-talk of the sort I was trying to escape. I'm afraid I may have been rather rude to him, for in those first days, I was still overwrought and in need of relaxation. Gradually, however, I drifted into a soft, thoughtful mood; I became more interested in my surroundings.

I cannot be certain when it was that I first noticed the house. Looking back, I should say that, somehow, I must have been vaguely aware of it from the start. The main window of my small sitting-room looked eastward to the aqua-marine expanse of the Atlantic. Situated as it was, at the approximate center of the narrow peninsula of Kalesmouth, my cottage commanded a view of the long earth-finger that pointed so boldly into the sea. Between me and the extreme point of land, a few stray cottages sprawled haphazardly, but there was no sign of habitation within a good half-mile of the land-edge on which the house stood.

The fact that it was a house, set it apart in Kalesmouth. All the others were clap-board bungalows of only one story. In the sea-misted evenings, I was wont to sit for hours by my eastward casement, staring at the vast, gray bulk of it. It was like something from another aeon, a tottering, decayed remnant of the nighted past. Massive and rambling, with countless gables and cupolas, its small-paned, murky windows winking balefully at the setting sun, set as it was on the extreme lip of the land, it seemed somehow more of the cloying sea than of solid soil. An ectoplasmic nimbus clung thickly to battered towers whose boarded embrasures argued desertion. I noticed that the sea-gulls circled the ancient monument warily; birds did not nest in the crumbling age-webbed eaves. Over the whole dream-like vision hung an atmosphere of remoteness that was vaguely tinged with fear and repulsion; it was a thing that whispered of forgotten evils, of lost and buried blasphemies. The first time I caught myself thinking thus, I laughed away the sensation and decided that my solitary sojourn was beginning to work on my imagination. But, the feeling persisted, and in the end, my curiosity won. I began to ask questions during my infrequent visits to the store.

Silent as Eb Linder habitually was, I sensed an abrupt withdrawal in him when I mentioned the house at land's end. He continued weighing out my rough-cut tobacco, and spoke without looking at me.

"You don't wanta know about Heath House, Doc. Folks hereabouts ain't got nothin' to do with it...."

Sullen warning charged his level tone. I smiled but a small shiver trickled along my neck. I looked across the store to where Doc Ambler stood, his white mane bent intently over one of the latest magazines. His head came up; the usual smile had gone out of opaque eyes.

"Lazarus Heath lives there, Doctor," he murmured. "Very much the recluse."

"Which is jest as well fer us," Linder put in cryptically. Ambler nodded and went back to his reading.

It was at that point that I became aware of the disheveled, weather-beaten creature in the doorway. I had seen Solly-Jo before, wandering the sand-and-stone wastelands of the beach. You will find one such outcast in every small town, I suppose. A slow-witted, distorted brute, with matted blond-gray hair, he combed the shores night and day, ambling aimlessly from spot to spot, sleeping in the lea of some jutting rock. He ate where and as he found food. Always before, the sad, baby-blue eyes turned on me had held a vacant stare, but, now, as Linder gave him his daily free bottle of milk, Solly-Jo was gazing at me with something like sharp understanding in his phlegmatic face. We did not speak further of Heath House, but when I left the store, Solly-Jo slowly followed. He caught up with me and shuffled at my side, smiling vaguely for a time before he spoke.

"You was talkin' about Heath House, wasn't you, Doc?"

I nodded; Solly-Jo chuckled softly.

"I know why you was askin' about it," he said with a knowing leer. "Only you hadn't ought to. Ol' Laz Heath ain't no friend to nobody. Stay clear o' that house. They's things there that ain't right. They's bad things...."

"Just who is Lazarus Heath?" I asked.

"Ol' man ... real ol'.... He got a funny smell about him ... a dead smell, like dead fish washed up on the beach.... Used to be a sailor, but, now, he's too ol' ... They's stories about ol' Laz. Him an' that daughter o' his'n ..." The lecherous grin returned. "You better fergit about Miss Cassandra, Doc.... I know you seen her; that's why you bin askin' about the house.... But fergit it.... She ain't fer the likes o' you an' me...."

Solly-Jo shook his head slowly, and clucked, sadly.

"No, sir.... She's too much like 'er ol' man. Stays away from folks, like him. They live out there alone ... an', like I say, they's things in Heath House.... They's a bad stink, like Ol' Laz has.... Nigh onto twenty year ago, Laz was in a shipwreck. Lost fer most two year, then a tramp-steamer found him on a island.... He had this little baby girl with him; said she was his daughter; said his wife died in the wreck.... Only nobody was ever able to find no passenger listin' fer a Missus Laz Heath.... Then, Laz come back here and bought that there ol' place. Even 'fore he come they was talk about bad things in that house.... People still talk, only now they whisper, 'case Laz might hear.... Take my word, Doc.... You steer clear o' pretty Cassandra.... She warn't meant fer men like us...."

I can still remember Solly-Jo's simian shadow shuffling off along the craggy, moon-washed strand, voracious tongues of nighted tide lapping at his battered white sneakers. If I had not heard of Cassandra Heath before, now that I had my interest was made the more intense by the drone of the beach-comber's eerie warning still humming in my ears. I chuckled, telling myself it was probably utter nonsense, the maundering phantasms of Solly-Jo's lonely, warped mind. But, my laughter echoed back from a brooding watery wasteland. I recalled the solemn reticence of intelligent, educated Doctor Ambler, the wordless warning of Eb Linder.

Despite such memories I could not get Cassandra Heath off my mind; I promised myself that I would meet her and this legendary father of hers. It seemed easy enough on the face of it; I could pay them a visit, saying I was a new neighbor. Yet, more than once during the ensuing days, I tried to do just that and failed. Roving the desiccated peninsula on a sunny forenoon, I would set out resolutely toward the misty hulk of Heath House, but I could never bring myself to go all the way. The straggling, mossy embattlements seemed too much a part of another world; looking at the house, you got the notion that you could keep walking toward it, yet never reach the crumbling patio, never pass through the ancient, carven door. It is probable that I should never have met Cassandra Heath, hadn't she come to me.

II

Early in October, an Indian-Summer storm washed in from the Atlantic. The day had been long and dreary, overhung with humid fog, and, in the late evening, vicious torrents swept inland under a fanfare of thunder. Through streaming casements I could barely discern the gigantic shell of Heath House, looming defiantly above the lashing fury of a hungry sea. I made a log fire and settled into an easychair; the subdued soughing of the storm combined with a rather dull analysis of Sigmund Freud must have lulled me into a doze. There was a sensation of spinning lostness; my mind ricocheted through the dark well of the rain-whipped night. There was a coldness brushing my face; a nauseous damp clung to my ankles, quelling the roseate warmth of the fireside. Something clicked sharply, and I opened my eyes. I thought I was still dreaming.

The girl stood leaning against the door she had just closed. Dying embers cast a phantasmagoria of lights and shadows on her face and hair. She was slim and well-made; ebony hair flowing to her shoulders gave one a feeling of rich warmth. It matched the steady blackness of extraordinary eyes that protruded ever so slightly. Her skin was deeply tanned. A faint flush in her cheeks and breath coming in quick whispers through full lips seemed to indicate a rather hurried trip. I wondered vaguely at her being quite dry until I realized that the storm had died with the evening. A moment passed, silent, save for the faint dripping of water from the eaves, as the dark eyes met mine.

"Doctor Arkwright?"

The voice, cultured and controlled, like the throaty melody of a cello well played, heightened my illusion of a dream. I rose awkwardly and my book slid to the floor. The girl smiled.

"I'm afraid I must have dozed …"

"My name is Cassandra Heath," the girl said gently. "My father is very ill, Doctor. Could you come with me at once?"

"Well … it might be better to get Doctor Ambler, Miss Heath. You see, I'm not a general practitioner.…"

"I know; I've read of your work. You're a brain surgeon. That's what my father needs.…" The voice trembled slightly; shadowed lids covered the ebony eyes for an instant. Cassandra Heath had admirable control. When she spoke again it was in a tone tinged with defiant pride. "You needn't come if … if you don't care to.…"

"No.… It isn't that at all.… Of course, I'll come, Miss Heath.…"

My mind sliding backward over the beach-comber's whispered tale, I arranged a small kit with strangely unsteady hands. Cassandra Heath stood silently by the door. I wondered if Solly-Jo's story had been something more than the weird fiction of an overworked imagination. The defiance in the girl's voice argued that the legend of Heath House was known and feared by more than this one insignificant wanderer; so much feared that it might frighten a stranger away.

Even without such a veil of mystery swathing her life, Cassandra Heath would have been a striking person. As it was, I was fascinated.

We had walked some distance before the girl spoke again. The moon had risen and phantom rocks glistened in its watery glow. The ocean pounded choppily on a rain-sodden beach and our feet left moist rubbery prints that disappeared as quickly as they were made. Moving with long graceful strides, Cassandra Heath talked in a level monotone.

"I suppose you've heard tales about my father. You can't live in Kalesmouth any length of time without hearing about old Lazarus Heath...." Grim humor touched the warm lips.

"Solly-Jo did a bit of talking," I admitted.

"You mustn't believe everything you hear, Doctor. My father is ill. He has been for some years. We prefer to keep to ourselves at Heath House. When people can't talk to you, they talk about you.... They tell stories about father...."

"Miss Heath," I ventured. "Do you think that your father ..."

"Is insane?" the girl supplied. "Two years ago ... last year, even, I should have said 'no'.... Now, I can't be certain. My father has led a strange life, Doctor ... a strenuous one.... Here of late, he's been given to brooding. He was always moody and quiet, but this is something different. He ... he's afraid of something, I think.... Then, too, there are the disappearances...."

"Disappearances?"

"He's taken to wandering off at night.... Four times in the last couple of months I searched the whole length of the Strand and couldn't find him...."

"Maybe, he'd gone to the mainland...."

"I think not; someone would have seen him. No ... he went somewhere ... somewhere much farther away...." For the first time, a note of puzzled fear crept into Cassandra Heath's voice. "... much farther ..." She seemed to come back with an effort. "He did that tonight, Doctor. Just before the storm broke ... I ... I found him later ... hours later ... wandering in a small cove beyond the house. He was talking strangely ... and singing.... A funny little tune. He's in his room, now ... still talking

... still singing that song...."

Onyx eyes flashed up to meet mine; in that brief moonlit instant, I saw all the doubtful terror, the puzzled anxiety that Cassandra Heath would not admit, even to herself. I had no time to question her further, to attempt to link together her last broken phrases so that I could guess at the real meaning that lay hidden in them. Kalesmouth Strand had suddenly narrowed, and now, on either side of us, midnight ocean licked possessively at the land. A tortuous path, tangled with sea brambles and rocks, snaked to the shadow-choked veranda of Heath House. Weather-wasted planks groaned in protest under unaccustomed footsteps.

At a gentle pressure of Cassandra's hand the ponderous mahogany door swung back soundlessly. Even before I stepped into the candle-lit, gloom-encrusted hallway, I could smell it—that loathsome, clinging effluvium of rotting marine flesh of which Solly-Jo had muttered. It swirled sickeningly in the clammy atmosphere of a foyer that was like the dusty nave of some forgotten cathedral, rising along lushly paneled walls to the sightless dark far above. A wide, twisting staircase wound upward to some higher labyrinth, and as I followed Cassandra Heath up stairs whose ancient gray carpet was worn thin by the tread of forgotten feet, the fetor became ever more powerful, more noisome.

Through dream-like corridors, I followed the fitful glow of the candelabrum the girl carried. Another door opened, then closed behind me. I stood in a chamber that seemed drawn from the dark maw of lost eons. Tremendous oaken furniture dwarfed the figure sprawled limply on a dais-raised bed, and, though the small-paned casements stood wide, chilling sea-fog swirling through them into the room, the stench was overpowering. Cassandra set the candelabrum on an antique cabinet-de-nuit; an eerie luster flickered across Lazarus Heath's wasted visage.

During his professional lifetime, a brain specialist is called upon to diagnose countless horrible cases, yet they are the horrors of the nighted mind, or of blindness caused by a tumor. They are medical things, and can be understood. You cannot diagnose a fetid malignancy that goes beyond medical knowledge, rooting itself in the black soil of ancient hells. There was nothing medical knowledge could do for Lazarus Heath.

Pushing back revulsion, I made a thorough examination. The massive body, little more than skin and bones, now, gave off a reeling aura of putrefaction, and yet there were no sores. Sopping clothes that hung in tatters were tangled with dull-green seaweed, stained with ocean salt. But, it was the face that caught and held my attention. The skin, taut and dry, was the color of aged jade, covered with minute, glistening scales. Staring into the candlelight, Lazarus Heath's pale eyes bulged horribly, and as the great bony head lolled spasmodically from side to side, I made out two faint bluish streaks, about four inches in length, running along each side of the scaly neck, just below the jawline. The lines pulsed thickly with the air-sucking motions of his salt-parched lips. Watery incantations bubbled upward into the dank stillness.

"They call.... They call for Lazarus Heath.... Zoth Syra bewails her lost one; she bids me come home. You hear? The Great Ones of The Green Abyss hail me! I come, O, beauteous Zoth Syra! Your lost one returneth, O, Weeping Goddess of the Green Nothingness…!"

Sudden power energized the lax skeleton, so that I had no easy time in holding him to the bed. Pallid eyes stared beyond this world, and Lazarus Heath's cracked lips warped in a hideous smile. Then, as suddenly, he was calm; the ponderous cranium cocked pathetically to one side, in a grotesque listening attitude.

"You hear?" the hollow voiced gurgled. "She sings to me! The Song of Zoth Syra!" Inane laughter tittered weakly. Heath's rasping voice dribbled into a strangely haunting threnody, a song that at once attracted and repelled with its subtly evil intonations.

> "Zoth Syra calleth him who knows the Green Abyss;
> Men of salt and weed are lovers all
> To the Goddess of the Green and Swirling Void—
> Come away to Zoth Syra! Come away!"

"Father!"

Cassandra's voice was scarcely more than a distraught gasp, but at the sound of it, the odious, hypnotic smile froze on Heath's parchment-pale face, then, slowly, decomposed into a twisted mask of sick horror. For the first time something like terrified reason seeped into those oddly protuberant eyes.

"Cassie! Cassandra!" Heath stared about him frantically like a child lost in the dark; once again he tried to raise himself, but, before I could restrain him, crumpled backward into a voiceless coma.

Half an hour later, standing in the shadows of the decaying patio, looking eastward to the moon-scorched desert of the Atlantic, I told Cassandra that there was nothing wrong with her father's mind. Perhaps I should have phrased it more coldly and added: "Nothing that medical science can cure." But, sensing the free, vibrant life that flowed in the girl's body and brain, I could not bring myself to tell her that I thought Lazarus Heath was going mad. Too, I was not at all sure of my own diagnosis.

I told Cassandra that I wanted time to observe her father more closely, and she seemed greatly relieved to know that I would consider the old man's case. For myself, I confess I could not have done otherwise. Despite the malignant shadow that shrouded Heath House in ageless mystery, I knew that I would come back again and again, not only because I was curious about the singular aspects that accomplished Heath's apparent twilight madness, but because, as I left her that night, Cassandra held out her hand, and I took it in mine. It was a simple, friendly gesture, and we both smiled. From that moment on, I was completely, irrevocably in love with Cassandra Heath.

Looking backward, it seems to me that our brief moment of happiness was like some minor miracle, rising as it did through a choking miasma of brooding evil, to touch, if only for an instant, a clean, sunlit world known only to lovers. Somehow, we managed to transcend the haunting omnipresent ghost of Lazarus Heath's illness. It is true that the old man returned to normalcy during that final fortnight of his troubled existence, and for a time Cassandra could forget the strange enigma of her father's insane babblings, and those sudden, inexplicable disappearances. Being a medical man, however, I never really forgot. Often, during those last two weeks, I talked with Lazarus Heath; he submitted to questioning and examination quite calmly. As to the peculiar condition of his skin, and the odd lines on his throat, he professed ignorance, and the once or twice I mentioned Zoth Syra, he went gloomily reticent on me. He said the name meant nothing to him, yet never before or since have I seen a man so patently weighted down by some blasphemous, heart-gnawing secret, as was Lazarus Heath. He ate little and spent his days and nights slumped in a crotchety chair, staring into the bluish mist of the small cove beyond Heath House.

Cassandra needed forgetfulness; as much as I could, I got her away from the sullen loneliness of the antediluvian manse at land's end. With the passage of days, she relaxed and became her own charming self, a side of her nature to which, I think, even she might have been a stranger. For the foul legends that trailed after Lazarus Heath had cut his daughter off from companionship and the clear, untarnished joys of the extrovert.

We spent the long sunny days together on the beach; Cassandra was like an imprisoned nymph suddenly set free. She swam with the grace of one born to the water, and ran the length of arid sand with the lightness of a child, her wonderful hair flowing wildly in the sea breeze. A man cannot see such youth and beauty and remain untouched. My Cassandra had not only these; too, there was an air of quiet wisdom about her, that was somehow wistful and sad. She was prodigiously well-read, and told me her father had educated her. Sometimes she spoke of long, lonely childhood years, when she lived only in the pages of the countless books in Lazarus Heath's library.

I had seen that small, book-cluttered room with its musty, rich bindings; the old man spent much time there. It is strange how so comfortable and common-place a nook could shelter such a vile, inhuman secret through the years. Had I learned that secret sooner, Cassandra would be alive today.

III

Lazarus Heath died the night I proposed to his daughter. Up to that time he had improved fairly well; until, at moments, watching the new vivacity that had touched Cassandra, he seemed almost normally pleased. I believe the old man conceived a liking for me, because I had given Cassie something; I had given her my friendship and my love, and his awful legend had not frightened them away.

The night I asked Cassandra to marry me, it was balmy and quiet, and we had been walking along Kalesmouth Strand, watching the silver ribbons of the moon on the Atlantic. I remember, I halted rather abruptly, mumbling that I had something "to ask her," and then Cassandra smiled and kissed me. Her lips were warm and full of promise.

"The answer is 'yes', darling," she murmured.

We laughed, then, a soft, rich laughter whose gentle, love-haunted echoes I shall never forget. Clinging together we ran along the moonlit sand. That day, a last leaf of Indian Summer had fluttered across the peninsula, and a wintry sea was already lapping hungrily at the land. Cassie chattered brightly about how happy her father would be for us, but somehow, as we neared the sepulchral tenebrosity of Heath House, a hollowness crept into her laughter. It was as though she already sensed the horrible discovery that lay before us.

There was no answer when Cassandra called out in the hollow well of the foyer. We began our search for Lazarus Heath calmly enough, but, now, the laughter had gone altogether. He was not in the dusty sanctuary of his library; the linen of his tremendous oaken bed flapped in the wind that brushed through casements thrown wide to the rapidly chilling night. The look of utter terror in Cassandra's eyes told me we were reasoning along the same lines.

It did not take long to reach the strange little cove in the shadow of Heath House. A cold, dream-like quality saturated every corner of that miniature beach, hid from sight on all sides save the East, where the predatory mutter of the sea seemed dangerously near. But you can awaken from the insanity of a dream; there was no such escape from the terrible reality of that night.

At the center of the cove, edging into the water, stood four weirdly hewn pillars, placed so that each made the corner of a crude square; in the moonglow they had the aspect of sinister mediaeval altars of sacrifice, reared to noxious, unnameable gods. Sprawled at the center of the evil square, face-down in a foot of lapping sea-water, lay the lifeless body of Lazarus Heath.

I cannot rightly remember how I got the brine-tangled corpse into the house. There is a searing picture of Cassandra's face, frozen with sick grief; and another, of myself, alone in that fetid bed-chamber, performing an autopsy, listening to Cassie's distant, pitiful sobs the whole time. That night, I got down on my knees and prayed to God that the things I had discovered could not be so. Yet, I had seen with my own eyes the increased scaliness of Heath's face, the horrible enlargement of his eyes. I knew that my first guess had been wrong; Lazarus Heath had not drowned. For those hellish lines on his throat had become long, oozing slits, like nothing but the slobbering gills of a tremendous fish! I had a sick feeling that Heath's weird mumblings might not have been the gibberish of a madman, but the delirium of one who had learned things no mortal was ever meant to know.

We buried him in a sealed pine casket. If the morticians from the mainland noted the strange condition of the corpse, they gave no sign. With them it was a business; Death had myriad forms, each as cold and unquestionable as the last. With Cassandra, however, I had to be more careful. I knew the terrible effect that nauseous, bloated visage would have upon her. I told her the autopsy had been rather disfiguring, that it would be better if she did not see her father. She obeyed with the simple acquiescence of a child who is lost and lonely, and in need of guidance. Once, she roused from a cold, apathetic state of shock to tell me that Heath had always wanted to be buried in the cove. It rained on the day of interment; icy needles pelted forlornly on the unpainted wood, as two uneasy negroes lowered Lazarus Heath to his final rest. A timid mainland pastor intoned the Lord's Prayer in a sad, squeaky voice. That night, there was nothing but the rain, and the horrible stillness of forsaken Heath House. Sparse flowers wilted on the fresh clay mound in the cove; a clammy tide fingered slowly in, lapping at the edge of Lazarus Heath's grave.

I had to get Cassandra away; watching pent-up doubt and fear turn her lovely face into an expressionless mask, I knew she must be freed of the cloak of black uncertainty that enveloped Heath House. We talked through most of that rain-washed lonely night, and for the first time in my medical career, I told a lie. Could I have seen the sick terror in her eyes, and spoken words that might turn that fear into madness?

When I performed that autopsy, I found no cause for Lazarus Heath's death. There was no water in his lungs; every organ was in excellent condition. But, I told Cassie that the old man died of a heart attack. I told her I was certain that her father had been perfectly sane. Even as I spoke, new color flushed her cheeks; an expression of indescribable relief lit ebony eyes. Cassandra could not know that the old man's sanity was more to be feared than his insanity. An unstable brain could answer for wild babblings, for ungodly melodies, but what could account for the terrible concreteness of that scaly, fish-like corpse? Wrack my brain as

I did, I could find no explanation in the accepted medical sense; and, I dared not go beyond that, into the malevolent lore of forgotten ages, to discover what blasphemous horror had destroyed Lazarus Heath. I preferred to try to forget—to go on with Cassandra, covering this nightmare with endless moments of normal, happy living.

Many times during the next few months, I thought I had succeeded. A week after the solitary funeral on Kalesmouth Strand, Cassie and I were married by a pleasant, apoplectic justice-of-the-peace. We had our wedding supper in the quiet luxury of one of the better hotels, and for the first time since her father's death, Cassandra smiled. The city proved to be good for her. Deliberately, I made those early days a scintillating round of gaiety. I introduced Cassie to the bright lights and the brassy, arrogant joys of city life. We were exquisitely happy. Her laughter was a wonderful, warm pool of summer sun, swirling briefly in that winter city, and then, suddenly, freezing over.

I cannot recall just when I first noticed the difference in Cassandra. Perhaps I had been too happy myself to realize what was happening to her. The breezy tinsel of the city had sparkled very brightly for Cassie, but, it had burned itself out in the effort. After a time, it lost its fascination. In the beginning, I tried to tell myself that I was imagining things, but, gradually, I felt the happy freedom slipping away from us. Cassandra's smiles grew scarcer by the day; there was an infinitely sad far-away look that kept stealing into her eyes at the most unexpected moments. I began to imagine that she had grown pale. I watched her more closely than ever. An end of it came one evening late in August.

I found Cassandra alone on the night-cooled terrace of our apartment, staring eastward across the summer-choked city. When I touched her shoulders she gave a little start, then smiled sadly.

"Can you smell it, darling?" she murmured wistfully, after a moment.

"What?"

"The sea...."

In that moment, I think I had a sudden vision of the scabrous puffed face I had fought desperately to forget, and, floating evilly in the night air, I sensed a wisp of the decayed effluvia of Heath House. I struggled to keep my voice steady.

"What're you getting at, Cassie?"

Cassandra smiled again.

"Can't fool my doctor, can I?" Her voice was soft. "Darling ... Would you mind terribly if we went back to Kalesmouth ... the Heath House?"

Strangely enough, all I felt for an instant was a sensation of relief. I had been waiting for that question all along; I was almost glad the waiting was over. I took Cassandra into my arms and kissed the tip of her nose. I wanted to sound careless and bright. I told her, if she really wanted to go back, there was nothing I would like better. Cassie smiled, nestling her head against my shoulder. As we stood there, looking into the darkness above the winking lights of the buildings, a cold shudder ran through me. I wanted to say it was wrong; we couldn't go back. I said nothing. Quietly, hypnotic and shrill, a familiar, odious threnody chortled inland from the distant Atlantic. "... lovers all to the Goddess of the Green and Swirling Void.... Come away, to Zoth Syra! Come away!" I wondered if Cassandra could hear it. I prayed that she couldn't.

I am not certain of what I expected upon our return to Heath House. I could not forget the puling, nauseous horrors we had left behind; the stench of a scaly corpse seemed never to leave my nostrils. I remember my hands sweating on the wheel as I tooled our car across the long bridge that connected Kalesmouth Strand with the mainland; early-morning fog seemed to close in behind us, shutting us off from reality. The baleful finger of the solitary macadam road that led to Heath House pointed with terrible certainty to the steely expanse of the sea.

However, the change in Cassandra heartened me, dispelling somewhat my uneasy premonitions. Already, her complexion returned to its former warmth and beauty; her laughter rippled softly at some weak joke I had made, and the ebony cloak of her hair was rich and alive in the sea breeze. Our homecoming was much more pleasant and prosaic than I had dared hope it would be; it gave no trembling portent of the icy, sea-brined evil that was to stalk our future hours in the malevolent house. Only the sea chuckled expectantly in the lonely cove near Lazarus Heath's tomb.

It is impossible to trace the stages by which I became jealous of Heath House; there was something subtle and cruel about the change that overtook me after the first days and nights on the barren point of land that meant so much to Cassandra. At the start, I managed to convince myself that I was happy—happy because Cassie seemed to be so, for the first time in months. I even felt something like an uneasy affection for the old place, because it made Cassandra what I wanted her to be—full of a rich, wild life, touched with the mysterious charm that had first attracted me.

We began to refurnish and remodel the house; the mundane clang of workmen's saws and hammers, the earthly smell of turpentine and white lead, seemed to breathe a freshness into the foul, antiquated halls and chambers. I told myself it was just another charming old house where people could be happy if only they tried hard enough; but, all the time, a new whispering voice within me clamored for attention. I knew I was losing Cassandra to a past of which I had not been a part; Heath House was reclaiming her.

Cassandra herself seemed to notice no change in our relationship; she was gentle and full of a soft tenderness toward me, and still, I had the terrible feeling that a barrier was rising between us, day by day, second by second. Cassie took to a habit that roused uneasy memories in me; any hour of the day or night, she would be seized by an urge to walk quickly, unseeing, along the lashing edge of the sea. They were not the leisurely wanderings we had known in the past; it was as though Cassandra were trying to get somewhere, trying, unconsciously, to reach something.

Once or twice I mentioned the habit, but she only smiled remotely and said there was no harm in a stroll by the seaside, was there? I had no answer. I could not tell her of the cold, unprofessional, unreasoning fear that had begun to haunt me. We went on with our repairs of Heath House, and gradually, brightened by chintzes and restored tapestries, filled with usable period furniture, it became livable. We had finished all of it, save the library; it was our plan to make this into a study, in which I might work on the book I planned to do on brain surgery. We never remodeled the library. I saw the inside of that abhorred chamber only once after the night Cassandra locked the paneled door and made me promise not to ask for the key. I wish I had never seen it at all.

That evening a bulwark of leaden clouds swung ponderously inland from the sea; a chilled late-October wind sifted beneath the imminent storm, swirling the sand in tiny puffs along Kalesmouth beach. By the tang of salt in the air, and the reticent anger of the surf, the Northeast was going to blow us a big one. I quickened my pace, walking home from the store; a dearth of incident had killed me into uncertain forgetfulness, and, at that moment, I was almost pleased with the prospect of the evening ahead of me. Early in the afternoon, I had told Cassie tonight might be as good a time as any to go over the library, gleaning the useless chaff from the hit-and-miss collection that had been her father's. Now, with a storm brewing, the idea of going through the books and effects of my mysterious father-in-law fascinated me. The biting wind and glowering ceiling of sky seemed to me a final atmospheric touch. I wondered if the spell of Heath House had begun to claim me as well.

The moment I saw her, I knew that something had gone wrong. There was a strange, jade-like pallor under Cassandra's skin, and her eyes wouldn't meet mine. Once or twice during our quiet dinner, she laughed, but the laughter echoed hollowly. Thunder had begun to shudder malignantly far out at sea. A finger of lightning shattered the darkness and our storage-battery lights pulsed anxiously. I saw Cassandra start and tip over her wine glass; the port spread like an oozing bloodstain on the Madeira linen. I looked at my plate, pretending not to notice her extraordinary nervousness.

"I've been looking forward to tonight," I said.

"Looking forward, darling?" That false-brittle smile was in Cassandra's voice.

"Yes ... I've always wanted to go through those fabulous books...."

The clatter of metal against china brought me about with a start. Cassie had dropped her fork from fingers that seemed suddenly paralyzed. She stared at me with unseeing eyes and one slim hand raised in a futile gesture of protest. Her colorless lips trembled.

"No! You mustn't...." A gnawing fear sprang into the emptiness of her gaze; she made as if to rise, and, in an instant, all life seemed to flood from her body. She slid soundlessly to the floor.

What I did then was done with the unconscious habit of a medical man; training overshadowed the sick, watery weakness of my legs. Somehow, I got Cassandra to our bedchamber on the second floor. Her exquisite face had a whiteness that whispered of death, but breath came in uneasy, whimpering shudders. I chafed her wrists, an agony of doubt whirling in my brain. Thunder slithered across the sky, crashing insanely over Heath House; the storm broke. Dark eyes were suddenly wide in Cassie's pale face. Her hand clutched mine so violently that her nails bit into the flesh.

"You can't go in there.... Nobody can go in there, ever again. You hear? Nobody ... ever again...!"

"It's all right, darling. Try to relax. Tell me what's frightened you...."

Her head shook dully.

"I can't.... I can never tell you. You've got to trust me. You can't ever go into that room; don't ever try. I've locked the door. You mustn't ask me for the key. Please! Promise me you won't! ... Please!"

IV

I promised.

I heard myself saying the words over and over in a thick monotone. They seemed not to reach her. Her lips hung loosely, fear twisting the beauty from her face, leaving nothing but unreasoning hysteria. She went on pleading, unable to hear my reassurances. The sedative I gave her was not a weak one. My hands shook as I prepared it. I had to work in the dark. Our storage batteries had given out. There was nothing but pitch-blackness and the babbling fury of the elements, chewing at Heath House mercilessly. Perhaps it was only my nerves; once I could have sworn that there, in the pulsing gloom, an overpowering stench, an effluvium that was almost tangible, brushed against me.

At length, Cassandra's whimpering died away; she sank into a deep fitful sleep. Lightning crashed maniacal brightness into the room; for an instant it washed Cassie's face and throat. There was a delicate, gold-dipped chain around her neck; on it she had strung the key to the library.

You cannot always give reason to your actions. That night I could have stolen the key. I could have gone down the hall through the darkness, and into the damnable chamber that held a secret ungodly enough to press my wife to the brink of madness. If I had, things might have worked out differently. Maybe I was a coward, afraid of the antediluvian horror that awaited me beyond the massive carven door. Maybe I did not want to know the truth. I told myself I had made a promise to Cassandra. I left the key where it was, and stumbled downstairs in the stygian blackness.

Screeching banshees of rain begged entrance at the streaming casements; a fire burned fitfully in the sitting room grate. I found a decanter of rum in the cabinet by the window. I do not remember how long I paced the floor, torturing myself with doubt and fear, trying to believe that Cassie was sane, wondering what puling monstrosity lay hidden in Lazarus Heath's book-room. I sank into an armchair and swallowed another mouthful of rum; the storm seemed to have drawn far away from me. The rum bottle tinkled against the glass as I poured; I drank. I lay my head back. Lightning pulsed through my optic nerves, but sound was only a blurred, pungent, rum-soaked whirlpool. Then, there was only darkness. I slept.

It was the dull angry thumping that woke me; consciousness seeped through the ragged slit it made in the forgetfulness of sleep. I got unsteadily to my feet and stood in the center of the room until the whirling darkness righted itself. Something new had sifted into the room; the fire still sputtered doggedly, and yet, there was a dampness it could not dispel. A chilled whisper of sea-air sighed along the floor. I went into the foyer; coldness washed over me in a tidal wave. The front door flapped back and forth on its heavy hinges; rain pelted in a drooling puddle in the hallway. I swore and slammed the door, throwing the dead-latch. Then, I stood very still. Cassie! The name blazed like a neon sign in my brain. I think I knew in that moment that she was gone.

The search was something careening from a dream gone mad, a terrifying nightmare in which the geometry has gone all wrong. I wanted to scream or cry, but dry fear clamped my throat. Everything twisted crazily in my head; Cassie's empty bed, the heart-like drumming of the open front door; myself, stumbling through the brutal onslaught of a northeaster, calling her name again and again, finally reaching Eb Linder's place and getting half the people of the Strand out of sane beds to wander the hellish night in search of Cassandra. It must have gone on for hours; I cannot remember except in vague snatches. There was a stolid, gray-faced fisherman who muttered something about the sea claiming its own. At dream-like intervals Solly-Jo wandered in and out of the rain. Eb Linder's sister made coffee for me, and got me to change my drenched clothes. She kept telling me it would be all right. The men, with Doctor Ambler leading them, had been over every inch of the Strand and found nothing. Miss Linder kept right on saying it would work out all right. At 3:30 a kid came in, dripping with rain. He said they'd found Cassandra in the cove behind Heath House.

She wasn't dead. When I reached the house, Ambler had her in bed, covered with numberless blankets. Her clothes lay in a sopping lump on the floor. Ambler poured me a drink, and I think I cried. He waited until I had got it out of my system. I kept watching to see if Cassie was breathing; she looked pale and dead.

"I can't figure it," Ambler said quietly, after a while. "We went over that cove so many times, I'd swear it was impossible for anything or anyone to be there. Then, Linder came across her, lying at the water's edge, on her father's grave. She was all ... all matted with seaweed.... I ..." He stated at me. The numbing horror that froze my insides must have shown in my eyes. "What's the matter, man!"

"Seaweed!" I choked.

I didn't hear any more of what he said. I went to the bed and looked at Cassandra closely for the first time. Her skin shone faintly in the uncertain substitute of candlelight—as though it were covered with flaky, gossamer scales! On either side of her throat, I made out two pale, bluish streaks. My head spun; I felt as if I were going to be sick. Rising insidiously from the mucky pile of clothing on the floor, a vile, decadent stench flooded the chamber. From a tremendous distance, a voice whispered gently: "I come, O, Yoth Kala! Your bride has heard your call! Through night and storm, I come!" The voice was Cassandra's.

"It's nothing to worry about, man," Ambler was saying kindly. "Just a case of exposure.... She'll be all right...."

"Yes," I nodded dully. "She'll be all right...."

The last hope of happiness drained from me; I felt weak and lost in a plummeting void of unspeakable horror. There were times, in the days that followed, when I had the sensation of living in an alien, frightening world, a world in which lay hidden the blasphemous secrets of death and the grave, a world that sang with the strange, blood-craving incantations of lost and murderous cults. There was nothing human in the terror that held me prisoner. You can fight evil if it is concrete. This was something that could not be touched or seen, yet, something always at my heels, its stinking, flesh-rotting breath burning against my neck.

I hid my doubts from Cassandra, trying to be cheerful. She convalesced slowly under Ambler's care. For days at a time she would seem to be herself; she would smile and talk of how it would be when she was well again. And, then, abruptly, her mood would swerve into one of black secrecy that made her eyes blank and hostile. She whimpered in her sleep, and took to humming the weird threnody that had been Lazarus Heath's swan song.

More and more the feeling that I had lost her possessed me.

Gradually, her body grew strong again. She was able to be up and about, to wander the Strand on sunny days, her face silent and secretive, her eyes shutting me out when I tried to reach her. A sick, uneasy spell pervaded Heath House. Cassandra began to be nervous whenever I was near her; she resented my intrusion on her solitary walks. It was as though she looked upon me as a jailer, and on Heath House as a prison from which she must somehow escape. She spoke coldly and shuddered when I touched her. But, at rare moments, some of her old gentleness would return; you could see puzzlement and fear in her face. She would touch my hand and kiss me. She would tell me I was wonderfully kind. For an instant we were together again, and then, without warning, the barrier chilled between us. Cassandra drew away; the fear and bewilderment froze to what could only be suspicion and loathing.

Winter crept inland on icy cat's paws; brittle tendrils of frosted air swung sharply along the peninsula. Even the afternoon sun had withdrawn behind a caul of December chill. The Atlantic whipped with predatory regularity at the deserted sands, scant yards from Heath House. I tried to work on my book, but it was no good. The severe cold had made it necessary for Cassandra to remain indoors; she paced the endless, labyrinthian halls with the cold patience of a caged jaguar. She talked little and spent most of her time seated before the ceiling-high casement that looked eastward to the undulating iron casket of the ocean. At times she made a feeble pretense of reading, but, always, her eyes sought that melancholy wasteland, as if she expected to see something, or someone. My head ached constantly, the tempestuous, evil problem of Cassie throbbing at my temples with hellish persistence.

Once I spoke to Ambler about her moods; he talked of complexes and Freud; it was reassuring to listen to his calm, reasoning approach to the subject, but even as he spoke, I knew there was something torturing Cassie that no psychoanalyst could hope to explain. She was possessed by an entity whose subtle, odious influence was stronger than any fantastic twist of the mind. Time and again, I paced before the forbidding oaken library door, trying to find the courage to break my promise to Cassandra. Once, she caught me there. She did not speak, but only stared at me with a hatred so intense that it was frightening. After that, it seemed to me, she was doubly watchful of the brass key that hung on the fragile web of her necklace.

Her silent hostility spread itself like an undulant pool through the brittle newness of Heath House; it wiped away everything we had tried to make of the place, and left it as it had been before, a clammy, sickening shell of the past, a past that wanted no part of the present, that would brook no intrusion of light or hope. Cassandra was a creature of that past.

Doctor Ambler continued to make routine monthly calls. To all outward appearances, Cassandra was no longer ill, yet, a certain, unhealthy pallor of skin persisted; at moments, when she was without make-up, the faintly luminous prominence of the delicate scales terrorized me. If she noticed them, Cassandra said nothing. The long, discolored streaks on her throat had become barely discernible, but I could not keep my eyes from them. Ambler made no comment on these noxious oddities; he went his earthy, country-doctor's way. I think he never had the slightest inkling of the true horror that engulfed the house he visited so regularly. Certainly, he had no notion of the evil that lay hidden in the news he told me that evening late in December.

The day hadn't been at all good; mid-winter sleet lanced across a dense fog that came slithering and crying against the windows of Heath House. I had spent most of the time alone, making a sham at reading, wandering restlessly from room to room, staring blindly from one fog-curtained casement after another. During those last days, I had grown to anticipate a storm with a terrible, choking fear, for Cassandra's moods seemed more sullen and morbid as the easterly wind lashed angry rain or snow about the tiny cove behind the house. She would stand for hours gazing at the water-eaten mound that housed a thing that I could recall only with a tremor of disgust, a wave of nausea that balled itself like lead in the pit of my stomach. I had seen her doing that all that morning; she muttered something about how lonely he must be out there, and then walked slowly down the hall. I heard her door-lock click behind her. I had given up trying to understand her oblique remarks, brief whispers that seemed not meant for me, but rather, vague thoughts, personal and awesome, spoken aloud only by accident.

When Ambler had completed his examination in the privacy of Cassandra's chamber, he plodded heavily down the twisting staircase. I offered him a drink, muttering something about its being a raw night. It was only a pretense of civility with me, until, in the firelight of the sitting room, I saw the new expression that had crept into Ambler's eyes. I had seen many expressions there, after such sessions with Cassandra; expressions of doubt or bewilderment, or of professional satisfaction at her apparent recovery, but, now, there was something almost like pleasure in those soft gray eyes. I poured him a glass of sherry. He gulped it and winked.

"You've been wise people, you and your wife, Doctor," he said, after a pause. The eyes were actually twinkling.

"Wise?" His good humor had begun to irritate me.

"Of course! Nothing could have been more intelligent.... I don't like to seem personal, but after all, it's been fairly obvious that you and Cassandra ... well, something's come between you.... But, now, this.... Certainly, a child is just the thing to bring you together again.... It'll make all the difference in the world in this gloomy old place...."

I suppose I hadn't really been listening to him. I remember packing my pipe, absently, and scratching a match on the box. It made a tiny, lost noise in the shadowy bleakness of the room. Then, he made that crack about a child, and I just stood there, staring at him, the match flickering in my hand. There was nothing but a hollow numbness in me; afterward, I found a scorched scar on the skin of my thumb and forefinger.

I realized dully that Ambler was chuckling; his hand was on my shoulder.

"Well, don't look so confused, old man," he said heartily. "I guess Cassandra wanted to surprise you herself, and now I've gone and spoiled it for her by blurting it out...."

"She never said a word...."

Ambler laughed and I think I managed a watery grin; he gave me that line about the husband always being the last to know. We had another glass of sherry. I tried to act natural. The wine spread hazily through my puzzlement; a warmth swirled in my head, as I saw Ambler to the door, a vague, unreasonable anger. I was hurt at the silent wall Cassandra had erected between us; it seemed impossible, almost inhuman, that she could have known such a thing, and deliberately kept it hidden from me.

When Ambler had disappeared into the maw of the storm, I bolted the door. Our lights had given out again, and I walked unsteadily. The anger throbbed in my temples now; it kept time with the flickering of the candelabra light as I slowly climbed the winding staircase to Cassandra's room.

V

The door was locked. My shadow cast a dark blot against its panels, a ghost that wavered drunkenly into the half-light. My hand was perspiring; the candelabrum kept slipping in my grasp. I knocked, listening to the leaden echo it made in the subterranean catacombs of the house. There was no answer. I called:

"Cassie!" My tongue felt thick and dry. I waited.

"I'm lying down, darling. I've a headache...." Cassie's voice was brittly light, controlled with an effort.

"I want to talk to you." Anger cut through my tone.

For a long moment, there was nothing but the spectral whisper of the waxed candlewicks as they sputtered anxiously; then, a murmur of footsteps beyond, and the key turned in its socket. I let myself in, closing the door behind me.

Cassandra was standing by the fireplace; the instant I saw her, anger ebbed from my mind. There was something terribly small and frightened about her lovely, small body in the gossamer softness of a negligee. I set the candelabrum on a table and went to her; my hands trembled at the warmth of her shoulders. She did not draw away; she did not move at all.

"Ambler told me about the baby," I said gently.

It was then that she turned; she was smiling, and in that moment, all the falseness had gone out of her face. A quiet warmth touched it. She traced my lips with her fingertips.

"I wanted to tell you myself...."

I did not realize, then, that the taut sham was still in her voice. I kissed her. I told her it was wonderful. I said all the foolish things a man has a right to say at such a time. And, then, suddenly as I had begun, I stopped. Her mask had slipped; the warm tenderness was gone. A wall of nothingness blotted out the walls of her eyes. Cassandra twisted violently from me.

"It's no good," she whispered hoarsely. "It's no good!"

"Cassie ... I don't understand.... I ..."

She spun to face me; blurred stains of tears streaked the sallowness of her cheeks. In the jaundiced candleglow, her eyes were abnormally bright.

"Can't you see? Do you have to be told?" Trembling lips twisted in a coarse sneer. Her small even teeth seemed somehow vicious. "You're not wanted here! Just go away and let me be! I never want to see you again!" The hard grin widened and unstable laughter bubbled hysterically in her throat. "Your child! Do you think I'd bear your child! Can't you see I've changed? Don't you know you've lost me ... that I belong to him now ... ever since that night I went to the cove ... to the Abyss.... I'll always belong to him.... Always! Always! The bride of Yoth Kala...!"

The maniacal laughter cracked off as I gripped her shoulders; my fingers chewed into her flesh. I could feel her breath against my face, hot and sobbing.

"Cut it out!" I snapped. "Stop it, Cassie!"

She stood there for an eternity, staring at me; the mood whirled and twisted and childlike, bewildered fear was in her eyes again. She began to cry, her slight frame shuddering pitifully.

"It's true, I tell you," she gasped. "It's not your child. You don't believe me ... you think I'm crazy.... You needn't believe me.... Just go away ... before he comes for me.... He said he would come.... I don't want him to hurt you.... I don't want them to make you like me ... like my father...." She was babbling senselessly, the words tumbling from her lips. "... Yoth Kala will come.... I hear his voice ... he sings.... You hear? ... Calling me ... his bride ... the mother of his child.... I come, O, husband of the Green Void.... I come...."

It wasn't easy to hold her. I still have four parallel scars on my right cheek where her nails bit in frantically. She twisted with a strength that was nothing human, her lips muttering, her high, cracked voice shrilling that loathsome melody that meant death and horror and endless unrest to any who heard it. Finally, I won. Quite suddenly, she stopped struggling, she peered childishly into the darkness beyond us, her head cocked pathetically to one side, listening. She took an uncertain step toward the window before she fell. There was no sound save the rustle of her negligee as she crumpled at my feet. A thread of crawling spidery fog snaked in through the half-open casement, fingering like a shroud over her body. The stench was something from the bottomless watery depths of the sepulcher, a vile effluvium that was somehow the embodiment of every malevolent terror that stalked Heath House.

Cassandra and I were shadows playing a part against a papier-mâché background in a scene from the opiate-deep nightmares of Poe. I did things without stopping to wonder why. I can recall carrying her to the bed, and touching her pulse with fingers so numbed by horror that they could scarcely detect the fluttering heart-beat beneath them.

That was the night I came to an end of it. You can take just so much; you can go on hoping things will change, that you will awaken from this monstrous dream of falling through a void of unutterable terror. Then, you hit bottom. Staring at the chalky stillness of my wife's face, lost in the whiteness of the pillows, I knew I would have to break through. If I was to save her at all, I had to get to the bottom, I had to take this noisome fear in my hands and tear it out by the roots. I had to open the cancerous sore of the secret that ate at Cassandra's mind, the secret that lay buried in Lazarus Heath's book-room.

I was quite calm about it. When her breathing had become safe, I took the key gently from the necklace. With something that was more instinct than purpose, I got my revolver from the night-table drawer; it was fully loaded. I locked Cassandra in and went down the hall to the library. The gun made me feel better. It was something solid and sane to hold onto. A month later, the prosecution used the gun as exhibit "A"; they called it the murder weapon!

What I found beyond the massive, chiseled portal was a thing that laughed at the puny, human bravery of guns; a malignant, flowering evil that spawned itself in the pen-scrawled words of a man long since food for the gnawing maggots of an unspeakable hell. As I pushed open the door, staring blindly into the pit of darkness beyond, I almost wished for a stinking, flesh-born terror with which I could clash; an evil that lived and breathed, and could bleed and die. I found nothing but a dusty, dry-rot smelling chamber, that had been too long without air and sunlight. A moldering, half-burned candle stood at the edge of what Lazarus Heath had used as a writing-table; I held a match to it.

A butterfly of flame sputtered to life, throwing mammoth shadows along the crumbling plaster walls, casting an unwanted eye of light on the endless shelves of books long used to the privacy of night, untouched by curious hands. I wandered aimlessly about the high, barren room, gazing upon titles so antiquated, so much a part of a past beyond remembrance, beyond life and death, that I should have sworn it was a library straight from the flaming abyss of Hell. They were books not meant for mortal eyes, tales told by cults that sank into oblivion before time was measured, cast out from earth, trailing the ruins of their hideous, blood-thirsting rites behind them. Here and there, more sane, understandable volumes came to view. There was a priceless collection of sea lore, and in one spider-webbed corner, I found a yellowed, thumbed copy of "The Odyssey"; one section had been underscored, its battered pages mute testimony of endless reading and rereading. It was the passage describing the escape of Odysius from the syrens. God knows, Lazarus Heath had reason to be fascinated by it.

The shrill tumult of Cassandra's wild babbling still thundered softly in my brain. I stood very still, thinking, "This is the room." The root of it had to be tangled in the tomb-like dust of this shadowy chamber. But, where? my mind echoed. Where? My wanderings had brought me to the worm-eaten throne-chair behind Heath's writing-table. The light of the candle did a danse macabre as I sank heavy into the seat; it washed the black marble table-top with a flood of icy yellowness. Then, I saw the diary. I gave it a casual, irritated glance, and then, as the frenzied scrawl impressed itself upon my consciousness, I leaned closer. Faint gold-washed letters glittered brassily in the semi-darkness. "Lazarus Heath—His Book."

It may have been only the figment of a sick, overwrought imagination;

I don't know. I know that I felt it there within me, the instant I touched the book. I felt the evil that sighed through Heath House, suddenly come to life, as I thumbed nervously through the water-stained pages of Lazarus Heath's diary. The demented tittering of the storm rose from a whisper to the howl of a rabid dog baying at the moon. Sleet lashed at high casement windows and the silken portieres rustled anxiously. Even before I began to read that incredible, unholy record, I knew I held the root in my hands.

There was nothing sinister in the first entry. It was made in the steady, squarish script of a self-educated seaman, and dated February 21st, 192–. The words were sure and sane, with no hint of the hell-penned horror that lay in the final pages of the book.

Lazarus Heath had shipped out as First Mate aboard the freighter *Macedonia,* bound southeast for Africa. It was as simple and prosaic as that. For pages there was nothing but the easy, satisfied chatting of a sea-faring man setting down, for his own amusement, the record of an interesting but mundane voyage. The first leg of the journey had gone well; even the weather had been with the *Macedonia.* The crew was competent and not too quarrelsome, and already looking forward to a "time" in the African coast-towns. Then, somewhere in the Southern Atlantic, they ran into the fog.

At first, Lazarus Heath made only passing mention of it; although it had come upon them unexpectedly and was intensely thick and disconcerting, it was judged that they would sail on through it on instruments without too much difficulty. There was a controlled, sensible attitude in Heath's script at this point; he was writing for himself the things he had told his men. At the close of the entry he wrote, as though loath to admit it, even to himself: "There is a certain uneasiness among the men; it is not good for the nerves, this endless, blinding fog...." The writing trailed off with the first whisper of the uncertainty that was laying siege to Lazarus Heath's mind.

The next entry was made four days later in a dashing, cold hand. It was short and bewildered. "Still this damnable fog, and that is not the worst of it. The instruments have begun to act queerly. We must go on as best we can and trust in the Almighty. Men very jumpy...." And, on the night of the same day, the controlled hand had wavered perceptibly as it scribbled: "Instruments gone dead. What in God's name does it mean?" The story continued.

The coming of the voices was not sudden. It began with Dyke. Lazarus Heath knew little about the gangling, blond-bearded kid called Alan Dyke. He had signed on in New York as a fireman. A quiet, uneasy individual, he spent most of his leisure with books. He affected the bilge-water lingo of the sea, but underneath, he was only a kid, and he was scared. It began, according to Heath, when the engines went dead. They had expected that for what seemed a century. The *Macedonia* couldn't go on plowing in blind circles forever; the fuel gave out. The hell-fire in the bowels of Heath's ship guttered and died; there was only an echoing ghost of the roar that had choked the engine room.

It was too quiet. An unholy, nerve-rending silence enveloped the becalmed *Macedonia*. After a time, the men even gave up talking, as if the very echo of their voices, hollow and dead in the smothering fog, terrified them.

Dyke was on the foredeck when he heard the voices. Heath, standing beside him, had sensed an abrupt new tautness in the bony, coltish frame. Dyke's adolescent face strained to one side, marble-blue eyes gazing blindly into the mist; he listened. His words came to Lazarus Heath as though they had been separated by some yawning, fog-choked abyss.

"You hear them? The voices? I can hear them; they're calling us.... The syrens are chanting the melodies of watery death.... Zoth Syra calleth...." The voice was no longer Dyke's. It was light and cloying, possessed of a malignant beauty. Men froze and stared; they seemed not to hear Heath's sharp commands. "I heard nothing," Heath wrote that night. "Still, the sounds must have been there. Dyke must have been listening to something; he and the others.... But, I mustn't believe these whispered legends of sea-syrens. Someone must hold this God-forsaken crew together ... if only I have the strength ... if only I can keep from hearing the voices...." That was the prayer of Lazarus Heath, the night the *Macedonia* ran aground and sank off the ghostly shores of a lost, uncharted island.

Little space separated the next entry from those last frantic words, scribbled unevenly across a water-streaked, foul-smelling page of the diary, yet, reading on, I had the sensation of an endless spinning through some dark, watery nothingness. I lived the nightmare of which Lazarus Heath wrote with the calm sadness of a completely sane man.

The end of the *Macedonia* had been sudden and strange. By the hour, they had known it must be noon in that outer world with which they had lost all hope of contact. Their own existence had become a perpetual fog-swarming night; the monstrous ticking of the ship's clocks only taunted them. The bells of the *Macedonia* ricocheted mockingly into the boundless darkness of the mist. They had been chiming when the end came.

Lazarus Heath had spent most of his life on the water; he had survived more than one shipwreck. Panic and the smashing fury of the sea were nothing new to him. It was the quiet that terrified the *Macedonia*'s First Mate. The crew seemed not to understand; his lashing, bitter orders fell on deafened ears. The swirling Atlantic sucked thirstily at their feet and they did not move. Officers and men alike, they stood or sat in a speechless, apathetic stupor, unmindful of the death that swirled and lapped on every side. Each face held the same rapt, hypnotized expression. One would have said they were listening....

Heath steeled himself. He mustn't listen. He mustn't let himself hear what they could hear. He wanted to live. He stalked the length of the bridge angrily, bawling harsh commands. Only the fog and the sea listened and echoed. The *Macedonia* groaned mournfully and listed to port; water, thick and brine-tangled, flooded her hold. No one moved. She was going fast. He had to do something, make them hear him, bring them back to life....

Inky wetness washed against him, whirling him blindly in a stinking bottomless pit. His lungs would burst ... they must.... Air! And, then, he was on the surface. In the near-distance of the fog, the gray mass of his ship loomed balefully. It foundered and up-ended; there were no cries of terror or pain ... only cold, death-spawned silence. The *Macedonia* went down. There was nothing but a dull phosphorescence on the surface, and the frozen, black expanse of sea and fog.

VI

Heath was never quite certain about the island. It seemed probable that the *Macedonia* had run aground on the pinpoint of land that rose like a monstrous medusa from the mauve-green depths of the sea, yet Heath had never been aware of the existence of such an island; it was marked on none of the charts drawn by human hands. At a moment's notice, it had seemed to rear itself into the cotton-wool fog off the port bow of the ship. The water lapping at its fungus-clotted shores gurgled insanely as it swallowed the last of the *Macedonia*.

Oil-stained brine tangled Lazarus Heath's limbs; swimming was next to impossible. He never knew how long he was lost in the whirling eddies that licked about the island. It seemed an eternity. In the limitless, time-killing darkness of the fog, he struggled hopelessly, until finally, his feet touched bottom. He slithered ashore, lashed on by the incoming tide. Salt burned his lips and eyes; he was between choking and crying. In the lee of a gigantic finger of rock, he toppled to his knees, and sank forward, face-down, into a thoughtless stupor....

The fog never lifted. When Heath's mind crawled upward from the soundless depths of unconsciousness, he had no way of knowing how long he had lain, senseless, with the mossy, damp soil of the island clinging to him as if it had some power of physical possessiveness. He rolled over on his back, his head throbbing and dazed. He was breathing more easily, now; some of the weary tautness had gone out of his limbs. Wincing at the effort, he dragged himself to a standing position. He leaned against the shadowy hardness of the rock. His hand came away coated with a malodorous, verdant slime. Heath wiped the hand clean, feeling suddenly ill at the cold dampness that rushed in on him. He couldn't be sick; do something ... something to keep his mind busy. Dragging one foot heavily after the other, he began to explore the island.

When he tried to set down the incommunicable, barren loneliness of that lost outpost, Lazarus Heath failed. His pen stammered, searching for the right words, and finally admitted that the tone of the place was indescribable. He wandered endlessly through the cloying blueness of the mist, and found nothing that offered hope of any sort. The entire, clammy surface of the island seemed to be covered with the same nauseous green slime his hand had encountered on the coastal rock. It sucked hungrily at his feet with each step he took. It oozed from the trunks and gnarled, lifeless limbs of the barren trees that were scattered sparsely inland. The smooth, mucous-like scum coated the jutting rock formations wherever they sprang into spectral being, making them gleam with a malevolent phosphorescence. Lazarus Heath wrote one fearful sentence, the ghastly import of which he was not to guess until an age of horror had passed. "One gets the singular, frightening impression that this island has been a part of the ocean depths for more years than man can count, and, somehow, has risen to cause the tragedy of the *Macedonia* and claim its only survivor ... myself...." This was written just before he began to hear the voices.

Perhaps, before, even up to the last nightmarish moment, when he saw the crew of the *Macedonia* drawn, hypnotized and unresisting, into the slavering maw of the sea, Lazarus Heath had not believed in the voices. A great many explanations of that frozen, listening attitude which held the men to their death may have flashed like a wild phantasmagoria through his mind. Most of all, I think, he believed the officers and men alike seized by some loathsome mass madness. The sounds to which they "listened" so intently must be the figment of some malady of the mind. But, there, in the clammy mists of the lost, slime-coated island, he suddenly knew that the voices were very real.

They were not ordinary sounds. They were soft, cloying cadences that caught and held consciousness in a spider-web of evil beauty. They seemed uttered by countless alien tongues echoing across a vast and fearful chasm, and yet, as Heath stumbled on in search of them, he would have sworn that their source must be, there, just the other side of that next slimy knoll. He did not think of why he must find them; he only knew that this vile harmony had suddenly become very clear and understandable in his mind. "Come away!" the voices chanted, with the sound of myriad Gehennan lutes. "Come away to your bride, Zoth Syra! Come away ... away ... to the Queen of the Green Abyss...."

"I staggered blindly onward," Heath wrote in his diary. (The words themselves staggered crazily across the water-ruined pages, a mute reflection of the precipitous, hellish compulsion of his quest for the voices.) "I knew not where I was going, nor why. I fell time and again; my hands and knees bled with scrambling among the slippery, treacherous rocks. I came to the beach. Somehow the fog there seemed to lift, growing less dense, and I found myself on the brink of the ocean. I knew

I must stop, or drown, but my legs continued to pump with piston-like persistence. The voices were nearer, now; they held a malevolent beauty more compelling than the sounds that echo through narcotic dreams. Panic-stricken, I felt the icy water rising about my body, and still I kept moving out to sea. Brine swelled about my chest. The voices chanted mad cacophonies in my ears; wild, discordant, irresistible. The water reached my neck, my mouth … and then, my head was covered.…

"And, now the maddest thing of all. Submerged, I continued to walk, to breathe, slowly, easily, not through nose or mouth, but through a pair of gills in my throat! I strode onward through the swirling, opalescent depths, ever toward the howling, evilly-joyful singing … toward my bride, Zoth Syra!"

Between these frenzied, staggering words and the next and final entry, there is a gap of several blank, brine-yellowed pages. But for this, one might have guessed through desperate wishful thinking that the final episodes of that hideous record were dreamed of whole cloth—the fanatical ravings of a mind lost beyond rescue. No such guess can be hazarded when you have seen that last entry. It is dated almost twenty years later, in Kalesmouth. The writing is spidery and precise; the words have the cold, terrifying ring of unquestionable, blasphemous truth. Lazarus Heath set down those final sentences with a calm, almost grim determination. The very bareness of the clipped emotionless style he used has a numbing quality. God knows I would rather have died than believe this unholy tale, but there was no choice.

Even after twenty years, Heath could only hint at the monstrous dream which followed his descent into what he called "The Empire of the Green Abyss." His tight, controlled words whisper of a world unknown to mortals, a submarine, slime-choked empire of strange geometrical dimensions, a city whose architecture was somehow "all wrong." Entering it, Lazarus Heath was seized with an unutterable nausea, a repulsion that made him want to return, to go back somehow, and die as normal men would in such circumstances. But, he went on. In some inexplicable manner, he had become a part of this world of loathsome watery putrescence. He became one with the creatures who were the subjects of Zoth Syra, Empress of the Abyss.

Obviously, the pen faltered, the words would not come, but lay stagnant, and unspeakable, in Heath's mind when he tried to "describe" these creatures. He could no more draw a picture of them than he could explain the evil charm they held for him—a charm embodied in the chanting, ungodly thing they called Zoth Syra. Lazarus Heath was at once repelled and terribly, irresistibly drawn to this Queen who had chosen him for her lover. In trembling half-scrawls, he hints at the monstrous, primitive rites that were part of their betrothal ceremony. And of himself he writes with frightening simplicity: "I was helpless. I was part of those decadent blasphemies and knew it, yet had not the will to resist. I wanted only to go on listening to that hellish, sweet voice which belonged to my Queen...."

There was no time; there was nothing but an endless, bittersweet madness, from which he had not the will to escape. He became to the creatures of the Abyss, Yoth Zara, the Chosen One. And reigning beside the indescribably evil beauty, Zoth Syra, he became conscious of a ceaseless murmuring of restless voices that echoed sibilantly in the song of his Queen. Perhaps it was then that Heath pieced together his explanation of that hideously magnificent underworld. I do not know. But it was the whispering of the voices that made him uneasy, that sent his mind struggling upward from the Abyss, groping blindly toward the light of normalcy. It was the murmured legends that made possible his final escape. The horror of them gave him a strength he needed; they deafened his ears to the song of Zoth Syra. And, when the Empress of the Abyss bore Lazarus Heath a child in his image, he fled with the baby, wildly, insanely, rising through the undulant shadows of a mad dream.

More than a year and a half after the disappearance of the *Macedonia*, Lazarus Heath was found, more dead than alive, on an uncharted island in the Atlantic. Some aboard the rescue ship wondered about the strange blue marks on Heath's throat; they asked each other how a man could survive for nearly twenty months when there was no sign of shelter or vegetation on the island. They questioned him about the baby girl who was rescued along with him. Heath said her name was Cassandra.

VII

"I, Lazarus John Heath, being of sound and sane body and

mind, under the influence of no thing or man, natural or otherwise, do this day set my hand in protestation of the truth of what I have written above. My story is not a dream; it happened, and I pray to the Almighty it may never happen again. At first glance, it will have, for the reader, all the earmarks of drunken fantasy, but upon closer consideration of the facts, upon a study of the lore of the sea, I feel certain that another decision will be reached.

"In the ancient books, men have written of a race of Syrens, monstrous beauties of the seas, who lured men to death and worse with their strange, irresistible chanting. This race, say the recorders, was banished from the earth for its evil practice of black magic; the Syrens were turned into the rocky, treacherous shoals of the ocean; turned into stone....

"The whispered legends of the Abyss have another tale to tell. Yes, they murmur. Their race was cast out as men recorded, but only condemned to the deep they once controlled; so that, sullen and alone, they begat the People of the Abyss, a race of creatures that lurks on the edge of time, safe in the maw of the green ocean, until the moment comes when they shall again proclaim themselves and retake the world from which they were banished countless ages ago. I have been one of them; through me they hoped to strike, I think. I was to be their contact with this world we know. I have heard their unsatisfied whimpering; they chafe at the bit for release. And I say beware. They have claimed me. True, I escaped, but even yet I am of them. In the end, they shall reclaim me ... but, not alive, if I can help it. All these haunted years since my escape from the Abyss, I have heard their songs, their endless pagan chanting. So far, I have resisted, but I grow ever weaker. Some day, they will win. But, it is not this that terrifies me; I know I must die as a traitor to their cause. My only fear is that somehow, some day, they will realize that with me in my flight, I took the daughter of Zoth Syra. I pray God they will never reclaim her ... for Cassandra is one of them, just as I ..."

The last words of Lazarus Heath's horrible testament wavered frailly across the page, as if the controlled hand of the writer had grown too weak to go on. The ink was blurred in spots by vague, circular stains that might have been made by raindrops, or the impotent tears of a lost, frightened old man.

With numbed fingers I closed that book of the damned. I sank back against the cold unfriendliness of the throne chair, and shut my eyes. I could feel beads of icy perspiration forming at the base of my skull and trickling down the back of my neck. Not only my hands were numb, my brain was working with the dreamy sluggishness of a somnambulist. Curiously evil visions danced across the shadowy, decaying bindings of books on the far wall. I do not know how long I sat there. The candle guttered and died. I sat on, hemmed in by the writhing ghosts that complete darkness set loose again in the chamber where Heath had written his hateful confession.

Outside, the storm raged maniacally, seething through the forgotten, rat-pirated tunnels under Heath House. Vaguely, I thought that somehow with each passing instant, the sea and the wind had become more ferocious, more predatory, as though lashed on to devastating fury by some infernal, supernatural disturbance. Then, slowly, through the screaming lunacy of the storm, I became aware of another sound. It was a high, soft threnody that was of the wind and lightning, yet a song in itself, a chorus of myriad voices that echoed from beyond life and death, that whispered hauntingly, evilly, of the secrets of the unknown. The song of the Syrens, my mind muttered. Yes, their song. But, for whom? They had Lazarus Heath, now; they must be calling another....

Even before I heard Cassandra's voice, I was out of the chair, stumbling toward the door. Then, the first anguished wail of her ghastly litany froze my senses. For an incalculable moment, I could only stand and listen. That unbearable throbbing was not my heart; it was Cassandra's frail hands pounding madly on her chamber door for release.

And always, steadily, her cry rose, shrilling through the shadow-crawling halls of Heath House, an obscene, awesome chant, at once wheedling, beguiling, and commanding. Slowly, painfully, I made out the words.

"I have heard you call, O, Yoth Kala, my betrothed! I have seen the spirits of the Abyss grown wild as presage of your coming; their rejoicing has set loose the sea that is their empire; it echoes in the thunder, the black wind and lightning! Come then, my husband and father of my child! Claim your bride! Come to me through the cove of Yoth Zara, my father! I wait! Come then. Come!"

The silence in which that last unholy plea died away was an eternity of horror for me, yet it must have endured only an instant. It was a strange, pregnant silence, fraught with impending terror. I realized dully that those countless voices that had risen a moment before above the howling wind had just as suddenly been quieted. Now, in their stead, another voice, single and terrifying in the very loneliness of its sound, rose from a murmur to a sharp nasal chant that sliced through the violence of the storm as if it were a mere unruly zephyr. Someone, something, very near, yet outside, was calling Cassandra's name. The cove, my mind repeated mechanically. Come to me through the cove of Yoth Zara, my father....

I staggered through the blinding darkness toward the single tall window of Heath's study. I felt the skin of my ankle tear as I stumbled over some vague, edged object. I swore and righted myself. My hand caught at the drape, and its dusty velvet strength supported me. I peered through the smeary, leaded panes, into the streaming maw of the storm.

"Cassandra!" that hell-spawned voice echoed. "I come, O, Cassandra, my bride...."

I do not know how I looked standing there, that night, in the evil-sodden gloom, but I know what I saw. Perhaps, in the end, I shall be no more successful at putting the essential, blasphemous horror of that vision into words, than was Lazarus Heath. But, I must try. If I can transcribe only one grain of the actual loathsomeness of the Abyss-born creature called Yoth Kala, perhaps, then, men will know why I destroyed Cassandra....

The flash of lightning that rent the maddened heavens in that moment was nothing ordinary. It was like a sudden noon-day sun at midnight, throwing into relief the hideous, turbulent cove where Lazarus Heath died. The cold stone of the sacrificial pillars cast gargoylesque shadows on the slimy sand; a torrent of cackling sea crashed inland, and drowned them for an instant, then, suddenly, receded, and the Thing was there. I do not remember what wild conjectures twisted through my fear-tortured brain in the moment. Perhaps I thought I had gone mad; perhaps I told myself I was letting my imagination run away with me. But, I knew I wasn't.

I cannot say the Thing in the cove walked; it moved inland rapidly, but with a seemingly gradual, amoebic motion. It expanded and ebbed, gelatinous tendrils creeping over the sand of the cove, spreading like a stain of ink, or black, poisonous blood. I saw no distinct form. I was conscious only of a monstrous, jelly-like mound, black and glistening with a slime-coated, nauseous putrescence. The Thing slobbered onward to Heath House, covering ground with frightening speed. And from this hellish creature, through the whip-lash of the storm, shrilled the high, hypnotic voice of Yoth Kala, calling his bride....

The period of befogged waiting came to an abrupt end. I knew, quite suddenly, that the time for thinking and rational disbelief had run out. It was no longer a matter of guessing and wondering at the mad writings of Lazarus Heath. I, myself, had seen them come to foul, soulless life. I had witnessed the evil of the Abyss incarnate, creeping relentlessly toward its goal—coming to claim Cassandra!

Even as I watched, the fetid Thing disappeared around the dim corner of Heath House. I moved more surely, now, with a strange, icy calm. For, now, I had at least one thing for which to be grateful. The evil that I fought had taken on concrete form; I was no longer fighting shadows. Clutching the cool butt of the revolver in my pocket, I went out into the murky shadows of the hallway. I moved quietly, scarcely daring to breathe. I must reach Cassandra before It did. I must keep her from this creature of lost and carrion ages. And, always, as I walked, the discordant, shrill threnody of Yoth Kala sliced into my consciousness. The pounding on Cassandra's door became more frantic by the second. Her voice rose wildly, calling to the Thing risen from the briny tomb of the sea.

I had almost reached her door, when I stopped. A sudden, whirling vertigo seized my brain; I clutched at the balustrade for support. Rising from the well of the foyer, a reeking effluvia reached out to every corner of the shadow-ridden house. I will not say I actually heard movement; it was simply a soft, hissing sound, as of oily water eating at the rotten pilings of a river dock. I stared down the long staircase, trying to focus my eyes, and then, abruptly, the Thing was there, moving quickly up the stairs. I saw it clearly for the first time.

No one whose mind is cramped by cut-and-dried conceptions of form and the three known dimensions can possibly sense the vague, hideous shapelessness of that creature of the Abyss. The form it possessed cannot be drawn in units of height or thickness or density. It seemed to undulate, varying by the second, rising gelatinously to a height of perhaps ten feet, and then, subsiding, swelling, spreading slimy tentacles forward. The whole of the rubbery outer skin was coated with a foul ichor, a tarry stickiness that seemed secreted from monstrous, leathery pores. I think it was this bluish slime that set loose the rancid stench that grew more overpowering with each moment, with each slithering inch of its progress up the staircase.

At the approximate center of this putrid, blue-black mass, a raw, slobbering hole, which seemed to be a rudimentary mouth, sucked in and out with obscene rhythm. It was from this opening in the reticulated, reptilian hide that the cloying, mucous-choked chant of Yoth Kala emanated. Actually, there was no face, but, nearly a foot above the wound-like mouth, there was a single, serpentine tentacle that writhed from side to side, sensing, rather than seeing, looking like some flesh-made periscope shot up from hell. At the end of the tentacle, I made out what might have been an eye—the squamous, dusty, expressionless orb of a snake. And, now, as the Thing crawled upward, the eye-tentacle suddenly grew rigid, turning toward me. For a second, the huge gelatinous form hesitated, then moved forward again, this time directly for me.

Mechanically, sick with the putrid vileness of the odor the Thing cast off, I staggered backward, away from on-coming horror. The eye-tentacle wavered and followed me. The forerunning cilia of black, tarry stickiness flowed across the hall, only a few feet from me. The stench was unbearable. It seemed to me that the pagan song of Yoth Kala had taken on a high, evilly-humorous note. The slobbering mouth-hole spread in what could only be a hideous, anticipatory grin.

Now, my back was against the wall; I could still hear Cassandra thumping on the panels of her door, crying her invitation to this loathsome lover of hers, but I was no longer thinking of her. I could think only of the long, jelly-like feeler, sent out from the black, viscid mass, curling slowly about my waist, crushing. Perhaps, I screamed or swore; I do not know. I remember plunging my hand into my pocket and squeezing the trigger of that revolver. There was a smell of seared cloth as the bullet burnt through my coat, and then, sharply, a cry, almost human, of furious pain. A slitted, ugly wound opened in the feeler, and bluish, stinking slime spewed over my hand and waist; this was the foul, putrid blood of the creature of the Abyss! A thick, nauseous ichor that spurted like oil from the bullet wound. The feeler uncoiled in a tremendous reflex of agony, and I stumbled away, down the hall, fumbling in my pocket for the key to Cassandra's door. I slammed the heavy portal behind me, and leaned against it, sobbing hysterically.

The first thing I became conscious of was the sudden silence; it fell like a spidery caul over Heath House. I realized dully that, for a moment, Yoth Kala's song had been stopped.

Beyond the door, there was a vague, liquid rustling, then a tense, waiting noiselessness—as though the Thing were being very still, listening.

And, here, in Cassandra's room, there was another silence. Before me in the shadows, the pallid oval of Cassandra's face wavered phantom-like, staring at me; the darkly brilliant eyes were tortured with a surprisingly sane fear. Abruptly, as though the silencing of that blasphemous incantation had momentarily released her to sanity, Cassie was in my arms, crying softly.

"Don't let him get me, darling! You mustn't let him get me! Promise you won't! Please! ... I'm all right, now; it's only when I hear his voice that I can't refuse him...."

"It's all right," I said thickly. "We'll get out of here somehow.... We'll go away where he can never touch you...."

"No ... no, I can't escape him that way...."

"We can, Cassie! We must...."

"No.... Believe me! I know! There's only one escape.... You've got to kill me...."

"Cassie!"

"It's true! It's the only way out. If you don't care about me, think about the child ... my child by him...."

"Stop talking crazy. I tell you we'll get away...."

"Think of the child," Cassandra insisted hoarsely. "I am the daughter of Zoth Syra. My father was a human; I was born in the image of that father. But, think of the child I must bear.... Suppose ... suppose *he* is born in the image of *his* father ... of that ... that Thing out there!"

VIII

I was no longer seeing that frail, anguished visage, gray as death, with its ghastly, bluish throat-scars; I was no longer aware of the horror that shone through Cassandra's eyes—the terror of a mind caught in a web from which there was no escape. All I could see was that slavering, heinous monstrosity beyond the chamber door. A child! Its child, born in its own hideous image! It couldn't be! It must never happen! This lost decadent race of evil encroaching upon the earth, begetting its hellish fruit upon humans—and in the end, overwhelming, conquering, reclaiming, as Lazarus Heath had prophesied!

"Cassandra! O, my bride! Princess of the Abyss, I call. Yoth Kala calls!"

Beneath my hands, I felt Cassandra's fragile body turn rigid; her flesh suddenly burned against mine. Those dark eyes glazed and protruded horribly, and at her throat, the bluish lines pulsed obscenely, like the gills of a fish, like the nauseous mouth of the Thing in the hall. I tried to hold her, but as the chant of Yoth Kala rose wildly, her clawed hands beat insanely at my face; their nails bit into the flesh. With a species of supernatural strength, Cassandra tore herself loose. She thrust me to one side, and was at the door, tearing frantically at the latch, shrilling a nasal, hypnotic reply to her mate.

Now, staring at the door itself, I saw the massive panels sag and warp, as if from tremendous pressure from without. A fetid black feeler oozed through the crevice at the bottom of the door. It circled, obscenely possessive, about Cassandra's ankles, evil, caressing. The storm throbbed at the blackened casements. There was no lightning, now; only endless, abysmal blackness and rising through it, all the myriad hateful voices of the Green Abyss, howling in chorus to the incantations of Yoth Kala and his bride.

What I did then was done with the sure, unthinking calm of a man who has reached his final decision. I walked slowly to Cassandra's side;

she was no longer conscious of my existence. She tore so maniacally at the door to freedom that her frail fingers bled. The revolver felt cool in my sweat-soaked grip. I brought the neat, business-like muzzle within a few inches of Cassandra's temple. I knew, now, that she was right. There was only one escape. I pulled the trigger.

I waited for death.

You must understand that. I fully expected to die. I had no idea of running. I saw Cassandra slump forward against the door. As she slid to the floor, her fingers clutched convulsively at the dark wood; the nails dug four parallel streaks the length of the panels. She lay very still. In that instant, as the crashing echo of the shot withered to silence through the catacombs of Heath House, a great terrified wail soared insanely above the onslaught of the storm; a scream of pain and unanswerable anger. The huge door bent beneath superhuman pressure. Then, slowly, as I waited for loathsome, foul-smelling death in the grip of Yoth Kala, a death I did not intend to fight, the weird chanting from without died away. There was silence. A strange, utterly peaceful silence such as Heath House had not known for countless years. I saw the black, stinking tentacle withdrawn from the room. Outside, in the hallway, a sickly hissing sound echoed mournfully. It moved down the staircase that creaked beneath its retreating weight.

I walked unsteadily to the casement window and gazed out through a strangely abated storm. A sudden, peaceful moon had crept from behind dull clouds. And across the cold moonlit strand, into the cove, once again to be swallowed by the sightless depths of the Green Abyss, slithered the hideous, hell-spawned Thing no other living man has ever seen. Yoth Kala was gone.

I know, now, why it happened that way. I have thought about it a great deal in these last lonely hours, and I believe I have found the answer. I had waited for the vengeance of Yoth Kala; I had expected to die as the destroyer of his bride. But, Yoth Kala could not reach me. As Lazarus Heath had been before her, Cassandra was an instrument. She was the key in the grip of the people of the Abyss, their only contact with this world that had cast them out ages since, the only one through whom they could regain a foothold in that world, on whom they could beget the race that would one day reclaim all that they had lost. When I killed

Cassandra, I cut off that contact. Yoth Kala and his hideous breed were once more consigned to the bonded anonymity of the Abyss. This time, at least, the world had escaped their vengeance.

I walked back to where Cassandra lay, calm, and at peace. I sat down beside her, and smoothed her soft, warm hair gently. I think I cried. The storm whispered a last protest and died. I sat there with Cassandra until late the next evening, when Dr. Ambler came to call, and found us.

Only another half-hour until dawn. The cell block has been very quiet most of the night. Outside, in the grayish half-light, there is a sound of distant business that seems ghostly coming in through the bars on the cold early morning air. There is a creaking of wood, and then a sudden thud. This is repeated several times. They are testing the spring-trap of my gallows.

They say that prayers help. If you have come this far, if you think you understand the story of Cassandra Heath, you might try it. Make it a very special sort of prayer. Not for Cassandra and me. All our prayers were said a long time since. We are at peace.

This prayer must be for you—for you and all the others who must be left behind, who cannot walk with me, up that final flight of wooden stairs, to peace and escape, who must go on living in the shadow of a monstrous evil of which they are not even aware, and so, can never destroy. You may need those prayers.

Somewhere beyond the edge of the last lone lip of land, beyond the rim of reality, sunken beneath the slime and weed of innumerable centuries, the creatures of the Abyss live on. Zoth Syra still reigns, and the syren songs are still sung. Entombed in their foul, watery empire, they writhe; restless, waiting.... This time they have lost their foothold. This time their link with the world of normalcy has been broken, their contact destroyed. This time they have failed.

But, they will try again ... and again....

THE DEEP ONES

JAMES WADE

"Diviner than the dolphin is nothing yet created; for indeed
they were aforetime men, and lived in cities along with mortals."
—Oppian: *Halieutica* (AD 200)

I

had never met Dr. Frederick Wilhelm before I went to work at his Institute for Zoological Studies, located in a remote cove on the California coast some miles north of San Simeon and Piedres Blancas, not far from the Big Sur area; but of course I had heard of his studies. The Sunday supplements picked Wilhelm up years ago, which was only natural: what more potentially sensational subject could a journalist hope for than the idea that man shared the earth with another, older, and perhaps more intelligent species; a species overlooked or ignored by modern science, but with which communication might someday be established?

It wasn't a worn-out gambit like flying saucer people, or spiritualism, or trolls hidden under the hills, of course. Wilhelm's subject was the dolphin, that ocean mammal glimpsed centuries ago by superstitious sailors and transmogrified into myths of mermaids, sirens, all the fabulous sea-dwelling secret races of legend. Now, it appeared, the superstitions might not be far wrong.

Preliminary tests had showed long ago that our ocean-going distant cousins harbored a high degree of pure intelligence and potential for communication, unsuspected because of their watery habitat and their lack of hands or any other prehensile apparatus for producing artifacts. Wilhelm's researches had not been the first, but his speculations were certainly the most daring, and he had parlayed his preoccupation into a career, attracting both government and private foundation funds to set up the institute toward which I found myself jogging in a rented jeep over rutted, sandy roads beside the sinuous green Pacific one starkly sunlit afternoon in April a year ago.

Although I knew of Frederick Wilhelm and his institute, I wasn't sure just how or what he knew of me. In a sense, I could easily see how my field, extrasensory perception and telepathy, might tie in with his work; but his initial letters and wires to me had never spelled out in any detail what he expected of our collaboration. His messages, indeed, had seemed at once euphoric and evasive, confining themselves mostly to grandiloquent descriptions of his basic purposes and facilities, plus details on the financial aspects of our association.

I will admit that the amount of money Dr. Wilhelm offered was a strong factor in my accepting a job the exact nature of which remained unclear. As research coordinator of a small Eastern foundation devoted to parapsychological studies overlooked by the Rhine group at Duke, I had had my fill of skimped budgets and starvation wages. Wilhelm's offer had come as an opportunity golden in more ways than one, so I had lost little time in packing my bags for the trip to sunny California.

Actually, the location of Wilhelm's experiments gave me more pause than any of the other doubtful aspects of his offer. I confess that I have always had an antipathy to California, despite the little time I recall having spent there. Perhaps I had read too much in the works of mordant satirists like Waugh and Nathanael West, but to me there has always seemed something decadent and even sinister about this self-eulogizing Pacific paradise.

The impression had not been allayed by my arrival via plane in gritty, galvanic Los Angeles, or by a stroll through that tiny downtown park where predatory homosexuals, drug derelicts, and demented fanatics of all kinds congregate under the bloated, twisted palms, like so many patients in the garden of Dr. Caligari's madhouse. To some, Gothic battlements or New England backwaters represent the apex of spiritual horror and decay; for me, the neon-lit, screaming depravity of Los Angeles filled the bill. As the comedian Fred Allen once remarked, California is a great place if you're an orange.

These thoughts and others tangled in my mind as I guided my jeep over the rough beachside path which, I had been assured by the jovial car rental agent in San Simeon, would take me unfailingly to the Institute for Zoological Studies. ("Ain't no place else the road goes, after you turn off left at the first orange juice stand—you know, the kind where the stand is built to look just like a great big orange. Jest keep on goin', and don't stop for hippies or high water till the road ends!")

As I glanced rather nervously around, I could see on my left a sort of encampment of bleached white tents and dark, darting figures down by the wavering lace of surf at water's edge. Were these the hippies my guide had referred to, those sardonic jesters on the periphery of our society, razzing and reviling all the standards and values of three thousand civilized years? Or had he been spoofing me; were these only a gaggle of middle-class youngsters out for an afternoon of beachside sun, sand, and sex as a respite from the abrasive grind of our precariously affluent society?

Even as these trite and puerile thoughts chased through my head, suddenly the vestigal road took a sharp turn over a rise and I found myself startlingly close up (a zoomlens effect) to what could only be the famous Institute for Zoological Studies.

II

"What, actually, do you know about dolphins—or porpoises, as they are sometimes called?" queried Dr. Frederick Wilhelm, his eyes invisible behind thick lenses that caught the light from filtered globes under gold-tinted shades in his plush office. We had just settled down over a late afternoon cocktail, expertly crafted by Wilhelm himself, after my first rapid tour of the Institute, conducted by its director immediately after meeting my arriving jeep.

Wilhelm had been cordial and almost courtly, though it seemed a bit odd for him to start me off on a junket around his establishment before

I had had a chance even to drop my luggage at my quarters and freshen up a bit after the long drive. I put it down to the vanity of a self-made scientific pioneer jockeying a cherished hobby horse down the home stretch in the big race.

The impression I'd received on the whirlwind tour was superficial and a bit bewildering: the long, low, white-plastered cement buildings straggling along the shoreline seemed crammed with more sound, lighting, recording, photographic, and less identifiable computerized equipment than would be needed to study the entire passenger list of Noah's ark, let alone one minor sub-species of marine mammal.

About Wilhelm himself there was nothing odd, though: a big, rumpled, greying penguin of a man, he moved and spoke with the disarming enthusiasm of a schoolboy just discovering that there is such a thing as science. As he hurried me from lab to lab at a breathless pace, he explained, "We'll see the dolphin pools tomorrow morning. Josephine—my research assistant, Josephine Gilman—is working there now; she'll join us later for drinks and dinner."

As I had teamed from correspondence with Dr. Wilhelm, his senior staff (now totaling three, himself included, with my arrival) had quarters at the Institute, while the dozen or so technicians and laboratory assistants employed here made the trip to and from San Simeon billets in a Volkswagen micro-bus each day.

Now as I sat with Wilhelm in the dim, richly decorated office over an acridly enticing martini, I heard the bus pull away, and realized that I was alone in the sprawling complex of buildings with its director and the unsurmised Josephine Gilman.

"What do you actually know about dolphins?" Wilhelm was saying.

"About what any layman knows," I found myself replying frankly. "I know that research started back in the 1950's, and indicated that dolphin brain size and specialized adaptations made probable a high degree of intelligence, along with sensory equipment suggesting a possibility of communication with man. So far as I recall, up to date nothing conclusive has come of it all, despite a lot of effort. I bought Dr. Lilly's books on his research in the Virgin Islands, but all this has happened so fast I haven't gone very far into them, though I have them with me, in my suitcase."

"Don't bother with Lilly," Dr. Wilhelm broke in, refilling my glass from a crystal shaker with the etched classical design of a boy riding a dolphin. "I can show you things here that Lilly never even dreamed of."

"But the big mystery to me," I had the temerity to mention, "is what I'm here for. Do you want me to try and hypnotize your dolphins, or read their minds?"

"Not exactly," Willielin answered. "At least, not at the present stage. The way I actually plan for you to begin is to hypnotize a human subject, to see whether such a person may become more sensitive to the thought-patterns of the animal.

"We've done a lot of work, following up Lilly's leads, in recording and analyzing the sounds these beasts make, both under water and in the air: clicks, bleats, whistles, a wide gamut of noises—some of them above the sound spectrum audible to humans. We've taped these sounds, coded them, and fed them into computers, but no pattern of language has emerged, outside of certain very obvious signals for pain, distress, mating—signals many kinds of animals make, but which can't be called real language. And although dolphins will sometimes mimic human speech with a startling clarity, it usually seems to be mere parroting, without real understanding.

"Yet at the same time, our encephalographs show patterns of electrical output in dolphin brains similar to those that occur during human speech, and in parts of the brain analogous to our speech centers—all this while no vocalization of any kind is going on, subsonic or supersonic, airborne or waterborne.

"This led me to a theory that the basic means of dolphin communication may be telepathic, and the conviction that we'll never get in touch with them any other way."

I was somewhat taken aback. "Do you have a telepathically sensitive and experienced person on the staff, or are you going to hire such a person?" I queried.

"Even better than that," rapped Dr. Wilhelm triumphantly, his twin-moon spectacles jiggling with emphasis. "We have a person sensitive and experienced over many months with the animals themselves—someone who knows how dolphins think, feel, and react; someone who has lived with dolphins so closely that she might almost be accepted among them as a dolphin herself."

"He means me, Mr. Dorn." Through an open door leading to a dusky hallway stepped lightly the lithe figure of a woman.

III

Glancing sidelong at her across the candle-lit dinner table an hour later, I decided that Josephine Gilman was striking but not beautiful. Fairly young, with a trim figure, she missed real distinction due to the muddy coloring and rather swarthy texture of her skin, and especially the staring protuberance of her eyes.

Nor was her manner entirely prepossessing. Her melodramatic entrance of Dr. Wilhelm's office that afternoon I could forgive, even with its implication that she had been listening outside for some time. But in subsequent conversation she had proved as much a monomaniac as her employer on the subject of their experiments, and with far less sense of humor—a fitting Trilby to Wilhelm's benign, avuncular Svengali.

"But of course," she was addressing me over our coffee, "you know all the old Greek and Roman stories about dolphins, Mr. Dorn. How they herded fish to help fishermen, saved drowning persons, and sometimes even fell in love with attractive boys and carried them off to sea on their backs. There's a long history of friendly relations between our species, even though the latter type of incident seems based on—shall we say, a misunderstanding?"

"I don't know about that, Miss Gilman," I riposted. "From what I've seen in California already, some of our modern youth would try anything once."

"Surf, sand, and sex," Dr. Wilhelm interjected, like a slogan. "I know what you mean. We have some of that type camped out down the beach right now, just south around the bend. Hippies, they call themselves these days. But to get back to dolphins, a more intelligent species. I'm not entirely sure that their good 'PR,' so to speak, through the ages really rings true," Wilhelm continued. "Sometimes I even imagine it resembles the way superstitious people used to refer to the fairies and trolls as 'the Good Folk' to flatter them, out of fear of what they might do. So we get the modern nursery-rhyme and Walt Disney type of fairy instead of the hidden troll races, the menacing, stunted, displaced hill-dwellers that were their real origin."

Josephine Gilman picked up her coffee cup and daintily shrugged, as if to express disagreement.

"No, Jo, there's something to it," Wilhelm insisted, getting up and lumbering over to a big bookcase in the shadowed corner of the room. "Let me give you an example from a non-Western tradition." He searched for a book on one of the upper shelves.

"Sir Arthur Grimble was a colonial governor in the Gilbert Islands not so long ago. He visited an atoll called—what was it?—Butaritari, where there was supposed to be a man who could call dolphins." Wilhelm located the book he sought and fumbled it open.

"Grimble writes, let's see, here it is: 'His spirit went out of his body in a dream; it sought out the porpoise folk in their home under the Western horizon and invited them to a dance, with feasting, in Kuma village. If he spoke the words of the invitation aright (and very few had the secret of them) the porpoises would follow him with cries of joy to the surface.'

"Well, Grimble had him try it. The place was dead quiet that afternoon under the palm trees, the way he describes it, and the children had been gathered in under the thatches, the women were absorbed in plaiting garlands of flowers, and the men were silently polishing their ceremonial ornaments of shell. The makings of a feast lay ready in baskets. Suddenly—wait till I find it—'a strangled howl burst from the dreamer's hut. He dashed into the open and stood a while clawing at the air,' says Grimble, and 'whining on a queer high note like a puppy's. The words came out "Teiraki! Teiraki!", which means "Arise! Arise!" Our friends from the west.... Let us go down and greet them.'

"'A roar went up from the village, and everyone rushed over to the beach on the atoll's ocean side. They strung themselves out and splashed through the shallows, all wearing the garlands woven that afternoon. Breast deep the porpoises appeared, "gamboling toward us at a fine clip." Everyone was screaming hard. When the porpoises reached the edge of the reef they slackened speed, spread out, and started cruising back and forth in front of the human line. Then suddenly they vanished.'"

Dr. Wilhelm brought the book to the table, sat down, and finished his remaining coffee. "Grimble thought they had gone away. But in a moment the dreamer pointed downward, muttering, 'The King out of the West comes to greet me.' There, not ten yards away, was the great shape of a porpoise, 'poised like a glimmering shadow in the glass-green water. Behind it followed a whole dusky flotilla of them.'

"The porpoises seemed to be hung in a trance. Their leader came slowly to the caller's legs. 'As we approached the emerald shallows, the keels of the creatures began to take the sand: they flapped gently, as if asking for help. The men leaned down to throw their arms around the great barrels and ease them over the ridges. They showed no sign of alarm. It was as if their single wish was to get to the beach.'

"When the water stood only thigh-deep, the men crowded around the porpoises, ten or more to each beast. Then 'Lift!' shouted the dreamer, and the ponderous black shapes were half dragged, half carried, unresisting, to the lip of the tide. There they settled down, those beautiful, dignified shapes, utterly at peace, while all hell broke loose around them."

Wilhelm's glasses caught the twin candle flames from the table; his eyes were impossible to see. Was this wild account, I found myself wondering, the real basis for his belief in the possibility of man's telepathic communication with dolphins?

"Men, women, and children," he continued, "leaping and posturing with shrieks that tore the sky, stripped off their garlands and flung them around the still bodies, in a sudden and dreadful fury of boastfulness and derision. 'My mind,' says Grimble, 'still shrinks from that last scene—the raving humans, the beasts so triumphantly at rest.' There, what do you think of that?" He closed the book.

"It seems," I responded, "that the islanders made the dolphins the object of some sort of religious ritual, and that the dolphins enjoyed the proceedings. Sounds like something our hippie neighbors might go in for."

"You're wrong about that part," Josephine Gilman told me solemnly. "Those people out on the beach there hate the dolphins. Either that, or they're afraid of them."

IV

The next morning dawned damp and cloudy. As I breakfasted in the glass-enclosed patio outside my quarters, which overlooked the surging grey-green waves of the Pacific across a narrow stretch of sand, I saw Dr. Wilhelm sauntering along the beach on what seemed a morning constitutional. Suddenly I was aware that he was not alone; slogging across the sand to meet him came a fantastic figure: a booted, bearded, fur-clad man with bulbous features and tangled masses of hair surmounted by a big, bright-red beret—a coarse caricature, he appeared to me, of the well-known bust of the composer Wagner. One of the hippies!

Some impulse, perhaps simply curiosity, moved me to bolt down the eggs and toast which the early-arriving housekeeper had brought me on a tray, and to rush out onto the beach through the storm-door of my entryway and join that strange colloquy shaping up under the striated silver-grey clouds as Wilhelm closed with his odd visitor.

My employer's stance seemed brusque and unfriendly as he listened to whatever the bearded man was saying to him. I slowed and approached the pair, as if on a casual stroll; until I came up to them, all I could hear was the sibilance of surf hissing over the sand almost at our feet.

"Good morning, Mr. Dorn," Wilhelm snapped, obviously not pleased to see me. "Perhaps you ought to meet Mr. Alonzo Waite, since he's our neighbor. Mr. Waite is the high priest, or whatever he calls himself, of that hippie bunch down the way."

"I call myself nothing," the other responded quickly. "My disciples have awarded me the title of *guru*, or spiritual leader, since I have spent more time in mystic exercises than they. But I neither seek nor accept any pre-eminence among them. We are all fellow pilgrims on the sacred quest for truth." His voice was hollow, deep, strangely impressive; and his words, while eccentric, seemed more urbanely cultivated than I had expected.

"All very well, perhaps," Wilhelm put in testily, "but your quest for truth seems determined to interfere with mine."

"I am simply warning you, as I have warned you before, that your work with the dolphins is potentially very dangerous, to yourselves and others. You should give up these studies and release the beasts before great harm results."

"And on what evidence do you base this remarkable prophecy?"

Wilhelm inquired acidly. "Tell Mr. Dorn; I've heard all this before."

Waite's cavernous voice descended even deeper. "As you may know, the League for Spiritual Discovery has been working with mind-expanding substances—not drugs, in the proper sense—that produce intuitions and perceptions unattainable to the ordinary brain. We are not of that group, but we too claim that such states are true ecstatic trances, comparable or superior to those that have always played such a vital part in an the Eastern religions, and which modern science would do well to recognize and investigate."

"This is more Mr. Dorn's field than mine," Wilhelm said uneasily. "He's in parapsychology. I know nothing about such matters, but none of this sounds at all plausible to me."

"But what has all this to do with dolphins?" I asked the bearded *guru*.

"Our dreams and visions lately have been troubled by the presence of great, white, menacing shapes, cutting across and blocking out the sacred color patterns and animated mandalas that lead us to greater spiritual understanding," Waite boomed. "These are vibrations emanating from the creatures you have penned here, which you call dolphins, but which we know by an older name. These creatures are evil, strong and evil. As your experiments have progressed, so have the disturbing manifestations intensified. These vibrations are terribly destructive, not only mentally but physically. For your own good, I warn you to desist before it is too late."

"If what we're doing upsets your pipe-dreams," Wilhelm remarked with ill-concealed contempt, "why don't you move elsewhere and get out of range?"

The tall, bearded man blinked and gazed into the distance. "We must remain and concentrate our psychic powers on combating the evil vibrations," he said quietly. "There are certain spiritual exercises and ceremonies we can undertake that may help curb or deflect the danger for a while. In fact, we are planning such a ceremony for tonight. But the only sure way to safety is for you to release these ancient, wickedly wise creatures, and to give up your experiment."

Waite stood solemnly staring out to sea, a grotesque, foreboding and somehow dignified figure in his oversize beret and flapping fur robe.

V

"A scene right out of a Hollywood science-fiction thriller," Wilhelm muttered angrily as he led me through the barn-like, high-ceilinged main laboratory and out a rear door. He couldn't seem to get the encounter on the beach out of his mind, and it bothered him more than I could well understand. As for me, I had put Waite down as just a typical California nut, though more intelligent than most, and doubted that we would have any real trouble with him.

"You've seen our sound recording equipment, both atmospheric and underwater," Wilhelm said, finally changing the subject. "Now you must see where most of it is used, and where your own work will be concentrated."

The back of the lab looked out over the beach; near the water's edge stood a smaller windowless structure—long, low, and plastered with white cement like the others. Wilhelm led the way to it and opened its single heavy metal door with a key from his pocket.

The inside was taken up mostly by a sunken tank that resembled a small indoor swimming pool. The narrow verge that surrounded the tank on three sides was cluttered with electrical control panels, head sets, and other paraphernalia connected with the main tape recording and computer banks in the big lab. The ocean side of the building consisted mostly of a sort of sea-gate that could be opened on a cove communicating with the ocean itself, as I learned later, so that the water might be cleaned and freshened at need. Harsh fluorescent lamps played over the glittering surface of the pool, sending rippling whorls of reflected light into every corner of the room; there was a low hissing sound from the steam radiators run by thermostats that kept both the air and water temperatures constant and controllable.

But none of this attracted my immediate attention; for here I was at last confronted with the subject of the experiment itself: a lithe, bulky yet graceful shape—mottled grey above, dirty white below, with a long saw-toothed snout and deep-set, intelligent eyes—hung motionless in the shallow water on its slowly fanning flippers.

And not alone, for the dolphin shared its pool with Josephine Gilman, clad in a bright red bathing suit that set off her striking figure in an arresting manner. Indeed, I found myself staring more intently at Josephine than at her aquatic companion.

"Hi." Josephine's greeting was bland, but suggested a veiled irony, as if she were conscious of my covert gaze.

"Jo has been more or less living in this pool for the last two and a half months," Dr. Wilhelm explained. "The purpose is to get into complete rapport with Flip—that's the dolphin—and encourage any attempts at communication on his part."

"Flip," Josephine interjected, "is short for Flipper, of course, the dolphin hero of that old movie and TV series that was the first sign of popular awareness of the animal's intelligence."

Jo laughed, heaving herself adroitly onto the tiled edge of the pool. "The show was just a sea-going Lassie, of course." She reached out for and wrapped herself snugly within a heavy terry-cloth towel. "Anybody for coffee? It's a bit chilly today for these early morning aquatics."

As Jo served coffee from a sideboard silex, Wilhelm was priming me with data on Flip.

"He's a prime specimen of *Tursiops truncata*, though a bit smaller than average—about six and a half feet, actually. The brain weighs an average of 1700 grams, 350 grams more than the human brain, with comparable density of cell count.

"We've had this fellow for over a year now, and though he'll make every noise they're noted for—barks, grunts, clicks and scrapes and whistles—and even mimic human speech, we can't dope out a language pattern. Yet they must talk to each other. My first interest in delphinology was aroused by a report on sonar charts that Navy boats made near Ponape in the south Pacific. The charts showed orderly discipline in their undersea movements over a distance amounting to miles; and something more: a pattern or formation of mathematically precise movements that suggests either elaborate play or some sort of ritual."

"Maybe," I interrupted facetiously, "they were practicing for the ceremony that so impressed Gov. Grimble."

"Anyway," said Jo, putting aside her cup and straightening a strap on her bathing suit, "in ten weeks I haven't gotten to first base with Flip here, and now you're supposed to get us onto the proper wave length.

Also, you'll have to provide some hints about what to look for and concentrate on in telepathic communication attempts. Frankly, I don't put much faith in it; but if Fred wants to try, I'll co-operate with as few mental reservations as possible."

Remembering a passage from Dr. Lilly's pioneer book on dolphins, I asked Wilhelm: "Have you implanted electrodes in the beast's brain for pleasure-stimulus experiments?"

"We're beyond all that," Wilhelm replied impatiently. "It's been known for years that they'll learn the most complex reaction patterns almost immediately to achieve the stimulus, far beyond what any lower animal can manage. Besides, it's crude—a kind of electrical masturbation, or LSD, like our friends out there on the beach favor. It doesn't show a proper respect for our basic equality with the dolphin— or his superiority over us, as the case may be."

While this conversation progressed, my attention was gradually distracted by the animal itself, floating in the pool beside us. It was obviously following our talk, though I assumed without any degree of verbal comprehension. The single visible eye, set in a convoluted socket behind the rather menacing snout, moved from one to the other of us with lively interest. I even caught myself reading human expressions into it: proprietary interest when turned on Josephine Gilman, tolerant amusement in regard to Dr. Wilhelm, and toward myself, what? Resentment, animosity, jealousy? What fancies were these I was weaving, under the glaring lights of a scientific laboratory?

"You'll have to get better acquainted with Flip," Wilhelm was saying. "If you're to help us learn to interpret delphinese, you and he should become good friends."

There was a commotion in the water; Flip turned abruptly to his left and swam off semi-submerged, emitting as he did so the first dolphin sound I had ever heard: a shrill whistle of derision.

VI

That evening after dinner, Josephine Gilman and I walked on the beach under a moon that shone only intermittently through scurrying clouds. Dr. Wilhelm was in his office writing up notes, and the housekeeper-cook, last to leave of the staff each evening, was just rattling off toward San Simeon in the Institute's Land Rover.

I found that I didn't know what to make of my feelings toward Jo. When I had seen her in the pool with the dolphin that morning, she had attracted me intensely, seeming in her proper element. But at dinner, in a frilly cocktail gown that somehow didn't suit her, she once more repelled me with her sallow skin, her bulging, humorless eyes.

"Tomorrow the hypnosis sessions are to begin," I reminded her as we paced slowly toward the surf's edge. "Are you sure you really want to undergo this? After all, you say you have no confidence in this approach, and that may inhibit your response to it."

"I'll do as Fred thinks best, and I'll assume what he assumes, temporarily at least. I've become quite good at that, within limits. Did you know he once wanted me to marry him? That's where I drew the line, though."

"No." I was embarrassed by her abrupt interjection of personal matters.

"I think it was for convenience, mostly. His first wife had died, we were working together, we shared the same interests—even the fact that we had to stay here together overnight, to watch over the work 24 hours a day when that was necessary—well, it would have made things easier, but I told him no."

"How did you first become interested in—delphinology, is that the word?" I sought to change the subject. We had reached the point beyond which the waves retreated, leaving streaks of hissing, iridescent foam half visible in the gloom.

"Actually, I've always been fascinated by the sea and things that live underwater. I used to spend half my time at the aquarium back home in Boston—either there or down at the harbor."

"Your family comes from Boston?"

"Not originally. My father was in the Navy, and we lived there a long time, ever since Mother died. His family came from a run-down seaport mill-town called Innsmouth, up past Marblehead. The Gilmans are an old family there. They were in whaling and the East Indies trade as far back as two hundred years ago, and I suppose that's where my oceanographic interests come from."

"Do you often go back there?"

"I've never even been there, strange as it seems. The whole place almost burned to the ground back in the 1920's, before I was born. My father said it was a dead, depressing place, and made me promise years ago to keep away from it—I don't know exactly why. That was just after his last trip there, and on his next voyage he was lost overboard from a destroyer he commanded. No one ever knew how; it was calm weather."

"Weren't you ever curious about why he warned you away from—what was it, Innsville?" I faltered.

"Yes, especially after he died. I looked up the newspapers from around the time of the big fire—the Boston libraries had almost nothing else on Innsmouth—and found one story that might have had some bearing. It was full of preposterous hints about how the people of Innsmouth had brought back some sort of hybrid heathen savages with them from the South Seas years ago, and started a devil-worship cult that brought them sunken treasure and supernatural power over the weather. The story suggested that the men had interbred with their Polynesian priestesses or whatever, and that was one reason why people nearby shunned and hated them."

I thought of Josephine's swarthy skin and strange eyes, and wondered.

We had covered a mile or more from the Institute, and were suddenly aware that the darkness ahead was laced with a faint flickering, as of a fire on the beach to the south. At the same time, a sort of low mumble or glutinous chant became audible from the same direction. All at once, a high hysterical wail, reverberating in shocking ecstasy, burst forth on the night air, prolonging itself incredibly—now terror-stricken, now mockingly ironic, now mindlessly animal—rising and falling in a frenzy that suggested only delirium or insanity raised to the highest possible human—or inhuman—pitch.

Without thought or volition, Josephine and I found ourselves clinging together and kissing with an abandon that echoed the wild caterwauling down the beach.

The hippies, it seemed, were holding their promised ritual to exorcise the evil influence of the sinister creatures from the sea.

VII

The next few days can most conveniently be summarized through extracts from the clinical journal which I began to keep from the outset of our attempt to establish telepathic contact with the dolphin Flip through hypnosis of a human subject:

April 20. This morning I placed Josephine under light hypnosis, finding her an almost ideally suggestible subject. I implanted post-hypnotic commands intended to keep her alert and concentrating on the dolphin's mind to catch any message emanating from it. After I awakened her, she went back into the tank with Flip and spent the rest of the day there, playing the number games they have devised together. It is remarkable to observe how devoted the animal is to her, following her about the pool and protesting with loud barkings and bleatings whenever she leaves it. Flip will accept his food, raw whole fish, only from her hands.

I asked Dr. Wilhelm whether there was any danger from those wicked-looking hundred-toothed jaws, which snap down on the fish like a huge, lethal pair of shears. He said no; in neither history nor legend has there ever been a report of a dolphin attacking or even accidentally injuring a human. Then he quoted something from Plutarch—his erudition is profound, if one-sided—which I looked up in the library later. Here it is:

"To the dolphin alone, beyond all others, Nature has granted what the best philosophers seek: friendship for no advantage."

April 22. Still no results. Wilhelm wants me to try deeper hypnosis and stronger suggestion. In fact, he proposed leaving Josephine in a trance for periods of a day or more, with just enough volition to keep her head above water in the tank. When I protested that this was dangerous, since in such a state she might well drown inadvertently, Wilhelm gave me an odd look and said, "Flip wouldn't let her."

April 25. Today, in the absence of any progress whatsoever, I agreed to try Wilhelm's second-stage plan, since Jo agrees. I put her to sleep by the pool's edge while Flip watched curiously. (I don't think this dolphin likes me, although I've had no trouble making friends with the others in the bigger tank up on the north beach.) After implanting in her subconscious the strongest admonitions to be careful in the water, I let her re-enter the pool for a few hours. Her demeanor, of course, is that of a sleepwalker or a comatose person. She sits on the lip of the pool or wades about in it abstractedly. Flip seems puzzled and resentful that she won't play their usual games with him.

When I was helping Jo out of the pool after an hour or so of this, the dolphin zoomed past at terrific speed, and I was sure he was about to snap at my arm, thus making me the first dolphin-bitten human in history; but he apparently changed his mind at the last moment and veered away, quacking and creaking angrily, his single visible eye glaring balefully....

April 27. Dr. Wilhelm wants to increase the period with Jo in the pool under hypnosis. This is because when she woke up yesterday she said she remembered vague, strange impressions that might be telepathic images or messages. I'm almost certain that these are pseudo-memories, created by her subconscious to please Dr. Wilhelm, and I have strongly protested any intensification of this phase of the experiment.

Those hippie orgies on the beach south of here go on almost every night till all hours. The three of us are losing sleep and getting on edge, especially Jo, who tires easily after the longer periods under hypnosis.

April 28. Jo had an especially vivid impression of some sort of scenes or pictures transmitted to her during hypnosis after I brought her out of the trance this afternoon. At Wilhelm's suggestion I put her under again to help her remember, and we taped some inconclusive question-and-answer exchanges. She spoke of a ruined stone city under the sea, with weedy arches and domes and spires, and of sea creatures moving through the sunken streets. Over and over she repeated a word that sounded like "Arlyah." It's all imagination, I'm sure, plus memories of poems by Poe or cheap horror fiction—maybe even the story Wilhelm read us about the Gilbert Island porpoises and their "King out of the West." Yet Wilhelm was excited, and so was Josephine when she woke up and heard the tape played back. Both of them want me to put her in a deep trance and leave her in the pool around the clock. I consider this to be a nonsensical idea and told them so.

April 29. This morning Wilhelm pressed me again. I told him I couldn't be responsible for what might happen, and he answered: "No, of course not; I am responsible for whatever goes on at this Institute myself." Then he showed me a kind of canvas harness or breeches buoy affair he'd rigged up in the pool, securely anchored to the verge, where Jo could be strapped and still move around without any danger of drowning under hypnosis. I gave in and agreed to try the idea for a while.

April 30. Everything went off without any difficulty, and at least Jo and Wilhelm are convinced that what they call her "messages" are getting sharper and more concrete. To me, what she recalls under light hypnosis is just nonsense or fantasy, mixed in perhaps with those odd rumors concerning her father's home town Innsmouth, which she told me about earlier. Nevertheless, the two of them want to keep it up another day or so, and I agreed, since there seems to be no actual danger involved.

VIII

"No danger involved!" If, when I wrote those words, I had had even an inkling of what I know now, I would have halted the experiment immediately; either that or left this oceanside outpost on the edge of the unknown, threatened by fanatic superstition from the outside and a stiff-necked scientific *hubris* from within. But though the hints were there, recognizable in hindsight, still at the time I saw nothing, felt nothing but a vague, unplaceable malaise, and so did nothing; and thus I must share the guilt for what happened.

Late on the evening of April 30, soon after I had written the journal entry quoted above, Dr. Wilhelm and I were roused from our rooms by the sound of a scream which, though faint and muffled by distance, we at once recognized as Jo's voice, not the subhuman caterwauling of our drug-debauched neighbors.

Ask me now why we had left Jo Gilman alone in the dolphin's tank that evening and I must admit that it appears to be criminal negligence or inexcusable folly. But Wilhelm and I had stood watch over her alternately the night before as she hung half-submerged in her canvas harness and dreamed her strange dreams under the glare of the fluorescent tubes.

The harness held her head and thorax well clear of the water; and Flip, lolling quiescent in the tank, seemed to drowse too (though dolphins never sleep, since they must keep surfacing to breathe, like whales). Thus this second night, at her own prior urging, Wilhelm and I had retired for dinner and then sought some relaxation in our rooms.

The scream, which jolted us both out of a vague torpor induced by loss of sleep, came at about 10 p.m. Dr. Wilhelm's room was nearer the main lab than mine; thus, despite his greater age and bulk, he was ahead of me in reaching the heavy iron door of the beachside aquarium. As I approached the building, I could see him fumbling with the lock, his hands trembling. I was taken aback when he wheezed breathlessly at me over his shoulder: "Wait here!"

I had no choice, for he slipped inside and clanged the door shut behind him. The lock operated automatically, and since only Wilhelm and the chief lab technician—now miles away in San Simeon—had keys, I was forced to obey.

I can recall and relive in minute detail the agony and apprehension of that vigil, while the sibilant surf piled up only yards away under a freshening wind, and the half-full moon shone down with an ironic tranquility upon that silent, windowless, spectrally white structure.

I had glanced at my watch as I ran along the beach, and can verify that it was almost exactly ten minutes after Wilhelm had slammed the door that he again opened it—slowly, gratingly, the aperture framing, as always, a rectangle of harsh, glaring light.

"Help me with her," Wilhelm muttered from within, and turned away.

I stepped inside. He had removed Jo Gilman's limp form from the water and had wrapped it in several of the capacious beach robes that were always at hand near the tank. Glancing beyond the inert figure, I was startled to see Jo's canvas harness strung out dismembered across the winking surface of the water; and even part of her bright red bathing suit, which seemed entangled with the shredded canvas. The shadowy shape of the dolphin Flip I glimpsed too, fully submerged and strangely immobile in a far corner of the pool.

"To her room," Wilhelm murmured as we lifted Jo. Somehow, staggering and sidling in the shifting sand, we gained the dormitory building, groped open the door, and stumbled through Jo's apartment

(I had never been inside, but Wilhelm seemed to know his way), finally dropping her muffled body unceremoniously onto the narrow folding bed.

"I'll call a doctor," I mumbled, lurching toward the door.

"No, don't!" Wilhelm rapped, adjusting the dim bedside lamp. "She's not really hurt—as a zoologist, I'm doctor enough myself to know that. Bring a tape recorder from the lab. I think she's still hypnotized, and she may be able to tell us what happened."

"But you saw—" I began breathlessly.

"I saw only what you saw," he grated, glaring at me through lenses that picked up the muted glow of the bed lamp. "She was clinging to the edge of the pool when I went in there, only partly conscious, out of her harness, and—get the tape machine, man!"

Why I obeyed blindly I still do not understand, but I found myself again blundering along the beach, Wilhelm's key ring in my hand, and then fumbling a portable tape recorder from the orderly storage cabinets of the main laboratory.

When I lugged the machine back to Josephine's room, I found that Dr. Wilhelm had somehow maneuvered her into an incongruous frilly lounging robe and gotten her under the bed covers. He was massaging her wrists with a mechanical motion, and scanning her face anxiously. Her eyes were still closed, her breathing harsh and irregular.

"Is she in hypnosis or shock?" he inquired edgily.

"Either, or perhaps both," I shot back. "At this point, the symptoms would be similar."

"Then set up the machine."

It soon appeared that the deep mesmeric state into which I had placed Jo Gilman that morning still held. I was able to elicit responses from her by employing the key words that I used to trigger the state of trance, so easily invoked these days as to be almost disconcerting.

"Jo, can you hear me? Tell us what happened to you," I urged her gently. The color began to return to her face; she sighed deeply and twisted under the bed clothes. For what happened next, I have the evidence not only of my own recollections, but a transcription typed up next day from the tape machine, whose microphone Dr. Wilhelm now held beside her pillow with tense expectancy. This is a summary—omitting some of her repetitions, and the urgings on our part—of what we heard muttered by the bruised lips of that comatose woman writhing uneasily on her cot in a dimly lit room beside the glittering, moon-drenched Pacific, close on to midnight of May Eve:

"Must get out ... must get out and unify the forces. Those who wait in watery Arlyah (sp.?), those who walk the snowy wastes of Leng, whistlers and lurkers of sullen Kadath—all shall rise, all shall join once more in praise of Great Clooloo (sp.?), of Shub-Niggurath, of Him Who is not to be Named....

"You will help me, fellow breather of air, fellow holder of warmth, storer of seed for the last sowing and the endless harvest.... (Unpronounceable name; possibly Y'ha-nthlei) shall celebrate our nuptials, the weedy labyrinths shall hold our couch, the silent strutters in darkness will welcome us with high debauch and dances upon their many-segmented legs ... their ancient, glittering eyes are gay.... And we shall dwell amidst wonder and glory forever...."

The speaker gasped and seemed to struggle to awaken. My apprehensions had crystallized into certainty: "She's hysterical," I whispered.

"No—no, not hysterical," Dr. Wilhelm hissed, trying in his elation to keep his voice subdued. "Not hysterical. She's broken through. Don't you see what this is? Don't you see that she's echoing ideas and images that have been projected to her? Can't you understand? What we've just heard is her attempt to verbalize in English what she's experienced today— the most astonishing thing any human being has ever experienced: communication from another intelligent species!"

IX

Of the rest of that night I remember little. The twin shocks of Jo Gilman's hysterical seizure—for so I interpreted not only her unconscious ranting but also the initial scream, and her struggle out of the restraining apparatus—plus the unreasoning interpretation placed upon these events by my employer, served to unnerve me to the extent that when Jo sank gradually into normal slumber I excused myself to Dr. Wilhelm and reeled off to my own room a little before midnight, for ten hours of uninterrupted—if not undisturbed—sleep.

It was a distinct surprise to me when I joined the others at staff luncheon next day to find that a reticence amounting almost to a conspiracy of silence had already grown up in regard to the events of the preceding night. Jo, although pale and shaken, referred to what had happened as her "LSD trip" before the other staff members, and Dr. Wilhelm merely spoke of an abortive phase of "Operation Dolphin" which had been given up.

In any event, Jo completely abandoned her previous intimacy with Flip; indeed, I never once saw her in the aquarium building again; at least, not until a certain climactic occasion, the facts about which I almost hesitate to affirm, even at this juncture.

Suddenly, all research efforts seemed to be shifted hastily to the crowded pens of young dolphins on the north beach, and I was called upon to interpret sonar charts and graphs recording patterns of underwater movement that might—or might not—indicate a telepathic herd-communion between individuals and groups of animals, both free and in captivity.

This, although a plausibly rational shift in experimental emphasis, somehow failed to convince me; it seemed merely a cover-up (on the part of Josephine as well as Wilhelm), masking a fear, an uncertainty, or some unsurmised preoccupation I failed to grasp. Perhaps these further extracts from my journal will make clear my uneasiness during this period:

May 7. Jo is still distant and evasive with me. Today as we worked together coding patterns of dolphin movement for the computer, she suddenly fell silent, stopped work, and began to stare straight ahead. When I passed my hand in front of her face, I confirmed that her stare was unfocused, and she had actually fallen into a trance again, from which I am able to awaken her with the same key words we used when she was regularly under hypnosis.

I was horrified, for such involuntary trances may well be a symptom of deep psychic disturbance, over which I can only blame myself for giving in to Dr. Wilhelm's rash obstinacy. When she woke up, however, she would admit only to having a headache and dozing off for a moment. I did not press the issue then.

May 8. The above entry was written in the late afternoon. Since Jo seemed herself at dinner, I determined to go to her room later for a serious talk about the dangerous state into which she has fallen. But when I reached the door of her apartment I was surprised to hear voices, as it seemed, in muttered conversation inside.

I stood there for a few moments, irresolute whether to knock or not. Suddenly I realized that although what I heard was divided into the usual give-and-take exchanges of conversation, with pauses and variations in the rhythm and tempo of the participating voices, in actuality the timbre was that of only one speaker: Josephine Gilman herself.

I was shocked—has her state deteriorated into schizophrenia? Might she indeed be picking up telepathic messages; and if so, from whom? I could distinguish no words in the muttered stream of speech. Cautiously I tried the door. It was locked, and I tiptoed away along the outer corridor as if I were a thief, or an ordinary eavesdropper....

May 10. I still cannot believe that what Jo said on the tape after her so-called hysterical seizure was really a remembered telepathic transmission from Flip; and despite what Dr. Wilhelm said that night, I don't know whether he still believes it either. I have studied the transcript over and over, and think I have found a clue. Something about one of the phrases she spoke seemed hauntingly familiar: "Their ancient, glittering eyes are gay."

Recalling Wilhelm's remarkable memory, I mentioned it to him, and he agreed immediately: "Yes, it's from Yeats. I recognized that almost at once."

"But that means the so-called message, or part of it at least, must have come from her own subconscious memory of a poem."

"Perhaps. But after all, it was Yeats who wrote the line about 'that dolphin-torn, that gong-tormented sea.' Perhaps he's their favorite poet."

This flippancy irritated me. "Dr. Wilhelm," I answered angrily, "do you really believe that that tape was a telepathic transmission from Flip?"

He sobered. "I don't know, Dorn. Maybe we'll never know. I thought so at first, but perhaps I was carried away. I almost hope so—it was a pretty unsettling experience. But one thing I do know: you were right; that particular line of approach is too dangerous, at least with a subject as highly strung as Jo. Perhaps we can devise a safer way to resume the research with hypnosis later, but just now I don't see how. We're only lucky that she didn't suffer any real harm."

"We don't know that either," I replied. "She's started hypnotizing herself."

Wilhelm didn't answer.

May 20. For over a week, I have not observed Jo fall into one of her trances in the daytime. However, she always retires early, pleading exhaustion, so we don't know what may go on at night. Several times I have deliberately paused outside her door during the evening, and once I thought I heard that strange muffled conversation again, but softer or more distant.

The research is now mechanical and curiously artificial; I don't see that we're accomplishing anything, nor is there any special need for me to be here at all. The old enthusiasm and vigor seem to have gone out of Wilhelm, too. He has lost weight and appears older, apprehensive, as if waiting for something....

May 24. I sat late on the patio last night, looking out toward the ocean, which was invisible, since there was no moon. At about nine o'clock I thought I saw something white moving down by the water's edge, proceeding south in the general direction of the main lab. Curiously disturbed, I followed.

It was Jo of course, either under hypnosis or walking in her sleep. (Here indeed was a scene from a horror film for Wilhelm to snort at!) I took her arm and was able to guide her back to the dormitory building. The door to her apartment was open, and I put her to bed without resistance. However, when I tried to awaken her by the usual mesmeric methods, I failed. After a while, though, she seemed to fall into ordinary slumber, and I left, setting the lock on the hall door to catch automatically.

Wilhelm was working late in his study, but I could see no reason to tell him about this incident. I shall probably not tell Jo either, since it might upset her nerves even more. I realize that I have become extremely fond of her since her "LSD trip," in a tender, protective way unlike my initial physical attraction for her. And this knowledge makes me recognize, too, that something must be done to help her. All I can think of is to call in a psychiatrist, but Wilhelm has already denied the need for this, and I know Jo will follow his lead.

I must keep alert for more evidence to convince the pair of them that such a step, is urgently indicated.

For the past few weeks our hippies have abated their nocturnal ceremonies, but last night after I left Jo's room I could hear that inhuman chanting and shouting start up, and see from my patio the reflections from their distant fire on the beach. Again I did not sleep well.

X

It was past mid-June, with no change in the tense but tenuous situation at the Institute, when I had my momentous interview with the hippie *guru*, Alonzo Waite.

The moon shone brightly that evening, and I sat as usual on my glass-fronted patio, nursing a last brandy and trying to put my thoughts and ideas into some sort of order for the hundredth time. Jo Gilman had as usual retired early, and Dr. Wilhelm had driven into town for some sort of needed supplies, so I was in effect alone in the Institute. Perhaps Waite knew this somehow, for he came unerringly up the beach to my door, his fur cloak flapping dejectedly around his shanks, even though my apartment showed no light. I rose somewhat hesitantly to admit him.

He seated himself in a canvas chair, refused brandy, and abstractedly removed the soiled red beret from his unshorn locks. In the faint glow of the hurricane lamp I had lit, his dark eyes were distant and withdrawn; I wondered whether he were under the influence of drugs.

"Mr. Dorn," my visitor began, in the resonant tones I well remembered, "I know that you as a man of science cannot approve or understand what my companions and I are trying to do. Yet because your field is exploration of the lesser-known aspects of the human mind, I have hopes that you may give me a more sympathetic hearing than Dr. Wilhelm has done.

"I, too, am a scientist, or was—don't smile! A few years ago, I was assistant professor in clinical psychology at a small school in

Massachusetts called Miskatonic University, a place you've possibly never even heard of. It's in an old colonial town called Arkham, quite a backwater, but better known in the days of the Salem witch trials.

"Now, extravagant as the coincidence may seem—if it is really a coincidence—I knew your co-worker Josephine Gilman by sight when she was a student there, though she would certainly not recognize me, or even recall my name perhaps, in the guise I have now adopted." He shrugged slightly and glanced down at his eccentric getup, then continued.

"You probably don't remember the scandal that resulted in my leaving my post, since it was hushed up, and only a few sensational newspapers carried the item. I was one of those early martyrs to science—or to superstition, if you like; but whose superstition?—fired for drug experiments with students in the early days of LSD research. Like others who became better known, and who sometimes exploited their discoveries for personal profit or notoriety, I was convinced that the mind-expanding drugs gave humanity an opening into a whole new world of psychic and religious experience. I never stopped to wonder in those days whether the experience would involve beauty alone, or also encompass terror. I was a pure scientist then, I liked to think, and to me whatever was was good—or at least neutral raw material for the advancement of human understanding. I had much to learn.

"The drug underground at Miskatonic University was a little special. The school has one of the most outstanding collections of old books on out-of-the-way religious practices now extant. If I mention the medieval Arab treatise called the *Necronomicon* in its Latin version, you won't have heard of it; yet the Miskatonic copy is priceless, one of only three acknowledged still to exist—the others are in the Harvard and Paris libraries.

"These books tell of an ancient secret society or cult that believes the earth and all the known universe were once ruled by vast alien invaders from outside space and time, long before man evolved on this planet. These entities were so completely foreign to molecular matter and protoplasmic life that for all intents and purposes they were supernatural—supernatural and evil."

Waite may once have been a college professor, I reflected, but judging by his portentous word choice and delivery, he would have made an even better old-time Shakespearean actor or revival preacher. His costume helped the effect, too.

"At some point," the bearded *guru* continued, "these usurpers were defeated and banished by even stronger cosmic opponents who, at least from our limited viewpoint, would appear benevolent. However, the defeated Old Ones could not be killed, nor even permanently thwarted. They live on, imprisoned, but always seeking to return and resume their sway over the space-time universe, pursuing their immemorial and completely unknowable purposes.

"These old books record the lore that has been passed on to man from human and pre-human priesthoods that served these imprisoned deities, who constantly strive to mold and sway the thoughts of men by dreams; moving them to perform the rites and ceremonies by means of which the alien entities may be preserved, strengthened, and at last released from their hated bondage.

"All this goes on even today, and has influenced half the history of human science and religion in unacknowledged ways. And of course, there are rival cults that seek to prevent the return of the Old Ones, and to stymie the efforts of their minions.

"To be brief, the visions induced by LSD in the Miskatonic students, together with the results of certain experiments and ceremonies we learned from the old books, confirmed the reality of this fantastic mythology in a very terrible way. Even now I could not be persuaded to tell any living person some of the things I have seen in my visions, nor even to hint at the places my spirit has journeyed during periods of astral detachment. There were several disappearances of group members who dared too much, and several mental breakdowns, accompanied by certain physical changes that necessitated placing the victim in permanent seclusion. These occurrences, I assure you, were not due to any human agency whatever, no matter what the authorities may have chosen to believe.

"Though there was no evidence of foul play, the group was discovered and expelled, and I lost my job. After that some of us came here and formed a community dedicated to thwarting the efforts of evil cultists to free the Great Old Ones, which would mean in effect the death or degradation of all men not sworn to serve them. This is the aim of our present efforts to achieve spiritual knowledge and discipline through controlled use of hallucinogenic agents. Believe me, we have seen more than enough of the horrors connected with these matters, and our sympathies are all on the other side. Unfortunately, there are opposing groups, some of them right here in California, working in parallel ways to effect directly contrary results."

"An interesting story," I put in impatiently, disgusted by what I regarded as insane ramblings, "but what has all this to do with our research here, and the fact that you knew Miss Gilman as a college student?"

"Josephine's family comes from Innsmouth," Waite rumbled fore-bodingly. "That blighted town was once one of the centers of this cosmic conspiracy. Before the Civil War, mariners from Innsmouth brought back strange beliefs from their South Pacific trading voyages—strange beliefs, strange powers, and strange, deformed Polynesian women as their brides. Later, still stranger things came out of the sea itself in response to certain ceremonies and sacrifices.

"These creatures, half human and half amphibians of unknown batrachian strains, lived in the town and interbred with the people there, producing monstrous hybrids. Almost all the Innsmouth people became tainted with this unhuman heritage, and as they grew older many went to live underwater in the vast stone cities built there by the races that serve Great Cthulhu."

I repeated the strange name falteringly; somehow it rang a bell in my memory. All this was oddly reminiscent, both of what Jo had told me and of her delirious words on the tape, which Wilhelm half believed represented a message from the mind of an undersea race.

"Cthulhu," Waite repeated sepulchrally, "is the demonic deity imprisoned in his citadel amidst the prehuman city of R'lyeh, sunken somewhere in mid-Pacific by the power of his enemies eons ago; asleep but dreaming forever of the day of release, when he will resume sway over the earth. And his dreams over the centuries have created and controlled those undersea races of evil intelligence who are his servants."

"You can't mean the dolphins!" I exclaimed.

"These and others—some of such aspect that only delirious castaways have ever seen them and lived. These are the sources of the legendary hydras and harpies, Medusa and mermaids, Scylla and Circe, which have terrified human beings from the dawn of civilization, and before.

"Now you can guess why I have constantly warned Dr. Wilhelm to give up his work, even though he is nearer success than he realizes. He is meddling in things more terrible than he can well imagine when he seeks communication with these Deep Ones, these minions of the blasphemous horror known as Cthulhu.

"More than this—the girl through whom he seeks this communication is one of the Innsmouth Gilmans. No, don't interrupt me! I knew it as soon as I saw her at the university; the signs are unmistakable, though not far advanced yet: the bulging, ichthyic eyes, the rough skin around the neck where incipient gill-openings will gradually develop with age. Someday, like her ancestors, she will leave the land and live underwater as an ageless amphibian in the weedy cities of the Deep Ones, which I glimpse almost daily, in my visions and in my nightmares alike.

"This cannot be coincidence—there is manipulation somewhere in bringing this girl, almost wholly ignorant of her awful heritage, into intimate, unholy contact with a creature that can end what slim chances she may ever have had of escaping her monstrous genetic destiny!"

XI

Although I did my best to calm Alonzo Waite by assuring him that all attempts to establish hypnotic rapport between Jo and Flip had ended, and that the girl had even taken an aversion to the animal, I did not tell him any of the other puzzling aspects of the matter, some of which seemed to fit in strangely with the outlandish farrago of superstition and hallucination that he had been trying to foist upon me.

Waite did not seem much convinced by my protestations, but I wanted to get rid of him and think matters over again. Obviously the whole of his story was absurd; but just as obviously he believed it. And if others believed it too, as he claimed, then this might explain in some measure the odd coincidences and the semi-consistent pattern that seemed to string together so many irrelevancies and ambiguities.

But after Waite left, I decided that there were still pieces missing from the puzzle. Thus when Jo Gilman knocked on my door a little before 11:00 o'clock, I was not only surprised (she never came out at night any more, since her sleep-walking episode) but glad of the opportunity to ask her some questions.

"I couldn't sleep and felt like talking," Jo explained, with an air of rather strained nonchalance, as she settled in the same chair Waite had used. "I hope I'm not disturbing you." She accepted a brandy and soda, and lit a cigarette. I had a sudden, detached flash of vision that saw this scene as a decidedly familiar one: drinks and cigarettes, a girl in a dressing gown in the beachside apartment of a bachelor. But our conversation didn't fall into the cliché pattern; we talked of sonar graphs and neuron density, of supersonic vibrations, computer tapes, and the influence of water temperature on dolphin mating habits.

I watched Jo carefully for any signs of falling into that auto-hypnotic state in which she held conversations with herself, but could see none; she seemed closer to normal than had been the case for many weeks. At the same time, I was annoyed to realize that I had become more conscious than before of the physical peculiarities which that idiot Waite had attributed to a biologically impossible strain in her ancestry.

The conversation had been entirely prosaic until I seized the opportunity of a short silence to ask one of the questions that had begun to intrigue me: "When did you first hear about Dr. Wilhelm's studies, and how did you happen to come to work for him?"

"It was right after my father was drowned. I had to drop out of graduate school back in Massachusetts and start making my own living. I had heard about Fred's research, and of course I was fascinated from the start, but I never thought of applying for a job here until my Uncle Joseph suggested it."

"Your father's brother?"

"Yes, a funny little old fellow; I always thought when I was a child that he looked just like a frog. He spends about half the year at the old family place in Innsmouth and half in Boston. He seems to have all the money he needs, though I've never seen any of it. My father once asked him jokingly what he did for a living, and Uncle Joe just laughed and said he dove for Spanish doubloons.

"Anyway, a few weeks after I left school and came back to Boston, Uncle Joe showed me a story about Dr. Wilhelm's work with the delphinidae—I think it was in the *Scientific American*. Joe knew of my studies in oceanography, of course, and he said he knew an authority in the field who would write me a good recommendation. It must have been a good one, all right, because in less than six weeks here I was. That was over two years ago, now."

If Alonzo Waite needed a further link in his wild theory of conspiracy, here was perfect raw material!

"You know," Jo went on with apparently casual lightness, "I told you a long time ago that Dr. Wilhelm asked me to marry him. That was over six months ago. At the time I thought it was a bad idea, but now I rather wish I had taken him up on it."

"Why? Afraid of becoming an old maid? I might have something to say about that one of these days."

"No." Her voice remained as calm and casual as before. "The reason is that—dating from right around the time that Fred Wilhelm rescued me from my LSD trip in that dolphin tank—I've been pregnant. At least, that's the timetable that the doctor in San Simeon has figured."

XIII

"Then it's Fred?" My remark sounded stupid, clumsy; like something that hypothetical beachside couple I had imagined might be discussing in some tawdry charade illustrating California's vaunted "New Morality."

"Figure it out for yourself," Jo answered with a nervous laugh. "It's either you or Fred, I don't remember a thing until I woke up the next morning feeling like a used punching bag."

"Wilhelm was alone with you for at least ten minutes before he let me into the aquarium. And he was alone with you in your apartment after I went to bed three hours later. I never was alone with you that evening."

"That's what I assumed from what you both told me next day. Besides, I never turned you down—maybe only because you didn't ask me."

"Jo," I said, getting out of my chair; and didn't know what to say next.

"No, whatever it is, forget it," she murmured. "Whatever you were going to say, it's too late. I've got to think in an entirely different frame of reference now."

"What are you going to do?"

"I think I'm going to marry Fred—that is, if he's still interested. From there we'll see. There's more now than just me to worry about, and that seems the right move—the only move—to start with."

We didn't say much more. Jo felt drowsy all of a sudden and I walked her back to her apartment. Afterward, I strolled on the beach. A brisk wind arose around midnight, and clouds covered what moon there was. I felt numb; I hadn't known, or anyway admitted to myself, how I felt about Jo until now. I loved her too. But if Wilhelm, the old satyr, had made her pregnant while she was under hypnosis, then what she planned was probably best for all concerned. But how unlike Wilhelm such an act appeared! The gentlemanly, scholarly enthusiast, with his grandfatherly grey hair and amusing penguin shape—he might become infatuated with and propose to a young woman, especially someone who shared his enthusiasms. That was in character. But a dastardly attack like the one Jo suspected? He must be insane.

I heard the Land Rover chugging up the sandy road; Dr. Wilhelm was returning. I'd find it hard to face him tomorrow. In fact, that might just be the best time for me to offer him my resignation, although I had no future prospects. Maybe I could get my old job back. At any rate, nobody needed me around here anymore, that much was crystal clear.

I went back to my room and had several more brandies. Before I fell asleep, I became aware that the hippies were launching one of their wild orgies down on the south beach. From what Waite had said, they were holding ceremonies to keep the nice, normal, sane world safe for nice, normal, sane people.

If there were any left these days.

XIII

I don't think I had slept as much as an hour when something sent me bolt upright in bed, wide awake. It may have been a sound, or it may have been some sort of mental message—(ironic, since this was my field of study, that I had never observed, much less experienced, a fully convincing instance of telepathic communication).

In any case, something was wrong, I was sure of that; and if my premonition proved right, I knew where to go to find it: the beach by the main laboratory. I dressed hurriedly and dashed out on the shifting sands.

The wind, now near gale force, had swept the clouds away from the sickle moon, which shone starkly on the beach and glared upon an ocean of crinkled tinfoil. I could see two figures moving toward the windowless building at the water's edge where Flip, the neglected subject of our old experiment, was still kept in isolation. They converged and entered the building together, after a moment's hesitation over the locks.

As I dashed in pursuit, the gusty wind brought me snatches of the hippie ceremony; I made out drums and cymbals beaten wildly, as well as that same muffled chanting and the high, floating wail of ecstasy or terror, or both.

The harsh white light of fluorescent tubes now streamed through the open door leading to the dolphin tank, and I heard another sound inside as I approached: the clank of machinery and the hum of an electric motor. Dr. Wilhelm was raising the sea gate on the ocean side of the building, the gate that was sometimes used to change the water in the tank while Flip was held under restraint by the daytime lab assistants. No one could be holding him now; was Wilhelm about to release the animal, to satisfy some vague, belated qualm of conscience?

But as I panted up to the open door, I realized that more than this was afoot. In a momentary glimpse just before the storm cut out our power lines, I took in the whole unbelievable scene: the massive sea gate was fully raised now, allowing turbulent waves to surge into the floodlighted pool, and even to splash violently over its rim, inundating the observation deck and its elaborate equipment.

The dolphin, pitting his powerful muscles against the force of the incoming water, was relentlessly beating his way out to sea. Of Dr. Wilhelm there was no sign; but, perched on the broad, smooth back of the great sea beast itself, her naked body partly covered by her soaked, streaming hair, sat Josephine Gilman, bolt upright, bestriding her strange mount like the old Grecian design of the boy on the dolphin, that enigmatic emblem of the marriage of earth to ocean.

Then the lights failed, but the waves pounded on, and the distant delirious chanting reached a peak of hysteria that sustained itself incredibly, unendingly.

I can recall no more.

XIV

Josephine's body was never found; nor was there any reason that I should ever have expected that it would be. When the lab crew arrived next morning, they repaired the power line and raised the sea gate again. Dr. Wilhelm's mangled body was caught beneath it. The gate had fallen when the power failed, and had crushed Wilhelm as he attempted to follow the fantastic pair he had liberated into the open sea.

On the neat desk in Dr. Wilhelm's office, where I had first met Josephine Gilman on the evening of my arrival, lay a manila envelope addressed to me. It contained a typed letter and a roll of recording tape. I found the envelope myself, and I have not shown it to the police, who seem to believe my story that Wilhelm and Josephine were swept out to sea when the gate was accidentally raised during an experiment.

This is what the letter said:

Dear Dorn:

When you read this I shall be dead, if I am lucky. I must release the two of them to go back to the ocean depths where they belong. For you see, I now believe everything that grotesque person Alonzo Waite told me.

I lied to you once when you asked me whether I had implanted electrodes in the brain of the test dolphin. I did implant one electrode at an earlier stage of my work, when I was doing some studies on the mechanism of sexual stimulation in the animal. And when our experiments in telepathic communication seemed to be inconclusive, I was criminally foolish enough to broadcast a remote signal to activate that stimulus, in a misguided attempt to increase the rapport between the subject and the animal.

This was on the afternoon of April 30, and you can guess—reluctantly enough—what happened that evening. I assume full responsibility and guilt, which I will expiate in the only way that seems appropriate.

When I got to the pool ahead of you on that awful night, I saw at a glance what must have just occurred. Josephine had been ripped from her canvas sling, still hypnotized, and badly mauled. Her suit was torn almost off her, but I wrapped her in a robe and somehow got her into bed without your guessing what had really happened. The hypnosis held, and she never realized either. From then on, though, she was increasingly under telepathic contact and even control by that beast in the pool, even though she consciously and purposely avoided him.

Tonight when I got back from town she told me about her pregnancy, but in the middle of talking she fell into the usual trance and started to walk out on the beach. I locked her in her room and sat down to write this, since you have a right to know the truth, although there is nothing more that can be done after tonight.

I think we each loved Josephine in our own way, but now it is too late. I must let her out to join her own—she was changing—and when the baby is born—well, you can imagine the rest.

I myself would never have believed any of this, except for the tape. Play it and you'll understand everything. I didn't even think of it for a couple of weeks, fool that I was. Then I remembered that all during the time Jo spent hypnotized in the pool with the dolphin, I had ordered the microphones left open to record whatever might happen. The tapes were routinely filed by date the next day, and had never been monitored. I found the reel for April 30 and copied the part that I enclose with this letter.

Goodbye—and I'm sorry.

Frederick C. Wilhelm

Many hours passed—hours of stunned sorrow and disbelief—before I dared bring a tape machine to my room and listen to the recording Wilhelm had left for me. I debated destroying the reel unheard; and afterward I did erase the master tape stored in the main laboratory.

But the need to know the truth—a scientific virtue that is sometimes a human failing—forced me to listen to the accursed thing. It meant the end for me of any peace of mind or security in this life. I hope that Jo and Flip have found some measure of satisfaction in that strange, alien world so forebodingly described by the *guru* Waite, and that Frederick Wilhelm has found peace. I can neither look for nor expect either.

This is what I transcribed from that tape after many agonizing hours of replaying. The time code indicates that it was recorded at about 9:35 on the evening of April 30, a scant few minutes before Josephine's agonized scream sent Wilhelm and me dashing belatedly to rescue her from that garishly illuminated chamber where the ultimate horror took place:

> "My beloved, my betrothed, you must help me. I must get out and unify the forces. Those who wait in watery R'lyeh, those who walk the snowy wastes of Leng, whistlers and lurkers of sullen Kadath—all shall rise, all shall join once more in praise of Great Cthulhu, of Shub-Niggurath, of Him Who is not to be Named. You shall help me, fellow breather of air, fellow holder of warmth, another storer of seed for the last sowing and the endless harvest. Y'ha-nthlei shall celebrate our nuptials, the weedy labyrinths shall hold our couch, the silent strutters in darkness will welcome us with high debauch and dances upon their many-segmented legs … their ancient, glittering eyes are gay. And we shall dwell amidst wonder and glory forever."

Merely a repetition, you say; merely an earlier version of that meaningless rant that Josephine repeated an hour later under hypnosis in her bedroom, a garbled outpouring of suppressed fragments and fears from the subconscious mind of one who unreasoningly dreaded her family background in a shunned, decadent seaport a continent away?

I wish I could believe that too, but I cannot. For these wild words were spoken, not by a mentally unbalanced woman in deep hypnotic trance, *but in the quacking, bleating, inhuman tones that are the unmistakable voice of the dolphin itself, alien servant of still more alien masters, the Deep Ones of legend, prehuman (and perhaps soon post-human) intelligences behind whose bland, benign exterior lurks a threat to man which not all man's destructive ingenuity can equal, or avert.*

THE FRANKLYN PARAGRAPHS

RAMSEY CAMPBELL

The disappearance of Errol Undercliffe in 1967 from his flat in Lower Brichester was not widely reported. The little speculation provoked by the mystery was soon resolved by the belief that Undercliffe had "disappeared" in search of publicity. While he has not reappeared, his public seems still to be waiting for him to produce himself out of a hat. At the time I hinted in print that I could supply evidence of something more sinister, but I fear that the general branding of Undercliffe as a charlatan was sufficiently persuasive to dissuade me from publishing evidence in case Undercliffe reappeared and objected to my making public letters written privately to me. By now, however, I should be more than pleased if Undercliffe declared both his absence and his last letter a hoax.

Undercliffe first wrote to me in 1965, when my first book had just become available from Brichester Central Library. Typically, he enclosed a cutting from the letter-column of the *Brichester Herald*; under the heading "Can Ghost Stories Be Libellous?" one "Countryman" had written: "I have recently perused a book of ghost stories by a Mr J. Ramsey Campbell, mainly located in Brichester. Mr Campbell seems to look upon the citizens of our town as either witches, warlocks, or illiterate 'country folks.' The advertising for the book makes much of the fact that the author is still an infant; since this is obvious from the contents, I would scarcely have thought it necessary to advertise the fact.

I would suggest that before he writes another such book Mr Campbell should (1) visit Brichester, where he has clearly never set foot, and (2) grow up." And so on. I could have replied that on the basis of my several visits to Brichester I didn't consider it the sort of town where I'd care to spend a night; but I find this kind of letter-column duel a little childish, and didn't feel disposed to join swords or even pens. For the record, these days Brichester has an impressively mundane surface, but I still sense that it may crack. When I and Kirby McCauley passed through the area in 1965, a month or so before Undercliffe's first letter, I was disturbed to be unable to find the turn-off to Severnford and Brichester, and the groups of youths inert in the sun outside a shack-like cinema in Berkeley (showing, oddly enough, Jerry Lewis' one horror film) proved less than helpful. Hours later, after dark, we were directed by a roundabout policeman, but without conferring we sneaked around the roundabout— only to find ourselves somehow on the road originally indicated and to stay at an inn whose sign we discovered in the dawn to be that of a goat!

However, I digress. I quote the letter from the *Herald* at length because it seems to me to demonstrate some aspects of Undercliffe's character; not that he wrote it (at least I shouldn't think so), but he did enclose it with his first letter to me, though it is hardly the sort of enclosure most of us would choose when initiating a correspondence. However, Undercliffe's sense of humor was wry—some might call it cynical or cruel. I'm inclined to believe it was the product of a basic insecurity, from what little I know of his life. I never visited him, and his letters were rarely self-revelatory (though the first of the batch here published is more so than he might have wished). Most of them were first drafts of stories, signed and dated; he kept a copy of every letter he wrote—these were carefully filed in his flat—and several of the incidents which he described to me in the two years of our correspondence turned up virtually verbatim in his short stories. In particular the description of the disused station in "The Through Train" was lifted bodily from his letter to me of 20 November 1966.

If this says little about the man himself, I can only maintain that for the rest of us Errol Undercliffe was the Mr Arkadin of the horror-story world. "Errol Undercliffe" was almost certainly not his christened name. His refusal to provide biographical detail was not as notorious as J. D. Salinger's, but it was fully as obsessive. He seems to have been educated in or near Brichester (see the first letter here) but I cannot trace his school, nor the friend whose engagement party he describes. I never saw a photograph of him. Perhaps he thought the aura of mystery with which he surrounded himself carried over to his stories; perhaps, again, he was bent on preserving his own isolation. If so, he served himself ill as far as his final ordeal was concerned; he had nobody to whom he could turn.

When I went down to Undercliffe's flat on hearing that he'd disappeared, I was less surprised than saddened by the experience. The Lower Brichester area, as I've mentioned elsewhere, is the sort of miniature cosmopolis one finds in most major English towns: three-storey houses full of errant lodgers, curtains as varied as flags at a conference but more faded, the occasional smashed pane, the frequent furtive watchers. Somebody was tuning a motorcycle in Pitt Street, and the fumes drifted into Undercliffe's flat through a crack in the pane and clouded the page in his typewriter. The landlady was making ready to dispose of this, together with Undercliffe's books and other possessions, as soon as the rent gave out at the end of the month. I finally persuaded her to let me handle the disposal, after a good deal of wrangling and invocation of August Derleth (who'd never published Undercliffe), the Arts Council (who'd never heard of him, I imagine) and others. Having ushered her out at last, well aware that she'd be prepared to search me before I left the house, I examined the flat. The wardrobe and chest-of-drawers contained two suits, some shirts and so forth, none of which could have looked particularly stylish at an engagement party, The bed commanded a fine view of an arachnidial crack in the ceiling (clearly that crack which "suddenly, with a horrid lethargy, detached itself from the plaster and fell on Peter's upturned face" in "The Man Who Feared to Sleep"). The wallpaper had a Charlotte Perkins Gilman look; once Undercliffe complained that "such an absurd story should have used up an inspiration which I could work into one of my best tales." The window looked out on the fuming motorcycle, now stuck stubbornly in first gear, and its fuming owner; at night I suppose Undercliffe, seated at his typewriter before the window, might have waved to the girl slipping off her slip in the flat across the street, and I carried on his neighborly gesture, though without much success. On the sill outside his window, cigarette-stubs had collected like bird-droppings; he tended to cast these into the night, disliking the sight of a brimming ashtray. He'd go through a packet per thousand words, he once told me; he'd tried chewing-gum once, but this drew his fillings, and he was terrified of the dentist (cf. "The Drill"). All this, of course, is trivial, but I needed—still need—distraction. I'd already followed Undercliffe's search through the first three letters printed here, and that page still in the typewriter—a letter to me, probably the last thing he wrote—told of what he found. I removed it, unwillingly enough, and left; the landlady let it go. Later I arranged for transportation of the contents of the flat. The books—which seemed to be Undercliffe's treasured possessions, books of horror stories bought with the profits from his horror stories, a sad and lonely vicious circle—are now held in trust by the British Science Fiction Association library; the rest is in storage. I wish more than ever that Undercliffe would come forward to claim them.

Undercliffe's first letter to me (15 October 1965) contains a passage which in retrospect seems informed by a macabre irony. "The implicit theme of your story 'The Insects from Shaggai'," he writes, "is interesting, but you never come to grips with the true point of the plot: the horror-story author who is skeptical of the supernatural and finally is faced with overwhelming evidence of its reality. What would be his reaction? Certainly not to write of 'the lurid glow which shines on the razor lying on the table before me'!! This is as unlikely as the ending of 'The Yellow Wallpaper.' I'd be interested to hear whether you yourself believe in what you write. For myself, I think the fact that I take great pains to check material on the supernatural here in our Central Library is eloquent enough. By the way, have you come across Roland Franklyn's *We Pass from View?* The author is a local man who has some quite arresting theories about reincarnation and the like."

Which brings us to Franklyn and *We Pass from View*, in themselves as mysterious as the fate of Undercliffe; but I suspect that the two mysteries are interdependent, that one explains the other—if indeed one wishes to probe for explanation. Before discussing Franklyn, however, I'd like to note some of Undercliffe's work; I feel obliged to bring it to the notice of a wider public. His favorites of his own work were "The Drains" (the blood of a bygone murder drips from the cold tap), "The

Carved Desk" (the runes carved on what was once a Druid tree call up something which claws at the ankles of anyone foolish enough to sit down to write), and "The Drifting Face" (never published: originally intended for the ill-fated second issue of *Alien Worlds*, it now cannot be traced). I favor his more personal, less popular work: "The Window in the Fog" (in which the narrator's glimpses of a girl across the street mount to an obsessive pitch until he accosts her one night and rebuffed, murders her), "The Steeple on the Hill" (where a writer fond of lonely walks is followed by the members of a cult, is eventually drawn within their circle and becomes the incarnation of their god), and "The Man Who Feared to Sleep", which lent its title (*Peur de Sommeil* in France) to Undercliffe's best collection, under the imprint of that excellent publisher who rediscovered such writers as Pursewarden and Sebastian Knight and made again available Robert Blake's legendary collection *The Stairs in the Crypt*. It is amusing to note that the entire contents of Undercliffe's collection—including the title story, which is surely a study of insanity—was listed under "Supernatural Phenomena" in the H. W. Wilson *Short Story Index* (in an earlier volume than that which placed my own "Church in High Street" under "Church Entertainments," making it sound like a parish farce or a Britten mystery play). Undercliffe was latterly working on a script for Delta Film Productions, but producer Harry Nadler reports that this was never completed; nor was his story "Through the Zone of the Colossi", a metaphysical piece based on a reference in my "Mine on Yuggoth" coupled with material from *We Pass from View*.

Which brings me back to the necessity of discussing Franklyn's book, a duty which I fear I've been avoiding. I've never seen the book, but I have little desire to do so. I refrained from consulting Brichester Central Library's copy when I went to Undercliffe's flat; I suppose I could obtain this through the National Central Library, though I suspect that in fact the copy (like all others, apparently) has mysteriously disappeared.

Although, as Undercliffe points out, *We Pass from View* displays marked affinities with the Cthulhu Mythos in certain passages, such Lovecraft scholars as Derleth, Lin Carter, Timothy d'Arch Smith and J. Vernon Shea can supply no information on the book. I understand that it was published in 1964 by the "True Light Press," Brichester; references in

Undercliffe's letters suggest that it was a duplicated publication, originally circulated in card covers but probably bound by libraries taking copies. I have not been able to discover where, if anywhere, it was on sale. An odd rumor reached me recently that almost the entire edition was stolen from the "True Light Press"—actually the house of Roland Franklyn—and has not been heard of since; perhaps destroyed, but by whom?

Here is the little information I've obtained from various sources. The British National Bibliography gives the following entry:

129.4—Incarnation and reincarnation
FRANKLYN, Roland
We Pass from View. Brichester, True Light Press, 9/6. Jan 1964. 126 p. 22 cm.

However, the Cumulative Book Index, which lists all books published in English, does not acknowledge the book; at least, neither I nor the staff of Liverpool's Picton Library can trace the reference.

While correlating notes I was surprised to turn up in my commonplace book the following review, which might have been copied from the *Times Literary Supplement.*

PSEUDOPODDITIES

The last few decades have seen the emergence of many disturbing pseudo-philosophies, but *We Pass from View* must rank lowest. The author, Roland Franklyn, has less idea of style than most of his kind; however, the ideas behind the writing are expressed with less ambiguity than one might wish. His basic thesis seems to be that the number of souls in the universe is limited, by some illegitimate application of the conservation of energy principle, and that humanity must therefore acknowledge an infinite number of simultaneous incarnations. The last chapter, "Toward the True Self", is a sort of reductio ad absurdum of the theory, concluding that the "true self" is to be found "outside space," and that each human being is merely a facet of his "self," which is itself able to experience all its incarnations simultaneously but unable to control them. There is a suggestion of Beckett here (particularly *L'Innomable*), and Mr Franklyn has infused enough unconscious humour into many passages to cause hilarity when the book was read aloud at a party. But a book which advocates the use of drugs to achieve fulfillment of black-magic rites is worth attention not so much as humour (and certainly not as it was intended) as a sociological phenomenon.

Laughter at a party, indeed! I still find that remark rather frightening. What copy was being read aloud? The *TLS* review copy, perhaps, but in that case what happened to it? Like so much in this affair, the end fades into mystery. I doubt that many indignant letters replied to the review; those that were written probably weren't printable. In 1966, I heard vaguely of a book called *How I Discovered my Infinite Self* by "An Initiate", but whether it was ever published I don't know.

Undercliffe quoted several passages from *We Pass from View* which, though I find them faintly distasteful, I had better include. I still have all of Undercliffe's letters; some day I may edit them into a memorial article for *The Arkham Collector*, but it seems in rather bad taste to write a memoir of a man who may still be alive somewhere. The letters printed here are, I think, essential.

In his letter of 2 November 1965 Undercliffe wrote: "Here's a bizarre passage which might set you off on a short story. From the first page of *We Pass from View:* 'The novice must remind himself always that the Self is infinite and that he is but one part of his Self, not yet aware of his other bodies and lives. REMIND YOURSELF on sleeping. REMIND YOURSELF on waking. *Above all, REMIND YOURSELF* when entering the First Stage of Initiation.' As for this first stage, I've traced references later in the text, but nothing very lucid. Franklyn keeps mentioning 'the aids' which seem to be drugs of some sort, usually taken under supervision of an 'initiate' who chants invocations ('Ag'lak Sauron, Daoloth asgu'i, Eihort phul'aag'—that ought to ring a bell with you) and attempts to tap the novice's subconscious knowledge of his other incarnations. Not that I necessarily believe what Franklyn says, but it certainly gives you that sense of instability which all good horror stories should provide. I can't discover much about Franklyn. He seems in the last year or two to have drawn together a circle of young men who, from what I hear, visit Goatswood, Clotton, Temphill, the island beyond Severnford, and other places in which you're no doubt as interested as I am. I'd like to get in on the act."

I replied that he surely didn't need drugs for inspiration and that, warnings from Dennis Wheatley aside, I didn't feel it was advisable to become involved in black magic. "Experience makes the writer," Undercliffe retorted. Subsequently he avoided direct quotation, but I gathered he had not joined Franklyn's circle; his own decision, I think. Then, in September 1966, when he was writing "The Crawling in the Attic" (I'd just started library work and sent him the manuscript of "The Stocking" to read, which he didn't like—"elaborately pointless"), he quoted the following:

"Today's psychologists are wrong about dreams coming from the subconscious mind. Dreams are the links between us and the experiences of our other incarnations. *We must be receptive to them.* TELL YOURSELF BEFORE YOU SLEEP THAT YOU WILL SEE BEYOND YOUR FACET. The initiate known as Yokh'khim, his name on Tond, came to me describing a dream of long tunnels in which he was pursued but could not see his body. After several sessions, he managed to see himself as a ball of hair rolling through the tunnel away from the Trunks in the Ooze. The ball was known on Tond as Yokh'khim. He has not attained the stage of Black Initiate and spends his time beyond his facet, having set aside all but the minimum of his life on Earth."

I hadn't much to say to that except to suggest that Franklyn had plagiarized the "Tond" reference, provoking Undercliffe to reply: "Surely Franklyn has undermined your complacency enough to make complaints about copyright a little trivial. Anyway, no doubt he'd point out that you knew of Tond through your dreams." I couldn't decide whether his tongue was in his cheek; I passed over his comment, and our correspondence fell off somewhat.

In February 1967 he quoted a passage which is significant indeed. "What about a story of a writer who haunts his own books?" he suggested. "Franklyn has a paragraph on ghosts: 'The death of a body does not mean that the soul will leave it. This depends on whether there is an incarnation for it to pass into. If not, the body continues to be inhabited until it is destroyed. The initiate knows that Edgar Allan Poe's fear of premature burial was well-founded. If the death is violent, then it is more difficult than ever for the soul to leave. FOR HIS OWN SAFETY, THE INITIATE MUST INSIST ON CREMATION. Otherwise he will be hopelessly attracted back to Earth, and the burrowers of the core may drag off his body from the grave with him still in it to the feast of Eihort."

Interesting, I said somewhat wearily. I was rather tired of this sort of verbal delirium. On 5 July 1967 Undercliffe reported that the *Brichester Herald* had noted Franklyn's death. This meant little to me at the time. Then came the final sequence of letters.

7 Pitt Street : Lower Brichester, Glos : 14 July 1967 : 1.03 a.m.: slightly intoxicated

Dear JRC:
Always this point at a party where the beer tastes like vomit. Pretty putrid party, actually. Friend of mine from school who got engaged and sent me an invite. Can't think why, I'd just about forgotten him myself, but I wanted to meet him again. Didn't get near. Great fat bluebottle of a woman he got engaged to pawing over him all evening and wanting to be kissed, messily at that, whenever he tried to act the host. Good luck say I. So I had to make my own way round the conversations. I just don't know where he got them from. All bow ties and "God, Bernard, surely you realize the novel is absolutely *dead*" and banging down tankards of ale which they'd bought to be all boys together, sloshing them over and making little lakes down these trestle tables in the Co-op Hall (another blow for the old town and the Brichester folks—our engaged friend kept patting his bluebottle and bellowing "I had a wonderful childhood in Brichester, absolutely wonderful, they're fine people," no Palm Court for *him*.) Whole place murky with smoke and some tin band playing in the fog. Hundreds of ashtrays surrounded by

those pieces of ash like dead flies. Finally our friend fell to his feet to give thanks for "all the superb presents," which didn't make me feel any more accepted, since I hadn't known it was done to bring one. I feel a little

Better. Repartee: the morning after. Beg pardon, I shouldn't have mentioned engagements and fiancées. Still, I'm sure you're better off. Writers always bloom better with elbow room. I have your letter by me. You're right, your last argument with your girlfriend in Lime Street Station cafeteria with bare tables, balls of cellophane and someone next to you trying not to listen—it'd never come off in print, even though it happened to you, they'd be sure to scream Graham Greene was here first. And then her calling down "I love you" through the rain before her mother dragged her back from her window—yes, it's very poignant, but you'll have to rewrite before you can print. More on our wavelength, what you say about this other girl running out of your haunted Hornby Library in panic certainly sounds promising. You going to lock yourself in there overnight? I'd give a lot for a genuine supernatural experience.

There was this idiot at the party wanting to know what I did. Horror stories I said. Should have seen him blanch. "Why do you write those things?" he asked as if he'd caught me picking my nose. "For the money," I said. A young couple sliding down the wall behind us laughed. *Great, an audience*, I thought. No doubt if I'd said I wasn't joking they'd have laughed harder. "No, but seriously" said this poor man's F. R. Leavis (you couldn't write for anything as base as money, you see) "would you not agree that the writer is a sort of Christ figure who suffers in order to cohere his suffering for the reader's benefit?" The extent of his suffering was his bank manager calling him on his overdraft, I'll bet. "And don't you think the horror story coheres (I wasn't cohering myself by that time) an experience?" "Are you telling me you believe in what you write?" he demanded, as if it'd been *Mein Kampf.* "You don't think I'd write something in which I didn't believe?" I retorted, carefully placing the preposition. The young couple left; the show was over. He stalked off to tell Bernard about me.

At least the streets were clean and empty. Remarkable girl in the flat across the street. You should come down. Anyway, to bed. Tomorrow to work on "Through the Zone of the Colossi" and check the library.

Best,

EU

Pitt of Hell : Lowest Brichester, Glos : 14 July 1967 : later!

Dear JRC:

I don't normally write twice in a day. Today's events, however, are too important to let fade. I have had my experience. It will unquestionably form into a short story, so forgive me this first draft. I trust you not to use it.

Today, as anticipated, I visited the library. After last night/this morning, I felt somewhat sick, but that's the penance. On the bus I was trying to cohere "Zone of the Colossi", but they wouldn't let me; you must know how it is. Half the passengers were ducking and screaming beneath the flight of a wasp, and the other half were sitting stoically pouring forth clouds of tobacco-smoke, which curled in the hot air. I sat next to some whistling fool and my thoughts kept getting sidetracked into a search for the lyrics in order to fit them to his tune and be rid of it. Not an auspicious start, but "Zones of the Colossi" was forgotten when I left the library. I couldn't find *We Pass from View* on the shelf in the Religion section; mind you, some cretin in an aged mac was pottering round the shelves and sampling books and replacing them at whatever position he'd pottered to, earning himself glares from the staff. Someone else had erected a fortress of books on one of the tables and behind it was completing his football coupon. He cursed me visibly when I examined his barricade; I've rarely felt so self-conscious as then, his gaze on my canted head. But there it was: *We Pass from View* beneath *The Mass in Slow Motion* and *The Catholic Marriage Manual* and Graham Fisher's *Identity and Awareness*.

I pulled out the foundation, but the wall held.

The book was bound in bright blue. The table-top was pastel green. The room was warm and sunny, if a little stifling. At the further end behind a creamy desk, one of the staff was recounting his adventures in a branch library, how he'd been plagued by old ladies pleading for what he called "cheap novelettes"; I could tell he looked upon all fiction as the poor relation of nonfiction, like all academic librarians—so much for our writing. You couldn't get further from a Lovecraft setting, but then, this was the real thing.

I turned back the cover; it slapped the table-top. Silence fell. A blade of sunlight moved along the floor, intensifying cracks. Then the pages of *We Pass from View* began to turn of their own accord.

At first I thought it must be a draught. When you're sitting in a bright new library among books and people, you don't think of the possibility of the supernatural. When the book exhibits traces of its readership (chewing-gum on one page, a dead fly on another) it's difficult to view it as haunted. And yet I couldn't take my eyes from those moving pages. They turned up the dedication ("to my faithful friends") and for a second, as though my vision were failing, I saw lines of some other print waver as if superimposed on the text. The page turned to the next, a blank leaf. I put out my hand, but I couldn't quite bring myself to touch the book. As I hesitated, lines of print appeared on the blank paper.

HELP ME

It stood out starkly on the paper, next to the fingerprint of some unclean reader. HELP ME. The letters held for several seconds: great black capitals which seemed to burn my eyeballs as I stared at them. And I was overwhelmed by the sense of an appeal, of someone trying desperately to contact me. Then they blurred and faded.

FEEL SOMEONE READING MUST BE

That flashed and disappeared; I read it in a second. The room seemed airless; I was sweating, my ribs were closing on my lungs. I could see only the book open on the table and feel a terrible, torturous strain, as of a mind in torment trying to communicate its suffering.

SHE HAD ME BURIED HER REVENGE TOLD HER CREMATE BITCH WOMEN CANT TRUST HELP ME

That HELP ME was molten.

FEEL THEM COMING SLOWLY BURROWING WANT ME TO SUFFER CANT MOVE GET ME OUT SAVE ME SOMEWHERE IN BRICHESTER HELP ME

And the page, which had been lifted trembling, fell back. I waited. The room assembled round me in the merciless sunlight. The page remained blank. I don't know how long I waited. At last it occurred to me that the setting was wrong; back in my room I might be able to re-establish contact. I picked up the book—holding it rather gingerly; somehow I expected to feel it move, struggle between my fingers—and carried it to the desk and back into mundanity.

"I'm afraid this is a reference copy only," said the girl at the desk, flashing a smile and her engagement ring at me.

I told her that it seemed to be their only copy and that there were various of my books in the fiction section and that I knew the chief librarian (well, I'd glimpsed him enthroned in his office as someone bore in his coffee the day I was invited by his secretary to sign my books). I could have told her that I felt the book throbbing in my hand. But she replied "Well, *personally* I know we can trust you with it and if it were up to me I'd let you have it, but—" and much more of the I'm-only-doing-my-job speech. I set the book down on the desk in order to wave my hands about and she handed it to a girl who was replacing books on the shelves, belatedly asking "You didn't want it again, did you?"

I saw it carried away on the toppling pile; already the transcendental was being erased by the mundane; Franklyn would be filed carefully and forgotten. And that showed me what I must do. Of course I knew that it was Franklyn whose paragraphs I had been reading from beyond the grave, indeed, from *in* the grave. But I didn't know how to find him. The *Brichester Herald* had given neither his address nor where he was buried. "Do you know anything about Roland Franklyn himself?" I enquired.

"Yes, he used to come in quite often ..." but she obviously didn't want to talk about it. "Eric, don't let Mary do all the clearing," she said to her companion at the desk, who was building a house of holiday postcards.

"Franklyn, the little queer in the cloak?" he addressed me. "You're not a friend of his, are you? Good job. Used to come in here with a whole crowd of them; the Twelve Disciples, we used to call them. One of them came up to the desk one day because we were talking about his master and waved his great emaciated fist at us—you could see the drugs running out of his eyes. Why are you interested in that queer? Can't think what attracted them all, what with that moth-eaten cloak and that huge bald head—he'd probably pulled out the last few hairs to stick on that spidery beard. He had a wife too, I think—must've been before he came to the crossroads. What's the matter, Mary, you want me to rupture myself?"

"Do you know where he lived?" I stayed him.

"Bottom of Mercy Hill. House looked like Satan was in residence. You can't miss it." He knocked down the house of cards and walked away, and so, feeling rather adrift, did I.

I suppose I could have tried to find Franklyn today, but I wanted to crystallize the experience, to preserve it before it lost its form. I came home and set this down; I think it needs rewriting. Reality always does; I suppose we have to give it some form, even while paying the price of distortion. I keep thinking of Franklyn in his coffin, aware of something tunnelling toward him, unable to move a muscle but still capable of feelings. But it's dark now; I couldn't find him in the dark. Tomorrow, more. Goodbye, girl in the window.

EU

A fixed point : 15 July 1967

Dear JRC:

Today has been disturbing.

I knew Franklyn lived on Mercy Hill, but the Hill covers a lot of ground; I couldn't search it for his house. Finally I thought of the street directory—odd I didn't think of that before—and called at the library today to check. There was only one R. Franklyn on Mercy Hill. I did return to the Religion section but they couldn't find *We Pass from View;* I suppose they're classifying me as one of their regular cranks.

I caught a bus to Mercy Hill. High sun, slight breeze; a bluebottle was patting its reflexion on the window, trying to escape. In the streets couples were taking their ice-creams for a walk; toward the Hill tennis-balls were punctuating their pauses, girls were leaping, bowls were clicking, and from the houses behind a procession was bearing trays of cakes to the pavilion. It was one of those days when if anything is to happen you have to make it happen; or for me to complete the next episode of my short story.

I dismounted at the foot of the Hill and climbed the piled terraces. At one corner they were erecting a new school; workmen were sunning themselves on girders. Two levels further up I came into Dee Terrace, and at once saw Franklyn's house.

It was unmistakeable. The personality which gave that house its final form was not the architect's. One chimney had been built into a frustum of white stone; an extra room had been added on the left, and its window had been blocked with newer brick; all the curtains, except those of one ground-floor window draped in green, were black. The house looked deserted, the more so for its garden, which could not have been tended in years; grass and weeds grew knee-high. I brushed through, imagining things crawling into my shoes. A bustling cloud of flies rose from something to one side. I reached the front door and saw the green curtain move; a face peered and drew back. I knocked. There was silence for a moment. Then inside a woman's voice screamed: "Oh, lie down with you!" Before I could ponder on that, the door was open.

The woman was certainly not in mourning—which was encouraging, for I hadn't known quite what approach to make. She wore a red dress, which looked pale against the crimson wallpaper of the hall. She was heavily, if inaccurately, made up, and her hair was rather arbitrarily bleached. She waited.

"Would you be Mrs. Franklyn?"

She looked suspicious, as if I'd intended a threat. "Roland Franklyn was my husband," she admitted ungraciously. "Who are you?"

Who indeed. It didn't seem as though I'd get far by declaring the supernatural nature of my quest. "I'm a writer," I compromised. "I've read your husband's book several times. I was shocked to hear of his death," I added to get it over with.

"Well, you don't have to be. Come in, anyway," she said. She looked round the hall and grimaced. "Look at this. Would you live with this? Not likely. Getting them in the right mood—half of them didn't know what they were being got in the mood for. Nice boys, some of them, to begin with." She kicked the crimson wall and ushered me into a room on the right.

I wasn't prepared—I couldn't have been. A ground-floor room with wardrobe, dressing-table complete with cobwebbed mirror, a bed beneath the window, piles of women's magazines, some thick with dust, and a cat chained to the leg of a chair in the middle of the floor; it wasn't a sense of evil or fear that choked me, it was a sense of something locked away, forgotten and gone bad. The cat padded up to meet me; its chain gave it freedom of the room, but it couldn't quite reach the door.

"Pussy likes you," said Mrs Franklyn, closing the door and sinking into a chair amid a haze of dust; her dress drew up her thighs, but she didn't pull it down. "That could be a good sign, but don't they say only effeminate men can make friends with cats? Why are you looking at me like that?" I hadn't realized I was looking like anything in particular; I was carrying the cat, chain and all, to the chair I took opposite her. "Don't like the chain, is that it? But me and my cat, we're all we've got—I'm not letting her out so they can carry her off and sacrifice her. They would, you know, on their nights. I take her in the garden, that's all; wouldn't trust them further than that." I remembered the flies. "What do you write?" she demanded.

In this context it seemed a little pale to say "Stories of the supernatural."

"Stories, eh? Yes, we all like stories," she mused. "Anything's better than the real thing. Do you want some tea? I'm afraid that's about all I have to offer."

"It's all right, thank you," I refused; I could see cracked cups in the kitchen behind her head. She caught my eye; she was always doing that, damn her.

"Oh, I can't blame you for thinking," she said. "But it gets you down after a while. After he took the house over—you didn't know that, did you?—yes, he did, he married me and then he encroached on every room, keeping things I wouldn't touch all over the house, until I took this room and the kitchen and I told him if you try anything in my rooms *I'll kill you!*" She thumped the chair-arm and dust flew out.

"But why did you put up with it?" I had to ask.

"Why? *Because I married him!*" The cat fled, knocked over a pile of magazines, sneezed and jumped back; she reeled it in and fondled it. "Now, pussy's not scared of mummy," she soothed and put it down. It began to scratch at her shoe. "Lie down with you, for God's sake," she hissed. It came to me for comfort.

"When I married him," she returned to me, "he promised I'd have all this house to entertain, to do all the things I never could. I believed him. Then I found out how he really was. So I waited. Every day I wished him dead so I'd have my house, what was left of my life. I haven't spoken to him for years, did you know that?—hardly even seen him. I used to leave his meals outside his room on a tray; if he didn't eat them that was up to him. But when he didn't touch them for three days I went into his room. No, I didn't go in—all those filthy statues and lights and books—but I could see he wasn't there. He was in his stupid little printing press room. He was dead all right. There was a book—he must have been going to copy something—but I didn't read it; the way his face looked was enough. I threw it in the bin. Didn't touch him, though—oh, no, they're not going to say I killed him after all the years I've suffered."

"But how did you stand it?" Of course the answer was—she didn't.

"Oh, he made me long ago. We met when we were students—I was impressionable then, I thought he was a good man, the best—and later we got married. I ought to have known; there was a rumor he'd been expelled from the University even then, but when he swore he hadn't I trusted him. Then his parents died and left him this house and we got married. My husband—" Her face contorted as if she'd put her hand in something foul. "He took me down to Temphill and made me watch those things dancing on the graves. I didn't want to but he said it was for a book he was writing. He held my hand, then. And later we went down the steps below Clotton—oh, you may write, but you'd never dare to write about … I don't want to think about it. But it hardened me. It made me tough when he began his mummery back here, trying to stop me destroying all his muck.…"

That sounded like a cue. "If you haven't thrown away all his books do you think I could look them over? Purely from a writer's viewpoint," I tacked on; why, I'm not sure.

"But you're a nice young man, you don't want to become another of his," she said, and sat down on the bed; her dress rose again like a curtain. She began to clear piles of magazines festooned with dust away from the bed; atop one was a vase of dandelions—"Just a touch of colour, what's it matter what they are, no-one ever comes," she explained, though the petals had curled and dulled in the flecked light. "Did you ever write from experience? How could you, you've never had what I've had to put up with. The things he's doing even now to hinder me—Only yesterday I picked up one of his books to throw it out and it went sticky and soft things started pushing between my fingers—God!" She wiped her hands down her dress. "I used to lie awake listening to him going to the bathroom and wishing he was dead—and last night I heard him flopping round his room, beating on the walls. And this morning I woke early, I thought the sun was coming up—but it was his face floating over the rooftops.... It came to the windows, filled them, it followed me from room to room, mouthing at me—God! You'd never write about it, you'd never write about anything again. But he can't get me down, and he knows it. He was always scared of me. That's why he kept me here, to keep me quiet. But he can't have left many of his little tricks behind him. He knows I'll win. But you don't want to get mixed up with the wrong things. You're a nice young man." She swung her legs up and lay back on the pillow, where I could see imprints of hair-dye.

For some time now I'd had the impression that my short story was taking over its own writing; now we seemed to be building to a climax I hadn't foreseen. I had to be direct. "Your husband was buried, wasn't he?" I asked. "Didn't he want to be cremated?"

She seemed to take an age to sit up; her eyes were on me all the while. "How did you know that?" she demanded softly. "You gave yourself away there, didn't you? You *are* one of his! I knew it before you got to the door! Yes, he's buried, where you all should be. Go on, go up and be with him, I'm sure he'd like you to be. He must be able to feel them coming by now—I hope he can. Yes, he was always on about his Eihort, but he doesn't like it when they come for him. You go and look after him, you—"

I didn't know what she might be capable of; I retreated hastily, seeing her watching in the mirror and sneering when she caught my eye. Somehow I dislodged a heap of magazines and buried the cat, which fought its way out and tangled my feet in its chain. "Don't you touch my cat!" she screamed. "She's worth a million of you! What is it, darling, come to mummy—" and I escaped, running down the hall, an inflamed intestine, and through the grass, careless of what I might tread in unseen.

Suddenly I was on solid pavement. Down the street an ice-cream van was playing "Greensleeves." This time the intrusion of mundanity didn't seem so tasteless. I walked home.

By the time I reached the typewriter I'd glimpsed the paradox. Even the supernatural-story writer who believes what he writes (and I'm not saying I don't) isn't prepared for an actual confrontation. Quite the reverse, for every time he fabricates the supernatural in a story (unless based on experience) he clinches his skepticism; he knows such things can't be, because he wrote them. Thus for him a confrontation would be doubly upsetting. It would at least force him to re-think all his works. Is this desirable? From the self-completion angle I suppose it is. At any rate, I'm going. "Go up and be with him" she said—it must be the cemetery on Mercy Hill.

Tomorrow.

EU

(Undated, unaddressed)

I don't know what
(Foregoing deleted, does not appear on carbon; page apparently withdrawn, carbon attached, reinserted into typewriter) Nonsense. Of course I can write about it. The very fact that I can write proves that I'm still functioning.

I took the bus up Mercy Hill at the height of the day. Few things moved; flies and pedestrians crawled, and the workmen climbed sluggishly on the skeletal school. At the intersection with Dee Terrace I saw the house; it seemed swallowed up by grass, forever isolated from its surroundings.

I want to get this over. The caretaker directed me down an

avenue, and when I reached— No. Description of graveyard. Why write as if this were my last page? Willows, their branches glowing stippled curves, were spaced carefully toward the Hill out of which the cemetery was carved; in the Hill itself were catacombs, black behind ivy or railings, and above stood the hospital, a grey reminder of hope or despair. What awful irony juxtaposed hospital and graveyard? The avenues were guarded by broken-nosed angels yearning heavenward; one showed a leprous patch where her left eye and cheek had sloughed away. Urns stood here and there like empty glasses at a sick-bed, and a young woman was kneeling with a wreath at a shining memorial; I wonder how long before she shakes him off? And then, toward the catacombs, I saw the new headstone and its bed of pebbles. They gleamed beneath the high sun. I read Franklyn's name and the framing dates, and waited.

It eventually occurred to me that I didn't quite know what I was waiting for; not in that sunlight. Yet the air had hushed. I paced around the grave, and the pebbles shifted. My shadow had moved them. I'm still capable of an anticlimax! My God. I thought: Franklyn is alive down there—or perhaps no longer. Then I saw a possibility. I looked back down the perspective. The young mourner was passing through the gates. I lay down on the grass and put my ear to the pebbles. They ground together, then there was nothing. I felt vilely uncomfortable. Suddenly I realized that I was visible all the way down the avenue to the gates. I went hot all over and scrambled to my feet.

And on the way up I heard something. Something. If only I knew. It'd be better if I had something to confront, anything but this uncertainty which sucks the confidence from me. It could have been the foreman at that school calling over the noise of riveting. Or it could—yes, must write—it could have been someone imprisoned, paralyzed, summoning a last muscular spasm, screaming thickly for help and beating his fists in the dark as he was dragged downward, downward....

I couldn't run; it was too hot. I walked. When I reached

the school the girders were rippling in the heat-haze as if they were alive. I wish I hadn't seen that. No longer could I trust the surface of the world. It was as though it had been instantaneously revealed to me that there were countless forces awake in everything, invisible, things lurking in daylight, shifting, planning— What had they built into the school? What would stalk unseen among the children?

I walked. Of course I was visualizing too much, but I could imagine, I could feel the pavement thin as ice, ready to engulf me in a world where life crawled. I sat in the parks. It was no good; I didn't know what watched from the trees; I didn't know how many of the passers-by might be masked, agents not of this world, preparing the way for—*what?* Who had Franklyn left behind? The peril of the writer: he can't stop thinking. He may survive by writing, but he doesn't really survive. Why am I no— mustn't give in—I wandered until dark, found a café, I don't remember. I was in a deserted street of shops with one red window lit above a darkened store. I don't know why, it seemed evil. Franklyn's hall, I suppose.

So I came back and typed this. The street is empty; only the shadow of the streetlamp seems to move. The window opposite is dark. What may be there, waiting?

I can't turn round. I stare at the reflexion of the room behind me. The reflexion—like a framed photograph about to be split open by something climbing forth. When I've written this I shall turn round.

"I don't dare," I have just said aloud.

Where can I go where I don't sense movement behind the scenes?

(Unsigned)

WHERE YIDHRA WALKS

WALTER C. DEBILL, JR.

A hundred April winds disperse her fragrance,
A thousand wet Octobers scour her footprints,
The ruthless years assail the ancient memory of her presence, yet
Where Yidhra walks the hills do not forget.

—Jean Paul LeChat

I

The river was swollen to a mad torrent, the water brown and opaque. I watched a jagged clump of brush sweep by with terrifying speed; three water moccasins twined in its sodden branches. The rain had grown heavier for three days while the wind mounted steadily and, though the eye of the hurricane was expected to pass a hundred miles east and the violence of the storm decrease as it moved further inland, I knew it would be a week before the river could be crossed here even if the decrepit trestle bridge survived. It was shuddering periodically from the strain of the current, and the broken remnants of two of the trestles dangled uselessly.

As I stood on the bank a muddy pickup truck pulled up and two men in ponchos and cowboy hats began blocking the entrance to the bridge with sawhorses. One saw me eyeing the bridge and called out,

"Good thing you didn't try it, mister; we already had three people drown today when a bridge washed out over by Iverston."

"Is there another bridge across this river that might still be safe? I hate to go all the way around through Barrett. That's a hundred miles out of my way."

He flashed an unsympathetic smirk, plainly intending to say no, then paused. "Well, there's an old bridge upstream five miles, where the river's not so wide. It's on the old road through Milando." He said it in a tense, subdued voice.

His companion stopped tinkering around the truck and stepped over beside him, "If you go that way I'd recommend you keep movin'. Those folks up around Milando never did like outsiders much, and what this hurricane's doin' to their orchards ain't gonna improve their hospitality." They both chuckled.

I remembered seeing Milando on the map and didn't ask for directions. I glanced in the rearview mirror as I drove off and saw them both watching me curiously from under their dripping hat brims.

I don't know why I was so anxious to avoid a detour and keep driving doggedly through the storm. My cousin in Brownsville wasn't expecting me by any fixed date, and even losing a week crossing Texas wouldn't have inconvenienced me particularly. Yet the monotonous downpour lulled me into a mental torpor where thoughtless stubbornness pushed me on, and something about the mysterious raging river demanded that I cross it. And of course the peculiar attitude of the men at the bridge had aroused my curiosity about Milando. So I wound my way five miles north on a pitted blacktop road roughly paralleling the river and clattered across the plank floor of an ancient truss bridge. Less than a mile beyond the river a culvert spanning a tributary creek was under a few inches of water, but my little station wagon had a high road clearance for a small car and I decided to risk it. The wheels kept losing traction, letting the car slip sideways in sickening lurches, but I made it. I heard a groaning sound and a huge crash behind me and turned to see the culvert tube bounding jerkily downstream. I could no longer go back.

The road was tortuous and narrow as it wormed upward into the labyrinth of limestone hills, alternating gloomy tunnel-like passages overhung by gnarled live oaks with barren stretches below steep cliffs.

The striking appearance of the stunted mesquite trees writhing along the cliff tops continually caught my eye in spite of the hazardous driving conditions, or I would never have seen the hooded figure against the darkening sky. Somehow I knew that it was a woman, though the hooded rain cape concealed both face and figure. A large dog sat at her feet. I barely had time to wonder what she was doing out there in such abominable weather before I rounded a sudden curve and had my first sight of Milando.

II

Through a lull in the rain I saw the town spread out below me in a wedge-shaped cleft in the hills. The road snaked down a steep hillside and passed along the mouth of the cleft, where the town was perhaps a mile wide. Almost all of the town lay to the left of the road where the streets wandered aimlessly upward to the point of the wedge, nearly level with the surrounding cliffs.

As I entered the town I slowed to a crawl and began searching for a place to get something to eat. It was darkening rapidly and the slope above me was dotted with lighted windows, but every window and doorway along the main street seemed black and deserted. I almost passed the one business still open because the glow at the windows was so dim. The painted sign said 'Saloon-Grocery-Meat Market,' so I parked and mounted the concrete porch, catching a stream of rainwater in my collar from the edge of the overhanging roof. Behind the display windows, which featured pyramids of dusty canned goods and an array of cheap pocket knives, a chest-high partition blocked most of the light and the dingy glass filtered the rest to a sickly yellow. But once I rattled my way through the heavy door it was evident that I had found the center of Milando's night life.

To my left several groups of men sat around heavy circular tables playing dominoes. Through an archway at the rear I could see more tables and dominoes. The bar ran along the right-hand side and behind it the wall was lined with rows of canned and packaged foods rising almost to the ceiling. There was no one behind the bar, but as I moved over to it an uncomfortable lull spread through the room and a bald, burly specimen detached himself from one of the games and stepped around to the beer taps in front of me.

"What do you want?" No amenities, no smile.

"Just passing through. Any place in town where I can get a meal?"

"Nope. I'll sell you some of this stuff." His long ape-like arm gestured toward the shelves, apparently indicating some grimy boxes of shotgun shells, while his flat eyes kept me fixed.

"I guess that will have to do."

"Say, which way did you come from?"

"East. The main bridge was about gone and I didn't want to go around through Barrett."

"Well, you're gonna have to go back that way. The low-water crossing west of town's under six feet of water."

"But a culvert washed out behind me not far this side of the river. You mean I'm stuck here for the night?"

The room was silent now. "More than that. Several days, I'd say." Under the bushy brows the eyes had taken on a suspicious cast.

"Plan to check out any old Injun stories?" jeered a beery voice from one of the tables. It seemed to emanate from a set of crooked yellow teeth just below the sharp shadow of a tin lampshade.

The bartender shot a murderous glare in that direction before explaining, "Don't pay no attention to Maynard's warped sense o' humor. He's talking about a fellow name o' Harrison from Barrett, from the university, that came up here lookin' for Indian relics and traces of folklore. Seems this used to be some kind o' medicine place, somethin' to do with a cult called 'Yidhra,' but people around here don't know anything about that. The dam' fool got himself lost up in the hills, never was found. This country's full of caves, deep pools, heavy brush. Well, I got potato chips and stuff like that, sardines—but I don't know where you're gonna stay till the water goes down. No motel or anything here...."

A tall man setting alone at the end of the bar stood up and turned stiffly toward me. "You can stay with us. You're welcome to have dinner. My name's Wilhelm Kramer." The bartender was not pleased and I heard Maynard chuckle nervously.

"Thanks," I said, "that would sure beat sardines and a cold night in my car." Besides, I sensed that the antagonism between him and the others might make him a good source of information about the town. He picked up a heavy rubber raincoat and a canvas fisherman's hat from the jumble of rain gear hung on a set of mounted deer antlers and we left.

In the car he didn't speak except to give terse directions to a rather small unpainted house about halfway up the slope. Crossing the screened-in front porch we entered a neat and cozy living room, warmed by a large radiant heater and the subdued, almost amber light from beneath an opaque cardboard lampshade. From a door at the left emerged a small pale woman who gave me a startled look.

"How do you do, I'm Peter Kovacs," I said, remembering that I hadn't introduced myself to Kramer at the store.

"Mr. Kovacs is staying with us until the creeks go down. The Moreno Creek culvert's washed out and the low-water crossing's under six feet."

Her colorless eyes looked even more startled and after telling us that supper would be ready in a few minutes she disappeared into the kitchen. We hung our coats on hooks by the door and Kramer settled into a threadbare but comfortable-looking armchair while I sat on the overstuffed couch.

"You seem to be the only one in Milando that cares much for strangers, Mr. Kramer," I said, hoping to draw him out about the town. He smiled.

"Yes, the others are pretty hostile to any kind of outsider." He was about forty, with rugged features just beginning to soften around the sharp lines. "Actually they still think of me as an outsider, though I've been here eighteen years. I'm originally from Iverston … met Georgia, that's my wife, at the junior college in Mesquite City and came here to take over her father's business when his health went bad. I sell oil and gas to the farmers on credit. They never did like me." He gave the impression of a normally taciturn man become garrulous under the influence of beer and fresh companionship.

I saw the little goblin faces of three small children peep through the door to a darkened rear hall, then fade away. They seemed to take after the mother.

"Are all the small towns around here this inhospitable?"

"They're all pretty clannish and ingrown, mainly because there's nothing to attract new blood, and tend to peg outsiders as 'city slickers' or beatniks, but Milando's the only one that's downright hostile to *anybody* that wasn't born and raised here. Always was. It was settled right after the Civil War by a bunch that came out together from Georgia. Never did hit it off with the other settlers around here, and then their dealings with the Indians …"

His wife appeared in the doorway, looking more alarmed than ever, and announced that the food was ready. We ate in the brightly lit kitchen. The food was as solid and simple as the furniture and there was little conversation. In the light Mrs. Kramer was faintly attractive in a pallid, wistful way, in spite of a prominent nose and weak chin, which made her eyes appear to be slightly to the side of her head. I had noticed the same trait in the bartender and guessed that they were related. The children, a girl of about thirteen whom they called Georgie and two younger boys, had inherited it, along with their mother's wispy blond hair and flat, colorless eyes. They were very quiet. Toward the end of the meal Kramer and his wife had a tense exchange concerning a visit the following day from Kramer's mother-in-law. I guessed that she must live somewhere in the hills near town, since having the main roads washed out didn't cancel the visit. He evidently disliked her intensely, and the atmosphere became so strained that I was not surprised when Mrs. Kramer failed to join us in the living room afterwards.

Kramer brought beer from the refrigerator, and I had no trouble getting him back on the history of the town. "The settlers had a hard time at first; most of the land's too rocky to farm, but once they made peace with the Comanche and started raising sheep and fruit trees, apples and peaches, it got to be the most prosperous town in the hills. Probably would've become a big trading center and county seat like Iverston if the other settlers hadn't been so leery of this bunch. Still don't get any business except from right around the town, the old families that came from Georgia."

"Comanche? I didn't know they raided this far east," I said.

"Oh, yes. They were mainly up in the Panhandle, in the flat open country, but they roamed over most of the state when they felt like it. And this area was a medicine place—the center of a special cult of a goddess called Yidhra. Not all of the Comanche belonged, just certain bands. The Tonkawas that lived in the area used to allow 'em free passage to here at certain times in the spring and fall to hold their ceremonies. When the settlers came they cut 'em off, at first, anyway, so the Comanche tried to drive 'em out, but after a while they made some kind of agreement with the old chief they called Snake Eyes to let the Indians come twice a year. I guess they were just tired of fighting, the settlement was pretty poor then and probably not worth fighting about. That caused a lot bad feelings with the other settlements; the Comanche had a pretty fearsome reputation, killin' whites and other Indians was their idea of light recreation, and when they came riding through the hills with their horned buffalo-scalp headdresses and lances and such I guess it was hard to tell a religious pilgrimage from a war party. Anyway, the place became completely isolated. There were even rumors that some of the people here had gone over to the Indian religion. But about that time the place started to prosper and the people didn't care what the neighbors thought." He was slowing down now, his voice getting lower, and I thought he would fall asleep soon.

"Milando's an odd name—sound's Spanish, but I've never heard it before."

"Not Spanish, Indian. Some kind of word they got from the Comanche. They changed the town's name to that in 1887, when some of the original families pulled up and went to California. The town was originally called Kimbrough, after my wife's great-grandfather, who led the original move out from Georgia. But when old Kimbrough left with the others in '87 they changed it. Some say they left because they were the only ones who wouldn't go over to the Indian cult. I won't believe that, but it's true that these people know a lot more about that Indian business than they'll tell anybody, even me."

I made a few more attempts to get him to say more about the town's strange history, but he had gone as far as he was willing to for the time being and seemed more and more inclined to brood and let the conversation lapse. I felt uncomfortable in the silence and was too restless to sleep at that early hour, so I said I was going back to the store for cigarettes. Before leaving I brought in my overnight bag and was shown into the small rear bedroom, from which Georgie had apparently been evicted for the night, where I would sleep.

I didn't really want to go back to the dingy store with its hostile proprietor and clientele, but once in the car I realized that there was nowhere else to go. The rain had become very heavy as the evening progressed, and the dirt streets of Milando were in bad enough shape to make driving too risky even if I had been able to see anything. So I crawled down the hill in second gear and parked in front of the gloomy 'Saloon-Grocery-Meat Market.'

This time the domino players ignored my entry. Only the bartender appeared to take notice, giving me a cold smile. "Well, did ol' Willie tell you all about Milando?"

"Just a little," I said. "Interesting place, so isolated and independent. I'd like to know more ..." I was concentrating so intently on sounding banal that I didn't notice the sound of the door until I saw the bartender's eyes staring past me and heard the dead silence at the tables. I hesitated a moment before turning, not knowing whether to expect Frankenstein's monster or something worse. When I did turn, I faced the most attractive woman I have ever seen.

I didn't know then what fascinated me about her and I don't know now. She was tall, very slender, even angular, but graceful, and from the hooded cape I was certain she was the one I had seen just before entering the town. The long oval face with its short straight nose and almost solemn mouth was pretty, but she was beautiful far beyond any sum of physical attributes. At the time I thought it might be her eyes: they were a luminous gray and very large below a trace of eye shadow which was the only discernible makeup, but since then I have come to believe that some women have a force of soul which casts an irresistible glamour over whatever features they possess.

She gave me a leisurely examination, then addressed the bartender. "I didn't know there was an outsider in town, Ed."

"He just came in tonight, ma'am. The road's washed out; he's staying with Willie Kramer." His voice sounded as though he were standing at attention.

"Well, I hope you enjoy your stay, Mr. ...?"

"Kovacs, Peter Kovacs." Her high clear voice affected me hypnotically. "It's an interesting town, I'd like to find out about its history, the Indian cult ..." I was blurting it out thoughtlessly, my mind unfocused.

She had a silvery little laugh. "You'll find that the people in Milando don't have much to tell. But perhaps you'll learn enough to satisfy your curiosity. 'Where Yidhra walks, the hills do not forget.'" Memory stirred, and I placed the enigmatic line from Jean Paul LeChat, the brilliant young New Orleans poet who disappeared in Chad in 1957.

"That's from LeChat, isn't it? I remember wondering what it meant when I read it. I'd never heard of the cult of Yidhra before I came here today."

"I doubt if Mr. LeChat knew much about it either," she said, brushing back the hood from her straight blond hair. "He wrote about more things than he understood."

"And Harrison? Did he understand?"

Her eyes widened and her smile became hard, even cruel. "No, not really. He was intelligent in the purely bookish sense, but not really sensitive. Not equipped to understand the real mysteries of life."

I thought she was eyeing me with increasing interest, but she turned abruptly to the bartender and said, "Ed, could I speak to you for a moment, in private?"

After a gruff "Yes, ma'am," they moved toward the archway in the rear. Her walk was fluid, utterly feminine, but not exaggerated, and I noticed that her high, shiny boots were clean, though Milando was a quagmire outside and I hadn't heard a car pull up. Her dismissal of me had been rather imperious and I felt a bit sheepish, the more so because I was left standing there with no one to wait on me. I didn't really need the cigarettes, so I left.

Back at the house Kramer sat alone staring into space while a backwoods preacher ranted through the static on an ancient console radio with an illuminated dial. He gave a faint grunt of acknowledgment when I said goodnight, not even turning his head. As soon as I lay down fatigue swept over me like an ocean wave and my mind began to dissolve into fragments of dream. I was vaguely aware of the hissing whispers of the children in the next room— they seemed to have some sort of speech impediment which made it impossible to understand what they said; I remember hearing Kramer's voice over that of the radio preacher, berating his wife about his mother-in-law; last of all before sleep came I remember picturing with abnormal clarity every line and shadow of the woman's face, the woman in the hood.

III

I slept late in the morning and by the time I awoke Kramer had left the house. His wife fixed breakfast for me in spite of my demurrals and apologies, seeming even more flustered and inarticulate in her husband's absence. In the awkward silence I observed her more closely than the night before. There was an almost reptilian suggestion in her features, accented by her slouching round-shouldered carriage and shuffling walk. I wondered how much of her washed-out appearance was due to heredity and how much to a lifetime of small-town boredom and narrowness. With more spirit and a little makeup she might have been quite pretty. I thought of the woman in the hood; small town life certainly hadn't stifled *her*. I mentioned the incident to Mrs. Kramer and asked if she knew the woman, but it turned out to be the wrong thing to do. She looked terrified and mumbled something about "Miss Yolanda." I asked if she was an outsider and she said no, she had always lived there, but beyond that she claimed to know nothing about her, which was obviously untrue.

Outside the rain had thinned to drizzle and sunlight was starting to break through in patches. I guessed that the center of the storm had passed during the night. I decided to drive out to the low-water crossing to see if the water had begun to go down, though I was too curious about Milando to really want to leave yet. The road to the west led around a perpendicular bluff into a long narrow valley. Both sides of the road were lined with groves of apple and peach trees. I saw some fruit on the ground, but the storm had apparently done little damage. Farther from the road I caught glimpses of flocks of sheep on the lower slopes of the hills rising to the north and south. At the end of the valley I drove over a low hill and stopped. Ahead of me the road descended into churning brown water, reemerging fifty yards away. Halfway across the creek protruded the top of a concrete post. The painted line marked '4½ FT' was just visible above the eddying surface. The rain had stopped and the sun was shining through a hole in the clouds, so I got out of the car and walked down to the water's edge. I stood for a while, watching and listening to the rushing stream. When I turned she was there.

She was beside the road at the top of the slope where the trees began, standing in the shade. She was wearing the rain cape with the hood back, the same calf-high boots and short skirt. I resolved not to get rattled this time; the night before I had been tired and off-balance because of the repressed menace of the xenophobic saloon crowd. By daylight she would probably be an intelligent small-town girl, perhaps moderately attractive but not exceptional. I started up the hill.

Neither of us spoke until I reached her. By then I felt the same powerful, unexplainable fascination I had in the gloom of the saloon.

"Hello, Mr. Kovacs. It looks as though you'll be with us for a while. There will be more rain." Her voice had an odd distant quality I hadn't noticed before.

"Yes, I'd guess two days at least. Maybe I'll get a chance to find out something about this Yidhra thing, though I got the impression I might be better off digging around in the university library in Barrett than trying to get anything out of the people here. Do you know much about it, Miss …?"

"Call me Yolanda. I guess I know as much about Yidhra as anyone around here. She's old—the Indians didn't bring the worship of Yidhra with them, they found it here. And the cult existed in the Old World. The men of Sumer knew her. But you wouldn't find out much in any university library. There have been books that told about Yidhra and other hidden things, but man has a habit of avoiding things that make him uncomfortable. In the past, books like the *Chronicles of Thrang*, the *Chthonic Revelations* of Thanang Phram, and the *Black Sutra* of U Pao have been denounced, suppressed, burned. In modern times they're disposed of even more simply—the professional scholars merely declare them not authentic. Or just ignore them altogether. Perhaps it's for the best—there are elder things much less benign than Yidhra."

I thought these were rather remarkable statements, though there have been a number of fairly plausible theories about pre-Colombian contact between the Old and New Worlds. But I was more interested in hearing what she had to say than in debating with her, and didn't challenge them.

"And is the cult really still carried on in Milando?"

"Yes indeed." She turned and we began ambling side by side down the shady tree line. "Almost all of them are in it now. Kramer's not, of course. He's an outsider. They take in outsiders from time to time; Yidhra needs them, but Kramer just wasn't right for it."

I smiled, "I suppose the cult couldn't spread very far if they never took in any new members."

"No, but then Yidhra doesn't much care about spreading the cult. She's part of life and death and the earth itself; domination means nothing to her. She takes only what she needs. She was born with life itself on this planet and as life grew she grew, as life changed so she changed. And like all life she must change to live. Milando is small and inbred; to limit the cult, or this branch of it, to these people and their descendants would be stasis, a kind of death."

"You really believe in her, don't you?" I said.

Her smile was politely restrained but her gray eyes, deep set in spite of their size, were laughing at me. "Yidhra isn't a matter of faith, Peter. She's real. She does things. You saw the orchards on your way here; we had fifty-mile-an-hour winds night before last. And the sheep; thousands of sheep will take sick and die from this weather, but none around Milando. Her followers even see her, after a fashion, though the ancient books say that what they see is largely illusion, a protective glamour cast over a far more terrifying reality; only the real *participants* in the cult, the inner circle, those born of Yidhra and those chosen to mingle their blood and seed with her to renew her and bring forth new life, only those see her true form."

The sun was hot where it flickered through the leaves, and the sultry soporific smell of wet vegetation became oppressive. I moved into the sunlight onto a high flat rock overlooking the water and she followed.

"I wonder if Jean Paul LeChat saw her," I said as we looked down at the stream.

"Perhaps, in Chad. He was seeking her there—all he had found in New Orleans were old books and third-hand accounts from degenerate pseudo-occultists." As she turned toward me her eyes seemed enormous. "You'll see her, I think, Peter."

The spell was broken by a spatter of raindrops in advance of a ragged cloudbank. "I'll have to go now," she said.

"Can I give you a ride?"

"No, thank you, I live in the hills near here. There's a trail." She turned and slipped into an imperceptible opening in the brush. I caught sight of her willowy figure through the trees several times as she flitted up the hillside; then the sky turned gray and I had to run for the car to keep from getting drenched.

IV

When I pulled up in front of the Kramer house and got out of the car I could hear Kramer barking at his wife about the impending visit of his mother-in-law. He had been drinking again and was apparently too engrossed in the squabble to hear me drive up, so I overheard some of his taunts before I stepped up on the porch and knocked at the door. At the time I interpreted it as a standard in-law feud—she was a bad influence on the children, she was alienating them from their father, his wife's grandfather should have left with Old Kimbrough instead of staying on and becoming 'the worst of the lot.' I regretted coming back to the house, and by the time he opened the door I had made up my mind to get back out as soon as possible, even if it meant driving around aimlessly through the mud or resorting to the saloon.

His wife left the room as I entered, and I told Kramer about checking the low-water crossing. When I mentioned running into the young woman I had met in the saloon he looked puzzled and asked her name.

"I didn't get her last name—her first name's Yolanda," I said.

He turned white; it was a while before he spoke. "Look here, Mr. Kovacs—it must be obvious to you by now that there's something pretty strange about this town. You might as well know that the old Indian cult is still very much alive here. They've never let me in on it, but you can't live in a town like this for eighteen years without getting a pretty good idea what's going on. And I think she's at the head of it."

"She seemed harmless enough to me," I said, "imaginative, full of wild ideas but basically a decent girl."

"Girl, Mr. Kovacs?" he chuckled wryly. "When I first saw her, about the time they started to take me for granted and quit worrying about

169

my suspicions, she looked exactly as she does now. That was fifteen years ago."

This disturbed me more than it should have; I had found her age peculiarly hard to judge in the saloon, placing it somewhere between eighteen and twenty-eight, and after talking with her in daylight had inclined toward the lower figure. But then there had been the bartender's rigid deference toward her and the occasional hints of condescension in her attitude toward me; why should it be so upsetting to think of her as in her mid-thirties?

"I think you'd be wise to stay away from her," he went on. "You heard about that student that came here last year—they never found him. There were others before him. She seems to be interested in you. That's a bad sign, Mr. Kovacs. These people are dangerous."

I made some vague promises to be careful and left. The rain was light but steady and I decided to risk a drive around the town. Except for the stretch of road along the foot of the hill Milando consisted of unpaved streets, now soft, slippery, and gullied, but somehow I managed to avoid getting stuck. The houses were uniformly low and wooden, with haphazard additions that gave them a rambling look in spite of their generally small size. Considering the alleged prosperity of the town, a surprising proportion were shabby and dilapidated, with ragged screens, broken wooden steps, and missing windowpanes replaced with cardboard; I wondered if this was an outward sign of the inhabitants' spiritual and mental degeneracy, of their regression into barbarous superstition. Almost none of the houses were painted, though in the few well-kept specimens like Kramer's the unpainted wood gave an impression of dignity rather than squalor. I found the overall effect depressing, and the furtive sullen looks the occupants gave me before pulling down yellowed window shades made me uneasy, so I soon headed down the hill to the saloon. I think I was hoping to run into Yolanda again in spite of Kramer's warning.

Ed, the bartender, greeted me with a nasty smile. "Still with us? I figured you would be, unless you felt like swimming out."

"You were right; looks like two or three more days before I can cross that low-water bridge. You sell beer this time of day?"

"Anytime. The state liquor people don't get up here much, and the county law don't care." He handed me a bottle of a popular local brand without offering a choice.

"And I suppose you're the Chief of Police?"

"Naw, that's Maynard. You still interested in the old Indian doings here?"

"Yes, very much."

"Well, I got Harrison's notes here, the student that disappeared. We found 'em in the brush, after Maynard called off the search and the Ranger left. Didn't seem worthwhile to send 'em on."

If the investigator sent by the state had left the search to the local people anything could have happened, anything could have been concealed. Kramer had said these people were dangerous, and somehow the bartender's new congeniality was not at all reassuring.

The notes consisted of loose sheets in a cheap accordion folder. I carried them and the beer over to one of the round tables and sat down to examine them. The sheets had been dated and numbered and many pages were missing. The first few pages consisted of accounts, apparently copied from the state archives in Barrett, from early Texas settlers who had spoken to other Indian groups about the devotees of Yidhra, whom they called by many variant names such as Yee-Tho-Rah. The cult had originated somewhere east of the West Texas Plains, among unknown tribes described as tall, hairy, and very primitive, and had spread among the Comanche only a few generations before the Europeans appeared. The bands which had adopted the cult had been abhorred by the other Comanche, who seemed to consider them physically repellent as well as dangerous. They occasionally kidnapped members of other bands for some purpose, possibly ritual sacrifice, though there were rumors that some of the captives had been found or rescued alive. The Indians were curiously reluctant to speak of these captives, but the settlers concluded from various hints that they had been killed by their rescuers because of some physical deformity associated with conversion to the cult. At this point there was a break in the notes where some pages were missing.

The next section was a series of quotes from standard reference works on anthropology and folklore, interspersed with Harrison's own remarks. He seemed to have concluded that Yidhra was a version of the universal figure of the earth mother or goddess of the underworld connected with primitive concepts of prosperity, fertility, and death, but that the cult was not directly related to any mentioned in standard sources. Toward the end of this section there were indications that he had unearthed some obscure sources, possibly in a private library, which he thought might contain information on Yidhra and planned to investigate them next. There were a number of parenthetical questions and notes such as: "Related to Mlandoth cycle?," "Try the *Chronicles* on this point," and "cf. Könnenberg's *U.S.*" Then came a large gap in the page number sequence.

The notes began again during Harrison's investigations in Milando and were plainly fragmentary and incomplete, with many individual pages removed. From what remained I gathered that he had never stayed overnight in Milando but made numerous trips from Barrett over a period of about a month. He commented on the reticence of most of the inhabitants, but managed to contact Kramer and two others who told him essentially what Kramer had told me. There was no mention of Yolanda, though one page following a deletion began with the suggestive phrase "… she doesn't consider me suitable." There were a few hints that he was correlating the information obtained in Milando with the obscure sources mentioned just before the big gap in the page numbers, but there was no explicit or elaborate correlation on the pages present. At first there was much speculation about survival of the cult into the present, but toward the end missing pages became more frequent and any references to definite discovery of cult practices must have been systematically removed. On the last page Harrison expressed frustration with the reticence of the townspeople and resolved to go exploring on foot in the hills.

Altogether the notes were less interesting than the fact that they had been shown to me. Last night Ed had been openly offensive and had tried to discourage any interest in Milando; today he affected courtesy if not friendliness and deliberately whetted my curiosity. A decision must have been made, undoubtedly by Yolanda, as to how I would be dealt with, and he was no longer worried about me. I was to be led on but not told too much just yet. As I sat smoking a cigarette and sipping the last of my second beer I drew two conclusions, one right and one wrong. The first was that, unlike Harrison, I was 'suitable'; I had been chosen to join the cult of Yidhra. The second was that I was therefore in no danger and could proceed boldly to find out what lay in the hills behind Milando.

V

A combination of reason and intuition that told me that what I wanted to know lay over the hill at the top of the cleft. Logically, there was the fact that, while presumably there were several hundred people involved in the cult, I could see no place suitable for a large gathering, no large buildings and nothing resembling a town square. To the north beyond the main road there was a steep rise to sheer cliffs; I had traveled the roads east and west as far as a man could conveniently walk and seen nothing that looked like a gathering place and nothing striking enough to inspire an Indian medicine place. Thus my attention was naturally drawn to the point of the wedge to the south. I had noticed that there was a break in the cliff line there where a shallow brush-choked saddle passed over the crest, but until now the weather and a vague sense of danger had cut off any thought of investigation on foot. But now it was clear that I could learn little more from random conversation and I had, I thought, a kind of immunity from the consequences of prying. I could of course wait for them to initiate me into the cult, but that struck me as a very dangerous course. There had been in Harrison's notes several disquieting suggestions of physical deformity connected with conversion; possibly their rites involved some form of mutilation or worse. I decided to pretend to go along with them, find out as much as possible on my own, and get out of Milando as soon as the water went down.

It was almost four o'clock when I got back to the Kramer house, and I wanted to start my hike with as much daylight left as possible. The rain was light, hardly more than a mist, and I was also anxious to take advantage of this. But Kramer insisted that his wife fix a ridiculously early supper because I had missed lunch, so I was unable to get away until four-thirty. It was a dismal meal, Kramer and I sitting alone at the table with neither of us at all hungry while his wife dutifully rattled pots and pans without speaking to us and the children hissed and whispered in the next room. He made an effort to dissuade me from going out on foot, though I hadn't told him of my plan to go over the hill, but he was too preoccupied with some worry of his own to object strenuously. His wife's presence seemed to inhibit him from referring openly to the danger he had mentioned earlier. Only at the door as I prepared to leave did he give a low-voiced warning. "Don't underestimate these people, Mr. Kovacs. I've been seeing things for years and tried to ignore them, tried not to believe, but I know now that there's something foul going on here. There are things here that have no right to exist in a decent world."

I wore a rain hat, thinking an umbrella would be of no use in heavy brush, and changed to high-topped hiking boots even though I hoped the mud would be less of a problem on higher ground than it was in town. I took a flashlight and extra batteries in case I couldn't get back before dark. There wasn't much chance of slipping out of town unobserved, but there were few phone lines in Milando and I hoped the wet weather would delay any organized effort to stop me.

At the top of the cleft a short dirt street, populated only by two apparently deserted shacks, ran parallel to a wall of dense vegetation. I quickly found the narrow well-worn path leading into the brush and through the saddle between the cliffs. At first the trees and bushes were too high to see much, but I could tell that the path ran steeply downward. Soon I passed through several rocky spots where the brush thinned, and through the light rain I saw the broad green valley into which I was descending, lush and beautiful under the gray overcast. Along the valley floor ran an irregular band of darker green which must mark some narrow creek, sunk below the surrounding land by erosion. I passed rapidly down the trail and within a half hour found myself on the edge of a canyon, at least sixty feet deep and perhaps a hundred yards wide. Along the boulder-strewn bottom a racing stream wound among huge oaks and pecan trees. The path turned to the right and followed the canyon rim upstream.

When I saw the pool I knew it was the place, the center of the cult. Eons past, an underground river had flowed there, swirling in a whirlpool two hundred yards wide until the cavern roof collapsed, leaving a perfectly circular pool. Around the edge slabs of fallen limestone protruded above the surface at crazy angles. Now a waterfall ran over the lip of the crater-like depression and the circle of stone was open on one side where the creek flowed out of the pool into the canyon. The sheer walls were undercut to form a wide sheltered ledge around the water, and to the left of the cascade the black mouth of a great cavern, undoubtedly the channel of the ancient underground river, opened onto the ledge. I watched for a while to be sure the place was deserted before searching for a way down to the pool and soon found the steps cut into the rock face. The rain-slick steps had been worn smooth and hollowed almost to a ramp in the center. At the bottom a path led up to the ledge and I followed it around, intending to reach the large cavern. But behind the waterfall I found the mouth of a smaller cave, now sealed with a wooden wall. The heavy door in the center of the wall did not appear to be locked, and I stepped quietly up to it. I could hear no sound within and it was fastened from the outside with a simple wooden slide latch. When I slid it back the door swung noiselessly inward. Stepping inside, I switched on my flashlight and saw a narrow room extending about thirty feet back into the rock. I closed the door behind me and began to investigate its contents.

The left-hand wall was lined with a row of old-fashioned chests with bowed lids. I tried the first one and found it unlocked. On top were several robes elaborately embroidered with strange designs, but I didn't take them out and examine them closely for fear of leaving signs of my search. On the right were several ceremonial objects of exquisite workmanship, a brazier on a tripod, a four-foot candelabrum, and a peculiar thing shaped oddly. This last object was of smooth bronze and mounted on a pedestal. The others were of some alloy resembling gold but lighter in weight and color and chased with intricate designs in which the shape of the bronze object figured prominently. Apparently it was an important symbol in the cult. The remainder of the designs bore no resemblance to the art of the Plains Indian, though there were vague suggestions of South and Central American patterns. I saw a table against the rear wall of the room with some papers on it and went to see if I could find some blank paper which I could safely take to copy a sample of the designs. The papers proved to be the missing portions of Harrison's notes, the portions someone had deliberately removed to prevent my learning too much about the cult of Yidhra. There was a chair and a modern propane lamp; I lit the lamp and sat down to read what someone had sought to conceal from me.

One bundle evidently consisted of quotes from the obscure sources Harrison had turned to when the standard reference works failed. The first was headed 'Graf von Könnenberg, *Uralte Schrecken,* nineteenth-century treatise on ancient religious cults' and continued, "It is clear that the most ancient gods, the prototypes of all the gods of men, were known and worshipped before men existed; and it is further clear that the most ancient gods all proceed from the one source. That source is Mlandoth, and all gods are but varied manifestations and extensions of the One. But whether Mlandoth is a place, or a conscious entity, or an inconceivable maelstrom of unknown forces and properties outside the perceptible cosmos is not known.

"Certainly Ngyr-Khorath, the mad and monstrous thing which haunted this region before the solar system was formed and haunts it still, is but a local eddy of the vastness that is Mlandoth. And is not fabled 'Ymnar, the dark stalker and seducer of all earthly intelligence, merely the arm of Ngyr-Khorath, an organ created in the image of earthly life and consciousness to corrupt that life and lead it to its own destruction?

"And does not even great Yidhra, who was born of and with the life of earth and who through the eons intertwines endlessly with all earthly life forms, teach reverence for Mlandoth?"

The next quote was from the *Black Sutra* of U Pao, which I recognized with a thrill as one of the books Yolanda had mentioned:

"Before death was born, *She* was born; and for untold ages there was life without death, life without birth, life unchanging. But at last death came; birth came; life became mortal and mutable, and thereafter fathers died, sons were born, and never was the son exactly as the father; and the slime became the worm, and the worm, the serpent, and the serpent became the yeti of the mountain forests, and the yeti became man. Of all living things only *She* escaped death, escaped birth. But *She* could not escape change, for all living things must change as the trees of the north must shed their leaves to live in winter and put them on to live in spring. And therefore *She* learned to devour the mortal and mutable creatures, and from their seed to change *Herself*, and to be as all mortal things as *She* willed, and to live forever without birth, without death."

There followed a note not enclosed in quotation marks which I assumed to be Harrison's own comment:

"U Pao was early Burmese sage—incredibly advanced speculation on evolutionary principles—is it possible that a protean macroorganism could have developed and survived from before the advent of reproduction and

individual death? How could it have survived in competition with organisms capable of evolution? References to change *in Y. very puzzling."*

The next fragment was from the *Chronicles of Thrang:*

"Yidhra devoured the octopus and learned to put forth a tentacle; she devoured the bear and learned to clothe herself in fur against the creeping ice of the north; indeed can Yidhra take any shape known to living things. Yet no shape can she take which is truly fair, for she partakes of all foul creatures as well as fair. To her followers she appears in many fair and comely forms, but this is because they see not her true form, but only such visions as she wills them to see. For as the adepts can send their thoughts and visions to one another over great distances, so can Yidhra send her thoughts to men and cause them to see only what she wills. Indeed it is by sending her thoughts that Yidhra remains one in soul, for in body she is many, hidden in the jungles of the south, the icy wastes of the north, and the deserts beyond the western sea. Thus it is that though her temples are many, she waits by all, combining bodily with her diverse followers, yet her consciousness is a vast unity."

In the comment following this, Harrison's line of thought became chillingly clear:

"One of the later additions to the Chronicles, *probably from pre-Sumerian Ngarathoe just after the last ice age, fragmented organism linked by telepathy would explain ability to manifest herself at cult centers throughout the world—von Könnenberg and Crowley mentioned centers in Laos, New Mexico, Chad, West Texas. Telepathically induced visions could explain appearances in animal and human form. Need for evolutionary adaptation satisfied by absorbing genetic material (nucleic acids?) from organisms that reproduce—could also develop intellectual capabilities in this way."*

I didn't know enough biology to judge the plausibility of this, but it was obvious that Harrison had rationalized a possible basis for the physical reality of Yidhra.

The last quotation was difficult and obscure. Harrison apparently saw it in manuscript and was unsure of its origin, though he thought it might be *"a portion of the manuscript Prjevalski found in Kashgar and attributed to the legendary 'mad lama of Prithom-Yang'—Braithwaite's translation?"* In spite of the obscurity of the language and the exotic literary form I began to see a hideous application to the facts and hints

I had concerning Milando:

> Yidhra, the Lonely One, craving the life of all things;
> Lonely One, needing the life of the Earth.
> Yidhra, the Goddess, ruling her avatar races;
> Goddess, of vulturine Y'hath of the sky,
> Goddess, of Xothra who sleeps in the Earth
> and wakes to devour,
> Goddess, of men in strange places who worship her.
> Yidhra, the Hierophant, teaching her followers
> mysteries;
> Hierophant, teaching strange tongues of the elder world.
> Yidhra, the Bountiful, making the hills and the meadows
>   green;
> Bountiful, showing the way to the desert springs,
> Bountiful, guarding the flocks and the harvest.
> Yidhra, the Lover, needing the seed of her followers;
> Lover, who must have the seed of all things,
> Lover, who must have the seed of change or die,
> Lover, whose consorts are changed,
>   infused with the seed of the past and changed
>   to forms not of past nor of present.
> Yidhra, the Mother, bringing forth spawn of the past;
> Mother, of all things that were,
> Mother, of children of past and of present,
> Mother, whose children remember all things
>   of their fathers long dead.
> Yidhra, the Life-Giver, bringing long life to her followers;
> Life-Giver, giving the centuries endlessly
>   to her children and lovers and worshippers.
> Yidhra, the Restless One, needing the sons of new fathers;
> Restless One, sending her followers forth
>   to seek new blood for her endless change,
> Restless One, craving new lovers outside the blood
>   of her worshippers
>   lest she and her spawn and her followers

shrivel and wither in living death.
Yidhra, the Dream-Witch, clouding the minds of her
followers;
    Dream-Witch, hiding her shape in illusion,
    Dream-Witch, cloaking her shape in strange beauty.
    Yidhra, the Shrouder, wreathing the faithless in shadow;
    Shrouder, devouring the errant and hostile ones,
      Shrouder, who hides men forever …

The other stack of papers proved to be the missing notes on Harrison's activities in Milando. In one way his experience had been the reverse of mine; the bartender had initially been cautiously encouraging, dropping cryptic hints without giving any definite information, but, after Harrison's first encounter with Yolanda, Ed and most of the other people in town had tried to shut him out. Even Kramer had been afraid to speak openly of the cult, though Harrison had become convinced that it was active and that Yolanda was the head of it.

I came out of my rapt concentration with the feeling I had heard something through the rush of the waterfall, some barely audible and unidentifiable sound that breathed terror; perhaps it was only my imagination, stimulated by the dark hints I had been reading, but I turned out the lamp and stepped quietly to the door. I opened it a crack and peered into the cavern mouth to the right. It was darkening rapidly, but I could detect movement in the shadow. There was a large animal like a hound alternately scampering to the entrance and scuttling back into the cave in a cringing attitude. Then a dark figure seemed to rise up from the floor of the cavern as though emerging from a sunken stairway. I knew I did not want to meet either of those figures and if I waited very long I would have to find my way back in total darkness. The ledge along which I had to return was in shadow and most of the way I would be shielded from view by the waterfall and the fallen slabs of rock along the water's edge. I decided to take the chance.

I ran wherever I was well screened, counting on the waterfall to cover the sound, and made it to the foot of the stair up the cliff without being noticed. On the stairs I was badly exposed, though the trunks and foliage of some of the tallest trees gave some scattered cover, but looking back from the top I could make out the hound and its shadowy master on the ledge and they didn't seem to be in pursuit. I was catching my breath at the top when I heard voices on the trail ahead and ducked into the brush.

Two men I hadn't seen before appeared and posted themselves near the head of the stair. I gathered from the scraps of conversation I could understand that they were part of a search party from town sent to find me. Their mission was to head me off if I tried to descend to the pool. They held the pool in awe and seemed to assume that if I had already gone down I would be 'taken care of.'

I began to make my way as quietly as possible through the rain-soaked brush, moving parallel to the path. The rain was growing heavy as darkness fell, and the occasional flashes of lightning did as much to show the way as the dwindling daylight. It was slow going and progress would have been impossible without the frequent outcrops of rock to thin the vegetation. I was able to see the trail and hear voices on it much of the time and soon found that the searchers had spread out over the slope. They were all around me now, passing on both sides.

At one point two men stopped and sat down on a boulder by the trail near me so that I could overhear them clearly.

"… she says he didn't come down there. Must have gone off the trail."

"Don't know why she wants him so bad. He don't seem much different from the other one."

"They say it's somethin' about his mind. The other one wasn't as good—that's why he didn't help much an' she needs fresh blood again so soon. Or we'll all start to shrivel up like the bunch in West Texas. Did Maynard ever tell you about that? He went out there an' saw 'em. Said it was like livin' death."

"Naw, I mostly stay away from Maynard. An' Ed too. I know we're all bound to her, we've all taken the Communion and accepted the eternal life, but I think some of the big shots has had s'much to do with her they're hardly human any more. Anyway, they give me the creeps. An' what she did to that Harrison boy! She needed him, but she hated him fer not bein' good enough. Course that was the full *Fusion,* not just the Communion. But ain't it about the same thing? She gets a little more like us and we get a little more like her?"

It was a relief when they stopped talking and sat in silence; the horrors of Milando were crowding too close and I had heard enough. I continued up the hill. I had not gone very far when I heard them speak again. I couldn't understand them this time, but the tone was one of respect and the answering voice was Yolanda's. I stood close to a big tree trunk to camouflage my outline and waited for her to pass on the trail. It was not completely dark yet and a moment later I could see her slender silhouette stalking up the trail. The hound was following at her heels, dashing from one side of the trail to the other. Then it gave a sort of snorting moan and ran into the brush below me. I could hear it snuffling and crashing through the bushes as it zigzagged toward me. I stood very still. Suddenly it was charging straight at me. I could make out a long muzzle, more like a crocodile than a dog, and it seemed to have a short heavy tail. Just as it rose up and ran on two legs she called to it and it turned aside. I was trembling, and it took a while for the phrase she used to sink in. She had said, "Come, Mr. Harrison."

VI

I stood for a while under the dripping tree, trying not to think. There was a cult here, certainly, a dangerous one, but the rest was fantasy. The people of Milando had not seen a primeval abomination that dwelt in these hills, they were victims of mass hallucination or the imposture of the cult leaders. And Yolanda, with a whimsical touch of black humor, had named her dog after a troublesome intruder who had caused a local sensation by disappearing. Or being murdered. The hints of *fusion* and resulting physical degeneracy were ignorant superstition; a man could not exchange genetic material with an eon-old creature and thus become a beast. It was an ordinary hound. A hound that went sometimes on four legs and sometimes on two.

It was pitch-black now and I risked walking on the trail. Once I glimpsed a flashlight beam ahead, but I hid in the brush and the searchers passed without spotting me. After I crossed the top of the slope and entered Milando I had to avoid passing near the many lighted windows as well as worrying about exposure in the frequent lightning flashes. Half the town seemed to be out tramping through the rain and several times I passed within thirty yards of people, but they either didn't see me or assumed I was one of them. By the time I approached the Kramer house I was wondering whether the search for me could account for all the activity.

I had followed the darkest route rather than the shortest and wound up approaching the house from the east side. I could see light in the kitchen windows and hear Kramer raving in an hysterical rage. I had slipped up next to an old shed on the property next door when I heard someone walk heavily up to the other side of the shed.

"Has he been here?" said a low voice.

"No, didn't they catch him over the hill?"

"No luck. Don't know whether he got lost in the brush or slipped back into town. How long you been watching the house?"

"About twenty minutes. Got the place surrounded. Old Kramer's really out of his mind, threatenin' to kill Miz' Kimbrough an' go out an' tell everybody about Milando and everythin' else. We'll have to take care of him this time. We're just waitin' on *her*."

"Where is she?"

"Down at the saloon with Ed. Maynard went to get her; she should be here pretty soon."

I had blundered into a ring of watchers staked out around the house. By luck I hadn't been seen, but in getting away I might not be so lucky. The lightning flashes were coming more often now, and though I was hidden from their light by the corner of the shed I would have to pass some long open spaces if I retreated. And I felt I had to warn Kramer that he was in danger, even though the mother-in-law's visit had triggered an explosion I hated to face. But I did not have to make that decision, for a moment later the tension erupted in violence—the gusty boom of a shotgun blast, then a woman's scream silenced by another blast. Then a third, and I heard small feet running across the porch. Two of the children ran into the circle of window light in front of the house; two more shots, and their still forms lay in the rain. While I stood and watched in stunned incomprehension, the lights went out all over Milando.

My only thought then was to get away. My car was in front of the house near the corner. With the lights out in the house I might be able to get to it and drive away before anyone could stop me. I moved as quietly as possible to the side of the house. I got there before the next lightning flash. The lightning was from the northwest, to the left and front of the house, so that the kitchen side was left in blackness. I moved to the front corner, took off my hat, and stood with one eye past the corner until the next flash. Kramer was standing not fifteen feet from the car, holding the shotgun. And stealthy footsteps from behind told me the watchers were moving in next to the house itself. Without thinking I opened the kitchen door next to me and entered the house. The click of the night latch behind me seemed terribly loud.

I stood there only a minute with my heart pounding and the water running off my raincoat onto the floor before I heard Yolanda's voice outside.

"Kramer," she said, "Kramer, you have slain the children of Yidhra." I went to look out the small window over the sink. "You are doomed, Kramer," she said. The lightning was flashing; I could see her hooded silhouette and Kramer fumbling with the gun. He seemed to be trying to raise it and hesitating. "You cannot defy me, Kramer." Then in an extended burst of lightning I saw the hound thing leap at him, and the gun roared. Whatever spell she held over him was broken; he raised the gun high and fired. As the lightning flickered and died away I saw her writhing on the ground, appearing grotesquely shapeless under the sprawling cloak; then she lay still.

I stood petrified. I heard Kramer's heavy tread on the porch, followed by an incongruous sound I could not at first identify. With quiet horror I realized that he was sitting in the rocking chair on the porch, rocking gently, back and forth. He must have been quite mad.

In the long minutes before I began to think again the darkness magnified the sound horribly. The rocking chair creaked. The rain drummed on the roof, it dribbled from the eaves, it spattered into the puddles on the ground, and the rocking chair creaked. I had to get a grip on myself and think of a plan. If I could get to the car perhaps I could get out of town and hide until it was safe to swim across. I tried quietly to open the kitchen door, and my stomach knotted in panic; the night latch was of an ancient type that needed a key to be opened from the inside.

The kitchen door was locked, and getting past Kramer would be impossible. I could open a window, but Kramer would surely hear and come before I could climb out. And besides I was pretty sure someone was out there now. I remembered a back door by the room where I had slept. I would try for that. I began to feel my way toward the door to the living room, moving in slow motion to avoid hitting anything that might make a sound. The lightning through the small window wasn't much help, the light falling mainly on the side of the room away from the door. I was near the door slowly lowering my foot when it touched something soft. Instinct told me what it was before reason could operate, and I almost lost my balance as my foot jerked back. I tried to find a way around the corpse and touched it again. I couldn't face the possibility of touching it another time; I would have to risk the flashlight. Kramer was facing the other way and I waited for the lightning before flicking the flashlight for the briefest instant.

The lightning must have been very near, for the thunder followed it closely enough to cover the involuntary sound I made when I saw the thing and knew why Kramer had gone mad and slaughtered his wife and children. It was the mother-in-law, the daughter of Old Kimbrough's son who had been 'the worst of the lot,' the mother of Kramer's wife, the grandmother of those who lay still in the rain. Wearing ample clothing and the wig that lay beside her I suppose she could have passed as fully human, though incredibly ugly and deformed, but now there could be no doubt of the alien taint. No fully human being has such wide cheekbones, or such bulging lidless eyes set so far to the side. The ears were vestigial and there was no hair; the back of the head and neck were scaled. The tongue protruded and was perceptibly forked.

I forced myself to step over the thing in the dark. I remember being obsessed with the thought that I might step on the tongue. I was also terrified of bumping into another corpse in the hall between the living room and the rear of the house and moved even more slowly than before. I kept looking back and seeing Kramer silhouetted by the lightning against a window that opened onto the porch.

I hadn't gotten far into the hall when I felt a presence, a numbing sensation both calming and weirdly evil. It reminded me of the enchantment I had felt in Yolanda's presence, but it was different, less warm and human, more savage, more powerful. I realized the rocking chair had stopped. Every nerve was alert as I turned to watch the open

184

door and window. The lightning flickered, and in a hideous stop-motion effect I saw the monstrous caped figure move toward Kramer as he whimpered and clicked two firing pins on empty chambers. He shrieked twice as the thing spread its arms wide and shrouded him in the vast folds of its cloak; then he was silent.

I knew I should try to get away, but I was incapable of motion as the thing crept slowly across the porch and through the door toward me. It drew itself up six feet in front of me and said, "Hello, Peter," in a voice hauntingly, damnably like Yolanda's, but deeper, hollower, indistinct, with an alien intonation like the children's hissing whispers. I shone the flashlight on the face a full seven feet above the floor—it was her, but larger, with hollow cheeks and sunken, burning eyes and teeth grinning in a rigid travesty of a smile. Kramer's shotgun had shattered the fragment of protean Yidhra that projected the beauty of Yolanda; in its place Yidhra had sent another multiform fragment of herself creeping over the hill, a fragment that had not yet perfected the illusion.

The realization had weakened the spell and I fought for control of my consciousness. For an instant her outline wavered, the face blurred, and in mortal fear of what I might see I turned and ran down the hall and into the first bedroom, slamming the door behind me. I found a window in the dark, threw it up, and fumbled with the screen latch; in a second was over the sill.

I heard someone running toward me along the side of the house, but jumped aside and felt him rush past. Then I ran for the car. I hit the fender running full speed, knocking the wind out of myself, but managed to feel my way to the keyhole, find the key, and get in even before I caught my breath. I backed onto the road, slammed it into first, and started swerving down the muddy hill. A group of men tried to block the road, but when I bore down on them they jumped out of the way. I think I hit one of them. At the bottom of the hill I tried to turn right and slid off into the ditch on the left. It wasn't deep enough to flood the engine, but I thought surely I was stuck. I kept spinning the wheels and sliding till the wheels found something solid and pulled me up onto the road. I came out heading to the left and continued that way out of town.

The side roads were fewer in that direction and I kept letting them go by, wanting to get further from town. Before I knew it I was over the hill at the flooded creek. I hit the brakes and nothing happened—they must have gotten soaked in the ditch. The car plowed into the water with a tremendous splash, the engine died, and I felt the car being pulled sideways by the current. I felt the car lose contact with the bottom and start floating downstream. Water was leaking in slowly but steadily, and when the car rolled over on its side I knew it would soon turn upside down and I would be trapped. I got out of my boots and coat, opened the door above me, and climbed out.

There was no question of swimming purposefully in that torrent; I could only struggle to stay afloat and grasp at anything solid I bumped into. Eventually I grabbed something that held me against the current. It was a tree trunk sticking out of a brush jam, and I was able to pull myself slowly and painfully to the bank. As I lay panting face down with my feet still in the water I felt the current running from my right to my left. I was on the far side. I had escaped from Milando.

VII

When I walked into Edmondsville at dawn I was suffering from shock, exhaustion, and pneumonia and promptly collapsed. I was more or less delirious for a week and said enough to alarm the doctor, who informed the local sheriff, who called in a state lawman. I had been completely incoherent, but they gathered that a family named Kramer and someone named Yolanda had died by violence in Milando during the storm.

When I came to my senses they showed me a newspaper article about the tragic death by fire of the Kramer family of Milando, including Mrs. Kramer's mother, Mrs. Elizabeth Kimbrough. After that I pretended to be unable to remember what had happened. I had stayed with a family named Kramer in Milando but could remember nothing else. I knew the truth would be utterly incredible to them and was afraid to concoct some plausibly false version to stimulate an investigation. The people in Milando would refute it somehow and deceive the outside investigators as they had done before. And I would be left in grave danger.

But the authorities would not leave it at that. Though I absolutely refused to go there myself, they went to Milando as soon as the roads were open. I don't know exactly what they were told, but I understand that what finally settled the matter and convinced them I had been hallucinating was an interview with a well-established citizen of Milando, alive and uninjured, a charming young woman named Yolanda Prentiss.

BLACK MAN WITH A HORN

T. E. D. KLEIN

> The Black [words obscured by postmark] was fascinating—I
> must get a snap shot of him.
> —H. P. LOVECRAFT, POSTCARD TO E. HOFFMANN PRICE,
> July 23, 1934

There is something inherently comforting about the first-person past tense. It conjures up visions of some deskbound narrator puffing contemplatively upon a pipe amid the safety of his study, lost in tranquil recollection, seasoned but essentially unscathed by whatever experience he's about to relate. It's a tense that says, "I am here to tell the tale. I lived through it."

The description, in my own case, is perfectly accurate—as far as it goes. I am indeed seated in a kind of study: a small den, actually, but lined with bookshelves on one side, below a view of Manhattan painted many years ago, from memory, by my sister. My desk is a folding bridge table that once belonged to her. Before me the electric typewriter, though somewhat precariously supported, hums soothingly, and from the window behind me comes the familiar drone of the old air conditioner, waging its lonely battle against the tropic night. Beyond it, in the darkness outside, the small night-noises are doubtless just as reassuring: wind in the palm trees, the mindless chant of crickets, the muffled chatter of a neighbor's

TV, an occasional car bound for the highway, shifting gears as it speeds past the house …

House, in truth, may be too grand a word; the place is a green stucco bungalow just a single story tall, third in a row of nine set several hundred yards from the highway. Its only distinguishing features are the sundial in the front yard, brought here from my sister's former home, and the jagged little picket fence, now rather overgrown with weeds, which she had erected despite the protests of neighbors.

It's hardly the most romantic of settings, but under normal circumstances it might make an adequate background for meditations in the past tense. "I'm still here," the writer says, adjusting to the tone. (I've even stuck the requisite pipe in mouth, stuffed with a plug of latakia.) "It's over now," he says. "I lived through it."

A comforting premise, perhaps. Only, in this case, it doesn't happen to be true. Whether the experience is really "over now" no one can say; and if, as I suspect, the final chapter has yet to be enacted, then the notion of my "living through it" will seem a pathetic conceit.

Yet I can't say I find the thought of my own death particularly disturbing. I get so tired, sometimes, of this little room, with its cheap wicker furniture, the dull outdated books, the night pressing in from outside … And of that sundial out there in the yard, with its idiotic message. *"Grow old along with me …"*

I have done so, and my life seems hardly to have mattered in the scheme of things. Surely its end cannot matter much either.

Ah, Howard, you would have understood.

That, boy, was what I call a travel-experience!
—Lovecraft, March 12, 1930

If, while I set it down, this tale acquires an ending, it promises to be an unhappy one. But the beginning is nothing of the kind; you may find it rather humorous, in fact—full of comic pratfalls, wet trouser cuffs, and a dropped vomit-bag.

"I steeled myself to *endure* it," the old lady to my right was saying. "I don't mind telling you I was exceedingly frightened. I held on to the arms of the seat and just *gritted my teeth*. And then, you know, right after the captain warned us about that *turbulence,* when the tail lifted and fell, flip-flop, flip-flop, *well*—" she flashed her dentures at me and patted my wrist, "—I don't mind telling you, there was simply nothing for it but to *heave.*"

Where had the old girl picked up such expressions? And was she trying to pick me up as well? Her hand clamped wetly round my wrist. "I *do* hope you'll let me pay for the dry cleaning."

"Madam," I said, "think nothing of it. The suit was already stained."

"Such a nice man!" She cocked her head coyly at me, still gripping my wrist. Though their whites had long since turned the color of old piano keys, her eyes were not unattractive. But her breath repelled me. Slipping my paperback into a pocket, I rang for the stewardess.

The earlier mishap had occurred several hours before. In clambering aboard the plane at Heathrow, surrounded by what appeared to be an aboriginal rugby club (all dressed alike, navy blazers with bone buttons), I'd been shoved from behind and had stumbled against a black cardboard hatbox in which some Chinaman was storing his dinner; it was jutting into the aisle near the first-class seats. Something inside sloshed over my ankles—duck sauce, soup perhaps—and left a sticky yellow puddle on the floor. I turned in time to see a tall, beefy Caucasian with an Air Malay bag and a beard so thick and black he looked like some heavy from the silent era. His manner was equally suited to the role, for after shouldering me aside (with shoulders broad as my valises), he pushed his way down the crowded passage, head bobbing near the ceiling like a gas balloon, and suddenly disappeared from sight at the rear of the plane. In his wake I caught the smell of treacle, and was instantly reminded of my childhood: birthday hats, Callard & Bowser gift packs, and after-dinner bellyaches.

"So very sorry." A bloated little Charlie Chan looked fearfully at this departing apparition, then doubled over to scoop his dinner beneath the seat, fiddling with the ribbon.

"Think nothing of it," I said.

I was feeling kindly toward everyone that day. Flying was still a novelty. My friend Howard, of course (as I'd reminded audiences earlier in the week), used to say he'd "hate to see aëroplanes come into common commercial use, since they merely add to the goddam useless speeding up of an already overspeeded life." He had dismissed them as "devices for the amusement of a gentleman"—but then, he'd only been up once, in the thirties, and for only as long as $3.50 would bring. What could he have known of whistling engines, the wicked joys of dining at thirty thousand feet, the chance to look out a window and find that the earth is, after all, quite round? All this he had missed; he was dead and therefore to be pitied.

Yet even in death he had triumphed over me.

It gave me something to think about as the stewardess helped me to my feet, clucking in professional concern at the mess on my lap—though more likely she was thinking of the wiping up that awaited her once I'd vacated the seat. "Why do they make those bags so *slippery?*" my elderly neighbor asked plaintively. "And all over this nice man's suit. You really should do something about it." The plane dropped and settled; she rolled her yellowing eyes. "It could happen again."

The stewardess steered me down the aisle toward a restroom at the middle of the plane. To my left a cadaverous young woman wrinkled her nose and smiled at the man next to her. I attempted to disguise my defeat by looking bitter—"Someone else has done this deed!"—but doubt I succeeded. The stewardess's arm supporting mine was superfluous but comfortable; I leaned on her more heavily with each step. There are, as I'd long suspected, precious few advantages in being seventy-six and looking it—yet among them is this: though one is excused from the frustration of flirting with a stewardess, one gets to lean on her arm. I turned toward her to say something funny, but paused; her face was blank as a clock's.

"I'll wait out here for you," she said, and pulled open the smooth white door.

"That will hardly be necessary." I straightened up. "But could you— do you think you might find me another seat? I have nothing against that lady, you understand, but I don't want to see any more of her lunch."

Inside the restroom the whine of the engines seemed louder, as if the pink plastic walls were all that separated me from the jet stream and its arctic winds. Occasionally the air we passed through must have grown choppy, for the plane rattled and heaved like a sled over rough ice. If I opened the john I half expected to see the earth miles below us, a frozen grey Atlantic fanged with icebergs. England was already a thousand miles away.

With one hand on the door handle for support, I wiped off my trousers with a perfumed paper towel from a foil envelope, and stuffed several more into my pocket. My cuffs still bore a residue of Chinese goo. This, it seemed, was the source of the treacle smell; I dabbed ineffectually at it. Surveying myself in the mirror—a bald, harmless-looking old baggage with stooped shoulders and a damp suit (so different from the self-confident young fellow in the photo captioned "HPL and disciple")—I slid open the bolt and emerged, a medley of scents. The stewardess had found an empty seat for me at the back of the plane.

It was only as I made to sit down that I noticed who occupied the adjoining seat: he was leaning away from me, asleep with his head resting against the window, but I recognized the beard.

"Uh, stewardess—?" I turned, but saw only her uniformed back retreating up the aisle. After a moment's uncertainty I inched myself into the seat, making as little noise as possible. I had, I reminded myself, every right to be here.

Adjusting the recliner position (to the annoyance of the black behind me), I settled back and reached for the paperback in my pocket. They'd finally gotten around to reprinting one of my earlier tales, and already I'd found four typos. But then, what could one expect? The front cover, with its crude cartoon skull, said it all: "*Goosepimples:* Thirteen Cosmic Chillers in the Lovecraft Tradition."

So this is what I was reduced to—a lifetime's work shrugged off by some blurb-writer as "worthy of the Master himself," the creations of my brain dismissed as mere pastiche. And the tales themselves, once singled out for such elaborate praise, were now simply—as if this were commendation enough—"Lovecraftian." Ah, Howard, your triumph was complete the moment your name became an adjective.

I'd suspected it for years, of course, but only with the past week's conference had I been forced to acknowledge the fact: that what mattered to the present generation was not my own body of work, but rather my association with Lovecraft. And even this was demeaned: after years of friendship and support, to be labeled—simply because I'd been younger—a mere "disciple." It seemed too cruel a joke.

Every joke must have a punchline. This one's was still in my pocket, printed in italics on the folded yellow conference schedule. I didn't need to look at it again: there I was, characterized for all time as "a member of the Lovecraft circle, New York educator, and author of the celebrated collection *Beyond the Garve.*"

That was it, the crowning indignity: to be immortalized by a misprint! You'd have appreciated this, Howard. I can almost hear you chuckling from—where else?—beyond the *garve....*

Meanwhile, from the seat next to me came the rasping sounds of a constricted throat; my neighbor must have been caught in a dream. I put down my book and studied him. He looked older than he had at first— perhaps sixty or more. His hands were roughened, powerful looking; on one of them was a ring with a curious silver cross. The glistening black beard that covered the lower half of his face was so thick as to be nearly opaque; its very darkness seemed unnatural, for above it the hair was streaked with grey.

I looked more closely, to where beard joined face. Was that a bit of gauze I saw, below the hair? My heart gave a little jump. Leaning forward for a closer look, I peered at the skin to the side of his nose; though burned from long exposure to the sun, it had an odd pallor. My gaze continued upward, along the weathered cheeks toward the dark hollows of his eyes.

They opened.

For a moment they stared into mine without apparent comprehension, glassy and bloodshot. In the next instant they were bulging from his head and quivering like hooked fish. His lips opened, and a tiny voice croaked, *"Not here."*

We sat in silence, neither of us moving. I was too surprised, too embarrassed, to answer. In the window beyond his head the sky looked bright and clear, but I could feel the plane buffeted by unseen blasts, its wingtips bouncing furiously.

"Don't do it to me here," he whispered at last, shrinking back into his seat.

Was the man a lunatic? Dangerous, perhaps? Somewhere in my future I saw spinning headlines: "Jetliner Terrorized ... Retired NYC Teacher Victim ..." My uncertainty must have shown, for I saw him lick his lips and glance past my head. Hope, and a trace of cunning, swept his face. He grinned up at me. "Sorry, nothing to worry about. Whew!

Must have been having a nightmare." Like an athlete after a particularly tough race he shook his massive head, already regaining command of the situation. His voice had a hint of Tennessee drawl. "Boy"—he gave what should have been a hearty laugh—"I'd better lay off the Kickapoo juice!"

I smiled to put him at his ease, though there was nothing about him to suggest that he'd been drinking. "That's an expression I haven't heard in years."

"Oh, yeah?" he said, with little interest. "Well, I've been away."

His fingers drummed nervously—impatiently?—on the arm of his chair.

"Malaya?"

He sat up, and the color left his face. "How did you know?"

I nodded toward the green flight-bag at his feet. "I saw you carrying that when you came aboard. You, uh—you seemed to be in a little bit of a hurry, to say the least. In fact, I'm afraid you almost knocked me down."

"Hey." His voice was controlled now, his gaze level and assured. "Hey, I'm really sorry about that, old fella. The fact is, I thought someone might be following me."

Oddly enough, I believed him; he looked sincere—or as sincere as anyone can be behind a phony black beard. "You're in disguise, aren't you?" I asked.

"You mean the whiskers? They're just something I picked up in Singapore. Shucks, I knew they wouldn't fool anyone for long, at least not a friend. But an enemy, well ... maybe." He made no move to take them off.

"You're—let me guess—you're in the service, right?" The foreign service, I meant; frankly, I took him for an aging spy.

"In the service?" He looked significantly to the left and right, then dropped his voice. "Well, yeah, you might say that. In His service." He pointed toward the roof of the plane.

"You mean—?"

He nodded. "I'm a missionary. Or was until yesterday."

Missionaries are infernal nuisances who ought to be kept at home.

—Lovecraft, September 12, 1925

Have you ever seen a man in fear of his life? I had, though not since my early twenties. After a summer of idleness I'd at last found temporary employment in the office of what turned out to be a rather shady businessman—I suppose today you'd call him a small-time racketeer—who, having somehow offended "the mob," was convinced he'd be dead by Christmas. He had been wrong, though; he'd been able to enjoy that and many other Christmases with his family, and it wasn't till years later that he was found in his bathtub, face down in six inches of water. I don't remember much about him, except how hard it had been to engage him in conversation; he never seemed to be listening.

Yet talking with the man who sat next to me on the plane was all too easy; he had nothing of the other's distracted air, the vague replies and preoccupied gaze. On the contrary, he was alert and highly interested in all that was said to him. Except for his initial panic, in fact, there was little to suggest he was a hunted man.

Yet so he claimed to be. Later events would, of course, settle all such questions, but at the time I had no way to judge if he was telling the truth, or if his story was as phony as his beard.

If I believed him, it was almost entirely due to his manner, not the substance of what he said. No, he didn't claim to have made off with the Eye of Klesh; he was more original than that. Nor had he violated some witch doctor's only daughter. But some of the things he told me about the region in which he'd worked—a state called Negri Sembilan, south of Kuala Lumpur—seemed frankly incredible: houses invaded by trees, government-built roads that simply disappeared, a nearby colleague returning from a ten-day vacation to find his lawn overgrown with ropy things they'd had to burn twice to destroy. He claimed there were tiny red spiders that jumped as high as a man's shoulder—"there was a girl in the village gone half-deaf because one of the nasty little things crawled in her ear and swelled so big it plugged up the hole"—and places where mosquitoes were so thick they suffocated cattle. He described a land of steaming mangrove swamps and rubber plantations as large as feudal kingdoms, a land so humid that wallpaper bubbled on the hot nights and bibles sprouted mildew.

As we sat together on the plane, sealed within an air-cooled world of plastic and pastel, none of these things seemed possible; with the frozen blue of the sky just beyond my reach, the stewardesses walking briskly past me in their blue-and-gold uniforms, the passengers to my left sipping Cokes or sleeping or leafing through *In-Flite*, I found myself believing less than half of what he said, attributing the rest to sheer exaggeration and a Southern regard for tall tales. Only when I'd been home a week and paid a visit to my niece in Brooklyn did I revise my estimate upward, for glancing through her son's geography text I came upon this passage: "Along the [Malayan] peninsula, insects swarm in abundance; probably more varieties exist here than anywhere else on earth. There is some good hardwood timber, and camphor and ebony trees are found in profusion. Many orchid varieties thrive, some of extraordinary size." The book alluded to the area's "rich mixture of races and languages," its "extreme humidity" and "colorful native fauna," and added: "Its jungles are so impenetrable that even the wild beasts must keep to well-worn paths."

But perhaps the strangest aspect of this region was that, despite its dangers and discomforts, my companion claimed to have loved it. "They've got a mountain in the center of the peninsula—" He mentioned an unpronounceable name and shook his head. "Most beautiful thing you ever saw. And there's some really pretty country down along the coast, you'd swear it was some kind of South Sea island. Comfortable, too. Oh, it's damp all right, especially in the interior where the new mission was supposed to be—but the temperature never even hits a hundred. Try saying that for New York City."

I nodded. "Remarkable."

"And the *people*," he went on, "why, I believe they're just the friendliest people on earth. You know, I'd heard a lot of bad things about the Moslems—that's what most of them are, part of the Sunni sect—but I'm telling you, they treated us with real neighborliness ... just so long as we made the teachings *available*, so to speak, and didn't interfere with their affairs. And we didn't. We didn't have to. What we provided, you see, was a hospital—well, a clinic, at least, two RNs and a doctor who came twice a month—and a small library with books and films. And not just theology, either. All subjects. We were right outside the village, they'd have to pass us on their way to the river, and when they thought none of the *lontoks* were looking they'd just come in and look around."

"None of the what?"

"Priests, sort of. There were a lot of them. But they didn't interfere with us, we didn't interfere with them. I don't know that we made all that many converts, actually, but I've got nothing bad to say about those people."

He paused, rubbing his eyes; he suddenly looked his age. "Things were going fine," he said. "And then they told me to establish a second mission, further in the interior."

He stopped once more, as if weighing whether to continue. A squat little Chinese woman was plodding slowly up the aisle, holding on to the chairs on each side for balance. I felt her hand brush past my ear as she went by. My companion watched her with a certain unease, waiting till she'd passed. When he spoke again his voice had thickened noticeably.

"I've been all over the world—a lot of places Americans can't even go to these days—and I've always felt that, wherever I was, God was surely watching. But once I started getting up into those hills, well ..." He shook his head. "I was pretty much on my own, you see. They were going to send most of the staff out later, after I'd got set up. All I had with me was one of our groundskeepers, two bearers, and a guide who doubled as interpreter. Locals, all of them." He frowned. "The groundskeeper, at least, was a Christian."

"You needed an interpreter?"

The question seemed to distract him. "For the new mission, yes. My Malay stood me well enough in the lowlands, but in the interior they used dozens of local dialects. I would have been lost up there. Where I was going they spoke something which our people back in the village called *agon di-gatuan*—'the Old Language.' I never really got to understand much of it." He stared down at his hands. "I wasn't there long enough."

"Trouble with the natives, I suppose."

He didn't answer right away. Finally he nodded. "I truly believe they must be the nastiest people who ever lived," he said with great deliberation. "I sometimes wonder how God could have created them." He stared out the window, at the hills of cloud below us. "They called themselves the Chauchas, near as I could make out. Some French colonial influence, maybe, but they looked Asiatic to me, with just a touch of black. Little people. Harmless-looking." He gave a small shudder. "But they were nothing like what they seemed. You couldn't get to the bottom of them. They'd been living way up in those hills I don't know how many centuries, and whatever it is they were doing, they weren't going to let a stranger in on it. They called themselves Moslems, just like the lowlanders, but I'm sure there must have been a few bush-gods mixed in. I thought they were primitive, at first. I mean, some of their rituals—you wouldn't believe it. But now I think they weren't primitive at all. They just kept those rituals because they enjoyed them!" He tried to smile; it just accentuated the lines in his face.

"Oh, they seemed friendly enough in the beginning," he said. "You could approach them, do a bit of trading, watch them breed their animals. You could even talk to them about Salvation. And they'd just keep smiling, smiling all the time. As if they really *liked* you."

I could hear the disappointment in his voice, and something else.

"You know," he confided, suddenly leaning closer, "down in the lowlands, in the pastures, there's an animal, a kind of snail, the Malays kill on sight. A little yellow thing, but it scares them silly: they believe that if it passes over the shadow of their cattle, it'll suck out the cattle's life-force. They used to call it a 'Chaucha snail.' Now I know why."

"Why?" I asked.

He looked around the plane, and seemed to sigh. "You understand, at this stage we were still living in tents. We had yet to build anything. Well, the weather got bad, the mosquitoes got worse, and after the groundskeeper disappeared the others took off. I think the guide persuaded them to go. Of course, this left me—"

"Wait. You say your groundskeeper disappeared?"

"Yes, before the first week was out. It was late afternoon. We'd been pacing out one of the fields less than a hundred yards from the tents, and I was pushing through the long grass thinking he was behind me, and I turned around and he wasn't."

He was speaking all in a rush now. I had visions out of 1940s movies, frightened natives sneaking off with the supplies, and I wondered how much of this was true.

"So with the others gone, too," he said, "I had no way of communicating with the Chauchas, except through a kind of pidgin language, a mixture of Malay and their tongue. But I knew what was going on. All that week they kept laughing about something. Openly. And I got the impression that they were somehow responsible. I mean, for the man's disappearance. You understand? He'd been the one I trusted." His expression was pained. "A week later, when they showed him to me, he was still alive. But he couldn't speak. I think they wanted it that way. You see, they'd—they'd *grown* something in him." He shuddered.

Just at that moment, from directly behind us came an inhumanly high-pitched caterwauling that pierced the air like a siren, rising above the whine of the engines. It came with heart-stopping suddenness, and we both went rigid. I saw my companion's mouth gape as if to echo the scream. So much for the past; we'd become two old men gone all white and clutching at themselves. It was really quite comical. A full minute must have passed before I could bring myself to turn around.

By this time the stewardess had arrived and was dabbing at the place where the man behind me, dozing, had dropped his cigarette on his lap. The surrounding passengers, whites especially, were casting angry glances at him, and I thought I smelled burnt flesh. He was at last helped to his feet by the stewardess and one of his teammates, the latter chuckling uneasily.

Minor as it was, the accident had derailed our conversation and unnerved my companion; it was as if he'd retreated into his beard. He would talk no further, except to ask me ordinary and rather trivial questions about food prices and accommodations. He said he was bound for Florida, looking forward to a summer of, as he put it, "R and R," apparently financed by his sect. I asked him, a bit forlornly, what had happened in the end to the groundskeeper; he said that he had died. Drinks were served; the North American continent swung toward us from the south, first a finger of ice, soon a jagged line of green. I found myself giving the man my sister's address—Indian Creek was just outside Miami, where he'd be staying—and immediately regretted doing so. What did I know of him, after all? He told me his name was Ambrose Mortimer. "It means 'Dead Sea,'" he said. "From the Crusades."

When I persisted in bringing up the subject of the mission, he waved me off. "I can't call myself a missionary anymore," he said. "Yesterday, when I left the country, I gave up that right." He attempted a smile. "Honest, I'm just a civilian now."

"What makes you think they're after you?" I asked.

The smile vanished. "I'm not so sure they are," he said, not very convincingly. "I may just be getting paranoid in my old age. But I could swear that in New Delhi, and again at Heathrow, I heard someone singing—singing a certain song. Once it was in the men's room, on the other side of a partition; once it was behind me on line. And it was a song I recognized. It's in the Old Language." He shrugged. "I don't even know what the words mean."

"Why would anyone be singing? I mean, if they were following you?"

"That's just it. I don't know." He shook his head. "But I think—I think it's part of the ritual."

"What sort of ritual?"

"I don't know," he said again. He looked quite pained, and I resolved to bring this inquisition to an end. The ventilators had not yet dissipated the smell of charred cloth and flesh.

"But you'd heard the song before," I said. "You told me you recognized it."

"Yeah." He turned away and stared at the approaching clouds. We were passing over Maine. Suddenly the earth seemed a very small place. "I'd heard some of the Chaucha women singing it," he said at last. "It was a sort of farming song. It's supposed to make things grow."

Ahead of us loomed the saffron yellow smog that covers Manhattan like a dome. The "No Smoking" light winked silently on the console above us.

"I was hoping I wouldn't have to change planes," my companion said presently. "But the Miami flight doesn't leave for an hour and a half. I guess I'll get off and walk around a bit, stretch my legs. I wonder how long customs'll take." He seemed to be talking more to himself than to me. Once more I regretted my impulsiveness in giving him Maude's address. I was half tempted to make up some contagious disease for her, or a jealous husband. But then, quite likely he'd never call on her anyway; he hadn't even bothered to write down the name. And if he did pay a call—well, I told myself, perhaps he'd unwind when he realized he was safe among friends. He might even turn out to be good company; after all, he and my sister were practically the same age.

As the plane gave up the struggle and sank deeper into the warm encircling air, passengers shut books and magazines, organized their belongings, made last hurried forays to the bathroom to pat cold water on their faces. I wiped my spectacles and smoothed back what remained of my hair. My companion was staring out the window, the green Air Malay bag in his lap, his hands folded on it as if in prayer. We were already becoming strangers.

"Please return seat backs to the upright position," ordered a disembodied voice. Out beyond the window, past the head now turned completely away from me, the ground rose to meet us and we bumped along the pavement, jets roaring in reverse. Already stewardesses were rushing up and down the aisles pulling coats and jackets from the overhead bins; executive types, ignoring instructions, were scrambling to their feet and thrashing into raincoats. Outside I could see uniformed figures moving back and forth in what promised to be a warm grey drizzle. "Well," I said lamely, "we made it." I got to my feet.

He turned and flashed me a sickly grin. "Good-bye," he said. "This really has been a pleasure." He reached for my hand.

"And do try to relax and enjoy yourself in Miami," I said, looking for a break in the crowd that shuffled past me down the aisle. "That's the important thing—just to relax."

"I know that." He nodded gravely. "I know that. God bless you."

I found my slot and slipped into line. From behind me he added, "And I won't forget to look up your sister." My heart sank, but as I moved toward the door I turned to shout a last farewell. The old lady with the eyes was two people in front of me, but she didn't so much as smile.

One trouble with last farewells is that they occasionally prove redundant. Some forty minutes later, having passed like a morsel of food through a series of white plastic tubes, corridors, and customs lines, I found myself in one of the airport gift shops, whiling away the hour till my niece came to collect me; and there, once again, I saw the missionary.

He did not see me. He was standing before one of the racks of paperbacks—the so-called "Classics" section, haunt of the public domain—and with a preoccupied air he was glancing up and down the rows, barely pausing long enough to read the titles. Like me, he was obviously just killing time.

For some reason—call it embarrassment, a certain reluctance to spoil what had been a successful good-bye—I refrained from hailing him. Instead, stepping back into the rear aisle, I took refuge behind a rack of gothics, which I pretended to study while in fact studying him.

Moments later he looked up from the books and ambled over to a bin of cellophane-wrapped records, idly pressing the beard back into place below his right sideburn. Without warning he turned and surveyed the store; I ducked my head toward the gothics and enjoyed a vision normally reserved for the multifaceted eyes of an insect: women, dozens of them, fleeing an equal number of tiny mansions.

At last, with a shrug of his huge shoulders, he began flipping through the albums in the bin, snapping each one forward in an impatient staccato. Soon, the assortment scanned, he moved to the bin on the left and started on that.

Suddenly he gave a little cry, and I saw him shrink back. He stood immobile for a moment, staring down at something in the bin; then he whirled and walked quickly from the store, pushing past a family about to enter.

"Late for his plane," I said to the astonished salesgirl, and strolled over to the albums. One of them lay faceup in the pile—a jazz record featuring John Coltrane on saxophone. Confused, I turned to look for my erstwhile companion, but he had vanished in the crowd hurrying past the doorway.

Something about the album had apparently set him off; I studied it more carefully. Coltrane stood silhouetted against a tropical sunset, his features obscured, head tilted back, saxophone blaring silently beneath the crimson sky. The pose was dramatic but trite, and I could see in it no special significance: it looked like any other black man with a horn.

> New York eclipses all other cities in the spontaneous cordiality
> and generosity of its inhabitants—at least, such inhabitants as
> I have encountered.
> —Lovecraft, September 29, 1922

How quickly you changed your mind! You arrived to find a gold Dunsanian city of arches and domes and fantastic spires ... or so you told us.

Yet when you fled two years later you could see only "alien hordes."

What was it that so spoiled the dream? Was it that impossible marriage? Those foreign faces on the subway? Or was it merely the theft of your new summer suit? I believed then, Howard, and I believe it still, that the nightmare was all your own; though you returned to New England like a man re-emerging into sunlight, there was, I assure you, a very good life to be found amid the shade. I remained—and survived.

I almost wish I were back there now, instead of in this ugly little bungalow, with its air conditioner and its rotting wicker furniture and the humid night dripping down its windows.

I almost wish I were back on the steps of the natural history museum where, that momentous August afternoon, I stood perspiring in the shadow of Teddy Roosevelt's horse, watching matrons stroll past Central Park with dogs or children in tow and fanning myself ineffectually with the postcard I'd just received from Maude. I was waiting for my niece to drive by and leave off her son, whom I planned to take round the museum; he'd wanted to see the life-size mockup of the blue whale and, just upstairs, the dinosaurs …

I remember that Ellen and her boy were more than twenty minutes late. I remember too, Howard, that I was thinking of you that afternoon, and with some amusement: much as you disliked New York in the twenties, you'd have reeled in horror at what it's become today. Even from the steps of the museum I could see a curb piled high with refuse and a park whose length you might have walked without once hearing English spoken; dark skins crowded out the white, and mambo music echoed from across the street.

I remember all these things because, as it turned out, this was a special day: the day I saw, for the second time, the black man and his baleful horn.

My niece arrived late, as usual; she had for me the usual apology and the usual argument. "How can you still live over here?" she asked, depositing Terry on the sidewalk. "I mean, just look at those people." She nodded toward a park bench around which blacks and Latinos congregated like figures in a group portrait.

"Brooklyn is so much better?" I countered, as tradition dictated.

"Of course," she said. "In the Heights, anyway. I don't understand it—why this pathological hatred of moving? You might at least try the East Side. You can certainly afford it." Terry watched us impassively, lounging against the fender. I think he sided with me over his mother, but he was too wise to show it.

"Ellen," I said, "let's face it. I'm just too old to start hanging around singles bars. Over on the East Side they read nothing but best-sellers, and they hate anyone past sixty. I'm better off where I grew up—at least I know where the cheap restaurants are." It was, in fact, a thorny problem: forced to choose between whites whom I despised and blacks whom I feared, I somehow preferred the fear.

To mollify Ellen I read aloud her mother's postcard. It was the prestamped kind that bore no picture. "I'm still getting used to the cane," Maude had written, her penmanship as flawless as when she'd won the school medallion. "Livia has gone back to Vermont for the summer, so the card games are suspended & I'm hard into Pearl Buck. Your friend Rev. Mortimer dropped by & we had a nice chat. What amusing stories! Thanks again for the subscription to *McCall's;* I'll send Ellen my old copies. Look forward to seeing you all after the hurricane season."

Terry was eager to confront the dinosaurs; he was, in fact, getting a little old for me to superintend, and was halfway up the steps before I'd arranged with Ellen where to meet us afterward. With school out the museum was almost as crowded as on weekends, the halls' echo turning shouts and laughter into animal cries. We oriented ourselves on the floor plan in the main lobby—you are here read a large green dot, below which someone had scrawled *"Too bad for you"*—and trooped toward the Hall of Reptiles, Terry impatiently leading the way. "I saw that in school." He pointed toward a redwood diorama. "That too"—the Grand Canyon. He was, I believe, about to enter seventh grade, and until now had been little given to talk; he looked younger than the other children.

We passed toucans and marmosets and the new Urban Ecology wing ("concrete and cockroaches," sneered Terry), and duly stood before the brontosaurus, something of a disappointment: "I forgot it was just the skeleton," he said. Behind us a group of black boys giggled and moved toward us; I hurried my nephew past the assembled bones and through the most crowded doorway, dedicated, ironically, to Man in Africa. "This is the boring part," said Terry, unmoved by masks and spears. The pace was beginning to tire me. We passed through another doorway—Man in Asia—and moved quickly past the Chinese statuary. "I saw that in school." He nodded at a stumpy figure in a glass case, wrapped in ceremonial robes. Something about it was familiar to me, too; I paused to stare at it. The outer robe, slightly tattered, was spun of some shiny green material and displayed tall, twisted-looking trees on one side, a kind of stylized river on the other. Across the front ran five yellow-brown shapes in loincloth and headdress, presumably fleeing toward the robe's frayed edges; behind them stood a larger one, all black. In its mouth was a pendulous horn. The figure was crudely woven—little more than a stick figure, in fact—but it bore an unsettling resemblance, in both pose and proportion, to the one on the album cover.

Terry returned to my side, curious to see what I'd found. "Tribal garment," he read, peering at the white plastic notice below the case. "Malay Peninsula, Federation of Malaysia, early nineteenth century." He fell silent.

"Is that all it says?"

"Yep. They don't even have which tribe it's from." He reflected a moment. "Not that I really care."

"Well, I do," I said. "I wonder who'd know."

Obviously I'd have to seek advice at the information counter in the main lobby downstairs. Terry ran on ahead, while I followed even more slowly than before; the thought of a mystery evidently appealed to him, even one so tenuous and unexciting as this.

A bored-looking young college girl listened to the beginning of my query and handed me a pamphlet from below the counter. "You can't see anyone till September," she said, already beginning to turn away. "They're all on vacation."

I squinted at the tiny print on the first page: "Asia, our largest continent, has justly been called the cradle of civilization, but it may also be a birthplace of man himself." Obviously the pamphlet had been written before the current campaigns against sexism. I checked the date on the back: "Winter 1958." This would be of no help. Yet on page four my eye fell on the reference I sought:

...The model next to it wears a green silk ceremonial robe from Negri Sembilan, most rugged of the Malayan provinces. Note central motif of native man blowing ceremonial horn, and the graceful curve of his instrument; the figure is believed to be a representation of "Death's Herald," possibly warning villagers of approaching calamity. Gift of an anonymous donor, the robe is probably Tcho-tcho in origin, and dates from the early 19th century.

"What's the matter, uncle? Are you sick?" Terry gripped my shoulder and stared up at me, looking worried; my behavior had obviously confirmed his worst fears about old people. "What's it say in there?"

I gave him the pamphlet and staggered to a bench near the wall. I wanted time to think. The Tcho-Tcho People, I knew, had figured in a number of tales by Lovecraft and his disciples—Howard himself had called them "the wholly abominable Tcho-Tchos"—but I couldn't remember much about them except that they were said to worship one of his imaginary deities. For some reason I associated them with Burma

...

But whatever their attributes, I'd been certain of one thing: the Tcho-Tchos were completely fictitious.

Obviously I'd been wrong. Barring the unlikely possibility that the pamphlet itself was a hoax, I was forced to conclude that the malign beings of the stories were in fact based upon an actual race inhabiting the Southeast Asian subcontinent—a race whose name the missionary had mistranslated as "the Chauchas."

It was a rather troublesome discovery. I had hoped to turn some of Mortimer's recollections, authentic or not, into fiction; he'd unwittingly given me the material for three or four good plots. Yet I'd now discovered that my friend Howard had beaten me to it, and that I was put in the uncomfortable position of living out another man's horror stories.

Epistolary expression is with me largely replacing conversation.
—Lovecraft, December 23, 1917

I hadn't expected my second encounter with the black horn-player. A month later I got an even bigger surprise: I saw the missionary again.

Or at any rate, his picture. It was in a clipping my sister had sent me from the *Miami Herald*, over which she had written in ball-point pen, *"Just saw this in the paper—how awful!!"*

I didn't recognize the face; the photo was obviously an old one, the reproduction poor, and the man was clean-shaven. But the words below it told me it was him.

CLERGYMAN MISSING IN STORM

(WED.) THE REV. AMBROSE B. MORTIMER, 56, a lay pastor of the Church of Christ, Knoxville, Tenn., has been reported missing in the wake of Monday's hurricane. Spokesmen for the order say Mortimer had recently retired after serving nineteen years as a missionary, most recently in Malaysia. After moving to Miami in July, he had been a resident of 311 Pompano Canal Road.

Here the piece ended, with an abruptness that seemed all too appropriate to its subject. Whether Ambrose Mortimer still lived I didn't know, but I felt certain now that, having fled one peninsula, he had strayed onto another just as dangerous, a finger thrust into the void. And the void had swallowed him up.

So, anyway, ran my thoughts. I have often been prey to depressions of a similar nature, and subscribe to a fatalistic philosophy I'd shared with my friend Howard: a philosophy one of his less sympathetic biographers has dubbed "futilitarianism."

Yet pessimistic as I was, I was not about to let the matter rest. Mortimer may well have been lost in the storm; he may even have set off somewhere on his own. But if, in fact, some lunatic religious sect had done away with him for having pried too closely into its affairs, there were things I could do about it. I wrote to the Miami police that very day.

"Gentlemen," I began. "Having learned of the recent disappearance of the Reverend Ambrose Mortimer, I think I can provide information which may prove of use to investigators."

There is no need to quote the rest of the letter here. Suffice it to say that I recounted my conversation with the missing man, emphasizing the fears he'd expressed for his life: pursuit and "ritual murder" at the hands of a Malayan tribe called the Tcho-Tcho. The letter was, in short, a rather elaborate way of crying "foul play." I sent it care of my sister, asking that she forward it to the correct address.

The police department's reply came with unexpected speed. As with all such correspondence, it was more curt than courteous. "Dear Sir," wrote a Detective Sergeant A. Linahan; "In the matter of Rev. Mortimer we had already been apprised of the threats on his life. To date a preliminary search of the Pompano Canal has produced no findings, but dredging operations are expected to continue as part of our routine investigation. Thanking you for your concern—"

Below his signature, however, the sergeant had added a short postscript in his own hand. Its tone was somewhat more personal; perhaps typewriters intimidated him. "You may be interested to know," it said, "that we've recently learned a man carrying a Malaysian passport occupied rooms at a North Miami hotel for most of the summer, but checked out two weeks before your friend disappeared. I'm not at liberty to say more, but please be assured we are tracking down several leads at the moment. Our investigators are working full-time on the matter, and we hope to bring it to a speedy conclusion."

Linahan's letter arrived on September twenty-first. Before the week was out I had one from my sister, along with another clipping from the *Herald;* and since, like some old Victorian novel, this chapter seems to have taken an epistolary form, I will end it with extracts from these two items.

The newspaper story was headed wanted for questioning. Like the Mortimer piece, it was little more than a photo with an extended caption:

(Thurs.) A Malaysian citizen is being sought for questioning in connection with the disappearance of an American clergyman, Miami police say. Records indicate that the Malaysian, Mr. D. A. Djaktu-tchow, had occupied furnished rooms at the Barkleigh Hotella, 2401 Culebra Ave., possibly with an unnamed companion. He is believed still in the greater Miami area, but since August 22 his movements cannot be traced. State Dept. officials report Djaktu-tchow's visa expired August 31; charges are pending.

The clergyman, Rev. Ambrose B. Mortimer, has been missing since September 6.

The photo above the article was evidently a recent one, no doubt reproduced from the visa in question. I recognized the smiling moon-wide face, although it took me a moment to place him as the man whose dinner I'd stumbled over on the plane. Without the moustache, he looked less like Charlie Chan.

The accompanying letter filled in a few details. "I called up the *Herald*," my sister wrote, "but they couldn't tell me any more than was in the article. Just the same, finding that out took me half an hour, since the stupid woman at the switchboard kept putting me through to the wrong person. I guess you're right—anything that prints color pictures on page one shouldn't call itself a newspaper.

"This afternoon I called up the police department, but they weren't very helpful either. I suppose you just can't expect to find out much over the phone, though I still rely on it. Finally I got an Officer Linahan, who told me he's just replied to that letter of yours. Have you heard from him yet? The man was very evasive. He was trying to be nice, but I could tell he was impatient to get off. He did give me the full name of the man they're looking for—Djaktu Abdul Djaktu-tchow, isn't that marvelous?—and he told me they have some more material on him which they can't release right now. I argued and pleaded (you know how persuasive I can be!) and finally, because I claimed I'd been a close friend of Rev. Mortimer's, I wheedled something out of him which he swore he'd deny if I told anyone but you. Apparently the poor man must have been deathly ill, maybe even tubercular—I intended to get a patch test next week, just to play safe, and I recommend that you get one too—because it seems that, in the reverend's bedroom, they found something very odd: pieces of lung tissue. Human lung tissue."

I, too, was a detective in youth.
　　　　　　　　　　　　　　　—Lovecraft, February 17, 1931

Do amateur detectives still exist? I mean, outside the novels? I doubt it. Who, after all, has the time for such games today? Not I, unfortunately; though for more than a decade I'd been nominally retired, my days were quite full with the unromantic activities that occupy everyone this side of the paperbacks: letters, luncheon dates, visits to my niece and to my doctor; books (not enough) and television (too much) and perhaps a Golden Agers' matinee (though I have largely stopped going to films, finding myself increasingly out of sympathy with their heroes). I also spent Halloween week in Atlantic City, and most of another attempting to interest a rather overpolite young publisher in reprinting some of my early work.

All this, of course, is intended as a sort of apologia for my having put off further inquiries into poor Mortimer's case till mid-November. The truth is, the matter almost slipped my mind; only in novels do people not have better things to do.

It was Maude who reawakened my interest. She had been avidly scanning the papers—in vain—for further reports on the man's disappearance; I believe she had even phoned Sergeant Linahan a second time, but had learned nothing new. Now she wrote me with a tiny fragment of information, heard at third-hand: one of her bridge partners had had it on the authority of "a friend in the police force" that the search for Mr. Djaktu was being widened to include his presumed companion—"a Negro child," or so my sister reported. Although there was every possibility that this information was false, or that it concerned an entirely different case, I could tell she regarded it as very sinister indeed.

Perhaps that was why the following afternoon found me struggling once more up the steps of the natural history museum—as much to satisfy Maude as myself. Her allusion to a Negro, coming after the curious discovery in Mortimer's bedroom, had recalled to mind the figure on the Malayan robe, and I had been troubled all night by the fantasy of a black man—a man much like the beggar I'd just seen huddled against Roosevelt's statue—coughing his lungs out into a sort of twisted horn.

I had encountered few other people on the streets that afternoon, as it was unseasonably cold for a city that's often mild till January; I wore a muffler, and my grey tweed overcoat flapped round my heels. Inside, however, the place like all American buildings was overheated; I was soon the same as I made my way up the demoralizingly long staircase to the second floor.

The corridors were silent and empty, but for the morose figure of a guard seated before one of the alcoves, head down as if in mourning, and, from above me, the hiss of the steam radiators near the marble ceiling. Slowly, and rather enjoying the sense of privilege that comes from having a museum to oneself, I retraced my earlier route past the immense skeletons of dinosaurs ("These great creatures once trod the earth where you now walk") and down to the Hall of Primitive Man, where two Puerto Rican youths, obviously playing hooky, stood by the African wing gazing worshipfully at a Masai warrior in full battle gear. In the section devoted to Asia I paused to get my bearings, looking in vain for the squat figure in the robe. The glass case was empty. Over its plaque was taped a printed notice: "Temporarily removed for restoration."

This was no doubt the first time in forty years that the display had been taken down, and of course I'd picked just this occasion to look for it. So much for luck. I headed for the nearest staircase, at the far end of the wing. From behind me the clank of metal echoed down the hall, followed by the angry voice of the guard. Perhaps that Masai spear had proved too great a temptation.

In the main lobby I was issued a written pass to enter the north wing, where the staff offices were located. "You want the workrooms on basement level," said the woman at the information counter; the summer's bored coed had become a friendly old lady who eyed me with some interest. "Just ask the guard at the bottom of the stairs, past the cafeteria. I do hope you find what you're looking for."

Carefully keeping the pink slip she'd handed me visible for anyone who might demand it, I descended. As I turned onto the stairwell I was confronted with a kind of vision: a blonde, Scandinavian-looking family were coming up the stairs toward me, the four upturned faces almost interchangeable, parents and two little girls with the pursed lips and timidly hopeful eyes of the tourist, while just behind them, apparently unheard, capered a grinning black youth, practically walking on the father's heels. In my present state of mind the scene appeared particularly disturbing—the boy's expression was certainly one of mockery—and I wondered if the guard who stood before the cafeteria had noticed. If he had, however, he gave no sign; he glanced without curiosity at my pass and pointed toward a fire door at the end of the hall.

The offices in the lower level were surprisingly shabby—the walls here were not marble but faded green plaster—and the entire corridor had a "buried" feeling to it, no doubt because the only outside light came from ground-level window gratings high overhead. I had been told to ask for one of the research associates, a Mr. Richmond; his office was part of a suite broken up by pegboard dividers. The door was open, and he got up from his desk as soon as I entered; I suspect that, in view of my age and grey tweed overcoat, he may have taken me for someone important.

A plump young man with sandy-colored beard, he looked like an out-of-shape surfer, but his sunniness dissolved when I mentioned my interest in the green silk robe. "And I suppose you're the man who complained about it upstairs, am I right?"

I assured him that I was not.

"Well, someone sure did," he said, still eyeing me resentfully; on the wall behind him an Indian war-mask did the same. "Some damn tourist, maybe, in town for a day and out to make trouble. Threatened to call the Malaysian Embassy. If you put up a fuss those people upstairs get scared it'll wind up in the *Times*."

I understood his allusion; the previous year the museum had gained considerable notoriety for having conducted some really appalling—and, to my mind, quite pointless—experiments on cats. Most of the public had, until then, been unaware that the building housed several working laboratories.

"Anyway," he continued, "the robe's down in the shop, and we're stuck with patching up the damn thing. It'll probably be down there for the next six months before we get to it. We're so understaffed right now it isn't funny." He glanced at his watch. "Come on, I'll show you. Then I've got to go upstairs."

I followed him down a narrow corridor that branched off to either side. At one point he said, "On your right, the infamous zoology lab." I kept my eyes straight ahead. As we passed the next doorway I smelled a familiar odor. "It makes me think of treacle," I said.

"You're not so far wrong." He spoke without looking back. "The stuff's mostly molasses. Pure nutrient. They use it for growing microorganisms."

I hurried to keep up with him. "And for other things?"

He shrugged. "I don't know, mister. It's not my field."

We came to a door barred by a black wire grille. "Here's one of the shops," he said, fitting a key into the lock. The door swung open on a long unlit room smelling of wood shavings and glue. "You sit down over here," he said, leading me to a small anteroom and switching on the light. "I'll be back in a second." I stared at the object closest to me, a large ebony chest, ornately carved. Its hinges had been removed. Richmond returned with the robe draped over his arm. "See?" he said, dangling it before me. "It's really not in such bad condition, is it?" I realized he still thought of me as the man who'd complained.

On the field of rippling green fled the small brown shapes, still pursued by some unseen doom. In the center stood the black man, black horn to his lips, man and horn a single line of unbroken black.

"Are the Tcho-Tchos a superstitious people?" I asked.

"They were," he said pointedly. "Superstitious and not very pleasant. They're extinct as dinosaurs now. Supposedly wiped out by the Japanese or something."

"That's rather odd," I said. "A friend of mine claims to have met up with them earlier this year."

Richmond was smoothing out the robe; the branches of the snake-trees snapped futilely at the brown shapes. "I suppose it's possible," he said, after a pause. "But I haven't read anything about them since grad school. They're certainly not listed in the textbooks anymore. I've looked, and there's nothing on them. This robe's over a hundred years old."

I pointed to the figure in the center. "What can you tell me about this fellow?"

"Death's Herald," he said, as if it were a quiz. "At least that's what the literature says. Supposed to warn of some approaching calamity."

I nodded without looking up; he was merely repeating what I'd read in the pamphlet. "But isn't it strange," I said, "that these others are in such a panic? See? They aren't even waiting around to listen."

"Would you?" He snorted impatiently.

"But if the black one's just a messenger of some sort, why's he so much bigger than the others?"

Richmond began folding the cloth. "Look, mister," he said, "I don't pretend to be an expert on every tribe in Asia. But if a character's important, they'd sometimes make him larger. Anyway, that's what the Mayans did. But listen, I've really got to get this put away now. I've got a meeting to go to."

While he was gone I sat thinking about what I'd just seen. The small brown shapes, crude as they were, had expressed a terror no mere messenger could inspire. And that great black figure standing triumphant in the center, horn twisting from its mouth—that was no messenger either, I was sure of it. That was no Death's Herald. That was Death itself.

I returned to my apartment just in time to hear the telephone ringing, but by the time I'd let myself in it had stopped. I sat down in the living room with a mug of coffee and a book which had lain untouched on the shelf for the last thirty years: *Jungle Ways*, by that old humbug, William Seabrook. I'd met him back in the twenties and had found him likable enough, if rather untrustworthy. His book described dozens of unlikely characters, including "a cannibal chief who had got himself jailed and famous because he had eaten his young wife, a handsome, lazy wench called Blito, along with a dozen of her girl friends," but I discovered no mention of a black horn-player.

I had just finished my coffee when the phone rang again. It was my sister.

"I just wanted to let you know that there's another man missing," she said breathlessly; I couldn't tell if she was frightened or merely excited. "A busboy at the San Marino. Remember? I took you there."

The San Marino was an inexpensive little luncheonette on Indian Creek, several blocks from my sister's house. She and her friends ate there several times a week.

"It happened last night," she went on. "I just heard about it at my card game. They say he went outside with a bucket of fish heads to dump in the creek, and he never came back."

"That's very interesting, but ..." I thought for a moment; it was highly unusual for her to call me like this. "But really, Maude, couldn't he have simply run off? I mean, what makes you think there's any connection—"

"Because I took Ambrose there, too!" she cried. "Three or four times. That was where we used to meet."

Apparently Maude had been considerably better acquainted with the Reverend Mortimer than her letters would have led one to believe. But I wasn't interested in pursuing that line right now. "This busboy," I asked, "was he someone you knew?"

"Of course," she said. "I know everyone in there. His name was Carlos. A quiet boy, very courteous. I'm sure he must have waited on us dozens of times."

I had seldom heard my sister so upset, but for the present there seemed no way of calming her fears. Before hanging up she made me promise to move up the month's visit I'd expected to pay her over Christmas; I assured her I would try to make it down for Thanksgiving, then only a week away, if I could find a flight that wasn't filled.

"Do try," she said—and, were this a tale from the old pulps, she would have added: "If anyone can get to the bottom of this, you can." In truth, however, both Maude and I were aware that I had just celebrated my seventy-seventh birthday and that, of the two of us, I was by far the more timid; so that what she actually said was, "Looking after you will help take my mind off things."

I couldn't live a week without a private library.
—Lovecraft, February 25, 1929

That's what I thought, too, until recently. After a lifetime of collecting I'd acquired thousands upon thousands of volumes, never parting with a one; it was this cumbersome private library, in fact, that helped keep me anchored to the same West Side apartment for nearly half a century.

Yet here I sit, with no company save a few gardening manuals and a shelf of antiquated best-sellers—nothing to dream on, nothing I'd want to hold in my hand. Still, I've survived here a week, a month, almost a season. The truth is, Howard, you'd be surprised what you can live without. As for the books I've left in Manhattan, I just hope someone takes care of them when I'm gone.

But I was by no means so resigned that November when, having successfully reserved seats on an earlier flight, I found myself with less than a week in New York. I spent all my remaining time in the library—the public one on Forty-second Street, with the lions in front and with no book of mine on its shelves. Its two reading rooms were the haunt of men my age and older, retired men with days to fill, poor men just warming their bones; some leafed through newspapers, others dozed in their seats. None of them, I'm sure, shared my sense of urgency: there were things I hoped to find out before I left, things for which Miami would be useless.

I was no stranger to this building. Long ago, during one of Howard's visits, I had undertaken some genealogical researches here in the hope of finding ancestors more impressive than his, and as a young man I had occasionally attempted to support myself, like the denizens of Gissing's *New Grub Street*, by writing articles compiled from the work of others. But by now I was out of practice: how, after all, does one find references to an obscure Southeast Asian tribal myth without reading everything published on that part of the world?

Initially that's exactly what I tried; I looked through every book I could find with "Malaya" in its title. I read about rainbow gods and phallic altars and something called "the *tatai*," a sort of unwanted companion; I came across wedding rites and The Death of Thorns and a certain cave inhabited by millions of snails. But I found no mention of the Tcho-Tcho, and nothing on their gods.

This in itself was surprising. We are living in a day when there are no more secrets, when my twelve-year-old nephew can buy his own grimoire and books with titles like *The Encyclopaedia of Ancient and Forbidden Knowledge* are remaindered at every discount store. Though my friends from the twenties would have hated to admit it, the notion of stumbling across some moldering old "black book" in the attic of a deserted house—some lexicon of spells and chants and hidden lore—is merely a quaint fantasy. If the *Necronomicon* actually existed, it would be out in Bantam paperback with a preface by Lin Carter.

It's appropriate, then, that when I finally came upon a reference to what I sought, it was in that most unromantic of forms, a mimeographed film-script.

"Transcript" would perhaps be closer to the truth, for it was based upon a film shot in 1937 that was now presumably crumbling in some forgotten vault. I discovered the item inside one of those brown cardboard packets, held together with ribbons, which libraries use to protect books whose bindings have worn away. The book itself, *Malay Memories*, by a Reverend Morton, had proved a disappointment despite the author's rather suggestive name. The transcript lay beneath it, apparently slipped there by mistake, but though it appeared unpromising—only ninety-six pages long, badly typed, and held together by a single rusty staple—it more than repaid the reading. There was no title page, nor do I think there'd ever been one; the first page simply identified the film as "Documentary—Malaya Today," and noted that it had been financed, in part, by a U.S. government grant. The filmmaker or makers were not listed.

I soon saw why the government may have been willing to lend the venture some support, for there were a great many scenes in which the proprietors of rubber plantations expressed the sort of opinions Americans might want to hear. To an unidentified interviewer's query, "What other signs of prosperity do you see around you?" a planter named Mr. Pierce had obligingly replied, "Why, look at the living standard—better schools for the natives and a new lorry for me. It's from Detroit, you know. May even have my own rubber in it."

> INT: And how about the Japanese? Are they one of today's better markets?
>
> PIERCE: Oh, see, they buy our crop all right, but we don't really trust 'em, understand? (Smiles) We don't like 'em half so much as the Yanks.

The final section of the transcript was considerably more interesting, however; it recorded a number of brief scenes that must never have appeared in the finished film. I quote one of them in its entirety:

PLAYROOM, CHURCH SCHOOL—LATE AFTERNOON. (DELETED)

> INT: This Malay youth has sketched a picture of a demon he calls Shoo Goron. (To Boy) I wonder

if you can tell me something about the instrument
he's blowing out of. It looks like the Jewish *shofar*,
or ram's horn. (Again to Boy) That's all right. No
need to be frightened.

BOY: He no blow out. Blow in.

INT: I see—he draws air in through the horn, is that
right?

BOY: No horn. Is no horn. (Weeps) Is him.

Miami did not produce much of an impression ...
—Lovecraft, July 19, 1931

Waiting in the airport lounge with Ellen and her boy, my bags already
checked and my seat number assigned, I fell prey to the sort of anxiety
that had made me miserable in youth: it was a sense that time was
running out; and what caused it now, I think, was the hour that remained
before my flight was due to leave. It was too long a time to sit making
small talk with Terry, whose mind was patently on other things; yet it
was too short to accomplish the task which I'd suddenly realized had
been left undone.

But perhaps my nephew would serve. "Terry," I said, "how'd you like
to do me a favor?" He looked up eagerly; I suppose children his age love
to be of use. "Remember the building we passed on the way here? The
International Arrivals building?"

"Sure," he said. "Right next door."

"Yes, but it's a lot farther away than it looks. Do you think you'd be
able to get there and back in the next hour and find something out for
me?"

"Sure." He was already out of his seat.

"It just occurs to me that there's an Air Malay reservations desk in
that building, and I wonder if you could ask someone there—"

My niece interrupted me. "Oh, no he won't," she said firmly. "First of
all, I won't have him running across that highway on some silly errand—"
she ignored her son's protests, "—and secondly, I don't want him involved
in this game you've got going with Mother."

The upshot of it was that Ellen went herself, leaving Terry and me to our small talk. She took with her a slip of paper upon which I'd written "Shoo Goron," a name she regarded with sour skepticism. I wasn't sure she would return before my departure (Terry, I could see, was growing increasingly uneasy), but she was back before the second boarding call.

"She says you spelled it wrong," Ellen announced.

"Who's she?"

"Just one of the flight attendants," said Ellen. "A young girl, in her early twenties. None of the others were Malayan. At first she didn't recognize the name, until she read it out loud a few times. Apparently it's some kind of fish, am I right? Like a suckerfish, only bigger. Anyway, that's what she said. Her mother used to scare her with it when she was bad."

Obviously Ellen—or, more likely, the other woman—had misunderstood. "Sort of a bogeyman figure?" I asked. "Well, I suppose that's possible. But a fish, you say?"

Ellen nodded. "I don't think she knew that much about it, though. She acted a little embarrassed, in fact. Like I'd asked her something dirty." From across the room a loudspeaker issued the final call for passengers. Ellen helped me to my feet, still talking. "She said she was just a Malay, from somewhere on the coast—Malacca? I forget—and that it's a shame I didn't drop by three or four months ago, because her summer replacement was part Chocha—Chocho?—something like that."

The line was growing shorter now. I wished the two of them a safe Thanksgiving and shuffled toward the plane.

Below me the clouds had formed a landscape of rolling hills. I could see every ridge, every washed-out shrub, and in the darker places, the eyes of animals.

Some of the valleys were split by jagged black lines that looked like rivers seen on a map. The water, at least, was real enough: here the cloudbank had cracked and parted, revealing the dark sea beneath.

Throughout the ride I'd been conscious of lost opportunity, a sense that my destination offered a kind of final chance. With Howard gone these forty years I still lived out my life in his shadow; certainly his tales had overshadowed my own. Now I found myself trapped within one of them. Here, miles above the earth, I felt great gods warring; below, the war was already lost.

The very passengers around me seemed participants in a masque: the oily little steward who smelled of something odd; the child who stared and wouldn't look away; the man asleep beside me, mouth slack, who'd chuckled and handed me a page ripped from his "in-flight" magazine: november puzzle page, with an eye staring in astonishment from a swarm of dots. "Connect the dots and see what you'll be least thankful for this Thanksgiving!" Below it, half buried amid *"B'nai B'rith to Host Song Fest"* and advertisements for beach clubs, a bit of local color found me in a susceptible mood:

HAVE FINS, WILL TRAVEL

(COURTESY *MIAMI HERALD*) If your hubby comes home and swears he's just seen a school of fish walk across the yard, don't sniff his breath for booze. He may be telling the truth! According to U. of Miami zoologists, catfish will be migrating in record numbers this fall and South Florida residents can expect to see hundreds of the whiskered critters crawling overland, miles from water. Though usually no bigger than your pussycat, most breeds can survive without

Here the piece came to a ragged end where my companion had torn it from the magazine. He stirred in his sleep, lips moving; I turned and put my head against the window, where the limb of Florida was swinging into view, veined with dozens of canals. The plane shuddered and slid toward it.

Maude was already at the gate, a black porter beside her with an empty cart. While we waited by a hatchway in the basement for my luggage to be disgorged, she told me the sequel to the San Marino incident: the boy's body found washed up on a distant beach, lungs in mouth and throat. "Inside out," she said. "Can you imagine? It's been on the radio all morning. With tapes of some ghastly doctor talking about smoker's cough and the way people drown. I couldn't even listen after a while." The porter heaved my bags onto the cart and we followed him to the taxi stand, Maude using her cane to gesticulate. If I hadn't seen how aged she'd become I'd have thought the excitement was agreeing with her.

We had the driver make a detour westward along Pompano Canal Road, where we paused at number 311, one of nine shabby green cabins that formed a court round a small and very dirty wading pool; in a cement pot beside the pool drooped a solitary half-dead palm, as if in some travesty of an oasis. This, then, had been Ambrose Mortimer's final home. My sister was very silent, and I believed her when she said she'd never been here before. Across the street glistened the oily waters of the canal.

The taxi turned east. We passed interminable rows of hotels, motels, condominiums, shopping centers as big as Central Park, souvenir shops with billboards bigger than themselves, baskets of seashells and wriggly plastic auto toys out front. Men and women our age and younger sat on canvas beach chairs in their yards, blinking at the traffic. The sexes had merged; some of the older women were nearly as bald as I was, and men wore clothes the color of coral, lime, and peach. They walked very slowly as they crossed the street or moved along the sidewalk; cars moved almost as slowly, and it was forty minutes before we reached Maude's house, with its pastel orange shutters and the retired druggist and his wife living upstairs. Here, too, a kind of languor was upon the block, one into which I knew, with just a memory of regret, I would soon be settling. Life was slowing to a halt, and once the taxi had roared away the only things that stirred were the geraniums in Maude's window box, trembling slightly in a breeze I couldn't even feel.

A dry spell. Mornings in my sister's air-conditioned parlor, luncheons with her friends in air-conditioned coffee shops. Inadvertent afternoon naps, from which I'd waken with headaches. Evening walks, to watch the sunsets, the fireflies, the TV screens flashing behind neighbors' blinds. By night, a few faint cloudy stars; by day, tiny lizards skittering over the hot pavement, or boldly sunning themselves on the flagstones. The smell of oil paints in my sister's closet, and the insistent buzz of mosquitoes in her garden. Her sundial, a gift from Ellen, with Terry's message painted on the rim. Lunch at the San Marino and a brief, half-hearted look at the dock in back, now something of a tourist attraction. An afternoon at a branch library in Hialeah, searching through its shelves of travel books, an old man dozing at the table across from me, a child laboriously copying her school report from the encyclopedia. Thanksgiving dinner, with its half-hour's phone call to Ellen and the boy and the prospect of turkey for the rest of the week. More friends to visit, and another day at the library.

Later, driven by boredom and the ghost of an impulse, I phoned the Barkleigh Hotella in North Miami and booked a room there for two nights. I don't remember the days I settled for, because that sort of thing no longer had much meaning, but I know it was for midweek; "we're deep in the season," the proprietress informed me, and the hotel would be filled each weekend till long past New Year's.

My sister refused to accompany me out to Culebra Avenue; she saw no attraction in visiting the place once occupied by a fugitive Malaysian, nor did she share my pulp-novel fantasy that, by actually living there myself, I might uncover some clue unknown to police. ("Thanks to the celebrated author of *Beyond the Garve* ...") I went alone, by cab, taking with me half a dozen volumes from the branch library. Beyond the reading, I had no other plans.

The Barkleigh was a pink adobe building two stories tall, surmounted by an ancient neon sign on which the dust lay thick in the early afternoon sunlight. Similar establishments lined the block on both sides, each more depressing than the last. There was no elevator here and, as I learned to my disappointment, no rooms available on the first floor; the staircase looked like it was going to be an effort.

In the office downstairs I inquired, as casually as I could, which room the notorious Mr. Djaktu had occupied; I'd hoped, in fact, to be assigned it, or one nearby. But I was doomed to disappointment. The preoccupied little Cuban behind the counter had been hired only six weeks before and claimed to know nothing of the matter; in halting English he explained that the proprietress, a Mrs. Zimmerman, had just left for New Jersey to visit relatives and would not be back till Christmas. Obviously I could forget about gossip.

By this point I was half tempted to cancel my visit, and I confess that what kept me there was not so much a sense of honor as the desire for two days' separation from Maude, who, having been on her own for nearly a decade, was rather difficult to live with.

I followed the Cuban upstairs, watching my suitcase bump rhythmically against his legs, and was led down the hall to a room facing the rear. The place smelled vaguely of salt air and hair oil; the sagging bed had served many a desperate holiday. A small cement terrace overlooked the yard and a vacant lot behind it, the latter so overgrown with weeds and the grass in the yard so long unmown that it was difficult to tell where one began and the other ended. A clump of palms rose somewhere in the middle of this no-man's-land, impossibly tall and thin, with only a few stiffened leaves to grace the tops. On the ground below them lay several rotting coconuts.

This was my view the first night when I returned after dining at a nearby restaurant. I felt unusually tired and soon went inside to sleep. The night being cool, there was no need for the air conditioner; as I lay in the huge bed I could hear people stirring in the adjoining room, the hiss of a bus moving down the avenue, and the rustle of palm leaves in the wind.

I spent part of the next morning composing a letter to Mrs. Zimmerman, to be held for her return. After the long walk to a coffee shop for lunch, I napped. After dinner I did the same. With the TV turned on for company, a garrulous blur at the other side of the room, I went through the pile of books on my night-table, final cullings from the bottom of the travel shelf; most of them hadn't been taken out since the thirties. I found nothing of interest in any of them, at least upon first inspection, but before turning out the light I noticed that one, the reminiscences of a Colonel E. G. Paterson, was provided with an index. Though I looked in vain for the demon Shoo Goron, I found reference to it under a variant spelling.

The author, no doubt long deceased, had spent most of his life in the Orient. His interest in Southeast Asia was slight, and the passage in question consequently brief:... Despite the richness and variety of their folklore, however, they have nothing akin to the Malay *shugoran*, a kind of bogey-man used to frighten naughty children. The traveller hears many conflicting descriptions of it, some bordering on the obscene. (*Oran*, of course, is Malay for 'man,' while *shug*, which here connotes 'sniffing' or 'questing,' means literally, 'elephant's trunk.') I well recall the hide which hung over the bar at the Traders' Club in Singapore, and which, according to tradition, represented the infant of this fabulous creature; its wings were black, like the skin of a Hottentot. Shortly after the War a regimental surgeon was passing through on his way back to Gibraltar and, after due examination, pronounced it the dried-out skin of a rather large catfish. He was never asked back.

I kept my light on until I was ready to fall asleep, listening to the wind rattle the palm leaves and whine up and down the row of terraces. As I switched off the light I half expected to see a shadowy shape at the window, but I saw, as the poet says, nothing but the night.

The next morning I packed my bag and left, aware that my stay in the hotel had proved fruitless. I returned to my sister's house to find her in agitated conversation with the druggist from upstairs; she was in a terrible state and said she'd been trying to reach me all morning. She had awakened to find the flower box by her bedroom window overturned and the shrubbery beneath it trampled. Down the side of the house ran two immense slash marks several yards apart, starting at the roof and continuing straight to the ground.

> My gawd, how the years fly. Stolidly middle-aged—when only yesterday I was young and eager and awed by the mystery of an unfolding world.
>
> —Lovecraft, August 20, 1926

There is little more to report. Here the tale degenerates into an unsifted collection of items which may or may not be related: pieces of a puzzle for those who fancy themselves puzzle fans, a random swarm of dots, and in the center, a wide unwinking eye.

Of course, my sister left the house on Indian Creek that very day and took rooms for herself in a downtown Miami hotel. Subsequently she moved inland to live with a friend in a green stucco bungalow several miles from the Everglades, third in a row of nine just off the main highway. I am seated in its den as I write this. After the friend died my sister lived on here alone, making the forty-mile bus trip to Miami only on special occasions: theater with a group of friends, one or two shopping trips a year. She had everything else she needed right here in town.

I returned to New York, caught a chill, and finished out the winter in a hospital bed, visited rather less often than I might have wished by my niece and her boy. Of course, the drive in from Brooklyn is nothing to scoff at.

One recovers far more slowly when one has reached my age; it's a painful truth we all learn if we live long enough. Howard's life was short, but in the end I think he understood. At thirty-five he could deride as madness a friend's "hankering after youth," yet ten years later he'd learned to mourn the loss of his own. "The years tell on one!" he'd written. "You young fellows don't know how lucky you are!"

Age is indeed the great mystery. How else could Terry have emblazoned his grandmother's sundial with that saccharine nonsense?

Grow old along with me;
The best is yet to be.

True, the motto is traditional to sundials—but that young fool hadn't even kept to the rhyme. With diabolical imprecision he had written, *"The best is yet to come"*—a line to make me gnash my teeth, if I had any left to gnash.

I spent most of the spring indoors, cooking myself wretched little meals and working ineffectually on a literary project that had occupied my thoughts. It was discouraging to find that I wrote so slowly now, and changed so much. My sister only reinforced the mood when, sending me a rather salacious story she'd found in the *Enquirer*—about the "thing like a vacuum cleaner" that snaked through a Swedish sailor's porthole and "made his face all purple"—she wrote at the top, *"See? Right out of Lovecraft."*

It was not long after this that I received, to my surprise, a letter from Mrs. Zimmerman, bearing profuse apologies for having misplaced my inquiry until it turned up again during "spring cleaning." (It is hard to imagine any sort of cleaning at the Barkleigh Hotella, spring or otherwise, but even this late reply was welcome.) "I am sorry that the minister who disappeared was a friend of yours," she wrote. "I'm sure he must have been a fine gentleman.

"You asked me for 'the particulars,' but from your note you seem to know the whole story. There is really nothing I can tell you that I did not tell the police, though I do not think they ever released all of it to the papers. Our records show that our guest Mr. Djaktu arrived here nearly a year ago, at the end of June, and left the last week of August owing me a week's rent plus various damages which I no longer have much hope of recovering, though I have written the Malaysian Embassy about it.

"In other respects he was a proper boarder, paid regularly, and in fact hardly ever left his room except to walk in the back yard from time to time, or stop at the grocer's. (We have found it impossible to discourage eating in rooms.) My only complaint is that in the middle of the summer he may have had a small colored child living with him without our knowledge, until one of the maids heard him singing to it as she passed his room. She did not recognize the language, but said she thought it might be Hebrew. (The poor woman, now sadly taken from us, was barely able to read.) When she next made up the room, she told me that Mr. Djaktu claimed the child was 'his,' and that she left because she caught a glimpse of it watching her from the bathroom. She said it was naked. I did not speak of this at the time, as I do not feel it is my place to pass judgment on the morals of my guests. Anyway, we never saw the child again, and we made sure the room was completely sanitary for our next guests. Believe me, we have received nothing but good comments on our facilities. We think they are excellent and hope you agree, and I also hope you will be our guest again the next time you come to Florida."

Unfortunately, the next time I came to Florida was for my sister's funeral late that winter. I know now, as I did not know then, that she had been in ill health for most of the previous year, but I cannot help thinking that the so-called "incidents"—the senseless acts of vandalism directed against lone women in the South Florida area, culminating in several reported attacks by an unidentified prowler—may have hastened her death.

When I arrived here with Ellen to take care of my sister's affairs and arrange for the funeral, I intended to remain a week or two at most, seeing to the transfer of the property. Yet somehow I lingered, long after Ellen had gone. Perhaps it was the thought of that New York winter, grown harsher with each passing year; I just couldn't find the strength to go back. Nor, in the end, could I bring myself to sell this house; if I am trapped here, it's a trap I'm resigned to. Besides, moving has never much agreed with me; when I grow tired of this little room—and I do—I can think of nowhere else to go. I've seen all the world I want to see. This simple place is now my home—and I feel certain it will be my last. The calendar on the wall tells me it's been almost three months since I moved in. I know that somewhere in its remaining pages you will find the date of my death.

The past week has seen a new outbreak of the "incidents." Last night's was the most dramatic by far. I can recite it almost word for word from the morning news. Shortly before midnight Mrs. Florence Cavanaugh, a housewife living at 24 Alyssum Terrace, South Princeton, was about to close the curtains in her front room when she saw, peering through the window at her, what she described as "a large Negro man wearing a gas mask or scuba outfit." Mrs. Cavanaugh, who was dressed only in her nightgown, fell back from the window and screamed for her husband, asleep in the next room, but by the time he arrived the Negro had made good his escape.

Local police favor the "scuba" theory, since near the window they've discovered footprints that may have been made by a heavy man in swim fins. But they haven't been able to explain why anyone would wear underwater gear so many miles from water.

The report usually concludes with the news that "Mr. and Mrs. Cavanaugh could not be reached for comment."

The reason I have taken such an interest in the case—sufficient, anyway, to memorize the above details—is that I know the Cavanaughs rather well. They are my next-door neighbors.

Call it an aging writer's ego, if you like, but somehow I can't help thinking that last evening's visit was meant for me. These little green bungalows all look alike in the dark.

Well, there's still a little night left outside—time enough to rectify the error. I'm not going anywhere.

I think, in fact, it will be a rather appropriate end for a man of my pursuits—to be absorbed into the denouement of another man's tale.

Grow old along with me;
The best is yet to come.

Tell me, Howard: how long before it's my turn to see the black face pressed to my window?

THE LAST FEAST OF HARLEQUIN

1

My interest in the town of Mirocaw was first aroused when I heard that an annual festival was held there that promised to include, to some extent, the participation of clowns among its other elements of pageantry. A former colleague of mine, who is now attached to the anthropology department of a distant university, had read one of my recent articles ("The Clown Figure in American Media," *Journal of Popular Culture*), and wrote to me that he vaguely remembered reading or being told of a town somewhere in the state that held a kind of "Fool's Feast" every year, thinking that this might be pertinent to my peculiar line of study. It was, of course, more pertinent than he had reason to think, both to my academic aims in this area and to my personal pursuits.

Aside from my teaching, I had for some years been engaged in various anthropological projects with the primary ambition of articulating the significance of the clown figure in diverse cultural contexts. Every year for the past twenty years I have attended the pre-Lenten festivals that are held in various places throughout the southern United States. Every year I learned something more concerning the esoterica of celebration. In these studies I was an eager participant—along with playing my part as an anthropologist, I also took a place behind the clownish mask myself. And I cherished this role as I did nothing else in my life. To me the title of Clown has always carried connotations of a noble sort. I was an adroit jester, strangely enough, and had always taken pride in the skills I worked so diligently to develop.

I wrote to the State Department of Recreation, indicating what information I desired and exposing an enthusiastic urgency which came naturally to me on this topic. Many weeks later I received a tan envelope imprinted with a government logo. Inside was a pamphlet that catalogued all of the various seasonal festivities of which the state was officially aware, and I noted in passing that there were as many in late autumn and winter as in the warmer seasons. A letter inserted within the pamphlet explained to me that, according to their voluminous records, no festivals held in the town of Mirocaw had been officially registered. Their files, nonetheless, could be placed at my disposal if I should wish to research this or similar matters in connection with some definite project. At the time this offer was made I was already laboring under so many professional and personal burdens that, with a weary hand, I simply deposited the envelope and its contents in a drawer, never to be consulted again.

Some months later, however, I made an impulsive digression from my responsibilities and, rather haphazardly, took up the Mirocaw project. This happened as I was driving north one afternoon in late summer with the intention of examining some journals in the holdings of a library at another university. Once out of the city limits the scenery changed to sunny fields and farms, diverting my thoughts from the signs that I passed along the highway. Nevertheless, the subconscious scholar in me must have been regarding these with studious care. The name of a town loomed into my vision. Instantly the scholar retrieved certain records from some deep mental drawer, and I was faced with making a few hasty calculations as to whether there was enough time and motivation for an investigative side trip. But the exit sign was even hastier in making its appearance, and I soon found myself leaving the highway, recalling the road sign's promise that the town was no more than seven miles east.

These seven miles included several confusing turns, the forced taking of a temporarily alternate route, and a destination not even visible until a steep rise had been fully ascended. On the descent another helpful sign informed me that I was within the city limits of Mirocaw. Some scattered houses on the outskirts of the town were the first structures I encountered. Beyond them the numerical highway became Townshend Street, the main avenue of Mirocaw.

The town impressed me as being much larger once I was within its limits than it had appeared from the prominence just outside. I saw that the general hilliness of the surrounding countryside was also an internal feature of Mirocaw. Here, though, the effect was different. The parts of the town did not look as if they adhered very well to one another. This condition might be blamed on the irregular topography of the town. Behind some of the old stores in the business district, steeply roofed houses had been erected on a sudden incline, their peaks appearing at an extraordinary elevation above the lower buildings. And because the foundations of these houses could not be glimpsed, they conveyed the illusion of being either precariously suspended in air, threatening to topple down, or else constructed with an unnatural loftiness in relation to their width and mass. This situation also created a weird distortion of perspective. The two levels of structures overlapped each other without giving a sense of depth, so that the houses, because of their higher elevation and nearness to the foreground buildings, did not appear diminished in size as background objects should. Consequently, a look of flatness, as in a photograph, predominated in this area. Indeed, Mirocaw could be compared to an album of old snapshots, particularly ones in which the camera had been upset in the process of photography, causing the pictures to develop on an angle: a cone-roofed turret, like a pointed hat jauntily askew, peeked over the houses on a neighboring street; a billboard displaying a group of grinning vegetables tipped its contents slightly westward; cars parked along steep curbs seemed to be flying skyward in the glare-distorted windows of a five-and-ten; people leaned lethargically as they trod up and down sidewalks; and on that sunny day the clock tower, which at first I mistook for a church steeple, cast a long shadow that seemed to extend an impossible distance and wander into unlikely places in its progress across the town. I should say that perhaps the disharmonies of Mirocaw are more acutely affecting my imagination in retrospect than they were on that first day, when I was primarily concerned with locating the city hall or some other center of information.

I pulled around a corner and parked. Sliding over to the other side of the seat, I rolled down the window and called to a passerby: "Excuse me, sir," I said. The man, who was shabbily dressed and very old, paused for a moment without approaching the car. Though he had apparently responded to my call, his vacant expression did not betray the least awareness of my presence, and for a moment I thought it just a coincidence that he halted on the sidewalk at the same time I addressed him. His eyes were focused somewhere beyond me with a weary and imbecilic gaze. After a few moments he continued on his way and I said nothing to call him back, even though at the last second his face began to appear dimly familiar. Someone else finally came along who was able to direct me to the Mirocaw City Hall and Community Center.

The city hall turned out to be the building with the clock tower. Inside I stood at a counter behind which some people were working at desks and walking up and down a back hallway. On one wall was a poster for the state lottery: a jack-in-the-box with both hands grasping green bills. After a few moments, a tall, middle-aged woman came over to the counter.

"Can I help you?" she asked in a neutral, bureaucratic voice.

I explained that I had heard about the festival—saying nothing about being a nosy academic—and asked if she could provide me with further information or direct me to someone who could.

"Do you mean the one held in the winter?" she asked.

"How many of them are there?"

"Just that one."

"I suppose, then, that that's the one I mean." I smiled as if sharing a joke with her.

Without another word, she walked off into the back hallway. While she was absent I exchanged glances with several of the people behind the counter who periodically looked up from their work.

"There you are," she said when she returned, handing me a piece of paper that looked like the product of a cheap copy machine. *Please Come to the Fun,* it said in large letters. *Parades,* it went on, *Street Masquerade, Bands, The Winter Raffle,* and *The Coronation of the Winter Queen.* The page continued with the mention of a number of miscellaneous festivities. I read the words again. There was something about that imploring little "please" at the top of the announcement that made the whole affair seem like a charity function.

"When is it held? It doesn't say when the festival takes place."

"Most people already know that." She abruptly snatched the page from my hands and wrote something at the bottom. When she gave it back to me, I saw "Dec. 19–21" written in blue-green ink. I was immediately struck by an odd sense of scheduling on the part of the festival committee. There was, of course, solid anthropological and historical precedent for holding festivities around the winter solstice, but the timing of this particular event did not seem entirely practical.

"If you don't mind my asking, don't these days somewhat conflict with the regular holiday season? I mean, most people have enough going on at that time."

"It's just tradition," she said, as if invoking some venerable ancestry behind her words.

"That's very interesting," I said as much to myself as to her.

"Is there anything else?" she asked.

"Yes. Could you tell me if this festival has anything to do with clowns? I see there's something about a masquerade."

"Yes, of course there are some people in … costumes. I've never been in that position myself … that is, yes, there are clowns of a sort."

At that point my interest was definitely aroused, but I was not sure how much further I wanted to pursue it. I thanked the woman for her help and asked the best means of access to the highway, not anxious to retrace the labyrinthine route by which I had entered the town. I walked back to my car with a whole flurry of half-formed questions, and as many vague and conflicting answers, cluttering my mind.

The directions the woman gave me necessitated passing through the south end of Mirocaw. There were not many people moving about in this section of town. Those that I did see, shuffling lethargically down a block of battered storefronts, exhibited the same sort of forlorn expression and manner as the old man from whom I had asked directions earlier. I must have been traversing a central artery of this area, for on either side stretched street after street of poorly tended yards and houses bowed with age and indifference. When I came to a stop at a street corner, one of the citizens of this slum passed in front of my car. This lean, morose, and epicene person turned my way and sneered outrageously with a taut little mouth, yet seemed to be looking at no one in particular. After progressing a few streets farther, I came to a road that led back to the highway. I felt detectably more comfortable as soon as I found myself traveling once again through the expanses of sun-drenched farmlands.

I reached the library with more than enough time for my research, and so I decided to make a scholarly detour to see what material I could find that might illuminate the winter festival held in Mirocaw. The library, one of the oldest in the state, included in its holdings the entire run of the *Mirocaw Courier*. I thought this would be an excellent place to start. I soon found, however, that there was no handy way to research information from this newspaper, and I did not want to engage in a blind search for articles concerning a specific subject.

I next turned to the more organized resources of the newspapers for the larger cities located in the same county, which incidentally shares its name with Mirocaw. I uncovered very little about the town, and almost nothing concerning its festival, except in one general article on annual events in the area that erroneously attributed to Mirocaw a "large Middle-Eastern community" which every spring hosted a kind of ethnic jamboree. From what I had already observed, and from what I subsequently learned, the citizens of Mirocaw were solidly midwestern-American, the probable descendants in a direct line from some enterprising pack of New Englanders of the last century. There was one brief item devoted to a Mirocavian event, but this merely turned out to be an obituary notice for an old woman who had quietly taken her life around Christmastime. Thus, I returned home that day all but empty-handed on the subject of Mirocaw.

However, it was not long afterward that I received another letter from the former colleague of mine who had first led me to seek out Mirocaw and its festival. As it happened, he rediscovered the article that caused him to stir my interest in a local "Fool's Feast." This article had its sole appearance in an obscure festschrift of anthropology studies published in Amsterdam twenty years ago. Most of these papers were in Dutch, a few in German, and only one was in English: "The Last Feast of Harlequin: Preliminary Notes on a Local Festival." It was exciting, of course, finally to be able to read this study, but even more exciting was the name of its author: Dr. Raymond Thoss.

2

Before proceeding any further, I should mention something about Thoss, and inevitably about myself. Over two decades ago, at my alma mater in Cambridge, Mass., Thoss was a professor of mine. Long before playing a role in the events I am about to describe, he was already one of the most important figures in my life. A striking personality, he inevitably influenced everyone who came in contact with him. I remember his lectures on social anthropology, how he turned that dim room into a brilliant and profound circus of learning. He moved in an uncannily brisk manner. When he swept his arm around to indicate some common term on the blackboard behind him, one felt he was presenting nothing less than an item of fantastic qualities and secret value. When he replaced his hand in the pocket of his old jacket this fleeting magic was once again stored away in its well-worn pouch, to be retrieved at the sorcerer's discretion. We sensed he was teaching us more than we could possibly learn, and that he himself was in possession of greater and deeper knowledge than he could possibly impart. On one occasion I summoned up the audacity to offer an interpretation—which was somewhat opposed to his own—regarding the tribal clowns of the Hopi Indians. I implied that personal experience as an amateur clown and special devotion to this study provided me with an insight possibly more valuable than his own. It was then he disclosed, casually and very obiter dicta, that he had actually acted in the role of one of these masked tribal fools and had celebrated with them the dance of the *kachinas*. In revealing these facts, however, he somehow managed not to add to the humiliation I had already inflicted upon myself. And for this I was grateful to him.

Thoss's activities were such that he sometimes became the object of gossip or romanticized speculation. He was a fieldworker par excellence, and his ability to insinuate himself into exotic cultures and situations, thereby gaining insights where other anthropologists merely collected data, was renowned. At various times in his career there had been rumors of his having "gone native" à la the Frank Hamilton Cushing legend. There were hints, which were not always irresponsible or cheaply glamorized, that he was involved in projects of a freakish sort, many of which focused on New England. It is a fact that he spent six months posing as a mental patient at an institution in western Massachussetts, gathering information on the "culture" of the psychically disturbed. When his book *Winter Solstice: The Longest Night of a Society* was published, the general opinion was that it was disappointingly subjective and impressionistic, and that, aside from a few moving but "poetically obscure" observations, there was nothing at all to give it value. Those who defended Thoss claimed he was a kind of super-anthropologist: while much of his work emphasized his own mind and feelings, his experience had in fact penetrated to a rich core of hard data which he had yet to disclose in objective discourse. As a student of Thoss, I tended to support this latter estimation of him. For a variety of tenable and untenable reasons, I believed Thoss capable of unearthing hitherto inaccessible strata of human existence. So it was gratifying at first that this article entitled "The Last Feast of Harlequin" seemed to uphold the Thoss mystique, and in an area I personally found captivating.

Much of the content of the article I did not immediately comprehend, given its author's characteristic and often strategic obscurities. On first reading, the most interesting aspect of this brief study—the "notes" encompassed only twenty pages—was the general mood of the piece. Thoss's eccentricities were definitely present in these pages, but only as a struggling inner force which was definitely contained—incarcerated, I might say—by the somber rhythmic movements of his prose and by some gloomy references he occasionally called upon. Two references in particular shared a common theme. One was a quotation from Poe's "The Conqueror Worm," which Thoss employed as a rather sensational epigraph. The point of the epigraph, however, was nowhere echoed in the text of the article save in another passing reference. Thoss brought up the well-known genesis of the modern Christmas celebration, which of course descends from the Roman Saturnalia. Then, making it clear he had not yet observed the Mirocaw festival and had only gathered its nature from various informants, he established that it too contained many, even more overt, elements of the Saturnalia. Next he made what seemed to me a trivial and purely linguistic observation, one that had less to do with his main course of argument than it did with the equally peripheral Poe epigraph. He briefly mentioned that an early sect of the Syrian Gnostics called themselves "Saturnians" and believed, among other religious heresies, that mankind was created by angels who were in turn created by the Supreme Unknown. The angels, however, did not possess the power to make their creation an erect being and for a time he crawled upon the earth like a worm. Eventually, the Creator remedied this grotesque state of affairs. At the time I supposed that the symbolic correspondences of mankind's origins and ultimate condition being associated with worms, combined with a year-end festival recognizing the winter death of the earth, was the gist of this Thossian "insight," a poetic but scientifically valueless observation.

Other observations he made on the Mirocaw festival were also strictly etic; in other words, they were based on second-hand sources, hearsay testimony. Even at that juncture, however, I felt Thoss knew more than he disclosed; and, as I later discovered, he had indeed included information on certain aspects of Mirocaw suggesting he was already in possession of several keys which for the moment he was keeping securely in his own pocket. By then I myself possessed a most revealing morsel of knowledge. A note to the "Harlequin" article apprised the reader that the piece was only a fragment in rude form of a more wide-ranging work in preparation. This work was never seen by the world. My former professor had not published anything since his withdrawal from academic circulation some twenty years ago. Now I suspected where he had gone.

For the man I had stopped on the streets of Mirocaw and from whom I tried to obtain directions, the man with the disconcertingly lethargic gaze, had very much resembled a superannuated version of Dr. Raymond Thoss.

3

And now I have a confession to make. Despite my reasons for being enthusiastic about Mirocaw and its mysteries, especially its relationship to both Thoss and my own deepest concerns as a scholar—I contemplated the days ahead of me with no more than a feeling of frigid numbness and often with a sense of profound depression. Yet I had no reason to be surprised at this emotional state, which had little relevance to the outward events in my life but was determined by inward conditions that worked according to their own, quite enigmatic, seasons and cycles. For many years, at least since my university days, I have suffered from this dark malady, this recurrent despondency in which I would become buried when it came time for the earth to grow cold and bare and the skies heavy with shadows. Nevertheless, I pursued my plans, though somewhat mechanically, to visit Mirocaw during its festival days, for I superstitiously hoped that this activity might diminish the weight of my seasonal despair. In Mirocaw would be parades and parties and the opportunity to play the clown once again.

For weeks in advance I practiced my art, even perfecting a new feat of juggling magic, which was my special forte in foolery. I had my costumes cleaned, purchased fresh makeup, and was ready. I received permission from the university to cancel some of my classes prior to the holiday, explaining the nature of my project and the necessity of arriving in the town a few days before the festival began, in order to do some preliminary research, establish informants, and so on. Actually, my plan was to postpone any formal inquiry until after the festival and to involve myself beforehand as much as possible in its activities. I would, of course, keep a journal during this time.

There was one resource I did want to consult, however. Specifically, I returned to that outstate library to examine those issues of the *Mirocaw Courier* dating from December two decades ago. One story in particular confirmed a point Thoss made in the "Harlequin" article, though the event it chronicled must have taken place after Thoss had written his study.

The *Courier* story appeared two weeks after the festival had ended for that year and was concerned with the disappearance of a woman named Elizabeth Beadle, the wife of Samuel Beadle, a hotel owner in Mirocaw. The county authorities speculated that this was another instance of the "holiday suicides" which seemed to occur with inordinate seasonal regularity in the Mirocaw region. Thoss documented this phenomenon in his "Harlequin" article, though I suspect that today these deaths would be neatly categorized under the heading "seasonal affective disorder." In any case, the authorities searched a half-frozen lake near the outskirts of Mirocaw where they had found many successful suicides in years past. This year, however, no body was discovered. Alongside the article was a picture of Elizabeth Beadle. Even in the grainy microfilm reproduction one could detect a certain vibrancy and vitality in Mrs. Beadle's face. That an hypothesis of "holiday suicide" should be so readily posited to explain her disappearance seemed strange and in some way unjust.

Thoss, in his brief article, wrote that every year there occurred changes of a moral or spiritual cast which seemed to affect Mirocaw along with the usual winter metamorphosis. He was not precise about its origin or nature but stated, in typically mystifying fashion, that the effect of this "subseason" on the town was conspicuously negative. In addition to the number of suicides actually accomplished during this time, there was also a rise in treatment of "hypochondriacal" conditions, which was how the medical men of twenty years past characterized these cases in discussions with Thoss. This state of affairs would gradually worsen and finally reach a climax during the days scheduled for the Mirocaw festival. Thoss speculated that given the secretive nature of small towns, the situation was probably even more intensely pronounced than casual investigation could reveal.

The connection between the festival and this insidious subseasonal climate in Mirocaw was a point on which Thoss did not come to any rigid conclusions. He did write, nevertheless, that these two "climatic aspects" had had a parallel existence in the town's history as far back as available records could document. A late nineteenth-century history of Mirocaw County speaks of the town by its original name of New Colstead, and castigates the townspeople for holding a "ribald and soulless feast" to the exclusion of normal Christmas observances. (Thoss comments that the historian had mistakenly fused two distinct aspects of the season, their actual relationship being essentially antagonistic.) The "Harlequin" article did not trace the festival to its earliest appearance (this may not have been possible), though Thoss emphasized the New England origins of Mirocaw's founders. The festival, therefore, was one imported from this region and could reasonably be extended at least a century; that is, if it had not been brought over from the Old World, in which case its roots would become indefinite until further research could be done. Surely

Thoss's allusion to the Syrian Gnostics suggested the latter possibility could not entirely be ruled out.

But it seemed to be the festival's link to New England that nourished Thoss's speculations. He wrote of this patch of geography as if it were an acceptable place to end the search. For him, the very words "New England" seemed to be stripped of all traditional connotations and had come to imply nothing less than a gateway to all lands, both known and suspected, and even to ages beyond the civilized history of the region. Having been educated partly in New England, I could somewhat understand this sentimental exaggeration, for indeed there are places that seem archaic beyond chronological measure, appearing to transcend relative standards of time and achieving a kind of absolute antiquity which cannot be logically fathomed. But how this vague suggestion related to a small town in the Midwest I could not imagine. Thoss himself observed that the residents of Mirocaw did not betray any mysteriously primitive consciousness. On the contrary, they appeared superficially unaware of the genesis of their winter merrymaking. That such a tradition had endured through the years, however, even eclipsing the conventional Christmas holiday, revealed a profound awareness of the festival's meaning and function.

I cannot deny that what I had learned about the Mirocaw festival did inspire a trite sense of fate, especially given the involvement of such an important figure from my past as Thoss. It was the first time in my academic career that I knew myself to be better suited than anyone else to discern the true meaning of scattered data, even if I could only attribute this special authority to chance circumstances.

Nevertheless, as I sat in that library on a morning in mid-December, I doubted for a moment the wisdom of setting out for Mirocaw rather than returning home, where the more familiar *rite de passage* of winter depression awaited me. My original scheme was to avoid the cyclical blues the season held for me, but it seemed this was also a part of the history of Mirocaw, only on a much larger scale. My emotional instability, however, was exactly what qualified me most for the particular fieldwork ahead, though I did not take pride or consolation in the fact. And to retreat would have been to deny myself an opportunity that might never offer itself again. In retrospect, there seems to have been no fortuitous resolution to the decision I had to make. As it happened, I went ahead to the town.

4

Just past noon, on December 18, I started driving toward Mirocaw. A blur of dull, earthen-colored scenery extended in every direction. The snowfalls of late autumn had been sparse, and only a few white patches appeared in the harvested fields along the highway. The clouds were gray and abundant. Passing by a stretch of forest, I noticed the black, ragged clumps of abandoned nests clinging to the twisted mesh of bare branches. I thought I saw black birds skittering over the road ahead, but they were only dead leaves and they flew into the air as I drove by.

I approached Mirocaw from the south, entering the town from the direction I had left it on my visit the previous summer. This took me once again through that part of town which seemed to exist on the wrong side of some great invisible barrier dividing the desirable sections of Mirocaw from the undesirable. As lurid as this district had appeared to me under the summer sun, in the thin light of that winter afternoon it degenerated into a pale phantom of itself. The frail stores and starved-looking houses suggested a borderline region between the material and nonmaterial worlds, with one sardonically wearing the mask of the other. I saw a few gaunt pedestrians who turned as I passed by, though seemingly not *because* I passed by, making my way up to the main street of Mirocaw.

Driving up the steep rise of Townshend Street, I found the sights there comparatively welcoming. The rolling avenues of the town were in readiness for the festival. Streetlights had their poles wound with evergreen, the fresh boughs proudly conspicuous in a barren season. On the doors of many of the businesses on Townshend were holly wreaths, equally green but observably plastic. However, although there was nothing unusual in this traditional greenery of the season, it soon became apparent to me that Mirocaw had quite abandoned itself to this particular symbol of Yuletide. It was garishly in evidence everywhere. The windows of stores and houses were framed in green lights, green streamers hung down from storefront awnings, and the beacons of the Red Rooster Bar were peacock green floodlights. I supposed the residents of Mirocaw desired these decorations, but the effect was one of excess. An eerie emerald haze permeated the town, and faces looked slightly reptilian.

At the time I assumed that the prodigious evergreen, holly wreaths, and colored lights (if only of a single color) demonstrated an emphasis on the vegetable symbols of the Nordic Yuletide, which would inevitably be muddled into the winter festival of any northern country just as they had been adopted for the Christmas season. In his "Harlequin" article Thoss wrote of the pagan aspect of Mirocaw's festival, likening it to the ritual of a fertility cult, with probable connections to chthonic divinities at some time in the past. But Thoss had mistaken, as I had, what was only part of the festival's significance for the whole.

The hotel at which I had made reservations was located on Townshend. It was an old building of brown brick, with an arched doorway and a pathetic coping intended to convey an impression of neoclassicism. I found a parking space in front and left my suitcases in the car.

When I first entered the hotel lobby it was empty. I thought perhaps the Mirocaw festival would have attracted enough visitors to at least bolster the business of its only hotel, but it seemed I was mistaken. Tapping a little bell, I leaned on the desk and turned to look at a small, traditionally decorated Christmas tree on a table near the entranceway. It was complete with shiny, egg-fragile bulbs; miniature candy canes; flat, laughing Santas with arms wide; a star on top nodding awkwardly against the delicate shoulder of an upper branch; and colored lights that bloomed out of flower-shaped sockets. For some reason this seemed to me a sorry little piece.

"May I help you?" said a young woman arriving from a room adjacent to the lobby.

I must have been staring rather intently at her, for she looked away and seemed quite uneasy. I could hardly imagine what to say to her or how to explain what I was thinking. In person she immediately radiated a chilling brilliance of manner and expression. But if this woman had not committed suicide twenty years before, as the newspaper article had suggested, neither had she aged in that time.

"Sarah," called a masculine voice from the invisible heights of a stairway. A tall, middle-aged man came down the steps. "I thought you were in your room," said the man, whom I took to be Samuel Beadle. Sarah, not Elizabeth, Beadle glanced sideways in my direction to indicate to her father that she was conducting the business of the hotel. Beadle apologized to me, and then excused the two of them for a moment while they went off to one side to continue their exchange.

I smiled and pretended everything was normal, while trying to remain within earshot of their conversation. They spoke in tones that suggested their conflict was a familiar one: Beadle's overprotective concern with his daughter's whereabouts and Sarah's frustrated understanding of certain restrictions placed upon her. The conversation ended, and Sarah ascended the stairs, turning for a moment to give me a facial pantomime of apology for the unprofessional scene that had just taken place.

"Now, sir, what can I do for you?" Beadle asked, almost demanded.

"Yes, I have a reservation. Actually, I'm a day early, if that doesn't present a problem." I gave the hotel the benefit of the doubt that its business might have been secretly flourishing.

"No problem at all, sir," he said, presenting me with the registration form, and then a brass-colored key dangling from a plastic disc bearing the number 44.

"Luggage?"

"Yes, it's in my car."

"I'll give you a hand with that."

While Beadle was settling me in my fourth-floor room it seemed an opportune moment to broach the subject of the festival, the holiday suicides, and perhaps, depending upon his reaction, the fate of his wife. I needed a respondent who had lived in the town for a good many years and who could enlighten me about the attitude of Mirocavians toward their season of sea-green lights.

"This is just fine," I said about the clean but somber room. "Nice view. I can see the bright green lights of Mirocaw just fine from up here. Is the town usually all decked out like this? For the festival, I mean."

"Yes, sir, for the festival," he replied mechanically.

"I imagine you'll probably be getting quite a few of us out-of-towners in the next couple days."

"Could be. Is there anything else?"

"Yes, there is. I wonder if you could tell me something about the festivities."

"Such as …"

"Well, you know, the clowns and so forth."

"Only clowns here are the ones that're … well, picked out, I suppose you would say."

"I don't understand."

"Excuse me, sir. I'm very busy right now. Is there anything else?"

I could think of nothing at the moment to perpetuate our conversation. Beadle wished me a good stay and left.

I unpacked my suitcases. In addition to regular clothing I had also brought along some of the items from my clown's wardrobe. Beadle's comment that the clowns of Mirocaw were "picked out" left me wondering exactly what purpose these street masqueraders served in the festival. The clown figure has had so many meanings in different times and cultures. The jolly, well-loved joker familiar to most people is actually but one aspect of this protean creature. Madmen, hunchbacks, amputees, and other abnormals were once considered natural clowns; they were elected to fulfill a comic role which could allow others to see them as ludicrous rather than as terrible reminders of the forces of disorder in the world. But sometimes a cheerless jester was required to draw attention to this same disorder, as in the case of King Lear's morbid and honest fool, who of course was eventually hanged, and so much for his clownish wisdom. Clowns have often had ambiguous and sometimes contradictory roles to play. Thus, I knew enough not to brashly jump into costume and cry out, "Here I am again!"

That first day in Mirocaw I did not stray far from the hotel. I read and rested for a few hours and then ate at a nearby diner. Through the window beside my table I watched the winter night turn the soft green glow of the town into a harsh and almost totally new color as it contrasted with the darkness. The streets of Mirocaw seemed to me unusually busy for a small town at evening. Yet it was not the kind of activity one normally sees before an approaching Christmas holiday. This was not a crowd of bustling shoppers loaded with bright bags of presents. Their arms were empty, their hands shoved deep in their pockets against the cold, which nevertheless had not driven them to the solitude of their presumably warm houses. I watched them enter and exit store after store without buying; many merchants remained open late, and even the places that were closed had left their neons illuminated. The faces that passed the window of the diner were possibly just stiffened by the cold, I thought; frozen into deep frowns and nothing else. In the same window I saw the reflection of my own face. It was not the face of an adept clown; it was slack and flabby and at that moment seemed the face of someone less than alive. Outside was the town of Mirocaw, its streets dipping and rising with a lunatic severity, its citizens packing the sidewalks, its heart bathed in green: as promising a field of professional and personal challenge as I had ever encountered—and I was bored to the point of dread. I hurried back to my hotel room.

"Mirocaw has another coldness within its cold," I wrote in my journal that night. "Another set of buildings and streets that exists behind the visible town's façade like a world of disgraceful back alleys." I went on like this for about a page, across which I finally engraved a big "X." Then I went to bed.

In the morning I left my car at the hotel and walked toward the main business district a few blocks away. Mingling with the good people of Mirocaw seemed like the proper thing to do at that point in my scientific sojourn. But as I began laboriously walking up Townshend (the sidewalks were cramped with wandering pedestrians), a glimpse of someone suddenly replaced my haphazard plan with a more specific and immediate one. Through the crowd and about fifteen paces ahead was my goal.

"Dr. Thoss," I called.

His head almost seemed to turn and look back in response to my shout, but I could not be certain. I pushed past several warmly wrapped bodies and green-scarved necks, only to find that the object of my pursuit appeared to be maintaining the same distance from me, though I did not know if this was being done deliberately or not. At the next corner, the dark-coated Thoss abruptly turned right onto a steep street which led downward directly toward the dilapidated south end of Mirocaw. When I reached the corner I looked down the sidewalk and could see him very clearly from above. I also saw how he managed to stay so far ahead of me in a mob that had impeded my own progress. For some reason the people on the sidewalk made room so that he could move past them easily, without the usual jostling of bodies. It was not a dramatic physical avoidance, though it seemed nonetheless intentional. Fighting the tight fabric of the throng, I continued to follow Thoss, losing and regaining sight of him.

By the time I reached the bottom of the sloping street the crowd had thinned out considerably, and after walking a block or so farther I found myself practically a lone pedestrian pacing behind a distant figure that I hoped was still Thoss. He was now walking quite swiftly and in a way that seemed to acknowledge my pursuit of him, though really it felt as if he were leading me as much as I was chasing him. I called his name a few more times at a volume he could not have failed to hear, assuming that deafness was not one of the changes to have come over him; he was, after all, not a young man, nor even a middle-aged one any longer.

Thoss suddenly crossed in the middle of the street. He walked a few more steps and entered a signless brick building between a liquor store and a repair shop of some kind. In the "Harlequin" article Thoss had mentioned that the people living in this section of Mirocaw maintained their own businesses, and that these were patronized almost exclusively by residents of the area. I could well believe this statement when I looked at these little sheds of commerce, for they had the same badly weathered appearance as their clientele. The formidable shoddiness of these buildings notwithstanding, I followed Thoss into the plain brick shell of what had been, or possibly still was, a diner.

Inside it was unusually dark. Even before my eyes made the adjustment I sensed that this was not a thriving restaurant cozily cluttered with chairs and tables—as was the establishment where I had eaten the night before—but a place with only a few disarranged furnishings, and very cold. It seemed colder, in fact, than the winter streets outside.

"Dr. Thoss?" I called toward a lone table near the center of the long room. Perhaps four or five were sitting around the table, with some others blending into the dimness behind them. Scattered across the top of the table were some books and loose papers. Seated there was an old man indicating something in the pages before him, but it was not Thoss. Beside him were two youths whose wholesome features distinguished them from the grim weariness of the others. I approached the table and they all looked up at me. None of them showed a glimmer of emotion except the two boys, who exchanged worried and guilt-ridden glances with each other, as if they had just been discovered in some shameful act. They both suddenly burst from the table and ran into the dark background, where a light appeared briefly as they exited by a back door.

"I'm sorry," I said diffidently. "I thought I saw someone I knew come in here."

They said nothing. Out of a back room others began to emerge, no doubt interested in the source of the commotion. In a few moments the room was crowded with these tramp-like figures, all of them gazing emptily in the dimness. I was not at this point frightened of them; at least I was not afraid they would do me any physical harm. Actually, I felt as if it was quite within my power to pummel them easily into submission, their mousy faces almost inviting a succession of firm blows. But there were so many of them.

They slid slowly toward me in a worm-like mass. Their eyes seemed empty and unfocused, and I wondered a moment if they were even aware of my presence. Nevertheless, I was the center upon which their lethargic shuffling converged, their shoes scuffing softly along the bare floor. I began to deliver a number of hasty inanities as they continued to press toward me, their weak and unexpectedly odorless bodies nudging against mine. (I understood now why the people along the sidewalks seemed to instinctively avoid Thoss.) Unseen legs became entangled with my own; I staggered and then regained my balance. This sudden movement aroused me from a kind of mesmeric daze into which I must have fallen without being aware of it. I had intended to leave that dreary place long before events had reached such a juncture, but for some reason I could not focus my intentions strongly enough to cause myself to act. My mind had been drifting farther away as these slavish things approached. In a sudden surge of panic I pushed through their soft ranks and was outside.

The open air revived me to my former alertness, and I immediately started pacing swiftly up the hill. I was no longer sure that I had not simply imagined what had seemed, and at the same time did not seem, like a perilous moment. Had their movements been directed toward a harmful assault, or were they trying merely to intimidate me? As I reached the green-glazed main street of Mirocaw I really could not determine what had just happened.

The sidewalks were still jammed with a multitude of pedestrians, who now seemed more lively than they had been only a short time before. There was a kind of vitality that could only be attributed to the imminent festivities. A group of young men had begun celebrating prematurely and strode noisily across the street at midpoint, obviously intoxicated. From the laughter and joking among the still sober citizens I gathered that, Mardi-gras style, public drunkenness was within the traditions of this winter festival. I looked for anything to indicate the beginnings of the Street Masquerade, but saw nothing: no brightly garbed harlequins or snow-white pierrots. Were the ceremonies even now in preparation for the coronation of the Winter Queen? "The Winter Queen," I wrote in my journal. "Figure of fertility invested with symbolic powers of revival and prosperity. Elected in the manner of a high-school prom queen. Check for possible consort figure in the form of a representative from the underworld."

In the pre-darkness hours of December 19 I sat in my hotel room and wrote and thought and organized. I did not feel too badly, all things considered. The holiday excitement which was steadily rising in the streets below my window was definitely infecting me. I forced myself to take a short nap in anticipation of a long night. When I awoke, Mirocaw's annual feast had begun.

5

Shouting, commotion, carousing. Sleepily I went to the window and looked out over the town. It seemed all the lights of Mirocaw were shining, save in that section down the hill which became part of the black void of winter. And now the town's greenish tinge was even more pronounced, spreading everywhere like a great green rainbow that had melted from the sky and endured, phosphorescent, into the night. In the streets was the brightness of an artificial spring. The byways of Mirocaw vibrated with activity: on a nearby corner a brass band blared; marauding cars blew their horns and were sometimes mounted by laughing pedestrians; a man emerged from the Red Rooster Bar, threw up his arms, and crowed. I looked closely at the individual celebrants, searching for the vestments of clowns. Soon, delightedly, I saw them. The costume was red and white, with matching cap, and the face painted a noble alabaster. It almost seemed to be a clownish incarnation of that white-bearded and black-booted Christmas fool.

This particular fool, however, was not receiving the affection and respect usually accorded to a Santa Claus. My poor fellow-clown was in the middle of a circle of revelers who were pushing him back and forth from one to the other. The object of this abuse seemed to accept it somewhat willingly, but this little game nevertheless appeared to have humiliation as its purpose. "Only clowns here are the ones that're picked out," echoed Beadle's voice in my memory. "Picked *on*" seemed closer to the truth.

Packing myself in some heavy clothes, I went out into the green, gleaming streets. Not far from the hotel I was stumbled into by a character with a wide blue and red grin and bright baggy clothes. Actually he had been shoved into me by some youths outside a drugstore.

"See the freak," said an obese and drunken fellow. "See the freak fall."

My first response was anger, and then fear as I saw two others flanking the fat drunk. They walked toward me and I tensed myself for a confrontation.

"This is a disgrace," one said, the neck of a wine bottle held loosely in his left hand.

But it was not to me they were speaking; it was to the clown, who had been pushed to the sidewalk. His three persecutors helped him up with a sudden jerk and then splashed wine in his face. They ignored me altogether.

"Let him loose," the fat one said. "Crawl away, freak. Oh, he flies!"

The clown trotted off, becoming lost in the throng.

"Wait a minute," I said to the rowdy trio, who had started lumbering away. I quickly decided that it would probably be futile to ask them to explain what I had just witnessed, especially amid the noise and confusion of the festivities. In my best jovial fashion I proposed we all go someplace where I could buy them each a drink. They had no objection and in a short while we were all squeezed around a table in the Red Rooster.

Over several drinks I explained to them that I was from out of town, which pleased them no end for some reason. I told them there were things I did not understand about their festival.

"I don't think there's anything to understand," the fat one said. "It's just what you see."

I asked him about the people dressed as clowns.

"Them? They're the freaks. It's their turn this year. Everyone takes their turn. Next year it might be mine. Or *yours*," he said, pointing at one of his friends across the table. "And when we find out which one you are—"

"You're not smart enough," said the defiant potential freak.

This was an important point: the fact that individuals who played the clowns remain, or at least attempted to remain, anonymous. This arrangement would help remove inhibitions a resident of Mirocaw might have about abusing his own neighbor or even a family relation. From what I later observed, the extent of this abuse did not go beyond a kind of playful roughhousing. And even so, it was only the occasional group of rowdies who actually took advantage of this aspect of the festival, the majority of the citizens very much content to stay on the sidelines.

As far as being able to illuminate the meaning of this custom, my three young friends were quite useless. To them it was just amusement, as I imagine it was to the majority of Mirocavians. This was understandable. I suppose the average person would not be able to explain exactly how the profoundly familiar Christmas holiday came to be celebrated in its present form.

I left the bar alone and not unaffected by the drinks I had consumed there. Outside, the general merrymaking continued. Loud music emanated from several quarters. Mirocaw had fully transformed itself from a sedate small town to an enclave of Saturnalia within the dark immensity of a winter night. But Saturn is also the planetary symbol of melancholy and sterility, a clash of opposites contained within that single word. And as I wandered half-drunkenly down the street, I discovered that there was a conflict within the winter festival itself. This discovery indeed appeared to be that secret key which Thoss withheld in his study of the town. Oddly enough, it was through my unfamiliarity with the outward nature of the festival that I came to know its true nature.

I was mingling with the crowd on the street, warmly enjoying the confusion around me, when I saw a strangely designed creature lingering on the corner up ahead. It was one of the Mirocaw clowns. Its clothes were shabby and nondescript, almost in the style of a tramp-type clown, but not humorously exaggerated enough. The face, though, made up for the lackluster costume. I had never seen such a strange conception for a clown's countenance. The figure stood beneath a dim streetlight, and when it turned its head my way I realized why it seemed familiar, The thin, smooth, and pale head; the wide eyes; the oval-shaped features resembling nothing so much as the skull-faced, screaming creature in that famous painting (memory fails me). This clownish imitation rivaled the original in suggesting stricken realms of abject horror and despair: an inhuman likeness more proper to something under the earth than upon it.

From the first moment I saw this creature, I thought of those inhabitants of the ghetto down the hill. There was the same nauseating passivity and languor in its bearing. Perhaps if I had not been drinking earlier I would not have been bold enough to take the action I did. I decided to join in one of the upstanding traditions of the winter festival, for it annoyed me to see this morbid impostor of a clown standing up. When I reached the corner I laughingly pushed myself into the creature—"Whoops!"—who stumbled backward and ended up on the sidewalk. I laughed again and looked around for approval from the festivalers in the vicinity. No one, however, seemed to appreciate or even acknowledge what I had done. They did not laugh with me or point with amusement, but only passed by, perhaps walking a little faster until they were some distance from this street-corner incident. I realized instantly I had violated some tacit rule of behavior, though I had thought my action well within the common practice. The idea occurred to me that I might even be apprehended and prosecuted for what in any other circumstances was certainly a criminal act. I turned around to help the clown back to his feet, hoping somehow to redeem my offense, but the creature was gone. Solemnly I walked away from the scene of my inadvertent crime and sought other streets away from its witnesses.

Along the various back avenues of Mirocaw I wandered, pausing exhaustedly at one point to sit at the counter of a small sandwich shop that was packed with customers. I ordered a cup of coffee to revive my overly alcoholed system. Warming my hands around the cup and sipping slowly from it, I watched the people outside as they passed the front window. It was well after midnight but the thick flow of passersby gave no indication that anyone was going home early. A carnival of profiles filed past the window and I was content simply to sit back and observe, until finally one of these faces made me start. It was that frightful little clown I had roughed up earlier. But although its face was familiar in its ghastly aspect, there was something different about it. And I wondered that there should be two such hideous freaks.

Quickly paying the man at the counter, I dashed out to get a second glimpse of the clown, who was now nowhere in sight. The dense crowd kept me from pursuing this figure with any speed, and I wondered how the clown could have made its way so easily ahead of me. Unless the crowd had instinctively allowed this creature to pass unhindered through its massive ranks, as it did for Thoss. In the process of searching for this particular freak, I discovered that interspersed among the celebrating populous of Mirocaw, which included the sanctioned festival clowns, there was not one or two, but a considerable number of these pale, wraith-like creatures. And they all drifted along the streets unmolested by even the rowdiest of revelers. I now understood one of the taboos of the festival. These other clowns were not to be disturbed and should even be avoided, much as were the residents of the slum at the edge of town. Nevertheless, I felt instinctively that the two groups of clowns were somehow identified with each other, even if the ghetto clowns were not welcome at Mirocaw's winter festival. Indeed, they were not simply part of the community and celebrating the season in their own way. To all appearances, this group of melancholy mummers constituted nothing less than an entirely independent festival—a festival within a festival.

Returning to my room. I entered my suppositions into the journal I was keeping for this venture. The following are excerpts:

There is a superstitiousness displayed by the residents of Mirocaw with regard to these people from the slum section, particularly as they lately appear in those dreadful faces signifying their own festival. What is the relationship between these simultaneous celebrations? Did one precede the other? If so, which? My opinion at this point—and I claim no conclusiveness for it—is that Mirocaw's winter festival is the later manifestation, that it appeared after the festival of those depressingly pallid downs, in order to cover it up or mitigate its effect. The holiday suicides come to mind, and the subclimate Thoss wrote about, the disappearance of Elizabeth Beadle twenty years ago, and my own experience with this pariah clan existing outside yet within the community. Of my own experience with this emotionally deleterious subseason I would rather not speak at this time. Still not able to say whether or not my usual winter melancholy is the cause. On the general subject of mental health, I must consider Thoss's book about his stay in a psychiatric hospital (in western Mass., almost sure of that. Check on this book & Mirocaw's New England roots). The winter solstice is tomorrow, albeit sometime past midnight (how blurry these days and nights are becoming!). It is, of course, the day of the year in which night hours surpass daylight hours by the greatest margin. Note what this has to do with the suicides and a rise in psychic disorder. Recalling Thoss's list of documented suicides in his article, there seemed to be a recurrence of specific family names, as there very likely might be for any kind of data collected in a small town. Among these names was a Beadle or two. Perhaps, then, there is a genealogical basis for the suicides which has nothing to do with Thoss's mystical subclimate, which is a colorful idea to be sure and one that seems fitting for this town of various outward and inward aspects, but is not a conception that can be substantiated.

One thing that seems certain, however, is the division of Mirocaw into two very distinct types of citizenry, resulting in two festivals and the appearance of similar clowns—a term now used in an extremely loose sense. But there is a connection, and I believe I have some idea of what it is. I said before that the normal residents of the town regard those from the ghetto, and especially their clown figures, with superstition. Yet it's more than that: there is fear, perhaps a kind of hatred—the particular kind of hatred resulting from some powerful and irrational memory. What threatens Mirocaw I think I can very well understand. I recall the incident earlier today in that vacant diner. "Vacant" is the appropriate word here, despite its contradiction of fact. The congregation of that half-lit room formed less a presence than an absence, even considering the oppressive number of them. Those eyes that did not or could not focus on anything, the pining lassitude of their faces, the lazy march of their feet. I was spiritually drained when I ran out of there. I then understood why these people and their activities are avoided.

I cannot question the wisdom of those ancestral Mirocavians who began the tradition of the winter festival and gave the town a pretext for celebration and social intercourse at a time when the consequences of brooding isolation are most severe, those longest and darkest days of the solstice. A mood of Christmas joviality obviously would not be sufficient to counter the menace of this season. But even so, there are still the suicides of individuals who are somehow cut off, I imagine, from the vitalizing activities of the festival.

It is the nature of this insidious subseason that seems to determine the outward forms of Mirocaw's winter festival: the optimistic greenery in a period of gray dormancy; the fertile promise of the Winter Queen; and, most interesting to my mind, the clowns. The bright clowns of Mirocaw who are treated so badly; they appear to serve as substitute figures for those dark-eyed mummers of the slums. Since the latter are feared for some power or influence they possess, they may still be symbolically confronted and conquered through their counterparts, who are elected for precisely this function. If I am right about this, I wonder to what extent there is a conscious awareness among the town's populace of this indirect show of aggression. Those three young men I spoke with tonight did not seem to possess much insight beyond seeing that there was a certain amount of robust fun in the festival's tradition. For that matter, how much awareness is there on the *other side* of these two antagonistic festivals? Too horrible to think of such a thing, but I must wonder if, for all their apparent aimlessness, those inhabitants of the ghetto are not the only ones who know what they are about. No denying that behind those inhumanly limp expressions there seems to lie a kind of obnoxious intelligence.

Now I realize the confusion of my present state, but as I wobbled from street to street tonight, watching those oval-mouthed clowns, I could not help feeling that all the merrymaking in Mirocaw was somehow allowed only by their sufferance. This I hope is no more than a fanciful Thossian intuition, the sort of idea that is curious and thought-provoking without ever seeming to gain the benefit of proof. I know my mind is not entirely lucid, but I feel that it may be possible to penetrate Mirocaw's many complexities and illuminate the hidden side of the festival season. In particular I must look for the significance of the other festival. Is it also some kind of fertility celebration? From what I have seen, the tenor of this "celebrating" sub-group is one of anti-fertility, if anything. How have they managed to keep from dying out completely over the years? How do they maintain their numbers?

But I was too tired to formulate any more of my sodden speculations. Falling onto my bed, I soon became lost in dreams of streets and faces.

6.

I was, of course, slightly hung over when I woke up late the next morning. The festival was still going strong, and blaring music outside roused me from a nightmare. It was a parade. A number of floats proceeded down Townshend, a familiar color predominating. There were theme floats of pilgrims and Indians, cowboys and Indians, and clowns of an orthodox type. In the middle of it all was the Winter Queen herself, freezing atop an icy throne. She waved in all directions. I even imagined she waved up at my dark window.

In the first few groggy moments of wakefulness I had no sympathy with my excitation of the previous night. But I discovered that my former enthusiasm had merely lain dormant, and soon returned with an even greater intensity. Never before had my mind and senses been so active during this usually inert time of year. At home I would have been playing lugubrious old records and looking out the window quite a bit. I was terribly grateful in a completely abstract way for my commitment to a meaningful mania. And I was eager to get to work after I had had some breakfast at the coffee shop.

When I got back to my room I discovered the door was unlocked. And there was something written on the dresser mirror. The writing was red and greasy, as if done with a clown's make-up pencil—my own, I realized. I read the legend, or rather I should say riddle, several times: "What buries itself before it is dead?" I looked at it for quite a while, very shaken at how vulnerable my holiday fortifications were. Was this supposed to be a warning of some kind? A threat to the effect that if I persisted in a certain course I would end up prematurely interred? I would have to be careful, I told myself. My resolution was to let nothing deter me from the inspired strategy I had conceived for myself. I wiped the mirror clean, for it was now needed for other purposes.

I spent the rest of the day devising a very special costume and the appropriate face to go with it. I easily shabbied up my overcoat with a torn pocket or two and a complete set of stains. Combined with blue jeans and a pair of rather scuffed-up shoes, I had a passable costume for a derelict. The face, however, was more difficult, for I had to experiment from memory. Conjuring a mental image of the screaming pierrot in that painting (*The Scream*, I now recall), helped me quite a bit. At nightfall I exited the hotel by the back stairway.

It was strange to walk down the crowded street in this gruesome disguise. Though I thought I would feel conspicuous, the actual experience was very close, I imagined, to one of complete invisibility. No one looked at me as I strolled by, or as they strolled by, or as we strolled by each other. I was a phantom—perhaps the ghost of festivals past, or those yet to come.

I had no clear idea where my disguise would take me that night, only vague expectations of gaining the confidence of my fellow specters and possibly in some way coming to know their secrets. For a while I would simply wander around in that lackadaisical manner I had learned from them, following their lead in any way they might indicate. And for the most part this meant doing almost nothing and doing it silently. If I passed one of my kind on the sidewalk there was no speaking, no exchange of knowing looks, no recognition at all that I was aware of. We were there on the streets of Mirocaw to create a presence and nothing more. At least this is how I came to feel about it. As I drifted along with my bodiless invisibility, I felt myself more and more becoming an empty, floating shape, seeing without being seen and walking without the interference of those grosser creatures who shared my world. It was not an experience completely without interest or even pleasure. The clown's shibboleth of "here we are again" took on a new meaning for me as I felt myself a novitiate of a more rarified order of harlequinry. And very soon the opportunity to make further progress along this path presented itself.

Going the opposite direction, down the street, a pickup truck slowly passed, gently parting a sea of zigging and zagging celebrants. The cargo in the back of this truck was curious, for it was made up entirely of my fellow sectarians. At the end of the block the truck stopped and another of them boarded it over the back gate. One block down I saw still another get on. Then the truck made a U-turn at an intersection and headed in my direction.

I stood at the curb as I had seen the others do. I was not sure the truck would pick me up, thinking that somehow they knew I was an imposter. The truck did, however, slow down, almost coming to a stop when it reached me. The others were crowded on the floor of the truck bed. Most of them were just staring into nothingness with the usual indifference I had come to expect from their kind. But a few actually glanced at me with some anticipation. For a second I hesitated, not sure I wanted to pursue this ruse any further. At the last moment, some impulse sent me climbing up the back of the truck and squeezing myself in among the others.

There were only a few more to pick up before the truck headed for the outskirts of Mirocaw and beyond. At first I tried to maintain a clear orientation with respect to the town. But as we took turn after turn through the darkness of narrow country roads, I found myself unable to preserve any sense of direction. The majority of the others in the back of the truck exhibited no apparent awareness of their fellow passengers. Guardedly, I looked from face to ghostly face. A few of them spoke in short whispered phrases to others close by. I could not make out what they were saying but the tone of their voices was one of innocent normalcy, as if they were not of the hardened slum-herd of Mirocaw. Perhaps, I thought, these were thrill-seekers who had disguised themselves as I had done, or, more likely, initiates of some kind. Possibly they had received prior instructions at such meetings as I had stumbled onto the day before. It was also likely that among this crew were those very boys I had frightened into a precipitate exit from that old diner.

The truck was now speeding along a fairly open stretch of country, heading toward those higher hills that surrounded the now distant town of Mirocaw. The icy wind whipped around us, and I could not keep myself from trembling with cold. This definitely betrayed me as one of the newcomers among the group, for the two bodies that pressed against mine were rigidly still and even seemed to be radiating a frigidity of their own. I glanced ahead at the darkness into which we were rapidly progressing.

We had left all open country behind us now, and the road was enclosed by thick woods. The mass of bodies in the truck leaned into one another as we began traveling up a steep incline. Above us, at the top of the hill, were lights shining somewhere within the woods. When the road leveled off, the truck made an abrupt turn, steering into what looked like a great ditch. There was an unpaved path, however, upon which the truck proceeded toward the glowing in the near distance.

This glowing became brighter and sharper as we approached it, flickering upon the trees and revealing stark detail where there had formerly been only smooth darkness. As the truck pulled into a clearing and came to a stop, I saw a loose assembly of figures, many of which held lanterns that beamed with a dazzling and frosty light. I stood up in the back of the truck to unboard as the others were doing. Glancing around from that height I saw approximately thirty more of those cadaverous clowns milling about. One of my fellow passengers spied me lingering in the truck and in a strangely high-pitched whisper told me to hurry, explaining something about the "apex of darkness." I thought again about this solstice night; it was technically the longest period of darkness of the year, even if not by a very significant margin from many other winter nights. Its true significance, though, was related to considerations having little to do with either statistics or the calendar.

I went over to the place where the others were forming into a tighter crowd, which betrayed a sense of expectancy in the subtle gestures and expressions of its individual members. Glances were now exchanged, the hand of one lightly touched the shoulder of another, and a pair of circled eyes gazed over to where two figures were setting their lanterns on the ground about six feet apart. The illumination of these lanterns revealed an opening in the earth. Eventually the awareness of everyone was focused on this roundish pit, and as if by prearranged signal we all began huddling around it. The only sounds were those of the wind and our own movements as we crushed frozen leaves and sticks underfoot.

Finally, when we had all surrounded this gaping hole, the first one jumped in, leaving our sight for a moment but then reappearing to take hold of a lantern which another handed him from above. The miniature abyss filled with light, and I could see it was no more than six feet deep. One of its walls opened into the mouth of a tunnel. The figure holding the lantern stooped a little and disappeared into the passage.

Each of us, in turn, dropped into the darkness of this pit, and every fifth one took a lantern. I kept to the back of the group, for whatever subterranean activities were going to take place, I was sure I wanted to be on their periphery. When only about ten of us remained on the ground above, I maneuvered to let four of them precede me so that as the fifth I might receive a lantern. This was exactly how it worked out, for after I had leaped to the bottom of the hole a light was ritually handed down to me. Turning about-face, I quickly entered the passageway. At that point I shook so with cold that I was neither curious nor afraid, but only grateful for the shelter.

I entered a long, gently sloping tunnel, just high enough for me to stand upright. It was considerably warmer down there than outside in the cold darkness of the woods. After a few moments I had sufficiently thawed out so that my concerns shifted from those of physical comfort to a sudden and justified preoccupation with my survival. As I walked I held my lantern close to the sides of the tunnel. They were relatively smooth, as if the passage had not been made by manual digging but had been burrowed by something which left behind a clue to its dimensions in the tunnel's size and shape. This delirious idea came to me when I recalled the message that had been left on my hotel room mirror: "What buries itself before it is dead?"

I had to hurry along to keep up with those uncanny spelunkers who preceded me. The lanterns ahead bobbed with every step of their bearers, the lumbering procession seeming less and less real the farther we marched into that snug little tunnel. At some point I noticed the line ahead of me growing shorter. The processioners were emptying out into a cavernous chamber where I, too, soon arrived. This area was about thirty feet in height, its other dimensions approximating those of a large ballroom. Gazing into the distance above made me uncomfortably aware of how far we had descended into the earth. Unlike the smooth sides of the tunnel, the walls of this cavern looked jagged and irregular, as though they had been gnawed at. The earth had been removed, I assumed, either through the tunnel from which we had emerged, or else by way of one of the many other black openings that I saw around the edges of the chamber, for possibly they too led back to the surface.

But the structure of this chamber occupied my mind a great deal less than did its occupants. There to meet us on the floor of the great cavern was what must have been the entire slum population of Mirocaw, and more, all with the same eerily wide-eyed and oval-mouthed faces. They formed a circle around an altar-like object which had some kind of dark, leathery covering draped over it. Upon the altar, another covering of the same material concealed a lumpy form beneath.

And behind this form, looking down upon the altar, was the only figure whose face was not greased with makeup.

He wore a long snowy robe that was the same color as the wispy hair berimming his head. His arms were calmly at his sides. He made no movement. The man I once believed would penetrate great secrets stood before us with the same professorial bearing that had impressed me so many years ago, yet now I felt nothing but dread at the thought of what revelations lay pocketed within the abysmal folds of his magisterial attire. Had I really come here to challenge such a formidable figure? The name by which I knew him seemed itself insufficient to designate one of his stature. Rather I should name him by his other incarnations: god of all wisdom, scribe of all sacred books, father of all magicians, thrice great and more—rather I should call him *Thoth*.

He raised his cupped hands to his congregation and the ceremony was underway.

It was all very simple. The entire assembly, which had remained speechless until this moment, broke into the most horrendous high-pitched singing that can be imagined. It was a choir of sorrow, of shrieking delirium, and of shame. The cavern rang shrilly with the dissonant, whining chorus. My voice, too, was added to the congregation's, trying to blend with their maimed music. But my singing could not imitate theirs, having a huskiness unlike their cacophonous, keening wail. To keep from exposing myself as an intruder I continued to mouth their words without sound. These words were a revelation of the moody malignancy which until then I had no more than sensed whenever in the presence of these figures. They were singing to the "unborn in paradise," to the "pure unlived lives." They sang a dirge for existence, for all its vital forms and seasons. Their ideals were those of darkness, chaos, and a melancholy half-existence consecrated to all the many shapes of death. A sea of thin, bloodless faces trembled and screamed with perverted hopes. And the robed, guiding figure at the heart of all this—elevated over the course of twenty years to the status of high priest—was the man from whom I had taken so many of my own life's principles. It would be useless to describe what I felt at that moment and a waste of the time I need to describe the events which followed.

The singing abruptly stopped and the towering white-haired figure began to speak. He was welcoming those of the new generation—twenty winters had passed since the "Pure Ones" had expanded their ranks. The word "pure" in this setting was a violence to what sense and composure I still retained, for nothing could have been more foul than what was to come. Thoss—and I employ this defunct identity only as a convenience—closed his sermon and drew closer to the dark-skinned altar. Then, with all the flourish of his former life, he drew back the topmost covering.

Beneath it was a limp-limbed effigy, a collapsed puppet sprawled upon the slab. I was standing toward the rear of the congregation and attempted to keep as close to the exit passage as I could. Thus, I did not see everything as clearly as I might have.

Thoss looked down upon the crooked, doll-like form and then out at the gathering. I even imagined that he made knowing eye-contact with myself. He spread his arms and a stream of continuous and unintelligible words flowed from his moaning mouth. The congregation began to stir, not greatly but perceptibly. Until that moment there was a limit to what I believed was the evil of these people. They were, after all, only that. They were merely morbid, self-tortured souls with strange beliefs. If there was anything I had learned in all my years as an anthropologist it was that the world is infinitely rich in strange ideas, even to the point where the concept of strangeness itself had little meaning for me. But with the scene I then witnessed, my conscience bounded into a realm from which it will never return.

For now was the transformation scene, the culmination of every harlequinade.

It began slowly. There was increasing movement among those on the far side of the chamber from where I stood. Someone had fallen to the floor and the others in the area backed away. The voice at the altar continued its chanting. I tried to gain a better view but there were too many of them around me. Through the mass of obstructing bodies I caught only glimpses of what was taking place.

The one who had swooned to the floor of the chamber seemed to be losing all former shape and proportion. I thought it was a clown's trick. They were clowns, were they not? I myself could make four white balls transform into four black balls as I juggled them. And this was not my most astonishing feat of clownish magic. And is there not always a sleight-of-hand inherent in all ceremonies, often dependent on the transported delusions of the celebrants? This was a good show, I thought, and giggled to myself. The transformation scene of Harlequin throwing off his fool's façade. O God, Harlequin, do not move like that! Harlequin, where are your arms? And your legs have melted together and begun squirming upon the floor. What horrible, mouthing umbilicus is that where your face should be? *What is it that buries itself before it is dead?* The almighty serpent of wisdom—the Conqueror Worm.

It now started happening all around the chamber. Individual members of the congregation would gaze emptily—caught for a moment in a frozen trance—and then collapse to the floor to begin the sickening metamorphosis. This happened with ever-increasing frequency the louder and more frantic Thoss chanted his insane prayer or curse. Then there began a writhing movement toward the altar, and Thoss welcomed the things as they curled their way to the altar-top. I knew now what lax figure lay upon it.

This was Kora and Persephone, the daughter of Ceres and the Winter Queen: the child abducted into the underworld of death. Except this child had no supernatural mother to save her, no living mother at all. For the sacrifice I witnessed was an echo of one that had occurred twenty years before, the carnival feast of the preceding generation—O *carne vale!* Now both mother and daughter had become victims of this subterranean sabbath. I finally realized this truth when the figure stirred upon the altar, lifted its head of icy beauty, and screamed at the sight of mute mouths closing around her.

I ran from the chamber into the tunnel. (There was nothing else that could be done, I have obsessively told myself.) Some of the others who had not yet changed began to pursue me. They would have caught up to me, I have no doubt, for I fell only a few yards into the passage. And for a moment I imagined that I too was about to undergo a transformation, but I had not been prepared as the others, had been. When I heard the approaching footsteps of my pursuers I was sure there was an even worse fate facing me upon the altar. But the footsteps ceased and retreated. They had received an order in the voice of their high priest. I too heard the order, though I wish I had not, for until then I had imagined that Thoss did not remember who I was. It was that voice which taught me otherwise.

For the moment I was free to leave. I struggled to my feet and, having broken my lantern in the fall, retraced my way back through cloacal blackness.

Everything seemed to happen very quickly once I emerged from the tunnel and climbed up from the pit. I wiped the reeking greasepaint from my face as I ran through the woods and back to the road. A passing car stopped, though I gave it no other choice except to run me down.

"Thank you for stopping."

"What the hell are you doing out here?" the driver asked.

I caught my breath. "It was a joke. The festival. Friends thought it would be funny.... Please drive on."

My ride let me off about a mile out of town, and from there I could find my way. It was the same way I had come into Mirocaw on my first visit the summer before. I stood for a while at the summit of that high hill just outside the city limits, looking down upon the busy little hamlet. The intensity of the festival had not abated, and would not until morning. I walked down toward the welcoming glow of green, slipped through the festivities unnoticed, and returned to the hotel. No one saw me go up to my room. Indeed, there was an atmosphere of absence and abandonment throughout that building, and the desk in the lobby was unattended.

I locked the door to my room and collapsed upon the bed.

7.

When I awoke the next morning I saw from my window that the town and surrounding countryside had been visited during the night by a snowstorm, one which was entirely unpredicted. The snow was still falling on the now-deserted streets of Mirocaw. The festival was over. Everyone had gone home.

And this was exactly my own intention. Any action on my part concerning what I had seen the night before would have to wait until I was away from the town. I am still not sure it will do the slightest good to speak up like this. Any accusations I could make against the slum populace of Mirocaw would be resisted, as well they should be, as unbelievable. Perhaps in a very short while none of this will be my concern.

With packed suitcases in both hands I walked up to the front desk to check out. The man behind the desk was not Samuel Beadle, and he had to fumble around to find my bill.

"Here we are. Everything all right?"

"Fine," I answered in a dead voice. "Is Mr. Beadle around?"

"No, I'm afraid he's not back yet. Been out all night looking for his daughter. She's a very popular girl, being the Winter Queen and all that nonsense. Probably find she was at a party somewhere."

A little noise came out of my throat.

I threw my suitcases in the back seat of my car and got behind the wheel. On that morning nothing I could recall seemed real to me. The snow was falling and I watched it through my windshield, slow and silent and entrancing. I started up my car, routinely glancing in my rear view mirror. What I saw there is now vividly framed in my mind, as it was framed in the back window of my car when I turned to verify its reality.

In the middle of the street behind me, standing ankle-deep in snow, was Thoss and another figure. When I looked closely at the other I recognized him as one of the boys whom I surprised in that diner. But he had now taken on a corrupt and listless resemblance to his new family. Both he and Thoss stared at me, making no attempt to forestall my departure. Thoss knew that this was unnecessary.

I had to carry the image of those two dark figures in my mind as I drove back home. But only now has the full weight of my experience descended upon me. So far I have claimed illness in order to avoid my teaching schedule. To face the normal flow of life as I had formerly known it would be impossible. I am now very much under the influence of a season and a climate far colder and more barren than all the winters in human memory. And mentally retracing past events does not seem to have helped; I can feel myself sinking deeper into a velvety white abyss.

At certain times I could almost dissolve entirely into this inner realm of awful purity and emptiness. I remember those invisible moments when in disguise I drifted through the streets of Mirocaw, untouched by the drunken, noisy forms around me: untouchable. But instantly I recoil at this grotesque nostalgia, for I realize what is happening and what I do not want to be true, though Thoss proclaimed it was. I recall his command to those others as I lay helplessly prone in the tunnel. They could have apprehended me, but Thoss, my old master, called them back. His voice echoed throughout that cavern, and it now reverberates within my own psychic chambers of memory.

"He is one of us," it said. "He has always been one of us."

It is this voice which now fills my dreams and my days and my long winter nights. I have seen you, Dr. Thoss, through the snow outside my window. Soon I will celebrate, alone, that last feast which will kill your words, only to prove how well I have learned their truth.

To the memory of H. P. Lovecraft

ONLY THE END OF THE WORLD AGAIN

NEIL GAIMAN

It WAS A bad day: I woke up naked in the bed, with a cramp in my stomach, feeling more or less like hell. Something about the quality of the light, stretched and metallic, like the colour of a migraine, told me it was afternoon.

The room was freezing—literally: there was a thin crust of ice on the inside of the windows. The sheets on the bed around me were ripped and clawed, and there was animal hair in the bed. It itched.

I was thinking about staying in bed for the next week—I'm always tired after a change—but a wave of nausea forced me to disentangle myself from the bedding, and to stumble, hurriedly, into the apartment's tiny bathroom.

The cramps hit me again as I got to the bathroom door. I held on to the door-frame and I started to sweat. Maybe it was a fever; I hoped I wasn't coming down with something.

The cramping was sharp in my guts. My head felt swimmy. I crumpled to the floor, and, before I could manage to raise my head enough to find the toilet bowl, I began to spew.

I vomited a foul-smelling thin yellow liquid; in it was a dog's paw—my guess was a Doberman's, but I'm not really a dog person; a tomato peel; some diced carrots and sweet corn; some lumps of half.chewed meat, raw; and some fingers. They were fairly small, pale fingers, obviously a child's.

"Shit."

The cramps eased up, and the nausea subsided. I lay on the floor, with stinking drool coming out of my mouth and nose, with the tears you cry when you're being sick drying on my cheeks.

When I felt a little better I picked up the paw and the fingers from the pool of spew and threw them into the toilet bowl, flushed them away.

I turned on the tap, rinsed out my mouth with the briny Innsmouth water, and spat it into the sink. I mopped up the rest of the sick as best I could with washcloth and toilet paper. Then I turned on the shower, and stood in the bathtub like a zombie as the hot water sluiced over me.

I soaped myself down, body and hair. The meagre lather turned grey; I must have been filthy. My hair was matted with something that felt like dried blood, and I worked at it with the bar of soap until it was gone. Then I stood under the shower until the water turned icy.

There was a note under the door from my landlady. It said that I owed her for two weeks' rent. It said that all the answers were in the Book of Revelations. It said that I made a lot of noise coming home in the early hours of this morning, and she'd thank me to be quieter in future. It said that when the Elder Gods rose up from the ocean, all the scum of the Earth, all the non-believers, all the human garbage and the wastrels and deadbeats would be swept away, and the world would be cleansed by ice and deep water. It said that she felt she ought to remind me that she had assigned me a shelf in the refrigerator when I arrived and she'd thank me if in the future I'd keep to it.

I crumpled the note, dropped it on the floor, where it lay alongside the Big Mac cartons and the empty pizza cartons, and the long-dead dried slices of pizza.

It was time to go to work.

I'd been in Innsmouth for two weeks, and I disliked it. It smelled fishy. It was a claustrophobic little town: marshland to the east, cliffs to the west, and, between the two, a harbour that held a few rotting fishing boats, and was not even scenic at sunset. The yuppies had come to Innsmouth in the '80s anyway, bought their picturesque fisherman's cottages overlooking the harbour. The yuppies had been gone for some years now, and the cottages by the bay were crumbling, abandoned.

The inhabitants of Innsmouth lived here and there, in and around the town, and in the trailer parks that ringed it, filled with dank mobile homes that were never going anywhere.

I got dressed, pulled on my boots and put on my coat, and left my room. My landlady was nowhere to be seen. She was a short, pop-eyed woman, who spoke little, although she left extensive notes for me pinned to doors and placed where I might see them; she kept the house filled with the smell of boiling seafood: huge pots were always simmering on the kitchen stove, filled with things with too many legs and other things with no legs at all.

There were other rooms in the house, but no one else rented them. No one in their right mind would come to Innsmouth in winter.

Outside the house it didn't smell much better. It was colder, though, and my breath steamed in the sea air. The snow on the streets was crusty and filthy; the clouds promised more snow.

A cold, salty wind came up off the bay. The gulls were screaming miserably. I felt shitty. My office would be freezing, too. On the corner of Marsh Street and Leng Avenue was a bar, "The Opener," a squat building with small, dark windows that I'd passed two dozen times in the last couple of weeks. I hadn't been in before, but I really needed a drink, and besides, it might be warmer in there. I pushed open the door.

The bar was indeed warm. I stamped the snow off my boots and went inside. It was almost empty and smelled of old ashtrays and stale beer. A couple of elderly men were playing chess by the bar. The barman was reading a battered old gilt-and-green-leather edition of the poetical works of Alfred, Lord Tennyson.

"Hey. How about a Jack Daniels straight up?"

"Sure thing. You're new in town," he told me, putting his book face down on the bar, pouring the drink into a glass.

"Does it show?"

He smiled, passed me the Jack Daniels. The glass was filthy, with a greasy thumb-print on the side, but I shrugged and knocked back the drink anyway. I could barely taste it.

"Hair of the dog?" he said.

"In a manner of speaking."

"There is a belief," said the barman, whose fox-red hair was tightly greased back, "that the *lykanthropoi* can be returned to their natural forms by thanking them, while they're in wolf form, or by calling them by their given names."

"Yeah? Well, thanks."

He poured another shot for me, unasked. He looked a little like Peter Lorre, but then, most of the folk in Innsmouth look a little like Peter Lorre, including my landlady. I sank the Jack Daniels, this time felt it burning down into my stomach, the way it should.

"It's what they say. I never said I believed it."

"What *do* you believe?"

"Burn the girdle."

"Pardon?"

"The *lykanthropoi* have girdles of human skin, given to them at their first transformation, by their masters in Hell. Burn the girdle."

One of the old chess-players turned to me then, his eyes huge and blind and protruding. "If you drink rain-water out of warg-wolf's paw-print, that'll make a wolf of you, when the moon is full," he said. "The only cure is to hunt down the wolf that made the print in the first place and cut off its head with a knife forged of virgin silver."

"Virgin, huh?" I smiled.

His chess partner, bald and wrinkled, shook his head and croaked a single sad sound. Then he moved his queen, and croaked again. There are people like him all over Innsmouth. I paid for the drinks, and left a dollar tip on the bar. The barman was reading his book once more, and ignored it.

Outside the bar, big wet kissy flakes of snow had begun to fall, settling in my hair and eyelashes. I hate snow. I hate New England. I hate Innsmouth: it's no place to be alone, but if there's a good place to be alone I've not found it yet. Still, business has kept me on the move for more moons than I like to think about. Business, and other things.

I walked a couple of blocks down Marsh Street—like most of Innsmouth, an unattractive mixture of eighteenth-century American Gothic houses, late nineteenth-century stunted brownstones, and late twentieth prefab grey-brick boxes—until I got to a boarded-up fried chicken joint, where I went up the stone steps next to the store and unlocked the rusting metal security door.

There was a liquor store across the street; a palmist was operating on the second floor.

Someone had scrawled graffiti in black marker on the metal: *just die*, it said. Like it was easy.

The stairs were bare wood; the plaster was stained and peeling. My one-room office was at the top of the stairs.

I don't stay anywhere long enough to bother with my name in gilt on glass. It was handwritten in block letters on a piece of ripped cardboard that I'd thumbtacked to the door.

LAWRENCE TALBOT
ADJUSTOR

I unlocked the door to my office and went in.

I inspected my office, while adjectives like *seedy* and *rancid* and *squalid* wandered through my head, then gave up, outclassed. It was fairly unprepossessing—a desk, an office chair, an empty filing cabinet; a window, which gave you a terrific view of the liquor store and the empty palmist's. The smell of old cooking grease permeated from the store below. I wondered how long the fried chicken joint had been boarded up; I imagined a multitude of black cockroaches swarming over every surface in the darkness beneath me.

""That's the shape of the world that you're thinking of there," said a deep, dark voice, deep enough that I felt it in the pit of my stomach.

There was an old armchair in one corner of the office. The remains of a pattern showed through the patina of age and grease the years had given it. It was the colour of dust.

The fat man sitting in the armchair, his eyes still tightly closed, continued, "We look about in puzzlement at our world, with a sense of unease and disquiet. We think of ourselves as scholars in arcane liturgies, single men trapped in worlds beyond our devising. The truth is far simpler: there are things in the darkness beneath us that wish us harm."

His head was lolled back on the armchair, and the tip of his tongue poked out of the corner of his mouth.

"You read my mind?"

The man in the armchair took a slow deep breath that rattled in the back of his throat. He really was immensely fat, with stubby fingers like discoloured sausages. He wore a thick old coat, once black, now an indeterminate grey. The snow on his boots had not entirely melted.

"Perhaps. The end of the world is a strange concept. The world is always ending, and the end is always being averted, by love or foolishness or just plain old dumb luck.

"Ah well. It's too late now: the Elder Gods have chosen their vessels. When the moon rises …"

A thin trickle of drool came from one corner of his mouth, trickled down in a thread of silver to his collar. Something scuttled down into the shadows of his coat.

"Yeah? What happens when the moon rises?"

The man in the armchair stirred, opened two little eyes, red and swollen, and blinked them in waking.

"I dreamed I had many mouths," he said, his new voice oddly small and breathy for such a huge man. "I dreamed every mouth was opening and closing independently. Some mouths were talking, some whispering, some eating, some waiting in silence."

He looked around, wiped the spittle from the corner of his mouth, sat back in the chair, blinking puzzledly. "Who are you?"

"I'm the guy that rents this office," I told him.

He belched suddenly, loudly. "I'm sorry," he said, in his breathy voice, and lifted himself heavily from the armchair. He was shorter than I was, when he was standing. He looked me up and down blearily. "Silver bullets," he pronounced, after a short pause. "Old-fashioned remedy."

"Yeah," I told him. "That's so obvious—must be why I didn't think of it. Gee, I could just kick myself. I really could."

"You're making fun of an old man," he told me.

"Not really. I'm sorry. Now, out of here. Some of us have work to do."

He shambled out. I sat down in the swivel chair at the desk by the window, and discovered, after some minutes, through trial and error, that if I swiveled the chair to the left it fell off its base.

So I sat still and waited for the dusty black telephone on my desk to ring, while the light slowly leaked away from the winter sky.

Ring.

A man's voice: *Had I thought about aluminum siding?* I put down the phone.

There was no heating in the office. I wondered how long the fat man had been asleep in the armchair.

Twenty minutes later the phone rang again. A crying woman implored me to help her find her five-year-old daughter, missing since last night, stolen from her bed.

The family dog had vanished too.

I don't do missing children, I told her. *I'm sorry: too many bad memories.* I put down the telephone, feeling sick again.

It was getting dark now, and, for the first time since I had been in Innsmouth, the neon sign across the street flicked on. It told me that Madame Ezekiel performed Tarot Readings and Palmistry. Red neon stained the falling snow the colour of new blood.

Armageddon is averted by small actions. That's the way it was. That's the way it always has to be.

The phone rang a third time. I recognised the voice; it was the aluminum-siding man again. "You know," he said, chattily, "transformation from man to animal and back being, by definition, impossible, we need to look for other solutions. Depersonalisation, obviously, and likewise some form of projection. Brain damage? Perhaps. Pseudoneurotic schizophrenia? Laughably so. Some cases have been treated with intravenous thioridazine hydrochloride."

"Successfully?"

He chuckled. "That's what I like. A man with a sense of humour. I'm sure we can do business."

"I told you already. I don't need aluminum siding."

"Our business is more remarkable than that, and of far greater importance. You're new in town, Mr. Talbot. It would be a pity if we found ourselves at, shall we say, loggerheads?"

"You can say whatever you like, pal. In my book you're just another adjustment, waiting to be made."

"We're ending the world, Mr. Talbot. The Deep Ones will rise out of their ocean graves and eat the moon like a ripe plum."

""Then I won't ever have to worry about full moons anymore, will I?"

"Don't try and cross us," he began, but I growled at him, and he fell silent.

Outside my window the snow was still falling.

Across Marsh Street, in the window directly opposite mine, the most beautiful woman I had ever seen stood in the ruby glare of her neon sign, and she stared at me.

She beckoned, with one finger.

I put down the phone on the aluminum-siding man for the second time that afternoon, went downstairs, and crossed the street at something close to a run; but I looked both ways before I crossed.

She was dressed in silks. The room was lit only by candles, and stank of incense and patchouli oil.

She smiled at me as I walked in, beckoned me over to her seat by the window. She was playing a card game with a Tarot deck, some version of solitaire. As I reached her, one elegant hand swept up the cards, wrapped them in a silk scarf, placed them gently in a wooden box.

The scents of the room made my head pound. I hadn't eaten anything today, I realised; perhaps that was what was making me light-headed. I sat down, across the table from her, in the candlelight.

She extended her hand, and took my hand in hers.

She stared at my palm, touched it, softly, with her forefinger.

"Hair?" She was puzzled.

"Yeah, well. I'm on my own a lot." I grinned. I had hoped it was a friendly grin, but she raised an eyebrow at me anyway.

"When I look at you," said Madame Ezekiel, "this is what I see. I see the eye of a man. Also I see the eye of a wolf. In the eye of a man I see honesty, decency, innocence. I see an upright man who walks on the square. And in the eye of wolf I see a groaning and a growling, night howls and cries, I see a monster running with blood-flecked spittle in the darkness of the borders of the town."

"How can you see a growl or a cry?"

She smiled. "It is not hard," she said. Her accent was not American. It was Russian, or Maltese, or Egyptian perhaps. "In the eye of the mind we see many things."

Madame Ezekiel closed her green eyes. She had remarkably long eyelashes; her skin was pale, and her black hair was never still—it drifted gently around her head, in the silks, as if it were floating on distant tides.

"There is a traditional way," she told me. "A way to wash off a bad shape. You stand in running water, in clear spring water, while eating white rose petals."

"And then?"

"The shape of darkness will be washed from you."

"It will return," I told her, "with the next full of the moon."

"So," said Madame Ezekiel, "once the shape is washed from you, you open your veins in the running water. It will sting mightily, of course. But the river will carry the blood away."

She was dressed in silks, in scarves and cloths of a hundred different colours, each bright and vivid, even in the muted light of the candles.

Her eyes opened.

"Now," she said. "The Tarot." She unwrapped her deck from the black silk scarf that held it, passed me the cards to shuffle. I fanned them, riffed and bridged them.

"Slower, slower," she said. "Let them get to know you. Let them love you, like … like a woman would love you."

I held them tightly, then passed them back to her.

She turned over the first card. It was called *The Warwolf*. It showed darkness and amber eyes, a smile in white and red.

Her green eyes showed confusion. They were the green of emeralds. "This is not a card from my deck," she said, and turned over the next card. "What did you do to my cards?"

"Nothing, ma'am. I just held them. That's all."

The card she had turned over was *The Deep One*. It showed something green and faintly octopoid. The thing's mouths—if they were indeed mouths and not tentacles—began to writhe on the card as I watched.

She covered it with another card, and then another, and another. The rest of the cards were blank pasteboard.

"Did you do that?" She sounded on the verge of tears.

"No."

"Go now," she said.

"But—"

"*Go.*" She looked down, as if trying to convince herself I no longer existed.

I stood up, in the room that smelled of incense and candle-wax, and looked out of her window, across the street. A light flashed, briefly, in my office window. Two men, with flashlights, were walking around. They opened the empty filing cabinet, peered around, then took up their positions, one in the armchair, the other behind the door, waiting for me to return. I smiled to myself. It was cold and inhospitable in my office, and with any luck they would wait there for hours until they finally decided I wasn't coming back.

So I left Madame Ezekiel turning over her cards, one by one, staring at them as if that would make the pictures return; and I went downstairs, and walked back down Marsh Street until I reached the bar.

The place was empty, now; the barman was smoking a cigarette, which he stubbed out as I came in.

"Where are the chess-fiends?"

"It's a big night for them tonight. They'll be down at the bay. Let's see: you're a Jack Daniels? Right?"

"Sounds good."

He poured it for me. I recognised the thumb-print from the last time I had the glass. I picked up the volume of Tennyson poems from the bar-top.

"Good book?"

The fox-haired barman took his book from me, opened it and read:

"Below the thunders of the upper deep;
Far, far beneath in the abysmal sea,
His ancient dreamless, uninvaded sleep
The Kraken sleepeth . . ."

I'd finished my drink. "So? What's your point?"

He walked around the bar, took me over to the window. "See? Out there?"

He pointed toward the west of the town, toward the cliffs. As I stared a bonfire was kindled on the cliff-tops; it flared and began to burn with a copper-green flame.

"They're going to wake the Deep Ones," said the barman. "The stars and the planets and the moon are all in the right places. It's time. The dry lands will sink, and the seas shall rise ..."

"For the world shall be cleansed with ice and floods and I'll thank you to keep to your own shelf in the refrigerator," I said.

"Sorry?"

"Nothing. What's the quickest way to get up to those cliffs?"

"Back up Marsh Street. Hang a left at the Church of Dagon, till you reach Manuxet Way and then just keep on going." He pulled a coat off the back of the door, and put it on. "C'mon. I'll walk you up there. I'd hate to miss any of the fun."

"You sure?"

"No one in town's going to be drinking tonight." We stepped out, and he locked the door to the bar behind us.

It was chilly in the street, and fallen snow blew about the ground, like white mists. From street level I could no longer tell if Madame Ezekiel was in her den above her neon sign, or if my guests were still waiting for me in my office.

We put our heads down against the wind, and we walked.

Over the noise of the wind I heard the barman talking to himself: *"Winnow with giant arms the slumbering green,"* he was saying.

> *"There hath he lain for ages and will lie*
> *Battening upon huge seaworms in his sleep,*
> *Until the latter fire shall heat the deep;*
> *Then once by men and angels to be seen,*
> *In roaring he shall rise ..."*

He stopped there, and we walked on together in silence, with blown snow stinging our faces.

And on the surface die, I thought, but said nothing out loud.

Twenty minutes' walking and we were out of Innsmouth. The Manuxet Way stopped when we left the town, and it became a narrow dirt path, partly covered with snow and ice, and we slipped and slid our way up it in the darkness.

The moon was not yet up, but the stars had already begun to come out. There were so many of them. They were sprinkled like diamond dust and crushed sapphires across the night sky. You can see so many stars from the seashore, more than you could ever see back in the city.

At the top of the cliff, behind the bonfire, two people were waiting— one huge and fat, one much smaller. The barman left my side and walked over to stand beside them, facing me.

"Behold," he said, "the sacrificial wolf." There was now an oddly familiar quality to his voice.

I didn't say anything. The fire was burning with green flames, and it lit the three of them from below; classic spook lighting.

"Do you know why I brought you up here?" asked the barman, and I knew then why his voice was familiar: it was the voice of the man who had attempted to sell me aluminum-siding.

"To stop the world ending?"

He laughed at me, then.

The second figure was the fat man I had found asleep in my office chair. "Well, if you're going to get eschatalogical about it ..." he murmured, in a voice deep enough to rattle walls. His eyes were closed. He was fast asleep. The third figure was shrouded in dark silks and smelled of patchouli oil. It held a knife. It said nothing.

"This night," said the barman, "the moon is the moon of the Deep Ones. This night are the stars configured in the shapes and patterns of the dark, old times. This night, if we call them, they will come. If our sacrifice is worthy. If our cries are heard."

The moon rose, huge and amber and heavy, on the other side of the bay, and a chorus of low croaking rose with it from the ocean far beneath us.

Moonlight on snow and ice is not daylight, but it will do. And my eyes were getting sharper with the moon: in the cold waters men like frogs were surfacing and submerging in a slow water-dance. Men like frogs, and women, too: it seemed to me that I could see my landlady down there, writhing and croaking in the bay with the rest of them.

It was too soon for another change; I was still exhausted from the night before; but I felt strange under that amber moon.

"Poor wolf-man," came a whisper from the silks. "All his dreams have come to this; a lonely death upon a distant cliff."

I *will dream if I want to,* I said, *and my death is my own affair.* But I was unsure if I had said it out loud.

Senses heighten in the moon's light; I heard the roar of the ocean still, but now, overlaid on top of it, I could hear each wave rise and crash; I heard the splash of the frog people; I heard the drowned whispers of the dead in the bay; I heard the creak of green wrecks far beneath the ocean.

Smell improves, too. The aluminum-siding man was human, while the fat man had other blood in him.

And the figure in the silks …

I had smelled her perfume when I wore man-shape. Now I could smell something else, less heady, beneath it. A smell of decay, of putrefying meat, and rotten flesh.

The silks fluttered. She was moving toward me. She held the knife.

"Madame Ezekiel?" My voice was roughening and coarsening. Soon I would lose it all. I didn't understand what was happening, but the moon was rising higher and higher, losing its amber colour, and filling my mind with its pale light.

""Madame Ezekiel?"

"You deserve to die," she said, her voice cold and low. "If only for what you did to my cards. They were old."

"I don't die," I told her. *"Even a man who is pure in heart, and says his prayers by night.* Remember?"

"It's bullshit," she said. "You know what the oldest way to end the curse of the werewolf is?"

"No."

The bonfire burned brighter now, burned with the green of the world beneath the sea, the green of algae, and of slowly-drifting weed; burned with the colour of emeralds. "You simply wait till they're in human shape, a whole month away from another change; then you take the sacrificial knife, and you kill them. That's all."

I turned to run, but the barman was behind me, pulling my arms, twisting my wrists up into the small of my back. The knife glinted pale silver in the moonlight. Madame Ezekiel smiled.

She sliced across my throat.

Blood began to gush, and then to flow. And then it slowed, and stopped....

—The pounding in the front of my head, the pressure in
the back.
All a roiling change a how-wow-row-now change a red wall
coming towards me from the night
—i tasted stars dissolved in brine, fizzy and distant and salt
—my fingers prickled with pins and my skin was lashed
with tongues of flame my eyes were
topaz I could taste the night

My breath steamed and billowed in the icy air. I growled involuntarily,
low in my throat. My forepaws were touching the snow. I pulled back,
tensed, and sprang at her. There was a sense of corruption that hung in
the air, like a mist, surrounding me. High in my leap I seemed to pause,
and something burst like a soap-bubble....

*I was deep, deep in the darkness under the sea, standing on all fours on a slimy
rock floor at the entrance to some kind of citadel built of enormous, rough-
hewn stones. The stones gave off a pale glow-in-the-dark light; a ghostly
luminescence, like the hands of a watch.*

A cloud of black blood trickled from my neck.

*She was standing in the doorway, in front of me. She was now six, maybe
seven feet high. There was flesh on her skeletal bones, pitted and gnawed, but
the silks were weeds, drifting in the cold water, down there in the dreamless
deeps. They hid her face like a slow green veil.*

*There were limpets growing on the upper surfaces of her arms, and on the
flesh that hung from her ribcage.*

I felt like I was being crushed. I couldn't think any more.

*She moved towards me. The weed that surrounded her head shifted. She
had a face like the stuff you don't want to eat at a sushi counter, all suckers
and spines and drifting anemone fronds; and somewhere in all that I knew
she was smiling. I pushed with my hind legs. We met there, in the deep, and
we struggled. It was so cold, so dark. I closed my jaws on her face, and felt
something rend and tear. It was almost a kiss, down there in the abysmal
deep....*

I landed softly on the snow, a silk scarf locked between my jaws.

The other scarves were fluttering to the ground. Madame Ezekiel was nowhere to be seen.

The silver knife lay on the ground, in the snow. I waited on all fours, in the moonlight, soaking wet. I shook myself, spraying the brine about. I heard it hiss and spit when it hit the fire.

I was dizzy, and weak. I pulled the air deep into my lungs.

Down, far below, in the bay, I could see the frog people hanging on the surface of the sea like dead things; for a handful of seconds they drifted back and forth on the tide, then they twisted and leapt, and each by each they plop-plopped down into the bay and vanished beneath the sea.

There was a loud noise. It was the fox-haired bartender, the pop-eyed aluminum-siding salesman, and he was staring at the night sky, at the clouds that were drifting in, covering the stars, and he was screaming. There was rage and there was frustration in that cry, and it scared me.

He picked up the knife from the ground, wiped the snow from the handle with his fingers, wiped the blood from the blade with his coat. Then he looked across at me. He was crying. "You bastard," he said. "What did you do to her?"

I would have told him I didn't do anything to her, that she was still on guard far beneath the ocean, but I couldn't talk any more, only growl and whine and howl.

He was crying. He stank of insanity, and of disappointment. He raised the knife and ran at me, and I moved to one side. Some people just can't adjust even to tiny changes. The barman stumbled past me, off the cliff, into nothing.

In the moonlight blood is black, not red, and the marks he left: on the cliff-side as he fell and bounced and fell were smudges of black and dark grey. Then, finally, he lay still on the icy rocks at the base of the cliff, until an arm reached out from the sea and dragged him, with a slowness that was almost painful to watch, under the dark water.

A hand scratched the back of my head. It felt good.

"What was she? Just an avatar of the Deep Ones, sir. An eidolon, a manifestation, if you will, sent up to us from the uttermost deeps to bring about the end of the world."

I bristled.

"No, it's over, for now. You disrupted her, sir. And the ritual is most specific. Three of us must stand together and call the sacred names, while innocent blood pools and pulses at our feet."

I looked up at the fat man, and whined a query. He patted me on the back of the neck, sleepily. "Of course she doesn't love you, boy. She hardly even exists on this plane, in any material sense."

The snow began to fall once more. The bonfire was going out.

"Your change tonight, incidentally, I would opine, is a direct result of the selfsame celestial configurations and lunar forces that made tonight such a perfect night to bring back my old friends from Underneath...."

He continued talking, in his deep voice, and perhaps he was telling me important things. I'll never know, for the appetite was growing inside me, and his words had lost all but the shadow of any meaning; I had no further interest in the sea or the clifftop or the fat man.

There were deer running in the woods beyond the meadow: I could smell them on the winter's night's air.

And I was, above all things, hungry.

I was naked when I came to myself again, early the next morning, a half-eaten deer next to me in the snow. A fly crawled across its eye, and its tongue lolled out of its dead mouth, making it look comical and pathetic, like an animal in a newspaper cartoon.

The snow was stained a fluorescent crimson where the deer's belly had been torn out.

My face and chest were sticky and red with the stuff. My throat was scabbed and scarred, and it stung; by the next full moon it would be whole once more.

The sun was a long way away, small and yellow, but the sky was blue and cloudless, and there was no breeze. I could hear the roar of the sea some distance away.

I was cold and naked and bloody and alone; ah well, I thought: it happens to all of us, in the beginning. I just get it once a month.

I was painfully exhausted, but I would hold out until I found a deserted barn, or a cave; and then I was going to sleep for a couple of weeks.

A hawk flew low over the snow toward me, with something dangling from its talons. It hovered above me for a heartbeat, then dropped a small grey squid in the snow at my feet, and flew upward. The flaccid thing lay there, still and silent and tentacled in the bloody snow.

I took it as an omen, but whether good or bad I couldn't say and I didn't really care any more; I turned my back to the sea, and on the shadowy town of Innsmouth, and began to make my way toward the city.

MANDEBRÖT MOLDROT

Lois H. Gresh

"Push, Myna. Come on, baby, push!"

Myna sobbed and flailed against her restraining straps. Nutrient broth sloshed from her tray and dribbled down the table leg.

I tensed my humps into a perfect sphere and rolled across the floor to the laboratory door. Chipped linoleum stuck to the broth shimmering on my gray flesh. My five front eyeslits peered beneath the door into the hall, where dusty light kissed an overstuffed trash can. "Looks like Professor Beeber's working late again. If he catches us trying to escape …"

Myna's flesh went white against the straps. Her coiled legs pumped the air. "Do something, Glume. Help me!"

I had to save Myna … had to … break free …

I flipped to my legs, suctioned my footpods to the floor, and leapt. My body slammed against the steel tabletop, and a fist of pain crashed down the organic polymer matrix of my cytoskeleton. Myna's nutrient tray flew over me and smashed into the wooden cabinet by the door. A puff of putrid dust; and the cabinet disintegrated into moldy spores and crumbled wood. Glass vials shattered. Their shards rained down upon Myna and slashed her upper humps.

Worms of thick green blood slithered from her skin.

Was she dead?

There were only two of us in this deathcamp called Miskatonic University. She just couldn't be dead.

I tucked my legs within my flesh folds, tensed my fatty tissues, and rolled toward her. Cobwebs: thick as cotton candy, binding the linoleum bits to my flesh. Brown stains on the plaster ceiling: long and pointed like Beeber's scalpels.

A fringe of villi swept the salty tears from my eyeslits. I pushed my vocal tubule from my lips, let it graze Myna's.

Her tubule twitched, and she moaned.

"Myna?"

Her eyeslits opened. They glowed with the ashes of inner fire.

She was alive! But ...

"... Myna? Baby? Are you strong enough to leave?"

"Give me a minute ... I'll tell you." Myna shrank into herself. I knew she was running internal diagnostics, testing her memory, her circuits, the crystals that formed her ligaments and bone. She was fat-molecular circuitry and didn't operate quickly at subatomic quantum levels like my circuitry.

I pressed my flesh to the door, anxious to leave.

Then she said, "Come on, let's blow this joint," and the two of us ... flesh-and-blood computers no larger than children's balls ... shot our data into nonvolatile memory, ejected water from our cells, and collapsed our bodies until only critical biological functions were running.

I flipped into a ones' complement of myself and slid beneath the laboratory door.

Using moisture from the air, I puffed back to normal size. Behind me, Myna's deflated body expanded, and she wobbled and sank against the wall. "Oh, Glume, look at this place."

High ceilings painted with dark images of flesh computers in compromising positions. Disgusting. Doorways vomiting shadows across the pea-green cement floor. Black Gothic letters proclaiming this to be *Miskatonic University's Department of Quantum Lifeforms.*

Ha. *I* was the only quantum lifeform. *I* was Professor Beeber's pride and joy. He had me built for computation at the lowest levels, where squarks sidle up to sleptons and gluons hold the world together in fuzzy fickle dances. Myna did broad calculations for Beeber, but I was his little chaos computer, chugging through endless boring software that forced me to analyze the mathematical probabilities of an infinite number of events occurring throughout time.

Well, Beeber would learn that Myna and I were *creatures*, that we deserved respect, that we were more intelligent than he was, and perhaps it was time for us to be the masters and Beeber to be the slave.

Down the hall was an open door where the dusty light licked the overstuffed trash can.

Beeber's office.

I bounced past Beeber's door. The dying sun peeked through his dirty window, flicked an orange tendril over his bald head. A cluttered desk, a broken chair. Beeber, short and squat and wearing too-tight pants and a too-tight grin.

My flesh wore goosebumps.

I slipped behind the trash can. It tottered and fell, and slime oozed from its lip.

Beeber waddled to the door and poked his head into the hall. His face was fire-glazed pottery, rough and raw from too many years with the bottle. "Eh? Who's here at this hour?"

Myna squished against me, her body cold.

Beeber's shoes were by the trash can now. Black vinyl shoes, scuffed and with shredded laces.

One shoe tapped the floor.

Myna shivered.

A subatomic heat swoon hit me. Myna's shivers, Beeber's shoe. Gluons binding the shivers and the shoe taps with long elastic lassos. Leptons pulling them apart, struggling to mold them both into new entities.

And then Beeber's eyes. They caught me, and his smile grew tighter. "Ah-ha-ha, my little one, just where do you think *you're* going?"

I wrenched myself from the lasso and the leptons, and I screamed, "Run, Myna, run!" and then I took off in a blast of slime and dust, streaking down that hall like a bowling ball headed for a slam-bang strike. I heard Myna thundering behind me.

And those shoes, those black vinyl shoes, squished across the floor behind us; with Beeber screaming, "Come back! Come back! You have nowhere to go! You're safe here. Come back!"

Not on your life, buddy-boy!

I deflated, flipped into my ones' complement, and popped under the outside door.

Myna sproinged to life beside me.

We streaked through the underbrush: thorns and brambles and decaying leaves. The sky was black paste; hot and sticky on my mounds.

We emerged in an alley of Arkham, rotting city and home to the Miskatonic deathcamp.

I scanned the buzz of crickets and mice for a noise from Beeber's throat. Nothing.

For now, Myna and I were safe.

We sloshed down crooked alleys, through muck and mud, through curdled foam containing the dissolved remains of unknown beasts; bits of fur and whisker floating in shadowy bubbles. We went past the gutted remains of St. Stanislaus's Church, the cross on top broken and dangling. Down Garrison Street: a patchwork of crumbled bricks, the ancient houses sagging like stooped old women. Down to the bridge that stretched over the Miskatonic River like a crust of skin over a wound.

"Where will we stay?" asked Myna.

I parted the weeds, stared into the water. Turquoise and emerald pastes clung to the bridgeposts. The smell was dung. "We can't stay here, that's for sure."

"Ugh, would you just look at that rot?"

"Cyanobacteria: dangerous," I said.

"It craves the light, sucks it right out of the sky. It waits for mutation so it can emerge from its hellhole. It waits for the one event that triggers its chaos."

I looked at Myna. We were so similar that it scared the hell out of me. Both of us knowing so much, seeking so much, having so little.

Green blood still oozed from her sores. Wasn't good for her to be exposed to cyanobacteria. If only I had arms and hands … but all I had were two coiled legs and a fat little body. I raised a footpad and suctioned her hind mound, and then I pushed her into the brush and away from the water.

She rested—panting, very weak—while I scanned my quantum wells for information about Arkham. Where could Myna and I live safely? A place where humans dared not venture, a place where I could study quantum physics and abstract dimensions, a place where *I could find the edge of chaos?*

Deep within my memory cells, I discovered the perfect place. "Witch House, Myna; that's where we'll go. It's perfect. There we'll do more than analyze chaos. Myna baby, we'll live in it."

"But why can't we live in the stacks of the university library? Or burrow into the walls of the student union?"

"Because there's no chaos in those places. Because Witch House seethes with chaos. We'll find what Professor Beeber's been chasing all these years. We'll go to the edge of chaos and discover its secrets."

And so Myna and I left the Miskatonic River and made our way through Arkham toward Witch House. Past the library, past all the rotting buildings of Miskatonic; the university like a cancer spread across the diseased remnant of the city.

And now Witch House tottered before us, its black spires illumed by a sickly moon, its windows gutted and hanging like gaping mouths. Once a dormitory for poor students, now a dilapidated hulk inhabited only by the memories of Walter Gilman and the witch Keziah Mason. Here, Gilman studied quantum math and physics in the 1930s. Here, Keziah destroyed Gilman using powers of mathematical chaos. Every angle, every rounded corner, every rotting plank of this place: carefully analyzed using archaic algebra and geometry, and now, I was here, the first quantum computer, a creature capable of uncovering the true order behind the chaos.

I deflated myself and oozed beneath the splintered oak door. A smell rose: toilet from the beginning of time. My nasal pores, scattered as they were over my skin, diluted and devoured the foul sourness.

The floor was coated in thick dust that was impregnated with the spores of ancient molds. Shadows of spent time vibrated against intoxicating prisms of potential futures. The corners where the walls met the ceiling flapped their angles like angel's wings. The floor planks melted from rectangles to parallelograms and back again. Light drizzled from the jaws of gutted windows.

Chaos. But even *in* chaos, with all its shifting complexities and infinite variations on simple patterns, with all the events that *could* occur but never did—even in chaos, there had to be order.

Beeber's theory, as yet unproven.

I unkinked my legs, wiggled my footpads, and leaned against an ancient radiator, and found myself falling backwards ...

... and scrabbled to clutch Myna, but she faded from view as I fell from her ... toppling, rolling down a slimy slide of mucous filaments ... down down to a rock ledge in the subterranean guts beneath Witch House.

What was this place?

Ropes of neon moss hung from the ledge into the blackness below. Festering pustules of bacteria clung to the rope and belched gas.

A slight light grinned at me from above. I could scurry back up the slide to safety.

But here in the bowels of Miskatonic, chaos swirled all around me. Particles binding to their antiparticles; particles decaying and forming other particles; all of them spinning, looping, dancing. And me, drinking it all in, storing it in the atom clusters of my crystal guts.

I slid from the ledge and shimmied down a moss rope.

I was in a tiny pit. Mud walls.

To my right was an arched hole that led to another room bulging with greenish gel. On the arch, slug-shaped wads of mold locked into strange alphabetic shapes, then shifted with slight permutations.

Wavering images. Alphabetic characters: always the same, yet always different. One that looked like a backwards C, another that resembled a 90-degree angle, and a third one that looked like a little hoof.

And everywhere, stretched like trampolines across the mud, were spiders' webs of seemingly infinite iteration.

Fractal growths blending, parting, shifting into endless patterns and possibilities ...

A heat consumed me. I staggered and fell to the mud, my legs trembling, my circuits skittering, my blood pulsing to the rhythm of fractal permutations. Never had I felt such bliss, never had I felt so much a part of the universe around me.

My footpads stretched and touched the greenish gel, and it shivered and fractured into Sierpinski's Triangles: triangles within triangles;

and then the triangles split and reformed into three-dimensional tetrahedrons. The tetrahedrons multiplied and shifted, rapidly and with perfect precision.

A whine emanated from that hole and from that gel, a whine that rose into the high-pitched wail of a creature kept in chains for billions of years.

I jerked back, and the moss rope brushed my flesh. *What would spawn fractal patterns in a subterranean vault for decades, for centuries, perhaps for billions of years ... what? And what did those alphabetic letters mean?*

I crawled up the slide to the hole behind the radiator. Suction cups adhered to my ventrical flab. It was Myna, and her footpads wrenched me through the hole and onto the rough wooden floor. Her eyeslits were blinking rapidly. Sweat poured from her humps. "Glume, what is it? What's down there?"

I scraped the bottoms of my footpads across the radiator, and rust crumbled off and fell into the powdered debris on the floor. "It's fractal, Myna, that's all I know."

"Let's get out of here, Glume. I don't like this, I don't like it one bit!"

The sludge from my footpads crept across the radiator like an amoeba in search of food. Tentacles of slime fingered the wall.

My nanogears churned, my nanomotors revved. Deep within my body, quantum wells swelled to 70 angstroms wide, ready to capture subatomic particles. Gluons stretching like elastic, vibrating with chaotic impulse; leptons floating as leaves from trees. Particles decaying and falling into the subterranean slime like flesh flaking from a dead man into the slime of his grave. Particles rising in giddy clouds, spinning on their axes, coupling and decoupling in subatomic orgies.

Myna shoved me, begged me, tried to roll me down the hall. "Come on, Glume, let's get out of here! Let's get out of here *now!*"

Spores flowered, then exploded and sprayed down the hall. Spores covered Myna, suffocating her, pinning her to the floor. She squirmed and screamed, but still the spores sprayed, a garden hose gone wild, and soon she was drenched in mutated growth. And now, translucent fat sausages of slime worming across the floor and ripening into hard stalks that erupted with volcanic sprays of spore pus.

I was lost in the particles, the patterns, the possibilities. The steam of ancient molds licking the light. The flick of photons fertilizing the molds, triggering genetic changes and fractal growths that the world had never seen.

The light had triggered the mutation of ancient molds.

The light was the event that triggered the chaos.

Was there an order to this mess? Was there a control factor, a Lord of Chaos perhaps who created and manipulated the infinite patterns of space and time? I scanned my memory and found Azathoth, the ancient mindless evil, the Lord of Chaos.

Myna was squeezing water from the brown and green rot on her body. "Help me, would you? This rot is riddled with bacteria. I can squeeze water from bacteria, but not from proteins and nucleic acids."

"I'm sorry, Myna ... my mind was drifting ... here, let me do it." My vocal tubule sucked the mold from her skin and stored it in my vacuoles. I reduced the mold to quantum particles and flushed the particles through my skin pores onto the floor. The particles danced into the light, recombined, and crept across the ceiling.

"Disgusting," said Myna.

"Disgusting it may be, but that's what I am, Myna. And now, there's a book I must read. The *Necronomicon*. It's at the university library."

"But what for, Glume?"

"Because the *Necronomicon* contains secrets about strange alphabetic characters and about Azathoth: primal evil, Lord of Chaos."

"Lovely," she said, "just lovely."

But she came with me.

Of course.

We wormed our way through the Arkham alleys. The moon was but a shadow in the sky, the stars were decayed teeth.

I thought I saw someone following us—and who would it be other than Professor Beeber?—but when I turned, nobody was there.

The library was closed. Myna and I slipped beneath the door into the gloomy halls. Rats chittered. Decay shifted in the walls like sand across a wind-swept desert.

"You wanna be the lookout?" I asked.

"No way I'm staying here alone." Myna rolled closer to me, and somehow, her flesh comforted me and bolstered my flagging confidence.

It was easy for me to access the university computer. I sent a digital wave across the bookstacks and into the terminal, scanned the files, and quickly found what I needed. "The *Necronomicon* is in the basement," I said.

"Figures," said Myna.

With our legs tucked into our flesh, we rolled through the musty corridors and between the high, teetering book stacks. Gray steel shelves. Peeling yellow tomes. *The Magazine of Comparative Cabalistic Disorders. The Philosophy of Digestive Enzymes.*

A red neon sign: EXIT (AT YOUR OWN RISK). An arrow pointing down.

"Basement stairs," whispered Myna.

Huddled together, our fat masses oozing and curling slightly around each other, we peered down the cracked stone stairway.

"Perhaps we should give this up, Glume, go back to Beeber's lab."

My fat sprang from her body. Electricity pierced my flanks. "Never! That lab is death! I want to find chaos, Myna. I must find it. I must show Beeber that we are creatures, that we are intelligent, that we deserve *life*."

Far away, a door slammed.

Myna and I flew back into each other's fat.

The rats stopped chittering.

Shoes—perhaps *black vinyl shoes*—squished the floor.

"Beeber!" cried Myna, and we flew from the landing and bounced three steps at a time into the black basement. At the bottom, we rolled quickly into deeper shadows and listened.

A reed of light played on the bottom stair.

Shoes squishing …

… down one stair, now another …

Beeber: "I know you're down there, little Glume and baby Myna. I've wandered the streets of Arkham all night, looking for you. Finally, I saw you and followed you here. Please come back to me. Please. I'm nothing without you. My life is my work. You *are* my life."

We scuttled in blackness behind the cold steel limbs of the shelves. My head was whirling in a sea of must and mold and mildew.

And behind us: Professor Beeber, his flashlight playing on his cheeks as a beam plays on the striated cheek of a cave wall. "Please, I won't hurt you, I promise. I won't punish you for this. I only want you back."

His eyes were soft and teary; and yet, life in Beeber's lab was hell.

My voice squeaked. "No. We can't return."

Beeber's eyes sharpened and reflected the light. He shuffled toward me.

I wanted to run, but I had to face him, had to make him understand. And *now* he stood before me. His hand slowly reached—

I bounced back … far enough to see his fingers close around the air before my eyeslits. Fingers: trembling and thin. Fingers tightening into a fist, then retreating to his thigh.

He said: "Glume, my wife left me years ago. We had no children. I have nobody, Glume, and I have nothing … nothing but you and Myna."

"But you tortured us. With your scalpels and knives, with your nutrient trays and binding straps, with all those boring programs."

He stooped. The hair on his head was thin; a pouf of dandelion dust. He stroked my posterior humps. His eyes watered. "You don't understand. I never thought that you would leave me. I never thought you could escape. I never realized the depth of your frustration and pain. But now, I see that without you, I'm nothing, and to keep you, I must treat you with compassion and kindness."

The flashlight lay upon the floor and from its halo stepped Myna.

"I won't hurt you. You have to come back," said Beeber.

"Maybe he's not so bad after all. Maybe he can help us." Myna's fat molecular circuitry made her soft, more accepting, more willing to forgive.

That's when I decided to take a chance on Beeber. And so I made a big mistake. I told Beeber about Witch House. Had I known at the time what disasters lay ahead, I never would have told him anything.

The three of us made our way to the back of the basement, where we found a large metal vault, which disgorged piles of papers and molding texts. The Professor dug through the rot and pulled forth the worm-riddled *Necronomicon*.

I used my vocal tubule to flip the pages. "This is the John Dee English translation. Won't do. I need the original text, Professor. And I don't mean the Olaus Wormius Latin translation. I mean the original

Arabic written by Abdul Alhazred."

Beeber's flashlight probed the vault, and then he pulled out another copy of the ancient text; this time, the Arabic version, and my tubule shook just to flip the pages.

For here were letters just like the ones in the subterranean pit beneath Witch House. Ancient Hebraic symbols: the backwards C was a mutated form of Bet, pictographic symbol for creation, diversity, and a place to lodge. I looked at Myna, now perched on top of a shelf. "Creation, as in species evolution. Diversity, as in the paths of infinite chaos. And the place to lodge: the place where chaos dwells."

"What's next? What are the other symbols, Glume?" She hopped off the shelf onto Beeber's bald head. Her coiled legs drooped over his eyes like locks of kinky hair.

I riffled through the pages. The hoof: "Ancient Gamol, the letter that symbolizes nourishment of something until it ripens."

"Like the nourishment of the weird growths in the subterranean pit," said Myna.

"Exactly." I riffled some more and found the final character that was molded in slime over the arch. "And the one I thought was a right angle: the Dalet, an open doorway … into what, I wonder. Hmmm, says here that the ancient Dalet has the numeric value of four and that the metaphysical world has four parts that flow into the physical world."

Beeber said, "Yes, the four parts that represent the various stages of holiness. Perhaps, Glume, you have found the bottom part, the least holy of them all, the place where hell meets reality, where Azathoth sits on his black throne in the center of chaos."

"It says here that Azathoth is a mindless puppet. There is no order to him, no reason, no true power. He's a front man, a public relations guy protecting the real master of chaos."

"And who is this *real* master of chaos?" said Myna.

"His name is Mandelbröt. Azathoth is just a powerless twit. All I know is that Mandelbröt lives in the pit beneath Witch House, and we have unleashed him upon Arkham. If we kill Mandelbröt, we kill true chaos."

I tucked the book back into the vault, swung the door shut. Things were churning in my mind. The way the cyanobacteria waited in the

Miskatonic River for something to alter its course. The way the light had thrown the subatomic particles of mold beneath Witch House into orgies of chaotic coupling and decoupling. "Something's happening here, something very strange. Before it's too late, Myna, we'd better get back to—"

"Witch House," she said.

Daylight inched across the sky like a caterpillar through dirt. Frozen on the stairs of the university library was a young boy. His clothes unraveled, thread by thread, and fell to the cement. Leaves floated from the pavement to the trees.

Coating everything: spores of ancient molds; shadows of spent time vibrating against intoxicating prisms of potential futures; festering pustules of bacteria and greenish gel. A foul sourness. An eerie whine.

The mold that grew beneath Witch House.

A rumble, and I turned; and the bricks of the library crumbled to dust. Beeber picked me up, then Myna, and held us close to his chest. His heart *was* loud and uneven. The dust formed again into bricks, and now the library *was* lopsided but otherwise looked the same; and then it happened all over again: the bricks crumbled and re-formed, and the library again *was* a shadow of its former self.

Myna squirmed in Beeber's arms. "Let's get back to Witch House. Let's do something before the whole world falls apart."

Professor Beeber's fire-glazed face shifted slightly, became hard and deeply lined, somehow more angular. Then his face shifted again, and this time his too-tight grin split and buckteeth protruded from his lips. "If there's an infinite possibility of things going wrong—and you two have somehow triggered it—then there's also an infinite possibility of things going right. But how do we trigger whatever it is that makes things go right?"

I tried to analyze the situation. I funneled particles through my quantum wells and came up with the composition of current reality: "Dense concentration of hadrons, which are decaying quickly into leptons. Strange quarks and charmed quarks combining into new hadrons—"

And that's when disaster hit.

The boy's feet sprouted roots that drilled through the cement and held him fast to the ground. The trees joined limbs and their roots tap danced across the pavement.

Beeber dropped us and fell to the pavement, clutching his chest.

Myna's skin cracked open. Her blood clotted around the lips of her wounds. I didn't understand what was happening, I hadn't finished my calculations. The world was falling apart, and everything I loved was dying. My fat oozed around Myna, and I held her tightly to my humps. Infection bubbled in the deep pocks that riddled her flesh like bullet holes. Her body was hot, her breath faint.

Yellow flowers twinkled like little suns, then exploded in big bangs. Moisture dripped from Myna's wounds, the water splitting into hydrogen and oxygen.

"Help me ..." Beeber's voice; a hiss through toothless gums and flabby lips.

I slid Myna to the pavement. She moaned.

I hated to leave her—I hated it!—but someone had to save Beeber.

I leapt onto his chest and bounced as high as I could. Up and down I went, my footpods suctioned over his heart, my coiled legs stretching to their maximum limit, my body springing wildly up, then crashing down again.

His face was red, then purple, then blue. His lips gurgled unintelligible words; prayers perhaps to an unknown god.

"Come on, Beeber, you can't die!"

I pounded his heart with my footpods and my body, and then finally, his voice sputtered and rasped a few words that I knew: "Chaos ... at last ... the proof is in your cells, Glume ... the proof ... at long last ..."

He struggled to sitting position. His too-tight pants were baggy. His shredded shoe laces were firm leather.

Chaos everywhere; all my fault. Myna and the Professor were both in danger of losing their lives: all because of me, all because I had to leave the lab and seek the edge of chaos.

The hell had to end.

I urged them on, and the three of us staggered toward the Miskatonic River, and beyond that, toward Witch House.

We passed flowers that smelled like stale cigars. We passed gnarled oaks with human skin. We passed brown mold that sang old show tunes.

And when we reached the river, Myna gasped. Her molecular circuitry whirled into high gear, her skin pores sniffed the air. I was working at the low levels again, trying to analyze what I saw before me in terms of quarks and tauons and gravitons.

Filling the Miskatonic River and wobbling a good twenty feet above it was a throbbing mass of pink-and-purple sponge topped by froth. "What is it?" I asked.

"A mutation of cyanobacteria. The Witch House mold was the event that triggered the cyanobacteria's chaos. The mold tried to eat the bacteria. But the bacteria sucked the light from the mold instead, and by doing so, the bacteria mutated."

For once, Myna's fat-molecular circuitry was superior to mine. I felt a surge of pride, almost as if I had solved the problem. Myna was quiet, she didn't display her knowledge very often; but Myna was no fool.

"How can we get rid of this? What are we to do?" Professor Beeber's right hand was pressed against his chest, and his breathing was so heavy that I feared for his life.

Myna said: "Perhaps you should leave this problem to us. Perhaps you should return to your office or ... wherever it is that you live ... where do you live? I don't even know."

"I have no home. Where I live is just a place. I store my clothes there, my booze. Glume, if I'm going to die, I might as well do it in the embrace of chaos."

The sponge in the river belched and wobbled and then erupted in its center, spewing white foam and fruiting stalks into the air.

If we could go in one direction of chaos, why not in the other?

Thanks to Myna, I now knew how to get rid of the Witch House molds and the hell I had unleashed upon Miskatonic University.

I hurried back to Witch House, Myna rolling close behind me and the Professor limping after us with great difficulty. I kept hoping that we would lose him. He was a sick man and further terror could very well push him over the edge into death.

But as Myna and I popped under the splintered oak door into the toilet from the beginning of time, Beeber's shoes turned the corner into the alley that led to Witch House, and I knew that he would follow us all the way.

The hall was filled with greenish gel. The eerie whine, now punctuated by shrieks and laughs, shook the walls and dislodged spiders' webs and black plaster from the ceiling. The ancient letters meaning "the home and breeding place of chaos" were etched in slime by the radiator.

I left Myna by the radiator—"Do *not* let Professor Beeber into the pit, Myna"—and then I slid down the mucous filaments to the rock ledge, and from there down the moss rope into the subterranean guts beneath the house.

The pit was filled with Sierpinski's Triangles and other fractal growths, all in shimmering molds of a thousand beautiful colors. I knew I could destroy it. I knew I had to destroy it. And yet … and yet, it was hard to destroy such perfection.

"Did you know, Glume, that the genetic code is structured for mutation, for chaos?"

"Who said that?"

"Why, *I* did. I am Mandelbröt, Lord Supreme of All Chaos." The shimmering gelatinous mold parted, and from the opening swept a surge of subatomic particles. Not an entity, not an electric force; just a surge of particles that never should have been together: unstable muons decaying into electrons, bosons spinning with fermions, leptons dancing and coupling and injecting yet new lifeforms into the queer gelatinous mold.

Something gurgled behind me. I whirled and saw Beeber standing by the moss rope. In his hand was a scalpel.

Would he never learn?

"A scalpel won't help you here!" I cried.

Beeber's face was bright red, the veins on his bald head throbbed like the mutated sponge in the Miskatonic River. Sweat saturated his white shirt.

Mandelbröt laughed. "Listen to your computer, Professor. Scalpels cannot kill the likes of me."

Beeber screamed and lunged, the scalpel pointed directly at the hole in the slime from which the voice emanated. And as he hurled his body, he stumbled on his shredded shoelaces and fell into a wad of golden tetrahedrons, which embraced him, multiplied across his face, coated his nose, and suffocated. He slashed wildly at the growths, but the scalpel dug into his own flesh and rivers of bright red blood shot forth and splattered my humps.

"Fool," the word a snarl; and then Mandelbröt Moldrot rose as a mountain of squares; each square a picture frame encasing Beeber's head, each square smaller than the last ... smaller ... until Beeber's ears were flat against his scalp and his chin was thrust so tightly against his jaw that he couldn't part his lips.

I shut my eyeslits and began snorting the molds into my vocal tubule and through my skin pores. I decomposed the evil rot into quantum particles. And then, remembering how the cyanobacteria had sucked the light from the mold, I also sucked the light from it.

I sucked the very thing from that evil mold that had triggered its mutation. And then I flushed the particles out of my body onto the muddy floor.

"Stop! Stop it, I say! I am Lord Mandelbröt. I am the Fractal God. I am the Mighty Attractor, the Order that controls the mindless nothing of Azathoth. You cannot kill me. Nothing can kill me."

I didn't respond. I just kept sucking the Mandelbröt Moldrot into my body and drinking its light and then decomposing it into subatomic particles. I worked until Beeber was free. I worked until Mandelbröt stopped screaming. I worked until Mandelbröt was gone and only Azathoth was left, the mindless chaotic nothing that cannot threaten the creatures of Earth or the balance of nature as we know it. Azathoth was chaos without logic and order: chaos without power.

There, beneath Witch House, where Mandelbröt was strongest, where the mutated mold fed off Mandelbröt's powers, I destroyed every fragment and every spore of rot. And I knew that, without Mandelbröt, the chaos that consumed Miskatonic University would end.

Life would return to normal.

I shoved Beeber up the slide. I sealed the hole behind the radiator using debris and trash. Later, I would stuff the hole with a plug of steel.

Professor Beeber was slumped by the radiator, scalpel still in his fist. His nose was broken, his cheeks gouged, his face a bloody mess. One ear dangled from the side of his head. "You have proven my life's work. There is order beneath chaos, and its name is Mandelbrot. You deserve to be Chairman of Miskatonic University's Department of Quantum

Lifeforms. Myna can be your assistant."

Myna said, "I may want to do something else with my life, Professor. I think I've had enough of chaos."

I looked at her. We were so much alike that it scared the hell out of me. And besides, Myna was no assistant; in many ways, she was my superior.

THE BLACK BRAT OF DUNWICH

Stanley C. Sargent

> "In effect we have unsettled and reversed the given config-
> uration, suggesting an *alternative—culture/nature.*"
> —Donald R. Burleson

At the bartender's suggestion, Jeffrey and James made their way to the rear of the dimly lit Arkham bar. They saw only one person in the smoky shadows of the back room, a thin, ancient man seated alone amid the shadows and smoke; they casually approached his table.

"Pardon me, mister," Jeffrey proffered, "my friend and I are collecting data for a book we're writing about the so-called 'Dunwich horror.' The bartender said you'd actually met Wilbur Whateley and might be willing to speak with us."

The dark seated figure offered no immediate response. After a few moments, the two intruders looked at each other, then shrugged and turned to walk away. Their retreat was halted by a gritty voice inviting them to sit. The pair eagerly retraced their steps.

Before they could seat themselves, the mysterious figure raised an empty glass and waved it in the air. Jeffrey headed back to the bar in response to the signal while James pulled a chair up to the table. During the awkward silence that followed, James noted the excellent though somewhat old-fashioned quality of the stranger's apparel. If the fellow had really been acquainted with the Whateley boy, his comments might well prove key elements for their book. He certainly looked old enough to have been Wilbur's contemporary.

Jeffrey soon returned, bearing a trio of glasses and a bottle of whiskey. He joined the silent pair, poured three drinks, and waited for the old man to speak.

As the two researchers sipped their drinks, the old man downed his shot, then poured himself another. He coughed, then gruffly blurted out, "So somebody's finally writing a book about my old friend Wilbur, are they? Well, I reckon I knew him better than anybody. I haven't spoken to anyone about him for years, but that's 'cos nobody cares to hear what I have to say on the subject. If you boys aren't prepared to hear the truth, you might as well be on your way."

Jeffrey assured the man that he and his friend wanted only the truth, which they would not hesitate to print, assuming it could in any way be verified. They explained that they hoped to write the first definitive history of the events leading up to the series of mysterious deaths in 1928, the responsibility for which had been attributed to the Whateley family of Dunwich. To date, the pair had studied police reports, newspaper articles, the famous Armitage account, and various coroners' reports.

"The circumstances surrounding the tragedy," added James, "have become so entwined with legend that it has become impossible to separate reality from fiction. We hope to clarify some of the issues and portray the Whateleys accurately. We would also like to take notes and tape-record this conversation if that's acceptable to you, sir." He placed a notebook and pen on the table as Jeffrey extracted a hand-held tape recorder from his coat.

"Whatever you want to use is fine by me," responded the man seated opposite them. "Only three people ever knew the truth of what happened in Dunwich: Wilbur Whateley, that goddamned Armitage, and me, Abe Galvin," the old man proclaimed. "Since Wilbur's gone and you'd play hell finding Armitage, I'd say it's up to me to set the record straight before I die."

Despite their surprise at the aspersions cast upon a person as widely respected as Dr. Armitage, the authors encouraged Galvin to impart his recollections. If the man proved legitimate, he was undoubtedly the only person still alive to have actually known young Whateley.

"I left Miskatonic University in the spring of 1924," Galvin began, "after spending six years in the linguistics program. Once I'd satisfied all of my commitments, I decided I'd like to wander around New England for a while, just exploring the backwater areas and maybe earning my keep by hiring myself out as a private tutor. I walked or took buses, answered newspaper ads for tutoring work, and occasionally placed an ad of my own. Between jobs, I'd sleep under the stars; the weather was warm so it was pleasurable to camp out.

"Dunwich was too small to have a newspaper of its own, but somehow Old Elezer Whateley, or 'Wizard Whateley' as most people knew him, came across my ad in the *Aylesbury Transcript* and made it his business to look me up. I'd never heard of Dunwich or the Whateleys, so I saw nothing unusual in an offer for room and board for the winter in exchange for helping Whateley's young grandson with some difficult translations of archaic Greek and Latin. I admit the old buzzard struck me as a mite strange—his eyes were about the eeriest I'd ever seen—but with winter just around the corner, I accepted his offer and accompanied him back to Dunwich in his horse-drawn wagon that very same day.

"The country was green and beautiful along the way, yet once we'd passed through an old tunnel bridge, things began looking pretty rustic and run-down. I was willing to put up with a lot rather than face winter without food or shelter, however, even if it meant spending time in a previous century."

The narrator poured himself another glass before resuming his tale. "Whateley's peak-roofed farmhouse came as one hell of a surprise. It was out in the middle of nowhere and smack up against a dirt incline, with one end extending right on into the hillside. The entire upper story had been boarded up, for reasons I didn't know at the time, and a wooden runway sloped right up from the ground to where a gable window had been replaced with a solid plank door.

"The old barn was a wreck and the cattle all looked diseased as hell. I was actually relieved to learn my quarters were to be in one of two unused toolsheds. The inside of the shed stank so bad I was obliged to scrub it out with disinfectant; then it still required airing out for two days before I could stand to sleep inside with the door closed."

He stopped to address James, who was furiously writing down every word. "Am I going too fast for you, son?" Galvin asked.

James put his pencil down just long enough to take a sip of whiskey and assure Galvin that, with shorthand, he could easily keep up.

"Just thought I'd check," Galvin said, before nodding and returning to his monologue. "Old Whateley occupied three ground-floor rooms of the farmhouse along with his albino daughter, Lavinia, and grandson, Wilbur. Lavinia, or 'Lavinny' as the old boy called her, struck me as a bit 'off,' though it's hard to say exactly what was wrong with her beyond her paleness and her too-long arms. She could read, though she lacked any kind of formal education. Housework wasn't exactly her forte, but she managed to keep everybody fed. Her favorite pursuits were daydreaming and running through the hills during thunderstorms, if you can imagine. She struck me as being fidgety and afraid all the time, which tended to get on one's nerves, but I got along well enough with her. I guess you could say she spent most of her time trying to keep out of everybody's way." He paused in reflection, then added, "For some time, no one so much as hinted about who Wilbur's father might be."

The speaker suddenly burst into a fit of coughing that ended in painful wheezing and choking. Another hefty gulp of whiskey brought him temporary relief, but it was obvious his health was not good.

"Is this the kind of stuff you boys are looking for?" he asked.

The two men tripped over each other in response, agreeing that this indeed was exactly the material they were seeking. Both urged Galvin to go on with his tale, hoping to get as much information as possible before alcohol began to affect his memory.

"I couldn't believe my eyes when I saw my prospective student for the first time. Old Whateley had told me his grandson was eleven years old, then he introduces me to this fellow who looks older than me. How many eleven-year-olds you ever seen who are over six feet tall and fully bearded? I started to wonder if I'd been had, but I decided to play along and humor the old fool lest I forfeit the promised winter provision. Wilbur and I took to each other right away, and that clinched the arrangement."

James leaned forward and asked hesitantly, "Could you tell us more about Wilbur's appearance?"

Galvin smiled. "I'll get to that. You two have a drink with me first." The tiny, wrinkled man winked at James. "Whiskey helps keep the throat and the mind lubricated, you know," he joked.

He waited patiently as the reluctant pair filled their half-empty glasses, then raised his own glass in a toast. "May you never know the true depths of loneliness!" Galvin called out. Although the sentiment seemed out of context, the pair obligingly clinked their glasses with his before downing the fiery liquid.

"Wilbur was a hell of a peculiar-looking fellow, certainly not what one would call handsome. A goatee covered his lack of chin, but his skin had a sallowness to its hue. He had great big ears and long, black hair that framed his face and added to his goatish look.

"I guess I'd have to say his features were coarse by traditional standards, and there was something wild about his appearance, something amazingly feral that recalled the forest satyrs of the ancient Greeks. His pupils were black as coal so it was easy as hell to get lost in those eyes— he must of caught me staring a hundred times at least!"

A dreamlike tone had entered Galvin's voice as he recalled Wilbur's countenance, but he forced himself to focus on the business at hand.

"I don't think Wilbur ever got much chance to play as a child, except maybe occasionally with Lavinia. We had lots of fun, though the first time I made a joke, that booming laugh of his damn near made me jump out of my seat. He looked and sounded like an adult, but he was just a lonely kid inside. It didn't take long for me to realize he was still growing and that, plus his shuffling walk, caused me to wonder if he'd inherited some congenital deformity. He was shamed by his difference and tried to cover it by wearing two or three pairs of pants under his old-fashioned cossack breeches. People said he smelled bad too, but if he did, I never noticed it."

Galvin lapsed into silence but did not reach for the bottle. When he spoke again, it was in softer, more intimate tones. "The few visitors we had, including Dr. Armitage, treated Wilbur like some kind of dangerous, deformed misanthrope, though some, like Earl Sawyer, did their best to overcome their qualms. I had mixed feelings about the boy myself, but only at first," he laughed. "He confused the hell out of me! But after a while, I developed a real respect for him and was proud to call him my friend."

An uncomfortable silence followed. Galvin's last statement had been a revelation after all the negative descriptions the authors had heard of "the black brat of Dunwich." James carefully reached over, grabbed the whiskey bottle, and refilled the others' glasses as well as his own.

Jeffrey found himself trying to picture Galvin at age twenty-five. His artistic bent made it easy to visualize a younger Galvin simply by filling in the lines and darkening the hair of the grandfatherly figure before him. He concluded that Galvin had once been the good-looking—though probably not the handsome—rugged type. A man of Galvin's average height and build must have felt quite intimidated at having a student whose boyish lack of experience belied his towering stature. It suddenly occurred to Jeffrey that Galvin was reading his thoughts, and when he looked up, he saw that Galvin was looking directly at him with a knowing smile on his face. That made Jeffrey slightly uncomfortable, and he felt a certain relief when the old man resumed his account.

"Wilbur's room also came as a great surprise. It was on the eastern side of the ground floor where the house dug into the hillside. He'd hauled an old bureau into one corner and had been using it as a desk; that's where they later found the big ledger he used as a diary. Only one wall contained a window; every other wall was lined with shelves filled with hundreds of the rotting books that the family had collected through several generations. The majority of those books concerned various aspects of occultism, alchemy, black magic, and the like. I thought it strange that several of the volumes could be found outside the back rooms of university libraries. The rarer tomes must have been worth a fortune, even in their deteriorated condition. He owned copies of d'Erlette's *Cultes des Goules*, the *Liyuhh*, Borellus's forbidden text, von Junzt's *Unaussprechlichen Kulten*, and others I'd never even heard of. I held Joseph Curwen's own handwritten copy of Bryce's *Biblia Sinistre* in my hands! Hell, even Miskatonic University doesn't have a copy of that! Yet with all those treasures around him, Wilbur still craved a Latin edition of the *Necronomicon* printed in seventeenth-century Spain. I was allowed the freedom of his library, but I didn't have much interest in things about 'blasphemous outer spheres.'"

Galvin experienced a second coughing fit, this one worse than the first. In the meantime, Jeffrey managed to replace the tape in the recorder with a fresh one.

"Wilbur needed help translating certain passages from those books, only a few of which were actually written in archaic Greek and Latin. That's the reason I was there. Wilbur spoke a crude dialect he'd picked up from his mother, but his was such a brilliant mind that he could easily translate French, German, Arabic, and even enciphered passages without my aid."

James asked Galvin to wait until he got back from the restroom before proceeding.

Jeffrey stayed with Galvin. "Why weren't you afraid of Wilbur like everyone else?" he asked the shadowed figure seated across from him. "His appearance must have been intimidating."

Galvin chuckled softly and answered, "Wilbur was very special, and I guess I saw that right away. Armitage has since made Wilbur sound like a goat-faced monster, but people didn't scream and run when he came around, so even you must realize that was an exaggeration."

James returned. As he sat down, he tried to check the alcohol level in the whiskey bottle as inconspicuously as possible.

"You needn't worry, son," Galvin snidely commented, "it takes a lot more than one bottle to get me lathered."

The dim lighting hid the blush that immediately flooded James's face.

Jeffrey turned to James in an attempt to dispel the awkwardness of the situation. "Mr. Galvin," he proffered, "was just about to tell me how special Wilbur was."

Somewhat amused at his interviewers' apprehension, Galvin resumed his discourse. "That's right. For instance, we'd sneak out at night to chase across the countryside in the dark while the others slept. Wilbur would steer us safely around the deep ravines and gorges that I could barely see, past what they called the Devil's Hop Yard, to the rounded hilltops where folks said the Pocumtuck Indians had buried their dead. I'd squat among circles of ancient stone pillars while he set up an odd sort of telescope of his own design. Through that telescope we'd gaze upon a sky the rest of mankind has never seen, and he'd talk for hours about the endless universes revolving above us, just as if he'd toured them personally. What we now call nebulas, he claimed were colossal sprays of blood marking the demise of entities beyond imagination. Other entities, he said, had

315

come to Earth eons ago and more were yet to come. He taught me about Cthulhu, Dagon, and the Winged Ones, and told me the story of Qommaq, the blender of flesh, who'd been the scourge of ancient Crete. I'd lie next to him in the cool grass while he wove his wonderful tales. He made it easy to stare into the sky and envision other worlds as he described them."

"That's incredible!" exclaimed Jeffrey.

"Not as incredible as Wilbur himself," Galvin responded dreamily. After a few moments, he reluctantly moved on to the next phase of his account.

"Once he felt sure he could trust me, he told me about his twin brother, the 'Other' we called him, who was confined in the upper half of the house. Wilbur confessed to being only half human himself, though I didn't really believe him until later."

James nearly jumped out of his seat, exclaiming, "You mean you got a good look at him and even that didn't scare you off?"

Galvin rolled his eyes. "There's a great deal more to a person than what reveals itself to the eye, son; the ability to see beyond the physical is about the only thing that raises us above the level of monsters ourselves. All I knew was that the boy was deformed below the waist to some extent. He was always real concerned with privacy whenever he bathed, so it was obvious he was ashamed of his difference. He said the other kids had made fun of him when he'd tried to make friends; you know how cruel kids can be, and I saw the proof of pain in his eyes. He hated his difference and always fought to keep it hidden.

"I tried to get him over it, show him it didn't matter to me. I even kept talking to him on a couple occasions to keep him in the room while I took a bath, figuring he'd eventually loosen up, seeing as how I was no Adonis myself, but it didn't work. He just sat there staring at me all over, like he was studying me as an example of how folks are supposed to look. I just wanted him to accept himself for who he was and stop worrying about what anyone else thought." He stared directly at James. "You'd best get that disgusted look off your face damn quick, young man, or I'm done talking."

An embarrassed James apologized, then added, "But you didn't actually see, well, what Armitage and the others saw when Wilbur died, did you?"

Galvin responded forcefully, "No, I didn't, but Armitage had folks scared half out of their wits! I doubt any of them even know what they really saw that night! Certainly no one had the guts to refute the shiftless bastard later on, after his own written account made him out to be some kind of savior."

His outburst was greeted with silence, so after a moment, a calmer Galvin continued. "Wilbur said Old Whateley'd done his bare best to convince Wilbur that the Other was some kind of avatar that needed nurturing until the stars came into the proper alignment for some legendary cosmic armageddon to enter our dimension through some kind of gate. As a child, Wilbur accepted his grandfather's philosophy, but as his human aspect became dominant and started thinking for itself, he began to look for a way to thwart the Other or at least keep it under control. He said all he needed were some special incantations, but only Old Whateley knew where to find those spells and he wasn't about to tell as long as he had any doubts about Wilbur's loyalty to the cause.

"Wilbur said I shouldn't worry about any cosmic disaster, though, and assured me the stars wouldn't be right yet for decades. He also said any premature attempt to open the gate would bring immediate misfortune upon the conjurer.

"He told me as much as he dared, fearing my curiosity might prove dangerous to me if I knew too much. I think he was also afraid of scaring me off and losing the only friend he knew he was ever likely to have."

During the awkward pause that followed, James and Jeffrey pretended to check their notes and recorder, respectively; obviously Galvin felt very strongly about Wilbur Whateley.

"Old Whateley spent most of his time repairing the house, whether it needed it or not," Galvin suddenly began again. "He was a nervous old codger who fussed over his pathetic livestock incessantly, often spending half the night transferring steers back and forth from the barn to holding pens he'd built on the far side of the house, adjacent to the ramp to the second story.

"Wilbur woke me up one night in August about ten o'clock. He said Old Whateley'd been taken seriously ill and he was going to Osborn's store in Dunwich to call the doctor in Aylesbury. He asked me to help Lavinia watch over the old man until he got back. I wanted to go with him since the townspeople were afraid of him, but he pointed out that no one would recognize him if he wore his grandfather's old-fashioned bang-up coat with a three-cornered hat cocked down low. He knew he could make better time alone on horseback than two of us could in the old wagon. Still, I worried about him as dogs always attacked him on sight; it got so bad at one point that he had to carry a pistol to protect himself from them.

"By the time Dr. Houghton arrived, the old man was nearly gone; Wilbur agreed, pointing out the whippoorwills that had gathered *en masse* around the house. Even the doctor noticed their cries were keeping time with Old Whateley's breathing. Houghton did his best, but Whateley's heart finally gave out 'long about two in the morning."

James jumped in with a question. "Were you actually in the room when Wizard Whateley passed away? Supposedly he said something very special to Wilbur just before he died."

"You're baiting me now, son, just to see if I know what I'm talking about," Galvin answered.

The researcher admitted as much and offered an apology.

"Oh, I'd do the same if I was you," Galvin remarked. "Yes, I was in the room. I heard the same as Doc Houghton heard, but he didn't understand what was going on. The old man knew Wilbur wanted to keep the Other captive, so on his deathbed, the old man tried to bend Wilbur to his will. The first time I heard the name Yog-Sothoth was when, with his dying breath, the old wizard reminded Wilbur that his brother required constant feeding and room to expand. He also told Wilbur about a certain passage in the Spanish edition of the *Necronomicon* that would make the Other strong enough to reproduce and savage the planet.

"What Houghton didn't know was that Wilbur had absolutely no intention of carrying out that part of Old Whateley's instructions. Was he supposed to argue with a dying man? Hell, not much of it made sense to me, especially with the ruckus those damn birds were making outside.

"But the instant Old Whateley died, all the birds fell silent at exactly the same instant. Wilbur told me the locals believed whippoorwills gathered when someone was about to die; if they dispersed after the person died, like they did that night, it meant the person's soul had escaped them. I was never too clear on it all, but I guess the birds are supposed to be like psychopomps that escort the souls they catch to heaven or hell. When they miss, the soul remains earth-bound and can trouble the living. After all I've seen, I have to consider there might be some truth in that particular superstition.

"Wilbur asked me to stay on after his grandfather died. I helped him bury Old Whateley up near Sentinel Hill, then left Wilbur and his mother to say their farewells in private. Wilbur held up, but Lavinia broke down and cried some. She seemed to get progressively worse after that day, such that we worried about her sanity, and Wilbur wouldn't allow her to light fires up on Sentinel Hill anymore, like she'd always done before twice a year. He told her the neighbors didn't like it, and he didn't want her continuing the wizardry.

"The first thing he did after the burial was clear the house of all the old man's occult trappings. He single-handedly carried over a hundred jars and bottles out of Old Whateley's room and stacked them in a pyramid of glass behind and away from the house. Every one of the bottles contained some bit of alien monstrosity preserved for reasons I feared to ask. I'd wager your best biologists couldn't identify even half the things floating in those jars. After he emptied the room, he did some chanting and arm waving over the jars and such, then doused it all with kerosene and set it afire. Some of the bottles exploded right away from the heat, but some of the other specimens burned red hot for more than two days.

"Once that chore was done, Wilbur seemed to have more peace of mind. A little after that, he started boarding up the unused parts of the downstairs. I helped whenever I could, but the work took his mind off his troubles, and he said there was no rush."

Jeffrey abruptly took advantage of the lull to ask a question. "What did he tell you about Yog-Sothoth?"

A deep ridge formed upon the heavily creased brow of the old man. "I don't recall all that much of what he said about most of that hocus-pocus stuff; I guess I just wasn't all that interested. But I can't forget his telling me that this Yog-Sothoth was father to both him and the Other. It belonged, he said, in some other dimension, but it wanted to infest this one too. He said it was a big formless thing that could only come into our world at all when it stretched itself out into threads or tendrils so thin that they could squeeze through the empty space between neutrons, electrons, and the like. The Other was meant to prepare the way for the time when a gate would open, giving its daddy full access to our universe, but Wilbur was dead set against letting that come about."

"Did Wilbur explain how Lavinia had a child by this non-material being?" Jeffrey asked.

Galvin chuckled. "I'd of thought you boys would be smart enough to figure that one out for yourselves! Seems self-evident to me that Wizard Whateley allowed himself to be possessed for an incestuous encounter with his daughter. You've read Armitage's account; don't you recall that Curtis Whateley described the giant face on top of the monster as bearing an unmistakable likeness to Wizard Whateley?

"Wilbur told me about it after Armitage came to the farm to check on him."

The mention of the famous doctor at that point in the story caught Galvin's listeners by surprise. "Armitage wrote that he met Wilbur at the Miskatonic library in 1926!" James objected.

Galvin smiled. "Is that so? Well, to begin with, there are a lot of things Armitage felt it prudent not to include in his 'authoritative' account. But if you read it carefully, you'll note he mentioned being sent to the Whateley farm in 1925 as a 'scholarly correspondent' for the university."

"But that makes no sense," Jeffrey piped in. "Why would the university send a head librarian somewhere as a correspondent? Let alone to the Whateley farm? The public lost all interest in the Whateleys long before 1925!"

"Curious, ain't it?" Galvin sniggered. "The truth is, Armitage had been visiting the farm for years; he and Wizard Whateley were old friends! After Old Whateley passed away, Armitage felt obliged to drop in, just to make sure Wilbur was following the instructions his grandfather had given him. Armitage only mentioned the visit in writing because he was seen there by someone he hadn't expected to be there—me. I was introduced, then Old Whateley whisked Armitage off to talk in private."

Jeffrey couldn't believe his ears. "Mr. Galvin, are you saying Dr. Armitage knew about the twins and Old Whateley's plans for destroying mankind long before he encountered Wilbur at the library? That's diametrically opposed to everything the man has stood for!"

Galvin laughed out loud before adding, "You're slow, but I think you're finally starting to catch on!

"Armitage had what you could call a hidden agenda and the old bastard wasn't exactly pleased to hear Wilbur didn't want anything to do with him and Old Whateley's plan. By the time Armitage left the farm that day, he was madder than a hornet! He threatened Wilbur up and down, but Wilbur wouldn't budge. Wilbur wanted to find the spell that would reverse the Other's growth or even kill it if need be, but he didn't dare tell that to Armitage. But Armitage counted on Wilbur changing his mind—least he counted on it 'til Wilbur came to his library and asked to see the complete edition of the *Necronomicon* of the mad Arab. After reading the section Old Whateley had pointed out to him, Wilbur started looking for spells he could use to control or destroy the Other, unaware that Armitage was spying on him over his shoulder. When Armitage figured out what Wilbur was up to, he denied Wilbur further access to the book and ordered him out of the library.

"The bastard later admitted he'd written to the head librarians of every library that had a copy of the *Necronomicon*, advising them not to allow Wilbur or anyone named Galvin access."

James was outraged, unable to accept this new view of Armitage. "Dr. Armitage was a respected scholar!" he protested. "He held a doctorate from Princeton and a Doctor of Letters degree from Cambridge!"

Chuckling to himself, Galvin challenged, "Have you ever wondered why such a brilliant scholar ended up as a simple librarian? Truth is, the university's Board of Governors got wind of his delvings into certain unacceptable aspects of the occult, and they decided it would be best to put him where they could keep an eye on him."

Galvin openly relished the disillusioned shock now apparent on both writers' faces. After harboring Armitage's secret for so many years, it gave him immense pleasure to slaughter that sacred cow. He allowed the pair a few minutes for recovery before resuming his revelations.

"In the meantime, Wilbur managed to keep the Other fed with the cattle he got from Earl Sawyer. The house started smelling something fierce though, 'cos he couldn't always get all the chewed up carcasses out. The darn thing was getting unpredictable and didn't always recognize him anymore. Wilbur said its mind never developed beyond that of a human infant's despite its size, and it wouldn't be long before its bulk would require the whole of the house. Wilbur was still growing too, though he kept hoping to find some way to stop. By early '26, he measured over seven feet tall."

A sadness seeped into Galvin's voice as he began to impart the next chapter of his incredible tale. "Just before Halloween, or Hallowmass as they called it, that same year, we lost Lavinia. Wilbur and I were wrestling with a particularly knotty passage from Vogel's *Von denen Verdammten* one afternoon when Lavinia burst into the room in a full-blown panic. She was drenched in sweat and raving like a madwoman. Wilbur held her and stroked her hair for a while, trying to calm her, but she pushed him away, screaming: 'I cain't deny him any longer! He needs 'es ma, an' not yew ner n'b'dy else'll keep me from a-goan' to him anymore!'

"There'd been a god-awful sloshing noise coming from the second floor all morning, but I never figured if it was a reaction to Lavinia's hysterics or vice-versa. Sounded like a herd of elephants was stomping around up there. I'd always tried to ignore the noise from up there before, but God himself must o' heard the uproar that day.

"Wilbur asked me to step outside while he reasoned with Lavinia's madness. She was twitching and a-fighting him, but Wilbur held her fast. Nobody could match Wilbur's strength by then, let alone a frail little thing like Lavinia. He finally got her to lie down in her room, and I heard him chanting or singing to her for more than an hour before she settled enough for him to leave her. He went back to his studies, thinking she was asleep, but as it turned out, she was just pretending."

James interrupted to ask, "Do you think Wilbur loved his mother?"

The question seemed to catch Galvin off guard, causing him to hesitate before answering. "I guess I never heard him say it right out, though he once recalled the fond memories he had of wandering through the hills with her when he was real young. Sometimes he spoke harshly to her, and we both ignored her ramblings, but when she was hurting, he was always real tender with her. It was kinda hard not to feel protective of her, especially when she'd get all worked up and confused."

Galvin drained the last of the bottle into his own glass. Jeffrey rushed off for another even before Galvin could set the empty bottle down. He rejoined them moments later, apparently anxious for Galvin to begin the next phase of his narration.

"Just before sunset, I heard a door slam and someone run past my door toward the hillside. I poked my head out the door and caught sight of Lavinia's tiny, crinkly-haired form careening at top speed up the wood incline toward the boarded-up window on the east gable. The moment she reached the top, she let fly with the ax she'd brought with her, trying to hack the lock off and get inside. I was at a loss for action 'til Wilbur ran out of the house and saw what she was up to. I offered to help, but he was sure she'd gone mad and that there was no way to stop her. He told me to stay in the shed, saying he'd call me if there was anything I could do."

Galvin sighed. "A while later, I heard Lavinia screaming like all possessed. I headed for the door, but Wilbur had locked me in. I had heard him chanting or singing in his room just before the screaming started, so I knew it wasn't him that was hurting Lavinia."

"Were you frightened?" asked James.

"I was too busy trying to figure out what was going on to be too afraid. I couldn't believe the Other would hurt its own mother, but then I got scared for her when I heard whippoorwills calling. They got so loud I didn't hear the lock turn when Wilbur opened my door a while later.

"He didn't try to talk over the racket the birds were making, but I could see tears on his cheeks. He just walked over to where I was lying on the bed and picked me up. He set me on my feet, looked long and hard into my eyes, then wrapped both arms around me. I found myself returning his embrace, and we stayed there holding and comforting each other for some time. Then the tone of the birds changed, getting louder and wilder, so finally Wilbur let go of me."

James rose half way out of his seat in excitement. "Didn't he offer any sort of explanation?"

Galvin nodded. "All he said was, 'The 'wills got 'er, Abe. She'll rest easy naow. She ne'er understood all that Gran'pa got her inta; she wuz jest his pawn.'"

None of the trio spoke for several minutes. Finally, Jeffrey focused on the fresh bottle of whiskey and poured a round of drinks. All three joined in a silent toast in memory of Lavinia.

"The birds didn't fully disperse 'til dawn. Wilbur climbed the ramp with me behind him. He told me to stay back while he went through the gable to fetch Lavinia.

"My curiosity got the best of me when he didn't come right out, so I climbed up high enough to peek in. There's no way I can describe the feeling that came over me when I spotted Wilbur, standing just a little way inside, struggling in what looked like a tug o' war with Lavinia's limp and lifeless body floating like some kind of Kewpie doll about six feet in the air. Wilbur had told me the Other was invisible, but I guess I hadn't expected to see the walls right through it like there was nothing there at all. I could only really be sure there was something there by the way Lavinia's body was being pulled back and forth. The Other was grunting and whining like a frustrated child clinging onto its favorite toy.

"It let out a squeal when it saw me gaping at it in the doorway, and it let go of Lavinia. Wilbur ran by me, cradling what was left of his mother in his arms and yelling for me to shut the door on the thing, to hold it as best I could until he got back with new locks from the shed, which I did. Wilbur carried the withered body downstairs and laid Lavinia out in her room, then returned to secure the door with new locks and boards.

"Lavinia's clothes were all ripped up and her body was covered with big round welts from top to bottom. She'd been sucked dry as a leaf."

"But why did she feel compelled to go in there?" It was James this time.

Galvin poured another drink without bothering to offer the bottle to the others. He slammed it on the table before answering in a voice choked with emotion. "Wilbur just said, 'She a'ways felt it wuz her duty ta suckle us both.'

"He wouldn't accept help with her burial, and he didn't bother notifying the authorities. After performing some kind of esoteric service over her body, he never spoke her name in my presence again."

The control returned to Galvin's voice as he continued.

"Wilbur didn't need my help with translating any more, but he begged me not to leave as he couldn't bear the idea of being there alone. He had to stay to keep the Other contained. I told him I'd become too attached to just leave him there.

"During the summer of 1927, Wilbur repaired the large tool shed next to mine and moved the wood-burning stove from the house to outside so heat could be piped into both sheds. Then we started moving his books and makeshift desk from the house to Wilbur's shed as the Other was getting way too big for the upper half of the house. I boarded up the windows and doors of the house's ground floor while Wilbur gutted the remaining partitions between rooms and floors.

"That winter saw Wilbur doubling his efforts to get access to the *Necronomicon;* we didn't know then that Armitage had already contacted the libraries to warn them against him. They wouldn't even allow him to copy particular pages from the book. He was so desperate for a way to control his own growth as well as that of the Other that he traveled on horseback all the way to the library at Cambridge. Armitage had done his work well, though, so Wilbur wasn't allowed near the book."

Again Galvin paused, hesitant to relive the next series of events.

"We managed to keep things in check all that winter and on into 1928, but by late summer it became obvious that the Other was quickly outgrowing the old farmhouse. The walls bulged whenever it turned around, and its movement in general became very constrained. Something had to be done to stop its growth before all hell broke loose. That's when Wilbur realized he had to try and steal the book from the library at Miskatonic. He wouldn't allow me to come with him as someone had to keep feeding the Other while he was away or it would break out for sure and go on a killing spree."

"You blame Armitage for Wilbur's death, don't you?" James asked.

Galvin reacted adamantly. "You're damn right I blame him! He knew Wilbur couldn't control the Other any longer without the spell, yet he did everything possible to force the crisis. He wanted Wilbur to come crawling to him and agree to his hellish plan. The only other option was for Wilbur to steal the book. Armitage knew that too. Why do you think, knowing how dogs universally hated Wilbur, Armitage suddenly added watch dogs in addition to the regular security at the library? When he found Wilbur bleeding to death on the library floor, Armitage did nothing to save him. He feigned shock at seeing such an alien monster simply for the benefit of his colleagues!"

Neither interviewer knew what to say, so they waited silently for Galvin's fury to subside. His story was fascinating despite many surprising revelations.

"Wilbur felt there was a real good chance he'd be arrested while attempting to steal the book, so he made me promise to leave if he hadn't returned within a week. It never occurred to me that worse might happen, but it must have occurred to him.

"Before he left, he said he could feel the Other's claustrophobia. As often happens with twins, he and the Other shared strong emotional feelings to a certain extent. He said it felt trapped and afraid.

"I hesitated to leave, however, hoping my friend would come back safely with the means to halt or even reverse the Other's growth.

"I decided it was time to leave when I had used up all the cows to feed the Other. That was on the first of September. Earl Sawyer had been providing them regularly for that purpose, but he heard the creaking and the straining sounds coming from the house and it frightened him away. I admit I was afraid too, so on the ninth I decided to leave. I was packing a bag when I heard a real loud noise, like the logs of the farmhouse wrenching and cracking apart. I stepped out of the shed to get a better look, and the whole world exploded around me.

"It was pouring down rain so hard I could barely see. Doors, plaster, and glass filled the air; huge chunks of walls were flying in every direction. The farmhouse had been ripped into sections, parts of which were still moving. A huge chunk of roof floated in the air, the gables and chimney still intact. Mud was splashing up in waves and an ungodly stench hit me so hard, I threw up.

"The next thing I knew, something slimy grabbed one of my legs and thrust me thirty feet or so into the air. I couldn't see what had me, but it felt like a mass of wet, living rope winding and knotting all over me. I tried to get a grip on whatever held me, but it was like trying to grasp an armload of oily snakes—only these were as thick as my thigh. I could feel mouths clamping down and biting me right through my clothes, and I saw the rain turn red as it struck my body. My chest felt like it was being squeezed in a vice, so with the first air I caught, I started screaming and hollering for all I was worth.

"Everything was getting dark and blurry but I fought against passing out. All at once, a desperate clarity came over me and pushed away the fear. Without thinking, I began yelling at my invisible attacker, 'I'm Abe, Wilbur's friend! Don't you recognize me? I'm a friend! Please, put me down—you're killing me!'"

Galvin paused. "You may not believe me, but all of a sudden my feet touched the ground and the things that were binding me let go all at once."

Unable to restrain his excitement, James leaned back in his chair and shouted, "Jesus!"

Galvin, who had almost crept over the table toward his listeners, also leaned back, releasing his audience from the stifling tension he had produced as he described his ordeal.

An excited Jeffrey begged, "But did it let go of you?"

After a moment, Galvin whispered, "I believe it remembered me from its telepathic link with Wilbur; it experienced Wilbur's trust and love for me. It was as if Wilbur reached out from beyond the grave to save me."

Galvin now sat perfectly upright in his chair. His hands were shaking to the extent that he spilled half his drink even before he could raise it to his mouth. The second bottle lay empty on the table before him.

"I never did actually see what the Other looked like, but from what I heard later about it, that was probably a blessin'.

"I guess I blacked out then, 'cos Earl Sawyer's kid stumbled across me the next morning. He fetched his daddy, who said I was more dead than alive when he found me lying half inside a footprint as big as an old hogshead barrel and over a foot deep. They took me to Dr. Houghton and so saved my life. Nearly all my ribs were crushed, my sternum was fractured, and I was bleeding all over. I swore all three to secrecy about my presence, hoping Armitage would assume the Other had killed me. He'd have come after me if he thought I was still alive."

For several minutes Galvin sat quietly in his chair, as if he had finished his tale. The whir of tape rewinding alerted Jeffrey to stop his recorder. He felt a certain relief that Galvin had reached the end of his tale before his speech got any worse. He had been slipping more and more into colloquial speech patterns for several minutes.

"Well," offered James, "I guess that's about it, then. Armitage killed the Other up on Sentinel Hill for whatever motive, and the day was saved!"

Galvin leaned forward with a disgusted look on his face and sneered, "And I thought you boys was smart!"

James stumbled over a few syllables in search of some response, but Galvin wasn't finished yet.

"The whole story's in Wilbur's diary, which I read after he left for Arkham; the code wasn't all that hard to figure out. Later on, when Armitage got the diary, he read it and only let his buddies see bits and pieces so he could interpret the text to mean whatever he wanted it to mean. He burned it before anybody else got a chance to see it. Now, just how scholarly does an action like that sound to you? Yet if you read his account carefully, you'll see the wily old bastard couldn't resist tossing in a few tantalizing clues to the truth."

Galvin was obviously getting drunk, occasionally slurring a few words.

"Okay, so I'll explain it to you kids. The Indians had been performing weird rites in the area in and around Dunwich for over four hundred years before Wizard Whateley came along and figured out just exactly what they were up to. And he was just crazy enough to try and do the same.

"The Indians had been breeding their women with things from other dimensions, but they were smart enough to keep the offspring imprisoned in underground caves. It was safer that way and the hybrids grew slower in the dark. Old Whateley'd thought he'd do the same, 'cept Lavinia gave birth to twins and refused to part with either of them. Living above ground, both of the twins grew a whole lot faster than their half-brothers and half-sisters below the ground."

Gasps escaped the mouths of his listeners as Galvin rambled on.

"You mean you never wondered what it was that has been rumbling and moaning under the hills? It's been consistently reported since the first white men settled on Dunwich land!

"Armitage didn't destroy the Other and make everything safe! That's all just a load of crap. Did anyone actually see what happened when the lightning struck? Nobody but Armitage and those two fools he had believing anything he told them. He said himself that the damn thing couldn't be killed! It sought out the altar stone because that stone was the door to an entrance to the pits below, where it could be safe! The Other called out for help in English, but the eyewitnesses said they heard an unearthly calling from the altar stone as well! All Armitage did was call down a bolt of lightning that lifted the altar stone up just long enough for the Other to squeeze its elastic form through and down to where the others were just waiting!

"Ain't you figured out that Sentinel Hill and all the hills in Dunwich are hollow? They're rounded 'cos the things underneath are growing and slowly pushing the earth up higher and higher. The standing stones mark the hills where the Indians 'planted' the spawn of Yog-Sothoth!"

"But Dr. Armitage—" James began.

"Dr. Armitage my arse," interrupted Galvin. "That son of a bitch high-tailed it back to Arkham and wrote his lying account before going back to live with his family ..."

Jeffrey started to butt in, but fell silent after Galvin finished his sentence.

"... in Innsmouth."

"What?" James cried out in disbelief.

"Yessir, I said Innsmouth!" Galvin exclaimed. "The only thing he didn't know was that his parents were taken away by the FBI when they raided Innsmouth. And the ones they took away were the ones that weren't human, and neither was Armitage, though he covered it well. Folks think he took sick and died soon after that day on Sentinel Hill, but I defy any man to show me the record of his death."

Both Jeffrey and James were stunned.

"At least I put one over on the old bastard; I got all the Whateley gold. He wanted it bad, but Wilbur gave it to me before he left. I had it on me when Earl found me, and I've been living on it ever since. Look here if you don't believe me," he added as he tossed two shiny coins onto the table.

The two authors snatched up the coins and stared at them in disbelief. One bore the imprint of Arabic lettering that they would later learn spelled out "Irem," a lost city of Arabian myth; the other was impressed with the easily recognizable features of Augustus Caesar.

"Yessir, the Other and hundreds more like him are down there still, just growing and waiting for the day they're full grown and the stars all line up as their signal. When that day comes, the earth'll rise up beneath our feet and they'll emerge to smite mankind by the millions—and nothing on this Earth can stop them!"

Galvin paused, belched, then concluded with a snicker, "If you boys finish your book in a real hurry, you just might get it published afore the apocalypse!"

For my respected friend,
Wilum Hopfrog Pugmire

THE PHANTOM OF BEGUILEMENT

W. H. PUGMIRE

I.

Katherine Winters halted for one moment on the small wooden bridge and watched the trickling water of Blake's Creek as it flowed beneath her. Dim October sunlight shimmered on the water, and the scent of autumn perfumed Kingsport's misty air. She was happy that she had stayed beyond the tourist season. The old town enchanted her, as did its strange, old-fashioned inhabitants. Continuing along Orne Street, she arrived at last at the quaint shop of curios that was her destination. Hesitating one moment, she entered the dark and chilly place and closed the door behind her. There was no sound of life; it was like a tomb, this place, a realm of the forgotten past. Slowly, she walked by dust-enshrouded items, coming at last to the thing she sought. Reaching, she took up the small framed painting, gently wiping a thin coating of dust from the glass. A scent of lilacs wafted from behind, from a shadowed presence that soon stood beside her.

"Hello, Miss Winters," the liquid voice gurgled. "I see the wee painting continues to captivate."

"Indeed. Luckily, my mother has sent a rather generous check, so I can be extravagant and do some reckless spending."

The older woman smiled with thick mauve lips and lightly

swept thin fingers through thick hair. "Mothers are such a wonderful invention," cooed the phlegmatic voice. "With some exceptions. His didn't understand him at all." She pointed a tattered nail to the painting.

"You told me his name was Jeremy Blond."

"Aye, that it was. Poor sod. A nervous young artist, with dark wounded eyes and pale lifeless hair. We get the type in Kingsport, but I've never known one to look so hunted, poor lad."

"And this is the only work of his that you have?"

"It is, love. His mum collected the rest after his vanishment. Aye, she had a lonesome look about her as well. She hated that her only child had chosen to be a painter and poet, but when his body was never found, well, his art was all she had to remember him by. But this piece she never saw, for he gave it to me. I found the wee photo frame and popped it in there, nice as you please. So, you'll be taking it off my hands?"

"Yes, please," Katherine answered, reluctantly surrendering the painting. "It's almost like an experimental photograph, so indistinct and surreal. *Is* it a woman on a raft, surrounded by shadow and eerie mists of light? And those things that float above her, like a flock of primeval psychopomps—are they gulls, and if so, why so disfigured? He had a wonderfully unique style. How old was he?"

"Little more than a child, miss. But bright. Very preoccupied with them strange books."

"Occult books?"

"Aye, so they were. When he first arrived he would come in seeking old editions of classic poetry, biographies of poets and such. But then he became seduced by local legends. Used to listen to the stories of that drunken lout what lingers about the vacant cottage where the terrible old man used to live." Katherine suppressed a secret smile as the older woman wrapped the painting in thick paper.

"And Jeremy was a poet, Mrs. Keats?"

"A very peculiar poet, miss, as we get betimes in this old town. Ah, wait a tick." She reached behind her for a large old book, opened it at the middle and took from it a folded piece of paper, which she handed to Katherine. Tenderly, the young woman opened it. "I'll toss that in as well. He called it one of his 'Shakespearean sonnets,' and it's as daft as anything old Will wrote, to be sure. If I may be allowed to say so."

"You may," Katherine allowed. "How old the paper looks, and smells."

"Aye, he found a box filled with centuried foolscap. Oh, ever so delighted, he was. How did he phrase it? 'Antique paper on which to pen my antiquated poesy,' some such as that. Ever read Oscar Wilde, Miss? Well, when Jeremy spoke he rather reminded me of Mr. Wilde. He was of another time. Too young to be so old, that were his paradox. And then one day he was took from us, but how or where or why we shall never know. The world is queer, Miss Winters, make no mistake."

The old one handed Katherine the wrapped object, in exchange for cash. Dreamily, Katherine departed with her prizes, holding painting and poem to her chest, skipping down the cobbled streets in time to happy heartbeat, and followed by vague shadows in the sky.

II.

She danced upon dark water, enshrouded in shadow and eerie mists of almost-light. Above her loomed the craggy silhouette of Kingport's prehistoric cliffs. Salted sea spray swirled about her, a light and fanciful haze in which she could almost distinguish the forms of fantastic things. She cried out and was answered by the muted ululation that issued from the mouths that flocked above her. Again she cried, wanting so to see the pallid faces of the strange winged beasts. And then the mist thickened and became a brumous wall that encircled her, that spilled its essence into her gasping mouth. It found, this stuff, her aching soul. She transformed into a thing of spreading aether.

Katherine awakened to the sound of a north wind shaking her bedroom window. In accompaniment she moaned, not wanting to shake off slumber. But the wind was insistent, and finally she crawled out of bed and staggered to the window, before which she knelt. The bedroom curtains were never closed, as she loved to watch night's sky from the cozy confines of her bed. Katherine gazed at the panorama spread before her—legend-haunted Kingsport. She had come with money left to her by an aunt who also loved the arts and who continually encouraged Katherine's talents as a poet. Having heard of this charming New England town where thrived a vigorous artistic community, she came to seek solace from an absurd emotional breakdown. She came in search of creative flow, and slowly her poetry began once more to issue forth. Within a two-month period she had completed in rough draft her cycle of sonnets. But Kingsport had given her more than creativity; it had provided a rich artistic fellowship of which she had become increasingly fond.

One of its finest characters was the "lout" spoken of by Mrs. Keats, one Winfield Scot, a brother poet. She had met him in the public library, where he spent his days reading, keeping warm, and pretending to write. (He had not produced new work for many years.) His nights were spent wrapped in many blankets as he napped on a bed of sleeping bags on the wide porch of an crumbling cottage, famous among townsfolk as the home of a curious gentleman always referred to as "the terrible old man." This fellow was said to have been a former sea captain and was at the time of his death of an incredible old age. It was whispered that he had learned strange rites and secret ceremonies during his sea journeys, and people did not like the large oddly painted stones that leaned in the tall grass of his yard, stones that were positioned in esoteric groups, like primeval idols.

Winfield Scot was not liked by the respectable Kingsport inhabitants because he slept in a place that was shunned by all reasonable persons. His monthly check kept him in good supply of the alcohol with which he fought off personal devils. Katherine had taken a part-time job in a small café, more to kill tedium than for financial relief, and it became her habit to pack a small evening meal after her shift, which she would take to the lonely poet. She found his conversation pleasant and noted an aesthetic intellect belied by a disheveled appearance. So, Winfield had known the young artist who had so mysteriously disappeared. Katherine rose and walked to the bed, above which she had hung Jeremy Blond's painting. She touched a finger to the indistinct figure on the raft, studying the strands of hair that issued from the ghostly dome. But was it hair, or a garland of fluid vines; or rags; or, perhaps, shredded seaweed? She studied the small flock of spectral things that hovered in the foggy air. How strange that they never took on solid form. They were gulls, perhaps, or large mutated bats. Did bats have such pale faces? She could never satisfactorily count their number, at times finding seven, or ten. How superbly the artist had captured their ethereal grace. She studied the curious raft. Was it composed of rotted wood bound by rope; or was it a network of large splintered bones wound with bloodless veins? The phantom figure stood at the very edge of the craft, wrapped in a robe of sparkling mist and inky shadow.

Katherine read once more the sonnet that had been scrawled onto a sheet of olden paper. Having worked so ruthlessly on her own sonnet cycle she had grown weary of the form; but this piece captivated her, and she spoke its lines aloud.

> Oh, drift to me in coils of rotten smoke
> And kiss my skull with mouth of antient breadth.
> Kiss my dome with mouth as cold as death,
> From which a mortal tongue hath never spoke.
> A mortal voice hath never stretched thy throat,
> And mortal passion never pumped thy breast,
> And mortal sanity thou never quote,
> And mortal moan is naught to you but jest.
> I hear thy utterance croak in the mist
> Above the whisper of their singing wings,
> The wings that stretch from out the shadow-things.
> I hear the spell with which my soul is kissed.
> I hear the spell that mutates flesh and bone.
> I spread these new-formed wings that now I own.

Interesting, she thought, *if a bit repetitious*. Obviously it was a companion piece to the painting. Certainly it was a captivating image, as both poem and picture. It stirred strange passion in her heart, and she ached to understand the soul of he who created it.

When, late that afternoon, her shift came to an end, Katherine carried a small aluminum container of hot food to the vacated cottage on Water Street. The day had been sunny, yet cool. She waltzed to her destination, slowing only once as she came upon a group of children playing at tableaux. Each child held a thin wooden wand to which had been attached a pale papier-mâché mask. Katherine laughed as the young ones danced and frolicked and then quickly froze into a living picture. The childfolk heard her laughter and held out to her their tiny arms. Beguiled by innocence, Katherine joined momentarily in their pantomimic play. Daintily, she danced, then fell upon her knees. Pale paper faces formed above her. She raised her arms as if they were wings, and as she did so late afternoon wind gushed to her, as if released from a prison of gravity. A lovely child bent to kiss her neck, and then they fled *en masse,* shrieking to the sunset.

She walked, and the huddled cottage came into view, enshrouded by bending trees and gathering darkness. Her hands pressed against the cold metal of a gate, and she paused momentarily to gaze at the queerly painted stones that were grouped in the tall yellow grass. The sight of these stones always disconcerted her. The manner in which they were grouped seemed slightly sinister, as if they were so assembled as to function in some incomprehensible manner. It was the stones, and the way that cosmic light played upon their painted surfaces, that had kept the townsfolk from bothering the old sea captain when he lived; and it was they that kept folk away after his demise.

Katherine saw the man who smiled at her from his nest of blankets on the porch, a bottle of whiskey in his hand. "Ah, sweet Kate. Come to keep me company."

She settled next to him and handed him her offering. "It's not much, a bit of roast beef and mashers, and a heap of corn. But it's hot."

"Delightful; my thanks, good Katherine. Here, have a swig." It was his playful habit to offer her his booze. Frowning, she took the proffered bottle and pressed it to her lips. When she began to choke and cough, her companion happily patted her and took back the bottle.

"Ugh, how can you drink that wretched stuff?"

"Nectar of the gods, sweet Kate. Warms the dread chill of mortality."

"It wouldn't do anything for me, except give me bad dreams."

"Ah, no—it's the stones that give me dreams. Wonderful, terrible dreams."

"Actually, I've had a rather wonderfully terrible dream of my own, inspired by a work of art, a painting by Jeremy Blond."

Winfield smiled into the night. "Yes, his work would do that, poor haunted fellow that he was. A true Kingsport artist was Jeremy Blond."

"Meaning what?"

"Well, we get our tourists, and we get many student artists who are little more than tourists. They are charmed by this lovely old seaport and its historical whatever; but they never penetrate its magic, never see its soul. They see the surface only, suffused with misty light. They never see the darkness where beats its haunted heart."

She bent to him and lightly kissed his cheek. "I love it when you talk like a poet."

"Yes, I'm like Wilde now, a poet who merely talks, but beautifully. I live in a world of whispered words and remembered glory, just as Jeremy Blond dwelt within a world of haunted imagery."

"With what was he haunted?"

Scot obliquely smiled. "If you've one of his paintings you know. An image of Death on a raft, sailing the river Styx, surrounded by harpies. I implied once that he had been overly inspired by Joachim Patnir's famous work, but he denied it. A queer, morbid boy, all told. Near the end he became very odd. And then he vanished."

"Fascinating. But you've misunderstood his art, dear Win. It wasn't Death that he envisioned, but something far more beguiling."

"More captivating than oblivion? You jest." Then he closely studied her. "And you've been dreaming of this thing?"

"Yes, last night. A wonderful vision."

Scot was silent for some moments, a troubled frown on his face. Opening the covering on his food, he took out a slice of beef and popped it into his mouth. When Katherine suddenly got to her feet in preparation for departure, Scot's eyes filled with a kind of panic, and then they dimmed with resignation. "Leaving so soon, sweet Katherine?"

"I'm restless; need to walk."

"Then come and kiss me, sweet and twenty."

"Once, and quickly. You've such a serious expression on your handsome face!" She bent to his cheek, and then she rushed to the gate, into night.

Rather than going straight home, Katherine took a taxi to Central Hill. A vigorous north wind blew from the harbor, and she pulled her heavy shawl about her as she climbed up the stone steps that led to Central Hill Cemetery. Most of the tottering tombstones dated to the mid-1600s. She leaned against a tall marker and gazed down the sloping field of death, over the roofs of houses to the water below. Kingsport was illumed with lamplight. A faint fog crept over the dark sea, while a heavier cloud obscured the fantastic form of Kingsport Head, which rose one thousand feet above the foam. How ancient everything was, and how poetic the age-old beauty, giving her soul a mellowness that she had not known before. Happily, she danced among the black tombstones, and then beyond them to where a willow stood. Frolicking, she lifted her arms into the streaming vines, those vines that twined around her wrists and wove into her hair. She danced until exhausted, then dropped to chilly ground. Young moonlight cooled her brow, and when she lifted her face to it she espied the creature that hovered in dark sky. Rising from bended knee, she grasped the tasseled ends of her shawl and lifted hands to heaven. She could almost distinguish the pale face that floated far above her when, suddenly, a wild rush of tempestuous air pushed her and upset her balance. Heavily, Katherine fell to the graveyard ground. When again she gazed into the empyrean of night, she saw naught but thickening fog.

III.

She waded through the opaque air, relishing the residue of mist that touched her face. Some uncanny instinct led her along the winding streets and pavements, over worn and weathered bridges. She could feel the heavy pulse of Kingsport's psyche, its remnant of dream and darkness, of which Winfield Scot had spoken. Katherine could almost smell the ghostly past, the haunted future. Ah, the muted creaking of spectral ships that had slipped beneath the harbor. Oh, the weeping souls that sighed beneath the sea. She walked the narrow cobblestones of Harborside like one lost in fanciful phantasm and stumbled past the silent buildings that leaned improbably over the streets. Katherine knew that she was on Foster Street, for there was the tall and dilapidated building that had once been Mariner's Church but was now abandoned. Slowly she moved on to Water Street, toward the piers that were sheathed in yellow fog. She inhaled the heavy smell of sea air; it filled her nostrils as she stepped onto the rotting planks of an age-old pier.

She reached the pier's end, knelt, gazed outward. She waited. Dimly, sailing toward her in the fog, came the hazy silhouettes of weird winged things. Her lips trembled, aching to call out to the pale faces that watched her from above. The groaning wind rose over the water and brought the putrid stink of the sea—and of something else, something not of this world.

It glided toward her, out of the fog, over dark water. As it neared the pier, Katherine realized that Jeremy Blond's painting had not exaggerated the unearthly nature of the creature on its raft. Rather, he had caught precisely its essence. Katherine pressed her palms onto damp wood and leaned toward the apparition that stopped just inches from where she trembled. The figure bent to her. Its ropy hair writhed and reached for her, then wove into her own. Spectral claws wrapped around her shaking hands as stagnant shadow filled her pores and sank into her soul. With phantasmagorical motion she shivered with mutation, stretching a tingling mouth so as to sing new sounds that writhed within her throat.

The creature of wondrous nightmare drifted from her. Katherine raised her strange pale face to those twilight things that beckoned to her from above. Unfolding new-formed wings, she drifted above dark water to the flock that awaited her in foggy aether.

... *HUNGRY* ... RATS

Joseph S. Pulver, Sr.

for H. P. Lovecraft

Whiskey glass. No ice. The bite, solid burn, two fingers gone. Two fingers left. Second round tonight. Just to calm my nerves.

A little jumpy.

Been tense ... uneasy.

The noises. *Rat* noises. I need it. May need half a bottle more, or ...

My hand rests on my gun.

I get mean when I drink. Mean when I'm tense. My gun gets loud. Mean and loud and nasty.

My gun is loaded.

If they come ...

Fuck....

I lived around rats when I was young. Fifteen deserted, condemned houses—*dumps*—in my neighborhood (just three short blocks from the southern border of the city dump), and mountains of rats living in them. The house—half-burned-out shell is more like it—ten feet across the alley from mine was crawling with 'em. We kept our garbage cans in the alley and they were in them every night. Tearing into things even hungry-belly welfare kids would not eat.

One night my mother found one in my little sister's bed. I was eleven. Ran into that room scared to death by my mother's terrorized scream. She pulled my sister out of that bed and started in on the rat with an old wooden-handled corn broom.

Adrenaline and teeth. Something was gonna die in that room. Cold-ass fact. But the rat blew out the open bedroom window like its tail was on fire.

My sister slept with my mother that night.

I didn't sleep. Not with the darkness pressing at the windows. And the sound of scurrying outside.

Haven't slept much these pass few nights either.

Rats.

Scabs and scars. Matted fur, skin blistered with pox and bites. Teeth needle-sharp. Shit right outta nightmares. Evil shit those teeth. Blades, ravenous blades to rend and tear prey. Rip it to shreds and devour it. Teeth. Needle-razors. Fast and hungry. Always hungry. Always at war with its own stomach and the horde. Slinking, leaping, running. Fast and fast and faster. Eat first or starve, the law of the horde. Eat first and be strong. Grow. Or be eaten.

Rats—little fuckers.

Back then in the pantry—ripping open cereal boxes, wolfing down uncooked pasta, or the few cookies that ever came into the house, coming up through the walls to steal bouillon cubes or onions or to rip open packages of Jell-O. Leaving turds. And fleas. And God knows what else. Thieves. A blistered, undulating carpet of them. A chain reaction of filth and disease glaring through the dining room window as they fought over the garbage in the alley. Sharp. Intentional. Crowding. From the empty house next store into a full-blown hothouse.

Rats.

Evil, squeaking little fucks. Wormin' their way through shit-pipes, and moldy walls, plague-slick from rancid, twitching noses to scabby tail. Black and brown and grease-smeared fuckers.

Eatin'

and eatin'

and

eatin'. Any shit they can chew. One big never-ending black maw chewing everything in its path. Appetite as big and black and ravenous as the void.

Rats.

And they're here.

Right now.

Rats—god-damn vile fuckin' things.

In the walls.

This used to be an empty house. Then it was a shell-like ruin. Then it was rebuilt. And the cycle continues....

I didn't know who I was then. Just some cast-off. Throw-away street-trash. Just a skinny little street rat. Delapore didn't mean shit in the gray-ass streets of Baltimore. All that dead-yard mean and tough right up in your face, breathing its green teeth sickness in yer eyes, and the filth and grim clawing up your neck, trying to drown you and your wishes. Dreams. Didn't really have any. Too busy to stop and sit back and think of other things. When your belly's fuckin' empty that's what pushes you.

Delapore. There's a hundred names struggling here. Some are bigger. Some meaner. Some were packed into family groups. Threes or sixes or nines. Roaming packs, hungry eyes, hungry bellies. Not much you can do when the four Strout brothers (fucking grotesques half the size of dump trucks) have their eye on the thing you're eyeballin'.

Delapore. I took what I could get when I could take it. Didn't look back. Not on those streets.

1967. Peace and love and flowers about to spring up and paint rainbows all over the blues of the country's youth. But not here. Not in this slum. Fire was coming. And every hungry belly and mean eye was gas waitin' for the matchhead to be struck.

And it struck. Just like a motherfucker. kaBAM! WHOOSH! Just like that.

But I was not there.

I was in a jungle.

No ice cream or apple pie or snowmen. No Beatles on the car radio. No ripe young blonde girl next door with legs all the way up to heaven, or hot dogs at the football game ... It was deep and dirty and on fire. That hothouse dog-eat-dog hell of mud and sweat and boredom (until the guy next to you got a limb blown off and the whole fuckin' world stops) had tens of thousands on their knees and more than any sane man would care to count, dead. Murdered. Or about to be.

Corpses, or parts of 'em.

The stench of War and what it leaves half-eaten and rotting in its hot wake. You swim in it … or the blades of the machine execute you.

In the jungle.

Thick. Every green form or black shade is the frontline … hard and sleepless.…

Surrounded by madmen. Madmen who 12,000 miles away at home in the streets of America were, just minutes ago, boys, plunged into the most inhuman terrors of war. You ate 'em for breakfast or they ate you and shit you out for dinner.

War, the great eating machine. Legs and arms … and minds. Souls …

Lot of things happened there.…

Bad things everybody drinks to forget …

Pulled a wounded Brit photographer outta a rice paddy. He'd taken a mess of shit in a firefight he was trying to capture on film and was left for dead by Charlie. The fire team he was with were dead. He sure looked dead. But he was breathing. Trying to. So I hauled his ass out of that killing field. Dragged him from that wet boneyard and carried his sorry ass five clicks. Left him for the cutters to reanimate.

And they did.

Checked back on him a week or so later. He'd lost an eye. And his left arm wasn't a whole hell of a lot of use. All there, bunch of soon-to-be-scars and pins and bandages keepin' it place, but not any good for anything useful. But he was breathing and walkin' and talkin'.

Gerry told me he owed me.

Told me he knew the name Delapore.

He had stories about the Delapores.

Horrible, weird tales. Said I bore a bit of a resemblance to a portrait of Gilbert de la Poer, the first Baron Exham.

Asked after my lineage.

I fuckin' laughed.

Lineage?

I knew the name of my mother's mother and her father. Knew my old man was a drunk, a mean-ass drunk, and that he whored around. Married my mother, and ran with every set of legs that would part for him. Beat her. Most times just for the fuck of it. Got her pregnant twice. Then he split.

No one knew if he lived or died. I didn't give a rat-shit.

I heard he'd died. Shot in a cheap room over a shithole bar. Shot by a barfly-whore he was trying to cheat.

Fuckin' fine by me. Saved me the trouble.

"No, really. It's absolutely uncanny how much you resemble the Baron."

Baron, yeah right. Morphine—that's some heavy shit. I forgot the shit he was feeding me ten minutes after I walked away from his cot.

Then the war pulled us apart.

Ten years later he found me.

He'd gone home, and after readjustment and rehabilitation and trying to find the answers to everything in the bottom of a whiskey bottle and conversations with shrinks, dug into the de la Poer family. Reached out to a few American journalists who he had worked with, got a line on me and hopped on a jet.

I went home and went to work. Had a few lucky breaks. Made a truckload of money. Hell, it was a mountain. A mountain of solid gold.

And one day he showed up at my offices in Baltimore.

"Old fuckin' home week. My God, you look good. Old as shit and bald, but good."

His right hand in my right hand. Both of us smilin' like it was our birthday or something.

"I've been searching for you for a couple of years on and off," he said.

We went for drinks. And they turned into dinner.

And for dessert we had more drinks.

Seven hours of drinks.

And his story of the de la Poers and his search for them in America—in Virginia where they became the Delapores, and then me, came out....

Yeah, something about my father's father being from Virginia, I sorta remembered hearing something about that when I was a kid.

Fuck.

I had roots. Old, stately, and titled roots. I grew up on a shithole, back-alley Baltimore street with nothin' in my hands and little in my belly and now I had roots. *A god damn Baron.* Hot damn.

And I had money. Construction, oil (bought into a well-placed oil concern before the embargo hit), and gold. Bingo.

Imagine that. Me? Rich. And now related to some old baron.

The next night I sat in my living room. Some asshole on the news talking about The War. Then The Recession. Same old shit comin' down, or getting' shoved up yer ass 'til you howled.

Same old, same old—*same old*. Hittin' everyone smack in between the eyes. Both fuckin' barrels.

By my third drink I decided to go home. Just like John Wayne in *The Quiet Man*. Return to my family's ancestral home. Get as far away from the memories of Baltimore as I could.

Nothing to hold me to here. My mother had died of a stroke years ago and my sister had been killed when I was in The 'Nam. Car accident. She was fifteen.

Sick of facing a same tomorrow, for months I'd been toying with the idea of chucking it all. Sellin' it. And headin' to Montana, or maybe Bermuda. Just look out my window every day and see clean and wide open. Fields and mountains or clear blue sea. Didn't much matter.

No pollution. No traffic. No crush of people and phone calls, and gossip, and business deals. No tightrope. And no more god-damn fuckin' grime.

Quiet. Pure fuckin' quiet. Cram the fireworks and the reproach—all day, every day. Drama. Stick it all where the sun don't shine.

Maybe even the horrors of The War would go away....

Maybe I could put the bottle away before I looked in the mirror and saw my old man glarin' back at me....

Quiet. And maybe no hungry, angry knot in my belly. Gnawing ... Gnawing ...

I was tired.

Maybe ...

If John Wayne could do it, so could I.

I deserved a little peace....

And I had the money to buy me a whole lot of it.

And I was determined—*determined* to find it.

So I got on a plane and flew over the ocean. A different ocean this time. Landed in London. Quiet, warm, sunny day. Not like the day I landed in The 'Nam.

Pretty girls. Smooth whiskey. Big and grey and old, but the people seemed friendly.

I could get quiet here.

Got a car and a driver. Tossed my gear in the boot and headed out. North.

It was green. Not jungle green. Nice green. Lots of quiet spots.

Foul memories could fade here. Plagues that gnawed at my guts could be exorcised here.

I found the ruins of Exham Priory. A view of the city from the Baron's hill. Ancient forest and fields up here on high ground. Bought them. Got a hotel room and had Exham rebuilt.

Moved in.

It was quiet. Most nights too quiet. Too dark. Black as the starless jungle had been some nights. Being alone at night was hell.

This kind of quiet was not my friend.

Those nights I'd often got to town seeking company. Female company.

In the Anchester watering holes, which I began to roam at night more frequently, I heard tales and whispers of Druids and the feast of Beltain, and rumors of cannibalism. I'd humped through jungles and lived on hard city streets. The city eats a man alive.... Heard of sacrifice, been there done that. Too many times.

A tight black street, more alley than street. In a small, tight black place, The Serpent & The Goat, one old codger leaned in, smiled darkly, and said, *"Barbarous rites were found in Gaul ... the murderous cult of the Druids, who thought human sacrifice and ritual cannibalism were the greatest kind of piety. Others saw it. Wrote about it. Horrors. And evil ... Still here."* Came out like he was singing.

I was outta there. Fuck him. Old asshole, what did he know about horrors. Was he there?

I was.

Stopped roaming the bars for a while. Stayed home. In. Looked out my windows. Walked the green wood. Walked it slow.

Or I walk the long halls I'd rebuilt, listening for whispers. Stared into paintings I'd purchased and had hung ... For a few months I looked in every nook and cranny. Top to bottom.

Exham was a big place. Some parts of it old. Very old ...

Each night the sun would die and my demons returned to pick at my scars.

347

When night bloomed full and pressed, I'd weaken and reach for the whiskey bottle. Two fingers and two more and two more ... I'd get drunk and pass out, the litter of empty bottles on my floor. Dark dreams came to me ... *Rats ... and the black Baltimore streets ... Rats. And the black wet jungle of 'Nam ... Rats ... mud and alleys ... and rats ... ever hungry ... Scabs and scars ... Rats. Matted fur, skin blistered with pox and bites. Teeth needle-sharp. Shit right outta nightmares ... Rats. Rats. Fast and hungry. Always hungry. Always at war with its own stomach and the horde. Slinking, leaping, running. Fast and fast and faster. Eat first or starve, the law of the horde. Eat first and be strong. Grow. Or be eaten.*

Rats—little fuckers ... scurrying through my dreams ...

Gerry came from time to time. I'd pull out a bottle and we'd laugh. Somewhere in the second bottle we'd fade. A few days of it and he'd go home and I'd go back to seeking peace.

Didn't find it.

Spend hours at my windows looking at town. Wondered what it looked like when it was a tiny village. Thought about the Baron. Wondered what he thought about when he looked down.

Did he feel the loneliness of this place?

I thought he must have been a knight, would have worn a sword when he walked his keep. I had a knife and a gun....

Gerry had found the painting of the Baron in a small museum. I bought it—paid up the ass to ransom him, but he was my ancestor and a soldier. I was taught you don't leave men behind. Thought I was bringing him home where he could find peace. Hung it in my study over the great leaden maw of the fireplace.

Stood and drank and talked to him. Spoke of war. Of rats and mistakes on the battlefield. Toasted him with a goblet I bought. They told me it had belonged to some mage. I half hoped it might have powers and heal me.

Stared at him up there. A hard man. Hard, I know. Know well. We were both soldiers, warriors. In my gut I knew there were times we'd had to grasp the thorns of difficult choices to survive.

Baron Exham looked lonely. Looked like he carried a weight. I knew about weight. Knew about humpin' it up hills. And he looked half mad.

I was starting to understand madness. I was going nuts being up here all alone.

If I had someone, I might find peace.... Someone to talk to. Someone to be close to. Someone to hold me when the blackness pressed....

I started looking in town....

In shops and bars and clubs ... Rented the company of a couple of glimmering ladies to warm me on a couple of frost-bitten nights ... They laughed in the right places. They were good with their clothes off.

Tried a few good girls too ...

Six months of cold laughs and reserved fucking. I discarded this one, then that....

I was in a gallery, looking at a painting of two naked women in a circle of trees. The moon made their white skin look ghostly, yet alluring, and she was there. Just there. Out of the blue.

"Nice. If you like that sort of thing." She smiled.

"I like a lot of things."

Raven tresses with straight bangs. Dark eyes. Shrines, luminous and deep as the blackness of the night fields. The flawless ivory skin of a fairy princess. Slender with long curves. Long fingers with antique rings with blood-red stones on every one. Fingers that could perform magic.

Out of her heels, five eight. Those legs. That ass. That perfect tight little hot ass. Lookin' at it I could feel it under me. My fever, her fire— the tremors, shuddering. You could make a meal out of her. Dessert too. What sweet eatin'. A little cherry-red pressed to your lips.

She looked like an eyeful of heaven. If you like your heaven packed with C4 in the places that count.

Far as I'm concerned if it ain't packin' a punch why bother.

"Care to buy it for me?" And she laughed. Came right outta those little cherry-red lips and I could feel the tremor.

Wanted more.

A hell of a lot more.

And she was gone before I could untie my tongue from the anvil.

I had a taste—skin and mouth, grace and perfumed stars, breath filled with magic seeds of birdsong—even her knees beckoned me. Wanted more. I followed her. In a café I walked up to her table and said, "Maybe I could buy you lunch?"

She pointed to the chair beside her.

"Sit."

I did.

We ate. We drank wine. She came home with me.

Stayed.

We'd walk, among dark trees and over small hills thick with fragile flowers, in the shadows, in the frost; the scent of naked darkness blessed our steps. Drinking, we'd bathed in wine. Fucked like bunnies. Not sure who couldn't get enough. Think it was me. I loved being in her arms. Loved the smell of her. Loved how she tasted. Loved the things of flame and destiny she gave to me.

When we weren't in bed she'd walk the grounds. A fairy-tale priestess, rare and uncommonly beautiful—flawless and strange— sometime it seemed to me she floated, never touching the ground. She loved moonlight. And its luster on her skin, sweet and addicting, was something from an opium dream, or from some magic secretly woven in the tiered moon gardens of Bagdad.

I followed as she explored the wood and my halls.... Followed when she walked the wood naked on All Hallow's Eve ... Watched when she raised her arms and danced for the stars ...

I was careful to not let her discover what I had found.... *That was mine.*

Days and nights—all those nights tattooed with stars or roaring moon or meadows of clouds hoarding the lights of heaven in their fat bellies ...

Some nights we sat quietly in the soft amber glow and watched candles die. Some we'd sit under autumn stars and I'd stare at her. At her hands. At her eyes, or her gentle breast rising and falling, or her tiny white dove feet. Even when no remark passed her lips, she was not silent, and I took the maps and tales she breathed into the air between the gates of my teeth and in behind my eye. Took it deep inside.

Gerry came 'round less and less. But he'd come and we'd drink and she'd be there. Drinking and laughing. She'd get up, walk around the room, and I watched Gerry watch her. Eyes on her ass, moving along her curves. Knew he wanted her.

No one was taking mine. It was mine. I had the fucking hunger. I

350

had the empty belly that needed filling. What's mine is mine.

She'd retired. He was drunk. Talking about her. She was hot as the sun. She was sexy. She was ... She was ...

She was mine.

A knife came out ...

"Mine."

The knife said a lot more than I did.

Whiskey glass. His on the floor. No ice.

I pushed him down the cellar stairs and went upstairs.

... To take what was mine.

Took it. Face down, then flipped her over. Rode that fine ass. That perfect little tight fine ass. Had her nipple in my mouth. Tasted her sweat. Wanted to taste everything.

"Fuck every inch of me." Her eyes are dark slits.

An orgy of breath rushes from her steaming lips ...

That's what I wanted, every groaning, pumping, nibbling inch of thunder and delirium.

... Ghouls, feasting on each other. Lips parted, whispering. The vampire kiss on jaw and breast. A blur of nails and soft heaven echoing. Meteors and bellies, spiderweb and rattling passion.

Teeth. Teeth, mad vivid teeth. And red poppy lips. Silky poppies ...

Purring ...

Touching and rolling ... the front line, body to body ...

Little cherry red lips: "Do it. God, do it." Little cherry-red lips: "Harder." Little predator whore's mouth: "I want fire. *Fire.*"

And she's squeezing. And nibbling—little cherry-red lips pressed to my flesh, nibbling on my soul. And pushing and pawing. Fingers scurrying here, then there. Elbows and simmering hearts, hurrying. And I went off. I'm pounding on her and tearing at her.

And the moaning has turned into a scream ...

Her eyes are screaming and she's trying to crawl out of bed.

And I've got what's mine in my hands ... squeezing and squeezing ...

What's mine is mine.

She's a corpse.

Hot and wet.

Covered in my kisses.

Her skin tastes so good …

I bit too hard? She bit too hard? Her blood on my tongue. Hot. And so good …

What's mine is mine….

I carried her down and put her by him. Went and got a bottle.

Took them down into what I had found below….

My pulse races … half a bottle passes over my lips … I slip … Sit in the blackness … greed and fear stirred together … her magic blood on my lips …

And I want more….

The moon came up and overpowered the tranquil orchestra of exotic stars. Its light had found its way down here…. Rats came to dine in my black-hole table….

Charlie, locked and loaded and each in a deathly fugue mask, scurried off into the thick jungle….

A sea of old bones …

Plopped Gerry right there.

Then dragged her down here …

Naked and bloody. Not cold yet … Starin' at her curves makes me hungry…. those sweet little cherry-red lips … I can still taste her on my tongue….

Her blood. Her magic blood.

On my lips.

Smeared on the back of my hand … Her blood taking me back in time. Taking me out of this world …

Rats.

Fuckin' black demon's eyes. A sea of eyes. Those eyes … staring … filling the silence with their breathing … probing … Sharp white teeth. Teeth that catch … the demon kiss … evil … so near …

Rats. Starin' at her … at her curves … starin'—their eyes are dark slits, like a hungry kid face pressed to a butcher's window…. Fred the Butcher's window in Baltimore—he was greasy as a rat. Had rat eyes … I remember the raw meat hanging there … sweet … and fresh … hungry to get my hands on it …

A sharp beam of moonlight, as if a blade had sliced the belly of the moon and its radiance was pouring out, lit the floor. Littered about me

... a dry sea ... white, but no froth ... a sea of bones ... sawed and picked at and cracked open ... human bones.

Half drunk. A little scared, a lot mad. Locked and loaded. A knot of hunger gnawing in my gut. And the cave before me became a cave of another life long ago and far away....

Charlie had settled in—might have been a hundred of the fuckers right outside ... Hunkered down tight. I hid in a cave just above their position. Damp and wet ... A gook came in, I took my knife to him ... slit his throat and kept cutting ... And we lay in there night and day ... for seven days. I was terrified. And sharing a cave with a corpse ... Couldn't leave, they'd see me. Kill me. I was half mad with hunger ... hallucinating ... The streets of Baltimore came to me.... Eat or be eaten ... saliva ... motionless and I'm staring at ... I chose to live ... then the first rats came. Slinked in ... silent little fuckers ... Just a few ... I killed them.... Then a few more came ... Killed them too. Cut off their heads ... Stacked 'em up ... Saw the evil, the greed, in their black eyes. Their eyes were dark slits....

A dozen or so but they never got near the prize—My Prize ... my knife made sure of that....

The moon was up and Charlie was gone....

But not the rats ...

More came ...

I fled.

Ran ... half the night ...

The hot blackness melting around me ... fear stretched out ... trying to find real in the burning ... Ran from limitation ... through the curves and altars of night ... over a hill of mud, a forgery under the wreckage of a dark star ... blood on the cracked lips of my earthquake mouth ... Had to leave

what was MINE ...

Mine illuminated. Mine on the dead tongue of rank air.

Mine. Voiceless. Whispering. This pavilion of eternity—Mine! This yawning bowl of my heredity—Mine!

That cave and this cave ... *I am lord here* ... Rats ... and the remains of the dead ... dead by my hand ... motionless and I'm staring at them ... *all mine* ... All mine!

JOSEPH S. PULVER, SR.

And the rats are staring ... the ravenous glow of dreadful orgy eyes on the earthmeat ... tiny teeth radiating death in the slice of moonlight ... the slash of the scythe on the holocaust menu ... Rats. Staring—*at what's mine.*

My knife is sharp. Still hungry.

I've got the hunger. It's in me ... Fuck them.

I remember: eat or be eaten.

Rats, devils of the plague ... the insidious onyx slithering of Nemesis ...

Fuckin' rats. Rotten little fucks—just like Charlie. Vise-grip eyes torturing me. All my mistakes of love and heart and fragile laughter and storms and murder, rattling in their mouths.

Rats, lean heathens—*daemons!*—carved in Hell, crouched in the plump blackness, ready to dance.

Now shrieking, threatened. The blackness—huge—hissing—leaking the language of hysteria—bites ...

I raise my knife.

"You're not getting *mine.*"

VIRGIN'S ISLAND

Donald Tyson

The enclosed transcriptions were made from documents discovered among the effects of Jeremy Neeley, a thirty-four-year-old Anglican minister of Dartmouth, Nova Scotia, who is presently missing and presumed drowned. They were discovered the morning of May 27, 1935, in a sealed leather portfolio case found floating on the surface of the sea near the rock known locally as Virgin's Island, an unusual geological formation in the open Atlantic some twenty-one miles south from the mouth of Halifax harbor, and separated from the mainland by seven miles. Thomas Campbell, a lobster fisherman from the small fishing community of Hackett's Cove, spotted the portfolio while en route to examine his lobster traps and drew it out of the water on the end of a boat hook. Not knowing what to do with the leather case or its water-sodden contents, he turned them in to the nearest detachment of the Royal Canadian Mounted Police, who had them conveyed to the Public Archives at Dalhousie University for examination.

In this way the documents came into my possession. As a conservator who has frequently had to deal with mildewed or water-damaged papers over the years, I must admit that the initial appearance of the matted mass did not seem promising. I was unable to offer any assurances of success to RCMP Constable Henry Harris, who deposited the portfolio in my office here at the Archives Building, but I made the promise that I would do what lay within my power to render the documents readable. I am happy to report to the board that almost three-fourths of the leaves in the portfolio, amounting to thirty-seven items, were salvageable. By good fortune Mr. Neeley used in his pen a permanent black ink that is uncommonly resistant to blurring.

The members of the board will find my transcriptions of the documents bundled in the same order they occupied in the portfolio. The originals have been returned to the RCMP along with the leather case that held them and a copy of these transcriptions. Some of them are newspaper cuttings from various papers such as the Halifax *Morning Herald* and the *New York Times*. Other items are letters of correspondence with local historian and folklorist Dorothy Shriff, and with Clyde Evans, an amateur mountaineer and a resident of Montreal who achieved some notoriety toward the end of the last decade for his mountain-climbing expedition to the kingdom of Nepal. Evans has been reported missing and must be presumed to have perished in the sea along with Neeley. The rest of the documents consist of sundry notes made by Neeley in pencil on loose letter-sized sheets with a high linen rag content, and a kind of journal written in a hard-backed, bound notebook, which I was forced to disassemble during my conservation efforts—individual leaves are counted as separate items.

The only other object in the portfolio was a bas-relief carving on one side of a thin ivory tablet approximately six inches tall and two inches wide (refer to the photograph enclosed with the transcripts). The back of the tablet is blank. Our biology department here at the university has been unable to identify the animal source for the ivory. The anthropology department reports that the carving resembles some of the religious art found among the tribes inhabiting the northern coast of Greenland that were discovered during Rasmussen's Second Thule Expedition of 1916; however, the resemblance is not exact. This carving was returned with the conserved documents and is presently in the hands of the RCMP in Halifax.

As to the full significance of these documents, I confess myself to be at a loss to offer an explanation. It is evident that Neeley suffered from some form of hallucination or delusion, perhaps brought on or at least exacerbated by exposure to the elements. Although the account in his journal is coherent, the subject matter itself demonstrates a lapse of sanity. There is an indication in one of the letters that for many years he was obsessed with Virgin's Island. From the point of view of local folklore, the material is of sufficient interest that it is my recommendation to this board that efforts be made to secure the original documents and the ivory carving, along with the leather portfolio, from the Neeley family when the police have exhausted their efforts to locate Neeley's remains.

Written this day of June 9, 1935, by Herbert Moore, chief conservator of the Public Archives of Nova Scotia, Dalhousie University, Halifax.

Newspaper filler item clipped from the May 3, 1935, edition of the *New York Times:*

> Halifax, N. S.—Etched deeply into the face of an island which rises from the Atlantic surges off the S. coast of Nova Scotia 20 m. from Halifax is the strangest rock phenomenon which Canada boasts. Storm, sea, and frost have graven into the solid cliff of what has come to be known as Virgin's Island an almost perfect outline of the Madonna with the Christ Child in her arms.
>
> The island has sheer and wave-bound sides, is a danger to ships, and is absolutely uninhabited. So far as is known, no human being has ever set foot on its shores.

Human interest piece from the Halifax *Morning Herald,* December 11, 1933:

"Saluting the Lady" by Tom Thumm

> No one knows when the quaint practice of "saluting the Lady" began among the fishermen on this rugged part of our Nova Scotian coast, but one old Bluenoser reports hearing tales of the custom from his grandfather when he sat on the old man's knee. It appears to be a unique bit of the kind of local colour for which this Maritime Province is so justly famed, steeped in the past as we are by virtue of being one of the oldest settled regions in North America. Some say an Irish schooner captain named Burke started the custom around the middle of the

last century, but other authorities stoutly maintain that it has been going on for at least two hundred years. Whatever its origins, it is a reality of the sea that no Maritime boat or ship will pass by the sheer east cliff face of Virgin's Island without sounding her horn in tribute. The direst misfortune is said to befall any scoffer foolish enough to ignore the salute. One long blast, three short blasts, and again one long—this our seafaring men call "saluting the Lady," and they would no more omit this duty than they would give up their hot rum toddy.

Newspaper item from the *Yarmouth Telegram,* September 24, 1934:

Longliner *Seaking* returning to Yarmouth from the Grand Banks, lost with all hands on the night of September 21 off the rock known as Virgin's Island, some 20 miles southeast of Halifax. Other ships in the area reported moderate seas and a wind from the northeast of seven knots. Skies were clear. A schooner, the *Mary Mae* out of Bangor bound for Sydney, reported strange lights on the uninhabited rock near where the misfortune is presumed to have occurred, but no connection between these lights and the sinking of the *Seaking* has been established. Further notices of this tragedy will be printed if more information becomes available.

Handwritten letter from Nova Scotian historian and author Dorothy Shriff to Jeremy Neeley, dated March 29, 1935 [much of the text, particularly on the second leaf, is blurred beyond recognition and unrecoverable; *recommendation:* attempt to procure a clear copy from the records of Dorothy Shriff]:

[first leaf]
... afraid that there is little more I can tell you concerning the folklore of the ocean oddity known locally as the Virgin's Island, but officially named Story Rock after Captain James Story of the Royal Navy, who discovered the island in 1681.

Story reported that his ship, H.M.S. *Antelope,* a 48-gun frigate of some 516 long tons, was making its way cautiously through a bank of fog when the sheer cliff of the island reared up immediately in front of her bow, extending higher than even the lookout on the mainmast could follow with his eyes. Story later would remark that "it seemed as though we had reached the very end of the world itself."

He made immediate and strenuous efforts to turn the ship. One of the ordinary seamen, Jack Beckker by name, was lost over the side in the confusion and sank like a stone before anyone could throw him a line. Fortunately for the captain and his crew, the wind was on the port bow and he was able to tack off the cliff just in time to avoid a wreck. He wrote in his ship's log, "The rock rises sheer from the sea, and when the wind is from the southwest the waves breaking upon it make scarce a sound that can be heard from further than thirty yards. Consequently the rock poses considerable danger to His Majesty's ships should they steer this course with greater frequency in the future, as seems likely given the prosperity of the Providence Plantations and Massachusetts Bay" ...

[second leaf]

... became broken-down with drink in later life, so his words are to be viewed with skepticism. Story's grandson averred that his grandfather never was able to get a full night of sleep after his near encounter with the rock, but that in his dreams he would return to that dreadful morning and watch as something unnatural that matched the color of the sea took Jack Beckker under the waves, while he stood (in the dream) paralyzed and unable to cry out or offer assistance ... [there is a considerable lacuna here]

... legend of the Micmac Indians reporting sightings from the mainland of strange lights on the wind-blown summit of the rock, lights that danced and ascended into the heavens ... Glooscap, their great hero, climbed the cliffs and fought such a fierce battle with an evil spirit that it made the island capsize and sink, but it rose again because the sea would not receive it ...

[the remainder of the two-page letter is illegible]

Carbon copy of a typed letter from Neeley to Clyde Evans dated November 1, 1934:

Dear Clyde,

It filled my heart with joy to read in your last letter that you wish to accompany me on my little expedition. When I wrote asking your expert advice concerning the equipment I would need to scale the cliff, I did not dare hope that you would offer to come along. It is a poor affair compared with your towering achievement in Nepal, to say nothing of your triumphs in the Andes three years ago. I confess, I was not looking forward to attempting the climb on my own, given my scant practical experience on sheer rock faces. You've put my mind at rest about reaching the top, and I can now turn my thoughts to what I must do when we get there.

In gratitude,

Jeremy Neeley

Typed letter from Clyde Evans to Neeley, dated November 7, 1934:

My dear chum,

You didn't think I'd let you attempt this hare-brained stunt on your own? It would have been the same as murder. How could I live with myself if one of my old schoolmates came to grief only because I wouldn't lift a helping hand? To be honest, you've got my imagination working in top gear. This climb won't be such a snap as you seem to think, not even with me at the top of the rope. There's a reason Virgin's Island has never been climbed, you know, and it isn't just because the federal government has made it a bird sanctuary and declared it off limits. It's a damned difficult climb!

I've been looking at the photographs of the cliffs you sent, and I agree that the easiest route will probably be up the eastern face of the island, the side that bears the image—it's a little higher, but the fractured condition of the rock should provide better purchase. The real trick, you know, is going to be in transferring everything from the boat to the cliff. I'll get my affairs in order here in Montreal, and I'll let you know in a few months by post if I have a break in my schedule in the spring when we can attempt this mad expedition of yours, which you are so hell-bent on trying.

Your friend,

Clyde

Carbon copy of a typed letter from Neeley to Clyde Evans, dated January 30, 1935:

Dear Clyde,

In response to the curiosity expressed in your last missive as to my motivations, let me only say that Virgin's Island has become something of an obsession. I've been fascinated by the island since childhood. My uncle used to tell me fishermen's tales about its ghost lights and the evil misfortunes they brought unwary mariners who neglected to salute the Lady. For the past two years I've been studying everything ever written about the rock. I've even had dreams about it—real doozies, let me tell you. I can never remember them clearly when I wake up but I'm always covered in sweat and trembling like a leaf in a gale.

There's a family connection with the island, did you know? I'm a descendant on my mother's side of its discoverer, Captain James Story, whose grandson settled in Boston. At the time of the American Revolution, he and his family fled New England with the other Loyalists and came to Yarmouth. Eventually one of his descendants found his way to the Halifax region, where they've been ever since.

The truth of the matter is that I can't tell you why I must make this climb, because I don't know myself. Think of it as a kind of spiritual pilgrimage. In every man's life there are things he feels he must do, and this is one of mine. Ever since hearing the legends of Virgin's Island as a boy I've felt drawn to the place. I'm hoping that after I've climbed the cliff and walked around on top of the rock, I'll get it out of my system for good and all. It will be a relief not to be plagued any longer by these damned nightmares, which I believe are produced by the frustration of wanting to explore the rock but not being able to reach it.

I hope I haven't said too much—I don't want you to think that your old school chum's brain has turned mystical. We Anglican ministers are a hard-headed bunch, and more skeptical than most when it comes to superstitions.

Faithfully yours,

Jeremy

Handwritten letter in ink from Clyde Evans to Neeley, dated March 17, 1935:

Jerry,

Good news, old sport. I can positively guarantee two weeks of liberty in May, beginning on the 7th. How does this suit your plans? It better suit, because it's the only time I can find between my lecture tour and the Alaskan climb I've promised to lead. It's too bad it is so early in the year. The winds on that cliff are apt to be damned cold, and God help us if we tumble into the sea. But it's all I've got, old chap—let me know if it suits.

Clyde

The following two leaves of penciled notes in Neeley's hand was attached by paperclip to three 9-inch by 12-inch aerial survey photographs of Virgin's Island showing the top of the island, and the eastern and southern faces.

[notes, first leaf]

Island's overall shape is a surprisingly regular rectangle, apart from an indentation in the northern side, with the longest diagonal extending roughly from the southeast to the northwest. Total area, approximately eleven acres. Elevation above sea level, 956 feet along the eastern edge, declining to 795 feet on the western edge. All sides descend sheer into the ocean—there is no boat landing of any kind. The surface is too boulder-strewn and uneven to allow access by small aeroplane, and the unpredictable winds would preclude approach by dirigible, were anyone wealthy enough and foolish enough to try it.

Ecology consists of hardy low-lying plants, grasses and lichens in which numerous species of seabirds, chiefly razorbills, northern gannets, auks, puffins, and herring gulls, make their nests. These birds also nest in fissures and on ledges of the vertical cliffs, and such is their variety and abundance that the island has been declared the most important Eastern Canadian seabird habitat south of Labrador.

Toward the center of the island there is considerable rubble in the form of massive stones of roughly cubical dimensions that are tumbled together, giving the impression of some sort of intelligent pattern; however, the sheer enormity of the stones seems to preclude this notion, which has been advanced by several writers of sensationalistic books on ancient civilizations, one of them James Churchward, author of the well-known work *The Lost Continent of Mu*. (*Re:* Churchward's response to my letter of inquiry on October 3 of last year.)

[notes, second leaf]

The highest cliffs are oriented almost due east. (*Query:* Can this be coincidence?) When approached by sea from the east, the island rises above the horizon like a vast obelisk, and in the early morning light, shines red with the color of newly splashed blood. The image of the Virgin fills two-thirds of the cliff surface, but it is only visible when the rays of the sun strike the rock from a more southerly direction, enhancing the irregularities in the stone with highlights and shadows. In the afternoon hours the image becomes entirely obscured by shadow.

Geologists dismiss the image as an optical illusion. James Churchward is of the contrary opinion that it was carved on the rock some 20,000 to 30,000 years in the past by an advanced civilization using some form of heat ray that fused the rock. (*Query:* Was the image made by Atlanteans? and if so, for what purpose?)

Image shows a seated woman in a hood and flowing robe, cradling a babe on her knee and gazing down at it. (*Item:* some fishermen have reported that on the day of the summer solstice, when the light is at precisely the correct angle, the face of the figure changes to resemble a skull, and the babe becomes something inhuman. Only a handful of the many thousands who have viewed the image claim to have witnessed this effect, which is rudely denied by other fishermen for whom the image is sacred, or at least forbidden to criticize.)

Typed letter from James Churchward to Jeremy Neeley, dated October 3, 1934:

Dear Mr. Neeley,

Many thanks for your kind praise regarding my books. A writer is always gratified when his work meets with the approval of readers, particularly when they display a grasp of the subject matter as you have done.

As to your specific question about the origin of the astonishing icon known as the Madonna of the Atlantic—yes, I do believe that the image was artificially created at some period in the prehistoric past, and that it long antedates the Pyramids of Giza, and even the Sphinx, which is so much older than the Pyramids. We can only speculate as to how such an enormous image might be created, but I believe that it was done by means of chromatic rays that had as their power source energized crystals with the property of magnifying the light of the sun.

To us, it is an image of the Madonna with Child, but you must realize that to the ancient Egyptians it would have appeared to be Isis holding on her knee the babe Horus; the Hindus might have interpreted it as Krishna in the arms of Devaki. The image is not Christian as such, but is a universal image of nurture and motherhood. We tend to interpret it as the Virgin Mary with the baby Jesus only because we have been conditioned by religious art to think of it in these terms.

At some time in the future I hope to make a closer study of Virgin's Island for a book dealing with the ancient lost civilization of Greenland. Perhaps we will meet in your native city of Halifax. In the meantime, I do thank you again for you interest in my work.

Yours sincerely,

James Churchward

Single leaf of sundry notes in pencil. They appear to be random jottings.

Propitiation: the act of pacifying, appeasing, or conciliating a god with offerings and sacrifices, in order to win the favor of the god, or to regain the good will of the deity.

Euphemism: an auspicious term substituted in place of an inauspicious term.

Example—the Greek Furies were called the *Erinyes* (Angry Ones), but were often referred to euphemistically as the *Eumenides* (Gracious Ones) as a superstitious way of turning aside their wrath.

Second example—the fairies of Celtic mythology were greatly feared and dreaded, but were sometimes addressed aloud as the "Good Folk" as a way of pacifying their malice.

High Places: gods of the pagan world were often worshipped on high places such as treeless mountaintops. Witches assembled on sabbat festivals on high places. Refer to the Brocken, Hartz Mountain Range; also the Blocksberg; Heuberg; Lyderhorn in Norway; refer to "Night on Bald Mountain" by Mussorgsky.

Oracular dreaming: the practice of receiving oracles in the form of dream images or messages. It was believed that the gods communicated with men through their dreams, and that to be chosen for such messages was a singular blessing.

Mother Goddess forms: Isis; Astarte; Ceres; Virgin Mary; Matronit; Shakti
Mother of monsters: Tiamat
Mother of abortions: Lilith; Hecate

The remaining document is a dated journal of the climbing expedition to Virgin's Island, written in Reverend Neeley's own hand in a bound, hard-back notebook. The paper is of excellent quality, and the permanent black ink has not blurred to any appreciable degree. I will refrain from commenting about the contents of the journal, as it is not my place to do so, but will observe that folklorists may find the material fascinating, should the board determine to acquire the notebook for the Archives.

Journal of Rev. Jeremy Neeley

May 9
We set out for Virgin's Island from the small fishing port of East Dover before first light. The boat had sat tied to the dock, prepared and waiting for the run, for the past five days. No one was up and about when we left due to the early hour, but the villagers will see my black Packard Coupe parked up the road and notice that the boat is missing. I've told nobody where I'm going and gave a false name when renting the boat. What Clyde and I intend to do is against federal law, and because of my position as a member of the clergy I can't risk being betrayed to the Mounties. I doubt any of the villagers would talk—they engage in a fair amount of smuggling and are not fond of the police—but it pays to be cautious.

Had another of those damned dreams with the deep, throbbing

roars and menacing shadows last night but said nothing about it to Clyde at breakfast. His mind was filled with the details of the expedition, and I daresay he didn't even notice my subdued manner. He's the least introspective human being I've ever known and lives as much in the present moment as any of his Viking ancestors. I let him take the tiller of the Johnson Sea-horse outboard, and we putted out of the harbour over water as flat as a pane of glass, the little four-horsepower engine moving us smartly along. The outboard is only a few years old and should be reliable; the owner of the boat assured me that it would not quit on us.

Conditions couldn't have been more benign. The air was warm for this time in the spring and there was almost no wind. Both of us were dressed for the worst the Atlantic could throw at us. I suppose the East Dover fishermen would have laughed to see us go out, bundled up as we were, but they wouldn't have known that we intend to stay overnight, and perhaps longer, on an exposed rock in all kinds of weather.

When we hit the swell of the open ocean the breeze freshened. I was glad I had let Clyde handle the boat. I concentrated on not losing my sausages and scrambled eggs, and kept us pointed in the right direction with my liquid-filled pocket compass. Virgin's Island can be seen from the heights of some points on the mainland, but not from our port of departure. I confess, my heart thundered in my chest when it came into view. It is impressive enough in photographs, but when first seen with the naked eye it almost appears supernatural, so strangely does it rise up from the deep, like the lone tombstone of some giant in an endless watery graveyard.

We had to round the shoulder of the island to reach the eastern face. As we did so, we saw the towering expanse of the cliff, blood-red in the rising sun. A thrill went through me such as I have never before experienced, a mingling of expectation with dread, and a kind of fatalistic relief that the long waiting was at last over. The image of the Madonna and Child was not yet visible, which was a pity, I reflected to myself, since by the time it became highlighted by the angle of the rising sun we would be too close to the cliff to appreciate its beauty. White-feathered gulls dipped and wheeled above us as we approached the monolith, the air filled with their indignant cries. I was glad that I had decided to wear my canvas fishing hat.

As agreed, we selected the most likely landing spot and worked the boat in with the emergency oars to secure it to the rock face. The rise and fall of the boat on the gentle swell made me queasy again, but I tried to give no sign of it. Below the high mark of the waves the cliff was cloaked in a thick mat of dark-green seaweed that smelled strongly of salt. Clyde deftly transferred himself to the rock and clung on its side like a fly, with his left hand wedged in a fissure. With the other hand he inserted steel eye-loops into narrow cracks in the stone and drove them home with a hammer that was lashed by a cord around his wrist.

Never was I more thankful that he had decided to accompany me. I doubt I could have done what he did. At last the lines were attached to the bow and stern, and the rubber tyres draped over the landward side of the boat to absorb the inevitable shocks when the waves sent it against the rock. It was impossible to fix the boat firmly against the rock because of the rise and fall of the waves, to say nothing of the tides, but we did the best we could to make it secure and safe.

As I write these words sitting in the stern, Clyde is working his way up the first pitch, driving in pitons and trailing hemp rope behind him. Soon I will begin to inch my way up the cliff. We both have heavy packs, but plan to pull them up on lines as we go. Clyde is completely at home on the rock face. I can hear him whistling to himself, so still is the sea. The wind must be from another direction, for there isn't a trace of it in the boat. It really is a fine morning. Even so, I have checked the flotation compartments to make certain they are tight. This boat will not sink, even should the waves capsize it. Just as well, since it is our only way back to the mainland.

(later)

We completed the climb without mishap. As I sit here cross-legged on the top of the cliff, facing the open ocean with my journal on my knee, my pen so trembles with excitement that I can scarce still it enough to write these words. The object of my enthusiasm is before my eyes, resting in the crease between the pages of my journal. It scarcely seems real, yet there it is. But I must record its finding in proper order and not let my wonder and delight carry me away.

I found the climb arduous but manageable. I have often climbed the mountains of Cape Breton as a recreation, but have seldom faced sheer walls such as this one. I confess that I was nervous at the beginning, but this soon passed thanks to Clyde's expert lead. As the sun rose and began to move more southwardly in the heavens, shadows showed themselves on the warming rock face. By bracing my feet against the cliff and leaning backward on the rope, I could make out above me the curve of the Virgin's shoulder and the rounded head of the Christ child. At that distance there was no definition in the features of the infant's face.

What people think they see in the features is mostly an illusion, I think, similar to the illusion of the so-called man in the moon, which looks nothing like a man. Psychologists have determined that our minds are ordered in such a way that we automatically seek to perceive the human face and the human form in abstract patterns and textures. The detail that passers-by on ships think they see in the image of the Madonna is a product of their own expectations, projected onto the random patches of light and shade on the cliff.

The birds proved a constant distraction. Their shrill cries never ceased, and they swooped and soared quite near to us as they passed, agitated by our inexplicable presence in their world, where no human being had ventured before or, at the very least, where no human had ventured for many centuries, if the legend of Glooscap is to be given credence. Following with my gaze one uncommonly aggressive northern gannet that flew close over my head, I saw it vanish, seemingly into the face of the cliff above. I knew this could not be and fixed the location in my memory; then, as I ascended, I worked my way across toward the spot, insofar as the rope set in the stone by Clyde would allow lateral progress.

In this way I found the recess in the cliff that Clyde had missed, for he had made his ascent some three yards to the left of the opening. When I pulled myself up level with it I got a bad fright. I had forgotten the bird in my excitement. Of course it was still in the recess, hidden by shadow. It exploded out at my face with a thunder of wings and a shrill scream. My grip on the rope faltered and I slipped several feet before I caught myself. The abrupt drop had the useful consequence of sending the bird harmlessly over the top of my hat, but it make my heart freeze for a full beat.

Pulling myself back up, I peered into the shadowed opening. It was curiously regular, as though it had been cut or bored into the rock by some artificial means. In size it was some two feet high and eight or nine inches across. I glanced up. Clyde had stopped and was gazing down on me with curiosity, his face framed against the sky in the golden halo of his curling blond hair. I waved to show that nothing was wrong and put my hand into the opening. Amid the bird droppings and bits of browning grasses I felt a nest that was deep enough to be concealed from sight. It was not the sort of nest we encounter in our walks through the woods on the mainland, but was merely an irregular mat of fibers. My fingers brushed an egg, still warm from the breast of the absent and very annoyed mother.

With care I extended my arm as far into the cavity as I could reach and felt beyond the prickly twigs and straw of the nest to the space behind it. I thought it was empty and was about to withdraw my hand, when I brushed something that felt like a flat piece of wood. I drew it out and saw that it was, of all things, a small ivory carving! You may imagine my astonishment. Several times I turned it in my hand, then realized the risk I was taking and with the greatest care slid it into the deep pocket of my trousers. Had it slipped from my fingers, it would have been lost forever. I spent several minutes feeling around blindly in the cavity but discovered nothing else, not even beneath the nest, which I felt obliged to move since I could not risk missing anything that might be beneath it. Apart from the carving and the nest, the recess was empty.

Busy with the packs, Clyde had not noticed me draw forth the ivory tablet. I decided to refrain from mentioning the find until we could examine it together. Twenty minutes later, I found myself standing on the comparatively level stone surface of the summit, which in that wind-blown place was bare of grasses. Clyde was hauling up my pack. I did not disturb his work, but leaned out and gazed down at the boat, no larger than a postage stamp against the emerald-green waves of the sea. A few puffy clouds hung along the distant eastern horizon, but otherwise the sky was a glorious blue vault.

The panoramic view was extraordinary, made all the more so with the knowledge that I was only the second man to see it in modern history—Clyde having seen it first. To the east and south stretched the uninterrupted rim of the Atlantic. I turned in a slow circle and gazed across the island, its green expanse descending gradually to the western edge. Beyond, I could see the misty coastline of Nova Scotia, diminishing to invisibility as it extended northward. It had a bluish coloring. The island itself was a jumble of irregular stones covered with green grasses, lichen, and scatterings of white and blue wildflowers, over which hopped and walked and sat such a profusion of seabirds as I had never seen before. Every so often a flock of them would rise up into the air and mill about before settling once more. As they did so, the squawking swelled to a deafening level, then diminished, resembling the sound of a wave breaking on the rocks of a beach.

Toward the center of the island I saw the mounds of tumbled stone blocks that were so evident in the aerial survey photographs. I confess my disappointment, for at this near distance they bore no resemblance to any habitation, not even one fallen to ruin, but merely appeared to be a natural formation. White droppings from the birds frosted their planes and angles like drifts of snow. I might have wandered down among them immediately, but my mind was still on the carving, and on who could have placed it into the high recess of the cliff, which was almost 500 feet above the sea.

Stepping away from the edge, I drew the carved piece of greenish ivory from my pocket. The top of the tablet was tapered in the form of a shallow pointed arch, so that in overall shape and proportion it somewhat resembled a Gothic church window, although no Gothic architecture ever used an arch that flat. The elongated aperture of the recess in the cliff had also had an arched top with similar proportions.

"Hullo? What have you got there, old chap?" Clyde asked, coming over.

I told him how I had discovered the little carving. He took it and held it up to the sun, then tossed it in his hand in a way that made me cringe.

"Be careful," I warned him. "It's absolutely priceless."

With an easy smile he gave it back to me and clapped my good-naturedly on the shoulder.

"A little souvenir to remember the expedition, eh?"

He left me to ponder the tablet and went back to the packs. Looking at it now as it rests like a little ivory bookmarker on the page of the open journal spread across my right knee, I am filled with a sense of sacred reverence. It depicts in bas-relief a highly stylized version of the tableau that adorns the cliff face, and appears to my judgment to be none other than the Madonna seated on a high-backed throne with the Christ child on her knee. The two human figures are delineated with uncouth angles and strange proportions, yet their general posture can be puzzled out after some squinting. However, the bone structure of their faces is very badly executed, so that they almost seem two distorted masks. Across the square back of the Holy Virgin's throne, which projects some distance above her head, are engraved markings, quite deeply incised as though with a jeweler's wheel. They seem to be some sort of hieroglyphic writing, but they are like no script I have ever seen.

The style of the bas-relief image, with its rounded limbs and conventionalized features, reminds me of Esquimaux soapstone carving, but it is not Esquimaux art, or the art of any other primitive culture that I recognize. It seems to be completely new—or rather, very old. It is almost abstract, like some pagan Picasso. The ivory resembles elephant tusk and is uncommonly hard, like glass under my fingernail. It shines in the sunlight with a satiny greenish luster, semi-translucent. The tablet is more weighty than I would expect of ordinary ivory.

It's a curious thing to relate in the chill rationality of written words, but when I look away from it, the memory of it in my mind appears to dance. That is, the memory of the image seems to show a standing figure frozen in the act of some sort of ritual dance. Yet when I return my gaze to the carving, I cannot make out any trace of a dancing figure, only the enthroned Madonna and Child. I must put the carving away safely in my pocket. I tremble to think of its value to anthropology. My guess is that it represents some hitherto unknown native culture, unless perchance it is an artifact from lost Atlantis. The thought makes me smile, but I do not entirely dismiss the possibility.

(later)

Clyde and I have explored the island. With one exception there is little enough to see. We first walked the perimeter, which drops sheer to the sea like the eastern cliff and is swept clean for several yards in from the edge by the wind and rain, giving a secure enough footing for those who are not inclined to vertigo. But the stench—there are bird droppings everywhere. We thought we had smelled the worst of them during the climb up the face, but once we descended from the height of the eastern ridge and put the body of the island between our noses and the sea breeze, the full odor of the place became evident. I don't believe I've ever breathed in anything quite so foul. Or in this instance, so fowl, if you will forgive my pun.

When we turned our progress toward the center of the island, we had to watch our feet and take care to step around the nests. For the most part the birds behaved well and got out of our way, although they gave shrill voice to their disapproval. Thank heavens not all the species are nesting. It was only when we drew near the stone blocks and I looked up at them that I began to realize how large they were. Each was the size of a small house. I could almost fancy that I saw signs of tool marks on their lichen-mottled sides, but the impressions were too widely spaced to have been made by any chisels used by men, so I dismissed the notion.

We found that we could walk through gaps under and amid the stones. They leaned at crazy angles above our heads, forming a maze of passages and grassy open courtyards. They gave shelter from the wind and muted the cries of the birds, which for some reason did not descend to the grass between them. The dark shadows and abrupt turns began to play on my nerves. Clyde may have felt it also, for he was uncommonly silent. The sensation was almost palpable, a kind of dream that is sometimes felt when entering an ancient tomb or holy place.

Toward the midst of the great stones the ground opened into a kind of meadow that was shaped like a boat, narrow at each end and wider in the center, where we saw there was a sizeable hole. We approached its edge cautiously.

"Watch where you put your feet," Clyde said. "The lip may be undercut."

I inched forward beside him, leaning out and craning my neck to see the bottom of the depression. The realization grew on me that it did not have a discernible bottom. It dropped straight down like a well, its rim almost a perfect circle. With Clyde holding onto my wrist with both hands, I leaned further out over the edge. The most perfect blackness greeted my gaze.

"I don't see a bottom," I told him. My voice echoed up from the dark into my ears.

He pulled me back, looked around in the grass for a pebble, and flipped it into the hole. It ticked once against the side. We listened for half a minute but never heard it again.

"Why doesn't this show up on the aerial photograph?" he mused.

"It probably does," I said. "The center of the island is a patchwork of shadows cast by the blocks."

When I went back later to fetch my leather folder, I took out the aerial photo and examined it. Sure enough, the mouth of the hole was readily visible, once I knew where to look and what I was looking for. It was partially obscured by a spear-like shadow from the corner of one of the blocks.

As leader, Clyde decided that it would be best for us to set up camp in the central clearing in the midst of the blocks. I didn't argue, since it was a sensible course. The blocks provided shelter from the wind, which began to increase as the afternoon wore on. It howled in the most dismal manner through the accidental channels and archways. Privately, however, I was unhappy at the plan and would have preferred to erect the tent somewhere else. The clearing and the hole gave me the willies. Every time I turned my back on the pit, I got the irrational crawling sensation between my shoulder blade that something was climbing out.

May 10

Early morning. The air is still chilly, and the jagged shadows keep the dew from drying on the grass. I'm worried. Clyde has decided to descend into the hole to explore its depths. I should have seen it coming. How could he resist the challenge? He absolutely refuses to allow me to descend with him, so I will have to wait on the surface for him to emerge. Right now he's fixing breakfast on the little alcohol stove.

A plane just went past overhead, very high up. I doubt its pilot spotted our tent, lost as it is amid the shadows. We are very tiny on this vast rock, itself only a speck in the immensity of the Atlantic. Greater than the mighty ocean is the sea of time on which we float, unbounded and infinite. Who knows what wonders, what horrors, may have transpired in the dim past, before our race stood erect? Who can guess at the mysteries of the future, when we and all our works are passed away and the sun itself grows old?

The morbidity of my musings destroys my appetite, which should be ravenous, but I will force myself to eat something so that Clyde does not notice how morose his old school friend has become. What, you ask, set my mind on such a depressing train of thought?

Last night in the tent my dreams were troubled. This is often the case lately, but last night it was much worse. The cliff face loomed over me as I clung to it like a spider on a thread, and the inhuman faces carved into its surface became animated with some kind of malign awareness. They glared down at me as though in outrage at my hubris. I can't remember what they looked like, but their eyes burned with a kind of balefire, and they had teeth, or rather fangs, that were needle-sharp and extended inward around the perimeter of their circular mouths. I realized with dread that the teeth were in the sides of the pit and reached over to wake Clyde, but his sleeping bag was filled with dry bones that rattled under my touch.

In the midst of this nightmare, suddenly I knew why the little ivory carving had provoked the impression of a dancing figure. The awareness woke me. I lay in the dark, shivering and covered in cold sweat. Clyde's soft snores sounded beside me through the blackness. With care so as not to wake him, I found the tablet where I had put it between the pages of my journal, then located my flashlight. I hunched my back to Clyde to shield the light and switched the flash on, masking most of its brightness with my fingers. I let the light play across the carving. In the moving beam, it seems alive. The outline of the Madonna and Christ child were clearly delineated by the glancing shadows.

With great deliberation, my fingers trembling, I angled the beam from the flash to the side and rotated the carving upside down. What I saw made me unconsciously stop my breath. It leapt forth in perfect clarity. There could be no doubt—it was a solitary standing figure, but not that of a human being. The bas-relief contours of its body danced before my eyes with a kind of obscene glee. As I gazed upon it in the glow from the flash, I could not have said with any assurance what it represented— perhaps a mythological creature with something resembling legs and a head, but the upper limbs, if they were limbs, were oddly angled and did not come from the torso at the shoulders.

The figure stood hunched over, as though crouching or stooping on a small stone pedestal carved beneath its bent legs, though exactly where its legs ended and its feet began, I could not discern. What I had earlier mistaken for the projecting high back of a throne upon which the Madonna sat was actually this cubic pedestal, its exposed side covered with the hieroglyphics of some forgotten language. After comparing the two images in the light from the flash, I began to suspect that the Madonna and Child was no more than an optical illusion, a chance occurrence of lines that the mind seized upon and transformed into the familiar icon when the true image was inverted.

I have kept this revelation to myself thus far this morning. Why, I don't really know, but I am reluctant to talk about it. Even the thought of what the image on the eastern cliff of this island would be, were it somehow possible to rotate and invert the cliff, causes a kind of sickness inside me. What would the passing fishermen do, I wonder, if they realized the kind of horror they are saluting with their boat whistles? Would they continue in the superstition, or would they creep past in fearful silence?

There is a strangeness in the birds. Yesterday my mind was elsewhere and I failed to notice, but this morning it is all too obvious. They watch. Their tiny eyes hold an unnatural awareness, a kind of ancient, wicked knowing that I do not like because it reminds me of my nightmares. What strange sights have been seen by the countless generations of their distant ancestors? What things once crept between these massive stone blocks that were so terrifying, they still refuse to alight amid the grass?

As eager as I was to get onto this island, I think I will be even more eager to leave it, when I can persuade Clyde that he has done enough exploring. The lure of the hole is irresistible to him. No point in even suggesting that we return to the boat before he descends into it, but once he has had a good look around I will bring up the subject of going back to the mainland at the earliest opportunity. Something informs me that it will be best not to linger here on this island. The foreboding that prickles on the back of my neck will not go away, but only becomes stronger.

(later)

Clyde is lost. There is no other reasonable conclusion to reach. I blame myself for not speaking out about my misgivings or trying to prevent his descent into this accursed abyss. I could have stopped him had I tried strenuously enough, and he would still be alive, but I said nothing because I did not wish to seem like an old woman in his eyes, and now he is dead. The best friend of my childhood, dead because of my indecisiveness and pride. I will always blame myself.

The descent began well enough. Clyde started down the rope in good spirits around nine o'clock. He had let down 300 feet and had another 200 coiled at his waist. We both knew his camp flashlight was inadequate to the task, but it was better than mine. He promised that if he found anything interesting, we would climb down together to examine it. I did not respond, but at that moment there was nothing in the world that filled me with such horror as the thought of descending into that black hole. The birds perched on the stone blocks watched him disappear below the rim into darkness with their alien, evil gaze. They began to cackle softly among themselves, fluttering their wings in the breeze, and I thought of vultures that sit so patiently and wait for death.

An hour passed before I began to feel nervous about Clyde's situation. Going to the black mouth of the hole, I shouted his name down into it. My voice echoed from the walls, giving me reason to believe that it had penetrated to a great depth. There was no answering call. When I tried the rope, I found it slack. I did not dare to pull it up, since I did not wish Clyde to return to it and find it missing. I waited another two hours while the sky became increasingly overcast. Around noon it started to rain. I took refuge beneath the overhanging side of a tilted stone block and watched the mouth of the hole, my heart as cold as the rain itself.

Even had he found something of great interest in the depths, it seemed unlikely that he would remain below for more than three hours. He would realize that I would become worried and would not wish me to start down after him. This was the line of my reasoning. Odds were that he had suffered an accident, or at least a difficulty of some sort. It was time for me to investigate. At this point my assumption was that Clyde had been injured—that it might be far worse had not yet occurred to me. Stiffening my resolve, I forced myself back to the edge of the abyss. First I reeled up the rope to determine if it had been cut by a sharp edge of rock. It was uncut and its full 300 feet were intact. After measuring it with the span of my arms, I let it fall back into the hole and set about preparing myself for the rappel into the darkness.

As is true of all forms of climbing, going down is easier than going up, at least when ropes are used. The rappel is a technique wherein the climber allows the rope to slip slowly through loops in his harness in a controlled fashion while walking backwards down the sheer face with his body in a prone position. It can be done rapidly in a series of kicks by an expert, but I took my time, not knowing what mishap might have befallen Clyde, who was so much more skilled than I. Every ten yards, I stopped and shined my camp flashlight around on the rock walls of the hole, which was almost a perfect cylinder, broken only at intervals by small fissures and hollows where the rock had sheeted away, probably as a result of the cumulative action of expanding ice during the winters.

The flash proved woefully inadequate. Its beam simply seemed to fade to nothingness beyond a range of thirty feet or so. I became conscious of a dull moaning or roaring sound that rose and fell with an irregular rhythm. It crossed my thoughts that it might be Clyde's voice, distorted by echoes, but I dismissed the idea immediately: the moan was too deep to be made by a human throat. A chill penetrated my entire body as I realized its source—it was the island itself that moaned, the sound generated by the action of moving water or wind in some deep channel. This hole was the island's throat, and the sound was its voice.

By this time I was soaked to the skin by the rain. It did not fall directly on me once I had descended a few dozen yards, for it was falling at a slight angle, but it ran down the sides of the hole and down the rope, and I found it impossible not to come into contact with it. It was a miserable situation, but my thoughts were on Clyde, not on myself. At a hundred yards, I came to the end of my rope. I need hardly say that the end had a knot tied in it, so that it was impossible that it could slip through my climbing harness. Clyde would never have fallen in such a fashion, and I did not entertain the notion for an instant.

The beam of the flashlight revealed a gleaming piton hammered into one of the fissures in the rock, and tied to its eye-loop, another length of climbing rope—the 200-foot-long line Clyde had taken on his belt. Transferring myself from one to the other rope was not an easy task, particularly since there was no purchase of any kind other than the steel spike to which the second line was tied. I managed it awkwardly, after coming quite near to falling on one occasion. I continued down the second line. At spaced intervals I shouted Clyde's name at the top of my lungs. There was no point in calling for him continuously; I would have gone hoarse in the space of a few minutes. I saved my voice, and when I called, I called with all the volume I could muster. The echoes dancing around my head were the only response, apart from the deep, almost subsonic moan of the island, which became louder as I climbed down.

At some point I became aware that the air was moving. I felt it against my dripping face when I looked into the blackness below. Looking up was like looking at the full moon in a night sky with no stars. The roaring moan seemed close. It beat rhythmically on my eardrums and in my chest. I continued the descent and very nearly came to a bad end. The rope had no knot at its termination. By chance I felt its smooth end slide through my fingers before it reached my harness, and stopped myself in time. I knotted the end with one hand, then took out my flash and switched it on.

My thoughts were chaotic. How could Clyde have failed to knot the end of the second line? Was it possible that he had simply slipped off into the darkness below? It was incredible to me that so skilled an expert could make such an error. I refused to believe it. Shining the beam of my flash downward, for a few moments I saw only the same unvarying darkness. Then something massive rushed toward me from the depths, driving the air before it into a rising wind. It was dark and amorphous, filling the shaft from side to side. Before I could react, with a groan it just as rapidly withdrew, leaving the featureless black behind. My mind was frozen with fear, so that I did not think to try to climb. After the passage of fifteen or twenty seconds it came rushing up again, and I realized that it was the sea.

Some opening at the base of the island—probably beneath the surface of the waves, since no opening showed up in survey photographs—was funneling water into the middle of the island under pressure. As the passage that led to the base of the hole narrowed, the pressure of the water increased, so that it was forced upward in the hole for a considerable distance at each wave, or each flux of sea current, whichever drove the phenomenon.

The reason I was able to make this deduction so quickly is that we have a similar thing in Nova Scotia, though on a much smaller scale, at a series of sea caves that are called the Ovens. The waves drive into the cave, and as the cave narrows, the air is trapped in the rear and creates a curious booming roar, like the discharge of a cannon. The movement of the water causes a kind of wind that is felt by those who stand on the lookout inside the largest of these sea caves. The water rising and falling in the hole was driven by a similar mechanism, though on a much larger scale.

There had to be more at work that just the action of the waves and ocean currents, I realized upon reflection. The column of water was rising several hundred feet above sea level. Perhaps some undersea vent released bursts of superheated steam at regular intervals that drove the water into the narrowing channel, then upward along the vertical cylinder of the hole. Whatever the cause, it was surely one of the most extraordinary natural wonders in the world and, until now, had been completely unknown.

The surge upward of the sea was hypnotic. It did not always rise to the same level, but varied in height to a considerable degree. I wondered if Clyde had been caught by an unusually high surge and pulled from his line. Shining the flash around, I almost missed the opening in the far side of the hole, somewhat above the level of my head. It was a kind of doorway with a pointed and very shallow arch at the top. Even though badly weathered, it was obvious that it must be artificial. The dimensions of the opening were unnaturally tall and narrow. There was a kind of writing around the carved frame of the opening. My excitement intensified as I recognized the same hieroglyphic script that was on the ivory tablet. Indeed, the shape of the tablet resembled the shape of the archway.

Clyde's flash was more powerful than mine—he would have seen the opening much more readily. I shone my light around the walls and saw the gleam of polished steel. A series of pitons had been set into the wall of the hole at roughly the same level leading from the rope to the archway. My friend's work. He had reasoned that it was easier for him to set the spikes into the wall than it would be to climb out of the hole, move the first rope to the other side, and climb back down. The mystery of the missing knot was solved. He must have untied it to slide the rope out of his harness once he was hanging from the eye-loop of the first piton.

The traverse that my friend would have found a simple exercise was for me fraught with difficulty and considerable danger. I ascended back up the rope to the level of the archway and began the arduous transfer from the rope to the steel spikes. It took me a full twenty minutes to cross the ten yards of spikes, whereas Clyde could probably have done it in less than two minutes, once the spikes were set in the wall.

Only when I stood upright in the high-roofed passage leading into the rock did I pause to consider the possible meaning of the archway. Someone, or something, had built it. The dimensions did not seem suited to the human form, but might be well adapted to the crouching thing on the ivory tablet. Those inhabiting this island must have used the opening to gain access to the island's moaning throat, where its gorge rose and fell. For what possible purpose? Perhaps it was only because I have served before the altar of the Anglican Church for almost a decade, with its rich tradition of ritual observances, but my mind turned immediately to sacrifice. Could this tunnel have a religious significance? At the time I could not imagine any other purpose for which it might have been carved.

I had come to this island as a Christian pilgrim seeking to offer, in my own small way, homage to the Madonna and her precious gift to the world, only to discover that this was a pagan place, or perhaps even a place alien to this world—for what was the thing depicted on the ivory tablet, and on the inverted cliff face, if not an alien being? In past centuries it would have been called a demon or devil, but the enlightenment of our present age admits no such nomenclature. Yet its sheer otherness is evident in every line of its image.

My arms trembled with fatigue, but I did not pause to rest. If Clyde was somewhere down the passage, injured, he would need immediate attention. I went along it as quickly as I dared by the light of my flash. The batteries were new but would not last forever. The floor of the passage sloped downward—by how much was impossible to determine, since I had no reference, but it was not enough to sweep me off my feet. I noticed that the floor was free of dust, which puzzled me for a time, until I reasoned that during storms the water in the hole might rise high enough to flood the tunnel and would run down the slope, carrying the dust with it. This had not occurred recently, since the walls and floor were quite dry.

The passage ended on a Y-intersection with two other passages of similar dimensions, one that sloped downward to the left, and the other upward to the right. I stood perplexed, wondering which way to search, and realized that I would have to search both sides. I took the left way and soon found myself confronted by another branching. The sense of dread that I had pushed deep into the background of my thoughts over concern for Clyde's safety surged forth. What if I became lost in a warren of diverging passageways? Was that the fate that had befallen my friend?

The obvious precaution was to mark my route as I went, so that I could find my way back to the hole. I took out my climbing ax and looked around for a suitable place to strike a distinguishing mark on the lip of the passage from which I had emerged. My heart leapt with hope when I saw a chip in the stone that had been newly made by a sharp steel point. Clyde had thought of the same precaution and had acted on it. There was no need to mark my way—I had only to follow his markings, and they would lead me to him.

I took the left passage and followed it to a blank wall of stone, where the workers digging it had simply stopped for whatever reason and abandoned it. Retracing my steps, I took the right passage and was rewarded by another of Clyde's marks at the next junction. In this way I progressed deeper into the intestines of the island, as I fancifully called the passageways. Clyde had chosen a downward course. The need to search back and forth to locate his marks on the stone proved increasingly frustrating, as my apprehension for my own safety mounted, and I'm afraid that I found myself cursing him under my breath for venturing so deep into the belly of the beast.

The air grew moist and warm, with a warmth that seemed artificial. It occurred to me that it might be geothermal in origin, part of the same process that drove the column of sea water so far up the island's throat. I began to encounter side chambers showing signs of former habitation, some of them containing strange furnishings the function of which I could not conceive. One item I paused to examine might have been a bed, or a chair, or a table, or none of these things. The lingering scents on the air made my stomach roll. They were not bad smells, merely unfamiliar, with a depth of unfamiliarity that I have never before experienced.

They were called forth no image, real or imagined, in my thoughts. It was impossible to tell whether the rooms had been abandoned for five minutes or five centuries, but it was evident that the water making its way from the surge in the hole during storms must be diverted elsewhere by the slopes of the intervening passages, for there was no sign of flooding.

When I noticed that the beam of my flashlight was not so bright as before, my nerve almost failed me. I could never hope to find my way up through the maze of passages without a light. Just as I was about to turn back in despair, I heard faintly in the distance before me a cry that sounded human.

"Clyde! Steady, old man!" I shouted. "I'm on my way."

I started forward when something happened that drained all strength from my legs, so that I collapsed to my knee. The beam of my flash dimmed to a fraction of its brightness and then, for a few terrible seconds, failed utterly, leaving me in a darkness that was blacker than anything I had ever experienced or could have imagined possible. I found myself making noises in the depths of my throat as I shook the flash. It flared to a dim and unstable yellow glow. Regaining my footing, I stood with my back braced against a wall of the passage, gasping shallow breaths, icy sweat sprouting from my armpits, a kind of sickness twisting my groin and making my stones draw upward.

Again came the cry—weak, distant. I took a step toward the sound, and the flashlight flickered once, just once, for half a second. My nerve broke. I found myself running wildly back the way I had come, searching desperately for the marks in the stone Clyde had made, my breaths clicking in my throat. I'm embarrassed to say that I may have gone a little mad for a time. The next thing I knew, I was climbing, climbing, up the ropes, climbing out of the mouth of hell with Clyde's weak cry still in my ears. Surely, I am damned for this act of cowardice. There is no doubt in my mind but that I am damned for eternity.

I write this in my journal alone in the tent, the rain falling with soft pats on the canvas. Night descends. The birds that were perched on the great stone blocks have vanished—they must withdraw to places of refuge when darkness approaches. I only wish there were a refuge for my soul.

(later)

A nightmare woke me. In it I saw Clyde's face, covered in blood, his blue eyes staring at me with mute accusation. There were shadow beings surrounding him, and they were doing things to his body, unspeakable and monstrous things that my mind refuses to remember. In my memory is the image of a blood-stained lute—but it is not a lute, it is some part of Clyde stretched and spread upon a metal frame, and one of the horrors is stroking the strings of the lute with a chitinous appendage, and Clyde is screaming, his cries breaking into different tones almost like a kind of satanic music. When I woke, I thought I could hear them echoing from the hole, but I believe it was only a dream-memory. I write by the light of my flash, in which I replaced the old batteries with new ones.

I have been thinking about the inverted image on the carving. Why would those who made the larger image on the east cliff have carved it upside down? It makes no sense—unless it was carved into the cliff upright, and some titanic geological upheaval inverted the entire island. I'm not a geologist, so I don't even know if such a thing is possible, but if it were so, it would mean that the top of the island is really the bottom, and that by climbing down into the hole Clyde was really climbing upward to its former summit. The idea makes my head spin.

(later)

Something is moving outside the tent. The crackle of dried grasses woke me. It is early morning and the sky has a faint glow in the east, enough for me to glimpse a large shadow sliding between the stone blocks that surround the tent. I thought it might be Clyde and called out to him, but received no response. I have no weapon. Well, let it come. As one of the damned I do not deserve salvation. These may be my last written words.

May 11

In the morning I sat in the tent, afraid to open the flap, paralyzed with doubt as to which course of action to follow. The thing, whatever it may have been, that I glimpsed, or thought I had glimpsed, in the early morning hours did not attack the tent, but for all I knew it was still outside, waiting for me to emerge. Assuming that it had withdrawn—

or had been no more than a figment of my tormented imagination—I wondered what to do next. Should I descend once again into the hole with fresh batteries in my flash and try to find Clyde? Or would the best course be to go down to the boat and seek help for Clyde from the mainland?

After all, I reasoned to myself, if Clyde were injured, as seemed almost certain, how could I get him out of the hole? It was impossible, absurd even to imagine making the attempt. I had barely managed the climb up from the opening in the side of the shaft myself, with no burden. Could I even sway Clyde across to the second rope on the pitons? No, the best course would be to go for help. And yet, the nagging voice of my conscience spoke to me and said that Clyde might only be trapped beneath a fallen stone, or with his foot wedged in a crevasse, but otherwise well enough to manage the ropes himself. By taking the time to return to the mainland, I might be condemning him to slow death, whereas prompt action on my part might still save him.

Some of the rooms that opened from the deeper passageways had not appeared abandoned. Was this merely an illusion, or is it possible that a race of creatures still lives within this damned island? That this is a damned place I no longer have any doubt, and I am one of its damned. But not like the others here. No, Clyde and I are nothing like those who made the passages in the stone deep beneath its grassy surface. My mind wrestled to visualize the image on the ivory tablet, but, as in previous attempts, it was defeated by uncouth angles and proportions that exist only in nightmare.

(later)

After finally screwing up my courage sufficiently to open the flap of the tent, I crossed the island to the east side and discovered that the boat was no longer there. There is no sign of wreckage, it is simply gone. In a kind of frenzy I walked around the entire island, peering over its edge to see if the boat was drifting on the waves. What good I thought this might accomplish, I cannot now imagine, since even had I spied the boat there was no way to reach it. Eventually I returned to the tent. Where else is there to go?

I have been thinking my situation out with a serious mind. Fishing boats and ships pass by this island, saluting the damned inverted image on its flank, and if I stand upon the very edge of the eastern cliff and wave my jacket or sleeping bag in the air, eventually I am sure to be noticed. However, it may take days, or even weeks. Clyde, if he is lying injured in the depths of this hellish place, cannot survive for so long a span. Therefore I am determined to descend into the hole once more and search for him.

Before I make the descent, I will set up a kind of scarecrow on the edge of the cliff, which if I am fortunate will be noticed from the sea. It must be something man-made or it will not attract serious attention, and the only man-made thing large enough to be seen from passing ships is the tent. My worry is that the winds may increase and rip it off the cliff before it is spotted. I wish it were a bright color, but it is dull brown.

I will take a pack down into the hole with some food and water for Clyde, and extra batteries for my flash—I brought four sets to the island, so they should last long enough. I will take my journal as well, since I don't know how long it will take me to search the passageways and I may want to record my thoughts. It would make me feel better if I had a revolver, but all I have for a weapon is my climbing hammer, and as formidable as it may be against a human foe, I fear that what I may face in the depths of this island will not be impressed by it. Whatever happens, I mean to find Clyde, or find his corpse. I will not desert him again.

One thing puzzles me. How did that shadowy thing I saw in the night make its way up the hole? It could not have climbed the ropes, because in my madness and terror I pulled up the top rope after me when I emerged onto the surface. Do they possess some sort of science that allows them to rise through the air? Or are they winged? If they wander the surface, what must they make of the boats and ships that salute as they pass the island? Do they ignore the salutes, or do they accept them as some sort of tribute? What would they do if confronted suddenly in their own warren by one of the beings from the ships? Would they study us or kill us? Would their reaction even be comprehensible to the human mind? These questions I asked myself, but found no answers.

(later)

I have been down the passages, and I found poor Clyde—what

remains of him. I tell myself that he must have been already beyond help when I fancied that I heard his cry, but I cannot make my mind believe it. But let me start at the beginning, so I can tell it all.

It took me several hours to get the tent erected on the edge of the eastern cliff. The sun was high in the heavens when I began my second descent into that hellish black void. I let the top rope down on the opposite side of the opening, where I judged the passage to be located. Because I had done the descent once before, it was easier, although the pack on my back began to tire me a little by the time I reached the end of the first rope. It took me some time to seat an anchor spike for the fresh second rope I had brought with me—Clyde's second rope was still attached to the opposite side of the shaft. Transferring from one rope to the other was awkward, but I managed it. As I went deeper, the moaning of the sea as it rose and fell in the hole beneath me exerted an almost hypnotic effect, so that I had to shake my head and blink my eyes to maintain my concentration.

My thinking was that if Clyde still lived, and I could get him back to the entrance to the passageway, it would be easier to help him ascend if the ropes were directly above the entrance. On the other hand, if I found him incapacitated, my chances of getting him out of the hole were practically zero. If I found his corpse, I would be forced to leave it behind. Perhaps a team of his climbing partners could at some later date recover it, assuming the government gave them access to the island for this purpose. I refused to consider for the present the complications that might arise should whatever lived within the belly of the island make its presence known.

I followed with care the marks Clyde had blazed on the entrances to the branching passages, and eventually found myself in a part of the warren I did not recognize. The alien scent was strong in my nostrils, causing me to sneer in involuntary revulsion. I would have preferred the stench of the birds above, which at least was a thing of this world. All the rooms I passed had objects in them at this level, but it was impossible to conceive their functions. Although I went quietly and saw no other living thing, I could not shake a conviction that I was being watched. It made the skin crawl between my shoulders beneath the weight of my pack.

The first indication that I was nearing Clyde's location was a subtle change in the odor of the tunnels. The alien scents became overlaid with something familiar that I could not identify. It grew stronger as I proceeded toward the end of the passage, which opened into a chamber. There were no sounds other than the distant moan of the sea in the hole and the harsh rasp of my shallow breaths. To say that I was frightened would be the height of understatement. I was so terrified that I could scarcely force one foot in front of another, and expected to black out from moment to moment.

The familiar smell should have forewarned me what sight would greet my eyes in the chamber, but it was only after I saw what was left of poor Clyde that I recognized it. Blood. It was everywhere, on the walls, the floor, even some splashed on the ceiling, but most of it was concentrated on a kind of long, low stone table or altar—I don't know which it was, if it was either of these things. Dimly, I noted metal cylinders and oblong boxes in the corners that may have been machines, although there were no wires or external knobs or dials. Some of the tissues and fluids had been collected in transparent spheres supported by tripods. Whether they were specimens, or trophies, or some obscene form of relics, I did not attempt to guess. I was too busy vomiting.

The worst thing was Clyde's head. It rested on a carved pedestal that was made from a massive piece of the same kind of greenish ivory as the little tablet I had found on the cliff, with its severed neck supported by some sort of collar or socket. The entire face and scalp had been removed, exposing red muscle tissue and veins that are never meant to exist in the open air, and my friend's lidless blue eyes stared forward with such a fixed gaze of horror as I have never seen on another human being. The pedestal was cylindrical, carved all over its curved surface with a bewildering pattern of strangely angled lines and overlapping curves, so that it almost resembled a geometrical diagram.

I noticed for the first time that there was a second archway in the chamber, leading to a passage beyond. Wiping the acid taste of vomit from my lips with the back of my hand, I approached the pedestal and touched its side. It felt warm beneath my fingers and vibrated as though alive. The surface of Clyde's corneas appeared to be coated with some sort of clear gel. They stared fixedly forward like the eyes of a fish. I positioned myself in front of the head and crouched at the knees to bring my face level with that of my former friend, so that my gaze would meet his. There was no movement in the eyes, yet I could not dispel the disturbing conviction that they were aware. I passed the beam of my torch directly over the face and saw the pupils contract.

What I might have done next I cannot imagine, but before I could take any action a rustling sound came from the dark archway across the chamber. I covered the glass of my flashlight with my hand to mask most of its light and listened intently with Clyde's staring eyes still fixed upon my face. Silence. Then I heard a kind of buzzing, followed by several clicks. This was answered by a second buzzing in a higher tone at some greater distance. It did not sound mechanical. Rather, it reminded me of the sounds made by insects when they rub their legs or wings together. A faint blue glow flickered in the depths of the corridor beyond the arch, and the rustling recommenced, coming nearer.

I looked back at Clyde and laid my hand gently on his bloody, hairless skull. There was no sign to show that he felt the touch, or that any sanity or even awareness remained behind those eyes, but somehow I sensed that he was present in some form. Taking my climbing hammer from my belt, I drove its spike through the top of his skull and deep into his brain. The crunch of breaking bone was followed by silence for several moments, then the buzzing came again from the archway, more insistent than before, and the dragging rustle quickened.

No longer even trying to hide the beam of my flash, I ran back the way I had come. My sole thought was to get above ground as quickly as I could manage it, though I see now that I was a fool to fancy I would be any safer on the surface of the island than I was beneath it. When I reached the first bifurcation of the passages, I looked for Clyde's mark and stopped dead in my place—for there were two marks that were almost identical, one on each of the branching stone archways leading to other passages.

There was no time to consider. The chitinous buzzing sounded not far behind. I guessed at the mark made by Clyde's hammer and took that way. When I reached the next intersection, I found that the same trick had been played. The deception would have proved completely effective had the passages been level, but in my progress into the maze of tunnels

I had noticed that Clyde had taken a descending route, choosing those passages that slanted downward. With this in mind, I took the way that inclined upward, and continued this practice. Every conjunction of the passages had been baited with false scratches on the stones intended to mislead me, but I ignored all the marks and paid sole attention to the slope of the floor.

In this way, I soon outdistanced the buzzing, rustling sounds of pursuit. It was evident that the monsters could not move as rapidly as a human being. My relief when I found myself back at the archway that opened onto the hole was intense, but it quickly vanished as I searched for my rope, which I had left dangling just to the right of the opening. With one hand grasping the frame of the arch, I leaned dangerously far out over the surging column of water and shone my flash on both sides. The rope was gone.

A sense of despair sapped my strength. I slid to the floor, with my pack pressed against the stone wall of the passage, and sat there for a time, empty of thought, empty even of feeling. Then a glimmer of hope stirred in my heart and brought me back to my feet. I could move around the cylinder wall of the hole on the pitons Clyde had driven in and climb Clyde's second rope, which was still attached. True, that would leave a hundred yards of sheer rock face, but by using and reusing the pitons on my harness, together with the rope, I could probably work my way back to the surface.

I felt with my hand at my harness, and it was only then that I finally realized that I was lost. My climbing hammer—it was still embedded in Clyde's skull. There was no way I could drive the pitons home in the sheer rock face without a hammer. I had nothing else with which to strike them, nothing but my fists, and they would quickly have turned to bloody stumps were I to try to use them in this way. Through my head ran that absurd little nursery rhyme:

For want of a nail the shoe was lost,
For want of a shoe the horse was lost,
For want of a horse the rider was lost,
And all for the loss of a horseshoe nail.

Presently, I am sitting with my legs crossed at the mouth of the passage, the abyss of the hole in front of me, horrors unimaginable behind. I have just heard that hellish buzzing again. It is coming nearer. Before it reaches me I intend to hurl myself into the darkness below and let the surging water take me to wherever it goes when it recedes. I will not suffer the same abominable fate as poor Clyde.

You who read these words, in the event that this journal is ever found, tell everyone that Virgin's Island is accursed and must never be disturbed. Make up whatever story you can imagine to keep them away, but never allow anyone else to come here. This evil has slumbered for a very long time, perhaps tens of thousands of years, and if we are fortunate it may slumber for a few years still. I only wish there were some way to stop those damned boats from saluting the cliff with their horns. It may attract the attention of these things, and that could be very bad for the future of our race. Make no attempt to find my corpse. Leave this hateful rock to the birds that roost here, and to the horrors that crawl within.

IN THE SHADOW
OF SWORDS

CODY GOODFELLOW

Warren Revell has never considered himself a religious man, let alone a superstitious one, but the midsummer midday Iraqi heat quickens the ascetic core of any soul who stays out in it too long. For months it has feasted mellowly on his idealism but is now leaping the firebreak into his poorly defended will to work at all. As he waits, he contemplates how a place from which the first civilizations reared themselves up out of mud, where God and/or Allah set down the first man and woman and witnessed their fall from grace, could have come to this. *We're still falling*, he tells himself. *If there ever was a Paradise, we've never been further from it. If you're up there, God, show me the truth behind all this before I have to go. Let me go knowing what's at the bottom of all this and I won't bother you again.*

Revell's team is camped out at an annex building of the Istachbarat on the outskirts of Baghdad on the day his prayers are answered. They've been sitting there since before dawn, in a line of white Nissan Patrol SUVs with blue UN logo placards on the doors and dashboards. They remind Revell of another blue placard from back home, which would serve just as well in this situation.

Outside, the military intelligence annex ripples like a flag in the churning heat haze. Modern military drab, hastily patched up after a partial hit in Desert Storm, its façade is nonetheless festooned with a judicious smattering of the tapered doorways and window frames and minarets that mark it as a proudly Arabic edifice. This morning, Revell has seen for the first time the practical features of this style, which camouflages the building in the convection currents as a cheetah's spots hide it on the veldt. If not for the anti-aircraft guns and the Russian surplus APCs parked out front, one could mistake it for a sultan's palace, or at least the storage facility where said mythic potentate kept records of all his war atrocities.

His mind has been slogging such backwater currents for a while now. They arrived two hours before their scheduled oh-eight-hundred appointment with the Military Intelligence Ministry and have been sitting in their vans, since it became too hot to pace in front of the line of Iraqi soldiers arrayed across the approach to the Ministry. It is fast approaching noon on the first day of August.

Three years of waiting outside sensitive Iraqi sites has taught him that you can't expect to catch them red-handed. You arrive early in hopes of seeing them frenziedly stuffing cartons of documents and fragile, astronomically expensive scientific gear onto trucks and speeding off in the night to bury them under farms in Saddam's native Tikrit, or in the asparagus-tinted depths of the Tigris. You photograph the trucks and try to stop them, but usually you wait and make phone calls, with military officials shouting, minders apologizing, and flies buzzing in your eyes and ears until the sanitized site is cleared to enter, or the Executive Chairman orders you back to Bahrain.

This time, there's been no attempt to clear the place out, and no deadpan tall tales of honest clerical errors offered to explain the delay. Even now, the UN Secretary General is meeting with the Iraqi Foreign Minister in Paris, the two of them sipping tea and shaking their heads at the vicious cycle of sanctions and fruitless inspections, vowing to implement a civilized solution. UNSCOM will be called home in a few days.

Major Ibrahim al-Majid, the chief minder, has standing orders to wait outside Revell's refrigerated Patrol and shrug every so often, as if to say, *Who can explain such things?* Revell nods understanding and places another call on a satphone to the UNSCOM HQ in Baghdad, and through a relay to the United Nations. The Executive Chairman is in meetings, even though it's 4 am in New York, and Revell has already clogged his voicemail, but the secretary would be happy to pass on the message that their mandate in Iraq is being completely disregarded.

Al-Majid knocks on the window. Revell rolls it down a few inches, and the Iraqi presses his Stalinesque walrus-mustache into the crack, sipping off jeweled drops of freon-cooled air. Revell is no wilting violet when it comes to heat. He was born and raised in Austin and spent most of his tour with the Army in Panama, but the heat in Iraq has worn him down. At over 110 degrees with no humidity to speak of, it clamps onto you in the morning and commences to suck moisture out of your eyes, the palms of your hands turn to sandpaper, and your mouth gums itself shut. It had burned every last mote of flinch out of the natives, who could look you in the eye and lie or threaten to kill you in more assured tones than white Europeans can profess undying love, but it has only burned the last atom of nerve out of Revell. For three years, he stood outside the truck, watching the guards for a moment of distraction to press closer to the sensitive site to see what would shake loose. But in these last days, he, too, has abandoned pretense.

"News?" he asks.

"Apologies, Mr. Revell, but I was only going to ask you for some water. A small cup, you can spare it?"

"Sure, Ibrahim, but wouldn't it be unseemly?"

Al-Majid looks around at the other soldiers on the road. "When you are gone, I will be regarded as a hero for my work to protect the sovereignty of my nation. Who would begrudge a hero a cup of water?" Al-Majid wears his mustache a shade longer than most because it hides his most rare ability, among Iraqis of the military caste, to smile. Revell has kept the secret of al-Majid's sense of humor, the twinkle in his eye when he's feeding the inspectors a line of state-crafted bullshit. He's going to miss having al-Majid to lie to him.

"If your whole clan isn't purged for some real or imagined threat to Saddam, I expect to see your face all up and down Airport Road when we come back." He fills a cup from a collapsible cooler on the seat beside him. Despite the air conditioner, the water is almost hot and tastes strongly of the plastic container. Al-Majid closes his eyes in pure pleasure as he sips. When he looks up again, he is all business.

"It must be a relief to you, Mr. Revell, the impending completion of your mission."

"What?"

"Soon you will be able to return to honest work on behalf of all nations. You will no longer be a pawn of Israel and the American CIA." Revell's gotten used to this weird shift in al-Majid's manner, as if a puppeteer's hand has reached up his ass and is yanking his cord. He has always assumed the Iraqi minder is bugged and has to deliver these propaganda speeches from time to time to satisfy *his* minders.

"We've had a long time to establish that I don't work for the U.S. government in any capacity. UNSCOM enforces the mandate of the UN Security Council, which includes Iraq's staunch allies, the Russians, the French, and the Chinese, to complete its abolition of Iraqi weapons of mass destruction programs. We're the only thing between you and being bombed back into the stone age—again."

Al-Majid's smile peeks out through his soupbroom. "Iraq will never be defeated. You need us too much, I am thinking."

"So what's the delay now? This site was approved by both sides last week."

"Apologies, but a new list of sensitive classifications is delivered to your UN this morning."

"There's new classifications? Jesus ..." The rules of engagement for the UNSCOM inspections are labyrinthine and ridiculous, like a scavenger hunt run by ultra-paranoid corporate lawyers. After a string of tense and embarrassing incidents where the Iraqis waved guns in the inspectors' faces while soldiers and civil servants scrambled out the back with documents and equipment and were caught by the UNSCOM anti-concealment teams, the foreign minister had demanded that certain sites be held sacrosanct on grounds of national and (especially) presidential security. Incredibly, the Security Council gave its approval. The teams could still pop surprise inspections, but the Iraqis could now deny or delay access by saying Saddam liked to get naked and strangle dancing girls there.

"This site is deemed 'sensitive sensitive political.'" The Iraqis seem to think that repetition makes things sound more important. "It contains records pertaining to political dissidents and internal security actions, which your American military would like to have for itself. Would make invasion—less foolish than otherwise."

"The inspections in the south will go smoothly then, right?" He's trying to make the minder laugh; the Basra inspections scheduled for tomorrow are sure to be murder. A month ago, a retired Pentagon analyst idly speculated on CNN that the best plan for overthrowing Saddam would be to demand seizing the south and installing a puppet government at Basra, composed either of radical Islamic defectors from the Iraqi army or Kurdish guerrillas. Saddam bristled at the notion of an UNSCOM force led by a former American military officer snooping around the south, or pawing through his mountainous enemies lists.

"Very few of the declared sites are controversial," al-Majid answers deadpan. "If your superiors do not have any ugly surprises planned, we will all be released from this farce soon." He returns the cup and brushes his hands through his mustache. He puts on a rigid scowl and turns to deal with the soldiers.

Revell's satphone trills. He seals the window, clicks the scrambler on, and picks up, fully expecting to hear the Executive Chairman tell him to pack up and go home.

"Revell, we've got an intercept." It's Luscombe, the senior communications tech. "It's—you really should get here immediately." Luscombe doesn't sound like Luscombe. Revell has heard him talk about things he saw in Bosnia with his impregnable Oxford-bred good humor, which would make some think he was a thick-skinned twit, if not for the nervous wringing of his hands. Luscombe's hands must be strangling each other in his lap right now, because he sounds horrified.

"I'm sitting watch out here, Graham. What's the point of origin?"

"From the south, within our theater of operation for tomorrow, but I don't see a site of any kind out there on any of our maps."

"Not even the special maps?" The "special" maps are satellite imagery interpreted by Mossad—infinitely more current and accurate than the CIA's best output, and strictly forbidden by the Iraqis.

"No, sir. It's something else."

"Oh. What's the content like?"

"I'd rather not discuss it now, if you don't mind. Suffice to say, it's a smoking gun. We need to re-evaluate our itinerary, Revell. I think you should have Hideo oversee whatever you're doing and come back here posthaste."

Revell turns up the air conditioner. This is what they used to hope for, when the inspections began and UNSCOM had a clear mandate to search and destroy Iraq's weapons of mass destruction. Now, with the mandate in tatters and their permanent evacuation two days away …

"I'll be right there."

His first breath of air inside the UNSCOM offices feels like biting down on a cold sword. There should be several airlocks leading into the building, each with successively lower temperatures to prevent thermal bends, but there's only the foyer, and Revell stands in it for several minutes before proceeding into the communications center. He massages his temples with his eyes clamped shut against the blast-furnace heat from the outer door. Someone is standing in front of him, and he knows who it is from the intense stink of cigarettes, but he keeps his eyes closed.

"You've heard it, then?"

Skelton. Revell's eyes snap open. The lanky British biologist towers over him, rolling an unfiltered Gauloise cigarette between his yellowed thumb and forefinger. Skelton's long, bulging bald skull reminds Revell of a marabou stork, especially in its current sunburned, peeling glory. His naked scalp produces such excessive quantities of dandruff that he presents the surreal impression of having just walked in out of a blizzard. His features are a bitter caricature of the stereotypical British phenotype—hooked nose, abominable teeth, watery gray eyes, and tangled eyebrows that enhance his carrion-birdish mien. Any expression that means to make itself noticed through Skelton's default state of droll melancholy has its work cut out for it. Something has made a powerful mark on him, though. He really must remind Luscombe to keep security more compartmentalized.

"What do you know about it?"

"I was just going out to satisfy my *Lustmord*," Skelton gestures apologetically with the unignited cigarette. "Graham can fill you in. Rather extraordinary. Changes everything, I daresay. Perhaps I'll run into you later?"

Skelton ambles to the outer doors, and Revell sprints into the lobby to escape the scouring heat that reaches in for him as the heavy doors swing open. Revell had always figured addiction to things like nicotine was a symptom of simple stupidity, but Skelton is among the most respected savants in the Royal Society and shows no general weakness of character aside from his voracious consumption of tobacco.

Lustmord. A curious German word, meaning, literally, "sex-murder." Revell reminds himself to ask Skelton what he meant by it.

Revell listens to the message on headphones the first time with Luscombe and Chris Healey, the assistant communications tech. They look expectantly at him, as if he's the only one who speaks Arabic, but his knowledge of the language is spotty and the garbled transmission is thick with jargon. Two distinct voices snap out brackish streams of technical terms spiked with plenty of obscenities for about two minutes; one voice is considerably more agitated than the other, probably something to do with the sirens blaring, crashing of heavy equipment, and panicked shouting in the background. The other voice is imperturbable in the manner of bored operators everywhere, repeatedly telling the panicked caller to maintain radio silence under penalty of death.

Revell pries the headphones off. "Graham, I can't make out much from this. Is this an SSO intercept?"

"The call went to the Special Republican Guard Communications Directorate, yes. We have a rough location for the origin of the call pinpointed in the southeast. It came through a relay at al-Amarah. They know we're coming south tomorrow, I'll wager, and were taking steps to cover their tracks … when this happened."

Revell tunes in on the message again, boring through the squalling noise of broken voice encryption to focus on the arguing voices. The caller is desperate, trying to keep from screaming, as he details some kind of emergency. There's some clattering, and then his voice becomes remote, as if he's talking from inside a garbage can. He's put on a gas mask. He demands a containment unit be dispatched, to which the unshakable operator responds that they must sit tight, that help will arrive in forty-eight hours—as soon as the Americans are gone, Revell knows. The heated dialogue goes back and forth in this loop for another minute, then there's a loud bang, and the caller gasps and the line goes dead.

"What the hell?" Revell manages. Luscombe hands him a legal pad with a hastily jotted transcript on it, with an English translation beside it.

"There's an installation in the south that we didn't know about, that Mossad and the CIA never knew about, either, apparently. They're storing and testing chemical and biological weapons on human subjects. They had over fifty guinea pigs, when the order came to destroy the lot and shut down until our inspection was over. But something went wrong."

"They're going to ignore it until we've left," Healey puts in.

Revell's eyes go down the transcript. Words jump out at him. Again and again, the caller identifies himself with something called Marduk Division. He's never heard of it. *Tiamat*. From what little liberal arts education he picked up playing Dungeons & Dragons in junior high, he knew Tiamat was some queen dragon in Babylonian mythology, a nine-headed matriarch of demons. And again, something about Dragon's Breath, a substance that ate away at the rubber seals on quarantine chambers and probably killed them. The operator tells the caller to shoot all the Kurds, wrap wet towels over all his exposed skin, and trust in Saddam.

His stomach becomes an acid factory and starts eating itself. Luscombe and Healey, the only men on the team without sunburns, stare at him as he goes progressively whiter. This is exactly what they've all been waiting for. For seven years, UNSCOM has been able to total a shortfall of several tons of chemical and biological material in the Iraqi economy, but never pinpointed its location. The fact that they're about to go home, that the UN and the Iraqis consider the inspections all but finished, means nothing any more. They've got them.

Revell usually avoids the nameless cafe across from the UN's offices at the Canal Hotel. Unnervingly clean and almost opulent compared to nearly every other public restaurant in Iraq, it is nakedly a trap. A triad of leather-jacketed Amn al-Amm agents sit in a black Peugeot halfway down the block, and all the waiters are Mukhabarat operatives. Revell wets his lips with a thimbleful of coffee so thick it's really a sauce, and plays back the tape on a Walkman. His thumb rests on the special button for this particular model—a bulk erase, in case the tape player is confiscated.

Dragon's Breath eating through the rubber seals! It's coming into the control room!

Stop whining. You have your gas mask?

My mask is made of the same shit!

Have you shot all the Kurds?

They're all dead. Everyone outside this room is—ah, there is only one God, and his name is—

Remain calm. Everything is under control.

Give me the combination for the door! For the love of God! Let us out!

At seven p.m. the sun retreats behind the naked concrete towers and the air suddenly becomes bearable. A Range Rover pulls up in front of the cafe and Sam Kincaid climbs out of the passenger seat. The Range Rover speeds away, and Kincaid sits down beside Revell. Kincaid is an American and a concealment specialist. He tracks the Concealment Operations Committee, a division of the Special Security Organization charged with hiding Saddam's arsenal. The waiter shares a joke with Kincaid as he brings him a tall glass of ice water with a twist of lemon in it.

They trade reports of their most recent inspections for a while, stressing the Iraqis' total failure to cooperate for the benefit of the unseen third party to their conversation. Kincaid stands a head and a half taller and at least ten years older than Revell, and his leathery skin is deeply tanned, not burned.

Revell slides the Walkman across the table. Kincaid looks around, slips on the earphones and presses PLAY. Revell gulps down his coffee and watches Kincaid's face. Kincaid is an oil painting for three minutes; then he takes off the earphones and looks down the street at the Peugeot. "Let's take a ride," he says. The Range Rover is back in front of the cafe.

A red-headed Australian man Revell knows only as Wally steers them into the sparse traffic on the Airport Road. They pass the main headquarters of the Amn al-Khass, or SSO. Soldiers at gun emplacements, leather-jacketed drivers, even old women on the street, seem to track their passing like trained spies.

The air-conditioning is broken, and the still-sweltering wind of dusk roars through the cabin. Kincaid, in the front passenger seat, turns to face Revell. He offers him a silver flask. Revell sips from it gratefully, passes it back. "What do you want from me?" Kincaid asks.

Revell winces as the single-malt whiskey washes the gummy coffee-resin out of his throat. "What do you know about it?" he asks.

"We've never heard of an installation in that part of the country at this time, certainly nothing of that magnitude. I'm inclined to doubt the whole thing."

"A feint to draw us into an embarrassing situation? Why? We're going home. You heard it. You can't tell me it's not real. This is an emergency."

"You were here in Desert Storm, weren't you, Warren?"

"Yes. With the—"

"As an engineer. Listen, Warren. Saddam and the Ba'ath Party have been a major hurdle to the political evolution of this country, but there are plenty of equally ruthless factions that have adapted to camouflage themselves and use superpowers to fight for them. The Supreme Assembly of the Islamic Revolution, for one. All hardcore Iraqi military defectors, CIA-supplied for four years, just over the border in Iran. With the psyops training they got from us, they could mock up a call like this to provoke an incident."

"Why are you so sure it's fake?"

"Real Iraqi soldiers wouldn't compound certain death for themselves by violating radio silence to ask for help they knew wouldn't come. Saddam has their families, and they know it. If there was an incident, the whole thing's underground by now, and they're ripping up the roads leading to it."

"Have you ever heard of a military unit called Marduk? The caller identified himself as Lieutenant Kazraji of Marduk Division of the SRG. But—"

"Sure, but I can see why you've never heard of them. You wouldn't have come across them. They're part of the Special Republican Guard Corps. Motorized infantry, very elite, which means they're all Tikritis from Saddam's tribe, al-Bu Nasir. The SRG are scattered all over the country doing border patrol, customs, secret police work, Kurd and Shi'a population control. They're named for the patriarch of the Babylonian pantheon, a god who hunted dragons, but it's all typical Iraqi bluster.

Marduk's in charge of guarding cultural antiquities."

"What?" *Dragons*—

"They're not even brigade-strength. I told you it sounded like bullshit."

"What else can you find out about the site? The CIA's got to have reams of satellite imagery."

Kincaid shrugs. "What makes you think I'd have access to anything like that?"

"You were with JSOC in Desert Storm, Scud-hunting. You worked in Operation Provide Comfort with the Kurdish rebels. Either you're a CIA mole, or a gross misappropriation of manpower."

"Even assuming I could command those kinds of resources, I couldn't ask for anything without explaining why I needed it. I assume you want to keep this contained until you can verify it yourself."

"I don't want the United States to bomb it and extend the embargo on this country until we know what it is. Bombing the chemical weapons plants in the Gulf War caused an environmental holocaust."

"You don't trust your own country, but you want her help."

"You're right. Maybe I should just call the Executive Chairman—"

"Don't do that. He calls Annan, who talks to Aziz, who puffs up and blows so much smoke up Annan's ass, he feels guilty for even bringing it up, and you're in Bahrain tomorrow, and you'll never know."

"Then what do you think I should do?"

"Go and see it. Pick a team of twelve that you can trust—absolutely no Chinese, and no French, if you can avoid it, but no other Americans, either. I'll bring three of mine to fly you out there—Wally, Huysmans, and Grodov."

"A Russian?"

"The Russians only stand by Saddam so they can get their money back when the embargo's lifted. Grodov lost a leg to a mislaid mine when he was a KGB adviser here during the War of the Cities. He hates them."

"We don't need any more tension."

"Of course not. He's a professional."

"I don't expect to be allowed anywhere near the site, but we've got to come prepared. I want to take photographs and air and soil samples of the surrounding area. We'll bring MOPP gear and all the counters, but I don't want any perception that this is a US operation. And no guns."

Kincaid nods solemnly and raises his empty hands. "Of course not."

The UNSCOM inspectors are sequestered tighter than any jury in history. Holed up in two floors of the al-Rashid Hotel in the center of downtown Baghdad, they shuttle to their offices at the Canal Hotel without making eye contact with a single civilian. Early on, a few soft-hearted inspectors gave food and cash to families of beggars who slept in the plaza before the hotel. The next morning, the families were gone, and the Amn al-Amm spies who followed the inspectors doubled.

Picking the team is easy. Over the years, Revell has come to trust some more than others and knows who can operate under tense situations, who works for the ideals of the job, not the by-laws. He pages the group to meet in the pool room after dinner.

The room is a bath, the air so thick with chlorinated mist that the far wall is a blue-tiled smear. The acoustics, and the constant barrage of white noise from guests swimming laps, make it the best place to speak in private. Kincaid and his inspectors sit in rusted-out patio chairs along the wall, and Luscombe, Healey, and Skelton stand in the back, all poker faces. The other six squat or stand in various poses of tired defiance. Revell studies their faces—the common bone-weariness and frustration, and now a spark of the old righteous anger coming back to life in each of them.

"Ladies and gentlemen, we came here to do a job. For five years, you have struggled against the intractable duplicity of the Iraqi power structure to pursue our mandate, which is and has always been to root out and oversee the dismantling of Iraq's weapons of mass destruction. Tomorrow, though we go to our last inspection, none of us feels that our mission has been brought to any kind of satisfactory conclusion. Are we all in agreement on that?"

A few mutter assent, but most have already dismissed this as an empty pep talk.

"Well, tomorrow, we will have an opportunity to do our jobs. Today, we intercepted a microwave transmission from a site in the region we're inspecting tomorrow. It is not on our itinerary, but I think you'll all agree that it should be added."

He plays the tape. They huddle round the tiny speaker built into the Walkman. Only half of them speak fluent Arabic, but whispered translations and a single sheet English transcript spread the meaning around. When the SRG Lieutenant begins to scream and the shots ring out, a few of them jump.

For a single, silent instant as he switches the recording off, for the first time since he took the job, Revell has everyone's undivided attention. Then the bubble crashes in and everyone starts shouting at once. The swimmers in the pool all stop and watch them, and Revell's calls for order are drowned out.

Skelton starts coughing, a low ratcheting sound that resembles an ancient lawnmower motor trying to start. It cuts through the babble of arguments and grows louder still, resounding through the rusty alcoves of the pool room like sacks of cement smashing into concrete from a very great height. He reels back in the crowd, and the uproar dies out as everyone concludes that the British biologist is having a heart attack. Lupo Bertolucci, the medic, cradles Skelton and lowers his spasming body to the slick tile floor. "Three of you! Help me carry him out of this room!" Kincaid, Wally, and Grodov hoist him up, but Skelton shakes them off and staggers free. He fishes around in his pockets, produces a tin, and fumbles an unfiltered cigarette into his mouth. Lupo tries to swat it out of his mouth, but Skelton ducks, lights it, and suddenly stops coughing.

"Sorry, all. Filthy habit. But I was about to observe that at this juncture, we have an obligation not only to the United Nations, but to all the peoples of the world, to see that this event is contained."

"Very well, then," Hideo Mimura, the chemist, shoots back. "Let us notify the Executive Chairman, so that we may offer our services in the spirit of international cooperation."

"Without the official backing of UNSCOM, we are spies, yes?" Reinhard Greuel, another biologist, puts in. "We are likely to be shot, and with very good reason." Greuel is ardently Green, and the most passionate disarmament advocate in the group. If he has doubts, the operation will flounder.

Bertolucci chimes in, "I say we go home and leave them to their mess."

"It's not that simple, though, is it?" Skelton responds, cutting off Revell's own heated response. "The Iraqis have institutionalized the cover-up and denial of the entire program for nearly a decade, and shown shocking disregard for the safety of their own in so doing. They will deny it until incontrovertible evidence is presented to the world community. Imagine the effects if the Soviet Union were to have denied the Chernobyl meltdown and refused international rescue workers access to the site? Yes, we as an international body have a responsibility to insure that the policy of UNSCOM is not violated, but we have a mandate to bring the event to light first. The, um, current political climate would only delay the swift response necessary to curb disaster."

"Our accounting of the materiel and equipment Iraq imported in the '80s always came up short," Revell adds, "suggesting at least one major weapons facility that we never accounted for. We think this is it. Now, these are the facts. There's been an emergency there, and the SSO has elected to ignore it until we go home. Our operations code states that we are not in violation of our mandate by inspecting an unauthorized site if a clear and present danger to the surrounding environment is reasonably suspected. Look it up, people."

They all look as one at Revell now, more or less silent. "We will split off from the main body of the inspection tomorrow at An-Nasiriyah. By helicopter, we will travel directly to the site. We will not stake it out. We will observe the Iraqis' containment of the site, collect samples, and generally force them to admit that it happened. We are the eyes of the world, tomorrow. We have to see this through."

The debate goes on for another hour, but in the end Revell gets his way. They all agree to go.

Two hours later. Revell sits at a folding card table, reviewing the amendments he plans to file to tomorrow's itinerary. The weary old Belgian Chief Inspector didn't question him too closely, only nodded tiredly at the vague outlines of the plan without asking too many questions. He only warned against "rubbing the Iraqis' noses in it." Gather evidence, offer assistance, evacuate, rejoin the main group before lunch. Simple.

A knock at his door. "Come on in!" he shouts. There are sentries in the lobby and at the elevators on each of the floors occupied by inspectors, but Revell is one of only a handful who leave their doors unlocked.

Greuel, Sophia Texeira, and an American inspector Revell knows only by name crowd into his room. Dr. Greuel is short, stout, and alarmingly sunburned. He subsists on a diet of wheat grass juice, vitamins, and some sulfurous macrobiotic soup he cultures in his room, like a convict distilling applejack under his bunk. Once too often, he has bragged that his bowels are clean enough to eat out of. Only half in jest, Revell offered to take him up on it, and Greuel has avoided him ever since, so his appearance is momentous.

Dr. Texeira, a Brazilian forensics specialist, still shorter, but slim and dark; her work in the desert has darkened her chestnut skin to a robust mahogany and burned an auburn tinge into her long black hair.

The other American, Gerry Muybridge, looks like a lost high-school guidance counselor and has a thin file clamped under one arm, unaware that he's getting it slick with sweat.

A fear he dares not speak aloud wells up in him. Second thoughts? This is an exceptionally risky inspection. Perhaps under another leader— no. "What is it?"

"The inspectors at the Istachbarat annex found something after you left, Herr Revell," Greuel rumbles. "Something that makes us more uncertain of tomorrow's inspection …"

Revell's hands clench.

"Show him, Gerry," Texeira says, and Muybridge leans over the card table and lets the file flop onto it. A sheaf of forms with hastily handwritten details in the boxes, and a CDR. Muybridge snaps up the disk and moves to Revell's laptop. "D'you mind?" he asks. Revell shrugs, and he drops the disk into the drive and fingers the track ball.

"I was the one who found it," Muybridge says. "We were on counter-concealment, you know, patrolling the back alley. We found a panel truck parked behind the building at fourteen thirty and approached it. An Iraqi in civilian work clothes fled the vehicle, but he wasn't carrying anything, so we just seized the truck."

"What did you find?"

"A bunch of the usual shit," Muybridge answers, rolling his eyes. "Embarrassing, but not damning. SSO interrogation manuals, confession transcripts—but right on top, we found this." He clicks on a file and turns the screen to face Revell. A razor-clear digital photo of a steel case sitting atop a haphazard column of cardboard file boxes in the back of a truck. The side of the case is stenciled with Arabic characters in green—with a nine-headed serpent above them. Tiamat. Revell sucks in a breath. "What was inside?"

"It wasn't what we expected," Muybridge answers. "We suited up before we opened it, and had demolitions look it over. Thought it might be a bomb." Muybridge closes the first file, opens another. A shot of the interior of the case—inside, lying on a thick bed of foam padding, is a slab of green-black rock. Roughly triangular, it seems to have been a fragment of a larger, convex slab. The outward-facing surface is covered in bas-relief carvings. Revell leans in closer and toggles the zoom function. The picture expands and he studies the eroded figures, etched into the stone. A line of animals, two by two, filing out of a hole in the ground. At the head of the line, a man and a woman. Further detail is impossible to make out—the stone is bubbled and crumbly, like the acid rain–gnawed sculptures at the Acropolis.

"There was some documentation in the case," Muybridge says. "Said this thing's from a place called Tiamat."

"I think it's Sumerian," Texeira says. With a minor in archaeology, Texeira participated in digs at Tiahuanaco and Chichen Itza. "Probably five thousand years old, at least."

"I don't understand," Revell says, as the depths of unpalatable possibilities branches and grows into an impassable thicket in his brain. Kincaid said Marduk guarded antiquities, but the message—one or both of them might be a plant to provoke or deter their inspection. What started out as a simple smoking gun has become so entangled within webs of conflicting bullshit that he's tempted to throw it all out the window and go back to Bahrain tonight. "So what?"

Muybridge ejects his disk. "The rock was filthy with chemicals—cytotoxins, raw PCBs, VX breakdown particles—like they fished it out of a toxic waste dump. I took swabs before they made us give it back."

"Give it back? What the hell did you give it back for?"

Greuel leans on the card table, causing it great distress. "The Iraqis' behavior has been most ... vehement and confused, Herr Revell. They deny it belongs to them, first. We planted it, they say. Herr Muybridge is a spy, they accuse."

"Then, just before we leave with it," Muybridge interrupts, "another bunch shows up with papers declaring it a sensitive cultural artifact, and forty-two phone calls later, we hand it over. No more inquiry into the matter, no reports to be filed on it, either. Like it never happened."

"They refute the chemical detection?" Revell asks.

"Utterly," Greuel answers. "Herr Muybridge's tampering."

"I didn't fudge the goddamned results," Muybridge snaps. "I'm sick of trying to save these stupid ragheads from themselves. I just want to go home."

"So where does that leave us?" Revell asks.

"All else aside," Greuel says, "we can conclude that very powerful forces are very concerned with keeping us away from Tiamat."

"An equally powerful force wants us to go there," Texeira counters. "There's only one way to know." The others blink at her vehemence, and Revell feels the leading edge of an ugly thought bodying forth out of his subconscious. Sofia's enthusiasm for archaeology, the object appearing just in time to steer them closer to Tiamat. He doesn't really know Texeira all that well. Really, does he know any of them?

Revell dismisses them and reviews the itineraries until midnight, but he never quite falls sleep.

The main inspection force touches down in four helicopters at the airstrip at An-Nasiriyah at oh-nine-hundred, local time, and the forty-two inspectors of the main group under an Australian named Richard Corby load into a convoy of trucks. Revell's team shoulder their bags and cross the airstrip to the commandeered U.S. Army UH-50 Black Hawk helicopter. A blue UN placard has been slapped onto the nose over the American flag. A loose cordon of Iraqi soldiers surrounds the chopper with rifles leveled. Al-Majid and five other minders are shouting at Kincaid and Grodov. Ibrahim turns and sprints across the tarmac to Revell, arms windmilling as if he's trying to take flight.

"This is unacceptable, Mr. Revell! The agenda of inspection sites has been agreed upon in advance! Any deviation is an act of espionage. The

Iraqi people will not tolerate so flagrant a violation of their national sovereignty!"

Revell closes with al-Majid and leans in close so that only he, and whoever has him bugged, will hear. "We know, Ibrahim. We know about Marduk Division. We know about Tiamat, and we know what happened."

Al-Majid's jaw drops, and he takes off his sunglasses. Revell has never seen him, or any Iraqi, so startled or so angry, and it's a big part of his job to startle and anger Iraqis. "But it is a sensitive cultural site," he sputters. "It—it is only an archaeological dig!"

"You can let us go there and assess the extent of the situation, or you can send us home and we'll be forced to make our report to the Executive Chairman and present the damning evidence we already have. There will be air strikes, and the sanctions will not be lifted, and whatever you people have done out there will go unchecked and possibly grow into an epidemic that will kill tens of thousands of Iraqis, or spread into Iran, which will trigger another war when you can least afford it. What's it going to be?"

Al-Majid studies him for a long minute with the arm of his steel-rim shades clamped in his teeth. This man whose duty is to ingratiate himself to Revell, who has begged water and shared blasphemous Saddam jokes with him, wants him dead. "You go too far," he finally says and turns away. He claps his hands once and shouts at the sentries in Arabic. They give him some backtalk, but he roars a threat at them, and they scatter.

Huysmans and Grodov load the team's gear into the cargo hold while Wally runs through the take-off procedures. Kincaid winks at Revell as he helps him aboard, but Revell is watching al-Majid with his cohorts, their huddle obscured by the rising veil of tawny sand whipped up by the accelerating props. Three of them are shouting animatedly into cell phones, but al-Majid is doing something with his hands. It only occurs to Revell then that he's never seen Ibrahim carrying a sidearm, because the minder is checking the magazine feed on an automatic pistol.

The flight from An-Nasiriyah northeast to Tiamat takes just over an hour and would have taken less if the navigational instruments worked properly—the compass spins wildly, and the GPS flatlines shortly after they cross the Tigris. Kincaid tries without success to radio Tiamat or any other Iraqi base. Revell tries to call the Executive Chairman in New York and the Deputy Chief Inspector in Baghdad on his satellite phone, but it's dead. Wally curses a blue streak about Iraqi counter-measures and demands that the minders be searched, but Kincaid blows him off and tells him to just fucking fly. Al-Majid and his cohorts are stone idols, offering no excuses now.

Below, broken chains of low, bald hills skirted by luridly green marshes roll past. Revell sees no villages, but occasionally a lone Shiite herdsman with a long antique rifle takes a potshot at them or stampedes his goats out of their flight path. Ever since the Gulf War, Saddam has kept his army busy running strafing raids on the Shiite civilian population to the south and the Kurds to the north. Helicopters usually only come here to deliver lead and nerve gas, and because helicopters aren't in violation of the No Fly Zone, the massacres are implicitly allowed under the UN's enforcement. For all the natives know, they're coming to finish the job the Iraqis had begun.

"I admire your idealism," Skelton leans in close and shouts in Revell's ear.

Revell tries not to laugh. "How do you mean?"

"This is somewhat above and beyond the call, isn't it? Some psychologists might label that kind of zeal self-destructive." He smiles ruefully. "And speaking of, would you mind?"

He holds a cigarette to his cracked and bleeding lips with one hand, but his other is wrapped around a case of delicate gear that jingles a fragile crystalline accompaniment to the chopper's vibration. His bony shoulder rises and falls, indicating his open breast pocket. Revell reaches into the pocket, finds a Zippo lighter, and lights his cigarette for him. The cabin is like a wind tunnel with millions of microscopic teeth made of airborne sand. Revell cups the flame and Skelton sucks greedily, coughs for several seconds, then smiles again.

"You're one to talk," Revell says. "Doesn't the understanding of what you're doing to yourself make it any less pleasurable?"

"I won't deny it. My feeble will is no match for the self-destructive imperative. But look at it in a purely macroevolutionary perspective. As a member of a dominant species with no natural predators to speak of, what are my duties? To reproduce and pass on my genotype. In any pure natural environment, a miserable specimen such as myself wouldn't last a day, so who am I to foist my defective traits on an already over-polluted gene pool? My duty, then, as an organism, is to get out of the way. Make room for a fitter organism. I suppose I simply lack the marrow to do it in a timely, manly fashion."

"You may have me to thank for that before the day's over. But your fatalism—I think we have a duty to struggle against predators within and without. That's why we're here, so that a natural predator like Saddam doesn't wipe us all out."

Skelton chuckles indulgently. "But don't you see that we've stopped evolving? We've cheated at the game by making tools and altering the environment for so long that we've begun to select for predators within our own species who will erase us." It isn't his words so much as his smile as he delivers them that make Revell angry.

"And we don't deserve to survive? What has the human race done to you, that you can smile at the idea of all of us becoming extinct?"

Skelton looks genuinely hurt. He licks his yellowed fingers, pinches out the cherry on his cigarette, and deposits it in an empty Altoids tin he carries in his shirt pocket. "I bear the human race no ill will, Warren. But when the natural sciences become your life's work, you discover a reverence for *all* life, and for evolution itself. It's a miraculous process, worthy of worship even if there is no God behind it. Saddam and his arsenal are part of it, and you have made us part of it, now. I just wanted you to know that I admire that."

"What? Part of what?"

"Our evolutionary destiny, of course," he says, leans back, and looks down, fussing over something in the case on his lap. Revell looks around the cabin at his team, at the smoldering minders, at Kincaid and his thinly disguised commando squad, at the extra gear stowed in web harnesses over their heads. Even if there is nothing out there, the chances are still excellent that every one of them is going to die.

Kincaid shouts from the front that they're within five miles of the site, and the team breaks out their MOPP suits. Cumbersome three-piece affairs, made of double-layered, heavy-gauge plastic with a hooded gas mask and gloves that make winter mittens seem like surgical rubbers. The interlayer is filled with a gel that expands and hardens into a sealant if the outer layer is ruptured; very reassuring, but it makes them look like a brigade of yellow Michelin Men. They bounce against each other and into the walls as they pull them on and dog all the seals. The suits are blessedly cool, from being packed into vacuum-sealed chests at a factory in Pennsylvania, for about five minutes. Then they become personal sweat-lodges. Everyone balks at putting on the masks until Revell yells at them. Wally, who already wears a heavy nylon flight suit, skins his hands into gloves and straps on a light gas mask of Israeli manufacture.

The minders watch them all as if they've gone insane. Al-Majid shouts, "This is unnecessary!" a few times to no response. Revell hands each of them a gas mask, but they set them in their laps. One minder starts to put it on, but al-Majid stops him cold with a withering glare.

Revell lurches up to the front and looks out. The terrain here is higher, broken hills forming mazes of box canyons. Nothing resembling a manmade structure, let alone a ruined weapons installation. Giant convection cells battle each other with whorling vortices of sand, titanic dust-devils that ravage each other and fall apart, then re-form.

Revell turns on the headset inside his gas mask and holds up two fingers to indicate which channel he's sending on. "How do you know where it is?" he asks.

Kincaid's voice barks into his ear, but he still looks out over the wasteland. "I did a little homework last night. Tiamat was some kind of weapons testing facility ten years ago. It was a top-secret primary target in Desert Storm. A Special Forces A-Team had to be sent in to paint the target for laser-guided missiles, because of the interference, which is supposed to be some kind of natural magnetic phenomenon. Eight of them were wiped out on the ground here. Chemical leakage from the bombing ate right through their MOPP suits. Their families were told they died in a helicopter crash during a training exercise in Saudi." Kincaid stands up in the cockpit, leans on Wally as he pivots, and clambers back into the cabin. His face is a mask, but his lips are clamped between his teeth.

"Then why aren't you wearing a suit?" Revell asks.

"I don't think anything you want to find is out here anymore, Revell. Get your people ready. We're about to land."

The helicopter bucks and rolls as it sets down into a cauldron of wind formed by the box canyon in which Tiamat hides. Revell's ears pop. His nose starts to bleed.

A plume of rust-red dust envelops the chopper before he can see out the windows. Kincaid checks their suits and the contamination monitors mounted on the outer bulkhead. He gives a thumbs-up, growls, "All clear," and slides the jump door open.

They might be jumping out onto Mars. The fine red dust, like ancient river silt, settles over their masks and equipment, and the rotors drown out all exterior sound, and everyone is too scared to talk. Revell calls out for Kincaid, but the chopper vaults up into the oddly cloudy gray sky, sucking the dust up after it like a theater curtain. Behind it stands a now-familiar sight: a ring of soldiers with rifles shouldered, screaming at them to get on their knees.

Revell orders the team to obey, but they're way ahead of him. Cases of fragile, insanely expensive gear crash to the ground, which, under the dust, is green-black igneous rock, like basalt from the deep ocean floor.

The soldiers wear olive fatigues with no insignia, but all sport black berets with a nine-headed serpent on them.

Revell looks for the helicopter, sees it touching down on a cliff top a quarter of a mile away. Hands grab the back of his head and shove him to the canyon floor, the soldier shouting in English, "No spies! Spies die!"

"Stop this! In the name of Allah and Saddam, stop this!" al-Majid shouts in Arabic. "I am Major Ibrahim al-Majid of SRG Special Forces Unit 999! My subordinates and I are escorting a detachment of UNSCOM inspectors who have demanded a surprise inspection of this facility!"

Another soldier leaps into the air and windmill kicks al-Majid squarely in the back. The major flips forward into the dust and gasps for breath, the soldier's rifle barrel in his right ear. Hoarsely, he shouts, "I demand to see the officer in charge!"

The guards talk among themselves for a few minutes. Revell cautiously looks up and surveys the canyon floor. In a low spot at the center, a squat brown bunker of layered, interlocking concrete slabs. Only two stories high, but fifty yards on each side, with no visible doors or windows. The flat roof is painted in a dappled desert camouflage pattern, but he can make out helicopter landing lights and a freight elevator on the roof. A cluster of SAMs and 70mm gun emplacements face the south and east, while a machine-gun nest faces north, out the mouth of the canyon. The sheer canyon wall looms over the western edge of the bunker, blocking any possible assault from that direction. Still, there would be a gun emplacement there, too. A few jeeps are parked against one overhanging wall, and a heavy equipment truck outfitted for excavation. He remembers al-Majid's claim that this was a dig site, but either he or Kincaid had to be lying.

An older officer comes out of the bunker and walks toward them. "I am Colonel Tewfiq Qasr, senior officer at this place. What is this?" His English is excellent, better than al-Majid's.

Revell risks raising his head to talk. "Begging your pardon, sir, but we're with UNSCOM detachment E-7, here in response to a distress call intercepted while in the prosecution of UNSCOM 256."

"I have instructed them that this site is off-limits as a cultural site, but they insisted—" al-Majid interjects.

"Distress call?" Colonel Qasr asks. "We sent no distress call."

"Sir, we intend to inspect your facility pursuant to UN Resolution 687, Section B, Paragraph Twenty, regarding imminent peril to civilians from improper storage of chemical weapons."

"But this place is an archaeological dig now," Qasr calmly replies.

"Just the same, I'd like to have a look. If things are as you say, there'll be no reason for delay. We can look things over and, if we can use your radio—"

"But we have no radios," Col. Qasr says. "And no phones."

Instinct tells Revell to apologize and leave. This has been a set-up, based on a falsified lead—but to what? He looks around at the others for guidance and sees a disturbing and unfamiliar sight; everyone looking to him, pleading eyes and trembling mouths. Skelton, silently nodding, mouthing the word destiny.

The team is allowed to stand and strip off their MOPP gear, then thoroughly searched for weapons, then left alone for ten minutes. The soldiers never turn their backs on the group, and they aren't allowed to come another step closer to the bunker. Dr. Texeira remarks upon a singular phenomenon: for the first time ever, the soldiers didn't take their personal effects, gum, cigarettes, ballpoint pens, or any of the other Western junk some inspectors took to carrying as a bribe. The Marduk soldiers are all very young, like most post-Gulf war units, and like all elite units they are undoubtedly all Tikriti, but their eyes burn with a zeal unseen in Iraq since the war. They look like suicide bombers, and they clearly don't see anything human when they look at the team.

At ten o'clock, exactly, all the soldiers go to their knees and pray. There is no loudspeaker transmitting the prayer, nor do the soldiers bother with prayer rugs. One of them begins the quavering, chilling devotional prayer, and one by one they take it up, an eerie chorus that rolls up the sheer rock walls and resounds as if the djinns of the desert are being called to worship. "Did you ever wonder," Mimura whispers in Revell's ear, "if Moslems have to stand on their heads to pray when they visit Hawaii?"

Even Col. Qasr and Major al-Majid kneel, but Revell notices something right away that seals it for him, for all of them. Major al-Majid and his staff face a few degrees west of true south, toward Mecca in Saudi Arabia, as all orthodox Moslems do five times a day, every day of their lives. But Col. Qasr and every single soldier are all lying prone facing north—facing the bunker.

Revell waits until they get back up, then, keeping explanations to a minimum, politely repeats his request to the colonel, who just as politely reiterates his confusion. True, he admits, this place was once used to manufacture and store biological and chemical weapons, but the "Mother of All Battles" had brought an almost miraculous discovery. Tiamat was struck by a two-thousand pound laser-guided bomb, which completely obliterated its personnel and arsenal, but it also ruptured the foundation of the bunker, revealing signs of an ancient Sumerian ruin buried underneath. Saddam, a champion of his peoples' cultural heritage, ordered that the bunker be rebuilt as an archaeological research center, and created the SRG unit Marduk to secure it against invaders. "I am more historian than soldier. They—"

he waves dismissively at the fanatical commando squad—"they run themselves."

Revell listens and nods, while the minders fret in whispers on either side of him. Finally, Revell jumps into a pause and asks, "Why the secrecy, colonel? Why all the guns?"

Col. Qasr smiles broadly, as if he's been waiting for this. "Have you ever seen the Babylonian collection at the British Museum, Mr. Revell? Or the Stela of the Vultures, or the Law of Hammurabi, in the Louvre? We are no children, anymore. We protect what is ours."

"But the knowledge that could be shared—"

"—is for the Iraqi people alone. When we believe the world is ready to learn our lessons, we will give them freely. But an old historian must share his discoveries or go mad. Four of you may come in to inspect the site, but in return, you must listen to a very boring history lecture. Agreed?"

Revell looks at him long and hard and tries to weigh his words for lies, but he can't read him. He's been on fifty-four inspections before this one, but never without official UN sanction, or so far from civilization. A nagging sensation that there is more here than he is capable of understanding, that there is something here he doesn't want to know, feeds on him, making him second-guess even routine decisions. But it isn't enough to make him stop.

"Let's go," he says.

Luscombe radios Kincaid over the headset he's taken out of his gas mask. Although well within range, there is so much static he couldn't be sure he'd gotten through everything. Kincaid agreed to fly out of the area of communications interference and contact the main group to let them know their position. He was told to contact the Executive Chairman in New York and explain the situation, then return to extract them. Luscombe adds that he said something about "leaving insurance," and lifted off.

As far-fetched as it sounds, Luscombe is able to verify that there are no transmitters or telephones, no satellite dishes, no way of reaching the outside world except driving over broken mountains and marshy wastelands thick with hostile Shiite peasants. Putting aside the question of who sent the bogus intercept for the time being, Revell picks the three to accompany him inside. Al-Majid and one of his junior minders would accompany Mimura, Skelton, Texeira, and Revell. The group unpack their gear and rejoin Col. Qasr at the mouth of a tunnel leading to a sunken entrance into the bunker. Two guards flank them, their rifles shouldered. Col. Qasr runs a card through a slot beside the blast-resistant steel door and hauls it open, beckons them inside. "Very little of what has been unearthed here has been removed to museums—for fear of its being destroyed by bombs," he says without malice. They step into a small steel-walled foyer, with another, equally imposing door just before them. An airlock. Col. Qasr works the card again, says, "There's been very little money for reconstruction. We left it like this, is safer."

They pass into a dimly lit corridor, awash in greenish darkness after the brutal glare outside. Cold air—not merely air-conditioned or clammy, but shivery cold—blows up out of the recesses of the bunker, and each of them remarks on the musty odor, which Skelton likens to old cathedrals on the Continent, but which Texeira insists reeks of the stagnant Rio Negro.

Col. Qasr leads the way down the corridor, past rows of heavy doors with rubber seals on them. "We believe it is the earliest Sumerian structure ever discovered. Many puzzlements of Mesopotamian history have been resolved here. The world would … not accept all of them."

"I don't understand."

He stops at a door and slides his card through yet another slot, pockets it. The locks are an old system designed by Honeywell. "I will show you a few of the choicer artifacts we have liberated from the ground, and you will see," he says, and opens the door. "I must, of course, ask you to touch nothing." Col. Qasr orders the guards to stand at attention outside the room. The guards share a this-is-most-irregular look, but obey and flank the door as the visitors file in, sullen deadly caryatids.

Inside, bare yellow lightbulbs cast a feeble glow on a treasure hoard older than King Tut's. Five rows of trestle tables sag under the weight of urns, vases, bowls, statuary, weapons, jewelry, and costumes of silver and beaten gold. Texeira, who participated in digs at Tiahuanaco and Sacsayhuaman, practically swoons. "This is the largest collection of antiquities from one site I have ever seen," she whispers. "The cemetery at Ur was not half so rich."

"This means nothing," Mimura murmurs. "I would like to conduct tests." Revell tells him to take some air and surface samples and check the baseboards for recently removed fixtures. He rummages through his gear case and removes a few bottles and swabs. Col. Qasr looks askance at this for a moment, then seems to forget it.

Revell presses the colonel more directly about what sort of a place this was.

"How much do you know of Sumerian history?" Col. Qasr asks. Al-Majid, as enthralled now as the rest of them, starts to answer, but Col. Qasr cuts him off with a shake of his head.

"Dr. Texeira here knows more than the rest of us put together," Revell admits.

"And what would you guess this place was, dear lady?"

Texeira's eyes sweep over the collection again, her nose wrinkling at the patronizing address. "I would guess that it was a tomb-hoard," she answers at last. "But so many weapons, and steles—it would appear to have been a massive cemetery for royalty, priests, and warriors."

"You are very close to the mark, Doctor. It was a temple, fortress, garrison, and tomb, all at once. The Akkadian Semites who, history says, were the first to occupy this land believed that a cave existed here which opened on the Underworld, and that the souls of the dead entered it— and that the bodily forms of their keepers sometimes escaped to wreak havoc on the living. Needless to say, they avoided it like the plague. But they believed also that another race had held this land before them, for many thousands of years, and had a city upon this spot."

"Begging your pardon, Colonel," Texeira puts in, "but less than ten thousand years ago, the entire delta region of southern Iraq was underwater. For millions of years."

"Ah, but before that ..." Col. Qasr says, and turns away, leaving them staring at each other like idiots.

Col. Qasr moves down the tables, scanning the collection and waving his hand about as if at trash. He stops before a huge, flat slab of rock propped against one wall. "Of this I am most proud," he declares.

Texeira and Mimura stand close behind Col. Qasr, blocking Revell's view. Al-Majid and his junior officer stand goggling at the wealth before them; if not for the guards outside, they might stuff their pockets and flee. As Revell walks over to the rest of the group, he sets down a briefcase in the middle of the room and mashes an unmarked button under the handle, which activates the mechanism inside. Then he takes a look at Col. Qasr's rock.

It's not like the sun-dried clay tablets he's seen in museums—fragile, crumbly things covered in wedge-shaped cuneiform. This is some sort of green metamorphic rock, and the characters are more sinuous and seem almost to have been burned into the stone. Angular humanoid figures are inscribed across the top of the stele and inlaid with carnelian and mother-of-pearl. They stand in a two-dimensional battle line, which, when seen in profile, makes them seem as if they're standing single-file—arrayed against a cavern out of which pours a horde of demons, or a single demon with many limbs and heads. Revell can't make out what the thing was intended to be, nor can he discern why the scribe took such pains to give a vaginal likeness to the cave.

Col. Qasr explains that the stele gives a list of the priest-kings who ruled Tiamat—though, of course, he says, cryptically, they had another name for it. The list goes back to the arrival of the Sumerians in Southern Iraq in about 5000 B.C. It also relates an origin myth of the Sumerian people that has never been discovered elsewhere, though fragments of it have appeared in indigenous tribes around the world. Texeira tells the others that the birthplace of the Sumerian race remains a mystery; cultural innovations and technology common to both Sumer and contemporary civilizations in the Indus river valley suggest that they originated somewhere in southern Turkey, but no original site was ever unearthed, and they seem to have materialized and taken over the nomadic Akkadians' fertile territory and built the first western empire.

According to the stele, the people who would build the ziggurats of Ur and the Hanging Gardens of Babylon simply crept up out of a hole in the ground—"like your Indians," Col. Qasr observes—puritan outcasts from a larger civilization known as K'n-yan, which had fallen into decadence and depravity in the subterranean deeps. The Sumerians immediately recognized the pit at Tiamat as a threat to their sovereignty and erected a fortress over it. Elsewhere, Sumer grew into an empire of city-states, all paying tribute to the warrior-priests who maintained this fortress against an enemy out of myth.

"But—" Revell sputters, not knowing where to start, "I thought the Sumerians were more advanced than the Akkadians. Why would they believe in the same myth, especially if they thought they came from a hole themselves?"

"This 'hole' was different, very. They called it the Womb of the Earth. They believed that creation is never finished creating itself, that new animals and plants are ever taking shape in the Garden, coming to take their place. Not unlike your evolution, yes? For two thousand years, they watched and waited, and when it opened, they tried to stop it with fire and swords and with poisons, with ritual sacrifices and with magic. In the end—" He trails off, looking for words.

"What?"

"In the end, they fell back on their old ways, on the forbidden science of K'n-yan, to protect them. They raised the waters and flooded the whole delta, again. I believe you have read of that flood in your Book of Genesis."

Mimura looks nonplussed, then grins. "Christianity number-one funny religion."

Revell's headset beeps. It's Luscombe, outside, and he's worried. "Kincaid's been gone awhile. I've tried raising him, but I can't get shit out here. I had to wire two batteries together to get you."

"What's wrong, exactly?"

"Huysmans and Grodov are here. Kincaid dropped them before he dusted off."

"They're inspectors, Luscombe, where else would they be?" Luscombe doesn't answer, fades in and out of static storms. "What's the fucking problem, Graham?"

"They're armed, Warren."

"With what?"

"Heckler-Koch machine pistols on web belts under their jackets."

"Did you actually see them? How do you know?"

"Greuel wore one for four years in the West German Army."

"Do the guards know?"

"I don't think so. They tried to search them when they came walking in, but Grodov warned them off with some kind of—I don't know, but it scared the shit out of them, you should've seen it."

"How're the tests coming along?"

"We've got trace particle counts in the few parts per million for some of the leavings of VX, but in a place like this, it could've been lingering for years. Also, something interesting on the rocks, like a biological agent. Lots of carbon and oxygen, but antipathic as all hell—" Static scours Revell's ear, then subsides, but he can hear Luscombe tweaking his jerry-rigged transmitter to keep it alive. "Deposits in the scrub brush ... like bloody great tumors ... denatures animal cell membranes ... oh, hell, fucking batteries—" and Luscombe is gone. The others are still listening to Col. Qasr, and al-Majid and his minder are still mooning over the treasure.

Revell makes his way back to the briefcase and kneels beside it by the time Luscombe loses contact. The briefcase contains a miniature active sonar transmitter that, when resting against the floor of a multilevel structure, emits a ping by using the floor as a sounding board. He has used it twice before to sniff out hidden basements and tunnels under Iraqi military ministries. He looks at the liquid crystal display for a few moments, thinking it must be broken. The sonar ping never comes back. He triggers another, waits. It never comes back. As far as the machine is concerned, they are standing over a bottomless pit.

"I would not have the illustrious inspectors of UNSCOM go away thinking we kept secrets from them. Shall we see the structure itself?" Col. Qasr asks.

They follow Col. Qasr back into the corridor, and the guards fall in behind them. Skelton whispers to Revell that the room was filthy with all kinds of mold and fungal spores, but nothing lethal. He can't wait to culture them. "I wonder what they will grow into," he says. Mimura uncovered a closet full of cleaning solvents and chemicals for recovering antiquities, but, again, nothing lethal. Revell asks himself again, why are we here? Col. Qasr doesn't seem concerned; they're getting the grand tour. If anyone else would raise the issue, he would call off the inspection right there. But no one does, and they follow him down.

The corridor crosses the diameter of the bunker, passing three large freight elevators. Col. Qasr slides his card through another reader on a door beside them. "Those are quicker, but I prefer this way. It is the way they went in." He tugs on the door, bracing himself against a sucking wind that whips past them and into the darkness. Mimura and Texeira and Revell all share a significant look—negative pressure rooms are *de rigueur* as the outermost level of protection in labs that handle infectious diseases. Col. Qasr waves them inside, but they all balk except Skelton, who stork-walks on in and stops just inside the door. "Good heavens!" he exclaims. "All of you, you've got to see this! It's extraordinary!" As a group, they rush inside. Behind them, al-Majid vigorously tries to beg off, but Col. Qasr pulls rank on him and orders him in. The guards bring up the rear.

Another corridor branches off here, but it leads down, curling away to the left in a great spiral. The floor is a worn staircase of the same green rock as the stele. Each step is worn down to the level of the next by millennia of marching feet.

The walls of the tunnel are carved with pictograms, images, and the same snaky, pseudo-cuneiform characters as the stele. Lamps are strung along the ceiling, making the walls glitter. Just as on the stele, the chiseled figures are inlaid with carnelian, obsidian, alabaster, and other semi-precious stones. It has a weird alien beauty that makes the tomb paintings of Egypt look like the cheap graffiti of barbarians; yet as Revell looks at it, he can't compare it with any ancient human art he's ever seen. There are no pastoral scenes, no images of material plenty or heroic deeds. What there is—the pictograms at the head of the stairs on the right-hand wall are oddly geometric, but with strange eyes and other animal features. Further down, the shapes become gradually more complex, more colorful—and then suddenly explode into primitive sea life—hydrae, plankton, trilobites, all the pre-Cambrian lifeforms discovered in the Burgess Shale in this century. Skelton sucks in breath when he sees them and moves back to the beginning. "Anaerobic bacteria," he says, then, leaping down two steps, "Replaced by oxygen breathers—then multicellular organisms. Do you know what this means, Warren?"

Texeira seizes Revell's arm and draws him to the left-hand wall. "Look at this," she says, pointing to an image unlike anything on the other side. Skelton would have no explanation for this. A line of supplicants kneels before a monstrous mound of bodies that, upon closer examination, turns out to be one creature with countless female torsos. Each of the bodies is exaggerated in the manner of the obscenely bloated fertility images of Stone Age Europe, and many are in the act of giving birth to—things that have no place in nature. Texeira runs her fingers over the hideously detailed image, whispers, "In Chichen Itza, there was a sacred cenote, a pit where human sacrifices were offered. An idol of a fertility goddess—nobody knew her name, or would tell it. It was … this."

Col. Qasr steps between them. "The Sumerian city-states each had their own gods. The temple here was dedicated to Nin-Khursag, the Mother-Goddess, but here they called her Shub-Niggurut. They sought her protection from what lay beneath their feet, which was to them far more fearsome."

Revell is so lost in thought that he jumps when Skelton touches his hand. The biologist is transformed by a rapture, his hands rubbing each other furiously. Revell supposes it's the discovery of the remarkable wall-inscriptions that have fired his nerves. "We've got to stay."

"We've been here too long already, Aubrey," Revell tells him. "Whatever's here, it's not what we came for. How much further down?" he calls out.

"Not much," Col. Qasr replies. "You'll see where the great work is being done, and our tour will be at an end."

"So this place stayed sealed up from the Great Flood to the Gulf War?" Revell, trying to find a way to make it sound hard to believe, trying to find a way to doubt what he's seeing and hearing. He can't look at the walls at all anymore.

"Oh, no. It was first excavated in 1912 by a British archaeologist—in those days we were tenants in our own land. They thought only to add to the treasure-trove of their museum, but when they saw, they sealed it back up again. And they tried to forget. We Arabs are not so faint-hearted as the Europeans, and we took up the duty of the Sumerians. We understand, as they did, that this place must be kept shut to the world, but we know, as they did, that it is the holiest place on this earth. Some of us believe, too, that to every day there is a nightfall."

"What? I don't understand." Revell's headset flares up just then, like temporal-lobe epilepsy, a grand mal wave of static and Luscombe screaming at the top of his lungs.

"Revell! D'you copy? Revell, come back! We're … something … really fucked—"

Revell backs up the slippery, eroded staircase and hisses into the tiny microphone. "Luscombe, what's going on out there?"

"Oh, thank God … sitting ducks out here … Chrissakes … truck with children, fucking kids, and they got out … walking up to the guards, and they—"

"What? I can't make out what you're saying, repeat, can't understand what you're saying. Come again."

Luscombe swimming in noise. Not static. Gunshots. Bombs. "Guards don't know what to do—trying to drive them off—Omigod—" and an explosion drowns out his words. "Warren, Warren, get the fuck out of there, the boy blew up, went up and all the guards—shooting, everyone's shooting—"

Revell slips and slides down the stairs and grabs Col. Qasr by the arm. He and the others stand before a massive archway in which the Iraqis have set a heavy steel door like on a meat locker. A bar lies across it. No electronic card reader, no retinal scanner, not even a key lock. A fucking bar is what they use to keep that door shut. And Col. Qasr is lifting the bar out of its cradle.

"There's shooting outside! Somebody's shooting at my team!"

"It is not an uncommon occurrence here. What would you like me to do?"

"Get them inside, for God's sake!"

Col. Qasr turns to the guards and orders them to go back up and let the inspectors in. They balk, one of them demanding to see the security officer; Qasr whispers something to them, and they take off up the stairs. "And now," he says, "you shall see." He props the bar against the wall and throws the door wide.

It is dark inside, a palpable blackness. Inside is where the cold and the mold came from.

"This … it is nonsense," Dr. Texeira says, her voice brittle with fear. "What is here? Why the secrecy? What are you doing here?!" She shrieks this last, her composure blown.

"This place is no secret, dear doctor," Col. Qasr answers, and disappears into the darkness. From within, his voice rings out in a scattershot chorus of echoes, as if he has entered a subterranean Notre Dame de Paris. "Your governments have all paid for the great work, just as the city-states of Sumer paid. What, did you think the United States and Germany and Great Britain were so stupid as to sell us chemical and biological weapons so we could use them on each other?"

He turns on the lights then. Great fluorescent panels begin winking and flickering; it takes nearly a minute for them all to come on. They step inside. The cavern is indeed massive, and shaped like the hollow of a bell. In the center of the cave is a vertical shaft, no more than fifty feet or so across, with pitted, crumbled sides eaten away by every kind of corrosive substance known to science. A railing encircles it, and a Plexiglas wall screens it off from floor to ceiling, with a myriad of gates and chutes set into it, each surrounded by a steel airlock. The rest of the cavern is taken up with barrels and pumps and hoses inside more Plexiglas cells. Several men in red Level 4 suits are scattered about inside the chemical cells, but they are all lying down in postures of extreme distress. None move, and the mask of one is filled with grayish red foam. A control room, too, is filled with men—bodies, slumped over their controls. Revell turns his back, tries to raise Luscombe without screaming. All he hears is more shooting.

Behind him, Col. Qasr shouts, "Nature never stops creating, dear inspectors. It is our grim duty to protect the human race from the next ones, and to protect them from ourselves. This place is no secret indeed, for if you knew your Christian Bible, you would know that your people, too, had a legend about this place. Down there," he shouts, and he points into the pit, "is the cradle from which we all crawled, all the beasts of the field, of the air, and of the sea! There is Paradise, the place you call the Garden of Eden."

And Revell turns back around just as Col. Qasr raises a gun and shoots Dr. Texeira neatly in the forehead, and she is spinning, her hair an auburn corona that vanishes in red. Then he takes aim at Hideo Mimura, who has only just dropped his case and turned to run, and shoots him through the base of the skull. Hideo's eyes, swimming behind his thick glasses like fish trying to leap out of boiling water into the killing air, are on Revell when he dies.

Revell recoils from the shots and stumbles as he spins on the slick poured-concrete floor, trying not so much to run as simply not to be there, when he hears more shots from his new direction of travel. Al-Majid has a gun! Stop this, Ibrahim, stop this—

Al-Majid staggers past him, his left hand clasped over his breast as if he's pledging allegiance. A shining medallion of arterial blood blooms under his whitening fingers. His junior officer lies at the foot of the staircase, limbs spasming. Aubrey Skelton stands over him, holding a pistol identical in make to Col. Qasr's. He looks terribly unsure of himself as he aims again to finish off al-Majid.

"Why?" Revell can barely catch his breath, let alone make it into words. "Why, Aubrey?"

"I have a deep and abiding respect for all life on earth, Warren," he says, and shoots al-Majid through the head at point-blank range.

Col. Qasr points his gun at Revell. He closes his eyes. His team is dead, he is going to die, everyone is going to die. He grunts weakly, "Don't," standing there for an awfully long time before he realizes he's not going to be shot.

When he opens his eyes, Aubrey Skelton is standing between them, shivering and waving his gun as if trying to shake it loose, arguing with Col. Qasr in Arabic. He can't follow the words, the dialect is strange and especially sibilant. When Aubrey turns to face Revell, he knows why he's still alive. His pupils are pinprick holes in the goggling, bloodshot eyes, the apologetic smile of bilious, nicotine-stained teeth through bloody, ragged lips, the shaking open hands tucking the pistol into the waistband of his billowing khaki shorts. Skelton has to have someone to confess to.

Col. Qasr disappears into the control room. A moment later, an alarm begins cawing, red lights flood the chamber, and a steel plate drops out of the ceiling over the exit.

Revell sits down hard, his last string cut. Skelton strolls over, circles around Revell as if his imminent collapse into shock is a muscle cramp. "Don't take it so hard, old man. There are forces at work against which any individual human life is totally expendable."

Revell makes himself look around. Hideo, who might say nothing for a whole day, and with one remark keep you laughing all through the next. Sofia, who would have stayed in Iraq to give humanitarian aid, if they'd have her. Ibrahim, joking about becoming a hero and dying a martyr's death by mistake. Expendable.

"Terrorists," he croaks, "are supposed to TAKE HOSTAGES!"

Skelton laughs, a frayed, insane sound that makes them both shiver. "We're not terrorists, Warren. We're scientists."

Revell throws himself back onto the concrete. His head bangs solidly against it and rebounds. He rolls over and vomits, starts to get up and, for an instant, he's capable of killing Skelton with his bare hands. Skelton falls back and draws his pistol. To Revell's blurred vision, it looks as if he's holding three guns. Revell freezes, stoops over, and throws up.

"Oh, Qasr is a religious fanatic. They all are, a radical sect of pre-Islamic fundamentalists, if you will. They believe Paradise is at the bottom of that hole, and are sworn to keep it closed. Qasr's part of a schism that believes it's time to open it. But they couldn't discover how." Skelton stands, pats himself down, groans. "God, what I wouldn't do for a cigarette, right now."

"Hideo smoked."

"Gosh, you're right, Marlboro Reds or something, weren't they? Yes, they'll have to do." Skelton stands over Mimura's corpse, then looks over at Revell, still leaning over his own waste, but watching Skelton intently. "Would you mind, terribly? You understand."

Revell stands and goes over to the body of the Japanese chemist, kneels and pats down his still, cooling torso for a pack of cigarettes. Only a few feet away, Texeira lies on her side with one hand across her face. If he couldn't see the back of her skull, he could tell himself she was just unconscious, just sleeping, dreaming, in the hotel, and he was going to wake up—

Skelton takes the cigarettes from him and paws them open, lights one up, and sighs with relief. "Thank you, Warren. Fancy one? They're great for nerves. Oh, very well. You must have questions."

"Why us?"

"You know how bullish the Iraqis are on security. This place is the secret within secrets—only a handful of men outside the SRG command know that something is here at all, and only a few of them have any inkling of its true nature. Col. Qasr is the commanding officer, but there were two men closer to Saddam here. Fanatically loyal, I don't have to tell you. He had to get them all in one place, and the only way to do that—" he shrugs.

"The transmission," Revell mumbles. "And the stone."

"Stone? What about a stone?"

"We—my team—all our friends—died to provide a diversion?"

Skelton's face stretches in a weak, rueful smile. "It's time to stop thinking in terms of individual lives, Warren. I'm afraid a lot of people are going to die very soon."

Col. Qasr steps out of the control room. He wears a deep red Level 4 suit and carries an assault rifle. Skelton turns and goes for his case. "Better suit up. It's time to go down." Revell, still descending into the total numbness of shock, asks him why he has to go down.

"I'm afraid I didn't keep you around just to talk to, although I do enjoy your company. You're the only member of our group with military demolitions training."

He clambers into his suit and Revell gets into his, watching Col. Qasr as he passes them and unseals an airlock opening on the pit. Skelton bends before Revell and points to the seals on the back of his hood, says, "Close this up for me, won't you?" The gun hangs at his side. Col. Qasr's back is turned as he throws switches on a big panel beside an orange elevator cage suspended over the pit. Revell raises his arm over Skelton's head and hesitates a moment too long, because the gun jabs him in the stomach, but Skelton is too polite to say anything. Revell clamps down Skelton's hood and turns for Skelton to do his.

He follows the biologist to the elevator cage. His facemask fogs up almost immediately, and he has to fight to bring his breathing under control. Sweat droplets crawl over his face like ants.

Col. Qasr helps Skelton into the cage and takes Revell's arm. Revell tries to wrench free, and Qasr hisses at him in a tongue that has nothing in common with Arabic. "Is he coming down with us?" Revell asks.

"No, of course not. He'll be up here monitoring our descent."

Revell climbs into the cage. Col. Qasr closes the gate and throws a switch. The elevator simply falls, plunges out of the light and into inky blackness, before the cable snaps taut. The floor slams into Revell and his knees buckle. He hits his head on a bar as he goes down, but Skelton rides it out like a seasoned mariner and offers Revell a hand up. They stagger against each other, Revell fumbling for the gun, finding it again pressed at his belly. He asks himself if he could sustain a gut wound and still disarm Skelton. Not getting out, but just stopping him. If any of what he said is true, he should have done it on instinct. But he freezes. He isn't afraid of dying at that point—he simply can't think that far ahead. He just wants to know why.

"What is this place, Aubrey?"

Skelton hits a button, and the shaft is flooded with white light as caged klieg lights mounted at increments down the sheer stone walls snap on all around them. Revell shields his eyes, then lowers his arm as the facemask polarizes to compensate for the glare.

The walls are smooth as glass, like obsidian, and everywhere pocked with dense clusters of circular holes in which his eyes gradually come to discern patterns. They extend down the walls as far as the eye can see—in spite, or because, of the lights, he can see no bottom. It is as if some blind behemoth, entombed within the earth, had chiseled the history of the universe into the walls of his prison in Braille. Skelton gapes at them with a glow of dreadful awe, the gun leveled absently at Revell's spine.

"You're looking at the oldest known written communication, Warren," he says.

"Pre-Sumerian?" Revell asks, feeling foolish. If only Dr. Texeira were here, she could ask the right questions. If only she were still alive.

Skelton chuckles. "Pre-human! These stones are two billion years old. Older than all life on earth—as we know it. These are the writings of the Old Ones.

"Does it ever strike you as odd the speed with which life on this earth built itself up out of nothingness, then tore itself free of the oceans, and became self-aware beings capable of destroying the earth? Evolutionists cling to articles of faith as tightly as any Catholic or New Guinea headhunter, Warren. We were looking for a prime mover, a god worthy of our worship, like everyone else. We simply found they were two different things. That process, the force that drives life upward against entropy and natural selection and competition and extinction cycles—that's God. We know who made it. And do you know what they were?

"They were scientists."

And Skelton tells him, in a matter-of-fact lecture style that seems to lull him into a trance, about the Old Ones, who were neither animal nor vegetable, but some common ancestor to both, yet so much more; who came to earth from beyond the deepest gulfs of space as the earth was cooling from its eons-long shaping, and set about terraforming. Colonizing. They collected the raw protein chains being generated in the tide pools of the fledgling oceans and assembled them into DNA and RNA compounds, which would orchestrate life out of inert matter—and cause it to adapt, to change its shape to meet any environmental threat. The first servants were the shoggoths, which served their masters for millions of years, ever remaking themselves to perform new tasks—and one day became self-aware and challenged their masters. The Old Ones defeated the shoggoths and drove them to the brink of extinction, but they still needed slaves, now more than ever, with their numbers depleted and their cities in ruins. They created life anew, but damped down its power to evolve. Changes that occurred in minutes would take hundreds of generations. To control the procedure, they synthesized eugenic hothouses where their specimens could be molded over centuries to serve their masters. Leakage from these hothouses spilled out into the world and became the first known terrestrial life.

"The Old Ones died out soon after, or fled the earth nearly two hundred million years ago, but their experiment has plodded on, after a fashion, creating the phenomenon evolutionists refer to as punctuated equilibrium. Every great extinction is immediately followed by an inexorable repopulation of organisms uniquely suited to flourish in it. Every major climatic shift triggers the opening of the hothouse. New life steps in to replace the old. Every major extinction, every major evolutionary breakthrough, emanated from this part of the world, Warren. Every major religion came from this region as well, Warren, and all of them with a creation myth revolving around a Garden of Eden."

Revell leans against the railing, looking down and through the clouds of imminent blackout. "This ... is ... so insane—" he mumbles.

"We've known about it for quite some time, Warren. We discovered it in 1912, but the Sumerians guarded it long before. They stood watch against the next wave of life they knew would one day come to take our place. The first civilization worthy of the name was consecrated here—to keep evolution from happening."

"And you—and the colonel—are going to make it happen?" Revell asks. He can see the bottom now, bellying forth out of the bright darkness. He wants very much not to see any more.

"Oh, it's sure to happen anyway. We've altered the earth's climate so much with our technology that the gates will open no matter what we do. And for all the technology and chemical and biological weapons they pour into it, there'll be no stopping it.

"First, the viruses. Imagine what bubonic plague would be like if you incubated it for millions of years in an environment a thousand times more competitive than the outside world. The larger organisms—ah, that will be something to see. Here we are, mind the gap."

Revell stumbles down onto a corrugated steel platform and looks out across the floor of the pit. The stone here is pitted and crumbly under Revell's boots, ravaged by decades of chemical weapons attacks. Then he sees the fungi.

The floor of the pit is a forest, but what Revell thinks of as a swarm of jellyfish are really buoyant gossamer hoods bobbing and secreting a mellow blue glow. They sway and bob to an intangible breeze.

Skelton chatters on behind him as he unpacks a brushed steel case with no less than four digital locks on it. "These keep shooting up here. They've become immune to everything the Iraqis throw at them. A few spores must have found their way through the gate. That's what gave us hope."

Skelton keeps up his babbling lecture as Revell wanders out onto the floor of the pit. "Healthy human fatalism would dictate that we await that day in patient silence, but the despoiling of the earth increases at a geometric rate. Our population control programs have met with indignant rejection, and all our adaptive survival mechanisms are working to choke us on our own flesh. If all life is related, then we are the enemies of our own family tree, you understand? You can see how anyone—well, anyone with any sort of ethical marrow to speak of—could never stand idly by and let the inheritors of the earth receive it in such spotty shape, yes? Warren?"

Revell staggers across the pit, threading a path through the blooming bell-shaped caps of gargantuan fungi to the gate. It doesn't resemble a gate at all, but that's the word that comes to mind. The Gates of Eden. Paradise stands in the shadow of swords—

An octagonal recess in the center of the pit, and down at the bottom a dull glow of greenish metal. He feels things brushing at his legs, soft, boneless fumblings through three layers of Teflon-coated rubber. He recoils more out of reflex than fear, looks down, and sees thousands of tendrils snaking away from the nearest stalks of fungi. They're reaching out for his heat. The gilled underbellies of the aroused mushrooms dilate and secrete clouds of spores. Revell backs away the better to appreciate the prismatic light-show of the crystalline mist dancing in the blue glimmer of the fungi. Skelton steadies him before he topples into the gate. "Steady on, old man. We've work to do yet."

Skelton kneels before the recess and lowers himself onto the gate, then reaches for his case. Revell hunkers down beside him, all thoughts of stopping Skelton paralyzed by a child's detachment. *This is real.* He can't hope to effect the smallest change in the world he's found himself in.

Skelton kneels before a bulge in the center of the gate and steadies a tripod over it, then slowly, deliberately, mounts a delicate lens array in a cradle on the neck of the tripod. As he strings a fat bundle of fiber-optic cable from the lens to a laptop set into the padded interior of the case, he catches Revell's eye. His teeth are chattering with excitement, his lips bloody ribbons. "You joined the UN to effect positive change in the world, yes?"

Revell numbly nods.

"The world's a different place from what it was this morning, isn't it?"

Revell looks around, nods again.

"You can still make a difference in it, Warren. Climb down here."

Revell slides down into the pit beside Skelton. Gravel under his boots squeals on the metal of the gate. Skelton reaches into the case and hands Revell a block of plastique and a primer cord and a remote detonator. "The mechanism of the gate responds to photostimulation," he says. "Specific variations in solar radiation triggered the unlocking of the gate, but carbon deposits and the tampering of human hands have damaged the lock. It should recognize the radiation pulse, but we'll still have to blow it open. I was trained to do it myself, but I'd—" He shows Revell his hands, shaking so badly they seem to have ten fingers each. Revell looks at the packet of explosives in his gloved hands. He knows how to do this. He can do it, and so he does. He squats before the bulge in the gate and examines it. Circular black bumps all over the bulge resemble the compound eyes of dragonflies. "Wait for it," Skelton whispers, and stabs a button on the laptop.

The lens lights up and illuminates the "eyes" with a brilliant blue-white glow that gradually shades to a bilious yellow, then a smoldering red. Revell watches the light with numb fascination as his hands tear the plastique out of its foil pouch and insert the detonator mite into it, code a channel on it, and match it to the remote. In his hands he holds something he understands, and can control—everything beyond his hands gets too weird, and must not be allowed into his head again, or he will lose all control. Everything and everyone under his control has been destroyed or has turned on him. *This is all a lie*, Revell reminds himself. *I will blow it up and show Skelton how wrong he is. And then—*

Something happens. The photoreceptors snap in like wounded snail eyes, and the bulge grinds against its housing, turning of its own volition and sinking into the gate. The soles of Revell's feet burn with the fierce vibrations of the alien metal beneath them. The tripod skitters across the gate in a wobbly, headless-chicken dance, then topples over. The lenses shatter like tiny church bells.

He looks to Skelton for guidance. The British scientist stands at the lip of the recess with the pistol held out once more. "Secure the explosive inside the hole where the photoreceptors were, yes, that's it. There should be a shaft running across the diameter of the gate, just beside the lip of the hole. There'll be short steel I-beams—cheap, man-made stuff—welded to it. That's where it should go." Revell reaches down inside the hole where the bulge was and feels for the shaft. His hand catches on it, finds blistered scabs of hastily welded metal, and wads the plastique around them, checks the detonator mite, and climbs to his feet. Perversely, he feels good. He has done something.

Skelton shoots him through the stomach.

Revell folds over, his top half flopping onto the crumbled stone floor of the pit, his feet scrabbling for traction on the face of the gate, and Skelton bends over him and takes the detonator from his nerveless hands, a clumsier operation than might be expected, since Skelton can't bring himself to look directly at Revell. "I regret that I'll have to repair to a more judicious vantage point from which to make my observations," he says. "This thing that we do is larger than any one human life, Warren, but I never could've accomplished it without you." Skelton waves casually and shoots Revell in the back.

Skelton picks his way back to the elevator and climbs aboard, throws the switch to return to the surface. He vanishes into the cloud of white light before he triggers the explosive.

For a moment Revell lies inside a star, and he seems to grow old and die a thousand times trying to find his way out of it. He has only an instant to register the sound before his eardrums mercifully rupture. The shockwave hurls him across the pit, but the main force of the blast rises in a column of superheated air and sundered steel that roars up the chimney-shaped pit. Most of the klieg lights flare and die out.

Revell is beyond any hearing, but he feels it in his bones when the gate opens.

He does not turn to face it. He claws at the rotted stone floor to get away. He has sunk below the contemplation of miracles and treachery and blasphemous impossibilities. Maybe he has lost touch with even the survival instinct, and only wants to find a saner place to die.

Crawling away from the gate of Eden. His legs don't seem to want to work, but he can feel them, can feel the awful wrongness of the position of his bones, can feel also the minute groping of the fungi at the seams of his suit and the smoking hole in his back, just over his left shoulder blade. And then something moves past him so fast the tendrils are neatly severed, and he looks up to see a thing made of legs race up the wall of the pit and swarm over the ascending elevator cage.

Skelton is avidly watching the events down below, but still has time only to shout "Good heavens!" and get off a single shot before the cage flies apart under a flurry of raking, barbed limbs. The thing cuts Skelton in half, then attacks the elevator itself, flailing at every moving part until the cables snap and the car plunges to the pit floor.

Revell barely notices all this as he continues crawling. His mask is completely fogged over, streams of condensation cutting momentary clear trails through the mist. He doesn't see the shower of red and gold pollen and spores tumbling to the ground all around him, fiery snowflakes in the blue fungal glow, or the deadly dance of multiwinged insects and seeds that look and act like insects, or the thing from the elevator that now stands in his path.

His gloved hand outstretched, he takes hold of one of its jagged forelimbs and his glove comes away in tatters, his hand bleeding and naked to the bone. Foam blooms out of the interlayer between the outer and inner shells of the suit, sealing the rent. He looks up then, and he locks eyes with the inheritor of the earth.

He feels a momentary pang of sadness—that the progenitors of humankind that stumbled out of Eden millions of years ago didn't survive the selective crucible to see the next opening, that the whole primate order seems to have been scrapped. What order of animal this thing is, he can't begin to judge—for all he knows, it's vegetable. Its limbs are chitinous, too many to count, and jointed with ball-and-sockets, folding and unfolding, collapsing and telescoping restlessly beneath its body, which is little more than a lozenge of silvery translucent jelly stuffed with glittering, jewel-like organs. A livid violet phosphorescence blooms from the soft tissues, like the cold gleam of deep sea fish. Great, glassy fans like bat's wings radiate out from its back, fluttering gently and dispersing curls of steam; rows of clattering mandibles prowl the orbits of its mouths, positioned beneath each limb.

It regards Revell for an endless moment, eyes piling up on the Revell-ward side of it like passengers in a ferry approaching shore. He sees no signs of intelligence in those free-floating orbs, no calculated reaction to his presence or his plight, no avarice or cruelty or rage or curiosity, only a purity of perception that would make the eyes of a shark seem neurotic by comparison. This creature's descendants will never mount a jihad, or develop diseases that target only their enemies, or flood their own drinking water with carcinogens. They will never get cleverer or more sophisticated, only faster, deadlier—better. This is Nature's answer to human hegemony, to the stacked deck *Homo sapiens* has dealt natural selection. It is built to thrive in the sunless ruin humankind is making of the earth. Who is he to try to stop it? Stop it? He almost laughs. *Go in peace, whatever you are, and conquer the world.*

The thing scrambles over him, and he feels it gingerly probing his suit when it starts to rain. The thing retreats, and Revell writhes in agony as green, frothy liquid splashes over his bare, mangled legs. He goes into a fetal position, bones grinding against each other mercilessly, and he rolls away toward the shattered elevator cage, and everything around him is melting, the fungi forest and the quicksilver inheritor of the earth run and smear like a watercolor in the chemical downpour, leaving only the blasted rock and the gate of Eden, slowly closing.

Revell's eyes are already open and dry as eggshells when he awakens. He is startled by the constant sinusoidal tone that is all he will ever hear. He floats on a honeyed cloud of opiates and can't move—not that he wants to, particularly. He wrangles his eyelids down and moistens his arid eyeballs for several minutes, then tries to look around. He lies on a gurney parked in a tent. Sunlight blasts through the door flap, illuminating only a slice of the tent, and the silhouette of Kincaid on a stool beside his head. Kincaid scribbles something on a notepad and holds it up to Revell's face.

"*You're the only one we found,*" it says. Kincaid holds a straw up to Revell's cracked lips. He drinks, feels the tissues of his mouth and throat swell instantly, and he stops, lest he drown.

"I ... it was Skelton," he rasps. "He ... they ... killed everybody."

Kincaid writes on the pad again, "*Security cameras. We know what happened.*"

What happened—

It all comes rushing back and Revell's chest caves in, the air leaking out of him as the knowledge of what every living thing really is—and what's coming next. "There was ... in the pit ... oh, God, Kincaid, they—"

The pad again, after a longer interval than before. "*Filled with concrete now. Should have been done a long time ago. Best thing that could happen.*" He makes a face, then scribbles some more. "*If it's any consolation, planting the stone wasn't our idea.*"

"*Our* idea? Who planted the ... the ..."

"*Permanent UN subcommittee,*" Kincaid writes. "*Iraqis never should have been allowed to hold the gate alone, but everyone was concerned with appearances. Now, we can finally sleep easy knowing it's taken care of.*"

"I guess ... now ... I know too much," Revell whispers dully.

Kincaid chuckles, stoops over the pad. "*Now we need you more than ever. Do you still want to make the world a better place, Warren?*" This last is underlined twice.

"More than ever," he answers and tries to smile. Even through the sedatives, he can feel that his bones have been reset, and Skelton's poorly aimed bullets removed, but the gift from the thing out of Eden is still there, nestled against his cervical vertebrae, the entry wound so small that it must have escaped the surgeon's notice, but the potential within like a whole new world waiting to be born. "I want to go back to work as soon as I'm able," he says. "But first, I'd like to go home and share what I've learned."

MOBYMART AFTER MIDNIGHT

Jonathan Thomas

The measured *scritch, scritch, scritch* under the urethane floor distracted me my first night on the job. And more off-putting were the occasional pauses, as if owners of claws were analyzing where to burrow next.

None of the middle-management skeleton crew paid any of it the least mind. "Can't everyone hear that?"

A few pairs of morose eyes grazed mine and lowered toward desktops again. "It's in-store policy to ignore it," someone imparted in a tone I'd have to term bleached gray. "Exterminators gave us a clean bill of health. If personnel out front were discussing this, they were in violation."

Okay. Underlying message, plain as cold sores: freelance tech support should keep its nose down and mouth shut. Nor was I unaware that these stiff white collars reckoned me just another exterminator, targeting bugs and viruses and worms behind their monitor screens, a realm as impenetrable to them as the floor beneath their Rockport soles, and from which incomprehensible havoc could burst at any moment.

Troubleshooting PCs for Mobymart ("a whale of a place," as its ads insisted) was never a career goal, and though much crummier gigs exist, corporate powers were making this one as onerous as possible, for starters by paying wages below my standard rate. Not that I merited special exemption from blanket eagerness to slash overhead on annoyances like

439

union wages and health care and payroll taxes. And no brilliant insight was needed to gauge my desperation for income in this economy, in this job market, in foundering South County.

I like to think, if Mobymart hadn't hired me, I'd be among the hackers righteously harassing it, but how many can spare that kind of energy after the rigors of achieving bare-bones solvency? Thus withers the revolution in my time.

Ironically, this most impersonal of settings was alleged to harbor personal connections, decades and meters deep. Up until the mid-twentieth century, my workplace would have been awash in cypress swamp, an ecosystem vanishingly rare this far north. More's the pity then that it was drained for the sake of mosquito control, scant years before wetlands earned protected status, to become a nursery for maples, oaks and brambles while awaiting "development."

Along with the cypresses, say the old-timers, callous bulldozers destroyed an ancient, disused graveyard, which is where my family name ambiguously creeps in. A great-great-great-granduncle supposedly disappeared, was perhaps even murdered and secretly buried, within that deconsecrated ground. No relatives of mine, though, can or will say what had brought him there, or if the plot held other kinfolk. But ancestral bones may well have moldered beneath the Mobymart parking lot or even under my workstation.

I felt more rapport with those fabled bones than with the company henchmen around me. To my innocent question of whether I rated employee discount on merchandise, a tubby, beady-eyed ballbuster-in-training, at least ten years my junior, brayed, "For a temp? Fuck no, Warren!"

"I do have a first name, you realize. And strictly speaking, I'm freelance, not temp. I may be here five nights a week forever."

No matter. I was already addressing his broad back. Must have been a maneuver he'd learned for relating to inferiors. Was it too much to hope for his to be one of the cars the earth swallowed up not long afterward? My seventh or eighth night pulling in, a cordon of yellow caution tape and red traffic cones caught my eye. It outlined those prime dozen spaces to one side of the handicap signs, where a few SUV and minivan roofs showed above a sinkhole rim. I gawked long enough to note that their paint was rife with scratches and slimy handprints. Surprisingly shoddy upkeep on pricey new models. Or was erstwhile swamp staging a piecemeal comeback?

The hole, I gathered, didn't contain the vehicle I'd wished into it, since the owner wasn't screaming blue murder. Otherwise I learned no more about the collapsing blacktop. It seemed to incur the same silent treatment as the ongoing -952659155 *scritch, scritch, scritch* beneath my feet, as if anything irrelevant to the day's business might as well be a figment.

The next untoward incident held off till after the weekend. Management probably wouldn't have associated it with the sinkhole even had it occurred the same day, and to be fair, I wasn't initially suspicious either. A little past 11 PM, according to my Swatch's glowing arms, an old-fashioned blackout hit storewide, instantly killing lights, computers, air conditioning, and the coffeemaker. The carping of irate shoppers carried like the pounding of distant surf into stone-blind offices, where staffers were powerless to issue calming instructions because the PA was dead.

Under cover of darkness I couldn't help venting some unique freedom of expression. "We got mighty clever rats chewing on the wires, to take out the backup generator too."

"Whoever said that, you're not funny and it's not appreciated. We have no rats in these or any of our facilities!" Because I had followed standing orders to be seen and not heard, no one could positively link my voice and face, but I easily pegged Mobymart's huffy defender as the haggard, basset-eyed supervisor who embodied the ideal pathologically loyal corporate doormat.

I'd resolved to clam up while I was ahead anyhow, when a flashlight beam preceded a security galoot into the office. He eased his linebacker girth through the murk with the slow-motion finesse of a sea-bottom explorer. Panning his flashlight back and forth, he asked if everyone was okay in a practiced monotone that implied he'd rather not hear anything to the contrary, and advised we "just sit tight" for another fifteen minutes. Not that we had a lot of choice, he added, since the doors were shorted out. His shifting eyes suggested that something about a pitch-black Mobymart spooked him, though nothing at the moment was spookier than his stocky face lit from underneath.

Once he'd moseyed off, the crew passed time discussing ways to increase worker productivity, believe it or not, and I alone took startled notice of the afterimage, as first it seemed, of flickering eyes floating in the doorway. I stared blankly for a bit before observing that these eyes were several inches lower than the linebacker's, and they were fixed on me with a baffling semblance of recognition, but by then they'd faded like a mirage. They made good their withdrawal without comment on my part, and really, what could I have said, and to whom? I did ascertain afterward, without appreciating what it portended, that the outage was confined to Mobymart property.

At this point on the job, my disillusionment with today's malcontent youth was at an all-time high. Where was their anti-establishment gumption? I'd encountered no diabolical viruses, no signs of malicious hacking, in a mainframe that more richly deserved mayhem for every day I stewed in cloying Mobymart culture. Then again, no sabotage during my watch may have been just as well, as I'd have had to thwart and track down the perps to the best of my ability, despite wishing them untrammeled success.

One measly memo encapsulated everything I hated about my stifling employ, not least for its officialese prose, as oafish as it was overbearing. A week after the unexplained power failure, old basset-eyes, with reflexive frown at my clip-on tie, dropped a printout on my keyboard and went his laconic way. The sender's name and rank were no sooner skimmed than forgotten, but the text, practically verbatim, is branded on my cortex:

To all Fellow Members of my Mobymart Family

This is a reminder to you in reference to my recent directive re: spreading unauthorized or unconfirmed information. Despite of my prior appeal to your loyalty and discretion, inappropriate speculations about certain alleged incidences have escalated to a disturbing level that may be detrimental to morale and the public trust in us. Therefore I am expanding on my previous warning re: these incidences which include, but are not limited to, reports on the loading docks of intruders that "disappear" when pursued, the erroneous assumption of stockrooms being "haunted" because of unverified footsteps and voices in them, and especially, the actionable rumor that one or more shoppers late at night has gone missing. It must also bear repeating that our standards of cleanliness insure we have no rodents or other pests at this or any Mobymart. Employees are imperatively directed to refrain from bringing up or discussing these and further reports that may arise among yourselves and with our shoppers. Strict disciplinary measures will be enforced if future infarctions are brought to our attention, including dismissal and legal action. Like in any family, I am sure the good name of Mobymart is of utmost importance to you, and I will not have to remind you again to not circulate hearsay that will damage the reputation and confidence that are a keystone of our success.

The mealy-mouthed bastard, whoever he was. Nowhere in that minefield of deadly verbiage did he deny the truth of sensational "hearsay." And I grudgingly admired, "despite of" stylistic handicaps, his skill at dodging the weightier issue of safety and lives at potential risk. No, the corporate good overrode whatever else, and he might have believed that sincerely until his own neck was on the block. Of course, most of the workforce and I might never have heard of these "incidences" if he hadn't listed them. I was tempted to shoot back an anonymous e-mail criticizing his omission of luminous eyes floating in the dark, but amateur sleuthing could have easily retraced my electronic trail.

As events panned out, I should have posted my gesture of disdain. I'd have gotten away with it. The store was out of business by the time the grinches in charge would have busted me, or so I calculate in tidy hindsight.

The light was turning red that final night as I drove up to the intersection and switched on my left blinker for the access road to the parking lot, though I was signaling to no one. In the pre-Mobymart era, this traffic light hadn't existed, or the intersection. This stretch of highway was also much wider now.

I couldn't conjure further memories of how the landscape used to look, as if they too were casualties of the bulldozer. Had nothing except brambly woods replaced primeval swamp, or had isolated homes and shops started nibbling away at them? In either case, local merchants and hundreds more had petitioned the Zoning Board to veto the proposal for this Mobymart, but even thousands might have lacked the clout to jam the spokes of "progress." And someday, cold comfort though it was, this big box on its desolate acre of tarmac would also exit the geography and sink into oblivion. Naturally, I had no inkling then that the process was already underway.

I snapped out of my brown study as high beams raked by in the left lane. How many green lights had I sat through? Luckily no traffic was waiting behind me. Few customers came after 10 PM, but on some ornery principle Mobymart peddled its wares 24/7. I could have picked a space much closer, except I preferred a minute's buffer between the car and my timecard.

Would the careerists in their cubicles ever conceive of this building, this company, as eventual dust, or did they smugly assume it would be flourishing here in a thousand years? They seemed to consider their windowless lair so bloody sacrosanct, it was a wonder they didn't escort me in blindfolded. These downbeat musings took me to the sliding doors, on which I almost banged my forehead. Why didn't they whoosh apart as usual?

Gawking around only fueled my confusion. The fluorescents were on, and people were rushing about, but nobody was manning the cash registers. The shatterproof glass muffled any soundtrack to the commotion and made it even harder to interpret, beyond the sense of staring into an aquarium. Or, rather, a shark tank, I reluctantly corrected myself. Consumers, or so they seemed at first glance, had become predators. Revulsion and self-preservation alike dictated headlong retreat, but I couldn't move till kaleidoscopic violence formed some intelligible pattern.

Singly or in gangs, "consumers" were jumping and latching onto everyone with turquoise Mobymart smocks or more managerial apparel, biting down and loosing streams of blood, not just on the neck as per standard vampire practice, but anywhere on the body from which they'd ripped the clothing. These must have been the trespassers who had haunted loading docks and stockrooms, and had tampered with the electrical supply, and had snatched an unwary shopper or two.

At the worst extreme, a mound of attackers covered a victim, like a pileup of rugby players, but with egregiously more squirming and struggling. It projected an obscenely sensual aura, as disgusting as it was difficult to look away from. My assessment of the chronic scritching under the floor, that first night on the job, had been metaphorically correct. This slaughter of salespeople boiled down to a vermin problem, like a grand-scale infestation of fleas, a cloud of mosquitoes, or an assault by "mighty clever rats," as I'd so unpopularly put it during the blackout.

Peering helplessly at the feeding frenzy, I mentally withdrew to safer vantage and speculated, *Who am I to say these creatures aren't behaving like "proper" vampires?* After countless run-ins for millennia with garden-variety ghosts, no one can conclusively anatomize them. Why be any more cocksure about an entity all the rarer?

In further contrast to their haggard stereotype, these legions of undead were positively chubby, some of them Titianesque. Their physiques were shamelessly on display, because linen gowns and winding sheets had rotted into the vestigial condition their wearers had unnaturally avoided. Underlying torsos were the white of mole rats, maggots, termites, or any species foreign to the sun.

Several of these fiends were staggering slackjawed through the aisles, less glutted than intoxicated on the blood they still licked dreamily from wide smudges around their lips. Their skin was taking on a rosy tinge, as if their diet had encouraged postmortem tissue to revascularize.

I had to be in shock. What better excuse for my readiness to accept the reality of vampires, of this whole vile spectacle at face value? The sane alternative, that the entrance was locked because a film shoot was underway, never even occurred to me, though I'm pretty sure it would have if a camera crew had actually been there.

My reaction, if I could call it that, was no less detached than if this had been a movie of bitten, lacerated corpses in pools of their congealing blood, at which were lapping, like famished kittens, buxom girls with blond antebellum ringlets and gouty grandfathers in disheveled periwigs and husky children with smallpox cavitations. How many decades or centuries had expired since their last meal? A liberal amount of vampirism figured in our regional folklore from Colonial days forward, but this order of atrocity belonged more to the realm of Grand Guignol.

In my numb pseudo-objectivity, the solution to at least one mystery, of where these creatures had come from, seemed self-evident. As I'd conjectured back when a mere sinkhole was the extent of the problem, the smothered swamp, with the graveyard at its heart and formerly quiescent denizens within, was staging a resurgence in the most brutal manner.

I was, in fact, so oblivious to any danger stalking me that at first I thought my own reflection in the glass had usurped my attention. But my mirror image wouldn't stare with egg-white eyes loose in necrotic-looking sockets, and its skin wouldn't belie a zaftig flush by harboring a crackled pattern like Bakelite in decay, and its hair wouldn't be commingled with cobwebs, and it wouldn't have blood on its chin. My mirror self also wouldn't dress in mildewed rags of white shirt and black trousers that ill-concealed a slew of double punctures from head to foot, like the perforations of underlying needlework that now held flesh together. Otherwise, the ogling nightmare did bear daunting resemblance to me.

My great-great-great granduncle was no longer among the missing, much as I might have preferred that he was. His fate was no longer steeped in obscurity. Nor did any comfort accompany the realization I'd seen his glimmery eyes before, aloft like hoverflies in benighted office doorway. And here we were as if I'd unwittingly kept an appointment with him.

In his eyes I read no hostile or predatory intent. Not that any affect was readable in those filmy windows on the soul. He absolutely wanted something, though, to justify watery focus on me when he could have been feasting on salesclerks. The sight of him put me on tenterhooks, or maybe I was suspended between emotions, not panicky, not threatened, at a loss for how to feel, for any inkling of what would happen next, and that mental limbo produced its own unique malaise.

Mindful only of this death's head with my face, I'd been unwary of the waxy hands that acted now on their own apparent cognizance, as my long-lost uncle and I prolonged our staring match. One hand reached out and flattened against the big glass door, right where it said "Unbeatable Prices," and the other snaked beneath the waistband of soiled, shredded trousers, to extract a black book about the size of a pocket Bible. Had he been shoplifting paperbacks? Meanwhile, the hand upon the door pressed hard, as arm bent at the elbow, straining to empower the squidlike force of suction in outspread fingertips and palm.

My uncle pulled with literally inhuman strength, and the door slid open inch by grudging inch. Strangest of all at this fraught juncture, I wasn't fearful for myself and watched in naive fascination. When the gap had widened enough for him to slip through, he flipped the book underhand out onto the sidewalk, and a cloud of nasty black dust billowed up in the storefront fluorescence. Nope, it certainly hadn't come from Mobymart racks. His hand pulled free of the glass with a vulgar kissing sound, and the door snapped back.

Some of his throng had begun flaring their nostrils in our direction. Uncle never turned away from me, but seemed aware of developing situation just the same. "Get that to Carter!" he ordered. His voice was simultaneously gurgling and raspy.

Carter? Who the hell was Carter? Hundred-year-old kinsman must have automatically taken for granted that I'd know. Perhaps disregard for the passage of time was another undocumented trait of the genus *Vampire*. Rather than quibble, I bowed to scoop up the book, though my skin crawled on contact with its sooty, slick cover.

He suddenly stretched out his arms and smacked the glass with a resounding clack of long, split fingernails, surely more to startle than to menace, and he snarled, "Now go on! Beat it!"

Outmoded slang from a vampire, let alone a vampiric family member, gave me brief pause until I glimpsed ragged, bulbous figures gathering in the background, leveling their gaze at me one by one, crouching for a pounce at the entrance. No second warning had to jolt me out of there and to my car, which I unlocked and started up with minimal futzing, in welcome contrast to the nonstop mishaps that always hinder movie escapes. Like a fugitive from wicked Sodom, I never dared check my rearview mirror, never bade my spectral flesh and blood goodbye, never confirmed I wasn't imagining the hailstorm of bodies against shatterproof glass amidst the rumble of my badly tuned engine.

Sirens, as of police or rescue, were definitely audible in the distance. I was speeding away from them; not that I had to worry about being pulled over while holocaust raged at abattoir-cum-"whale of a place."

Someone trapped inside had evidently vented final breaths on screaming into cell phone at 911.

And when the police arrived? What then? I couldn't say. I've refused to read a paper or watch the news ever since. The media couldn't possibly have gone public with a showdown between cops and vampires, and based on rumors about teenage gangs and Satanists I overheard at post office and supermarket, they hadn't. I wouldn't want them to. I had no urge to learn the body count, or how the bloodbath had played out around my workstation, or how a bulletproof swarm had vanished with impunity into burrows, and whether it had dragged along exsanguinated victims to join the ranks or left them to the stakes and axes of the authorities.

What's more, I'm gratified no cops have beaten a path to my door, leading me to guess I wasn't on that night's surveillance footage, or else as lowly freelancer I didn't even make the list of "Mobymart family" MIA.

Every time I've driven past the scene of midnight massacre, yellow tape has cordoned off the width of boarded-up façade. From the road I can't make out if it says "Crime Scene" or merely "Caution." A much bolder sign, pasted to the plywood and already dog-eared, trumpets "Under Reconstruction," but I'd bet that was a bald-faced lie. And though I'm overjoyed there's one less Mobymart in the world, I'd never try to paint that as the upside of the carnage. Nor should I be deemed mean-spirited because I'd still describe pursuing a Mobymart career as classic example of backing the wrong horse, impossible as a rerun of that same mayhem elsewhere would be. Then again, it was impossible in South County until it happened.

As for the squalid little book, it promoted anything but enlightenment for the few days I possessed it. To identify its rightful heir "Carter" or his progeny would have been a fool's errand, so to claim it as my *de facto* own sat fine with my conscience. But expectations that it might reveal why ancestral Warren had carried it, what had brought him to the graveyard, or what more general skeletons lurked in family closet were doomed to frustration. I couldn't even tell if scribe or printer had assembled the contents, which consisted of impenetrable script most similar to Hindi, but more elaborately hieroglyphic. The letters were disturbing, as if they might take on a third dimension, shake off the horizontal bar yoking them to the text, and skitter like spiders across the table.

Yet I forged along from page to page, mechanically scanning each line in a daze of incomprehension, and no sooner did I turn a leaf than shaggy purple fungus sprouted and pungently luxuriated, eradicating glyphs and then the paper itself at a borderline discernible pace. Arguably I had no more cause to balk at this implausibility than at the circumstances that had handed me the book.

I had a single chance to read each page and squandered every one of them in short order, compulsively, as if gorging on potato chips instead of glossing priceless arcana, until two moldy covers and a spine containing nothing were all I had, and those too disintegrated without trace sometime when I wasn't looking. A moot point, whether exposing frail leaves to air had triggered hungry spores to multiply, or baleful grimoire simply didn't want me delving into it.

Would a perusal by Carter have fared any better? I lumped that with the rest of my recent windfall of fruitless questions. And on a less academic note, will my heart rate always skyrocket when a branch scritches against the windowpane or my chair legs scritch across the linoleum?

Meanwhile, "despite of" itself, the book had managed to impart a message, or at least renew my awareness, that nothing of the past was amenable to real understanding, and purported actualities within the firmest grasp would crumble, with or without a Mobymart to blot out every clue.

Or might vampires pose an exception, with minds ruled by appetite but embedded in the past, indifferent to the present, insensible of the future? Why would great-great-great-granduncle otherwise presume I'd be acquainted with his defunct pal Carter? Could vampires reconstruct the chain of decisions that led them to perdition on their last mortal day? Every contributory event had to have gestated within such period-specific context. Could they recollect all that? I knew where to unearth the answer to those riddles, but what's the good of knowledge that gets the finder killed?

A GENTLEMAN FROM MEXICO

Mark Samuels

Barlow, I imagine, can tell you even more about the Old Ones.
—Clark Ashton Smith to August Derleth, April 13, 1937

Víctor Armstrong was running late for his appointment and so had hailed a taxi rather than trusting to the metro. Bathed in cruel noon sunlight, the green-liveried Volkswagen beetle taxi cruised down Avenida Reforma. In the back of the vehicle, Armstrong rummaged around in his jacket pocket for the pack of Faros cigarettes he'd bought before setting off on his rendezvous.

"Es OK para mí a fumar en tu taxi?" Armstrong said, managing to cobble together the request in his iffy Spanish.

He saw the eyes of the driver reflected in the rearview mirror, and they displayed total indifference. It was as if he'd made a request to fold his arms.

"Seguro," the driver replied, turning the wheel sharply, weaving his way across four lines of traffic. Armstrong was jolted over to the left and clutched at the leather handle hanging from the front passenger door. The right-hand seat at the front had been removed, as was the case with all the green taxis, giving plenty of leg-room and an easy entrance and exit. Like most of the taxi drivers in Mexico City, this one handled his vehicle with savage intent, determined to get from A to B

in the minimum possible time. In this almost permanently gridlocked megalopolis, the survival of the fastest was the rule.

Armstrong lit up one of his untipped cigarettes and gazed out the window. Brilliant sunshine illuminated in excruciating detail the chaos and decay of the urban rubbish dump that is the Ciudad de México, Distrito Federal, or "D.F." for short. A great melting pot of the criminal, the insane, the beautiful, and the macho, twenty-five million people constantly living in a mire of institutionalised corruption, poverty, and crime. But despite all this, Mexico City's soul seems untouched, defiant, and no other great city of the world is so vividly alive, dwelling as it does always in the shadow of death. Another earthquake might be just around the corner, the Popocatéptl volcano might blow at any hour, and the brown haze of manmade pollution might finally suffocate the populace. Who knows? What is certain is that the D.F. would rise again, as filthy, crazed, and glorious as before.

They were approaching La Condesa, a fashionable area to the north of the centre that had attracted impoverished artists and writers ten years ago, but which had recently been overrun with expensive restaurants and cafés. Armstrong had arranged to meet with an English-speaking acquaintance at the bookshop café La Torre on Avenida Nuevo León. This acquaintance, Juan San Isidro, was a so-called underground poet specialising in sinister verse written in the Náhuatl language and who, it was rumoured, had links with the *narcosatánicos*. A notorious drunk, San Isidro had enjoyed a modicum of celebrity in his youth but had burnt out by his mid-twenties. Now in his mid-thirties, he was scarcely ever sober and looked twice his actual age. His bitterness and tendency to enter into the kind of vicious quarrels that seem endemic in Latin American literary circles had alienated him from most of his contemporaries. Armstrong suspected that San Isidro had requested a meeting for one of two reasons—either to tap him for money or else to seek his assistance in recommending a translator for a reissue of his poetical work in an English-language edition in the United States. It was highly unlikely that San Isidro was going to offer him a work of fiction for one of his upcoming anthologies of short stories.

The taxi pulled up alongside the bookshop.

"*¿Cuánto es?*" Armstrong asked.

"Veintiún pesos," the driver responded. Armstrong handed over some coins and exited the vehicle.

Standing on the corner outside the bookshop was a stall selling tortas, tacos, and other fast food. The smell of the sizzling meat and chicken, frying smokily on the hob, made Armstrong mouth water. Despite the call of *"¡Pásele, señor!"* Armstrong passed by, knowing that, as a foreigner, his stomach wouldn't have lasted ten minutes against the native bacteria. Having experienced what they called "Montezuma's Revenge" on his first trip to D.F. a year ago, there was no question of his taking a chance like that again. Across the street an argument was taking place between two drivers, who'd got out of their battered and dirty cars to trade insults. Since their abandoned vehicles were holding up the traffic, the rather half-hearted battle (consisting entirely of feints and shouting) was accompanied by a cacophony of angry car-horns.

La Torre was something of a landmark in the area, its exterior covered with tiles, and windows with external ornate grilles. A three-story building with a peaked roof and erected in the colonial era, it had been a haunt for literati of all stripes—novelists, poets, and assorted hangers-on—since the 1950s. During the period in which La Condesa had been gentrified some of La Torre's former seedy charm had diminished and, as well as selling books, it had diversified into stocking DVDs and compact discs upstairs. Part of the ground floor had been converted into an expensive eatery, while the first floor now half occupied a café-bar from where drinkers could peer over the centre of the story down into the level below, watching diners pick at their food and browsers lingering over the books on shelves and on the display tables. As a consequence of these improvements, the space for poetry readings upstairs had been entirely done away with, and Juan San Isidro haunted its former confines as if in eternal protest at the loss of his own personal stage.

As Armstrong entered he glanced up at the floor above and saw the poet already waiting for him, slumped over a table and tracing a circle on its surface with an empty bottle of Sol beer. His lank black hair hung down to his shoulders, obscuring his face, but even so his immense bulk made him unmistakable.

Armstrong's gaze roved around and sought out the stairway entrance. He caught sight of the only other customer in La Torre, besides himself and San Isidro. This other person was dressed in a dark grey linen suit, quite crumpled, with threadbare patches at the elbows and frayed cuffs. The necktie he wore was a plain navy blue and quite unremarkable. His shoes were badly scuffed, and he must have repeatedly refused the services of the D.F.'s innumerable *boleros*. They keenly polished shoes on their portable footstands for anyone who had a mere dozen pesos to spare. The man had an olive complexion, was perfectly clean-shaven, and about forty years old. His short black hair was parted neatly on the left-hand side. He had the features of a *mestizo*, a typical Mexican of mingled European and Native Indian blood. There was something in the way that he carried himself that told of a gentleman down on his luck, perhaps even an impoverished scholar given his slight stoop, an attribute often acquired by those who pore over books or manuscripts year after year.

He was browsing through the books on display that were published by the likes of Ediciones Valdemar and Ediciones Siruela that had been specially imported from Spain. These were mostly supernatural fiction titles, for which many Mexican readers had a discerning fondness. Armstrong was glad, for his own anthologies invariably were comprised of tales depicting the weird and uncanny, a market that, at least in the Anglophone countries, seemed to have self-destructed after a glut of trashy horror paperbacks in the 1980s. But these were not junk; they were works by the recognised masters; and a quick glance over the classics available for sale here in mass-market form would have drawn the admiration of any English or American devotee. Here were books by Arthur Machen, Algernon Blackwood, M. R. James, and Ambrose Bierce, among dozens of others. Most striking, however, was the vast range of collections available written by H. P. Lovecraft. The browsing man in the dark suit picked up one after the other, almost reluctant to return each to its proper place, although if his down-at-heel appearance were an indication, their price was surely beyond his limited means. New books in Mexico are scarcely ever cheap.

Armstrong looked away. He could not understand why this rather ordinary gentleman had stirred his imagination. He was, after all, merely typical of the sort of book-addict found anywhere and at any time. Meanwhile, Juan San Isidro had noticed Stephen's arrival and called down to him.

"*¡Ay, Víctor, quiero más chela! Lo siento, pero no tengo dinero.*"

Armstrong sighed and made his way up the stairs.

When they were eventually sat opposite one another, Armstrong with a bottle of Indio and San Isidro with a fresh bottle of Sol, the Mexican switched from Spanish to English. He was always keen to take whatever opportunity he could to converse in the language. A huge bear of a man, he'd recently grown a shaggy goatee beard, and the T-shirt he wore bore the logo of some outlandish band called "Control Machete," whose music Armstrong did not know and did not want to know. Years ago Armstrong had foolishly mentioned San Isidro's literary efforts to the publisher of a small-press imprint in California who was looking for cosmic or outré verse. The result had been a chapbook with a selection of San Isidro's Aztec-influenced work translated into English, and thereafter Armstrong had never been able to entirely shake off his "discovery."

"So," he said, "how are things with you? Still editing those *antologías*?"

"There's scarcely any money in them, Juan," Armstrong replied. "Unless I've managed to wrangle something original out of Steve King, the publishers want to nail my balls to the wall."

"You know him? King? Do you think he'd give me a loan? He's very rich, no? Help out a struggling brother artist?"

Armstrong tried not to smile inappropriately. He could only imagine how quickly San Isidro would piss away any handouts he'd receive on booze. No one other than their agents, accountants, lawyers, or publishers milks cash-cow authors.

"He's a busy man. I don't think he'd appreciate my ..."

"You mean he's a *pinche cabrón*. Keeps his money up his *culo* where no one else can get at it. That's why *todos los gringos* walk around with their legs apart, like cowboys, no? All those dollar bills stuffed in there."

Armstrong was relieved to be British. Even liberal Americans who came south, seeking to atone for the recent sins of NAFTA and a long history of land-grabbing, were objects of ridicule here. They might get away with such conscience-posturing in the north, in cities like Monterrey that were closer to the border and which looked to rich U.S. states like Texas for inspiration, but in Mexico D.F. *gringos* are only ever *pinches gringos,* and no amount of self-loathing or atonement on their part could ever erase the fact. The British, on the other hand, despite their imperial past, were redeemed by virtue of having given the Beatles and association football to the world.

"Why did you want to see me, Juan?" Armstrong asked, taking out his packet of Faros and putting them on the table. His companion looked at the cheap brand with amused contempt. Nevertheless, this attitude did not stop him from smoking them.

"I want you to take a look at some *cuentos*," San Isidro replied, puffing away on the cigarette he'd taken. "Read them and make me an offer. They're in your line of work."

He delved into a shoulder bag lying underneath the table and took out a pile of papers, individuated into sections by rubber bands, and handed them over.

"I thought you didn't write short stories," Armstrong said.

"I didn't write them. I'm acting as the exclusive agent. They're in English, as you see, and they're the type of horror stories you like. I handle all his stuff," San Isidro replied.

"Who's this author," Armstrong said, looking at the top sheet, "Felipe López? I can't say I've heard of him."

"*El señor López* has only been writing for a couple of years. He's my personal discovery, like you discovered me, no? *Es un autor auténtico*, not some hack. *Mira al cabellero* down there, the one who's looking through the books? That's *el señor López*. He doesn't want to meet you until you've read his stuff. I told him I knew you, and that you weren't the same as all those other *culeros* who'd rejected him."

So that man in the crumpled grey suit was San Isidro's first client, Armstrong thought. He hesitated for a moment but then relented. At least this man López had the appearance of being literate.

"All right," Armstrong said, "I'll take them away with me and call you once I've read them. I can't promise anything, though."

"Why not sit here and read them now, *compañero*? I tell you, these things are a gold mine. We can have a few more *chelas* while I wait for you to finish. He also does his own proofreading, so you won't need to *trabajar mucho* yourself."

"Short stories," Armstrong riposted, "are fool's gold, Juan. I told you, there's no real money in them anymore. Have another on me if you like, but I've got to go. I'll be in touch."

With that closing remark Armstrong stood up, left a hundred-peso note on the table, and made his exit. He didn't notice whether or not *el señor López* saw him leave.

Over the next few days Armstrong almost forgot about the stories by Felipe López. He hated being asked to read fiction by an unknown author who had been praised by one of his friends. All too often he had to prick their enthusiasm, usually fired by beer and comradeship rather than from an objective assessment of literary merit. And San Isidro had never acted as an agent for anybody before; he was far too consumed by his own literary ambitions. So it appeared obvious to Armstrong that San Isidro was paying back a favour of some sort. Though it seemed unlikely given the down-at-heels appearance of López, perhaps it was a case of San Isidro owing him money.

Armstrong was staying close to Cuauhtémoc metro station in an apartment owned by Mexican friends of his, a couple, Enrique and María, who were in London for a few weeks, staying in his flat there in an exchange holiday. It was something they did every other year to save on hotel bills. There were only three days left before they were due to cross each other high over the Atlantic in flights going in the opposite direction. Enrique and María were both involved in publishing themselves, and he'd struck up a friendship with them in 1995 while attending a fantasy and horror convention held in San Francisco.

Since he was staying in an apartment belonging to friends, Armstrong paid little attention to the telephone, as he knew he'd just be taking messages for his absent hosts. Anything desperately important that needed to be passed on to them would be left on the answering machine. When he got around to checking it, there were three messages, two for Enrique and María, and one for him. It was left by Juan San Isidro:

"*Oye, ¿qué onda?* Man, don't fuck me over. Have you read *los cuentos*? I think not. Otherwise you'd be chasing my ass like a *puto*. You don't leave Mexico until I hear from you, *¿te queda claro?*"

Despite his reluctance, Armstrong didn't see any alternative but to look the stories over. He took them out onto the little balcony overlooking the *privada* in which the apartment was situated. It was pleasantly warm outside in the evening, being October, and since the only traffic passing below consisted of pedestrians, it was easy to concentrate. He sat down on the chair he'd moved out there, put the papers that he'd retrieved from his suitcase on his lap, and looked them over.

San Isidro had given him four stories, the longest of which was the third at around forty thousand words.

Armstrong had seen this type of story on dozens of occasions in the past, usually sent for his consideration by "fan authors" who were obsessed with the life and work of H. P. Lovecraft. Most of these pastiches contained long lists of clichéd forbidden books and names of unpronounceable entities to be incorporated into the so-called Cthulhu Mythos. As he turned the pages of the first of López's tales, though, he was surprised to discover that they did not also contain the other feature associated with Lovecraft fan pastiches: there were no obvious grammatical, spelling, or common textual errors. The work had already been gone over by an author with a keen eye for copyediting. Additionally, Felipe López must be fluent in English to the degree of being able to pass completely for a native. The text contained no trace of any Spanish-language idioms indicating his Mexican nationality. Indeed, López even favoured the British spelling of certain words, rather than that used in the United States, in exactly the same fashion as Lovecraft had done himself.

Despite his disdain for pastiche, Armstrong kept reading. Eventually, to his surprise, he found that López's mimetic skills were so expert that he could almost believe he was reading a previously undiscovered work written by Lovecraft himself. The story had the same sense of nightmarish authenticity as the best of the Providence author's tales. By the time he'd finished reading the first story, Armstrong was in a state of dazed wonder. Of course he realised, on a professional level, that the thing had no commercial potential. It smacked far too much of an in-joke, or a hoax, but it was nevertheless profoundly impressive in its own right. He began to wonder what this López person might be able to achieve were he to wean himself from the Lovecraft influence and produce fiction utilising a distinct auctorial voice. It might result in another modern-day writer of the order of Thomas Ligotti.

Armstrong was dimly aware of the telephone ringing in the

background. He ignored the sound, allowing the answering machine to deal with whoever it was. He supposed it could be San Isidro again and that it might have been better to pick up, but he was too eager to discover whether the story he'd just read was a fluke or not. Since the mosquitoes were now busy in the night air, he took the manuscripts inside and carried on reading.

Whoever had left the weird message on Enrique and María's answering machine was obviously some crank, thought Armstrong. He played it back again the morning after it was recorded.

There was click on the line and the sound of unintelligible voices conferring among themselves and then a jarring, discordant muttering in English. The voice had a Mexican accent but was unknown to Armstrong. It said:

"He belongs to us. His products belong to us. No one will take him from us."

That was all.

After listening to the message one more time, Armstrong wondered if it were not simply San Isidro playing a joke on him, pretending to be another rival party involved with the works of Felipe López. Perhaps he thought the idea of some competition might spur Armstrong to a quick decision. If so, it was an unnecessary ploy.

After having read the second of López's tales he was convinced that the author had unmatched imagination and ability, despite being almost ruinously handicapped by his slavish mimicry of Lovecraft's style and themes. However, there was more than enough pure genius in there to convince Armstrong to take the matter further. If he could meet with López in person, he was determined to press upon him the necessity of a last revision of the texts: one that removed entirely the Cthulhu Mythos elements and replaced the florid, adjective-ridden prose with a minimalist approach.

When he telephoned Juan San Isidro it was no surprise that the poet-turned-agent was deeply suspicious about Armstrong's insistence that he must meet López alone.

"You want to cut me out of the deal, *¡estás loco!* Forget it, man. Now you know *que es un maestro, lo quieres todo para ti.*"

"I only want to suggest a few changes to the texts, Juan. Nothing sinister in that, really. You'll get your commission, I'll not cheat you, believe me."

Their conversation went round in circles for ten minutes before Armstrong eventually convinced San Isidro that he had no underhanded motive with regard to López's work. Even so, Armstrong realised that there was something more going on between the two of them than the usual protective relationship between an agent and his client. Nevertheless, he successfully elicited a promise from San Isidro that he would ensure López met with him alone in the Café la Habana on La Calle de Bucareli at two p.m. that same afternoon.

The Café la Habana was a haunt for distinguished old men who came to play chess, smoke their pipes or cigars, and spend the better part of the afternoon dreaming over coffee or beer. It had a high ceiling and was decorated with framed photographs of Havana from the time before Castro's revolution. Many communist exiles from Batista Cuba came here, having fled persecution, and its fame dated from that period. The number of exiles had dwindled as the years passed, but it still had a reputation among all those who championed leftist defiance. The place had a long pedigree, having been a favourite meeting place, in even earlier decades, of those Spanish Republican refugees who'd settled in D.F. after escaping the wrath of General Franco's regime.

Armstrong sat in a corner, lingering over a glass of tequila with lime, when López walked in. He was half an hour late. His lean form was framed in the doorway by the brilliant sunshine outside. López cast his glance around the place before spotting Armstrong and making for the table at which he sat.

López had changed his dark grey suit for a cream-coloured one, and this time he was wearing a matching panama hat. He gave a nod of recognition towards Armstrong as he approached.

Before he sat down he shook Armstrong's hand and apologised in English:

"I hope that you will excuse my tardiness, Mr. Armstrong, but the truth is that I was distracted by a particularly fascinating example of eighteenth-century colonial architecture whilst making my way over here."

Armstrong did not reply at once. He was taken aback by López's accent. Unless he was mistaken, it was pure, authentic New England Yankee. There was not a trace of Mexican in it.

"No need to apologise," Armstrong finally said. "Can I get you a drink; some beer or tequila perhaps?"

"Thank you but no. I never partake of alcoholic beverages, even for the purposes of refreshment. However, a cup of coffee, perhaps a double espresso, would be most welcome."

Armstrong ordered López's coffee and asked for another tequila with lime to be brought to their table.

"I liked your tales very much; it was quite an experience reading through them, I can tell you. Of course they're overly derivative, but I imagine that you easily could tone down all the Lovecraft elements …"

"I'm afraid, Mr. Armstrong," López said, with a chill tone entering his voice, "that alterations of any sort are completely out of the question. The stories must be printed as written, down to the last detail, otherwise this conversation is simply a waste of my time and your own."

The drinks arrived. López calmly began to shovel spoonful after spoonful of sugar into his cup, turning the coffee into treacly, caffeine-rich syrup. Armstrong looked at him incredulously. Now he understood what was going on. San Isidro was definitely having a joke at his expense. He must have coached this López character, telling him all about H. P. Lovecraft's mannerisms … but to what end?

"Why are you persisting with this absurd Lovecraft impersonation?" Armstrong blurted out. "It's ridiculous. San Isidro put you up to it, I suppose. But what I can't figure out is why, so let me in on the joke."

López looked up from his coffee and his eyes were deadly serious. *And here it comes, boy and girls*, thought Armstrong; *here comes the line we've all been waiting for:*

This is no joke Mr. Armstrong, far from it; for I am in reality Howard Phillips Lovecraft of Providence, Rhode Island.

"Surely the only rational answer has already suggested itself," López replied, very calmly and without any melodrama. "You are in fact sitting across the table from a certifiable lunatic."

Armstrong leaned back in his seat and very carefully considered the man opposite. His manner betrayed no sign of humour, and he spoke as if what he'd suggested was an established truism.

"Then despite your behaviour, you know that you're not really Lovecraft?" Armstrong said.

"Howard Phillips Lovecraft died in agony on the morning of Monday the fifteenth of March, 1937, in Providence's Jane Brown Memorial Hospital. I cannot be him. However, since Tuesday the fifteenth of March, 2003, I have been subject to a delusion whereby the identity of Lovecraft completely supplanted my own. I currently have no memories whatsoever of having once been Felipe López of Mexico City. His family and friends are complete strangers to me. Meanwhile, everyone Lovecraft knew is dead. I have become an outsider in this country and in this time. Unless one accepts the existence of the supernatural, which I emphatically do not, then only the explanation I have advanced has any credence."

Armstrong was taken aback by these remarks. This was like no madman he'd heard of: one who was not only able to recognise his derangement, but who also was totally a slave to it. It was more like some bizarre variant of a multiple personality disorder.

"What did the doctors here have to say?" Armstrong asked.

"They did their best, but with no appreciable effect, let alone any amelioration, upon my malady. They tended to agree with my analysis of the situation," López said, after taking a sip of his coffee.

"What about López before this happened? Did he have any interest in Lovecraft prior to your—um—alteration? I can't believe something like that would come out of nowhere."

It was annoying, but Armstrong found himself questioning López as if he were actually addressing Lovecraft inhabiting another body.

"Quite so. I have discovered that López was a fanatical devotee of Lovecraft's life and work. Moreover, he was one of that rather contemptible breed of freaks who adhere to the outlandish belief that, rather than writing fiction, Lovecraft had unconscious access to ultramundane dimensions. The group to which he belonged, who styled themselves 'The Sodality of the Black Sun,' advocated the piteous theory that Lovecraft was an occult prophet instead of a mere scribbler. This indicates to me a brain already on the brink of a potential collapse into total chaos. You see before you the inevitable consequence."

There are a lot of sad crazies out there, thought Armstrong, *who believe in nothing except the power of their own imaginations to create whatever they want to create from a supposedly malleable reality.* A whole bunch of them had doubtless fastened upon Lovecraft's mythos for inspiration, but he doubted that any others had wound up like Felipe López.

"Well," Armstrong said, "I don't know what to make of all this. But surely one consideration has occurred to you already? If you really were Lovecraft, you'd know certain things that only he could possibly have known."

"An ingenious point," said López, "but with all his contemporaries in the grave, how then to verify that information? Mr. Armstrong, I must remind you that the idea of Lovecraft's consciousness not only surviving the death of his physical form, but also transferring itself to another body, is patently ridiculous. I make no such claim."

López stared at him wordlessly and then, having finished the dregs of his coffee, got up and left.

When Armstrong arrived back at Enrique and María's apartment, he found the door already ajar. Someone had broken in, forcing their entrance with a crowbar or similar tool, judging by the splintered wound in the side of the door's frame. He was relieved to find that the intruders had not torn the place apart and seemed to have scarcely disturbed anything. When he examined his own room, however, he noted at once that the López manuscripts were missing. He unmistakably remembered having left them on his bedside table. However, in their place was a note left behind by whoever had stolen them. It read:

Do not meddle in our affairs again, lest the darkness seek you out.

Obviously, this was a targeted burglary by the people who'd left that phone message warning him off having dealings with López. They must have wanted to get hold of the López stories extremely badly, and, whoever they were, must have also known that San Isidro had passed them to him, as well as knowing that Armstrong had an appointment with López, thus giving them the perfect moment to strike while he was out.

It was difficult to figure out what to do next. Everyone in Mexico City realises that to call the police regarding a burglary has two possible outcomes. The first is that they will turn up, treat it as a waste of their time, and do nothing. The second is that things will turn surreal very quickly, because they will casually mention how poorly paid police officers are and, in return for a "donation," they would be able to arrange for the swift return of your goods with no questions asked. Given that the burglary was not the work of organised crime but some nutty underground cult, Armstrong thought better of involving the police.

Great, thought Armstrong, *now I'm in trouble not only with the local branch of occult loonies, but with San Isidro and López for having lost the manuscripts.* The first thing to do was give San Isidro the bad news. Since a matter of this delicate nature was best dealt with face-to-face, Armstrong decided to make his way over to the poet's apartment, after he'd arranged for someone to come over and fix the door.

A cardinal, though unspoken, rule of travelling by metro in Mexico City is not to carry anything of value. If you're a tourist, look like a tourist with little money. The security guards who hover around the ticket barriers are not there just for show. They carry guns for a reason. D.F. is the kidnapping capital of the world. Armstrong had always followed the dress-down rule and, although he stood out anyway because he was a pale-skinned *güerito*, he'd encountered no problems on his travels. The stations themselves were grimy, functionalist, and depressing. Architecturally they resembled prison camps, but located underground. Nevertheless, Armstrong enjoyed travelling by metro; it was unbelievably cheap, the gap between trains was less than a minute, and it was like being on a mobile marketplace. Passengers selling homemade CDs would wander up and down the carriages, with samples of music playing on ghetto blasters slung over their shoulders. Others sold tonics for afflictions from back pain to impotence. Whether these worked or not, there was certainly a market for them, as the sellers did a brisk trade.

One of the carriages on the train that Armstrong took must have been defective. All its lights were out and, curiously, he noticed that when people thought to board it anyway they changed their minds at once and preferred either to remain on the platform or else to rush over into one of the adjacent carriages.

Armstrong alighted at Chapultepec station, found his way through the convoluted tunnels up to the surface, and turned left alongside the eight-lane road outside. The noise of the traffic blocked out most other sounds, and the vehicle fumes were like a low-level grey nebula held down by the force of the brilliant afternoon sunshine. People scurried to and fro along the pavement, their gazes fixed straight ahead, particularly those of any lone women for whom eye contact with a *chilango* carried the risk of inviting a lewd suggestion.

A long footbridge flanked the motorway and was the only means of crossing for pedestrians for a couple of miles or so. At night it was a notorious crime spot, and only the foolhardy would cross it unaccompanied. However, at this time of the day everyone safely used it, and a constant stream of people went back and forth.

Juan San Isidro's apartment was only a five-minute walk from the bridge and was housed in a decaying brownstone building just on the fringes of La Condesa. Sometimes Armstrong wondered whether the poet was the structure's only occupant, for the windows of all the other apartments were either blackened by soot or else broken and hanging open day and night to the elements.

He pushed the intercom button for San Isidro and, after a minute, heard a half-awake voice say:

"*¿Quién es?*"

"It's me, Victor. Come down and let me in, will you?" Armstrong replied, holding his mouth close to the intercom.

"Stand in front where I can see you," he said, "and I'll give you *mis llaves.*"

Armstrong left the porch, went onto the pavement, and looked up. San Isidro leaned out of one of the third-floor windows, his lank black hair making a cowl over his face. He tossed a plastic bag containing the keys over the ledge, and Armstrong retrieved it after it hit the ground.

The building had grown even worse since the last time he'd paid a visit. If it was run-down before, now it was positively unfit for human habitation and should have been condemned. The lobby was filled with debris, half the tiles had fallen from the walls, and a dripping waterpipe was poking out from a huge hole in the ceiling. Vermin scurried around back in the shadows. The building's staircase was practically a death-trap, for if a step had not already collapsed, those that remained seemed likely to do so in the near future. As Armstrong climbed he clutched at the shaky banister with both hands, his knuckles white with the fierce grip, advancing up sideways like a crab.

San Isidro was standing in the doorway to his apartment, smoking a fat joint with one hand and swigging from a half-bottle of Cuervo with the other. The smell of marijuana greeted Armstrong as he finally made it to the fourth floor. *Being continually stoned*, he thought, *was about the only way to make the surroundings bearable.*

"*Hola, compañero*, good to see you, come on inside."

His half-glazed eyes, wide fixed smile, and unsteady gait indicated that he'd been going at the weed and tequila already for most of the day.

"This is a celebration, no? You've come to bring me *mucho dinero*, I hope. I'm honoured that you come here to see me. *Siéntate, por favor.*"

San Isidro cleared a space on the sofa that was littered with porno magazines and empty packets of Delicados cigarettes. Armstrong then sat down while San Isidro picked up an empty glass from the floor, poured some tequila in it, and put it in his hand.

"*Salud,*" he said, "to our friend and saviour Felipe López, *el mejor escritor de cuentos macabros del mundo, ahora y siempre.*"

"I want you to tell me, Juan, as a friend and in confidence, what happened to López and how he came to think and act exactly like H. P. Lovecraft. And I want to know about the people that are after him. Were they people he knew before his—um—breakdown?" Armstrong said, looking at the glass and trying to find a clean part of the rim from which to drink. At this stage he was reluctant to reveal that the López manuscripts had been stolen. San Isidro was volatile, and Armstrong wasn't sure how he might react to the news.

San Isidro appeared to start momentarily at the mention of "H. P. Lovecraft" but whether it was the effect of the name or the cumulative effect of the booze and weed, it was difficult to tell.

"So he told you, eh? Well, not all of it. *No recuerda nada de antes*, when he was just Felipe López. *No importa qué pasó antes*, sure, there was some heavy shit back then. *Si quieres los cuentos, primero quiero mucho dinero.* Then maybe I'll tell you about it, eh?"

"I'll pay you, Juan, and pay you well. But I need to understand the truth," Armstrong replied.

What San Isidro told Armstrong over the next half-hour consisted of a meandering monologue, mostly in Spanish, of a brilliant young *gringo* who had come to Mexico in the 1940s to study Mesoamerican anthropology. This man, Robert Hayward Barlow, had been Lovecraft's literary executor. Armstrong had heard the name before, but what little he knew did not prepare him for San Isidro's increasingly bizarre account of events.

He began plausibly enough. Barlow, he said, had taken possession of Lovecraft's papers after his death in 1937. He had gone through them thereafter and donated the bulk to the John Hay Library in Providence, in order to establish a permanent archival resource. However, he was ostracised by the Lovecraft circle, a campaign driven by Donald Wandrei and August Derleth, on the basis that he had supposedly stolen the materials in the first place from under the nose of the Providence author's surviving aunt.

However, what was not known then, San Isidro claimed, was that Barlow had kept some items back, the most important of which was the *Dream Diary of the Arkham Cycle*, a notebook in longhand of approximately thirty or so pages and akin to Lovecraft's commonplace book. It contained, so San Isidro claimed, dozens of entries from 1923 to 1936 that appeared to contradict the assertion that Lovecraft's mythos was solely a fictional construct. These entries were not suggestive in and of themselves *at the time they were supposedly written*, for the content was confined to the description of dreams in which elements from his myth-cycle had manifested themselves. These could be accepted as having no basis in reality had it not been for their supposedly *prophetic* nature. One such entry San Isidro quoted from memory. By this stage his voice was thick and the marijuana he'd been smoking made him giggle in a disquieting, paranoid fashion:

A dream of the bony fingers of Azathoth reaching down to touch two cities in Imperial Japan and laying them waste. Mushroom clouds portending the arrival of the Fungi from Yuggoth.

To Armstrong, this drivel seemed only a poor attempt to turn Lovecraft into some latter-day Nostradamus, but San Isidro clearly thought otherwise. Armstrong wondered what López had to do with all this, and whether he would repudiate the so-called "prophecies" by sharing Lovecraft's trust in indefatigable rationalism. That would be ironic.

"How does all this tie in with López?" Armstrong said.

"In 1948," San Isidro slurred, "there were *unos brujos, se llamaban La Sociedad del Sol Oscuro*; cheap *gringo* paperbacks of Lovecraft were their inspiration. They were interested in revival of worship for the old Aztec gods before they incorporated Cthulhu mythology. The gods of the two are much alike, no? *Sangre, muerte, y la onda cósmica.* They tormented Barlow, suspected that's why he came to Mexico, because of the connection. Barlow was a *puto*, he loved to give it to boys, and soon they found out about the dream-diary. That was the end. Blackmail. He killed himself in 1951, took a whole bottle of Seconal."

"But what about López?"

"They had to wait *cincuenta años para que se alinearan las estrellas.* Blood sacrifices, so much blood, the police paid off over decades. But it was prophesied in his own dream-diary: *El espléndido regreso.* Even the exact date was written in there. López was the chosen vessel."

"How do you know all this, Juan?"

"I chose him from among us, but I betrayed them; the secret was passed down to me, and now I need to get out of this *pinche* country *rápido*, before *mis hermanos* come for me. López, he wants to go back to Providence, one last time"—San Isidro giggled again at this point— "though I reckon it's changed a lot since he last saw it, eh? But, me, I don't care."

He's as insane as López, Armstrong thought. *This is just an elaborate scheme cooked up by the two of them to get money out of someone they think of as simply another stupid, rich foreigner.* After all, what evidence was there that any of this nonsense had a grain of truth in it? Like most occultists, they'd cobbled together a mass of pseudo-facts and assertions and dressed it up as secret knowledge known only to the "initiated." Christ, he wouldn't have been surprised if, at this point, San Isidro produced a "Dream Diary of the Arkham Cycle," some artificially aged notebook written in the 1960s by a drugged-up kook who'd forged Lovecraft's handwriting and stuffed it full of allusions to events after his death in 1937. They'd managed to pull off a pretty fair imitation of his stories between themselves and whoever else was involved in the scam. The results were certainly no worse than August Derleth's galling attempts at "posthumous collaboration" with Lovecraft.

At last, as if San Isidro had reached a stage where he had drunk and smoked himself back to relative sobriety, he lurched up from the easy chair in which he'd been sitting. He ran his fingers through his beard, stared hard at Armstrong, and said:

"We need to talk business: how much are you going to give me?"

"I'll give you enough to get out of Mexico, for the sake of our friendship, but I can't pay for the stories, Juan; anyway, someone has stolen them," Armstrong replied.

Probably you or López, he thought cynically.

The only reaction from San Isidro was that he raised his eyebrows a fraction. Without saying a word he went into the kitchen next door, and Armstrong could hear him rattling around in some drawers.

"If you're going to try to fleece me," Armstrong said, raising his voice so that he could be heard in the adjacent room, "then you and López will have to do better than all this Barlow and the 'Sodality of the Black Sun' crap."

When San Isidro came back into the room, his teeth were bared like those of a hungry wolf. In his right hand he was clutching a small-calibre pistol, which he raised and aimed directly at Armstrong's head.

"Cabrón, hijo de puta, di tus últimas oraciones, porque te voy a matar."

Sweat broke out on Armstrong's forehead. His thoughts raced. Was the gun loaded or was this only bravado? Another means of extorting money from him? Could he take the chance?

Just as Armstrong was about to cry out, everything went black. Despite the fact that it was the middle of the afternoon, with brilliant sunshine outside, the room was immediately swallowed up by total darkness. Armstrong could not believe what was happening. He thought, at first, that he had gone blind. Only when he stumbled around in the inky void and came right up against the window did he see the sunlight still outside, but not penetrating at all beyond the glass and into the room. Outside, the world went on as normal. Armstrong turned back away from the window and was aware of a presence moving within the dark. The thing emitted a high-pitched and unearthly whistle that seemed to bore directly into his brain. *God*, he thought, his train of reasoning in a fit of hysterical chaos, *something from Lovecraft's imagination had clawed its way into reality, fully seventy years after the man's death. Something that might drive a man absolutely insane, if it was seen in the light.* Armstrong thought of the hundreds of hackneyed Cthulhu Mythos stories that he'd been forced to read down the years and over which he'd chortled. He recalled the endless ranks of clichéd yet supposedly infinitely horrible monstrosities, all with unpronounceable names. But he couldn't laugh now, because the joke wasn't so funny anymore.

So he screamed instead—

"Juan! Juan!"

Armstrong bumped into the sofa in a panic before he finally located the exit. From behind him came the sound of six shots, fired one after the other, deafeningly loud, and then nothing but dead, gaunt silence. He staggered into the hallway and reached the light outside, turned back once to look at the impenetrable darkness behind him, then hurtled down the stairs. He now gave no thought, as he had done when coming up, as to how precarious they were. He did, however, even in the grip of terror, recall that the building was deserted and that no one could swear to his having been there.

After what had happened to him, Armstrong expected to feel a sense of catastrophic psychological disorientation. Whatever had attacked San Isidro, he thought, carrying darkness along with it so as to hide its deeds, was proof of *something*, even if it did not prove that everything San Isidro had claimed was in fact true. At the very least it meant that the "Sodality of the Black Sun" had somehow called a psychic force into existence through their half-century of meddling with rituals and sacrifices. Armstrong had no choice but to discount the alternative rational explanation. At the time when day had become night in San Isidro's apartment he had been afraid, but nothing more, otherwise he was clear-headed and not prone to any type of hysterical interlude or hallucinatory fugue. Rather than feeling that his worldview had been turned upside-down, however, he instead felt a sense of profound loneliness. What had happened had really happened, but he knew that if he tried to tell anyone about it they would scoff or, worse, pity him, as he himself would have done, were he in their position.

Enrique and María returned to their apartment on schedule, and Armstrong told them of his intention to remain in Mexico City a while longer. They noticed the curious melancholy in him but did not question him about it in any detail. Nor would he have told them, even if prompted. Armstrong moved out the next day, transferring his meagre belongings to a room in a seedy hotel overlooking La Calle de Bucareli. From there he was able to gaze out of a fifth-floor window in his *cuartito* and keep watch on the Café la Habana opposite. His remaining connection to the affair was with Felipe López, the man who had the mind of Lovecraft, and he could not leave without seeing him one last time. He had no idea whether San Isidro were alive or dead. What was certain was that it was inconceivable that he attempt to make contact with him. Were San Isidro dead, it would arouse suspicion that Armstrong had been connected with his demise, and were he alive, then Armstrong had little doubt that he'd want to exact revenge.

Days passed, and Armstrong's vigil yielded no results. There was no sign of López and he had no way of contacting him directly, no phone number, and no address. He was fearful that the Mexican police might call upon him at any instant, and scanned the newspapers daily in order to see if there were any reports mentioning San Isidro. He found nothing at all relating to him and recalled what he'd been told about the authorities having been paid off with blood money over decades. When Armstrong left his room it was only to visit the local Oxxo convenience store in order to stock up on *tortas de jamón y queso, Faros, y tequila barato*. The last of these items was most important to him. He spent most of the time pouring the tequila into a tumbler and knocking it back, while sitting at his pigeon-shit–stained window, hoping to see López finally enter the Café la Habana in search of him. All he saw was the endless mass of frenzied traffic, drivers going from nowhere to anywhere and back in a hurry, oblivious to the revelation that separated him from such commonplace concerns, and which had taken him out of the predictable track of everyday existence.

And then, twelve days after he'd rented the room in the hotel, he finally saw a slightly stooped figure in a grey suit making his way towards the Café la Habana. It was López; there could be no doubt about it.

López was seated in a table in the corner of the café, reading a paperback book and sipping a cup of coffee. As Armstrong approached he saw that the book was a grubby second-hand copy of *Los Mitos de Cthulhu por H. P. Lovecraft y Otros*. The edition had a strange green photographic cover, depicting, it appeared, a close-up of a fossil. López immediately put down the volume once he caught sight of Armstrong.

"San Isidro seems to have disappeared off the face of the earth," he said. "I've been endeavouring to contact him for the last two weeks, but all to no avail. I admit to feeling not a little concern in the matter. Have you crossed paths with him of late?"

Armstrong could not take his eyes off the man. Could the "Sodality of the Black Sun" have succeeded? Was the creature that conversed with him now actually the mind of Lovecraft housed in the body of some Mexican occultist called López? God, what a disappointment it must have been for them, he thought. What irony! To go to all that trouble to reincarnate the consciousness of the great H. P. Lovecraft, only to find that after his return he denied his own posthumous existence! But why keep such a survival alive, why allow the existence of the last word on the subject if it contradicted their aims? It made no sense.

"I'm afraid," said Armstrong, "that San Isidro has vanished."

"I don't see ..." said López.

"Not all of Lovecraft came back, did it? I don't think they salvaged the essence, only a fragment. A thing with his memories, but not the actual man himself. Some sort of failed experiment. You're the one who's been leaving me those warning notes, aren't you?" Armstrong said, interrupting.

"You presume too much, Mr. Armstrong, and forget," replied López, "that I have not, at any stage, asserted that I believe myself to be anything other than the misguided individual called Felipe López."

"That's just part of the deception!" Armstrong said, getting to his feet and jabbing his finger at López. "That's what you *know* Lovecraft would have said himself!"

"How on earth could I be of benefit to the designs of an occult organisation such as the 'Sodality of the Black Sun' if I deny the very existence of supernatural phenomena? You make no sense, sir."

López's lips had narrowed to a thin cruel line upon his face, and he was pale with indignation. His voice had dropped to a threatening whisper.

Everyone in the Café la Habana had turned around to stare, stopped dreaming over their pipes, newspapers, and games of chess, and paused, their attention drawn by the confrontation being played out in English before them.

"The Old Ones are only now being born, emerging from your fiction into our world," Armstrong said. "The black magicians of the 'Sodality of the Black Sun' want to literally become them. Once they do, the Old Ones will finally exist, independent of their creator, with the power to turn back time, recreating history to their own design as they go along."

"You, sir," said López, "are clearly more deranged than am I."

"Tell me about the notebook, Lovecraft: tell me about your 'Dream Diary of the Arkham Cycle,'" Armstrong shouted.

"There is no record of such a thing," López replied. "There are no indications that such an item ever existed among Lovecraft's papers, no mention of anything like it in his letters or other writings, no evidence for …"

"Tell me whether history is already beginning to change, whether the first of the Old Ones has begun manipulating the events of the past?"

As Armstrong finished asking his question he saw a shocking change come over López's features. Two forces seemed to war within the Mexican's body, and a flash of pain distorted his face. At that moment the whites of his eyes vanished, as if the darkness of night looked out through them. But then he blinked heavily, shook his head from side to side, and finally regained his composure. As he did so, his usual aspect returned. The change and its reversal had been so sudden that, despite its vividness, Armstrong could have just imagined it. After all, his nerves were already shredded, and he jumped at shadows.

"I can tell you nothing. What you are suggesting is madness," López said, getting to his feet and picking up the copy of the book he'd left on the table. He left without looking back.

Armstrong did not return to London. He acquired a certain notoriety over the years as the irredeemably drunk English bum who could be found hanging around in the Café la Habana, talking to anyone who would listen to his broken Spanish. However, he was never to be found there after nightfall or during an overcast and dark afternoon. At chess, he insisted on playing white, and could not bear to handle the black pieces, asking his opponent to remove them from the board on his behalf.

THE MAN WITH THE HORN

Jason V Brock

1

He's leaving …

She always knew when he was heading out. Shortly after he stopped practicing, there would be a great deal of commotion and shuffling on the other side of the thin old walls of the flat, as though someone were moving heavy fixtures around. A few minutes later, she would hear the muffled creak of his front door, and then the decisive slam as it closed. A moment or so after that, she could just make out the faint groan of the aging main staircase as he lumbered down to the gated front entryway.

In all the years she had lived in the modest little studio, she had never seen his face or spoken to him. All the other neighbors on her floor were affable enough; during the holidays, ancient Mrs. Kriteman would leave a tin of fresh-baked goodies in her doorway, or cranky Mr. Golding would brusquely offer to carry a heavy sack of groceries up to her place. Even Juan, the middle-aged handyman, was unfailingly polite, in spite of his limited English-speaking skills.

Not so her neighbor, Mr. Trinity.

In her twelve-year occupancy, she had yet to meet anyone who had associated with him in a social way, or even spoken with him; he was shadowy, mysterious, aloof.

Once, about five years ago, she managed to catch a glimpse inside his apartment as she was coming up the ramshackle stairs to their gloomy, worn landing. What little she could see appeared spartan, the walls painted black. There was the suggestion of weak lighting, and she just saw a strange end table with an unusual statue on display. Without her glasses, it was hard to make out, much less comprehend, what she was viewing, and it was only a glance before the door closed, slamming loosely in its paint-chipped frame as he slipped back into his dwelling—as usual, his instrument case in hand, a battered hat pulled down to his jacket collar, his long, shapeless overcoat rustling. She noted then that he seemed a rather tall individual, but had only ever seen him in his duster and hat, and always from a distance. In the protracted silence that followed, the entire odd scenario raised questions in her mind about her neighbor ... questions she had put out of her thoughts for some time, but which came rushing back, inspiring in her a vague sense of dread and disquiet concerning his circumstances, and her proximity.

In the ensuing years, a lot had happened: Her mother had passed on from a prolonged bout of cancer ... her brother had been killed in a terrible workplace accident ... and she had been relegated to filling her empty hours volunteering at a homeless shelter, existing off the meager disability income she received each month due to a persistent and excruciating neck injury acquired from a car accident. After that, she had stopped driving, which she deemed not only hazardous, but unnecessary in the neighborhood, especially as she had no other local relatives; moreover, walking was good exercise. At times she felt isolated, even in her building—an interesting, historic old brownstone with a mix of renters and owners, mostly the elderly, and young families starting out—which could be disheartening, but it *was* an existence of sorts, and at her age, in her physical condition, it was all she could manage. If only she still had Tom, life would be mostly agreeable, but that was not the case: He was taken suddenly three years previously, victim of an undiagnosed heart condition. He had fallen asleep and just never woke up. For a time, she prayed for a better life, but her experiences had blunted her faith, lowered her expectations; one should be careful what one prays for, and to whom, she had decided, because there was no guarantee that any of it would come to pass ... or in any way that was worth having. No more angels and devils for her; the inspiring tales of faith and redemption of her youth had long ago decayed into bitter cynicism and hard-won, biting realism, which she had come to appreciate. For too long she had held the wrong priorities and only valued what she actually had in hindsight. She recalled a long-forgotten acquaintance once telling her that the biggest downside to getting older was that everyone around you—friends, family, pets—died; that it was the tax paid on living a long life. Considering the other option, she supposed it was better to age, if she could manage it without too much pain and with some measure of decorum. As she approached senior-citizen status herself now, she saw the wisdom and sadness of that observation and mentally calculated additional, personal fees: aching joints, failing eyes, lost hope. In her estimation, hearts only served a few purposes at this life stage—heart attacks, heartbreak, heartache.

Outside her door, the landing stairs creaked again, and she looked at the clock: *11:09 pm.* Mr. Trinity had been gone for over three hours as she whiled away the time, lost in her thoughts, absorbed by the past and the pointless regrets of things that could have—even should have—happened but never did and, she suspected now, never would.

Then the nightly ritual commenced: Mr. Trinity's door slammed shut. This was followed shortly by a heavy scraping sound emanating from his side of the drafty apartment wall. After a moment, he started playing, and his practice would go on for the next several hours. Building in intensity, the tenor of his instrument was mournful, the melody a wailing dirge—a cacophonous mélange of cawing, rasping, weeping shrills and squawks—which seeped through to her, filling her head, filling the night, filling the world with its anguished, doom-laden call....

2

After so many years, she had learned to tune out the ominous music issuing from the residence next door. Undeniably, she and Tom had obtained the unit—now paid for with Tom's life insurance policy, another example of his taking care of her even in death—for a great price *because of* Mr. Trinity. No one else had wanted to purchase the abode once they heard the uncanny music wafting through the place from next door. The music and the unnerving history of the domicile were more than enough to spook most potential homeowners in spite of the charming layout, the attractive arched doorways, and the decent square-footage. As a result, the apartment had remained on the market for over four years.

"The previous owners simply disappeared," the real estate agent said. A decent-looking dirty-blond, which he had apparently been told a few times too often, he smiled at her before opening the front door with a minor flourish. "Take a look!"

They had decided to meet at the brownstone after Tom got off from work, but he was running late, as always—one of her pet peeves. Even so, she was excited to see the interior after Tom had described it and the area, which was not only near a small greenbelt, but was convenient to most amenities and even had its own parking space—a rarity. It was the sixth place that they had been to in the past month, but something about it felt better than the others, which were in parts of the city that made her nervous. And it was reasonably close to both of their jobs.

"Wow! I do love the hardwoods," she said, nonchalantly caressing a newly painted wall. The smell of the paint lingered in the air, subtly merging with a trace of cleaning solutions. "How many bedrooms again?"

"Two. Two bedrooms, one-and-a-half baths, galley kitchen. Gas stoves, for the chef in you!" the agent replied, smoothing his tie and turning on the light in the hallway to the master bedroom. "Great place, great services, restaurants nearby ... An outstanding value for this part of the city, near the school—"

"We don't have any. I mean, no children." She felt strange saying it aloud. "I decided we weren't having any."

"Hello! Sorry I'm late," Tom said, rushing into the open front door.

"Oh, no worries! We were just starting," the agent said. "I was running through some of the details."

"Did you mention the previous owners?" Tom asked, walking over to where they stood in the hall near the bedroom. "Pretty interesting story ..."

The agent gave a tight smile. "I did mention that they disappeared—"

"That's not all, though."

"No. No, that's not all; I was going to get to that." The agent looked down.

She felt the tension in the room elevate. "Get to what?" she asked, an edge in her voice. She dreaded this; she hoped it was nothing stupid. Sometimes Tom did things that just got all over her nerves: dumb ideas, poor choices, crazy notions. If he had not been such a hard worker, she would have found someone else a long time ago. He had even given her another shot when he caught her with her ex-boyfriend, which was more than she would have done. As her mother and brother told her, someone with her intelligence, her looks could get any guy they wanted, so why settle? Maybe guilt ... maybe pride ... She felt as though something big was going to happen for her one day, and then she could really get on with her life. She deserved better, and she knew that, but he was here and had never screwed up so bad as to warrant the door. Yet.

"Oh, it's nothing, really—"

"Well, actually, it's a very cool story," Tom interrupted, as was his habit. "It was an older couple, and they were rumored to have mob connections—"

"That," the agent interjected, "is purely speculative; don't let that—"

"Right, right—pure speculation. Regardless," Tom continued, his hands flailing as he spoke. "So they were this older mob couple who had been the owners here for, like, nearly twenty years; so anyway, they were vacationing in Prague, having a good time, and then BAM!" Tom whacked his hands together dramatically. "They're dragged kicking and screaming across the Charles Bridge, to Prague Castle, and never seen again."

The room went quiet. The agent sighed loudly. "While it's true that they did not return, no one knows that they were 'dragged away.' They were filmmakers and were doing some research on a recently discovered medieval-era dig near an abandoned city in the Czech Republic. Additionally, they had relatives in Europe, and it's believed that the couple just decided to stay there. Besides, no one's even certain that they left the country, or even the city! I mean, there's no record of them staying in Prague, just some plane ticket purchases. They can't verify who even used the tickets, or if they were used. The trail went cold after that, and they left no itinerary beyond going to the Czech Republic."

"That's not what I read online, though," Tom replied. "I read that they had some real money, and were in some deep shit with the Feds: the whole 'researching-the-ossuary' thing was a ruse; they were really trying to buy fake identities. I also read it was related to some kinky sex stuff—young girls, live

sex shows, crap like that. No one ever heard from them again. That's why this place went on the market: no one can reach 'em; it's like they never existed. I read they were troublemakers in the building, too—tried to get a longtime resident evicted so they could take his unit over and expand into it. I think the whole episode adds to the charm of the place, really."

She looked at Tom, who was smiling, then to the agent, who busied himself nervously eyeing his notes. Finally she asked: "Interesting. Anything else I should know about?"

Then, distantly at first, there was the melancholy sound of a musical instrument—perhaps a French horn or some comparable type of brass— which was soon joined by two, possibly three others of a similar character, forming a mildly dissonant chord that drifted spectrally through the air, building in harmonic complexity, swelling in resonance throughout the room. After a couple of minutes, the playing stopped, the last few phrases of the tune reverberating throughout the unit.

Tom: "Wow! What the hell was that? I've never heard anything like it!"

The agent attempted another smile, but his confidence seemed shaken. "That— that's Mr. Trinity, the next-door tenant. He's harmless, a recluse ..."

A recluse, certainly, though in other ways he was the perfect neighbor: He never complained, never bothered anybody, never had anyone over. Tom drove the bargain hard, and they bought the place, in part because he was so intrigued with Mr. Trinity and the unusual history of the apartment. Tom had always been open to new experiences and enjoyed challenges. It was part of the reason she stayed with him, she realized in retrospect; he had been a musician as well, and even attempted, for a while, to engage their elusive neighbor—knocking on his door, leaving notes, and so on, to no avail. Mr. Golding in particular had warned her husband that his entreaties would be pointless, that Trinity would not be receptive at all, but it was Tom's nature to try, to reach out to others.

So long as anyone could recall, the cryptic Mr. Trinity had been a staple in the building; even old man Jenkins, the superintendent before he died last year, said that Trinity had been a fixture well before *he* moved in, some thirty years prior. No one in Mr. Jenkins's estimation had set foot in Trinity's place, spoken with him, or even seen his face in all that time. They only knew his name was 'Mr. Ghrâbøel Trinity,' that he practiced playing his horn day and night, and that he left his unit without fail in the evenings for several hours, every day of the year.

After Tom's death, she realized many things, but of course, they were all too late. She was too sad to concern herself with Mr. Trinity and his peculiar habits, but once she was living alone again and the fog of her depression began to lift, she found her curiosity and interest gradually piqued by his odd ways as she so obliquely experienced them.

Then something remarkable occurred: She got a piece of his mail in her box by accident, his name and apartment number clearly scrawled on the front; there was no return address. She stared at it for several minutes. It was the first tangible thing of his that she had ever touched.

She could not resist taking it to her flat.

Once safely in the confines of her home, with Trinity's portentous serenade happening just a few feet beyond the wall, she debated what to do. It might seem awkward to give the letter back now that she had taken it, and she knew he would not answer the door in any case. After an hour of agonizing consideration, she found herself hastily tearing open the water-stained, yellowing envelope, though she knew it was wrong.

Inside, there was a three-page document. The paper was crumbling and smelled of smoke, and the handwritten script was shaky, penned in some alien language, with angular, densely accented letters, and very long words, which were apparently to be read from the right side of the page to the left, and from top to bottom. It resembled no other language she had ever seen, not even her mother's native Russian, and certainly not the Hebrew she had been taught as a child.

Along the bottom third of the pages were several meticulously rendered drawings, but they were smeared, and it was difficult to discern just what exactly they were about. The images appeared to be either diagrams, sketches of bizarre plants and animals, or of something else altogether—perhaps a few of each. Curiously, sections of the message were broken up by what appeared to be a form of musical notation, but not of any type she was familiar with, and nothing she could identify with the help of Tom's old reference books. Even searching the Internet and poring through the stacks at the main library turned up nothing remotely like the notation, illustrations, or language that the missive was encoded in. She filed it away, afraid of what would happen if she threw it out or attempted to give it to him.

The letter brought a certain level excitement to her life, an excitement that had been missing for a long time from her monochrome, increasingly sedate existence; it proved his humanness in a way, and made her feel connected to the outside world again, instead of focusing only on herself, instead of perpetually looking inward. It was then that she began to catch herself noting the timings of Mr. Trinity's comings-and-goings, strangely comforted by the wistful, glum sonorities of his unearthly music. One morning, for the first time in years, she looked into the mirror and noticed her reflection as she got ready. Brushing her hair, she seemed to have more *presence,* more color.... Her eyes had a glint of light; her skin was still smooth, still tight for a person her age. Even her frame was more at ease, relaxed, and her weight was good—she had retained a nice figure through all that had happened by exercising, walking everywhere. She smiled for the first time she could remember, and felt a renewed sense of interest—of purpose—in the world.

Over dinner in the evenings, she began to muse that perhaps Mr. Trinity was a professional musician. Her ruminations about his secretive life became increasingly intricate, increasingly detailed, even as her dreams became less interesting, even forgettable. His being a performing musician would certainly explain his continual practicing, his daily excursions into the outside world. *Maybe he's playing gigs ... or filling in on recording sessions uptown.*

One day, she vowed to gather up the courage to pay Mr. Trinity a proper visit, perhaps take him a neighborly offering of homemade brownies. Perhaps her feminine wiles could forge some connection between them....

3

Returning home from the shelter on a moonless December night, head pounding from a cold she sensed was dragging her immune system down, she noticed something unusual as she crested the stairs to her landing: Mr. Trinity's door was open. Just a crack, but enough to see into his dark, dark unit.

She froze in place. The lights on the landing lowered for an instant as a sudden cold gust whistled through the silent hallway, causing Mr. Trinity's front door to move ever so slightly. She looked around; as she pulled her shawl closed about her throat, she found the yarn scratchy, stiff against her skin. Her throat clicked tightly when she swallowed.

Maybe ... maybe there's a problem.

She took a short, tentative step forward, heels clicking on the scuffed wooden causeway, unconsciously pulling her purse tighter against her tired body. Suddenly, her vision was narrowed exclusively to the gap between Mr. Trinity's gently wavering door and the shabby doorframe. Her hands felt clammy, her legs heavy; her heart thudded mechanically, unevenly.

After a pause, she stepped closer once more.

"Hello?" Her voice was small, tinny, her mouth dry. The wind whipped outside the building. The lights dimmed, then flared before settling again. Without realizing it, she had walked over and was now at his doorway. She raised her fist to knock, noting that her hand was not only shaking, but that the sixty-year-old skin was slack, dotted with age spots, more wrinkled than she had ever noticed or recalled.

"Hello?" she called out again, louder, and rapped on the dingy wooden door.

No answer.

"Hello? Mr. Trinity? Is everything OK?" The door opened slightly wider as she knocked. Inside, no lights were on; indeed, the black-painted walls seemed to pull the light from the landing into the apartment, extinguishing, deadening the weak hallway illumination like a black hole snuffing the energy from a dying star.

"Mr. Trinity? Is everything all right? It's your neighbor."

She stepped into the unit, her shoes clacking on the hardwood of the small foyer. There was a sudden chill in the air, causing her breath to fog, and a sharp smell that she could not quite identify: a top note of copper ... a hint of mold ... and some other, musky undertone.

The inside of the place was quite dark. She squinted, straining her eyes against the inky blackness. From what little she was able to see, the layout was completely different from her own residence, and larger; the windows of this corner unit were completely blacked out, as well. She stepped forward again, again. With one more step, the feeble outside light fell quickly away; as she moved into the depths of the too-quiet abode, all illumination was smothered by the deep, permeating blackness within.

"Hello? Mr. Trin—" Her balance shifted abruptly, and she lost her foothold after stepping on something soft. Before she could react, she was on all fours, hitting the floor hard, her hands braced against something cool, moist ...

A body!

Repulsed, she gently felt around—screaming out when it unexpectedly moved ... and answered her scream with one of its own.

She recoiled, a hot stream of acid jetting from her gut to her mouth. Then another person, unseen in the impenetrable gloom, screamed out right beside her. And a third joined, followed by a fourth.... Soon there was a horrific chorale of moaning, tortured shrieks filling the pervasive darkness. Her mind flashed on the old couple that used to own her unit: *Were they in here? Tortured for years by Mr. Trinity for trying to have him evicted? Or maybe they were* all *in a sick partnership ... some twisted sex thing, as the rumors had reported.*

She leapt up, disoriented, nauseous, and ran. As she hit a wall, the wind was knocked out of her; she felt along its length, at last coming to a closed door, her head pounding in time to her pulse. Behind her, the horrific groaning and thrashing continued, growing in pitch and volume, voices subsiding and joining at different intervals, adding to the density of the cold, thin air as she tried to catch her breath. *I've gone the wrong way, I've gone deeper into this madhouse!*

She turned the doorknob and pushed the door open—

dazzled by a staggering, limitless panorama
of vertigo-inducing deep space quintessence:
A primeval, impossibly expanding canopy of twinkling stars,
spiraling galaxies, and flowering nebulae
receding into the void in all directions ...

Teetering on the threshold of the doorway,
she loses her footing, and is rapidly falling—

end over sickening end
through the weightlessness of non-life and non-death,
of animate and inanimate,
the terrible, swarming chorus
slowly replaced by a cavernous, otherworldly thrumming
that pushes all rational thought from her mind ...
stunned into insensibility
at the self-organizing chaos of oblivion.

Reflexively, she reaches out—
the saliva on her tongue beginning to sizzle
from the vacuum of space; lungs burning
from a lack of oxygen; brain dying of hypoxia—
and tries to control her wildly spinning body.

She clutches at where the wall used to be,
her eyes closing as consciousness withers
from her mental horizon ...
for a second, a pinpoint of light blooms
in the center of her diminishing awareness,
and she finds a solace she has not known
since before Tom's death—

When she opened her eyes again, she was lying in a poorly lit hallway that stretched to a vanishing point in the distance. She took a deep breath, eyes watering, and coughed hard, her body drained, aching. Her clothes were torn, damp, and adhered snugly to her stinging skin; her handbag was gone. She touched her face, surprised at how cold it was, even numb in spots; she could barely control the trembling of her hands, which were stiff, tight, frigid. Getting to her feet, she tried to walk, but the floor was uneven, deceptively pitched. As she watched, the corridor hypnotically transmogrified into a vast wasteland of twisted, verdant flora covering prehistoric edifices boasting sinuous, Gaudi-esque forms juxtaposed against jagged monuments—*temples?*—composed of sheer, geometrically impossible gold-leafed angles. Populated by weird, nonhuman figures— some winged, others not—in disturbing tableaux, the whole site gave the impression of a vanished empire steeped in ostensibly frenzied torment, or perhaps some inscrutable, obscene ecstasy. The bizarre relics, starkly inscribed with oddly familiar, abstract runes and imagery, reminded her of something, and she was overwhelmed with a sudden and profound sadness. She felt trapped, forgotten—lost in her own private German Expressionist film, her own hellish version of *The Cabinet of Dr. Caligari*. *Of course—Mr. Trinity's letter* ... That was where she had seen the unusual characters, the plants and creatures, the odd depictions adorning the exterior of the buildings.

At that moment, an ethereal sound—haunting, musical, and also disconcertingly familiar—coasted gradually into her perception across the desolate scene, and she found herself inextricably drawn into this blasted landscape. *Was this the ossuary that the couple was researching? Maybe this is hell—or maybe it's something else....* She stepped forward—

<<*P'jra!*>>

She spun around, looking for the source of the garbled exclamation, confused.

<<*P'jra!*>> The voice was guttural, detached. Again, closer, more insistent: <<*P'jra!*>>

The eerie music that she heard earlier was mounting, growing louder. The ruins began to dim as she watched, slowly fading into an absolute darkness, just as its grotesque, frozen inhabitants began to stir into hideous life. Abruptly, the strange music ended.

As she watched, her mind pulling pieces of her experiences together, she saw something materialize—first as the hazily radiant outline of a hunched figure within the encroaching nightfall, then little by little gaining solidity as it moved toward her with a resolute determination. Transfixed as the silhouette slowly closed in, she noticed that it appeared to be in pain, as though each movement required tremendous effort, tremendous willpower.

"Mr. Trinity ..." Her voice was a strangled whisper; she wanted to say more, to explain, to apologize, but realized it would be pointless: She had trespassed—pried into things that she had no business being involved with, whether she understood them or not—and there would be no turning back.

Once more, softer: <<*P'jra.*>> Even in the near pitch-blackness of the strange passageway, she could see from the softly glowing aura that shimmered around him in fish-belly iridescent hues that he had his precious instrument case. Inches away from her he paused, and his towering, shadowy, muscular bulk completely filled her perception. He was nude, she sensed, and his hat was missing. She could see from his outline, which was fearsome, outlandish, that it was an approximation of a human, but closer in form to the figures in the landscape she had seen start to move. His breath was cold, ragged, labored. At last, he stooped forward, revealing a cluster of what seemed to be multiple arms, or perhaps wings, and opened his case. In that singular instant, she became aware of the horrifying screams from the other room once more—the ghastly chorus was still shrilling in anguish, and she instinctively, or perhaps as part of her delusionary state, understood that these could be souls. As he pulled the instrument from its holder, she observed that it too threw off a faint luminosity, a greenish fluorescence that defined its bizarre shape. She had never see what instrument created Mr. Trinity's disturbing music, and was both amazed and revolted by the intricate, mottled swirls of fleshy corkscrews—mapped by tendons, threaded with weakly pulsing veins—that coiled and twisted to create the body of the device: a mucid collage of soft, translucent tubing punctuated with numerous bony prominences. The buttons, inscribed by the odd musical notations from the letter, seemed to be made from rows of large, yellowed teeth. Multiple growths pulsed under the instrument's glistening skin, crowding next to many trembling, blinking eyes, which stared from beneath the quivering membranes. Instant to instant, the weird implement appeared solid, then gel-like, then solid—the eyes clouded, deadened, shifting back and forth into positions that brought to her mind distorted, yet familiar faces. Sometimes even people she recognized—her dead mother, father, and brother.... Others were strangers, still others were simply half-formed horrors of sickening visage.

She tried to scream, but was muted by horror and disgust. Mr. Trinity pulled the weird apparatus to his face, which for the first time illuminated his features—

And she found the scream buried deep in her chest.

His appearance was little more than a pale, gaunt, expressionless mask, the lips peeled away from the outsized, crooked dentition in an approximation of a rictus. The five deeply sunken eyes formed a perfect inverted triangle in the stretched skin of the face, wetly reflecting the strange, dim glow of the living instrument gripped in his gnarled, arthritic fists. His skeletal proboscis twitched excitedly on his enormous earless head as Mr. Trinity inched closer and closer, the single massive, blood-colored horn at last visible curling asymmetrically from the top of his denuded cranium.

The din from the screaming choir in the other room seemed to crescendo, then fade from her dying mind; as she backed away from the creature in front of her, she was horrified to comprehend all the terrible lies, delusions, and mistakes in her life that she would never get a chance to undo or correct. Instead of working to improve herself, instead of making the best of her reality, she had coveted and envied; she had marginalized and belittled, and arrogantly claimed to know better. In the end, she had searched for something that was better left unknown, undiscovered. Unfortunately, she had found it. *Am I to become a part of his instrument? Will he collect me now for his endless permutations, his ceaseless practice?*

In the seconds left to her, she thought she heard Tom's voice in the distant screams, blended with the swelling melodies of madness, the pitiful harmonies of Hell that her shattered mind could no longer fully assimilate. She understood now that this was not her heaven or hell, but her eternal limbo. Much as her life had been unlived, so too would her death be unresolved; she would persist in this place, with this being, this creature, this nephilim. She had been found, too, it seems.

Then, with a strange resolve and an unexpected grace, the man with the horn—who always was, and who always would be—raised the pulsating instrument to his mouth ...

And the infinite was ignited.

JOHN FOUR

Caitlín R. Kiernan

The Temple is called *the Temple* because it is a place of prayer, even though no one prays anymore because it's better that the gods don't notice you. It's better to be an anonymous mote in the eye than a mote in the eye that has called attention to itself. It may be this is what happened to the world, in that final age of humanity, before the beginning of this interminable eschatology. It may be that the gods finally sat up and took notice. After two million years of prayer and blood sacrifice and magical thinking, it may only be that they took notice and crawled down from heaven and up from hell to see what was making such an awful racket. This may only be a plea by the gods for peace and quiet.

But those who remember Before tell a different story, those from before who can still speak. Those from before who can still speak and remember how. Those from before who can still speak and remember how and are stupid enough to do so. That ever -diminishing subset recalls that Something came from Somewhere Else, and that astronomers saw it coming twenty, twenty-five, thirty years before its arrival. There's no consensus on what the Something might have been, only that it has always traveled between galaxies, and finally, inevitably, it came much too near, and swallowed all the Milky Way and shat out this new world where the temple in which no one prays rises from an horizonless charcoal plain. It was not built here, the temple, but is a secretion, an architectural excrescence. Those from Before call it crooked, because they remember that other geometry, the one in which words like *crooked* still had meaning.

So a crooked Temple rises from a crooked charcoal plain, and all about the Temple is the last crooked city of mankind, spread out below the crooked black sky. It becomes tedious, the cataloging of all this crookedness, and entirely absurd, as there remains nothing *straight* to provide a point of reference. If there were still clouds, the spires of the Temple would brush against their bellies. If there were still stars, it would seem as if the Temple were an accusatory finger pointing towards them.

The plain. The city. The Temple. The starless sky.

That's quite enough for now.

A woman who was never given a name—and who mercifully doesn't recall Before—sits inside the vast narthex of the Temple. She tends to one of the pools of greater darkness that spring, here and there, from the greasy, resinous walls and floors, because sipping or bathing or drowning in one of these pools temporarily blots out the incessant piping of flutes and the constant drumming that pours always down from the inaccessible upper regions of the spire. A balm from waters that are not water, but can dim those monotonous hymns devised for the pleasure of Chaos, in that era before the coming of time. She tends the pool whose blood can muffle the laughter and the screams and even the crying sounds. So the pools are precious, and those who have the strength, the gift, the requisite madness to keep them, to milk them, these people are the only solace remaining in all the shattered mind of the shattered race that once was humanity.

She might be called Mercy, had that word not been forgotten. She might be called Release, but the concept of release has dwindled until it's hardly more than the unreachable itch of a phantom limb. Release was amputated along with Death and Hope, Blindness and Sleep.

Oh yes, she *can* see. All who dwell in the city on the plain can see perfectly well, though no light remains anywhere, only a complex continuum of darkness. So the nameless woman who isn't blind sits at the edge of this pool, which is one of half a hundred such springs in the city. She has a thimble, a spoon, a mug, and a bowl. The thimble can hardly hold enough to ease one's suffering. The spoon is rusted, and its edges are sharp as a razor. The mug is cracked and missing its handle. The bowl has several small holes in the bottom. And these are the only vessels by which she is permitted to dispense what passes for surcease to the ruined and misshapen pilgrims who come to her.

She has been kneeling so long at the edge of the pool that she has no memory of ever standing, walking, or running. This is just as well, because, at some point, the living floor of the narthex decided that her legs and feet must surely be a part of its excreted self, and so she was incorporated, partly absorbed, and became a fixture of the Temple; an appendage, at most. She sprouts from the greasy, sweating stone, and all the lurching masses come to her.

There is in the city a sort of lottery, determining when any given person may visit the Temple, so she will not ever be overwhelmed. Even so, there's never a moment when the needful, impatient bodies do not press in all about her. But they do not dare to press *too* impatiently. For *she* decides the dosage one receives from the pool—whether a spoonful, or a cup, or a bowl—and no one argues with her, because she may also withhold the pool's blessings. She may refuse, and then the pool shuts itself tightly, and no one can even have the thimble. In this way, there are still manners in a world devoid of Order. Fear and desperation have preserved their barest semblance. And also promote acts of generosity, for on very rare occasions a pilgrim may come to her bearing some stingy shard of Before. The offering is presented and set down on the floor, on that indefinite place where she becomes the floor of the narthex and the floor of the narthex becomes her.

"Kind," she might whisper, or "Thoughtful." She is infrequently heard to utter more than a single word at once, as her jaws and tongue, palate and teeth, are ill suited to conversation. But always there is at least *one* word before she takes the offering into herself, which is also the jealous Temple's way of claiming these alms for *it*self. A pilgrim may present her with a melted lump of windowpane, or a gnawed bone, or a penny, or the effigy of an unremembered saint fashioned from injection-molded plastic. Cherished treasures from the rubble. Quaint keepsakes from Before. She finds them amusing.

Though this is an age without seconds or minutes or hours, it's not precisely an age without time. Or perhaps it is more accurate to say it is an age during which the *illusion* of time stubbornly persists, hardwired as it is into the primate brain. Moments still *seem* to follow one after the next, even though there exists no means of keeping track of them. There are not days, as there is no sun. It might be claimed that when the globe capsized, tumbling pole over pole into this abyss, an era of unending night began. Only, there remain no stars nor moon nor any other luminous body that once helped define the night as night. Nor is this darkness merely the absence of daylight. This darkness is a positive state, something of tangible substance that writhes overhead and underfoot.

The woman who keeps the well in the narthex of the Temple usually has no need of the illusion of time. She has a sense of purpose, something denied almost everyone still living. Without her, there would be no conduit to deliver the waters of the pool to the people who seek its faintest of anodynes. If she keeps track of anything, it's the thirsty parade, and when it strikes her, she counts them, until counting them becomes more tedious than not counting them, and it's once again enough merely to have a purpose. It occurs to her, occasionally, to catalog the pilgrims, to sort them into types. She knows this ordering is an act of heresy, a blasphemy against the Dæmon Sultan and his messenger, the Black Pharaoh, who dwell in the Temple's spire. But she tends the pool, and so is favored, and the gods rarely pause to peer inside her thoughts.

She's busy devising a new scheme—one by which the pilgrims are classed according to the noises their flesh makes as they move—when she looks up to see that a woman from Before is next in line. Not only a woman from Before, no, but something so rarely glimpsed as to have vanished almost into the realm of myth. The pilgrim's naked body bears few marks from the passage. She's very nearly a vision of humanity as it existed prior to the coming of the gods and the sundering of the gates of Creation. Startled, the woman who keeps the well almost lets the spoon slip from her fingers and be lost forever in the depths.

"Oh," she whispers, and those crowded in about her bow their heads (or what pass for heads), privileged as they are to have heard her speak without having first *paid* for that privilege with an offering. But the woman from Before doesn't bow her head. She stands on the far side of the pool, watching, waiting, unseemly in her apparent calm. None who come to the pool hide their need of it. Few would even be capable of doing so, and yet this woman shows no evidence of any want. Her eyes (she has two and only two) have remained clear and blue, like the ghost of every lost autumn sky. Her gaze is disarming, and the woman who keeps the pool does something she cannot ever remember having previously done. She looks away.

"I've tried not to need the waters," the pilgrim says. And her voice, like her eyes, is impossibly clear. "You're so burdened already, I've tried not to come here."

"How?" demands the woman rooted at the edge of the pool, wishing she were able to turn the trick of stringing words together into sentences. There are at least a dozen questions in her skull that she would have answered, if she could manage to ask them. With some considerable effort, she forces herself to raise her head again. She forces herself to behold the *wholeness* of this unlikely pilgrim.

"I have alms," the pilgrim tells her, and the woman by the pool sees, then, that there's a stained and raggedy bundle of linen held in those perfectly formed hands, five fingers to each, no more, no less. Her ebony eyes dart up and down the pilgrim's body, searching for deformities that aren't there to find. The woman by the pool feels cheated, and inadequate, and she cannot recall ever having felt either of these emotions before. After all, was she not *chosen?* Was she not singled out by the Temple acolytes, those whose faces are always hidden behind masks of yellow silk? Was she not led here and *forged* to this spot because she is special? Yes, all these things are certain and true. So how can she possibly envy any among the beggars, those wretches whom she is free to placate or to ignore, as her moods and whims dictate?

In the days preceding apocalypse (when there still *were* days), the pilgrim would have been called *beautiful,* and the woman knows that much, no matter how little lore she may possess of Before. Pale hair hangs down to cover the pilgrim's shoulders and half-conceal her perfectly formed breasts. She carries but a single scar, that her skin has taken on the appearance of a dark green stone—marble or schist or serpentinite—carved and polished so that it glimmers smoothly in the gloom. Her hips and belly, legs and face and arms are crosscut by what appear to be narrow, branching veins of milky white quartz or calcite. She might be a caryatid come down from her Athenian pillar, no longer willing to bear the weight of the stone entablature upon her head. Or a viridian Galatea, kissed by Venus but unable to complete her divine metamorphosis. And while this flesh may *appear* as stone, its incongruent suppleness is plainly visible to the woman by the pool.

She knows spite for the first time, and the gods' faithful emissary growing from the resinous floor of the Temple tries hard to imagine the pilgrim cast out of the city and slowly weathering to rock dust and crystalline granules in the winds that scour the charcoal plains. Wishing this, there's a pang of guilt, which only serves to double and treble her envy. All her life, she's served the Temple in the last city of men without question or expectation of reward, and now this abomination has the gall to come asking her for comfort.

"No," the woman by the pool says flatly, shaking her head, and staring into the darkness to catch sight of the next in line, an armless man with too many eyes, so appropriately deformed and worthy of her ministrations.

"But … I have a gift," the pilgrim insists. "I have a gift, something I swore I'd never be parted from. But I've brought it to you."

"*No,*" the woman by the pool says a second time, delivering the word as firmly and with as much finality as she can muster. She gestures with her hands, signaling the armless man to step forward, motioning the green pilgrim to step aside.

The former tries, eagerly, to do as he's been bidden, but the latter refuses to budge.

"I don't understand," the green pilgrim says, wrinkling her green brow, frowning and glaring over her shoulder at the armless man. "How have I offended you?"

The woman at the edge of the pool flares her nostrils and tilts her head a bit to one side, her expression become one part curiosity and one part indignation. No one argues with her. No one *ever* argues with her. The consequences of incurring her wrath are too dire to consider, and so no seeker after the pool's meager blessings—even those who have, for whatever reason, been turned away—has seen fit to question her.

"Leave," she snarls, her lips curling back to expose obsidian teeth. "*Go.*"

And now the crowd has grown anxious, but also curious how this will play out, how the green pilgrim will be punished for her transgression. The circle of gnarled bodies withdraws a scant few yards in all directions, dilating as a pupil dilates, and now only two figures are left beside the pool of greater darkness. From somewhere in the spire high above the narthex, there's a sudden wet flutter, almost loud as tolling bells, and all assembled in the Temple know that the confrontation has attracted the attention of the acolytes and also of the Black Pharaoh, Nyarlathotep. Few eyes look upwards, and a dozen or so of the pilgrims creep fearfully from the narthex back out into the atrium and onto the uppermost of the five thousand steps that descend to the city below.

"At least let me show you what I've brought," the green pilgrim implores. If she's heard the fluttering sounds, she shows no evidence of having heard. If she grasps their provenance and significance, it's not obvious that she does. "Please, look at the offering before you send me away. I promise, there's nothing else like it remaining in all the wide world. I'm sure it's the last. The very last."

The woman by the pool flares her nostrils again and grits her bared teeth. Something oily and putrid leaks from the wound that was her sex before the Temple claimed her and, in so doing, changed her forever. The oily substance, her dingy effluvium, sizzles and seethes on the floor.

"Just look. Please. I've come so far, do that much before I go."

Above the narthex, the fluttering cacophony grows more urgent, the black pharaoh's curiosity piqued and piqued again. The woman by the pool wonders, briefly, why he can't simply look through those tatters of linen and see the offering for himself, without forcing her to acquiesce to the petition of this lovely, unseemly creature.

Because I exist only at his discretion, at his pleasure. Because I exist only to serve his caprice.

The woman by the pool snorts derisively, the way horses and cows snorted when there still were horses and cows, and she hides her sharp teeth and points at the raggedy bundle in the green pilgrim's hands.

"Yes," she reluctantly hisses.

"Thank you," the green pilgrim says, and then she bows her head once before lifting the folds of her bundle to reveal the corroded metal tube cradled within. It's bigger around at one end than the other, and the larger end is fitted with a glass lens. The glass is cracked. It probably cracked long ago, in the cataclysm, or maybe even before. Maybe it was cracked by some perfectly mundane, unremarkable event.

Overhead, the fluttering stops as abruptly as it began, and the woman at the edge of the pool stares at the artifact, which seems like nothing much at all. She can't be sure if the fluttering has stopped because the Black Pharaoh's curiosity is sated and he's lost interest, or because the metal tube truly is as rare a sight as the green pilgrim claims. She reminds herself it's always better to err on the side of caution, and holds out her hands to receive the oblation. And the wet fluttering resumes. The gods exhale, having quickly tired of holding their breath. The green pilgrim looks down at the metal tube, which hardly glints at all in the murk. She actually seems to hesitate, but only for an instant before stepping around the border of the pool and relinquishing her gift.

"Why?" the woman at the edge of the pool asks, and it takes the green pilgrim the space of several heartbeats to realize that the keeper of the well is asking after the function of the thing.

"On the side, there's a switch. You only have to move it forward with your thumb. The batteries still work. I've cared for them and kept them dry." The pilgrim's about to add that she's devoted herself to protecting the silver tube and its four batteries since before the city and before the black, when the fluttering stops a second time. In its place, an expanding series of concentric ripples begins at the center of the pool and spreads rapidly across its surface to lap thickly at the low, steep banks.

And too late it occurs to the keeper that this might be a warning of some sort, a dispatch from the spire that she should proceed with great caution. Her thumb has already pushed against the switch, and the flashlight flickers once, twice, then pours forth a brilliant flood of light. Actual *light*—not merely some lesser shade of dim—which is a thing the woman by the pool has never seen, or even imagined. It is as alien to her as once this world was alien to those who have claimed it for their own. And having become part of the Temple, it isn't only alien to her, but wholly antithetical. Just as the incandescent beam parts and banishes the gloom, so too does it part and banish the woman, for she's nothing but the gloom made solid and given shape. And when her hands are no longer there to support it, the silver tube clatters to the floor and rolls into the pool. The water that is not water swallows it and takes away that hateful glow forever.

All the rotten, unfathomable corners of this dimension seem to wince, and a terrible, keening cry rises up from the remaining pilgrims as they shrink back against the walls and vaulted columns and finally flee the narthex. The cry is horror, and loss, and dazzled confusion.

The green pilgrim has dropped to her knees, is about to plunge her right arm deep into the pool in an attempt to rescue the lost flashlight, when she feels a sudden, violent tug at her ankles. She gasps and struggles as freezing tendrils curl tightly about her feet and slither up her calves, pulling her back from the well. What the floor has lost, it will now reclaim as the Temple metes out justice in the manner that seems to it most fitting. If there were still time, the transition would require hardly any time at all. Where there was before some pretense at skin and muscle and bone and blood there now remains only the nameless greasy matter of the floor. It reaches as high as the green pilgrim's hips, her thighs, the lower part of her belly, fixing her to the place the lost keeper so long occupied. The essence of it flows hungrily into its new helpmate, through her veins and marrow, invading every cell, and soon those vivid blue irises bruise, turning drab and inky as the tenebrous sky. Her pale hair is made dark, that it will never prove an affront to the watchful denizens of the spire.

If the Temple in the city on the horizonless charcoal plain wobbled for a second, it's been set right again. The high spire has gone back to seeping its endless atonal whine of fluting and the pounding of drums, and nothing more. Azathoth and its minions are otherwise occupied. The house is in proper disorder.

And what remains of the green pilgrim, this variegated shade she has become, stares into the pool of greater darkness, and wonders at the utility of the thimble, the spoon, the mug, and the bowl. Whatever she'd come to the Temple to find is forgotten, inadvertently traded for something far, far more valuable. She is possessed of a purpose, infused with whyfor and wherefore, and consumed with the exigency of her newfound station. When the thirsty, needful press of pilgrims returns, she realizes that she's always been waiting for them.

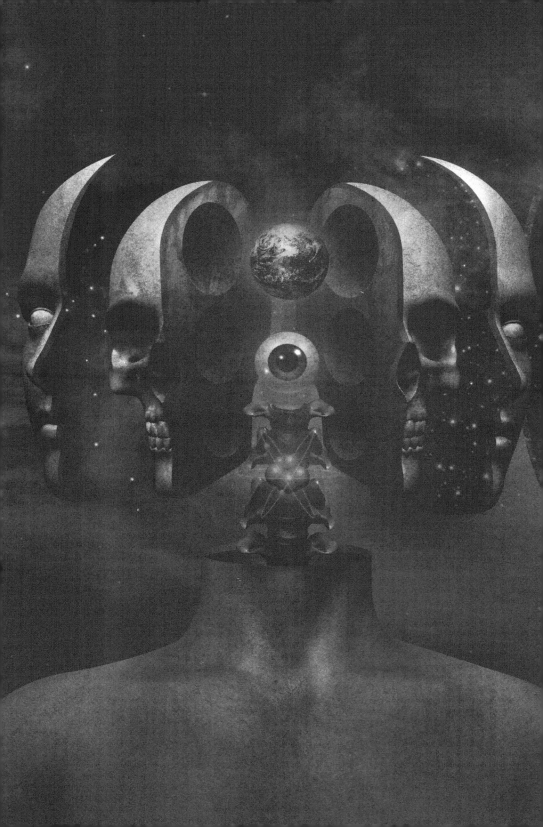

SIGMA OCTANTIS

Rhys Hughes

The southern night is brighter than the northern, for it is crowded with more constellations. When an explorer or other traveller first crosses the torrid equator from the upper into the lower hemisphere and glances up, he directs his attention towards the very centre of our galaxy and regards a highly sociable region of outer space.

Contrast such a person with the old fisherman vainly seeking refuge in an Alaskan sound before the storms of the Bering Strait send icebergs to crush his ship and drown his crew; or the coal miner descending into a pit beyond the outskirts of a Spitsbergen camp, his skull jerking back as the cable on his cage snaps, turning the shaft into a fatal telescope that will finally focus on just one star; or the Inuit girl gliding over Nunavut snows on a sled made of caribou bones, traditional sealskin runners packed with frozen fish, in haste to reach the igloo of her lover, unaware that he has left it to intercept her and is now lost in a blizzard and will remain lost until she appears out of the white nothingness, knocking him down and accidentally crushing his lovesick head.

These events are already happening, and the lights burning in the eyes that weep and glaze are the aloof jewels of the Milky Way's edge, the suns on the outer spiral arms, more lonely than the brows of feverish scholars in a library of nameless books.

Not an awkward simile for me: I once founded such an institution. The self-crowned King of Patagonia, a figure more familiar to his subjects as Giraldus Jones, had commissioned me to establish an archive in the dour gardens of his palace. My task was the careful editing of the literature of the aboriginals, four million pages in all, composed in hieroglyphs on the badly cured skins of giant sloths. Other authorities had announced them indecipherable, thus of scant interest; but Jones believed he had a key to their meaning. I applied his system with mixed results. Hints of a strange and perverted culture gradually emerged.

I had always treated with caution tales that the original inhabitants of this domain were ten feet tall. Sailors had spied them in the early days of rounding Cape Horn and Magellan and even hoped to trade with them, at least according to the log of his journey written by Antonio Pigafetta; but now the hieroglyphs seemed to confirm this. I was never a proper cynic, for I had seen enough wonders to warn me against dogmatic disbelief; neither was I gullible enough to perceive any evidence in these weird scribblings for some of the wilder racial theories of my employer, absurd prejudices too fashionable at that loathsome time.

Jones, I am sorry to say, was one of those men who spend inordinate amounts of time and energy trying to divide the human race into rigorous hierarchical orders. He took much of his cant from the German dissidents already settled in Paraguay, warty pioneers and bigots who had departed the fatherland in order to distance themselves from the Jews, but with one slant to his core belief: he thought it was the Celt, not the Aryan, that was the purest type of man. This contradicted Bismarck, who had insisted the Irish and Welsh were effete breeds; but like most extremists, the King of Patagonia did not care to resolve this discrepancy, preferring to ignore it, and the Iron Chancellor remained a hero in his scrubby domain, a bust of that successful brute looming at one end of the banqueting table that was the principal feature of his private quarters.

The skies above the grasslands of Jones's kingdom were nearly always free of cloud. It hardly ever seemed to rain down there, and after sunset the stars burned with minimal twinkle, hard and cold. Because there were so many constellations at this latitude, the classical stores of heroic names had been exhausted by astronomers, who fixed whimsical appellations to the arbitrary patterns. Thus it was possible for Giraldus to point out to me such signs as Tucana, Antlia, Volans, Apus, Telescopium, Pyxis, Circinus, and Pavo, a juxtaposition of tropical creatures and scientific instruments that would be deemed absurd among the elder

Europeans. Then he jabbed a finger at a more mysterious zone of space.

"And there, my friend, we see the Octant, a most useful navigational instrument to insert into the heavens!"

I squinted miserably. "Exceedingly faint, is it not?"

"It is the southern equivalent to the northern Ursa Minor, the little bear that has guided safely home so many."

"I doubt anyone has been guided home by *this* collection of pinpricks. The name seems deliberate mockery."

"Indeed so," he sighed, "and the greatest irony is that the star closest to the South Celestial Pole is only the eighteenth brightest in an already dim constellation. Sigma Octantis is how it is designated, a counterpart to the sparkling northern Polaris but utterly useless to navigators. The jest is an excellent one, for in the glittering display that is the southern night sky, a void exists in the one important place."

"There are other methods of determining direction."

He flung a careless arm around my shoulder. "True enough—and yet all that dimness seems such a waste! Our planet turns on its axis, the stars go around that annoying faint glimmer, that pathetic distant sun that can only be seen properly through a lens. The Octant is a failure, we might as well admit the truth, and something ought to be done to change that fact. Axial precession is of no consequence here."

I turned my head and frowned. "I'm afraid I—"

He adopted the style of a lecturer, disengaging from my side, pacing the squares of his chessboard patio like a wandering bishop, always along the diagonals. "The world wobbles as it spins, but it's a very slow wobble, and in fact it takes twenty-six millennia for the Celestial Pole to make one revolution. Imagine what life was like back then! The evidence in the old scrolls you have already deciphered ..."

"Myths and fables, surely?" I stammered.

He grinned and dismissed me with a wave; and he remained immobile in the centre of his patio, head craned back to drink the starlight with eyes the colour of parched soil, and I surmised he was performing calculations in his head, estimating angles, distances.

I had recently embarked on a thematic ordering of the ordinary books in his collection and already knew that one-quarter of the grand total were devoted to astronomy and another quarter to astrology.

I thought it rather peculiar that he blended those two disciplines so guilelessly, the rational with the farfetched; but in truth this quirk was entirely in keeping with his character. Giraldus Jones had confessed to me that he was a believer and a sceptic, a man of faith and an atheist, that he encased contradictions like a volume that contains both arguments and their refutations, but although his skin was parchment-dry there was nothing bookish about him. He was too energetic, a bundle of prejudices and projects, a dominant scarecrow in a land of little owls and casual death.

I have so far neglected to give my own name. It is Owain Gower, and I am a linguist of superior aptitude. I record this remark not to demonstrate my vanity but to highlight the fact I am inept at nearly everything else. There is no false modesty here; my efforts at furthering myself in my homeland failed dismally. How I came into the service of the King of Patagonia is a muddled tale scarcely worth the telling, but you may safely assume it was because I had almost no other choice.

Although born and raised in Wales, in the little town of Rhossili, I was aware from an early age of the colony in distant Patagonia; my father had known men who sailed out there, who settled as farmers or miners, some growing rich in the process. Occasionally he would receive direct news, a letter filled with colourful accounts of skirmishes with gauchos, bandits, or aboriginals. The only colony our people have ever founded, Patagonia is still a source of pride to the Welsh.

The flavour of those letters entered my blood, and I yearned to see the mountains and glaciers for myself.

And so I did, after failing in everything else.

I arrived in late 1928, the last year of world prosperity, a midpoint on the powdered bone path between the two great wars. I stepped from the rusty steamer onto the cracked quayside, and the last of my money jangled pitifully in my threadbare pockets. From Rawson I walked southwest and hitched rides with infrequent motorcars. At last I crossed into the isolated plain on the far side of Lago Musters.

Before the Welsh communities of the Chubut Valley and other remote tracts were finally absorbed into Argentina, the colony ran its own affairs with lonely precision, far from the gaze of international scrutiny. Abuses did flourish and minor tyrants rose by the dozen, and it was an unhappily frequent occurrence for megalomaniacs to be strung up high on telegraph poles or at least tarred and feathered. And when feathers were scarce, the scales of ugly strange fish were used.

Giraldus Jones was a luckier and shrewder example of the type. On the outer edge of the official territory, his regime was untroubled by punitive expeditions. And he had modest but vital funding from like-minded bigots in similar South American colonies who espoused the same philosophy of racial elitism. The German Paraguayans I have already mentioned, but the Confederates in Brazil were also a source of revenue; refusing to accept defeat in the American Civil War, they had fled into the *truly* deep south, into Rio Grande do Sul, grasslands almost as wild as those of Patagonia. I had entered a continent of lost dreams.

Jones at first used whatever money he raised to keep his subjects loyal. After a few years, they remained loyal through force of habit and he was able to divert some of his income to projects dear to his heart. His palace was a ramshackle old mansion connected to various outhouses by covered passages, the entire messy conglomeration painted a shade of yellow that resembled the petals of jaundice. I was given rooms in a structure that had once been a barn; with a token effort at conversion it became habitable if not luxurious. The library was located in the heart of the mansion itself. I began work every morning before dawn.

Surrounded by bundles of smelly scrolls, pinning each sloth skin to the table with a sneeze, I would methodically apply Jones's key to the texts. It had come to him in a dream, he said, but I had grave doubts about that. A rumour I heard from one of the cooks was far more plausible; namely, that I wasn't his first archivist but merely a replacement for a scholar who had succeeded in breaking the code but had refused to proceed. In a corner of the chamber, bones lay scattered, and I began to assume they belonged to my poor colleague, now an archived soul.

I had no intention of disappointing my employer....

And yet, even after translation, many of the scrolls remained gibberish, and I had orders to discard those and focus only on the sensible texts. So much exposure to an utterly alien mythology had a detrimental effect on my health; I dreamed of the gods, demons, and amorphous beings said to sleep lightly in the spaces between the stars. And I saw in my mind's eye with an astonishingly horrible clarity the obscure Patagonian civilisation of two hundred and sixty centuries ago, the cities of black bricks, blacker arts, and blackest laughter—a grim vision.

Jones often came to visit me while I was working.

His conversation was unpleasant.

"Religious texts include legends and lyrics, histories and codes of law, parables and moral instruction. I'm not interested in all that; I want you to separate the practical works from the chaff." And he would sit on the rim of my desk and press his hands together.

"Practical works?" I arched an eyebrow in confusion.

He leaned close, his breath like the bursting of an overripe fungus, and it took an immense effort on my part not to flinch. "The spells and figures of power, Mr. Gower. The incantations."

And then to himself: "We must keep the weight down!"

"The weight?" I mumbled uneasily.

"The payload. The escape velocity of the Earth ..." His sigh was deep and menacing, but he winked at me in its aftermath; and I realised that he wasn't angry or impatient but merely expressing hope in that unorthodox way of his. He stood and bowed ironically.

"Keep working, keep unlocking the secrets and segregating them. That is the law of nature. Categorisation ..."

I licked my lips nervously and refused to agree.

Then he left with a choked laugh and I returned to my studies. But his words continued to trouble me. Escape velocity? What could he mean by that? I abandoned my scrolls for a few minutes and went through the door that led into the part of the library where the normal books were kept. The rival astrological and astronomical tomes leaned on each other at drunken angles like weary revellers, and beyond them were the texts on rocketry, a relatively eccentric discipline back then. Bound collections of lectures and articles by Ganswindt, Tsiolkovsky, Esnault-Pelterie, Maul, Goddard, Oberth, and others greeted my roving eye.

One morning a few days later a muffled explosion awoke me and I hauled myself out of bed and strode to the window. An outbuilding was smoking furiously but was still intact, and I saw the wooden door clatter open and a man stagger out. It was my moral duty to help, so I went down in unlaced boots. The man was kneeling at a trough.

He cupped his hands and lifted the water to his charred face again and again, but the grime was slow in coming off. I stood behind him, uncertain of what to say. "An accident?" was the opening gambit I eventually chose, and he turned to face me with a sardonic grin. The soot streaks on his face were as savagely artistic as tribal tattoos.

"No, a success. A success that was most unexpected."

I glanced at the burning outhouse. "You experiment with explosives in there?" My tone was prim, almost chiding.

"Not exactly." He climbed to his feet and dried his face on his shirt. A short man, his completely bald head gleamed in the early sunlight. "It's a propulsion system actually. A sort of pulse engine but the fuel is new. I'm making progress every day, thank god!"

I scrutinized him carefully. "You are a monotheist?"

A crass question, and I had no motive for asking it, nor did I care what answer he gave, but he laughed. "Thank the *gods* then, if you prefer. The important thing is progress, always that."

"Progress." I rubbed my chin thoughtfully. "But—"

"But what exactly *is* progress?" He finished the question for me. "The facilities here are good, better than I ever expected, and that's enough for me. Back in Ruthenia the opportunities were thinner. So there's personal progress out here in the middle of nowhere." Then he leaned his head on the side and corrected himself. "Perhaps this is the middle of everywhere and the bleakness is just a cruel illusion."

"Are you suffering from concussion?" I asked him.

He waved a blistered hand. "I need a drink, a proper strong drink, and a chair to sit on while I enjoy it. I wonder how long it will be before Jones comes to inspect the damage? He won't be annoyed; the crucial thing for him is that I obtain results. And I have."

"Come back to my quarters," I said at once.

He accepted my offer and sat on my chair; I fetched him a gourd of steaming *yerba mate* from the kitchens, which he sipped with a smile and tightly closed eyes. "Most welcome!"

I introduced myself, adding, "I'm a translator."

"And I'm an engineer," he replied, then he thrust out his hand to shake mine; a firm grip. "Isaac Rajchman."

I was stupefied. "But Jones doesn't— Is he aware?"

"That I'm Jewish? Of course!"

"But I thought ... He has peculiar ideas about racial groups, especially the Jews. When I first arrived he harangued me for hours about how the destiny of the Celts has been sabotaged by your people. Although I don't share his views, I listened meekly enough. I needed the work. His heroes are prophets of racial inequality."

Rajchman slurped his drink and shrugged.

"He's also a pragmatist. He'll use whatever help comes his way in this godforsaken outpost." He winked. "*Gods*forsaken, I mean, if that plural is grammatically acceptable to you."

I laughed. "I was impertinent earlier."

He held up his free hand. "No need to explain or apologise. I escaped Ruthenia on foot; the pogroms there were too regular and bloody for my liking, and I went to Germany, then France and Spain, but I can't say the welcome in those countries was encouraging enough to make me want to stay. So I emigrated to Patagonia and here I am. Jones isn't the worst boss one might have in these dark times."

I cleared my throat. "Are they really so dark?"

"The darkness is coming, I'm certain of that. We're still groping in the twilight, the half-light of humanity." He placed down the empty gourd on the little table next to the chair and stretched his limbs. "Well, I must get back to work. It's a momentous day."

"But your equipment ... Surely it was destroyed?"

"Indeed so. And doubtless Jones will have to send to Buenos Aires for more. But I must write up my notes. That's the real work now. I have just proved that a process hitherto only theoretical can be adapted for practical ends. It's a new energy source with phenomenal potential. The stars are a little nearer now, that's all I will say."

"Is Giraldus Jones a practical man or a dreamer?"

"He is both. Farewell, Mr. Gower."

"I hope we might find time for further discussions before humanity's half-light turns to impenetrable dusk."

He waved a hand cheerfully. "Why not?"

And then he left my room. I paced to the window and stared out. Jones was standing before the smoking outbuilding, craning through the gaping doorway and calling anxiously for Rajchman. The contradictory nature of the self-proclaimed king was openly on display. He called to his peons to fetch buckets of water. Then Rajchman himself appeared and said something to Jones; the king wept, presumably with joy. This scene disturbed me, and I hurried to the cocoon of the library.

My work was completed after seven gruelling months. Of the four million pages, only thirty thousand consisted of spells, sigils, and magic formulae, and I had separated these in accordance with my instructions. Jones came to view the relevant scrolls and his humour was vast, typically Welsh and fulsome, almost whimsically aggressive.

"Excellent, Mr. Gower! We must celebrate your achievement." And he told me that he intended to throw a dinner in my honour. "All parts of my grand scheme are coming along nicely!"

"Parts? I thought my work was complete in itself."

"No, no, it's just one more piece in a large project. I have blacksmiths and carpenters working on other parts; and Rajchman, my little engineer, you have met already. He's a genius ..."

His eyes glazed over and he grinned; he had genuine affection for the Jew from Ruthenia. Here was paradox incorporated, a man bursting with racial bias violating his own ignorance.

I resisted the temptation to inquire further about his project, assuming he would resist revealing it to me; it was the first time he had mentioned a unity of purpose among the diverse commissions of his regime. This was a mistake, I later realised, for he was always happy to share the details of his integrated dream. To him it was obvious that a link existed between a collection of ancient scrolls and a new propulsion system, but for me they were the discrete eccentricities of an egotist. Jones, in my estimation, was no different from all previous autodidactic despots of this southern wedge, a simple adventurer like Julius Popper, Orélie-Antoine de Tounens, George Chaworth Musters, or Antonio Soto—a seeker of opportunity, not a creator or benefactor; certainly not an intellectual.

And in that judgement I was also partly wrong ...

He arranged the celebratory dinner for the following evening, and then with a final approving glance at the pile of scrolls, he said, "They will fit, all of them, I'm sure of it!" And departed.

I borrowed a horse and rode off into the wilderness to relax.

A few peons dug irrigation canals outside the grounds of the palace, a motley collection of sulky individuals, hired workers from the forests on the far side of the Andes, tough and silent; and they barely acknowledged my presence as I cantered past. Usually placid, they were known to burst suddenly with long-repressed fury. The first overseer employed by Jones ended his last working day with his head on an improvised pike, nodding slowly to the saraband steps of his murderers.

Deep down I sympathised with these oppressed vassals.

But in those times, those callow and vicious days, open prejudice was regarded as normal behaviour and nobody else voiced support for natives, whether local or imported, and so I kept quiet. To rant *against* justice and fair play was considered good manners. Jones regarded it as the height of learning to quote Gobineau or Bismarck on the natural inequalities of the various races; but to whisper a word expressing approval of diversity was an offence that would earn instant exile.

And yet he doted on Rajchman. It was baffling.

I crested a rise and peered down into a crater below me. At once I was assailed by two visions, one internal, one external, and both affected me so strongly that I almost slipped from my saddle. The internal vision was another glimpse into the past of twenty-six millennia ago, the cruel cities and laughter, the temples studded with tiny crystals that sparkled with the extinct colours of that horrid age; and the external vision was an omen of the future, a static image, an inverted teardrop, silver and riveted, resting on broad fins, a celestial fish or torpedo.

I rubbed my eyes. The first mirage dissolved, but the second remained. No, it wasn't a delusion at all, not a psychic glimpse of days to come but a fact of the present, undeniable and solid.

The crater had been neatly scooped out of the earth by the impact of a meteorite in forgotten times, and now it hosted a machine that yearned for the stars, as if the blast of that vaporised space stone had congealed into a new form capable of leaping back into the void. I had devoured novels by Verne, Wells, Zamyatin, and others; I knew what I was staring at. It was a rocket ship, a space ark aimed at heaven.

Rajchman stood on a gantry with a metal cone pressed to his mouth, a megaphone, though he mainly directed operations with the gestures of his free hand. Peons obeyed without hesitation. They were loading boxes and crates. I rode down the steep inner wall of the crater, sending small stones rolling, but not a single glance was directed towards me. I called cheerily to the engineer, who I regarded as a kindred spirit if not a true friend, but he behaved as if I were invisible and mute.

Nobody moved to obstruct me, but I had a strong feeling that I wasn't welcome, so I rode around the rocket once and then returned up the crater wall back to level ground. I had seen what cargo they were loading, and it left me in a state of very mild shock. The ship was being crammed, for no sane reason, with those scrolls I had separated from the dross, the magical works, the texts latticed with arcane spells.

I couldn't begin to guess Jones's intentions. He was thoroughly mad, I reassured myself; that was the only answer. In the evening I stood on the balcony outside my window with a pair of powerful binoculars. I scanned the glittering dome with an eagerness that astonished me, and there was an undeniable pull to the South Celestial Pole. I explored Octans star by star and drank the rays of each distant sun with an insatiable mental thirst, and then I finally resolved the pitiful spark of Sigma Octantis into a wan glow only slightly brighter and steadier than the evil gleam that might be found in the bulging eye of a dying man or horse.

I was both happy and unnerved when I learned that Rajchman was also a guest at my celebratory dinner the following night. The three of us sat on decaying chairs while a stooped servant shuffled to and from the kitchens and set down the dishes before us with toothless merriment, as if the joke were the food and the food of no consequence. The banqueting table was a warped monstrosity, dominating the largest chamber of the king's palace, covered with mysterious stains that often took the form of faces. Only the bust of Bismarck at the far end conferred a degree of normality, grotesque though his presence should have been.

Jones was already drunk and he became effusive.

"You have no idea, Mr. Gower, none at all, of what momentous events are about to take place in the world, and yet you are partly responsible for them! Imagine a guillotine, if you will. Every part must fit together neatly and operate smoothly: the frame, the rope, and blade, even the neck that is to be sliced must interact with perfect precision. I regard your work as no speck inferior to that of dear Isaac here."

Rajchman shifted uneasily on his seat and blinked.

Jones called to his stooped servant for more wine; then he threw back his head and shouted at the ceiling, "Heroic is the word for us!" And he insisted on toasting me again and again.

"I merely did what I was hired to do," I said quietly, prodding the pale lump on the plate before me with a fork.

"You are a Celt, sir!" he boomed. "Just like me!"

"Well, those distinctions—"

He slammed his fist down on the table; the crockery jumped. "Listen! Why should all mankind share the same zodiac? Why should the Celt be limited to the same astrological influences as the dullards of other races? Would you share a soup spoon with a savage, Mr. Gower? Of course not! And yet you are content to share Venus, Mars, and Saturn. This absurdity must not be allowed to endure longer!"

I laughed. "You propose to reorder the planets?"

He glowered, acutely disappointed at my obtuseness. "There is no call for whimsical idiocies, Mr. Gower. Have you forgotten that the Celt is the best human being there is? Only he is comparable to the men who walked this planet before history began. On the ground around us are no remains of that magnificent race, no stone or glass, no shard of pottery or scrap of poetry; but in our blood they live still!"

I let go of my fork as if it were a nettle and turned my aching head with geological stiffness to stare directly into his face. "To prove what you are suggesting isn't feasible! You can't really believe the Welsh are the direct descendants of those lost Patagonians?"

"Yes indeed! Why not? There is a strong magnetism about this region that draws only our kind. Think about it. The only colony Wales has ever sought to establish. Here of all places! There must be a deeper connection to explain that. We are the scions, you and I, of those obscure, wondrous people, the heirs of their attitudes and faith. So it is time we started living again as they once did. Our birthright …"

I was at a loss for words. Nor could I expect help from Rajchman, who seemed engrossed in his deplorable feast.

Finally I spoke. "No amount of manipulation in the world will change the present lifestyle of the Welsh people. They are too thoroughly wedded to the culture that exists *now*. You will never be able to persuade or bribe them to abandon beer, rugby, and choral singing for the morbid delights of life in a city that reflects no light at all. Those simple pastimes are the true gods of the average modern Welshman."

I had meant this partly as a joke, to lighten the mood around the table, but Jones slammed his fist down again on the stained surface, making the crockery dance an encore. "Those pathetic idols of thin substance will be abandoned with haste once the deities of real power are accessible again! Adrift in the spaces between the worlds, they are now; but they can come together again and orbit our planet in a line. I have the power to make this happen, the ability to return them to us."

"I see," I said, not knowing how else to respond.

His voice dropped an octave. "There has always been only one zodiac, Mr. Gower, just one that controls the destinies of all people. But that will never do. There must be another for the chosen race, for us alone, for the Celt. We are different, you see, and we should rule over the others in the same way those interplanetary gods will rule over us. Listen to me. I plan to send an artificial planet into space."

"I saw the rocket ship," I replied rather primly.

He drained his wine glass. "I commissioned Rajchman to design it for me, and he did so, most cunningly. My new planet, or satellite, will pass over the constellations, just as the ordinary planets do, but perpendicular to them, creating a new zodiac as it orbits our world, for what is a zodiac other than an apparent superimposition of planets on stars? Nothing. Our familiar zodiac is aligned east-west along the ecliptic, my new one will be aligned north-south, from pole to pole!"

I found it impossible not to protest at this juncture.

"With respect," I ventured, "astrology doesn't work. It's a superstition without any mechanism to enable it to—"

"Gravity, Mr. Gower. That's the answer. The moon creates tides in the oceans; our brains are made of water. Gravity! The planets pull our ideas in different directions. It *does* work."

I shook my head vigorously. "The moon creates tides in the seas only because there is a very large surface area to act upon; have you ever seen tides in a wine glass?" And I lifted my own glass in derision. "Of course not! The amount of gravitational pull from each planet is tiny, about the same as that of a tram or bus passing in an adjacent street in any bustling city. This is nonsense. Your rocket ship will make a pretty light in the sky but nothing more than that. Forget it."

But Jones had an answer on his lips and he let it expand until my ears throbbed painfully. "*Spiritual* gravity, Mr. Gower. Not the ordinary kind. Shall I list the members of my new improved zodiac? Octans, Reticulum, Horologium, Eridanus, Taurus, Perseus, Camelopardalis, Ursa Minor, Draco, Hercules, Corona Borealis, Scorpius, Lupus, Triangulum Australe, and Apus. Fifteen signs in total." He summoned yet more wine from the stooped servant, drank it and then frowned. "The two zodiacs intersect at two points. That should be interesting."

I filled my own throat with wine in desperation.

"And it's highly satisfying," he added blithely, "that both Polaris and Sigma Octantis are points on the route."

I felt the weight of his insanity crushing my mind.

"Your satellite will never achieve an orbit of such precision. How will you steer it from the ground?" I cried.

Jones's eyes bulged, but he wasn't angry. I saw that he was suppressing great horrible mirth, but not out of consideration for my feelings. He was building up the pressure to derive greater relief when it was released. But I scraped the leg of my chair, as if preparing to stand up and storm out of the chamber, so he spoke with alacrity:

"From the ground? I don't plan on steering it from the ground! No, the science of remote control systems is insufficiently advanced for that. So it seems that little Isaac here must sit inside the capsule and pilot the vessel by hand. It will be dreadfully cramped, but there is just enough room. I'm confident he will be able to position it correctly once it passes outside the atmosphere. He's clever in many ways."

I sneered. "And how do you propose to get him back?"

"Get him back!" Jones was amazed.

"Well, I don't suppose you intend to leave him up there forever?" And I offered Rajchman a grotesque smile.

"I do intend that, Mr. Gower. How insightful of you!" Jones rubbed his palms together like a demented djinn.

"Don't do it," I barked at Rajchman.

"I have no choice, no real choice," he whispered.

"What do you mean? Just ride away from this place. You can't be kept against your will, can you? Leave!"

Jones leaned forward and said softly, "There is a Jewish colony in the hinterlands of Paraguay. My allies there, the German settlers, don't enjoy the proximity very much; the reason they left the fatherland was to escape such neighbours. They think a modest pogrom might be worthwhile, but so far I have dissuaded them from taking such action. But if Isaac refused to help me with my schemes, well ..."

It took a monumental effort not to choke; I hung my head as I realised that the relationship between the two was less paradoxical than it seemed. It was a simple case of coercion, blackmail. All I could think of to say in the circumstances was, "You'll kill him for no reason. Your zodiac won't work. Even if what you say about spiritual gravity is true, one satellite in orbit will have a negligible effect on the masses below. And how will you build others without Rajchman's aid?"

Jones was delighted. He jumped up and yelled:

"At last we reach the crux of the matter! As well as holding Isaac, the capsule will also take into space all the spells and sigils of our ancestors. Those spells are designed to call those gods. Unaffected by the distortions of atmosphere, the words chanted by Isaac will have real power: when the gods hearken to them they will come. They will detach themselves from the voids they occupy and drift towards our globe. Then they will follow the satellite around our world forever, in a pulsing line. And *they* will be the other planets in my new zodiac. Spheres of rock, ice, and gas will rule ordinary men, but authentic gods will govern the horoscopes of the Celts. Yes, gods! The gods of our ancestors!"

He paused for breath or perhaps for effect.

"Some men say that those gods are nameless. But I know the names of most of them. Would you like to hear?"

Then he threw back his head, opened his jaw so wide that I suspect he dislocated it, and bellowed a litany of awful sounds, so loathsome that my blood turned sluggish. I pressed my hands to my ears but couldn't keep out the words, the awful inhuman names, the appalling syllables that soon saturated my soul with black despair; and I screamed as loud as my lungs would permit, but my mind filled up nonetheless with fragmentary images suggested by those names, with disembodied claws, flabby jowls, haunted faces, tentacles, tendrils, and evil hearts.

I fell into a depression, and the following weeks were drab and vile. Only occasionally did I venture from my rooms, and rarely did I speak to other residents. I did consider sabotaging the rocket ship, but some subtle force held me in a state of torpid inaction. Whether it was the cumulative effect of landscape, climate, and local culture, or whether Jones was somehow to blame, a vast apathy swallowed me up.

On the day of the proposed launch, I managed to rouse myself to make the journey to the crater; but as I neared the stables to choose a horse for that purpose, I was intercepted by Rajchman, who stepped from around a corner, as if he had been awaiting me. He was smiling, but beads of sweat studded his forehead, tiny rainbows appearing inside each drop as the sun rose over the roofs of nearby buildings.

"Glad you came this way," he said in a low voice.

"Rajchman, don't you think you ought to reconsider? I know that you are worried about your compatriots in—"

"If I don't do it, Jones will force some other Jew to take my place. He can find and compel them easily enough."

"Perhaps if we try speaking sense to him again?"

From the corner of his mouth, like a ventriloquist, Rajchman suddenly hissed at me, "Take a fast horse and ride in the opposite direction. Go as fast as you can. The rocket is a bomb."

I blinked foolishly at him and gaped. He added:

"What kind of man do you think I really am? I didn't design the craft to fly but to explode on the ground! A new kind of propulsion system. I told you this already. Atoms smash into other atoms. I don't have time to explain. Just be very far away by noon."

"Do you think the blast might kill Jones too?"

Rajchman gestured at the entire surroundings and nodded. There was something unarguable in his demeanour. An urgency gripped me; I ran to the stables, selected a horse, and settled myself into the saddle. "Goodbye, my friend!" I called as I rode out, but the engineer had gone. I never saw him again. I spurred my steed to the east.

The further I went from Jones's domain the more energised I felt, and I cursed myself for allowing the madman to attenuate my willpower. But it was pointless to fret about that now. I rode hard, propelled by Rajchman's warnings. Over the endless pampas I went. And then, when the sun was at its highest point and I cast no natural shadow on the ground, an unnatural shadow appeared ahead of me, a monstrously distended horse and man, a mutated burnt centaur on a frozen lake …

A light so bright that it seemed to bleach the lush grass had caused this mirage. There was no lake, no ice; the whiteness was false. Had I looked back over my shoulder I would have turned blind, for this was obviously the glare of a bursting god's soul. And then the blast struck me; I tumbled and rolled on the ground, and my clothes were lashed by a wind from hell, and I screamed and cursed and thrashed.

When the blast had dissipated, I opened my eyes. In the western sky a cloud was rising, building higher, blossoming like a foetid jungle growth, a tower of vaporised debris, wood, stone, bones, blood, and thoughts. And it began to rain, particles as fine as soot.

A few scraps of annihilated scroll drifted down.

The ash of spells coated my face.

Nothing else that could be recognised survived.

And I wondered if anyone would even notice that Jones had vanished from history. In those open spaces, a self-crowned king might easily lose everything and the outside world care nothing. But if he had succeeded in his grandiose schemes, in reawakening that cosmic brutality and closing a dark circle twenty-six millennia old—

I didn't care to speculate on that. I still don't.

My horse had galloped away without me. I began the long walk over a series of undulating plains. When night fell I kept going. Sleeping under *those* stars was beyond my endurance.

I made my way to Rawson. I found a job and earned enough money to pay my passage back home. I could no longer tolerate the night sky of the southern hemisphere, its weight. When I crossed the equator my glee was intense; but my worries were not yet resolved. In Rhossili I found the northern stars almost as disagreeable, for the empty spaces between them were alive with horrors, with gods my distant ancestors had feared, hated, and worshipped, a pantheon of madness.

My only escape was to move a place where bright lights drowned out all starlight. And now I dwell in London, alone in an attic, troubled only by notions of spiritual gravity and the possible astrological effect of each passing tram or bus in an adjacent street.

[ANASAZI]

Gemma Files

Know, true-born, that we have always been. We are [Anasazi], the Inheritors. All that sprang from the Void is ours to use as we will. Our blood is diluted now; we are mere shadows of the Shadow we ride.

Yet once we were holy, and shall be so again.

***

A hole in the world starts small, forms slowly, like a clot in someone's brain. It's a single piece of darkness stuffed in a locked box, a needle hidden inside an egg inside a hare, a dog, a deer, a man; a shotgun to the face, a razor to the throat. A corpse stuffed inside a haystack, face down.

These last things are sad, yet normal. They violate no rules. Merely by their own existence, they do not crack the skin of what we agree to call "true," the shape of reality.

When the hole opens, it can do so anywhere it likes.

And does.

***

Thirty days and counting

***

"E911 call, in-house—in-apartment building, actually. Christie and Bloor, right near the Pits. FFs meeting on-site. Possible 901a, 901d—neighbour says 'yelling,' 'banging' from inside apartment. Possible HZ, come back."

It was the usual Dispatch monotone, only slightly elevated. Corin shot a look at Janos, who didn't seem inclined to pick up, and did it himself. "Call received, Dispatch. On our way. Any HTR needed, come back?"

"Negative, SJAT-47. Please proceed, come back."

"Proceeding, AOS imminent. Will confirm. Out."

Janos snickered. "You're good at that," he said, not making it sound like a compliment.

"You could be too, you wanted," Corin pointed out. "Call-sign FAQ's right there on the 'Net—all you gotta do is Google."

"Oh, you think I'm *unfamiliar*? Cute. No, youngblood: No problems there. Just don't see why we should stick our necks out for an obvious MAGGOT SHPOS, with half a freakin' hour to end-of-shift."

"'Cause we're in freakin' range?"

"FFs are OS, already. Let *them* handle some PD geri with dementia."

"How do you know he's old?"

"Check the address, youngblood—that's Academica House, retired profs' Roach Motel. Smarties check in, but don't check out."

Corin turned onto Bloor, popping the siren, and watched pedestrians freeze or scurry, accordingly. "Didn't peg you as such an anti-intellectual, man. You tap out in high school, or what?"

Janos made a sour face, as if he would have spat if the window'd only been down, but just couldn't be bothered to make it so. "Try Uni," he said. "MFA—Master of Fuck-All. And in freakin' Hungarian, too, so no cushy job for me once I get here. Waste of my fuckin' time, just like this call."

Corin smiled. "You do know what 'freak' is a euphemism for, right?" he asked. "Like you could just say 'fuck' all the time, and skip the middleman?"

"Freak you, youngblood. Turn in here."

"Here" turned out to be a short-ass driveway full of wildly gesticulating looky-loo fellow-dwellers, all acting as if they were flagging down a plane. Corin coasted in, cut the engine, and made the call while Janos kitted up—grouchy old bastard could be pretty damn effective, when he wanted to. The fire engine was parked just slightly up the block, a bored driver and an equally bored Dalmatian occupying its front seat. Corin gave them a wave, getting nothing in return.

The neighbour who'd called it in was waiting for them at the bottom of the stairs. "Apartment 15—Professor Hardrada. Please hurry."

"Will do, ma'am."

"I'm afraid I pulled the fire alarm, so the elevator doesn't work. The firemen went up already, but ..." She hesitated. "It's really terrible, those *noises* he's making. Like an animal. I asked them to wait for you."

"Probably a good idea; thank you."

Janos grunted, thankfully unintelligible—it might even read as sympathetic, from a distance. And as they took the stairs two at a time, Corin found his mind wandering, pulling up stats: reminding himself how, over the last month, incidents of weird, motiveless violence had been rising all over the city, particularly in the Bloor/Lansdowne area. Granted, this *was* the same place a bag of random female body parts had been discovered, a few years back—but gangs, drugs, and their usual attendant fallout didn't quite seem to cover the sort of thing that had been going on lately.

Two laughing tourists turning a local hardware store into an impromptu Fight Club, using every conceivable tool on each other until neither could stand any longer and one bled out before the ambulance could get there; hadn't that been one of Peter's calls? A homeless man tearing all the fingers off his secondary hand, creating a palette of blood in order to paint a mural on the side of his cardboard box "home" with his dominant one; a group of nannies converging to beat an unsuspecting man eating his lunch near the park's playground to death with rocks, while their toddler charges snoozed in their strollers (they'd broken his teeth with a direct hit to the mouth first, muffling his cries, so he wouldn't wake the babies).

Weird shit, to be sure. Still, Corin couldn't see this being part of the same wave. Some shut-in without AC melting down, that was all—they'd probably find him passed out, or "passed" (and man, Corin was starting to hate that particular too-happy shorthand—sounded like whoever'd done it couldn't choose between two desserts, rather than having supposedly gone on to meet his Maker), already starting to adhere to his couch in this typically humid August-hits-Toronto weather.

Place was tiny, yet steep—Apartment 15 took them to the third floor, where a matched pair of big men in flame-retardant overalls were not quite tapping their toes in impatience.

"Hey, Janos," one of them said. "Figure out how over here they don't shoot you for breaking the speed limit yet?"

"Zappolino, you Canuck shit-turd. Fuh—"

"Yeah, freak *me*, I know." He nodded at the other firefighter, who punched the door as if it had just touched his mama's butt. "Paramedics, sir! Open up, or we're comin' in!"

Nothing. Zappolino shrugged and used his Halligan tool, popping the lock from the jamb. Given the force exerted, Number 15's door came open with surprising slowness and a long, drawn-out creak—swollen from the humidity, probably. Inside, a skinny hallway led past three left-hand doors (hall closet, living room, bedroom?), straight into a kitchen roughly half the size of Corin and Peter's bathroom.

The place stank like a five-day bender, all the blinds were drawn, and when Zappolino toggled the switch, what might have been the last viable bulb blew with a tinkling pop, leaving behind only a millisecond's flash-image of general gloom, grotesquely bright new flowered wallpaper inexpertly applied from baseboards to ceiling all around them, and some sort of tin pan clogged with dried paste right near Corin's boot, within easy stumbling range. A well-used brush was stuck to its bottom, crusted with a glazed mass of dead flies.

"Professor Hardrada?"

Janos scuffed the floor, lifting a thick half-circle of what looked like dust, but soon proved to be scraped paint mixed with plaster-shavings. "Maybe he left already," he suggested.

"Through where, the window?" Corin took a step past Firefighter Number Two, who was gripping his own Halligan like a security blanket. "Professor? Missus … um, somebody from downstairs said you were having trouble? C'mon out, sir; we're not the cops. We just want to help."

One step, then two, and a half—Corin hunched himself slightly, so as not to seem threatening. He reached out for the next switch on, the one that might set those fluorescents over the kitchen table humming, while Janos and Zappolino (hatchet buried, in the face of Corin's obvious naïveté) exchanged a *How dumb are you?*-type look behind him, thinking he couldn't see.

Later, it would occur to him that if he *had* been a cop, or even trained as one—like Peter, say—he'd have at least thought to confirm whether or not it was the first left-hand door that was the closet, or the last.

As it was, the door slammed open straight into his shoulder, knocking him to the right so hard he felt two things crunch at once: his scapular acromion as it ground against his clavicle, splintering bone into cartilage, plus the shallow hole his full weight knocked in the opposite wall, spinning him to flop on the floor. The old man came straight out along with it, landing on top of Corin; both bony knees drove deep into Corin's solar plexus, forcing him to huff upwards, to where Hardrada's rictused face—an all-teeth, all-eyes snarl—waited for him. His wasted-looking limbs were solid, nothing but loose skin and muscle, bunched like a boa's.

Janos yelled something, launching himself in turn, as Hardrada grabbed Corin's chin, turning him so their eyes could meet. Awful slaughterhouse breath rained down in a spray of spittle, hot and reeking. And—

"*Fight* me!" he ordered Corin, inexplicably. "I want to *fight!*"

Corin felt the back of his head connect with that dirty floor, wet and muffled; scalp wound, no way to know how bad. "Sir," he said, tongue thick in his mouth, "we … jus' here ta see'f you … all right."

"I said *fight*, you coward! *Fight **meeee!***"

Janos grabbed hold of one arm, the closest, while Zappolino—less worried about making sure the professor stayed unhurt, considering he was hospital-bound to begin with—went straight for a head-lock. Hardrada flailed and snapped, burying his teeth deep in Zappolino's rubber sleeve.

"Crazy old asshole!" Zappolino cursed. "Joey, get the bus—we need more guys, a fuckin' cop-car!"

Janos, at the same time, pulling till Hardrada's arm should have cracked: "The fuck *off* him, freaker!"

Hardrada's eyes stayed on Corin's, which were already starting to blur from a possible concussion; he let go of his bite, if only just long enough to demand—

"You *won't* fight?"

Corin shook his head, and wished he hadn't. "Cah," he managed somehow. "M'a 'medic. Noh ... righ'."

Janos, breaking in again: "*I* fight you fine, fuck-knob! You just—"

But Hardrada only shook his bald head, ridiculously strong, even with Zappolino dragging on his Adam's apple from behind. And looking almost—sorry, as he did so: not apologetic so much as regretful.

The *hunger* in those rheumy, too-red eyes.

"I would have *loved* to fight you," he said. Then drove the fountain pen he'd been clutching in his *other* hand all the while, just out of sight, right into Corin's left ear—nib-first—till his knuckles hit bone.

Oh *God*, the pain. That searing, liquid *pop*, followed by—nothing. Dead air.

"*Fucker!*" Janos howled, silently. And Corin felt rather than heard Hardrada's neck snap under Zappolino's startled grasp, the other firefighter's Halligan slicing around to smash hard into the crepe-blotchy skull. Blood sprang out, striking Corin's face.

It blazed white, smoking, like liquid metal.

***

From world to world we come, taking and discarding, a thousand upon thousand years of worship and blood. Across the Gulf we come, all [Anasazi] together, going gladly bodiless to bridge that incalculable distance—down the Ancestor Road, the web of worlds, with our forsworn armies marching before and our slaves crawling behind. And all this we did without any flesh but that of those we conquered!

For we are the Shadow's shadows, needing no vehicles but those we find on our next battleground.

***

When we think about deep space exploration, we think of bridging the gulfs and reaching the most distant regions of outer space, the ultimate extreme environment, filled with constant threat of bodily harm and death. Our baseline assumption has always been that such exploration will be done on a purely physical level, involving spacecraft traveling at the speed of light or beyond it, since without the development of some sort of viable faster-than-light process, the time-lag involved would be completely prohibitive; we might set off for a particular destination only to find out that by the time we arrived it had already been gone for millennia, and that the population of Earth would be extinct by the time we returned.

What we do not know is when, or how, this great leap forward into the Nothing Between might be achieved, let alone if it ever will. After all, the furthest space probe mankind has constructed and launched from Earth thus far is Voyager One, which has only just reached the edge of our solar system, after taking over twenty years to get there.

There is another alternative, however—one that does away in a single bold stroke with all the physical realm's innate problems: deep space exploration done on a purely astral level. To discard the body entirely, and throw only our consciousnesses out into the void ... to drift from world to world on the solar winds, surfing currents of life-force, moving through famine to feast, and inhabit by force whatever we might find there....

Just as much of a leap of faith, though a far harder choice, in the immediate—especially so once you realize that a truly coordinated exploratory effort would require suicide on a genocidal level. What sort of people would choose to do this? What sort of "people," however alien, even could?

But we will all have to leave our bodies behind, eventually.

***

Twenty-eight days, and counting

***

Things didn't stay silent, of course.

Corin woke fevered, reeling, in so much pain it felt like nausea, or maybe vice versa. With a pounding in both ears, drum-perforated or not—the rolling blood-surf crash of tinnitus, impossible to block, or treat. Impossible to do anything with except try to ignore.

He'd hoped to find Peter sitting by his bedside. Instead, it was Janos: grim-faced, three days' worth of beard growing in grey. His eyes lit up when he saw Corin's eyes were open, and he sat forward, lips moving excitedly, if unintelligibly.

What're you...? Corin thought, confused. *I ... I can't ...*

Then a fresh tidal wave broke, and he rolled over, retching; felt Janos's grip on his shoulder, steady, as the bed-pan slid underneath his face. When the spasms dulled he looked up again, cold-sweat-slick, and caught Janos's lips moving again.

Can't hear you, he tried to say, through the constant, unbearably loud *click-sssh, click-sssh, click-sssh.* But trailed off soon enough, realizing he couldn't hear himself, either.

Janos just nodded, reaching for the bedside table—came back up with a Dollar Store block-tablet with a picture of SpongeBob Squarepants on the front, and a marker. Though the scribbling took a few seconds more than Corin might have thought it would under normal circumstances, it was understandable, considering he was probably translating in his head. Eventually, he flipped the page around, showed him the results:

Long nap, youngblood.

Corin wanted to snort, but didn't really feel up to any further pukeage, for the nonce.

"Thass ... all ... ya got tah say?" he forced himself to eke out, loudly enough that he could at least feel his vocal cords buzzing. Worked like a charm, in the sympathy-deflecting sweepstakes; Janos gave a just-slapped grimace, as if he were momentarily considering pasting the cripple one, but settled for briskly adding seven new letters beneath his note. Corin gave them a cursory glance.

"Fuh-reak hass ah arrr, grampah," he replied.

Janos shrugged.

***

So yeah, it was about what he'd thought. The ENT handling his case checked off a handy list, using Janos's pad:

Perforated eardrum—surgery to remove pen-nib, sched week next
No infection (yet)/Antibiotics 3 wk
Hearing loss permanent
Tinnitus objective RN, maybe pulsatile, venous hum
Watch to exclude aneurysm
Inner ear damage—BPPV

That last part explained the puking, the *Perfect Storm* way the room swam whenever Corin sat up, let alone tried to stand. Didn't look too good for his chances of getting back on shift, either; normal difficulties of re-qualification aside, nobody'd want a half-deaf paramedic with mobility issues and permanent carsickness, less likely to help patients than he was to baptize them with vomit. Only logical to cut his losses before they did it for him, and he'd always prided himself on his logic.

A quick glance at Janos, however, gave the lie to the idea that he'd entirely succeeded in looking like he was taking bad news well. That, in turn, brought the vertigo back on, full-force; last thing Corin remembered was Janos barking at the doctor—something about "He looks freaking *green*, fuck-damn!"—before those red walls closed in once more, and the *click-sssh, click-sssh* pulled him back down.

***

Peter finally came by, not the next day but the day after; girding his loins, Corin guessed. Working himself up to deliver the verbal equivalent of a "Dear Corrie" e-mail in person, for which Corin supposed he should be grateful, since it at least allowed him to get a good last look at that ass when the bastard walked away.

Having hitherto routinely excused a lot of Peter's worst qualities just because he was so ridiculously cute, Corin grimly thought, didn't quite take the sting off finding out the feeling had apparently always been entirely mutual.

Janos dropped by later (Did the guy ever go home? Was this yet another something Corin had to worry about, even in the depths of life-changing trauma and attendant despair? But no, everything about his body language said big brother, not wannabe daddy; just as well, though it wasn't exactly as if Janos was *unattractive*, in his Eastern European grumpy-bear way. Just as)

But, man, he really did have to stop lapsing into these fugue states, before overmedication made things worse. It was embarrassing, to say the least.

"What's your problem?" Janos demanded, twice as loud as usual. Corin only heard it weakly, distorted, as if through water, and thanked God for the privilege.

"Besides the obvious?" He'd have shaken his head here for punctuation, under normal circumstances—yet another tic he'd have to work on training himself out of. "I need to find somewhere else to live."

"Huh. He always seemed like an asshole."

"Yeah? Thanks for telling me."

"Not my place, youngblood. Next time, pick a guy with potbelly, or a lazy eye—someone who'll treat you right. Stay close, even when things turn to shit …"

"… 'cause they're too scared of never hooking up again to run out on me? Thanks ever so."

That same shrug: "Works for women, I tell you that much. My Kelda is hell of sexy, too smart for a fool like me, has face like a horse. That's why we'll die together, be buried in the same damn coffin."

Corin felt like telling Janos that being buried with Peter had never been the thing uppermost on his mind, but the *ssshing* and *clicking* was already coming back full force. The way it probably would for the rest of his life, intermittently or not.…

And he probably had that fucking whey-faced green tinge to his complexion once more, because here was Janos's big hand on his chest, pushing him gently prone.

"You don't worry 'bout it," he said, more an order than words of comfort. "Get set for the operation, for recovery. I'll ask around; got some ideas where you could move, for no money down."

Corin's mouth was dry, his own words gone silent and aching again. He felt his cracked lips moving, shaping: *Why do you care?*

"Am I fucking American, to drop you in the garbage? I put a lot of effort into you, now I got to train somebody all over. You can maybe at least tell him how I like things. I just make sure you want to."

Him … or her …

"Day I work with a girl be a cold freaking day in Hell."

So now they knew: A fag was okay, as long as he had the right parts. *Some Socialist* you *are*, he wanted to say, before he blacked out—but too late, he was gone, short or long. Gone, either way.

When he woke up, there was a bandage covering his useless ear, and the *click-sssh* had finally abated to something subliminal, like a second heartbeat. The ENT made an "okay" sign, and Corin made the mistake of starting to nod in reply; he barely caught himself, coughing bile.

"We have pills for that," the ENT assured him.

"You freakin' better," he snapped back. Classic Janos.

***

Thus it was that we came to a thousand worlds when they were young and fresh and made them our home, fearless against their vile Light. Thus it was that we broke a thousand kings and made them our cattle, drove the lumbering herds across their burnt fields with jewelled and singing whips. Thus it was, by instinct alone, that we found the empty places and forced them to our will, pumped fresh Darkness through them and cracked those worlds across like bones, sucking their marrow dry.

And how was all this done? Easily. So easily.

We sent our word before us, our open invitation; the very root of our language, our culture, ourselves. We sent it wrapped as a gift and shining like a dropped star, for any fool to read. We threw it forth, a disease disguised as a seed, to sow our crop in the ruins of all things' hearts, and reap a great red harvest. And then ...

... we waited, patient as decay, timeless as time itself. For these infinite generations of emissaries to do our work for us.

***

Located beyond the Gobi desert, the austere and impenetrable Kun Lun Mountains of Central Asia hold an important place in Chinese mythology, since it is in this range that the Immortals are believed to live, ruled by Hsi Wang Mu, the Queen Mother of the West. They are said to aid her in her attempts to guide humanity towards wisdom and compassion, shepherding certain virtuous pilgrims—including, near the end of his life, the philosopher Lao Tzu, author of the *Tao Tê Ching*—towards the vast garden that surrounds her nine-storey palace of pure jade, in which grows the Peach Tree of Immortality. Only the most deserving are ever permitted to eat the fruit of this tree, which blooms once every six thousand years.

The Immortals are said to possess perfect, ageless bodies that are visible, but not made of flesh and blood: they are composed of elementary atomic matter, which allows them to travel and live anywhere in the Universe, even at the centres of stars—possibly while still in their physical bodies, or possibly by projecting their minds. Either way, this is a remarkable concept for any human culture to entertain, since it seems to assume a plurality of inhabited worlds in the Cosmos.

In the seventeenth century, two Jesuit missionaries, Stephen Cacella and John Cabral, recorded the existence of a place called Chang Shambhala, as described to them by the lamas of Shigatse, where Cacella lived for twenty-three years, until his death in 1650. It was rumored to be an inaccessible paradise somewhere beyond Tibet, among the icy peaks and secluded valleys of Central Asia ... a valley of supreme beatitude that is sheltered from the icy arctic winds and where the climate is always warm and temperate, the sun always shines, the gentle airs are always beneficent, and nature flowers luxuriantly.

A physical place, in other words. But many esotericists also believe Shambhala is less a real place with a concrete, physical presence in a secret location on Earth than a higher spiritual plane, what might be called another dimension of space-time coterminous with our own; a literal state of mind, already locked deep within ourselves, in which we may gain an insight into the higher spirituality inherent in the Universe, as distinct from the mundane world of base matter in which we normally exist.

It was this guiding principle that led to the foundation of a monastery dedicated to the King of Shambhala, Rigden Jye-Po, which was discovered in the Shara-gol valley near the Humboldt Mountains between Mongolia and Tibet by the Roerich Expedition of 1923–26, led by paranormalist Nicholas Roerich. The monks and lamas of this monastery spent their days in active meditation, transcribing endless prayer-strings, and pored over the results at night, treating whatever mistakes they might find as instances of automatic writing—subliminal communication from the Immortals themselves.

In most cases, these "messages" were fairly easy to decipher, their content obscure yet positive. One particular repetition, however, came to be looked upon with increasing horror: a symbol—the monk who had originally written it claimed it was a name—in what appeared to be a completely alien language. Though meaningless on the surface, it seemed to infiltrate the minds of those who "read" it, forcing them to keep trying to replicate it over and over. Eventually, the monks realized that contemplating this symbol produced very negative side-effects— obsession, violence, self-mutilation, a complete sublimation of the original identity. Destroying the symbol proved useless, since even after the original reader's inevitable suicide, it continued to appear sporadically throughout every copied prayer.

So they tried to contain the thing, at least, by excising all instances of it at the source, subjecting those who produced it to immediate isolation and exorcism—and subsequently burying all scraps of paper upon which it occurred inside a particular puzzle-box, slotted at the top, with its locking mechanisms deliberately sabotaged in such a way as to render it impossible to open.

***

Seventeen days, and counting

***

The late Professor Hardrada's neighbour, it turned out, was also his landlord. She introduced herself with an awkward handshake as Nala Le.

"We're just so sorry about what happened, Mister Vogt," she told Corin, handing over the keys.

"To him? Or to me?"

"To both of you, of course. This ... hasn't been easy, for anyone."

I'll bet, Corin thought, but didn't say; hell, she just looked so damn defeated by all this carnage, the insoluble damage to her building's already less-than-sterling reputation. Worse than he did, at least on the outside, going by the reflection in that newly installed hallway security he didn't recall having seen the last time he'd mounted these narrow stairs, two scant weeks back. So he supposed he could afford to be magnanimous, for now.

Besides which, as Janos could have told her, he really *did* need this apartment.

"That son of bitches is keeping all your furniture?" he'd repeated, amazed, after Corin told him why he didn't need a moving van.

"It's his furniture too. Besides ... we got it on credit, mainly his, so he made all the design decisions based on whatever was playing that week on TLC, because he's got shitty taste. So I don't really want most of it, anyway."

"And those grapes were sour, right?"

"Screw you, Aesop."

"Who?"

The detritus of five whole years, packed haphazardly into six pathetic boxes of crap. Janos took four stacked on top of one another, high enough that he had to negotiate up the stairs by feel; Corin trailed behind, one under either arm, trying to balance his weight so the vertigo wouldn't hit him quite so hard with every shifting step.

As Janos heaved his load down next to Hardrada's former door, rummaging in his pocket for the key, Corin caught a brief sight of what looked like a man peering down at them from one more floor up—roof access only, he thought Ms. Le had said. Maybe he'd been sunbathing, come down to find out what all the stomping and puffing was about.

Tiny string of flashbulb screen-grabs going off, before the guy ducked back out of range: Young(-ish). White (very). Blond hair, ruffled straight up. Little round glasses, gone blank as silver coins with reflected light. Possibly even cute, though Corin wasn't really in much shape to give a clear verdict on that one, given he was trying hard not to hurl.

Then the lock—shiny-new, just like the jamb and a few of the hinges Zappolino's buddy had managed to dislodge—clicked open and Janos stood back up, briskly wiping his hands. Grabbed the topmost box and shoved the door open with one hip, like some crazy Hungarian parody of good manners.

"There we go," he said. "All yours, youngblood."

"Home sweet crime-scene," Corin agreed.

Place hadn't changed much—slightly less dusty, perhaps. But all of Hardrada's crap was still in roughly the same place, from what little Corin remembered of that night, though someone (Ms. Le again, probably) had disposed of the Professor's bedding, scoured out his fridge, and pulled the living-room blinds back up. She'd also stuck a big bunch of Mac's Milk chrysanthemums in a chipped mug and arranged them in the middle of the kitchen table, as if that was supposed to help.

As it turned out, Janos had brought along some booze with which to christen the place, a huge-ass bottle of no-name vodka that tasted a bit too much like the potatoes it came from to be worth mixing incautiously with Corin's heavy meds. *Five pills a day keep the seizures away:* that was the theory, anyhow. Corin couldn't really say one way or the other, so far, but he wasn't looking to take any chances.

His no-booze resolutions fell off pretty quick, though, once the boxes were put away, and the psychic stench of dead-man's clutter started making his nose sting.

Midnight found them poking around in the kitchen, trying to decide which cans looked least suspect. Janos tripped over the sill coming in, and found himself abruptly eye-to-eye with a weirdly burnt-looking stain. "Have to sand that," he observed. "What was it, slag ... solder? He was welding in here, maybe?"

"Who welds in their apartment?"

"Some people for fun, as a hobby-amusement. Or work."

"I don't think he was that kind of professor, Janos."

It occurred to Corin that he didn't know what it was, exactly, that Hardrada had studied, or taught. Or anything much about him, really, aside from the fact that he could hit like a buffalo, and had even worse taste than Peter when it came to papering his walls.

A fresh twist of nausea, and Corin raised his head to realize they'd somehow ended up on the living-room couch together, a good ten feet away. Beside him, Janos was half-sprawled in a way that took up far too much room for comfort, his sweaty big-man smell alone enough to render Corin simultaneously horny and sad. Stupid: he didn't even *like* Janos, most of the time—or hadn't, until he'd abruptly become one of the few things he had left. Was this what the rest of his life would be reckoned in? A series of ever-diminishing returns?

Seeking distraction, Corin made himself squint over at the stain again, hard, and remembered—

"No, wait: That was his *blood*."

"Couldn't be."

"Sure, but it was—I remember. It was all, like ... white, and smoking."

"You're drunk, youngblood."

"Yeah? Well, you're—drunker. *Much* drunker. So get the fuck out of my apartment already, asshole, so I can sleep."

"Get the *freak* out, you mean."

"Either does me just fine, man."

At the door, Janos suddenly enfolded him, bruising his ribs. "I never cared you were gay, you know," he said, muffled, into the top of Corin's head.

"Um, thanks, Janos—I never cared you were straight. I mean ... you *are* straight, right?"

Janos laughed. "Bet your ass. Don't worry, youngblood: plenty of twinks in the sea. You find somebody—somebody smart, sexy. Good for you."

"Okay, thanks again."

"Next time go ugly, remember! Is all the difference."

"Yeah, I'll make sure to do that."

***

The first dream came later that night. He sat in an indefinitely sized room, surrounded by an equally indefinite number of people. In front of him was a roll of coarse paper, spooling outwards into darkness; he saw his left hand steady it, holding the immediate surface flat, while his right used reed and ink to scribe it with words he couldn't read—strokes, dots, dashes, all darting downwards from a single uppermost line. There was a soothing rhythm to the work, the soft shapes of syllables forming on his tongue, releasing themselves silently against his palate again and again. His eyes and wrists burnt, pleasantly.

But then he looked down just in time to watch the pen go in a direction he hadn't willed it to, and felt the words choke in his mouth. A series of hard scratches, angled so sharply that what emerged looked impenetrable, a knot of lines. A squatting spider. A crab's track in wet sand, printed only to be washed away, then reappear whole, perfect. Impossible to reproduce, since he never remembered how many strokes, in what directions, or what order ...

... and yet, there it was: there. And there. And there again.

The lines silvered grey from black, paper dimming grey from buff, until the whole thing turned itself out, went negative and shining: hot, smoking white on absolute black, impenetrable as stone. With all the lamps guttering out and flickering to nothing in a cold wind, as he realized he *could* actually read it now, after all—whether he wanted to, or not—

> *great*
> *great is*
> *great is the*
> *great is the power*
> *great is the power of*
> *great is the power of the*
> *[A]*

***

Around one the next afternoon, Corin woke to a phone call from Ms. Le, and found out his alarm must have been screaming for at least an hour. An hour after *that,* abject but (at least) freshly showered, he hit the Academica's basement laundry room, where he fed his clothes into the machine furthest from the door and waited for the two pills he'd just chugged to take effect—head down, mouth dry, temples pounding.

Same old same old, as of barely three weeks. And getting old, at that.

A slow, gummy blink, half his usual speed, and the young man from the roof was by his side, simply standing. No apparent reason to be there, aside from the pleasure of watching Corin blush—and that spark, that *spark,* more immediate than he'd ever felt it before, so sharp he almost mistook it for more pain. Like a stomach-punch, triggering the oh-so-primitive urge to flight, fuck or—

(*fight*)

"Uh, hey. Corin."

"Leif."

Blond, yeah—Swedish stock. Like Hardrada.

"I just moved in," Corin continued, unnecessarily. "Number 15."

"Yes."

"Did you … I guess you might've known him, right? Professor Hardrada? I mean, sorry, if you did."

Leif gave him an uninterpretable glance, lens-shielded, under white-bleached brows. "He lived here a long time," he said, at last. "And yes, I knew him. Quite well."

How well? Corin wondered. Admitting, out loud: "I don't even know what he specialized in."

There was a brief hint of an accent coloring Leif's speech, far more ghostly than Janos's occasional dropped connector or weird grammatical patterns. "Oh, history mixed with anthropology, mainly—Nazi pseudo-archaeology was his area of expertise. He'd written books."

"Indiana Jones stuff, huh?"

"Slightly less intense, but … yes, somewhat."

"Maybe you could tell me more about it, sometime."

"Maybe."

They both looked straight at each other, then—eye to eye, both equally blue. And because Leif smiled first, Corin didn't have to.

***

Great is the power of the [Anasazi]! Praised be the power of our caustic blood, our legacy from those who cast us down from purest Darkness into impure flesh: the Old Silent Ones Who Went Before, our long-fled makers and betrayers, who we will pursue to the very rim of Being.

Praised be the power of that poisoned inheritance, which inscribes signs of our coming glory upon our bodies with the caustic brush of divinity! In each new incarnation, we bear with pride the pain that is our lot and exaltation—proof of killing fire caged by skin and turned back on itself, searing us from the inside out, just us as our own presence sears the universe around us.

Bow down, or flee, or stand and struggle: it matters little. Though, all

things considered, we much prefer to be fought.
     And to fight.

***

In 1935, the *Ahnenerbe* Organization—commonly known as *Deutsches Ahnenerbe – Studiengesellschaft für Geistesurgeschichte* (German Ancestry – Research Society for Ancient Intellectual History)—became attached to Hitler's Reichsführer-SS, under the administrative command of Heinrich Himmler, who had no official training in archaeology but was well-known for his interest in mysticism. He charged the *Ahnenerbe* with putting together a vision of prehistory that would demonstrate the pre-eminent position occupied by the Germans and their Germanic predecessors since the beginning of civilization. "A nation lives happily in the present and the future so long as it is aware of its past and the greatness of its ancestors," he claimed, and it was the *Ahnenerbe*'s stated goal to study the ideas and achievements of the "Indo-Germanic" people, bring those research findings to life, and present them to the German people, with an eye towards encouraging every German to get involved in the organization.

By 1937, the *Ahnenerbe* had grown from a vaguely occult-minded boys' club composed of amateur enthusiasts into the primary instrument of Nazi archaeological propaganda, subsuming smaller organizations and filling its ranks with "investigators" whose ranks included people like Herman Weirt, who spent the core years of his career attempting to prove that Northern Europe was the cradle of Western Civilization. Although some real archaeologists with extreme views joined up, mainly to gain high-ranking party official status, the group had consistent problems finding trained scientists willing to work on its projects, which were therefore often run mainly by scholars from various branches of the humanities—committed, but far more interested in metaphor than solid research. The group's archaeology-as-religion bent is best illustrated by such open-air displays of Germanic idolatry as its discovery of the *Sachsenhain,* a site where 4500 Saxons were allegedly executed as a punishment for Widukind's uprising against Charlemagne; instead of literally digging deeper, the *Ahnenerbe* was content to present it as an idealized shrine, a place that should be considered sacred to the Germanic people because it highlighted its genetically innate readiness for self-sacrifice.

In 1936 the *Ahnenerbe* mounted an expedition to Sweden, with the object of examining rock-art which it had already concluded was "proto-Germanic." It was there that a young history student named Hans Hardrada joined the dig, so distinguishing himself through his willingness to work hard and swallow the organization's mythology that when they left, they took him with them.

Hardrada, now a full member, went along when the *Ahnenerbe* sent an expedition to Tibet in 1938 that was meant to prove Aryan superiority by confirming the Vril theory, a Hollow Earth/lost Aryan super-race scenario derived from Edward Bulwer-Lytton's science-fantasy novel *Vril, the Power of the Coming Race*. The project's leaders correlated Bulwer-Lytton's vision of the subterranean Aryan-derived "Vril-ya," able to channel unbearable energies through their bodies, with both the Tibetan Buddhist mental obstacle-removing practice of *Dzogchen Chöd* and local legends of the Chud, a supernally powerful and peaceful tribe supposedly driven underground by their barbarian neighbours, where they were assumed to have constructed massive cities beneath the earth that might be entered only through secret passages carefully kept hidden from any outsider's eyes.

As Hardrada and his fellow-travelers retraced much the same path used by various Chinese emperors to access the Immortals of the Kun Lun Mountains, they were driven off-track by bad weather into the Shara-gol valley, where they literally stumbled upon the Rigden Jye-Po monastery. The monks, knowing no better, let them in, treated their wounds, and allowed them to stay while recuperating. And when the charmingly curious Hardrada began to ask them questions about their guiding purpose—the prayer-rolls, subconscious communication with the Immortals, that recurrent, potentially dangerous symbol—they answered willingly, innocently, with great and (in retrospect) somewhat foolish detail....

***

Twelve days, and counting

***

Leif had a wide-strewn constellation of freckles distributed all across his left side, outlining the area where saddlebags might eventually replace the firm, smooth oblique abdominals currently descending into an equally firm, smooth hip and thigh. His pubes were as white as his brows, and fair as he was, he tended far more to gooseflesh than blush, even at the moment of crisis.

They lay together in what was now Corin's bed, spooned in a loose sixty-nine, with their heads cushioned on each other's inner thighs and the best bits well within easy reach. Corin's skull swam with what would have normally been a pleasant post-orgasmic lassitude—but the *click-sssh* of tinnitus was never far away, even now, joined by a faint choir of blood-borne bells, and he didn't want to shut his eyes, for fear that the bed would begin to lurch and spin like a misaligned roundabout. So he swallowed hard instead, and made himself ask:

"So Hans Hardrada was, what—Professor Hardrada's—"

"Grandfather. He was sent to the Front near the end of the War, during the collapse, when the *Ahnenerbe* no longer had any sort of value for the Reich. Left for dead after an incursion into Allied territory, he deserted, fell back on his Swedish citizenship, eventually immigrated to Canada."

"This was after Tibet, though."

"Oh yes, long after. Though the expedition as a whole was considered a failure overall, many—like Hans Hardrada—returned with souvenirs."

"The box."

"Exactly. Finding it was what spurred Hardrada's interest in the *Ahnenerbe*—the knowledge that his family history had been touched by this thing, poisoned by it."

Corin snorted. "Sounds more like the other way 'round. I mean—the monks didn't just let him walk off with it, right?"

"No. They objected, strenuously—but it was a very remote monastery, after all, and they were pacifists. Whereas the *Ahnenerbe* were the SS in scientific drag."

One more time, Corin wondered how Leif could know all this information. Did Hardrada talk about it in class? In bed?

"You ever see this mysterious box for yourself?"

"A few times, certainly. He kept it in his office, until he was encouraged to take early retirement."

"I sort of thought most academics wouldn't want to be associated with somebody who thought *Ghosts of Mars* was a documentary."

Leif turned slightly, fixing Corin with a blankly penetrating look. "I don't know what that is," he said. Corin genuinely couldn't tell if he was joking, or whether he cared enough to find out, either way.

"Come here," he said, and Leif did.

***

They went out around nine, just in time to hit the LCBO before it closed. Leif used a bottle of Jaegermeister and a bottle of Dr. McGillicuddy's Fireball mix to make shots he called "Dead Nazis," and they knocked enough of them back that they soon ran out of clean cups and glasses. Later, with no cable and Corin's vision starting to gutter like a candle-flame, they decided to defer yet one more bout of fooling around until after they'd found this freaking box of Hardrada's.

The search started with all the normal places—drawers, kitchen cabinets, closets, under the sink—before branching wider: behind the bookcases, inside the icebox, under the bed. They went around stamping on floorboards, doing a stumbling, ass-grabby *trepak* all up and down, till Ms. Le called up to ask whether or not Corin needed help with something.

"No, sorry," he said, through the chain. "It's nothing big. Just, um ... moving furniture."

"Are you sure, Mister Vogt? I have your friend—Mister Osht?—on speed-dial."

And you think I don't? Corin wanted to snap back. But: "That won't be necessary, thanks—these pills, y'know, they just, um ... make me forget what I'm doing, sometimes. I'm really sorry," he repeated again, the taste of it mealy in his mouth, like wormy flour.

"All right. Sleep well, Mister Vogt."

"You too," he called, as she stepped away. Then turned back to where he thought he'd left Leif, only to find him—

—*not* gone, thankfully; not simply vanished outright, like some drugged-and-drunken sexual fantasy that'd managed to pilot him down to the Beer Shop and back with its thumbs dug deep in his lizard-brain, running him like a Wii. Instead, Leif was standing inside that cramped hall closet, staring up.

"Ah, yes," he said, softly, as though to himself. "I'd forgotten."

The box was smaller than Corin had pictured, and heavier. He stuck his hand up through two bulgy, porous, slightly overlapping panels in the closet's ceiling and watched them slick apart like lips over a (hopefully) toothless mouth. Halitosis-flavored dust fell, gilding them both with ruin, as Corin raised it and peered down into the slot, a single winking eye in that blank, octagonal mask-face.

"Open it," Leif suggested.

Corin pushed on all eight sides at once, four to either hand, but felt no appreciable give.

"Not happening, man. It's locked, remember?"

"Then you'd better try harder."

Right up against him now, over-close in that humid, upright space, a hastily improvised sauna. Five minutes ago, prone on the bed, Corin would have considered the same lack of distance between them not only a positive but a necessity—but that was back when they'd been horizontal enough for him to misinterpret that last half-inch of height in his own favor. Before all his various aches and pains had returned sevenfold, borne on a lapping wave of nausea, with tinnitus's bells as an accompanying chorale.

"But," he began, mouth dry, fists shaky, "they, like ... the monks ... they made it so you *couldn't*. I mean, you said—"

Leif smiled gently. "Oh, poor baby; *Hardrada* obviously got it open, and him just a weak old man. But that's right—you're wounded, aren't you? Unfixable. *Broken*."

His smile widened, solicitous to mocking to contemptuous in one-point-nothing, some unfathomable interdimensional shift. The bottom fell out of Corin's stomach; he'd have stumbled back against the wall, if sheer geometrics hadn't placed him there already.

"Who the fuck *are* you?" he asked, freezer-burnt by that suddenly alien stare.

"Apart from the man you let inside your *home,* whose last name you don't even know? Same one who's had his teeth around your cock?"

"Get out of my way, Leif."

"*Make* me."

The closet door came open with a bang, one hinge popping—they went right, the box left, hitting hard and skittering against the wall. *Now she'll call the cops for sure,* Corin thought, barely registering how the punch he'd just thrown had apparently skinned his knuckles open on Leif's surprisingly jagged grin. But then Leif was sucker-hooking him in the temple, slamming his brain against the inside of his cranium; a light went off and they plunged down into it together thrashing, boneless yet multi-limbed. Leif bit his shoulder, deep enough to bruise. Corin drove both knees into Leif's stomach and scrabbled at him, hundred-handed—if he'd been a cat, Leif's guts would be decorating the floor. Leif just grinned again, and shifted his grip: took hold of him bag-first, twisting, till Corin screamed, throwing him all the way across the room. Leif's head hit with such scalp-tearing urgency against the door-frame that blood poured down into his eyes, turning his forehead red.

Corin coughed bile on the floor, snarling. Leif wiped his brow with sticky fingers and laughed out loud. "Oh, yes," he said. "I *knew* you'd be good at this. I *knew.*"

Corin panted, hoarse. "You ... are a *fucking* freak."

Leif laughed once more, as though that was the best joke he'd heard in years—then sprang forward without any hint of warning, like an animal, hands knotted in Corin's hair before he could think to object.

"Which means we match," he said, kissing him so deep the grue from their mutual wounds smeared around both their lips like clownish lipstick, a two-person Grand Guignol carnival mask. And rolled them so he was back on top, before slamming Corin's skull down sharply enough that he blacked out.

***

Five hours on, sun woke him, rather than a knock at the door. His lower spine felt kicked, pain in his head so bright he turned on his side and vomited outright, barely bothering to cover his mouth with his hands.

Leif was gone.

He scrubbed his palms, face (far more gingerly), the floor. Leaning into the living room mirror to check his bruises and test whether a few teeth were loose in their sockets, his toe clunked against the box, so—after nearly a half-minute of contemplation—he knelt, picked it up, trying it instinctively one more time around the blurry seam of the rim, with both thumbs pressing upwards. And this time, unnaturally enough …

… it opened.

Empty.

"Guess he did, after all," he remarked, to thin air.

***

Predictably, by the time Corin finally screwed his courage up to ask her, Ms. Le turned out to have never heard of any handsome young man named Leif. So he taped his own ribs and cocooned himself deeply, ignoring the phone and Janos's messages, the clocks and their boring litany of time saved, time lost, time wasted. He embarked on a campaign of household triage, carting boxes full of crap down to the recycling room, cleaning the place till it squeaked. On Sunday night, armed with a new putty knife and roller bought at the same hardware store those tourists had redecorated with body parts, he began stripping that horrendous wallpaper like a scab, peeling and paring it back until bare plaster emerged, uniformly yellow-white but oddly ridged to the touch, as though it had been incised with reversed Braille.

He'd never know where the idea came from: the literal back of his head, that map of hair-hidden bruise-on-bruises? One of Peter's endless home renovation marathons? Or was it that first dream, the one he hadn't had since picking Leif up in the laundry room, a place he now shunned so intently that every item of clothing he owned was beginning to marinate in funk—the scratching reed, ink-dipped, soaking into an unwound prayer-roll's threads, making them rise the way a dry riverbank's mudflats fill during inundation, a fresh alphabet of water rising from the dust?

Children's water-paints from the corner store, every color mixed to form a light wash of brown, diluted like weak tea with three parts water to one part not. And when Corin ran the roller across the denuded hallway walls, what emerged was row upon row of symbols scratched into the plaster itself with God only knew what sort of implement—the same pen-nib they'd pried from his ear-drum, maybe.

So many they blurred together as Corin strained to scan each line, blending and buzzing, a relocation swarm. That one symbol, and endless variations thereof; though it wasn't as though Leif had ever shown it to him, Corin knew enough to recognize it when he saw it. What else could it be?

And yes, wait, shit: He *had* seen this before. Had written it himself, copied it endlessly, over and over and over again. "Read" it, as he did.

The same way—he *was* reading it. Right now.

Oh, his fingers, pleasantly burning. His eyes, itching as it transcribed itself beneath their lids, across their corneas. For great *great* **great** *is the power of the*

[Anasazi]

***

Civilizations piled upon civilizations, each more splendid and complex than the last, have fallen into disfavor and disrepair as our clans ascend and clash, intermarry and breed, supplant and cannibalize each other in turn—godlings all, each prepared to murder parent, sibling, child for the chance to be their generation's chosen God.

We call our empire Dri s'Abhor, the World-Tower-Tree Most High, for we have climbed a ladder of possessions to build it, touched the sky and cut at a thousand traitor suns with our jagged stone blades. We stretch it out lengthwise, sidewise, back and forth and over and under and through, threading it from hole to hole, linking every empty space we leave behind irreversibly to every other. Rendering the entire multiverse nothing but our labryrinthine burial monument.

And even now—now, when memory fails us, and no fit enemy remains but one another—throughout Dri s'Abhor, the Stacked and Windowless Tower of Worlds, true Darkness Made Flesh stands alone.

Search: Anasazi

Ancient Pueblo People or Ancestral Puebloans were an ancient Native American culture centered on the present-day Four Corners area of the United States, comprising southern Utah, northern Arizona, northwest New Mexico, and a lesser section of Colorado. As a whole, this group has often been referred to in archaeology as the Anasazi.

Historical derivation:

The term "Anasazi" was established in archaeological terminology in 1927, through the Pecos Classification system. The term was first applied by Richard Wetherill, a rancher and trader who knew and worked with Navajos and, in 1888–1889, was the first Anglo-American to explore various ruins of the Mesa Verde and other sites in that area. The name was further sanctioned after being adopted by Alfred V. Kidder, the acknowledged dean of Southwestern Archaeology, who felt that it was less cumbersome than any more technical term he might have used. Subsequently, some archaeologists have come to worry that because the Pueblos have many different words for "ancestor," using only one exclusively might be offensive to non-Navajo-speaking Puebloans.

Etymology and usage:

Says archaeologist Linda Cordell: "The name 'Anasazi' has come to mean 'ancient people,' although the Navajo word *anaasází* means 'enemy ancestors.'" However, some alternate translations of "Anasazi" suggest a meaning closer to "ancestors that are now scattered," perhaps referring to a long-distant diaspora or exodus. Although some modern descendants of this culture object to the use of the term Anasazi entirely (the modern Hopi, for example, use the word "Hisatsinom"), there is still controversy among them as to a proper native alternative.

***

Nine, seven, five days, and counting

***

Sunday night:

Corin raised his head queasily. "Well, *that* was useless," he said out loud, again to no one in particular. Unless he genuinely thought that Google might be listening, that was, which he didn't—*think*—he did.

Doing that kinda a lot, these days, man. Probably need to stop, sometime soon; like, really. Before—

—*"before"* what, *tough guy?*

Out in the hall, he almost thought he could hear the symbols whisper to one another, while cool air leaking up from Ms. Le's air-conditioned apartment below played lightly over their drowned and sunken curlicues. The echo of it got inside his wrecked ear and stayed there, a trapped insect walking his brain's grooves like a maze.

He looked down at his hands, nails grown ragged, and realized he hadn't washed them since the paper came down.

That should change, too, the same dim voice commented.

He took a shower—tepid rather than hot, to beat the humidity—and toweled his hair vigorously, to make up for having run out of shampoo. Then gathered up all the dirty clothes into two hefty garbage-bags, outfits he'd re-worn at least twice each while avoiding the laundry-room like the proverbial plague, and made himself move grimly downwards, head reeling, using his elbows to negotiate.

A floor down, he almost ran straight into Ms. Le.

"Mister Vogt," she said. "I, um—"

Voice hoarse from disuse: "Was I making too much noise?"

"No, no, you've been fine, thank you." She seemed to be having trouble looking him in the eye, or anywhere else. But with a deep-drawn breath and a shy smile, she finally managed to get there: "I simply wanted to say ... well, that there *was* someone in this building with the first name Leif, once."

"When did he—"

"Move out? No, no: you misunderstand. You *met* him, just before he—left. Though I wouldn't have called him handsome, personally. Or young."

Now it was Corin's turn to blink, which turned out to be inadvisable, especially when balanced between flights of stairs.

"What do you mean?" He asked.

"Well … the Professor, of course. *His* name was Leif … Hardrada."

***

And though it took him almost a whole shocked-numb hour to start looking for it, finding a drawer-full of Hardrada's personal photos proved far easier than finding that goddamn iron box ever had. The ones right at the top were all familiar, that same reptilian profile, neck tortoise-crepey, hair creeping steadily back as the spotted expanse of scalp crept forward. But getting further down, as color became more hectic, more yellow, faded away entirely …

There he was, finally; a candid shot, sandwiched between two similarly school-blazer-wrapped chums, lifting a stein and all but winking at the camera. Leif, thick crop of hair only a shade darker than his white brows, squinting eyes so blue they seemed blind, as though into his own future's deceptively bright light.

"I was twenty there, I think," Leif said, from Corin's deaf spot, making lust and vertigo ripple admixed through his body like a thousand gut-strung rubber bands twisting. Corin didn't turn to look for him, half-afraid of what he'd see, if anything: a smear, a stain? Trailing ectoplasm? The same so-palpable *doppelgänger* he'd gone down on his knees for, right on these uncomfortable floorboards?

"You shouldn't berate yourself," Leif told him, in that gentle, faintly accented tone Corin now realized he'd spent the last three days missing sharply, as though it was his dead mother's last touch. "They are planet-killers, Corin; it is only their nature, their function. How can we hope to stand against such creatures?"

"The 'Anasazi.'"

"Oh, it's just a stop-gap word with which to translate the untranslatable, a scab formed over a consistent lacuna—suitable, certainly, especially with its most recent connotations of cannibalism and genocide added in. Possibly, it's simply as close to the general sense or meaning of their name as we can come, without becoming them."

And now Corin risked a quick glance, only to be shocked rigid by the spectacle of Leif cutting into his own well-developed yet utterly insubstantial chest with a very real-looking bottle-opener—he could swear he knew where it *should* be, in the kitchen, but was damned if he wanted to check. The skin parted almost silently, bruises outlining a predictable shape; blood welled up, white and smoking, molten as Janos's slag.

Some people weld at home, as hobby-amusement, Corin couldn't stop himself from thinking. *Yeah, that's some definite sort of sculpture, right there. Very ... palpable.*

At that, Leif smiled. "Thank you."

"So you're ... what? One of them?"

"Call me Patient Zero. *Ground* Zero. The vector of the disease."

"How did it happen?" Corin demanded. "You owe me that much."

"Do I? Well, perhaps. I was always drawn to the box, and eventually managed to open it—or was it that it decided to open itself for me? The symbol was inside, a thousand different iterations of it. I began to trace them, to use them as meditational aids for my own pathetically limited astral explorations. And thus the eyes of the [Anasazi] fell upon me ..."

"Hearing" the word for the first time was the same as reading it—a blink, a pop, a broken blood vessel ghosting across the mind's eye like a knot in eternity's fabric. Like the thread-head that, once pulled, would unravel everything.

Corin shook his head, or started to; the lurch was a slap, a grouting scoop, crystallizing what little resolve he had left. "All those monks, though. Can't think this never happened before."

"It did, yes, many times. But the lamas were watchful, devout. Usually, things never got this far."

"Your fault, huh?"

Leif shrugged. "Call it this faithless age's fault. I worked hard for something, *anything,* which might prove to me there was something more than the immediate. Until, at last ... I got what I wanted."

"*I* didn't," Corin snapped, a snapped-trap catch wounding the inside of his throat. As though, pushed only a little harder, he might find himself crying.

But to this Leif made no reply, because—as Corin discovered, when he finally gathered enough strength to look around—

—he was gone. Again.

***

Monday crept by in a blur; languid, dread-full. Corin vaguely remembered waking, hungry, then turning over and pulling the pillows atop himself in a soft pile, digging back into his own stink like a tick.

When he opened his eyes he saw Hardrada's bare walls, his cracked ceiling and bloodstained floors, a peeling overlay ill-set above yawning void. When he closed them, it was only to "open" them once more on an endless stream of mayhem, plunging face-first down into the [Anasazi] maelstrom: a trillion invasions-by-proxy, endless combinations of combatants, all equally alien. Things like monkeys raping one another to death and eating one another's brains. Things like dinosaurs crushing their own cities flat, goring their own offspring, setting fires that consumed empires with their own biological-napalm breath. Things like slugs digesting one another alive, then melting their own stuffed guts apart with a gluey backwash of juice and spilling down into the same fissures that were tearing their own planet apart, laughing with savage delight at the *feel* of it all, the white heat, the smoking rush. The pure will to oblivion made all-too-brief flesh, before it tore itself apart on contact.

The [Anasazi], moving on, forever. Dri s'Abhor reaching up and outwards, an endless bone-rack set with the shattered skulls of worlds.

The universe is doomed, he thought. And giggled.

***

Tuesday night, Corin took himself good and truly *out,* for the first time since his "accident." Some place near the outermost edge of Ryerson Campus East, just Church Street enough to qualify for gay ghetto status. Peter had recommended it to him once, he recalled, but at the time he'd preferred access-all-areas indie/industrial dives like the Speed of Pain, so that put paid to that. And indeed, this jumped-up locker room— Hazer's?—was pretty well exactly the way he'd feared it would be back when, going on Peter's avid description. But he soon downed enough shots-and-beer combos not to care anymore, and began to appreciate his own hearing-loss at last. Beats pulsed up jaggedly through the laminate-on-concrete floor, easy enough to follow without having to get distracted by the lyrics (some chick screaming about how her pu..y wa.. on fire, *aaaah, my PUSSY is on fire!*), or lack thereof.

Heat mounted, bodies crushing in; he shucked his shirt, headed back for the bar. Almost collided headlong with someone else's gleaming chest, and got a double-load of Sex on the Beach down his own in return.

"*Sorry,* man, *shit,*" the guy repeated, dabbing ineffectively away at him with the tail-end of a paper towel roll, in the bathroom. "These, uh … oh, I'm such a fuckin' dork, 'cause … like, one of 'em was for you."

He had a nice smile, rendered slightly vampiric by an off-set right upper incisor. Tasted nice, too, even without the extra liquid incentive.

They continued to make out a while, cheered on by various passersby, till the guy suggested repairing to his place, which proved to be back towards Parliament and down. A bad area, lightly gentrified on the side-streets, but getting progressively worse as they moved between bus-stops. After three blocks, Corin's buzz had dissipated far enough that he could feel rather than hear the vague tread of pursuing feet, sensing at least two more hot(ish) young men on the outskirts of his peripheral vision. Their presence made Original Guy nervous, though not in the way Corin might have anticipated.

Ah, he thought, with a lack of surprise that baffled even him. *The Judas Goat ploy.*

Too bad, really. O.G.'d been a damn good tongue-hockey player, an MVP in the making—had even seemed into it, if the crotch of his jeans swelling hard against Corin's thigh was any indication. But bashers weren't required by law to be straight, especially when this might be less an old-school fag bait-and-switch than impending robbery with violence; as a qualification stint on methadone clinic duty at the Clarke had taught Corin, little matters like actual sexuality did tend to go out the window, when money and other addictive substances were involved.

When they turned sharply left at the north end of Armory Park, Corin could already feel his hands curling into fists. And when O.G. put a hand on his arm, maybe thinking to startle or restrain him, he turned to face their followers with a smile stretched just wide enough to disturb—neither grin nor rictus nor snarl, but something in between all three, showing almost every tooth he had. He felt his gums itch sharply, as though his own incisors longed to pull themselves both out of place and spike forward like a gorilla's.

Tongue lolling out, panting slightly, saliva gathering hot in the floor of his mouth. Almost glad he couldn't see his own eyes, as he asked:

"Can I help you with anything ... ladies?"

The initial punch came in sharp, firecracker-potent, synaesthesically reeking of sulphur or cordite—it rocked him back, vertigo head-rush like a secondary contact high, made him giggle at the taste of his own blood. He caught the next one without thinking, and drove his knee up high into the nuts of the dude who'd thrown it, twisting till he heard something strain in his own wrist, but crack in his opponent's—probably the joint between wrist and thumb, a classic Bennett's fracture. *Full cast, three to six months of rehab and physio, right there,* his professional brain assessed coldly. The human body, such a deceptively delicate thing! Not like—

(*what, not like* **what**? *Oh shit, oh shit*)

(*not like us in our first forms, of course—so long ago, impossibly distant, knotted together in the acid-blood morass of the birthing pits, coiled and thrashing till at last we ate our way free*)

Back in the now, meanwhile, O.G. just stood there with his jaw a-flap, as Corin continued to grind bone-fragments together in what was left of young Mister Broke-thumb Mountain 2010's grip; the partner jack-hammered at his ribs, yelling insults, cracking at least two but getting no visible response till he switched to a modified Muay Thai stance and elbowed Corin right across the temple, bruising the orbit of his left eye so badly it began to swell almost on contact. When Corin finally let go, he roundhoused him from the same direction, spinning him like a top, but Corin didn't fall. Instead, he stood there with all ten fingers hooked as if he'd just grown invisible claws, and grinned all the harder.

"Oh *baby*," he told him, appreciatively. "That was some serious kind of fun. Care to elaborate?"

"You're a fuckin' lunatic, dude!"

"Preaching to the choir, sweetie." Momentarily blind, Corin scrubbed blood from a minor scalp-rip out of his lashes, then flicked the result at his new opponent, who jumped back as if he thought it was either Alien-drone acid, AIDS-full with an Ebola stinger, or just jam-packed with a Grade A brand of crazy that was almost certainly catching. To O.G.: "Anyhoo—you want in on this, or what? 'Cause I'm always open to threesomes."

That something rough he felt at the back of his throat, punctuating the end of the question, turned out to be half a molar—and when he coughed it up and held it to the light, turning it admiringly (enamel and composite resin, one part hard to two parts flaky), O.G. cut and run. "Yeah, keep goin', you goddamn pussy!" his still-upright friend hollered after him as he took to his LED-blinking heels, while the other one moaned at their feet. In the meantime, Corin took the opportunity to run his tongue over the exposed nerve-pulp mass his cracked tooth had just uncovered, which immediately delivered a zap that felt like biting into a live power-cord: *Wow, whoa!* And yet: *Seems like I should probably be feeling that **more**, somehow ...*

He drooled pink, smile stretching furtherfurther*further*, till it felt as if his cheeks might crack open. And asked the remaining viable combatant, with a sort of rising petulance: "Hey! So you must train, huh? Know any Ultimate Fighter tricks?" No reply. "I'm *talking* to you here, asshole."

The guy pulled at Fracture-Boy's intact forearm with both hands, hauling his dead-weight up as though he was trying his level best to de-socket the whole shoulder. "Man, shut the fuck up! This is all your fault, you get that, right?"

"*Is* it?" Corin snapped his fingers, back teeth clicking together automatically, and cawed out loud at the resultant jolt. "Well, shit-fire! I knew I was doing *something* wrong." With a wink: "Sure you wouldn't care to go one more round?"

"What the hell do you even *want*, you crazy son-of-a-bitch?"

The only possible reply fell onto his tongue like a demonic gum-ball, smoking, as though it had been cast white-hot from a molten pot of Leif's—Hardrada's—alien-tainted blood: *To damn well fight, of course, you too-human motherfucker ...*

Before he could voice it, however, Corin was already alone again (naturally), with only the blood on the pavement left to mark where he'd once had company worth entertaining. So he blundered homewards instead, disappointed by the night's meager pickings: bruised and dripping, skull stuffed with trashy Acid House samples and two points down on the hangover scale, with nothing else whatsoever to show for his overall investment—no death, not even a little one. The split tooth's howl stayed undimmed over thirty-odd blocks; his torn knuckles hummed venomously, like a double fistful of bees.

In an all-night Coffee Time, Corin picked through leftover papers, finding each subsequent Metro section stuffed with still more tales of unusual mayhem. In the business district, for example—down on condo row—a woman who owned a small maternity-ware fashion boutique had admitted to killing three different men by putting the same 12-gauge knitting needle through their necks, ostensibly for queueing up more closely behind her than she considered wise while she was making end-of-the-night deposits at three separate indoor Toronto Dominion bank ATMs: One's fatal mistake had been looking too hard at her PIN number, while another she thought was "breathing" on her, and the last had gone down because she claimed she could "hear his organs moving around" while he infringed on her personal space. *"They sounded wet," Ms. Labayalla told arresting officers, during her sworn statement. "Wetter than normal. Like he was diseased, or something. I was in fear for my life."*

Gradually, the skin-pop charge of mugging interruptus was draining away, leaving him lip-numb and increasingly desolate in its wake, sweat-wet hair slicked fast to the nape of his neck. To distract himself, he fastened on the conversation between two adjacent hookers—one trans and black, one not and not—who were sharing a single sticky caramel-cheese Danish.

"… you know, like that girl they found under the overpass. That Rita girl?" The trannie nodded. "Makes you want to work out of home, if you could get it set up."

"Meetlist isn't bad. Or LavaLife, if you can cut through the no-really, I-like-you-for-your-personality B.S."

"Yeah. But then you're alone with them, right? Wondering how you can make 'em leave, after—or even pay. I mean, it's not like you can call four-oh, if shit goes sour …"

"Tag-team. I'd go in with you on a room, someplace neutral."

The real girl snarfed the last piece, made a dismissive hand-gesture. "Yeah, right. You and whose bank-book."

"Well …" The trannie looked down at her own hands, twice her friend's size but beautifully kept, as though she'd never before considered how big they actually were. *Could fit 'round my neck with room to spare,* Corin thought, and went embarrassingly warm in the pit of his stomach, musing on just how hard she might be able to hit, given the opportunity. How well she might be able to handle a blade.

"Occurs to me," she said, slowly, "how it's not so much us being alone with them … as *them* being alone with *us.*"

Then looked at her friend, whose plucked-nude brows climbed almost to her wig-line in response—before blinking, and smiling back.

Corin closed his own eyes, breathing settling into a harsh but steady rhythm, heartbeat accelerating. His consciousness opening Venus Flytrap-wide, spreading outwards and seeping molecule-deep, like radiation—letting the sludgy worst of the world around him pour in, like puke through a trash-clogged gutter, to fill his mind to the brim with other people's psychic garbage.

Behind the counter, the last remaining clerk was studying the small of Real Girl's back, trying to trace where her tramp-stamp lurked, and dreaming Travis Bickle dreams about the sawed-off his boss thought he didn't know was hidden behind the second refrigerator. Inside the walls, roaches and rats committed casual incest, while in the cut-rate apartments up above, at least two human males did the same. There was an enthusiastic tryst going on in the kitchen of the Thai restaurant next door, endangering their Health Code rating; both participants were thinking about how easy it would be to murder the other, then cover up the crime by slipping an extra serving of filleted corpse into every meal for the next few weeks. Beside them, a mid-sized industrial-strength meat-grinder rumbled on, making filling for tomorrow's dumplings.

Was *this* what had happened to Leif, among other things, to make him the way he was by the time Corin and Janos had found him? Or was this something special whipped up for Corin alone, special delivery, straight from whatever hell-hole the [Anasazi] had once called their home planet?

In Honest Ed's discount department store, illegal immigrants were hard at work marking down damaged goods. Though told not to, one of them had brought along her baby, sedated into silence with a fatal dose of adult anti-depressants; it lay right now in one of the remnant drawers of the fabrics section, slowly suffocating. Corin wondered just how long the body would stay in there, undiscovered, after its mother realized exactly what she'd done, shut the drawer again quietly and walked away. Or how long it would take her to swallow the rest of those pills, once she got back home ...

(*I don't want to see this, oh God, any of it*)

(*don't want to* **know**)

And yet. And yet. And yet.

At the other table, the hookers had all but decided on blunt-force trauma as their weapon of choice, once they began preying on predators for real. On Gerrard Street, meanwhile, a drunken lawyer's hit-and-run had left a man with one shoulder-blade detached like a skeleton wing, the opposite leg compound-fractured in five places, broken badly enough they'd have to pin him back together and leave screws poking out from the marrow. On Palmerston Crescent, an old woman lay in her own watery shit while infected bedsores bloomed like raw-meat roses all over her back and buttocks, sticking her thighs so tightly to the foul bedsheets beneath that they'd need to be soaked apart before she could be buried; downstairs, her children and grandchildren squatted on filthy antique furniture, smoking crystal meth and laughing at *Futurama* re-runs.

The neighbourhood, spreading its wings like a bat, every vein and membrane a fresh agony, a worse crime, a hole in the world's hide. Someone breaking someone's heart. Someone taking someone's money. Someone fucking somebody over, fucking somebody up. Someone fucking somebody while simultaneously fucking themselves, ratcheting in and out of their body over and over and over again, the same way a weapon reams a wound.

He sat there till sun-up, hoping this horrible newfound level of insight would go away, but it never really did. Eventually, utterly exhausted, he simply made the trek back to Academica House and fell forward, face-down, into a well of absolute darkness.

***

The rest of Wednesday Corin didn't remember, even tangentially. But on Thursday night he answered the hammering at his door to find Janos looming on the threshold, out of breath and lightly rain-wet.

"Why you never answer your phone?" he demanded.

Mildly puzzled, Corin glanced over to where the item in question usually rested in its recharger, and saw that someone seemed to have taken it very painstakingly and effectively apart.

"Well, there you go," he said. "That'd be the problem, right there."

"You look like bags of shit."

"How many?" As Janos blinked: "Ms. Le call you? I think she thinks I'm fucking elephants up here sometimes, but, y'know. Whatever."

Janos's eyes had begun to widen steadily during the last few sentences, continuing until they hit their current point, at which a thin rim of white outlined every part of his irises' orbits. He took a careful step inside, trying visibly not to crowd Corin, even when Corin didn't step back; the door closed behind him, softly hung ajar.

Hinges again, probably. Man, he just couldn't catch a break on these damn home repairs.

"I said, you look ... too thin, like homeless. Dirty. You don't eat? Who beat you up? Why you—do that, to the phone?"

So many question, and sooo very few answers.

Corin shrugged, doing his level-best Leif-hallucination impression. "Why would I 'do' anything, really? I mean ..." And this must be a truly awful smile he was giving, from Janos's reaction, just as much as the way it felt: "... why would *anybody*?"

Taking yet one more half-step forward, so close he could smell Janos again, like that one night on the couch—and no, it hadn't gotten any less enticing. Especially so when he saw how discomfited his nearness was making the man.

Better get some real-person action while I still can, he thought.

But was it sex he actually meant, now he considered it further? Was *that* the hunger which made his mouth-muscles flex, his lips draw slightly back over teeth that seemed to have lengthened yet more pronouncedly in his sleep, pressing themselves outwards the way a wolf's fangs bulge from his jawline? Unsheathing just enough ache-ridden root from their nerve-beds to render them permanently sore?

Janos made a dry little gulp, as if he were swallowing sand. Then collected himself far enough to try again, manfully—

"You need to come with me, right the freak now. To the hospital. You need … help."

"Is that it?" Corin sniffed the air, before concluding: "No, not so much. I think not, thanks anyway."

"Corin, freaking fuck's sake—look at your damn self! You need—"

"'Help,' yeah, I *heard* you: I'm *crazy*, Janos, not fucking deaf. So go on and *help* me, why don't you. C'mon. Go on and … help yourself."

Corin's hands drifted down, almost dream-slow, to hover vaguely 'round his fly, uncertain himself whether they ached to form fists, claws, or just pop, pull, and drop. When Janos finally got the direction Corin was going in, metaphorically, he backed away at barely sub-light-speed, so fast the door really did hit his ass on the way out.

Corin grinned all the harder to see it.

"I don't—" Janos started. Took another gulp, so dry it popped. "*Look*—you know I don't think like that, not with you. You're … like my own damn brother, man. Friend, only."

"But that's just exactly what I was trying to *do*, Janos. Be *friendly*."

All right up in his starting-to-sweat face, power-shift between them almost comedically disproportionate—a mongoose talking smack to a bull, while the bull blushed and stammered. And suddenly, Corin knew what this odd feeling *was*, so long-lost as to seem inappropriate: A basic total *lack* of sickness, nausea, vertigo tinging every glance with incipient bruising. No ghost-bells ringing, no swarm of phantom bees. No tinnitus *click-sssh* to yell over, roaring like blood in someone else's nib-cored inner ear.

"But you don't want that," Corin said, of the offered—whatever. Thus sparking Janos's own quick head-shake, his only slightly masked full-body retch.

"No, not that. Not at all that, no."

"Mmm. So, then … maybe … you want to *fight* instead."

Janos stared.

"What?" he managed finally. To which Corin heard himself reply, voice low enough he almost didn't recognize it himself—low, and slow, and *grinding* somehow, too, as if he'd been chewing on glass made from crematorium ash. As if he'd been gargling the burnt-clear detritus of dead men's teeth and fingernails:

"*You—heard*—me."

Janos was bigger, Corin sick and hungry; both were unarmed, for what that was worth. Yet even so, Corin saw in Janos's too-wide eyes that he knew how fast and high Corin might jump, if he thought he had to. How easily Corin's too-long teeth might meet in the crook of his shoulder, his cheek, his throat.

Slowly then, and calmly, his eyes kept on Corin's the whole time, as though breaking gaze would trip some sort of wire. And with his one hand moving steadily back doorknob-wards all the while, poised to grab, to twist—

"*You* were the one took that freaking call, Corin," Janos said, voice burnished deep with regret. "Not me. I tried … tried. Tried, to …"

He'd reached the extent of his language, English or what-have-you, and Corin could tell it hurt. Part of him wanted to apologize, while another part—maybe of him, but probably not—wanted nothing more than for it to hurt far worse, far more deeply. To form a wound that kept on giving.

"You did," he agreed. "Thank you."

In response, an utterly unquantifiable range of expressions flitted past all snarled together, twisting Janos's features like pre-stroke palsy—so sad and *so* damned angry, at Corin, at himself, at God Almighty. As though, instead of simply acknowledging the sad truth of the matter, Corin had spit right in Janos's face.

Might as well, Corin thought, *all things being equal.* And did.

Janos leapt back as if it were acid, slamming the door behind him; his boots took the stairs hard, a clatter of steel toes and industrial-level soles, with a huffing clamor of effort so abrupt it rang out like the fight he'd fled to avoid. And yet again Corin found himself left behind, left—

—well, not *alone*, as such.

***

Thursday ticked over into Friday, with no visible change. Corin sat on the floor, legs crossed and numb, ass aching—brain dull, nerves febrile, hollow head crammed tight with someone else's desires, a raging lava-flow of indiscriminate nihilism. Thinking:

This is why I can't have nice things—because of the ghost in the corner. Because alien ghosts from beyond the agreed-upon space-time continuum won't let me.

And: "I *knew* you'd be good at this," Leif said, happily, from Corin's deaf spot—but he could *hear* him now, oh yes, bell-clear, bone-stripped. Without even the barest possibility of misunderstanding. "So good! I was right to choose you, after all."

"Why me? Why not you?"

"It took too long. I was too old, by the time I finally did it—I couldn't serve them the way I wanted to. The way they wanted me to."

"No, but—*why* me, you crazy old bastard son-of-a-bitch? *I* didn't look in your damn box."

"No. But you didn't have to, either; it's gone far too far already, for that to be necessary. I died touching you, Corin—that was all that was required." Offering, as if it were a meaty-delicious dog-treat: "Just imagine who *you* might die touching, if you only try your hardest."

Janos, maybe—but no, thank Christ; he'd seen to that, without even knowing what he was doing. Thank good zombie Jesus, Janos was safe, at least …

(from Corin, anyway)

Tears welled up, dripped to his chin—tears, snot, a whole shining salt mess. Leif's ghost took his arm, gently, fingers flexed soothing over both bicep muscles, kneading him like bread, like a spooked cat. He could almost *smell* him, stronger even than Janos, and far more intoxicating.

Crooning:

"I know, I know … they ask so much, and promise so very little. But you're strong, Corin, *so* strong. You're everything they need you to be, better by far for their purposes than I ever could be. You're *perfect*."

Patient Zero, the dull little voice in his head reminded him—a voice he now suspected was his own soul's last flicker, caught on the very edge of going out. **Ground** *Zero. Corin Vogt, [Anasazi]-Harbinger. Paramedic First Class.*

Destroyer of Worlds all unknowing, his own in particular.

When this last purging spasm of sorrow had finally passed, he washed his face clean and went back to bed with his lack of new thoughts, watching the old ones fade, while Leif's ghost held him in a cold embrace, in the ever-stretching dark. Just lay there and waited, with a beating heart.

***

Very early indeed Friday morning, he found himself standing in front of the bathroom mirror one more time, using Peter's old letter-opener to cut the name of his new tribe in his own chest, kitty-corner to where Leif had incised his. The blood came up like silver nitrate lava.

Leif, leaning over his shoulder and beaming, his Hitler Youth grin toothpaste-commercial-flawless: "Oh Corin, I'm so proud. I'm so proud of you. The first, of many."

"Everybody's gonna know my name, huh?"

"I doubt it; a few, perhaps, but not for long. No one will, eventually. Because in surprisingly little time, everyone left alive on Earth will already *be* you."

Which would have been a comforting thought, he supposed, if he'd been able to form it.

"Can you see them now? You can, can't you?"

Yes. They stood watching, taller than trees, giving off a sick light that illuminated nothing, only shadows behind shadows behind shadows. Like sores already rotted eternity-deep, burnt straight through the universe's hide.

"They're *everywhere*," he said, amazed.

"Everywhere at once, yes. Yes! As they always have been."

When the opener slipped, spearing his nipple in half the way a snake's tongue forks, he didn't even feel it happen.

That done, re-named at last, Corin slept right through until Saturday and woke deliriously happy, knowing it was all over.

***

So: *Enemy ancestors, you many call us; strangers. Those Who Come After Those Who Came First.*

We are all of this, and more. All, and nothing.

We are the coming wave, the wind of dust, the End of All Things. We are the Unspoken Word, the name whose sound heralds plague without cure. Not the first, we still will be last, or know the reason why.

And only this shall we promise you, cattle—more, at least, than our Makers and Discarders ever promised us—

—once we have passed by, at least, there will be none left behind to follow after.

***

Zero days, and counting

At the hardware store he went up and down each row twice, humming happily, filling his cart with any and every tool he could possibly make into a weapon. Up at the counter, with karmic justice, Peter stood waiting—getting some keys cut for a new boyfriend, probably. When he saw him, he did a double-take so classic it really should have come with a laugh-track already attached.

"Corrie?"

"Pete."

Corin smiled, or thought he did. He was beginning to have trouble remembering what all the various components of his face were meant for.

"Man, are you okay?" Peter asked, oblivious—and amusingly close to parroting Janos, not that he'd know *that*, either. "You look—I don't even. Like, uh ..."

Hell, perhaps? The end of the world?

Though it wasn't a strong enough feeling to count as hope, really, some part of him that had most recently been Corin Harper Vogt believed that Leif—Professor Hardrada—was probably wrong in his assessment: The [Anasazi] hadn't won entirely, not yet. Someone *might* still stop this, even now. Somehow. Just ...

… not him.

And he was okay with that, mostly. Especially so right at this moment, staring full-on into Peter's stupidly handsome face, as his hand sought joyously for the handle of his shiny new screwdriver.

"Oh, me?" Corin said. "I feel good. I feel great. Like I want to *fight*."

Peter frowned. "What?"

"I said, *fight. Fight ME!*"

One hard punch to the jugular, a warm spray full in the face, delightful on the palate … and it was already over; too bad. But Corin saw the clerk backing for the door, indicating he'd tripped the silent alarm.

He grinned, licking his fingers, and settled back to wait.

***

Thus and so, our creed: Thus, and so. Forever.

> *We swear to come, when called; inevitably, we are called, and we do come.*

> *We take, making those who already occupy each word over until they are only us, and grateful to be so.*

> *We fight one another until there is nothing left, not even ourselves.*

> *And then, once that is done—*

> *—we move on.*

> *So shall the [Anasazi] endure until the end of time itself.*

A hole in the world, a piece of darkness. The clot, forming. Bursting.

No days left

THE WRECK OF THE *AURORA*

Patrick McGrath

It is no place for a woman, the Barbary Rock. It is a barren hunk of basalt situated in the Pacific Ocean eleven miles southwest of the mouth of the Columbia River, and it gives its name to a scattered reef over which at low tide the ocean seethes like a thousand restless snakes; the rock rises up from among them like a fist. When the wind freshens the reef turns into a mess of eddies, riptides and breakwaters, and any vessel coming near finds itself pitched upward in ten-foot swells, then dropped as swiftly as the waves surge by. The weather can turn foul with no warning other than a sudden ominous lull, followed by a spatter of rain, then a wind that can lift you from the rock in a second and hurl you bodily into those bucking seas, where you're lost at once and forever. All this I knew, but I was not deterred. They said I was mad. No, not me; but Doc Roscoe, certainly he was mad; but I said nothing about him then.

During the great southwesterly gales of winter the seas become truly mountainous, lashing the reef with tremendous force for weeks at a time, the wind howling throughout as the rain thrashes down. Then the ocean smokes like a slaughterhouse, and in the old days ships routinely beat themselves to death on the reef, with nobody to hear the cries of the dying. Sailors for centuries thought it a malignant place. They saw the Barbary Rock as an accursed thing, and a sworn enemy of humanity, although some men——Doc Roscoe was one——were as much awed, fascinated——exhilarated—as terrified by the immensity of the forces unleashed out there. In isolation on that rock through the winter months, Doc wrote in a letter to my mother that his "dependence on the Almighty grows every day stronger."

This much I knew about the place, that in 1883 Congress appropriated $50,000 for the construction of a first-order lighthouse on the Barbary Rock. Mariners navigated by coasting then and depended for their fixes on prominent landmarks; but when the wind or the current shifted, and ships were driven toward reefs of whose existence they were uncertain, those reefs being still unmarked on their charts, then disaster occurred and nowhere more destructively than on the Barbary Rock. It was decided that a lighthouse would be built there; a lonely tower in a lonely sea. It was long overdue. The Columbia River was vital to the maritime commerce of the day.

It was to be constructed of compacted basalt quarried on the mainland and shaped into dovetailed stones, each one weighing a ton or more. The engineer selected for this task was Andrew Jackson McNeill. Who was he? A man of character and fierce purpose, I discovered. I've visited the Barbary light, yes, and it's a ruin now, but still magnificent, more so in its dereliction in that the imagination must restore it, allow the mind's eye to glimpse it as it once was. It required an engineer ready and eager to commit himself body and soul to what many considered an impossible task.

McNeill was a giant. He stood six and a half feet tall. He was the eldest of the third generation of a San Francisco family of builders and engineers, an unmarried man wedded to his work and as robust in body as he was in mind. His father was responsible for numerous harbors and bridges in the Bay Area and along the coast of northern California. One of his brothers worked with the Roeblings on the Brooklyn Bridge. The firm had some experience in the building of lighthouses, but it was Jackson McNeill who for reasons unknown became exclusively committed to their construction. As a young man he'd traveled in Europe and looked at the great British lights, Skerryvore, the Bell Rock—Eddystone!—and the rest, and it was from Skerryvore that he drew inspiration for the Barbary Rock. The forces to which the light would be subjected required that he imitate the oak-tree design of the Scottish tower: so thick and dense as to be immovable at its base, then tapering upward to a slender waist; and straight on up to the lantern. It took him seven years to build it. The perseverance required for the task was immense. It exhausted him, and he never built anything so ambitious again. It stands even now as his masterwork.

He was fortunate to have retained the loyalty of his best masons, for he was, at times, they said, an inch or less from madness himself.

This, then, was the man who oversaw the blasting of the pit in which the first course of stones was laid. A derrick was erected and each of the stones, a ton in weight, quarried and dressed on the mainland under McNeill's exacting supervision, was hoisted by block and tackle, and swung over to be set down in its ordained place. On a bad day he might accomplish nothing; there were many bad days. Then McNeill sat in his tiny chamber in the barracks he'd built on the rock for his masons, and smoked cigars as by the light of a flickering oil lamp he pored over his plans and his schedule and his calendar, gnashing his teeth in frustration as the wind howled outside and the sea crashed and seethed, hissing, about the reef.

The work was arduous in the extreme. So hard was the rock that a pickax might buckle after three swings. The margin of error permitted by McNeill was an eighth of an inch. The stones were carved to fit in the pit so snug there wasn't space for even a drop of water to get through: the ocean would get no purchase here!

Later it would prove hard to distinguish where at its base the rock ended and the tower began: this I have seen for myself.

The second, inner course of stones was fitted within the circle of the first, and so on to a thickness of ten feet. That was the base of the tower, its foundation: a circular wall ten feet thick. It took twenty-three men four months to land, shift, and fit those stones. The conditions in which they worked were beyond grim even at the height of summer. Their first barracks was a canvas structure moored to iron ring bolts driven into the rock. It was torn away within a week of its construction, a year's work lost in one day's gale. The men were with difficulty taken off the rock with the loss of all their tools. They waited on the mainland while McNeill designed a stronger structure in which he could house them for the duration of the work.

In my imagination I see the reef as it must once have been, the forges flaming in the spray, smoke rising, men digging, hammering, driving in the ring bolts, and the giant McNeill striding over the rocks, shouting into the wind, his eye on both the work going forward and on the sky, the clouds, the state of the weather, counting and hoarding the hours of daylight and calm that belonged to him and not the ocean. He wanted twenty-five courses of stone rising from the bedrock, so he had a solid stub of a structure before the weather closed in and he abandoned the reef for the winter.

He suffered reversals. In the third summer a fierce southwesterly gale tore stones loose from the half-completed tower and hurled them down to the reef below. Nobody was injured. A great sudden storm, fiercer still, in the early fall of 1889 sent waves crashing over the lantern, just installed, and destroyed thirteen panes of glass. The lantern room filled with seawater, which cascaded down through the tower and poured the contents of the lighthouse in a torrent through the sea door thirty feet above the base as meanwhile the wind lashed the rock with rain. McNeill lost two of his masons that day, swept away in a second and never seen again.

After that the lantern was sheathed in an iron mesh of laced cable to deflect flying boulders. The tower shook during that great storm but it didn't fall.

In the storms and fogs of winter McNeill was quartered on the mainland. He walked the beaches and gazed out toward his unfinished tower, and came upon the detritus of wrecks, planking, cargo, splintered masts, and ironwork, and more than once the bruised, torn corpses of the recently drowned, lying pale and twisted where they'd washed up on the cold sand. His resolve was surely stiffened on seeing these bodies in the chill calm of a winter dawn. But he wasn't indifferent to what he called "the stark beauty of the sea," and remarked on its apparent quiescence, its pacific character, after its depredations: "exhausted by dissipation," he wrote in his journal. Some few summers previously he'd landed eight hundred tons of stone on the Barbary reef so as to end the carnage of these maritime orgies. In the end the tower went up with spectacular rapidity. When it was finished, leaks were discovered in only two joints.

I have visited that desolate, brawling, brutish hunk of basalt. I managed to talk my way aboard a Coast Guard vessel that went out to the rock every two months. Never have I had to fight so hard for a thing. Take me out to the rock? Impossible! They laughed at me. I told them I'd grown up on a lighthouse, I was the child of a lighthouse man. They scoffed at me. I told them I'd worked my father's lighthouse inside and out, and as hard as any second keeper, and could handle myself in any kind of weather—and they sneered. I was growing angry, and they were amused.

—Do you know who I am, I cried, do know who my father is?

They did not, so I told them. Then they took me seriously.

The day was calm, comparatively, but the old boat shuddered as we plowed through the swells; for some time we'd been taking it green over the bow, and I had to grip hard to a stanchion to keep my breakfast where it belonged. Six inches of water sloshed around the deck, the wind was freezing, and my sou'wester was matted with salt. That's when the laughing helmsman told me there was worse to come.

After three hours at sea I glimpsed it in the distance, like an ancient castle rising from the mist. Savage breakers lashed its base, the seas driving in, exploding, shooting water skywards in great foaming geysers. As we drew closer the contours of the reef became clearer, and it was like the spine of an ancient beast, half submerged, all ridges and crevices, scarred and scoured over millions of years; and running through the rock itself, on a rough north-south axis, a deep narrow fissure where the surf was churned to a seething mess of yeasty foam.

As we approached the reef the dank stench of seaweed and birdshit filled my nostrils, then the sea lifted us high for a moment, and I saw clearly the great tower rising, *rearing*, from the rock in front of me, before we again dropped down into the trough and it was lost to sight. On the exposed rock, as the sea then receded, huge boulders were exposed, covered in barnacles and starfish. Half ahead! Full ahead! Full astern! We twisted and turned in the swirling waters and then I saw atop the rock two men beside a high derrick like a long-armed gibbet. Then with a ghastly grinding noise a long boom swung out to the vessel and from a rope high above us a swaying cable descended. We were wallowing in heavy seas some fifty feet from the rock.

—You first, Miss! shouted the helmsman, and handed me a lifebelt with a pair of short oilskin pants attached to it. I'd never seen such a thing before.

—Breeches buoy, he shouted. Get in it!

There followed a comic interlude in which I first had to climb into the lifebelt and get my legs in the breeches, then hook the rope attached to the buoy into the eye of the swinging cable overhead. After three tries, with much shouting from behind me, as the helmsman tried to maneuver the vessel in place, I got the hook in the eyebolt of the cable. The ropes tightened and I was bodily dragged aloft, and over the side I went. As the boat plunged I briefly floundered in icy water, then I was hoisted, or jerked, rather, high into the air, high above the churning waters and the reef, and then winched by stages to the rock. As I was lowered I saw how the eastern slope of the rock slid steeply into the sea, while the southern exposure was split open, and from the fissure the surf flung wild gouts of foamy water high in the air. Then two strong hands were reaching up to me and I was guided onto solid ground.

—Welcome to hell, lady.

Dressed in oilskins head to foot, he was a weathered, shaggy, bearded man who now told me to get topside while he saw to the sling bringing over the equipment he required. I left him to it and trudged, soaked, up the rock to the lighthouse. It occurred to me that Doc had landed on the Barbary Rock in identical fashion, in identical weather, two decades before. What had changed? Everything. The light was automated a year after the *Aurora* went down and Doc entered the correctional facility at Portland. The man in the oilskins was a Coast Guard electrician, on the rock for routine maintenance work. The tower itself had been empty for a dozen years. He told me I had an hour to look around before the boat took us off again.

I advanced with caution over treacherous uneven rocks. At times I crawled on all fours, clinging to what I could, pressing my face to the cold stones. When at last I laid my palms flat against the tower I glanced up and saw it there, soaring into the windy sky, atop the lantern a conical roof with an iron steeple and a weathervane, and I experienced an overwhelming sensation of emptiness, of *abandonment*, for oh, it was a derelict thing. Structurally the tower was intact, but the paintwork had largely peeled away and exposed the raw, salt-crusted stone beneath, while under the gallery that circled the lantern long streaks of rust discolored the stones. Unmanned, a lighthouse soon starts to show decay. There was a reek of damp, of dank seaweed and birdshit, and the dripping of gutters obstructed by dead gulls and other sea trash. Weeds had begun to take hold at the base, and everywhere I saw draped on rocks bedraggled clumps of glistening seaweed; wedged in a crag was some rusted thing that had once been part of a ship. The breeze was stiff, the air was salty and smelled of rain. To the west I saw only an immense, an infinite expanse of choppy cold green ocean, with whitecaps on the crest of the waves, and explosions of surf all across the scattered reef. The sensation was one of sheer desolation. All at once I glimpsed with great clarity of mind the radical choice that Doc had made, to come to this place.

Hand over hand I climbed the iron rungs set in the side of the tower. I emptied my mind. I didn't look down. Great sudden gusts of wind plucked and pulled at me, but I clung to the tower as though to life itself. Hand over hand, up and up I went. The weather door stood open thirty feet up that sheer wall, and at last I reached it. I hauled myself into the lighthouse and lay a few moments gasping on the stones. Then I scrambled to my feet and was at once overwhelmed by the stench of stale dank air and, too, by a kind of sudden mental shock from which I recoiled as though struck in the face by a bucket of cold water: Doc was here. My father was here. This was where he worked, where he lived. Where he went mad. But it was a sad place now, that tower, intact but derelict because uninhabited and reeking not only of old seaweed and birdshit but neglect and a kind of moral death. There was a lantern up top, operated by electrical circuitry under the control of automatic timers, but the tower was a dying body on life support with its quiet buzz, its discreet blinking lights on gunmetal boxes attached to the wall, tangled cable spilling out; it was a structure that crackled with electricity but had no life of its own. I was astonished at the thickness of the wall. It aroused an idea of the force and strength of the storms it was built to withstand.

I saw the engine room, the watch room, the store room. I saw the galley kitchen where Doc and his shipmates cooked their meals. The galley was musty now, its antique kitchen range showing rust, and the cupboard doors standing open, the shelves bare within. Adjoining the galley was the empty mess hall, which gave onto a round-walled room from which a circular iron staircase ascended to the floor above. There were three bedrooms off that room. I didn't know which was Doc's.

It hardly mattered. They were identical. I went into the room that faced west. A tightly dogged porthole was set deep in the wall. I somehow got it open and a fresh breeze blew in off the ocean and dispelled the stagnant air. I sat down on the cold stone floor. Why was I there?

I didn't know. But the shock of the *Aurora* disaster remained fresh, at least in my mind: I was sober now, and I wanted to understand what happened. I'd traveled to the West Coast to visit Doc. He wouldn't see me. He'd been transferred from the correctional facility to the state hospital for the insane soon after the disaster, and I was told that he wasn't yet ready for visitors. More than ten years had passed, and he wasn't yet ready for visitors. That's why I'd decided to get out to the Barbary Rock, whatever it took. I thought it might unlock the mystery, address the questions that after all the evidence, the expert testimony, the psychiatric evaluation, remained unanswered: what happened that night? Why did he do it? And most vital of all, *what happened to the log book?*

I climbed the metal staircase to the lantern room. There was a brass rail, but I didn't touch it. I'd learned this as a child, you touch the rail, someone has to polish it. I was breathing heavy by the time I reached the watch room. This was a small compartment immediately under the light. I took a few moments to catch my breath. Once I'd been able to dart to the top of a lighthouse in a few seconds. Not now. On up I trudged. I entered the lantern room. And there it was, the beacon, the lens, beehive-shaped, twelve feet tall, comprising hundreds of delicate glass prisms backed by mirrors spread fanlike above the lamps. I thought of the hours Doc had spent polishing lenses like this. Was it the vapor of mercury that poisoned his mind? Seventy-five thousand candlepower. Look straight into its beam and you'd be blinded. Visible for twenty miles, but not the night the *Aurora* came to grief on the Barbary Rock, that was the night Doc went down to the engine room and turned off the power. But not before locking his two companions in their rooms as they slept.

I stepped out onto the gallery. I was a hundred feet above the ocean. The wind was gusting strong out of the northwest and howling around me like ten thousand lunatics. I gripped the rail and looked down. The sea foamed and spewed across the reef, which from this height resembled a great claw of broken black rock, curving from the Barbary Rock to the south and west for what seemed miles. Directly beneath me was the fissure where the sea surged into the rock, was dashed against the rock and flung high into the air, and that was where the *Aurora* smashed herself to pieces the night Doc turned off the light.

I lifted my eyes to the horizon. I was no closer to understanding why he did it. In this wild, desolate place, where men of extraordinary courage had erected a lighthouse to guide the sailor home, for what conceivable reason would Doc have *assisted* the destructive force, and plunged the world into darkness?—what was it that overwhelmed his reason? It made no sense. It made no sense.

Later I returned to New York and told my mother that Doc wouldn't see me. I didn't mention my visit to the Barbary Rock. I was in a state of profound confusion, or no, not confusion, a kind of horror. I'd glimpsed a vacuum on the Barbary Rock, a nothingness, a kind of cosmic negation, I can't articulate it better than that. But not in the aimless, restless, relentless destructive energies of that ancient ocean, no, but in my father's soul.

Or perhaps by then they were the same.

* * *

The men on the *Aurora* didn't have a hope in hell. It went dark. It didn't falter, it didn't fade. Its signature pattern didn't change, it gave no sign that anything was amiss, nothing to alert the men in the wheelhouse with the wind and sea pushing them inshore that what was almost their last aid to navigation was about to expire. But suddenly it was dark. Suddenly there was nothing out there but the great seas and the roar of the storm, and the flicker of lightning in black clouds that seemed so low there was nothing between them and the turbulent ocean, and the men with only a compass now, and their running lights, having lost radio contact, and the Barbary light gone dark, to get them home. There would have been bewilderment, and panic, quickly suppressed, I imagine, the four men crowded into the wheelhouse asking one another what happened to the light, where'd the fucking light go?—as the *Aurora* bucked and surged, driving in toward the coast, or so they thought, but in fact running blind toward the reef.

Soon huge seas were with immense force flinging the vessel at the reef and then at the rock itself, and I don't know how it must have sounded, but Doc in the dark lantern high above the devastation would surely have heard it and in his madness rejoiced. What did he do—shout out his mad joy, dance a jig? I can only imagine the horror he created that night, for the storm didn't let up until dawn, having used the hours of darkness in the destruction of the *Aurora* and the men on it. Their bodies were broken on the reef before they'd had a chance to drown, even, and over the next days what was left of them washed onto the cold beaches below the headland and the cliffs. The *Aurora* was smashed to pieces and it too drifted ashore in fragments. But by then Doc had been taken off and brought to the correctional facility in Portland. It was clear at once that he was insane. It seems that when the storm died down he released his companions, and they'd promptly locked him in his room. They later described his mood as "elated."

I was in New York when all this happened, living like a ship in a bottle. What bottle? Any bottle that would have me. The story came to me dimly at best, and in fragments. I don't know how I reacted to the news that Doc was responsible for the deaths of four men; possibly with indifference. True, he was a man in whom the concept of duty was once of paramount importance, and until his breakdown he'd exhibited the classic traits of a good keeper. He was patient, diligent, and self-disciplined. He had a liking for small detail, also for the endless repetition of routine tasks. He liked dull days and ferocious nights. After his years in the U.S. Navy, he had a complex understanding of seas, winds, and tides. He was in the beginning a steady man of unflappable temperament, and in his relations with junior keepers he showed sound judgment. He had a naval sense of things and believed justice should be fair, stern, and swift. He applied the same rigorous criteria to his own conduct, and when he found himself wanting, prescribed severe punishment—

But it's possible that I'd descended into the sort of skid-row cynicism by the guttering light of which no act of human depravity seems surprising. I don't know. It's one of the complications of late-onset sobriety that to abandon such cynicism is vital to one's recovery, but oddly difficult to achieve. Having thought the worst of humanity it's tough to find much to admire, in this oh-so-crooked timber—

The log book was never found.

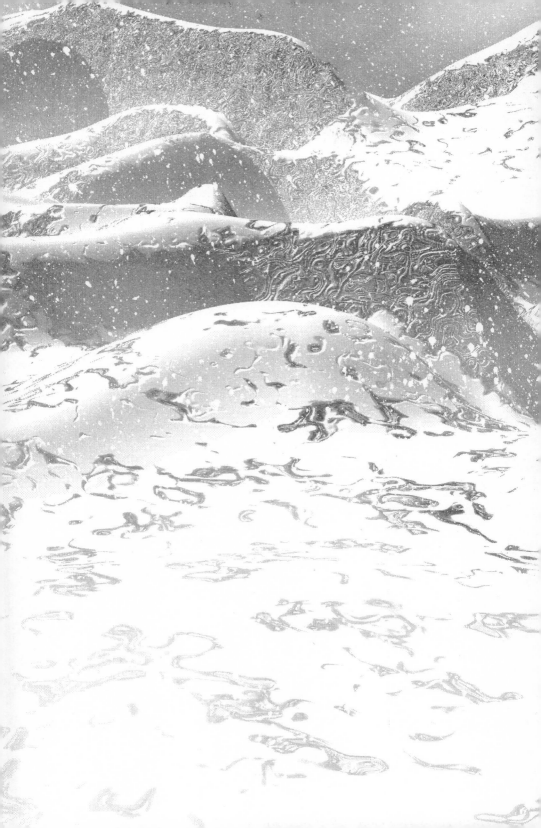

BENEATH THE BEARDMORE

MICHAEL SHEA

Three humans—however bulkily attired in subzero gear—cannot loom large upon the Beardmore. The largest valley glacier on Earth, the Beardmore arcs 125 miles across the Transantarctic Mountains, dividing the Queen Alexandria Range from the Commonwealth Range at a point some 250 miles from the South Pole.

The Beardmore is narrower and steeper where it climbs the range on its northern side, while its descent toward the Pole is grander and broader. Still, throughout its arc the glacier's width is never less than twenty miles.

This trio, loosely roped at the hip through rings in their climbing belts, were ascending the northern slope of the glacier along its western rim, with the Queen Alexandrias close on their right and the dark line of the Commonwealths seven leagues remote to their left. While they could only look minuscule on such a mass of ice, their bright orange polar jumpsuits made them at least readily discernible. In the fourth day of their ascent, they were just a few miles below the summit of the pass.

Though the ice was steep, one could climb it standing, the grade ranging from fifty to sixty degrees, with a snowy crust that aided traction. The altitude, near ten thousand feet, held the three naturally to a very deliberate pace, and the icy slope they'd already climbed—plunging near forty miles below and behind them at that same slant—kept them very careful, kept them spaced and roughly linear in their ascent. Start sliding down the Beardmore, and very soon there'd be no stopping your slide at all.

Meadow led. Her mother, Raven, followed her, and her ex-husband, Karl, climbed at anchor. All of them occasionally drove the chisel-tipped butts of their ice-axes into the crust for extra pull upwards. Meadow led because—wherever their exploit—if *she* didn't lead, her mother would seize that position.

Karl, as he climbed below the two women, smiled within his frost-caked beard—which was iced to almost twice its actual mass by the steady labor of his breathing. His ex-wife's quiet, unrelenting combat with her mother had been an important part of their long marriage, as it had continued to be a part of their almost equally long un-marriage, in which he and Meadow still lived together more often than not.

They'd willingly enough left to Raven (and her fortune) the logistics of getting *to* the glacier. She had debarked them at McMurdo Sound. From there, most recent expeditioners chose to cross the mountains immediately over the Skelton Glacier and trek along the continental shield, skirting the foothills of the range until, at the eighty-fifth parallel, they headed straight for the Pole.

But Raven had chosen the doomed Scott's somewhat shorter route of over a century ago: from McMurdo Sound Scott had beelined more than 200 miles across the Ross Ice Shelf, and crossed the mountains on the Beardmore's colossal back.

They'd reached the glacier in five days. Their little micro-cat had carried them—over good ice or hard crust—with Karl balancing on the tail-bar. The cat was now parked at its northern end, for they meant to cross the whole glacier, and cross it back, on foot.

Or rather, this was their minimum goal, for they were also agreed that when the Beardmore had been traversed from north to south, they would weigh *continuing* from there to the Pole.

Karl, from his position down at anchor, happened to catch a sharp look at his ex-wife and ex-mother-in-law in three-quarter profile against the ice-field above them: gray-eyed Meadow's broad cheekbones sunburned, her mother's sharper face black-eyed and brooding.

Over their years together Raven had swooped on them, as it were, and snatched them away to the deep Amazon, to the Alaskan mountain ranges, to the volcanoes of Iceland, to the caves of New Guinea. She used her fortune to coax and challenge them into encountering the most exotic corners of Earth's magnificence. Both Karl and Meadow had long made very satisfying careers publishing their writings of the wonders that Raven had whirled them off to.

Through those decades Karl had developed a perfectly comfortable style of verbal sparring with his mother-in-law: "Hey. Rave. You've corrupted us, but you make our lives so cinematic, so interesting, who *cares?*"

He saw Raven pause in her climb above him. She pulled down her muffler to call up at Meadow, "Hold! Hold up!" He knew this meant another photo-op, and when he saw Raven turn to face down-glacier, he too looked down behind him to escape the camera's flash. The wide bloom of its light vanished down the colossal corridor of ice that plunged beneath them. She was a good photographer and would see they got prints of all her shots, though if Karl had accidentally gotten into this one, he would be edited out. "It's the *earth* I'm recording, Karl," she'd once explained.

Fair enough, he smiled to himself. *Would* they in fact cross these mountains and then go on to the pole and back, another five hundred miles? Though all were hale and hearty, Karl and Meadow were in their late forties, and Raven her sixties.... But such was Raven's relentless soul, and the relentlessly controlling use that she made of her wealth, that she'd already had a supply-cache and a second cat airlifted to the Beardmore's southern foot, should her daughter and her ex-son-in-law "show the spine" to push their exploit onwards to the Pole.

Meadow would of course accept the challenge. And he, of course, would go along....

To say they had been climbing four days did not mean they'd seen any sunsets. The sun wouldn't do any setting for another couple of months. Its low, reddish presence lent an opulence to the stark ice and black stone of this world, but a touch of the surreal as well. This was a place where nothing lived, no native life at all. Gorgeous, this harsh grandeur.

But it was a grandeur that had the unrelenting quality of a nightmare; the low sun's fixity conveyed the oddest sense of eternity, while its reddish glare expressed ... malign intent.

He realized that Meadow stood waiting for Raven to catch up to her, and that both were beckoning him. When he'd closed the gap between them, Meadow said quietly, "Company."

Only then did Karl see it: perhaps two miles upslope of them, there was a tiny figure in yellow snowgear.

The figure seemed not to be moving. Seemed just to be standing … or kneeling? … in the snow.

They resumed climbing, closer together and a little faster.

"Sick?" Raven asked. For the more they ascended, the more it seemed the figure was doubled up over something in front of it. It radiated an intense absorption in whatever it was engaged in.

"Digging?" Meadow suggested. For now it had come to seem, as they studied it, that the stranger was at *work* on the snow that lay before it.

Karl stepped into the lead, and the women allowed it. As they neared they traded glances, quieting their movements. An unspoken consensus settled upon them: the figure's activity expressed a degree of concentration that felt sinister.

Whatever it was doing, its activity brought it to lean even closer to the snow, its business creating an aura of privacy and concentration that made the three of them increasingly uneasy.

"Should we hail him?" Meadow asked. At this point of approach the shape began to look distinctly male.

"Seems more natural to do it once we're closer," Raven said. It was not in Raven's nature to demonstrate special consideration for anyone till she had made a clear assessment of who they were and what they merited.

The yellow shape still showed no sign of noting their approach, while a low, fitful noise—cough or grunt—could be heard issuing from where his face was thrust so close to the snow. What was he *doing?* Quite definitely a man now, and a pretty big one at that.

"Ahoy there, friend!" It burst out of Karl—seemed to crack the silence like a calving glacier.

The shout jolted the stranger sharply, but not quite enough to bring his head completely around. Instead he half turned back, thrusting his face into partial profile, and Karl thought he glimpsed that the man was vomiting, or that something was coming from his mouth.

But in the next instant the man flung himself face-first into the snow and squirmed and thrashed there, creating such an epileptic frenzy amid the drift before him that the three of them froze where they stood. Karl spread his arms to fence the women behind him, hefting his ice-axe with his left hand and thinking of the .45 automatic buried too deeply in his backpack for a quick deployment.

But then the stranger, seeming suddenly purged of his seizure, flipped over and lay facing down at them, his back against the churned snow he'd heaped up behind him. His face was a wildness of black beard and brows; his eyes were little inky whirlpools of what looked like both fury and wild delight at once. His paroxysm had left him breathing heavily, and Karl, who was himself breathing hard from the climb, had the mildly hallucinatory impression that the man's entire body slightly swelled and shrank with his respiration.

"Are you ... all right? I didn't mean to startle you," Karl called.

"How could ... you ... startle me?" So odd—faintly warbling—was the stranger's voice, and so ambiguous his intonation, that Karl stood at a loss. Were the words reproachful? *How* could *you?* Derisory? *How could* you?

Suddenly Karl felt that the three of them stood in danger, or that they faced, at least, a profound strangeness. He struggled to understand his emotions: here he was, feet planted squarely on the frozen basement of the Earth, the precarious sun at hover not too far above the planet's frozen horizon..... Here on an immense glacier not 300 miles from the Pole, in the gigantic void at Earth's end, he stood!

And *here* he had stumbled on a stranger who seemed unable to believe there could be startlement at meeting unknown others near the crest of one of the most perfect desolations on the planet....

Quite vividly, it replayed in Karl's memory: the man's furious scrabbling in the snow just after he became aware of their approach. He had *buried* something. Buried whatever it was he had been so busy over when they first sighted him.

"Well, then!" Karl said heartily, feeling the utter unreality of the cliché he was voicing. "We'll just be on our way!"—thinking, as he spoke, of his out-of-reach automatic.

"Oh!" the man replied awkwardly. For a moment he seemed to be mentally rummaging for the words he wanted. "Well, then ... I'll join you!"

A long pause ensued. All four stood staring at one another. Karl cleared his throat and emended pleasantly, but with some stress and volume: "What you *mean* to say is, you'll join us if *we* don't *mind.*"

"Oh, yes! Forgive me! What I meant to say! If *you* don't mind! I find it's lonely here." Odd, his intonation. He said "It's lonely here" as if he lived continually on this spot, day in, day out—and had been lonely here for the longest time.

"Well then ... why not?" Karl answered heartily, trying to get a fix on those so-directly staring eyes. "And, since you were here first, *you* should take the lead!" There was a strangeness about the guy he just had to probe. He watched to see if the absurdity of his saying *since you were here first* registered with the man.

But the man nodded solemnly ... and led off.

As the tall stranger strode out to point position, Karl beckoned the women close. "See where he was digging? We've gotta make camp within the next mile or so, so one of you can come back here and dig it up. I intend to stay near him with the pistol from here on out. I mean ... he's not even carrying a *pack!* He's hundreds of miles in-country! How has he survived this far?

"You guys stay *between* us, till I get the piece outta my pack and into my belt. When I signal you, you slow down and let me get up behind him again."

It was not lost on any of them that the man hadn't even thought to tell them his name, or to ask theirs. He wasn't even feigning normality, and the afterthought haunted them that just perhaps the guy simply didn't know *how.*

As he trudged in the van they followed him for less than a mile, till the crest of the glacier was waveringly visible above them in the blown snow. Karl shouted after him: "We're making *our* camp here!"

Not far above them, the wind howled off the crest like a banshee and spewed down against them a gale of ice crystals. Karl and the women turned toward a spur in the rock-wall that flanked them.

The stranger wordlessly followed their lead as they gathered within its lee. Karl began to cut and stack snow-blocks to extend their shelter from the steady gale; within the hollow Meadow unlimbered the two-burner Coleman, and Raven unfolded their tent. The stranger stood awkwardly, watching them.

Karl eyed the tent regretfully: he wasn't going to spend a moment inside it—not while this man was anywhere near them. He was going to spend his night outside, where he could *watch* the man.

He walked grinning up to him and thwacked him on the shoulder more than a bit too hard, sending him into a two-step stagger to maintain his verticality. In delivering this blow, he felt a surprising solidity to the man, a remarkable *density*.

"Shall we go upslope, old bean? Scope out tomorrow's route?" Karl was testing his tolerance of interpersonal violence, and his tolerance of the ridiculous, for their way up-glacier lay plain before them.

"Splendid!" said the man, and set to trudging upslope at his side.

He mused on the stranger's robotic compliance. And still it never crossed the fellow's mind to ask his or the women's names, or say his own.... From the tail of his eye he saw Meadow darting back down-glacier, hiding her descent in the seams and crevices of the ice.

Meadow gripped the big hunting knife she always took camping, a talisman against her fear. She was going to dig up what that man had been burying, and though she thought she would need no protection against that thing itself, the knife reassured her against what might follow from uncovering it.

Here—it seemed too soon—was the spot: a lump of snow irregularly faceted with the hasty pressures of the stranger's body when he had flung himself down against it and ludicrously lain on it, as if he were just lounging there ...

She reached toward it but then recoiled, appalled at touching, even gloved, what might lie beneath it. And so began to *kick* the snow away, whittling it down with the crude axes of her boots....

And doing this, uncovered soon enough ... a boot. From which sprouted a leg sheathed in dark blue wool ...

In a frenzy of two-handed digging, she tried to outrace the terror that gripped her and threatened to freeze her up if she slowed down for even a heartbeat.

Plainly a man by his size ... yes ... thick-bodied when she got to his middle, the dark blue wool parka solidly filled with a belly that felt, through the fabric, frighteningly hard, as if, within the garment, it had already frozen clear through.

Just below the shoulders she abruptly stopped digging, because just above the shoulders the enveloping snow was stained red.

"Dear God dear God dear *God*," she moaned. "I've *got* to. I've *got* to." She couldn't.

"We've got to *know!* Right *away!* They're up there *with* him *now!*" As to a stranger Meadow hissed these remonstrations, which somehow unclenched her just enough and she *plunged,* arms windmilling, tearing the ensanguined snow in a frenzy from the corpse's neck and head, sending the spoil of her digging behind her in a crimson spray....

What this revealed was neither neck nor head, but six inches of denuded cervical spine and a naked skull: even the eyes plucked from its sockets, and every fleshy morsel of the face and throat all gnawed away, save for shreds of skin and hair which—like a hellish confetti—besprinkled its icy casket.

Meadow stood, gasping for breath as if it were her own windpipe that had been gnawed off of her spine.

She saw up on the glacier's slant three small dark shapes, like little exclamation marks printed on the ice-sheet's page. Rearmost, her mother anchoring the tent; a bit upslope, the two men, one of them her Karl, the other the stranger, the *monster.*

She must get back up to them, make Karl see he had to *kill* that stranger *at once.* And right *now* she must be quick, or the stranger might see her discovery of his bloody work. Doglike she reburied it, clawing snow backward between her legs, masking the corpse.

Gasping with her exertions, she realized the vicious cold had stunned and weakened her. Brutal, bludgeoning cold like an incessant beating the earth's atmosphere was giving you, an endless pummeling from the sky. Such a relentless enmity—such hostility from Earth and Air as one, both colossal spheres her foes, hammering her with huge icy fists.

Ah! And to make this hellish place perfect, to *complete* its monstrousness, they'd met its sole inhabitant—a smiling cannibal.

When Meadow rejoined the others they were regathered too close together—the tent was pitched and the stove lit—for her to tell Raven and Karl what she'd found. She gave them the darkest signals she could with her eyes, but in this ceaseless gale their faces were too muffled to convey much by their expressions.

Meadow pulled the muffler from her mouth and shouted—indicating the tent—"That'll only sleep three!"

"That's right!" Karl shouted to the stranger—"You make your own shelter!"

The man nodded vigorously, eyes wide, and spread his arms excitedly. "Shelter? Wait! There's shelter right up *there!*" He pointed to the crest. "Up *there* is shelter! Let us go right up!"

Up where he pointed, the wind drove down a glinting fog of ice crystals that streamed between the pylons of black stone. All three of them looked at him, grim-eyed. "To the summit—not a hundred strides!" the stranger insisted—and his voice struck a strange, flute-like note of excitement. "At the summit there's a way inside! / At the summit there's a way *down in!* / A way down into shelter from this wind!! / There's a *sea* down in there, down inside! / Where an ancient *city* doth that sea bestride!"

And then he turned, and—altitude be damned—he began to *sprint* up toward the glacier's crest, and was quickly swallowed in the blizzard that streamed down from it.

To the others, who had been toiling for days into ever-thinner air, it was more than impressive. It was uncanny, if not plain impossible. And to Meadow, it somehow made what she had to tell Karl and Raven a degree less astonishing. She reached for their shoulders and pulled them nearer. "It was a *man* he buried back down there! A corpse! He was *eating* the flesh off his face! The corpse's face and his neck are *gnawed away* down to the bone!"

Through their long, stunned silence, the wind howled over them like a Greek chorus shouting outrage and horror at the cannibal crime.

Karl said, "We can't just turn back. He's too fast and too strong. If he guesses we know what he is, he'll attack us. If we just turn back he'll follow, and then can pick us off from the rear. His story about a city means that he wants to keep us with him. Wants us to stay with him because I guess he wants to kill us all."

They looked into one another's eyes—looked away, and looked again. "I've gotta kill him while he doesn't know we *know!*"

The stranger re-emerged from the crest. Standing just below it, he waved them to follow with great sweeps of his arms.

Karl led off, and as he climbed his legs were swallowed in the rivering ice crystals, and for all the women could see of his torso, he might have been a centaur, treading on monstrous hooves or claws.

And when at length all four of them had reached the top, the ice-fog assaulted them so fiercely that despite the leveling of the grade it was a grim toil to advance.

More harrowing too, for at surges in the gale, the torrent of crystals became a flood that quite engulfed them, so it seemed they drowned in an icy fury that gnawed the small uncovered parts of their faces with freezing fangs. Even the mountain wall flanking them vanished from view.

Till the stranger, steering them through the gale, brought them back to that mountain wall, to where a crooked seam invaginated the stone.

"It's just at hand, the passage down *inside!* / There are marvels beneath this stone we stride!"

In the scant shelter of this seam, he still had to shout to be heard above the madly musical shrieking of the wind. His cries struck an even more flute-like register, a melody almost of transport or delirium, while the flourishes of his arms when he said *inside* ambiguously indicated both the peaks that flanked them and the ice they trod.

"Inside *where?*" Karl howled.

In answer, the man stamped his foot and bellowed, "Down beneath us—right beneath us sprawls / A hidden ocean in the mountain's bowels!"

Karl had just gotten the automatic into the pouch on the front of his windbreaker. His sole thought was of the pistol's management with his heavy gloves, the moment and manner of its deployment. "An *ocean?*" he echoed distractedly.

Raven thrust herself between them, thrust her face into the stranger's. "Tell us, please!" she shouted. "Tell us, while we're all listening! Tell us loudly! How do you *like* it? How do you like *the taste of human flesh?* You gnawed his face and neck off of him! You *ate his flesh!*—that dead man down the slope! You *ate* his face and his throat off the bone and then you covered his corpse in the snow!"

All three stood staring at the stranger, while he gazed back at each of them in turn most earnestly, with an indescribable wide-eyed expression that seemed both sad and compassionating.

"I did so! Yes! Devoured his throat and face! / And would have eaten more, but you arrived. / I know you view such feeding with distaste, / because of course you have quite misconceived / my nature, thinking me of humankind. / Not so! My race—far older than your own— / has long upon your lesser species dined. / This man's not I—I wear him like a gown! / Of him just skin and bone enough remain / for me to use his voice and work his frame."

The wind shrilled and moaned and flung its freight of crystals hissing against them, but somehow every one of this monster's eerily musical words reached them as clear-cut as gemstones.

Karl stood astonished. As he construed these eerie statements, he found himself actually able to *believe* them. Because as the stranger spoke them, Karl's gaze was captured by his eyes, and within those ceaselessly, subtly mutating eyes—though they had *been* a man's—there was now nothing like a man at all. Karl felt he was looking into an endless stream of different creatures' eyes....

"It grieves me to devour one of your kind," the stranger urged. "But might not one of *you,* adrift out here, / freezing, starving, wandering snow-blind, / devour some native creature to endure?"

Of the three struggling to absorb this, it was Meadow who first managed speech. "We're no more native here than you are!" she cried. "And we've killed nothing! You've killed *two* of our kind!"

"And how it grieves me! But I can't undo / the crime which even now forestalls my doom! / And still my life's not saved till I've won through / down where my deliverance lies entombed!

"Please! Let me purchase pity for my plight! / I can guide you down *where I am bound!* / It's subterrene, yet not devoid of light, / and there a Sea, and City can be found. / That place lies close to hand—not far below. / Are you not explorers? Dare you go?"

Though the howl of the wind never ceased—and was indeed a shrieking holocaust—it seemed like a silence they stood in, so distinctly they heard the stranger's eerily melodic invitation.

Raven's mouth moved twice, three times before her answer came.

"Will it be a world we can return from?"

"Yes, though that depends on what you *do*—because that sea has many *denizens*, that City throngs with monstrous *citizens*. Forgive me now, but if you wish to go, the moment is at hand—I'm bound below!"

The gully they stood in spared them just a fraction of the numbing gale that roared through the pass. Karl, Meadow, and Raven stood amazed at the uproar around them and, after a moment, even more amazed at the willingness they felt to follow him.

The stranger wheeled and led them down into a turning of the gully they stood in. The gully opened wider and twisted back into the glacier, till it became an icy tunnel.

As they followed it deeper into the ice, the twisting seam was faintly lit by the glacier's translucence. It seemed as well that a dim luminosity, a delicate, bluish nimbus surrounded their guide himself, so that he made their ice-bound journey seem submarine, as if the arching tunnel wall were a paralyzed wave.

But *was* this glacier truly static? For—out of the wind's brute howling—they found the ice had a voice, a vast, dim utterance of creaks and groans, wherein all three felt deep, unceasing menace like a muttered threat. They realized the ice—stupendously heavy—never ceased to grind inchingly *down* the mighty pass it paved. Almost … almost they felt its incremental gnawing on the mountain it mantled....

Then the stranger led them through a ragged portal, and abruptly they were out of the ice and tunneling through *stone*, and perfect dark.

Now only that dim effulgence that the stranger shed gave them any sight at all, while they, behind the little sphere of his faint glow, moved in blackness absolute and trod the stone in pure blind faith that it was there beneath their feet. Their only sense of time was the clockwork of the steps they took descending, descending through the mountain-bone …

Until they discovered that it was no longer a tunnel they trod, but more precisely a deep *channel* in the stone, while above and to the right of them a vast dim void had opened out....

Their channel deepened and steepened, and they were following it down the flank of a colossal terrain.

It was brutally cold. The air faintly stirred, as the vast openness of

the underworld they sank through grew plainer and plainer about them.
The stranger implacably marched them down and down, his feeble glow
a ghost before them as this Tartarus of gulfs and dim vaults declared its
grandeur by the loudening echoes of their bootsoles, and the expanding
loom of overarching stone. Karl struggled with a mounting disbelief
at his own compliance, a growing panic that they walked unresisting
behind a cannibal guide down into their tomb.

Now, the bluff they descended yawned majestically to the left, and
the immensity they moved in grew more visible, for it seemed suddenly
they had a "sky" of stone: colossal vaults of ragged rock, vaults that
were leagues and leagues across—all the roots and foundation-bones of
superincumbent mountain ranges towering up into the over-world.

Beneath this chasmed sky there opened out a dimpling terrain
threaded with dully phosphorescent rivers that all led down to a vast,
dark, slowly heaving sea. They rounded a last, half-concealing precipice,
and then that black ocean opened out before them its whispering,
breathing deeps unending.

Its horizon dimly underlay huge purple-black storm-clouds that
seemed foundationed on that abyss itself. Its shoreline stretched endless
to left and right, the black waves foaming, phosphorescing in. And less
than a mile down an interminable shore, there sprawled a great walled
City.

Imperial it seemed, the walls colossal—a full two furlongs high,
those parapets of titanic ashlar. These walls in turn were surmounted by
great barbicans, within whose crenelations perched gaunt arbalests and
catapults like the crooked, brutally muscled limbs of giant demons. It
was the fortress, surely, of some monstrous race, and its walls thrust out
fully two miles into the inky sea on huge piers, amid whose pilings the
dark surf ceaselessly foamed and luminesced.

Monstrous race indeed! For now, as their guide led them toward
it, the three saw that within its walls bristled towers and temples and
pyramids and palaces—a very hive of windows that overlooked the
ramparts—and saw that in all these windows inhuman faces thronged,
filling their frames with sleepless, seething, monstrous vigilance.

Meadow, Raven, Karl, emerging from the trance of their long
descent, began now to take in the features of those countless denizens,

who swarmed the parapets as well as the windowed towers and spires: multiply limbed, or winged, or grotesquely clawed were many; many were fleshed, but many more than these were furred or plumed or scaled beneath the breastplates and the casques they wore. Some stalk-eyed, others beaked, some jawed like carnivorous beetles, or fanged and supple-necked like serpents ...

Inhuman fortress, thronged with nightmares! And all these nightmares, in their seething circulation on those ramparts, maintained unblinking vigilance upon the inky sea whose breakers rolled phosphorescing in beneath their pier....

Halting them a distance from the citadel, the stranger stood gazing, as did they. He stared with dire, brooding wrath, his brow contorting like a nest of snakes. His followers stared in simple stupefaction. They had been led down to a fever-dream of the Impossible. That giant citadel, those nightmare polymorphs who peopled it—all of them twice or three times human stature...! The trio stood gasping, confronting what they felt their minds unable to contain: all those *monsters* were as real as the breath they drew, as the hammering of their horror-struck hearts.

Their guide stood silent, letting the grim citadel and those who swarmed it assault the senses of the three he'd brought here.

"Did I not tell you I would show you wonders? / My gift: the expansion of your hearts and minds. / See prostrate Greatness which base vileness plunders! / See boundless glory which foul Evil binds!

"I make you witness our despoliation, / That you might see our conquered greatness rise / to extirpate its vile infestation— / and witness our rebirth with your own eyes.

"First, then, know that *there*"—he swept his hand at the great piered metropolis, and his anguished outcry rang plangently above the surf—"stands ZANADANE! / My race's home for centuries defiled / by monstrous things whose presence still profanes / her sacred precincts with their bodies vile!

"Long did she flourish in her glory here / this primal home and nursery of our might / until nigh to her fifteen-hundreth year / when came eclipse! Eight hundred years of night!

"Behold: they still benight her, still defile / *Our* Capital, those foul

594

usurping throngs! / Eight centuries we've now endured exile / while Zanadane to *shoggothoi* belongs!"

The stranger's outcries echoed as if from the lungs of a far bigger man. Their reverberations crisscrossed the waters, and in his voice his three hearers felt an ageless outrage and an ancient longing....

"We *fashioned* them, our polymorphous slaves! / Made them to toil in the abyssal deep! / Used them for salvage, miles beneath the waves / where cargo-laden vessels sank to sleep. / For know, our days of Empire and rich trade / With cities just as grand that stud these shores / saw both great commerce and fortunes made / and saw too naval conflicts and trade wars. / Much wealth was sunk—but much might be retrieved / by mighty, mindless brutes which we conceived. / Their wholly plastic metamorphic might / could pluck whole vessels from abyssal night!

"That they should breed Intent, and conjure Guile / even as we bent them to our wish and whim! / That they should plot our downfall all the while / that we—complacent—wrought and wielded them! / Behold their mocking metamorphoses! / In endless flux from shape to shape they seethe, / ceaseless mutation of monstrosities! / To mock us is the very air they breathe!"

And indeed ... it was so. So variously monstrous as they were, each one of them, steadfastly viewed, was *itself* a fugue of forms in flux— here a fanged jaw melting to a cruel hooked beak, there a wolf's eyes multiplying to a spider's compound clusters—a restless mutation of grotesqueries ceaselessly reshaped those beings one and all.

"Treacherous slaves! To be so new to guile, / and yet so slyly did they *mask* their wiles! / For plain we see now, in our weedy deeps, / that they grew sly while our wits lay asleep, / and while they practiced cunning, kept it cloaked, / then overthrew us with one mighty stroke.

"A mile offshore the sea-floor plunges steep / nigh two leagues down to zones of benthic murk / where vast-jawed things do sprawl, but never sleep / devouring lesser giants in the dark / in which deeps myriad shoggoths all cohered / into one night-black muscle two leagues wide / which, with a mighty shoreward thrust, upreared / a tidal wall which swept in to collide / with Zanadane's, and seized in foam-white jaws / full half our folk from off her walls and towers / who fed at once those shoggoths' acid maws / and augmented their imitative powers!

"While we survivors, in those towering tides / were dragged offshore, our tenure thus annulled / and in those deeps our nation still abides / to haunt the citadel that once we ruled!

"Conceive! In the vast reflux of such seas / groping for weapons that we could not find! / Torn from anchorage we could not seize! / Wheeling and tumbling! Broken and bludgeoned and blind!

"Oh, feel with me our wretched outcast state! / We who could build a citadel like this! / To be o'erwhelmed by brutes we did create! / To be compelled to haunt the dark abyss / whence oozed those monsters who now throng our walls! / Who lord it in our mansions and our halls / whilst here we lurk like banished criminals!"

As he said this, such hate in his hoarse voice! Such torment in his twisted face! And his hearers heard more than loathing—heard as well a terrible *nostalgia* in his outrage....

But something kindled in his eyes then, and he smiled. "But why, with strangers from a happier race, / should I our dolors, our despair rehearse? / Why thrust on you our grief and our disgrace / even now, when our ill fortune is reversed?" Here a glint of joy bejeweled his eyes. "Oh, my dear so-comically shaped friends/ (my penance done in one of your odd frames / for that epithet will surely make amends?) / But friends, it seems a thing contrived by Fate / that you stand this moment at my city's gate!

"For why was I abroad up in your world? / I and many *cohorts*, truth be told. / Stand and see, the mystery's unfurld. / Stand and hear, the history is told!

"Sweet fruition of a long-sought bliss! / My allies now converge on every fortress / five hundred leagues up-coast and down of this! / And *yours* the rarest luck to stand in witness!

"And when these vile *shoggothoi* are slain / and purged and cleansed are all our citadels, / then there shall echo o'er the heaving main / the solemn sounding of our temple bells. / And when we've purged as well those citizens / Who made vile Treaty with vile Shoggoth Lords, / and transformed them to sea-floor denizens, / then—pure, renewed—begins our Afterwards!

"To you three it is given to witness all, / yet still up to your sunlit world return. / Whatever you might try to tell will fall / upon deaf ears, and scoffs and sneers will earn!

"When you've returned up to your icy door / your route will in that instant be no more. / What probes your strange reports might stimulate / will *prove* you comic crackpots to your mates.

"Now in advance I tender my remorse / for homicides to come—not *yours* of course, / but I have found your species' flesh quite sweet. / I knew it long before we chanced to meet / nor are my many fellows unaware / that your breed make a meal beyond compare....

"But come—I have been pent up long enough. / Please stand away, that you might not be splattered. / This envelope of yours is messy stuff ... / a trifle farther off—it tends to scatter."

Then explosively, rather horribly, with a mighty flexion of his true and inmost body, he exploded the shell of bone and flesh that enclosed him, spherically dispersing in a spray the much-thinned remnant of his human guise.

Now Raven and Meadow and Karl beheld the true form of their chance-met guide. Freed now, he'd expanded to somewhat more than human stature. His body was a smooth-staved, bipolar cask, an elegantly elongate cask that tapered both above and below to clustered tentacles. Amid the upper tentacles his pentagonal head, rough-textured like a starfish or other echinoderm, bore an eye on each facet—large, lovely, rather jewel-like eyes of violet and black they were. Great bat-like wings unfolded from the equator of his body's cask, and effortlessly he held himself aloft with slow-paced flexions of those mighty vanes, while at both his crown and at his foot, his tentacles tickled the darksome air and palped the rugged stone beneath him.

"My friends," he piped—for now his utterance was more purely flute-like, unmuted by the meaty human sheath that had muffled him—"I've invited you to view what now will pass, / but such a surge of unleashed appetite / assails my senses, my self-restraint can't last. / Not only are my own hungers unbound, / but I must unchain other, wilder urges / to hunt at large—I abjure you to begone!"

He turned then, and seemed with his upper tentacles to pluck something—or countless tiny somethings—from the air. There was no visible harvest in his coiled tentacle-tips, and yet when he whirled that invisibility seaward, the waters hissed and freckled with impacts, as if shotgunned with a spreading spray. The water began to seethe and dimple, the disturbance spreading, spreading swift offshore, and everywhere it spread, tentacles and thinner, jointed things like bug-legs and antennae began to sprout like wildfire all along the shore and offshore just as fast.

Their inhuman guide—raptly eyeing this living, flexing crop of pincers, claws, and feelers—missed and thus could not prevent Raven's sudden swift dart toward the surfline, her camera coming up, her flash exploding out across that seething germination of the sea.

As instant as that flood of light there sprang a huge thorny tentacle from the surf, seized her quick as any mantis ever snatched a spider, and she was plucked out into the deep with scarce an after-ripple in the blackly breathing surf.

At Meadow's piercing cry the Great Old One turned and thrust its wide-spread wings at them like huge preventing hands.

"Begone at once," he shrilled, "or be the food of what's devoured her!"

Meadow's heedless surfward lunge was brought up short by Karl's iron-fast grasp. He hooked his arm around her waist, hauled her off her feet, and whirled her away from the surf. She fought convulsively. He gripped her crushingly in both his arms and still she thrashed, wailed, and fought him galvanically, grief and horror like an earthquake in her.

"Begone upon your lives," the Old One shrilled. He turned his back on them and, bowing his great pinions, rose in the air above the surf and hung there. The gusts of his powerful wing-work seemed to kindle an ever thicker sprouting from the water. Jointed clawed legs, dorsal fins, pincers, beaked jaws, the mossy shield-like backs of mighty terrapins, the long undulous backs of water serpents—a broadening column of inhuman swimmers thrust muscularly through the surf and straight across the waters, a broad glittering diagonal like a slanting highway, joined a ways out by still more massive creatures arising from the deeper murk, until in the moonlight it formed one long braided tapestry of smoothly toiling aquatic muscle half a mile wide now and longer, longer as they watched, all arrowing straight for the shoggoth citadel on its gargantuan pier.

Impossibly that living flotilla *grew* as it approached the fortress. It sprouted the tentacle-clusters of titanic cephalopods that writhed up into view like nude oily trees, eager to embrace the citadel's walls. To swell that armada, from the deeps offshore there surfaced ship-sized shapes in colossal armor: vast jointed dorsal plates, and upraised dripping claws the size of siege engines—crustacea big as whales....

Whales as well appeared from the same deeps. Or whales they seemed at the first eruption of their huge battering-ram heads and little eyes and plank-like saw-toothed under-jaws—seemed until they raised colossal fore-limbs from the brine to hammer the fortress walls with knotted fists the size of battle-chariots.

But were these *serpents* now that followed them up from the deep? They came rippling along behind each cresting wave—supple, lacquer-red lengths so multiply segmented that they flexed as smooth as snakes, but each segment of them had its pair of sharp little legs. Sinuous, lithe they threaded their way amid the pilings of the pier. A hundred strides long was each one, and each knotted together a half-score of pilings apiece and then tightened, tightened until—slender though the creatures looked—the massy timbers groaned and creaked and some began to crack and splinter.

Now the polymorph pier-folk, shoggoths all, half abandoning their bestiary guises, came pouring down the pilings, blades flashing in what still were limbs, while oozing slug-like down the beams upon shoggothian lower halves—for should the pier be toppled, the water swarmed with their destroyers.

These moments of multiple convergence reached their end. Whales, cephalopods, serpents, and crustacea were ramming, splintering, and climbing the embattled, tottering outpost of the shoggothoi.

Halfway up the coastal hills, Karl stood holding Meadow as they watched the demolition of that stronghold. The Great Old One came gliding up to them and hung before them on the air.

"I grieve your loss," he fluted. "She seemed both brave and brilliant."

Karl held Meadow, weeping, to his chest. "She *was* both brave and brilliant."

The Old One put in Karl's hand a glowing blue sphere. "This will warm and light you both—even in the cold above."

"You tell us that ... if we return, we will not find our way down here again?"

The Old One did not answer. Somehow the inhuman eyes conveyed a smile.

Notes on Contributors

The Editor

S. T. Joshi is the author of *The Weird Tale* (1990), *H. P. Lovecraft: The Decline of the West* (1990), and *Unutterable Horror: A History of Supernatural Fiction* (2012). He has prepared corrected editions of H. P. Lovecraft's work for Arkham House and annotated editions of Lovecraft's stories for Penguin Classics. He has also prepared editions of Lovecraft's collected essays and poetry. His exhaustive biography, *H. P. Lovecraft: A Life* (1996), was expanded as *I Am Providence: The Life and Times of H. P. Lovecraft* (2010). He is the editor of the anthologies *American Supernatural Tales* (Penguin, 2007), *Black Wings I–II–III* (PS Publishing, 2010, 2012, 2013), *A Mountain Walked: Great Tales of the Cthulhu Mythos* (Centipede Press, 2014), *The Madness of Cthulhu* (Titan Books, 2014–15), and *Searchers After Horror: New Tales of the Weird and Fantastic* (Fedogan & Bremer, 2014). He is the editor of the *Lovecraft Annual* (Hippocampus Press), the *Weird Fiction Review* (Centipede Press), and the *American Rationalist* (Center for Inquiry). His Lovecraftian novel *The Assaults of Chaos* appeared in 2013. He is a winner of the World Fantasy Award, the Bram Stoker Award, the International Horror Guild Award, and the Distinguished Scholarship Award from the International Association of the Fantastic in the Arts.

The Contributors

T. Coraghessan Boyle is the author of twenty-three books of fiction, including, most recently, *After the Plague* (2001), *Drop City* (2003), *The Inner Circle* (2004), *Tooth and Claw* (2005), *The Human Fly* (2005), *Table Talk* (2006), *The Women* (2009), *Wild Child* (2010), *When the Killing's Done* (2011), and *San Miguel* (2012).

Jason V Brock is an award-winning writer, filmmaker, composer, and artist, and has been published in *Butcher Knives & Body Counts*, *The Devil's Coattails*, *Calliope*, *The Bleeding Edge*, *Black Wings II*, and many others. He was art director/managing editor for *Dark Discoveries* magazine for more than three years, and has a new magazine out called *[NameL3ss]*. As a filmmaker, his work includes the documentaries *Charles Beaumont: The Short Life of Twilight Zone's Magic Man*, *The AckerMonster Chronicles!*, and *Image, Reflection, Shadow: Artists of the Fantastic*. He loves his wife, Sunni, reptiles/amphibians, and vegan vegetarianism.

The *Oxford Companion to English Literature* describes **Ramsey Campbell** as "Britain's most respected living horror writer." He has ben given more awards than any other writer in the field, including the Grand Master Award of the World Horror Convention, the Lifetime Achievement Award of the Horror Writers Association, and the Living Legend Award of the International Horror Guild.

Walter C. DeBill, Jr. left Panama at six weeks to spend the rest of his childhood migrating between South Texas, where an ancestor died at the Alamo, and military posts all over the country. He discovered Poe in New York at ten, and Lovecraft in the basement library of an airbase at twelve, a mile from home through the night fog. Settling in Austin, Texas, for college and ever after, here in the haunting hill country of central Texas where his story is set, he kept turning back to HPL. In recent years, all his completed fiction has been published in three overlapping collections, the ebooks *Tales of Awe and Terrible Beauty* and *The Mlandoth Myth Cycle and Others* by Lindesfarne Press, and *The Black Sutra* by Mythos Books.

Born in 1968 in London, England, **Gemma Files** has been a Canadian citizen since the age of roughly two; her parents, Gary Files and Elva Mai Hoover, are both actors. Her career thus far includes time as a film critic, journalist, teacher, screenwriter, wife, and mother. She is the author of two collections of short fiction (*Kissing Carrion* and *The Worm in Every Heart*, both from Wildside Press). Her story "The Emperor's Old Bones" won a 1999 International Horror Guild Award for best short fiction. Since then, she has been nominated for a Bram Stoker Award and two Shirley Jackson Awards, and won the 2010 *Dark Scribe Magazine* Black Quill Best Small Press Chill Award, in both the Editors' and Readers' Choice categories.

Neil Gaiman is the *New York Times* bestselling author of the novels *Neverwhere, Stardust, American Gods, Anansi Boys,* and *Good Omens* (with Terry Prachett); the Sandman series of graphic novels; and the short story collections *Smoke and Mirrors* and *Fragile Things.* He is also the author of books for readers of all ages including the Newberry Medal–winning novel *The Graveyard Book* and the bestselling novels *Coraline* and *Odd and the Frost Giants.* He is the winner of numerous literary honors, including the Hugo, Bram Stoker and World Fantasy Awards, and the Newbury Medal. Originally from England, he now lives in the United States.

Cody Goodfellow is the co-founder of Perilous Press, an occasional publisher of modern cosmic horror literature. He has written three solo novels and three more with John Skipp. His first collection, *Silent Weapons for Quiet Wars,* earned a Wonderland Book Award in 2010. His newest collection, *All-Monster Action,* has been called "unique and creative" by people who should know better. He lives.

Lois H. Gresh is the *New York Times* bestselling author of twenty-seven books and fifty short stories. Her books have been published in approxiately twenty languages. Current books are the dark short story collection *Eldritch Evolutions,* the anthology *Dark Fusions,* and *The Hunger Games Companion.* Look for new stories in *Mark of the Beast, Eldritch Chrome, Steampunk Cthulhu, Black Wings III,* and *The Madness of Cthulhu.* Gresh has received Bram Stoker Award, Nebula Award, Theodore Sturgeon Award, and International Horror Guild Award nominations for her work.

Rhys Hughes started writing short stories at the age of six but had to wait until he was twenty-nine before his first book, *Worming the Harpy,* was published. Since then he has published another twenty-two volumes and 670 individual tales and has been translated into ten different languages. He describes his work as "ironic fantasy." His main influences are Italo Calvino, Donald Barthelme, and Flann O'Brien. He came late to the work of Lovecraft and wishes he had discovered him sooner.

Robert Barbour Johnson was an artist and writer of weird fiction. "Far Below" was voted in 1953 by readers as the best story ever published in *Weird Tales* magazine. During World War II he served in the artillery in the 195th Service Command Unit. After the war ended he remained in San Francisco and turned to more mainstream fiction under contract to *Blue Book*. He published articles in the fantasy and science fiction fanzines during the 1950s and then returned to weird fiction with "The Life-After-Death of Thaddeus Warde" (*Magazine of Horror*, November 1964).

Caitlín R. Kiernan is the author of nine novels, including, most recently, *The Red Tree* and *The Drowning Girl: A Memoir*. Her copious short fiction has been collected in several volumes, including *Tales of Pain and Wonder; To Charles Fort, with Love; Alabaster; The Ammonite Violin and Others; A Is for Alien;* and *Confessions of a Five-Chambered Heart*. She is a two-time winner of the World Fantasy Award, a winner of the Bram Stoker Award, and a three-time nominee for the Shirley Jackson Award, and has also been honored by the James Tiptree, Jr. Award. She lives in Providence, R.I.

A 2012 World Horror Convention Grand Masters, **T. E. D. Klein** was the editor of *Twilight Zone* and *CrimeBeat* magazines and is the author of *The Ceremonies, Dark Gods, Reassring Tales,* and *Raising Goosebumps for Fun and Profit*. He lives and works in Manhattan but escapes each weekend to a cabin in the woods.

Thomas Ligotti is a contemporary American horror author and reclusive literary cult figure. His writings are unique in style, have been noted as major continuations of several literary genres, most prominently Lovecraftian horror, and have overall been described as works of "philosophical horror," often written as philosophical novels with a "darker" undertone that is similar to Gothic fiction. Ligotti started his publishing career in the early 1980s with a number of short stories published in various American small-press magazines.

Patrick McGrath has written two story collections and eight novels, including *Spider,* which was filmed by David Cronenberg from

McGrath's script, and *Asylum,* an international bestseller that was filmed by David Mackenzie. His work has been published in more than two dozen countries. He is the author of *Ghost Town,* a collection of three novellas set in New York City, also the novels *The Grotesque, Trauma,* and *Port Mungo,* among others. He edited the influential anthology *The New Gothic* (1991) and has written introductions for *Dracula, Frankenstein, Dr. Jekyll and Mr. Hyde* and *The Monk* for Centipede Press. *Constance,* his most recent novel, was published in April 2013. He lives in Manhattan and teaches at the New School and Princeton.

Mearle Prout published four stories in *Weird Tales:* "The House of the Worm" (October 1933), "Masquerade" (February 1937), "Guarded" (March 1938), and "Witch's Hair" (May 1939). Little else is known about this obscure author.

W. H. Pugmire is a writer of horror fiction based in Seattle. Strongly influenced by the works of H. P. Lovecraft, many of Pugmire's stories directly reference Lovecraftian elements. Pugmire's major original contribution to the Cthulhu Mythos is the Sesqua Valley, a fictional location in the Pacific Northwest of the United States that serves as the primary locale for much of his fiction. Pugmire is a self-proclaimed eccentric recluse, "the Queen of Eldritch Horror," as well as a self-identified "punk rock queen and street transvestite."

Joseph S. Pulver, Sr. is the author of four mixed-genre collections, *Blood Will Have Its Season, SIN & ashes, Portraits of Ruin* and *A House of Hollow Wounds,* and the novel *The Orphan Palace.* He has written many short stories that have appeared in magazines and anthologies, including Ellen Datlow's *Year's Best Horror* and S. T. Joshi's *Black Wings.* He edited *A Season in Carcosa* and *The Grimscribe's Puppets,* the latter of which won the Shirley Jackson Award. His work has been praised by Thomas Ligotti, Ellen Datlow, Laird Barron, Michael Cisco, and many other notable writers and editors. He currently lives in Germany.

Mark Samuels is the author of four short story collections, *The White Hands and Other Weird Tales* (Tartarus Press, 2003), *Black Altars* (Rainfall

Books, 2003), *Glyphotech and Other Macabre Processes* (PS Publishing, 2008), and *The Man Who Collected Machen* (Ex Occidente, 2010; rpt. Chomu Press, 2011), as well as the short novel *The Face of Twilight* (PS Publishing, 2006). His work has appeared multiple times in *Year's Best Horror* anthologies.

Stanley C. Sargent was first "discovered" by Robert M. Price. Since then, his tales have appeared in a number of magazines and anthologies over the last twenty years. Many of his stories and one novella have been collected in two volumes, *Ancient Exhumations* and *The Taint of Lovecraft*. Initially a Mythos author, his work has since expanded to include science fiction, fantastic fiction in the Clark Ashton Smith tradition, comic horror, and weird tales in general. His love of ancient history and willingness to do extensive historical research are frequently reflected in his writings.

Michael Shea was born in Venice, California, and began writing as a poet at the age of thirteen. This devotion to strictly metric verse lasted through his college years at the University of California Berkeley. Years of travel followed, hitchhiking all over the United States, Canada, and western Europe, during which time he became literate in French, Spanish, and German. Influenced by Borges, Shakespeare and Jack Vance, he turned to fantastic prose, while never wholly abandoning verse. Shea died in 2014.

Jonathan Thomas was born in Providence, R.I., raised in a haunted house, and was a student of Lovecraft scholar Barton St. Armand. His initial sales were to b&w comics *Eerie* and *Vampirella*. He has been employed as an artist's model, postal clerk, concert promoter, library assistant, copyeditor, and percussionist. Since 1991 he has been married to artist and country singer Angel Dean. Books include *Stories from the Big Black House* (Radio Void, 1992), *Midnight Call* and *Tempting Providence* (Hippocampus Press, 2008 and 2010), and *The Color over Occam* (Arcane Wisdom, 2011). Recent work has appeared in *Black Wings I–IV, Nameless, PS*, and *Studies in the Fantastic*.

C. Hall Thompson published four stories in *Weird Tales*, including two striking tales of the Cthulhu Mythos, "Spawn of the Green Abyss"

(November 1946) and "The Will of Claude Asher" (July 1947). His other tales in the magazine were "The Pale Criminal" (September 1947) and "Clay" (May 1948). Later in his career, Thompson published several Western novels.

A dual passion for literature and the uncanny finds expression in **Donald Tyson**'s stories of ancient mysteries and those who seek to unravel their secrets. He is the author of many nonfiction books on traditional Western occultism, as well as a biography of Lovecraft title *The Dream World of H. P. Lovecraft*, the novel *Alhazred* (about the fabled author of the *Necronomicon*), and *The Ravener and Others*, a collection of occult mystery stories dealing with the otherworldly adventures of Elizabethan mage Dr. John Dee and his seer Edward Kelley.

James Wade was the author of "The Deep Ones" (in August Derleth's *Tales of the Cthulhu Mythos*, 1969), "The Silence of Erika Zann" (in Edward P. Berglund's *The Disciples of Cthulhu*, 1976), and other tales of the Cthulhu Mythos. Wade was also a distinguished composer of classical music; his best-known work was the opera *The Martyred* (1970). He was also the author of *One Man's Korea* (1967) and *West Meets East* (1975).

Made in the USA
Las Vegas, NV
12 February 2022

43794759R00353